MW00884334

The Angels' Pride

The Fallen Angels
Book 1

Steven Lindsay

For Mum, Dad and David
for always encouraging my love of reading
and for Marina
whose words put me on and kept me on this path

Part 1

A Fall From Heaven

Chapter 1

Sariel looked out her apartment windows, looking upon the beauty of Heaven from her confines. Rays of sunlight speared through cloudbanks to glance off the pastel buildings of the Citadel and the long white bridge that connected it to the palace. She watched with longing at the Angels that were free to roam as they pleased, walking and flying through the streets and the skies. She heard their songs and their laughter, the music of Heaven filled her ears. She watched them flirting, talking and kissing.

She saw them living free and she was jealous.

She knew that envy was one of the deadly sins, and that it had more power over her than an Arch Angel should ever allow, but she couldn't help it. She was jealous of the other Angels free to leave the palace, free to roam the Citadel and especially envious of those who were allowed to descend to the Surface. A place she had never been. She was rarely allowed to leave the palace, being able to count on one hand the number of times she had actually been allowed to visit the Citadel.

She understood her brother's concern. She had almost no magic of her own, lacking the basic defences afforded to even the weakest of Lesser Angels. Yet it was ridiculous that she was an Arch Angel who could not leave the palace without an escort. She found it weird that she was even an Arch Angel being almost powerless. But she was Michael's sister and she was the daughter of Samael and Lilith both of whom had also been Arch Angels before being killed in the War.

But that wasn't the only problem, not only was she practically powerless, something thought impossible for an Elder Angel, she was also the youngest. The Arch Angels babied her because she was one of their own, and she was at the bottom of that strict hierarchy. But the other Elders worried over her because she was the last of their kind. There had been no Elder Angels born for nearly two thousand years. Not an uncommon situation for the immortals but a troubling one nevertheless. Until Michael and Gabriel managed to conceive a child they would continue to baby her.

She wished that someone would birth another Elder, not just for her own sake but also for the sake of the Angels. The Elder were the most powerful Angels, but many of their numbers had been killed in the War of Heaven and the subsequent Fall. Despite well over a thousand years having passed since the War they had not recovered to the numbers they had once enjoyed. Many of the Arch Angels had been lost, forcing many of their children to step up. Including her, as stupid as it was.

She theoretically had the power of ruling Heaven and Earth, but in reality Gabriel and Michael ruled the world. The other Arch Angels were mostly family members, they simply compounded their ruling strength. But in reality she was powerless, having barely any magic of her own, no experience of the world below. She was being groomed by Michael and Gabriel to be all she could as an Arch Angel but she thought the point moot. She was simply expected to lend her vote to any decision they made.

That alone would spike anyone's envy but the fact that powerless Lesser Angels were allowed to the Surface to whisper in the ears of mortals to fight the waning faith simply stoked her jealousy. Why should they get to go and she not? They were more defenceless than she was, she at least was immortal, the Lesser were simply spirits. But as Gabriel said, they were expendable and she was not.

She agreed and disagreed. She was after all an Elder with the potential at least to conceive, they were dead and unable to reproduce. Lesser Angels were everywhere, Elders were much more of a rarity.

She sighed as she continued to gaze out the window, there was so much she wanted to see and do. She wanted more than anything to visit the Surface. To see real mortals, real land, to see the sea. She wanted to walk among the Humans in their swelling cities, to gaze upon the Heathens who undermined and resisted the will of Heaven. To marvel at the technology Humans had created. To see the night.

The palace and Citadel were a place of ever sunlight, it waxed and waned but never went dark. The skies would streak beautiful pinks, oranges and purples but otherwise it was near perfect azure skies all the time. Even storms rarely visited the Citadel.

There was so much she wanted to do, see and experience. Had wanted to do for over a thousand years. But had never been allowed. It just wasn't fair.

Gabriel slipped into Sariel's rooms, moving with all the silent grace inherent to the Elder Angels. She was a beautiful woman, a stand out beauty even among the immortal and flawless beauty of the Angels. She was tall and lean, with sun kissed olive skin and six glorious white and gold wings that managed to catch every ray of light. Even her brown-blonde hair seemed to float like liquid sunlight around her head. But above all it was her extremely rare violet eyes that made her unique.

Ironically enough most of the Arch Angels had violet eyes. Michael and his sister, their uncle Azrael and her own cousin Ariel all had similarly stunning violet eyes. But no other Angels did. It was a characteristic she found that helped subtly emphasize the difference between the Arch Angels and the other Angels.

Gabriel was the poster child of Angelic beauty, all sun kissed and reflections. Sariel, just like the rest of her family were almost polar opposites. Like her brother and uncle she had very pale skin that made them look like they had rarely seen the sun. It was hard to think that they lived in the eternal sunlight of Heaven. They also lacked the blonde or brown-blonde hair most of the other Elder Angels had. They had jet black hair that matched their six jet black wings, once again something completely unique to their family. But then their physical appearances were the characteristics of the Angels of Death.

For whatever reason that bloodline over powered all other inherited characteristics. It was however a pure breeding bloodline, producing some of the most powerful Arch Angels, all four of them had been Arch Angels. It was this unique power that had made Michael a good match for her own phenomenal powers.

Not that their powers were doing them much good. The world was changing, faith was dying out as science accelerated Humans' control of their own destiny. Every Angels' strength would be needed to reign back in their wayward subjects.

It was this thought process that accelerated her anger when she saw Sariel daydreaming out the window.

"Sariel, what are you doing?" she snapped. Elder Angels were far more valuable than any other Angel. They needed every trained Elder they could. Sariel might well be that crucial tipping point.

Sariel turned those surly violet eyes towards her, why did she always have such an attitude? "I'm watching people live. I'm watching people do everything I'm not"

Gabriel twitched her wings in annoyance "live!

Ha! The Lesser Angels are dead spirits rehoused in flesh, how much living are they doing? You are living Sariel, you are an Elder, real flesh and blood housing powers beyond reckoning."

"Powers beyond reckoning, I can barely light a candle. I have more in common with them than with the Elders."

"We are their masters. There are problems with your powers granted but you are still an Elder, still an Arch. You have control over them."

"Why should I govern them when I hardly know anything about them? Why should I govern over the Earth when I have never seen a Human let alone their cities? How can I understand the work of Demons when I cannot see it for myself? Instead I am stuck in this palace day after day, century after century. I'm not even allowed to visit the Citadel, the heart of Angel power."

"We're protecting you Sariel, you're not well."

"Not well! I'm perfectly fine. I can fly, I can walk. I'm not sick or weak. I'm naturally protected by my latent powers. I could fly down to the Surface and see the world for myself. Someone could come with me, half of Heaven could come with me if that is what it takes. You need to let me live!"

Great, another tantrum. "Sariel many things can go wrong on the Surface, there are a great many temptations and dangers."

"Stop judging me by your brother. I am not Lucifer!"

Even as she said it Sariel realised she had gone too far, Gabriel's face contorted with rage, her violet eyes seeming to burn. "No you are not, he at least cared about his duty." She spat as she stormed out the room. The door slammed shut and a pink shield bloomed across it. Sariel wasn't going anywhere.

Interesting, it was rare for Gabriel to make a slip but she had just praised Lucifer. Of course that was an indication of her anger if she had just favoured Lucifer over her. Gabriel loathed her brother with a fury that seemed to have no end.

But then he had divided Heaven with its civil war. He was the reason there were so few Elder Angels. The Fall had extracted a huge price on the Angels unloyal to Michael and Gabriel.

Sariel wondered what Heaven would be like now if Lucifer had won and Gabriel had lost.

Gabriel leaned against the door, trying to control her shaking. It was unseemly to appear so angry after visiting Sariel. In court when people failed her yes, when seeing an adolescent girl no. Damn her and damn Lucifer. Damn them both. Why couldn't either of them just do as they were told? Life would be so much easier if they just accepted their place. At least Sariel was controllable without her magic.

Lucifer was still someone to be feared. He might be trapped in Hell but she sometimes worried that he might one day escape. That was of course impossible, Hell would never fall. Lucifer would always be trapped as he was. It was a fitting punishment for his sins. Siding with the Gods they had fought so hard to overthrow, convincing so many that they could coexist. He had refused to see the error of his ways, had refused her logical reasoning. He had insulted her and had tried to take away her throne. He had been beyond foolish.

Now he was paying for that foolishness. But it had come at a terrible cost. One third of the Angels had Fallen with Lucifer into Hell. Another third had Fallen into Purgatory. They were only a third of the strength they should have been. Was it any wonder they were losing grasp on the world as Humanity thundered down the road to its own control. That could not be allowed.

Why could Sariel not see how vital she was, that as an Arch she had the power to shape the world, even if she couldn't access that power. She still had the latent abilities of the Arch Angels. She could invoke wars with simple whispers, she could condemn a nation with a single word. She could bend other Angels to her will with just her voice and aura. Yet she failed to appreciate what she still had. Always pining to see the Citadel and Surface. She was so sick of her whining. Just like a child she lived for the now with no appreciation for the future.

When she and Michael needed so much of their attention focused on the world, here they were chasing after a spoilt brat. Still she was his sister, he could deal with her. She had to see that they knew how to rule Heaven, she just had to lend her support to them. She didn't need to govern, Heaven was theirs.

Nothing would remove her from her throne. Of that she was sure.

Sariel looked at herself in the mirror. Did people really think she was unwell? She wasn't deformed or disfigured. She had two arms, two legs and six wings. Her skin was pale, but then so were Michael and Azrael's and so had her father's she had been told. Just like them she had jet black hair and jet black wings. An extreme rarity in Heaven where everything was synonymous with sunlight. The rest had sun kissed olive or darkened bronze skin, wings of white and gold. The rest of the Angels seemed to live and breathe light.

But her family were no ordinary Angels. They were the Angels of Death. Though of course she didn't actually get to do anything, and Michael was usually too busy running Heaven and Earth. Most of the duties of

Death fell to Azrael and his handpicked servants the Reapers.

Other than colouring she looked like every other Elder Angel. She was pixie like, delicate and defined but with the natural strength that was there for all Elders. She could lift more than any mortal, endure exertion, hunger and thirst for far longer. She healed very quickly, had need for little rest and glowed softly.

Her other rarity was her violet eyes, of all the Angels only her family and Gabriel's had them. Of the Seven Arch Angels only Raphael and Uriel did not have violet eyes. The other Elder Angels tended to have amber or light blue. The Ascended and Lesser Angels had a wide variety.

No she was definitely not deformed, she looked like an Elder Angel from her family. Though she would never admit it she did secretly long for Gabriel's sun kissed complexion.

It was times like these that she especially wished that her parents had survived the War. To have the normal family dynamic, to have Michael as her brother and not her keeper. Maybe then she's actually like him and Gabriel. Maybe not.

She sighed and sat down by the window, gazing out once again at the going ons of Heaven. The sky was streaking gold and orange. It was approaching dinner time. She hoped it didn't take Michael long to come and sort her out. She was hungry.

She opened her eyes when she heard the door open. It had been so long she had dozed off. A quick glance out the window showed violet and pink skies, it was just before dawn, not that the sun ever actually set or rose, but they still used the timelines mortals used. It was easier.

Her brother wore an annoyed expression as he walked over to her. Not that she expected any difference, but just one she would like him to side with her. He sat down next to her and studied her for a moment, looking for something in her eyes.

"Gabriel is very upset." He said softly.

Gabriel was always upset. There was a reason people did very little to annoy her. Her temper was legendary and frequent. "I cannot win. If I sulk I am being a spoilt child and if I actually form an adult argument then she gets upset."

"You shouldn't have mentioned Lucifer. You know she is extremely touchy on the subject."

"But that is who she is comparing me to. You both fear that I might be the next Lucifer and tear apart the fragile control of Heaven. That is the real reason you both tuck me away out of harm's way. There is nothing to worry about, I have no powers. How could I ever be a threat to Heaven? You are suffocating me with your fears. I am not living. I do not see the world, I do not see how even my own kind lives. Angels go about their lives and I barely know anything about it."

"You know how Angels live."

"I know how Elder Angels live, and just how different I am from that expectation. I do not know what the Lesser or Ascended get up to or do for Heaven. I'm one of the Arch Angels, ruling over Heaven and Earth yet I have never seen a Human. I do not know how they live, what they aspire for. I do not understand the merest details about the people I'm meant to rule."

"The Lesser were once Humans, their journals fill the archives."

"They are not Human any more. They have changed."

"The Surface is too dangerous for you."

"And not for the many Angels that have little or no magic? They survive fine."

"They are expendable, you are not. Elder Angels are the real might of Heaven, we are the magic that holds it together. The Lesser will never have our power. We are living they are not. We are infused with the essence of Heaven, they are not. They live here at our discretion."

Sariel fell quiet shocked by his words. She hadn't realised that the Elders viewed the Lesser as expendable. Were the Ascended saints and prophets viewed as equally expendable?

"You are irreplaceable Sariel. You will not be going to the Surface and that is final. Put such notions from your head, they will only cause you further problems. You will apologise to Gabriel. It is also clear you need to learn some humility. You will work with the servants until we have decided that you have learned your lesson." With that he turned on his heel and left.

She sagged against the window both furious and sorrowful. She wasn't being spoilt, she was genuinely concerned about her ability to govern. Why couldn't they seem to understand that? Yes she wanted to see the world but her reasons were more than just that.

The reason the War of Heaven had broken out was because of the cruelty and ignorance of the Gods. They had once ruled Heaven, had in fact made it. But they were cruel and vain. They lost touch with the world that they dominated. It was from their decaying reign that the Angels had stepped up to lead the world. Naturally the Gods had been unwilling to relinquish their absolute control and war had broken out. Eventually the Angels had won at a great cost. But Humanity had been given a new chance, a new era of expansion. It seemed to her that the Angels were now in danger of losing touch.

And if they did, what was to stop them being

overthrown by Humanity? Benevolent and understanding rulers remained in power. Those out of touch were so often overthrown.

Perhaps the greatest concern was the Elder view on the Lesser. It was chilling to hear two of the Arch Angels talk about how expendable they were. Did the other Arch Angels think the same? She knew she didn't, but then her voice fell on no one's ears. The Arch Angels were meant to look out for the wellbeing of Heaven and all who dwelled within it, but apparently there were divisions she had been unaware of. That was food for thought, but at another time.

Right now she had to go and apologise to Gabriel, which would be a trial in itself. Still she had learned a few things over the centuries of annoying Gabriel. She responded to respectability and appearances. Gabriel was always one for appearances. She was after all the most beautiful and most powerful Angel in all of Heaven. Appearances meant a lot to her.

She sat down in front of her mirror, trying to think what look would ease Gabriel's anger the most. She was stumped.

Chapter 2

It had been as bad as she had thought it would be. Gabriel had been in a really spiteful rage. The usual apologies had not been enough. Still it was partially her own fault, she knew just how touchy the topic of Lucifer was with Gabriel- she had been known to erupt at the very mention of his name- but she had wanted to prove a point.

It was true after all. Gabriel worried over her brother, his defection had done something to her mind. Michael had said when loved ones hurt you their cuts and scars ran much deeper than normal ones. She guessed she understood but she figured that she and Michael had a different relationship than the one Gabriel and Lucifer had once shared.

She wondered how Gabriel must have felt to have thought peace had finally come to Heaven after the War only to discover that her very own brother was stirring rebellion. And that the rebellion had stripped Heaven of two thirds of its numbers. She supposed she could sort of understand Gabriel's obsessive wrath.

After her torturous apology Gabriel had decided she needed extensive humbling. It was in punishments that Gabriel's vindictive nature was allowed full control. She had been assigned to cleaning- anything and everything, from the kitchens to the bathrooms to the armoury and library. If the sewers had ever needed cleaning or fixing she felt sure she would have been assigned to that. Thankfully they did what they did without ever needing fixing or cleaning, which was just as well because no one knew how they worked. It would have been most unseemly for streams of sewage to cascade from underneath the Citadel. Though it did leave many unanswered questions.

For Sariel though her punishment was more of a relief than anything else, for it allowed her to escape the mundane routine of her everyday life. She would be free from being force fed the books on the history of the War and Fall, the grimores on magic she couldn't learn. Every now and then she'd be given something different if equally boring- books on warfare, agriculture, weapon making, governance, architecture- though she had to admit, while the way it was written was incredibly boring, architecture itself she found fascinating.

Now she had access to the library, she doubted that either of them would understand that their punishment would delight her so much. Now she had the freedom to peruse the shelves while cleaning them. She was excited to find out what was contained within them.

But first she had to report to Mary for the other domestic duties. She knew it would be bathrooms first, before kitchens and once that was all taken care of she would finally get to be in the library.

As she had expected she had first been assigned to routine cleaning and maintenance of waste disposal. It was disgusting without the aid of magic, but she didn't hate it. The other Elders used magic for everything, it was their lifeblood, any that were given these tasks crumbled quickly. She was used to her lack of magic, her physical strength and stamina probably akin to the many warriors around.

As for the demeaning nature of it, well she was used to the pitying glances of the other Elders. What was one more step down in their eyes? She didn't care what they thought, but interestingly enough it gave her plenty of contact time with the Lesser and Ascended Angels.

Every day she had to report to Mary in the kitchens before being sent on her way. Every morning she was greeted with a smile and breakfast from her, as well as welcoming smiles from many of the other kitchen staff. They were used to whining Elders and Ascended being sent for humility, but she was no whiner and she was there far more frequently than any other Angel.

She had learned the most fascinating bits of information about various people around Heaven. Nariel had had a crush on Raphael for years, Gabriel was on a rampage again, but this time had trashed the throne room when some country had officially separated religion from its government. Even Michael had gone on a rage, fighting every Angel stupid enough to fight with him. His rage was based on homosexual marriage being legalised in yet another country. Ariel continued to haunt across the Angel countries with her Inquisitors, keeping the leash of control tight.

There were rumours about people worshiping the Old Gods again, in ever increasing numbers. The Hindus continued to deny the Angels' truth and clung to their dead Gods. One of the saints had accidently set a city on fire, but it was still under wraps as to who it was. Once again there was talk about sending Jesus or Mohammad for their second comings.

She even heard details of the Surface; the Pope was a weak man, caught between the fractured powers of the cardinals. The old Israel and Palestine conflict was flaring again. There were fights breaking out in America, Iran and Pakistan as the Angels' words were twisted by Humans. She had learned a lot about the religions the Angels had founded to replace the old debauched religions. She didn't think that they were any improvement at all.

Every day she was taken down into the bowels of

the Palace to scrub dirtied walls, oil and clean magical machines and repaint sigils. It was a long tiring job but she found the days passed quickly in the company of John. He had been permanently put on these duties after he had called Gabriel a stupid bitch and refused to apologise. He said he was happier out of her glare, and not being made to do unsavoury tasks he found reprehensible.

At the end of her days she could go back to her rooms, crawl into her bath and allow all the grease and muck to soak away. It was here that her small access of magic was highly useful, cleaning was a breeze no matter how grotty she got. And the time she floated in her bath allowed her to mull over everything she had learned in her days. Whether it simply be some piece of gossip about an Angel, or a more significant piece of gossip about Human politics and religion. She was learning a lot about the dynamics of Heaven. Michael and Gabriel really did have near total control. The other Arch Angels with the exception of Azrael always backed them up, as did much of the Council of Elders. Azrael was only really safe because he was the eldest Arch Angel, scared nearly everyone and was absent so frequently because of his duties. The other Archs had a tendency just to let him do his own thing.

She felt guilty, she had never really spent much time with her uncle. Whether it was him always being busy or her never getting around to it she wasn't quite sure. Rumour held it that he had never recovered from the loss of his brother, retreating into his death duties as a way to avoid the world around him. She would have to visit him.

Chapter 3

Sariel couldn't believe that it was finally time to start her duties in the library. She couldn't believe that several months had passed either. But both were true. She had worked her way through most of the palace, working amongst the servants who were surprisingly accepting of her. As they had mentioned time and time again, she didn't think she was better than them. She was willing to pull her weight without moaning. There was quite a bit of resentment amongst the different levels of Angels.

The Arch Angels stood above everyone, ironic that she was cleaning the palace, next came the Elder, the most magical of the Angels and from where the Arch Angels could only ever come. They were the living, breathing magical citizens of Heaven. Under them stood the Ascended Angels, Lesser Angels who through various means of sainthood or duty had been returned to life, blessed with more magic and gained an extra pair of wings. On the bottom most rung were the most populous Lesser Angels, the spirits of Humans who had ascended to Heaven as payment for their good deeds on Earth. Most of them were powerless and lived at the beck and call of those above them.

It seemed akin to the regime that the Elder Angels had originally over thrown. Not that she was foolish enough to mention that aloud.

She had found her interest in the War had ever increased as she had worked her way through the Palace. Despite many attempts to remove and cover over all traces of the Gods there were still stunning artefacts of their legacy. Stunning murals, paintings and sculptures hidden away in forgotten rooms, they all bore remarkable resemblance to many of the stunning artwork gracing most of the palace. The so called art of the Angels. Most of the architecture was clearly of the Gods' design and magic, the Angels had only really done a rudimentary cover up of the Gods.

And now she stood outside the library staring at the massive wooden doors ornately decorated with carvings and gilding of owls, ravens, ibis and various other species of birds. There were symbols she didn't know and images of men and women she felt sure were not Angels, though some had wings. She was surprised it hadn't been replaced. Was its beauty its saving grace? That it could be assumed that the people gracing the doors were Angels.

She pulled one of the doors open, grunting at the effort. The door swung smoothly but it was damned heavy. No wonder the Elders used magic so much, Heaven was designed for it. She wondered how the poor Lesser managed to get about with their lack of magic and physical strength.

Inside was the stunning world she had only glimpsed in passing. Tall wooden shelves stacked full of books, scrolls and tablets reaching high up into the soaring ceiling far above. Dappled light danced across the marble floors and polished surfaces of the rich and dark woods. It was a place not of stunning white and blinding light like the rest of Heaven. It was a place of solace, of retreat and relaxation. Her glance hinted at many sights that were not traditionally Heavenly. There were even various plants in pots, casting more shade and scenting the air with subtle scents.

She walked casually along the main aisle to the desk she saw at the end, taking her time to absorb as much of the library with her eyes as she could. This was better than a dream, this was almost a different world. A tantalising world full of unimaginable knowledge she had never accessed before.

The desk was a beautiful construction of owls, ravens and ibis intertwined around each other, their wings spread wide, their claws clutching books and scrolls. They had been carved from different woods, the ravens from ebony, the ibis from pine and the owls from various woods of dark, light and golden hues. It was like light and shadows poured into one magnificent wood carving. The usual gold and white of Heaven seemed sparse and simplistic in comparison.

She was standing there marvelling at it when a young female Angel popped up from behind the desk.

"Can I help you?" she asked eying her warily.

"Mary sent me to assist Patrick, do you know where he is?"

She smiled "He pretty much lives in the Archives. Head down the main aisle until you reach the doors, you might have some trouble finding him though. He gets lost in there for days sorting through God knows what."

Sariel thanked her as she left, prompting a surprised smile from the girl, who ducked back behind the desk. Sariel glanced over as she walked past. The girl was sitting in a circle of books, apparently sorting through them, but she seemed to have gotten distracted with reading some of them.

The Archives doors were just as impressive as the outer doors, but to her surprise there were a wider variety of animals, and most surprisingly she glimpsed snakes. The snake was one of the symbols of Lucifer and Gabriel had done her best to remove every trace of him from Heaven.

These doors were clearly used far less often, moaning in protest as she pulled one open. Inside was a darker world. While the main library was all about the play of light and shadow, filled with the golden hues of polished wood, the Archives were all about shadows. The soaring shelves were all made of ebony, decorated with gold, silver or bronze. The floor was black marble, occasionally broken by crests and designs of various stones. Black marble and granite columns soared up to the vaulted ceiling, where white glass let in filtered light. She heard water running and was surprised to see fountains here and there.

She was more surprised when she walked up the main aisle and followed it around the corner to find not only a large fountain of what could only been Gods but a massive ebony desk sitting in front of it, carved entirely with the design of serpents.

It was a truly unusual creation, she was unused to dark features and snakes were completely alien to her. She was fascinated by the differences of them, some were huge, others seemed tiny in comparison, some even had ornate hoods. Coils plain and decorated with stripes or diamonds twisted around each other and the desk. Their dark eyes seemed to follow her as she moved, their open mouths ready to strike. It seemed terrifyingly lifelike. The workmanship was truly astounding.

Perhaps strangest of all was that it was warm to the touch as she ran her hands over some of them.

"Truly marvellous isn't it?"

She turned around to see an Ascended Angel walking towards her carrying a stack of scrolls. He was not the typical Ascended, pale skin, dark brown hair, skinny rather than muscular. But his brown eyes were warm and welcoming.

"Patrick I presume?"

"Indeed and you must be Sariel, Mary has told be so much about you."

She smiled "Yes it is marvellous, I haven't seen anything like it."

He smiled "I bet you haven't. It is very rare to see anything that bears a serpent or harks back to the Age of Gods."

"Yes Gabriel was very thorough in removing all traces of her brother."

"It wasn't just Gabriel, Michael was also very thorough at removing all traces of the serpent but of course the serpent must live on in the depictions of Eden."

She frowned in confusion, why would Michael bother unless Gabriel had demanded it. It seemed like it would have been a more personal goal of Gabriel's to remove all trace of her brother.

He looked at her funny thinking her confused "The serpent is an integral part to our history. Adam was the first man born solely into the Angels cause. He was born in Eden, our citadel on Earth. Lucifer and others were tasked with tempting him and his offspring to see how reliable they were."

"Was that what led Lucifer to his Fall? By tempting Humans he himself was tempted."

He gave her an assessing look "That is not a bad theory. You would do well to mention it to Gabriel, it will certainly put you in her good books. She will readily agree with your assessment."

"But you do not?"

"No. But then I am well read on my history. I may not have been there but others were and have left extensive journals in the archives. Journals that the other Arch Angels would be furious to learn about."

Sariel leaned forward her eyes wide with curiosity "Journals the other Arch Angels would not want me reading? I haven't been told the whole truth have I?"

He studied her for a moment, searching for something. Whatever it was he seemed satisfied. He propelled her down various aisles so fast she was instantly lost. He led her to a forgotten derelict corner. Dust coated everything, the wood more grey then black. The poor fern sitting next to a bench looked the worst for wear.

He stopped in front of the shelves, his hands hovering along the books until he found what he was looking for. He pulled out a black journal with a unique crest on it- a serpent on Venus.

"This is a copy of one of Lucifer's Journals, he kept extensive records of his life. I suggest you read it." He clicked his fingers and a box full of cloths and polish appeared. He smiled "just in case anyone comes looking for you."

"Like Michael or Gabriel?"

"Exactly. Now I shall leave you to read. Once you finish feel free to read any of the other journals around." She watched him walk away before turning her attention to the book. It was a copy, the product of a copy spell, everything would be exactly as the author wrote. A shiver ran down her spine as she ran her hands over the cover. Lucifer's Journal, she couldn't believe it. Gabriel would kill her.

She sat down on the bench and opened it to the first page, written in a neat masculine hand was *Lucifer* and underneath he had drawn a serpent on Venus. It seemed to be his personal crest. Excited and more than a little apprehensive she turned to the next page filled with neat line after neat line. She settled down and lost herself for hours in his journal.

She put down the last of his journals on the pile next to her, her hand shaking slightly as she wiped away stray tears.

She had lived a lie her entire life. If the journal was to be believed then Heaven was built on lies, pride and blood. Even if only half of it was true then the history of Heaven she had been told was nothing like the truth.

Heaven had existed before the Angels, being made by the Primordial Gods and Goddesses of Air and Sky. Their children the Gods had come into their inheritance as the Primordial Gods had disappeared one by one. They ruled Heaven and Earth as they saw fit. The Angels had been their servants but more shockingly their bastard offspring. All Angels were descended from the Gods.

Whose bloodline ran in her veins? Would she ever know now that all the Gods had been killed or imprisoned in the Underworld?

That was another shocking fact. The Gods had not all been killed, the Rulers of the Underworld had been trapped within their own domains and many other Gods drained of their Lifeforce and thrown into either Hell or Tartarus.

Heaven was not of the Angels' creation, and neither was Eden. Heaven was the creation of the Sky Gods and their brethren, the beauty worked upon by generations of immortals- Primordial Gods, Gods, Angels and Nymphs. They had been born to it, just like the Sky Gods. As for Eden that had belonged to one of the Mother Goddesses as a meeting place for their kind, for them to share experiences. It had once been a place of creation, now it was hidden away by the Angels.

More shockingly were the Angels' religions on Earth. They did not follow the Angels, they followed a non-existent God. An omnipotent God who saw all. Little did the Humans know that God was an acronym for Governance Over Divine, the initial title for the Governing Council. She wondered how Humans would feel to find out they did not have an omnipotent God looking out for them but a bickering mass of Angels. God's messengers. How had Gabriel put up with that for so long?

Lucifer had once been an Arch Angel, which wasn't really surprising. He had tested the faith of Humanity along with Samael, her own father. Why had no one told her that he was the Serpent from the Garden of Eden? The Serpent crest was originally her father's, Lucifer had adopted it from him. Both of them had been ambassadors to the Gods from their faction, the faction calling loudest for peace with the Gods. He had written of his hope for a new future alongside the Gods. His vision for a brighter future of greater understanding where magic would once again flow freely across the world and her realms had made her eyes water.

Alas Gabriel had been his loudest opposition, calling for the war effort.

His last entries had been about his increasing worry and anxiety about his sister. His very last entry had mentioned being summoned before her. There were no more entries afterwards.

Curious she picked up the duster and headed back towards the desk. As she was approaching she detoured as she heard voices. Michael was interrogating Patrick in the middle of the main aisle. She wondered if Michael could see the desk from where he stood, that might explain why Patrick looked so agitated.

Patrick's eyes fell on her and relief swept through him.

"Sariel why are you in the library, you were assigned to Mary for cleaning duties." Michael asked without even looking at her.

"But I am on cleaning duties, I'm cleaning the shelves. I've been dusting all day." Michael glanced at her taking in her bedraggled appearance. Reading through the journals had covered her in dust. It coated her from head to foot. Patrick was relieved that she not only looked like she had been cleaning but looked the worse for wear for it.

Michael turned back to Patrick "Make sure she doesn't stop while she is here. She is here to clean not dawdle."

Bowing he said "Of course Arch Angel" To Sariel's surprise he cast a glare after Michael as he left.

They both remained silent until they heard the scrape of the doors signalling that Michael had left. "Are the journals true?" she asked rounding on him.

"More truthful than anything you will have read or been told. This is why the archives are limited to only the Elder Angels and a few select Ascended."

"Which select few?"

"The Ascended that have been unwavering in their support of Gabriel and Michael throughout their rise to Arch Angel. Or those that do not baulk at the tasks set them. Myself and Mary were assigned to our positions by the Old Council and the new one sees no reason to remove us."

"What really happened? How did Lucifer Fall from Heaven?"

"Gabriel. She cast him out of Heaven. He had nearly completed negotiations of peace between the Gods and Angels. He had single handedly offered a way to end the war and stop the centuries of conflict. But Gabriel charged him with High Treason and cast him from Heaven. He was ensorcelled to prevent him ever rising up against Heaven.

He has never been heard of since. For well over a thousand years no one has seen any trace of him. The Angels made the final push and the last of the Gods were driven into Hell and in some cases Tartarus. Since then there has been hardly any trace of them. There has always been the occasional Pagan group worshipping one of the Gods from time to time but the Gods have not been felt on the Earth in a long, long time."

"Until recently. Once again Heaven is talking of another cleansing. But if the Pagan groups have been around for so long then why now?"

"Humans, and other mortals. Their beliefs lend both the Gods and Angels strength and power. The power base Heaven needs to have supremacy relies nearly entirely on Human belief with a small amount of Jinn. It is why the lands of God have always felt the need to spread the message into other lands. But now Humans are turning away from the Angelic religions in droves, seduced as the Council would say by science. But science is not the only culprit, though it is one of the main reasons in the Western World. People are converting to the ever growing abundance of New Age Religions and beliefs which are a resurrection of forgotten Gods and rites.

The Human world is changing beyond Heaven's ability to control it. Thus Heaven's power is undermined, and the Elders powers weakened. That is why you as an Elder are so important to their plans."

"And just what are their plans?"

"To bring about the Apocalypse again and bring the Human world to heel. When the planet is scarred once more then the Humans will fear Heaven for a long time."

She shook her head in horror. The Apocalypse, that couldn't be. Even she knew that the Old Council had declared for it to never be used again. Its effects were uncontrollable and the Angels were not immune to its wrath. It had killed off a great deal of the Old Council, prompting their banning of it. It had killed off her parents, how could Michael even consider using it?

She backed away from Patrick very afraid of what he might have to say. Turning on her heels she ran out of the archives.

Patrick watched her go, she would be back. She had to but the seeds had been sown, she would hunger for the journals of other Angels. She would no longer trust Michael and Gabriel, and in her desperation she would turn to either Mary, John or himself. And once she did then the truth would no longer be hidden.

In the early morning, as the purple was being lined with streaks of pink and orange, Sariel made her way back to her rooms to find both Gabriel and Michael waiting for her. She was barely in the door before they both began yelling at her "Where have you been?"

"I was in the tower"

That stopped them momentarily. It was clear they had feared she had left the palace, the fact she had not seemed to placate them a lot. A new voice in her head started asking what the real reason they didn't want her leaving the palace might be.

"We were worried sick about you, you didn't turn up to your morning lesson." Her brother said as he wrapped his arm around her. It had been a long time since her brother had shown any sign of affection to her.

"When did I have to report day and night what I am doing? I needed to be alone and think?"

"You don't even have the common decency to turn up to our lessons when we go out of our way to train you" Gabriel yelled before Michael shushed her. She didn't know who was more surprised, her or Gabriel. He never told Gabriel to be quiet.

"What did you need to think about Sariel" he

asked kindly. She hadn't seen this side of him in a very long time. She gave in and leaned into his embrace.

"I was thinking about the War, the Fall and how important my place is here in Heaven and the responsibilities that I have."

That stunned them both, even Gabriel smiled at her.

"That is surprisingly mature of you Sariel, it is pleasing to see you embracing your responsibilities. Perhaps this means we can get past all this fighting and return to our normal relationships. I hate having to baby you Sariel, I'd rather have my sister with that sharp mind she used to have."

"In the future Sariel, please let us know where you are. We were worried." Sariel nearly collapsed from shock when Gabriel said it, and was even more shocked when she gave her shoulder a squeeze.

She smiled at them both as they rose and left the room hand in hand. But as soon as they had left she ran over to her door and opened it a crack. Sure enough she could hear their whispering.

"This is a good thing Gabriel, she is finally seeing what we have wanted her to see for centuries. She is starting to accept her roles. If she continues she can be handled better, she can be distracted with visiting the Citadel or something else as a token of our trust."

"She cannot stray too far from the palace or the spell will weaken. We cannot risk that." She hissed.

"We have to do something, otherwise she will revolt or run away. Then we would have a whole new set of problems."

Their whispers trailed away as they walked down the corridor. She closed the door again. Spell? What spell? And what would happen if it weakened? What did the spell do? She wondered but she had no idea, though her imagination ran wild with Heaven falling out of the sky.

Intrigued she decided to head back to the archives. Michael and Gabriel had far too many secrets, and while they may not be the same as what Lucifer or Patrick alluded to there was still something they were hiding. And she was going to find out what it was.

Chapter 4

Sariel read and read and read. She lost days and weeks reading, while she was apparently cleaning. Gabriel and Michael had decided the archives would be her last punishment.

She spent her days buried in journals across the ages. She had read and re-read Lucifer's journals so many times. She also devoured any journal Patrick gave her as well as the ones she chose to read. She saw the War and Fall from different sides. She had even stumbled across some of Michael's early journals, his later ones were presumably in his own library.

She also raided the library afterwards, but was highly selective of what she read and borrowed. Cassiel was under strict orders from Gabriel to note everything she read. Being one of Gabriel friends she was very thorough in her cataloguing of everything Sariel read in the main library. She was one of the reasons Sariel never removed any of the journals from the Archives. She did not want Gabriel or Michael to know what she had been reading.

It was in the archives that she learned the most, away from the prying eyes of Cassiel. Patrick was proving insightful beyond belief. One day she came in to find a stack of journals ready for her on the desk. One was her fathers, marked with his crest, a six winged serpent wrapped around a scythe. The other her mother's, a golden sun intersecting a silver moon. These were from their later life, and she read their joy of her and Michael's births. She learned a lot about the dynamics of the Old Council, the endless factions and politics as the War progressed. Her father's continual call for peace, and his pain over her mother leaving.

That was perhaps the most surprising. Lilith had left Heaven before the War finished, no one knew why. Which made her question if she had really been killed in the War or if that was just another lie.

One day she worked up the courage to ask Patrick about the selections she had been given. "All the journals you have given me are from the War onwards, but you haven't given me anything from before the War. What has been hidden from me that even you hesitate to show me?"

He studied her, hesitating. He had been increasingly impressed with her intelligence. He had questioned it initially but it had merely been suppressed by her family. Allowed to develop on its own accord it was thriving. He too had been keeping an eye on what she read, following both the journals and texts she read. Her selections were wide and careful. She had read her parents journals, Lucifer's, Michael and Gabriel's, various Arch Angels and a wide selection of Ascended and Lesser. She was keeping an objective view on it all.

He wondered at the risk he was taking "what have you been told about the Angels? How did the Elder originate?"

"The Elder Angels are the most powerful of all the Angels. Only they can form the Governing Council and it is the Council which is most affected by Human belief. Belief empowers us, but also binds us. Those who die and are accepted into Heaven become the Lesser Angels. They are weak but plentiful. The Ascended are Lesser who have been empowered by either being venerated as saints or prophets."

"Can anyone be an Angel? Can an Elder be born from non-Elder?"

"No" she said carefully "Only those accepted into

Heaven can become Angels and only the Elder can give rise to more Elder."

"What if I told you, you were wrong? That people can be made into Angels against their will. That not all Angels wish to remain that way and would do anything to remove all Angelic trace from themselves. That the Elder are the offspring of Gods and Demigods and even Demons."

"Where is your proof? The writings of deranged Angels?"

He hesitated before gesturing for her to follow. Confused she followed him in silence as he headed to the fountain. With a wave of his hand the middle stream parted to reveal a shadowy corridor behind. Once they were in the cave the only sound was of the water returning to its usual route.

She glanced around her surroundings as they crossed several corridors, heading ever downwards. Heaven was a place of eternal light; decorated in bright whites, cheerful pastels and shiny metallic. The hall was grey granite heavily veined with white, but it lacked any decoration. It had been smoothed and mounted with light globes.

She had never been here before and was curious as heavy gold doors started to appear. They passed dozens of them, turning into different corridors until finally they stopped before one. Its' simple bronze name plaque said *Brigid*.

"Behind these doors is all the proof you need. However once you have your proof you will not be able to unsee what you have seen. Beyond lies more questions than answers and you cannot turn back once you have seen beyond." He whispered, making her wings shiver.

She swallowed but was determined. She had to know the truth, so much of what she had been told was lies. This affected her and everything she had ever known. There were answers to her questions behind these doors. And besides it was an Arch Angels duty to always uncover the truth. She was meant to do this. "Show me"

He opened the doors, pushed her in then slammed them shut behind himself. He was scared, either of what he was showing her or because she was here. Curious she glanced around the room. It was a perfectly circular room, intricate patterns of blue and pink magic danced across the floor, all encircling an Angel who sat chained to the floor.

She was beautiful in the way of the Divine, that ethereal sense that permeated every pore of their skin. Her skin was pale compared to other Angels, with only the slightest of tanning, but it was slightly darker than her own skin. Six brown wings hung limp behind her. Her long brown hair covered most of her face, but two eyes glowing like emeralds shone through. She looked young but had the feel of someone old for some reason, an air of power as well as the wisdom and suffering in her eyes.

Her eyes were stunning, beautiful and haunted. They had seen so much, suffered so much. Hate blazed through them but overall resignation and defeat were the dominant emotions.

Who was she? And why was she chained? Was she one of the Fallen, captured in Heaven? A traitor against Gabriel, a supporter of Lucifer?

"This is the Goddess Brigid of the Celts. She was captured early in the War, but despite her absence her people adored her so much they would not revoke her when the church moved in. Despite all the persecution they endured they would not give her up. Facing defeat the Angels whispered in the cardinals' ears, Brigid was no Goddess but an Angel and her love benefitted the people. As their beliefs changed so in turn did she. She developed wings, her magic changed, all while she was chained up in here. She was one of the first casualties of the War, before the Gods even knew there was a war. She was imprisoned as a Goddess but was twisted into an Angel."

Sariel stared in horror at the Angel/Goddess before her. She had not realised the Gods were so vulnerable to Human belief. Were the Council as vulnerable to Human belief? She realised they were, it was why they were so desperate to remain in control of Humanity. If Brigid had once been a Goddess and was now an Elder Angel, where did the original Angels come from? Were they really the offspring of Gods and Demigods? Or possibly even Demons?

"How is this even possible?"

Brigid turned those remarkable emerald eyes to face Sariel, pinning her with that stare. "Because the Order has been changed. The Servants rose up against their Masters and took their place feeding on the prayers and beliefs of mortality. In turn they developed towards what they had overthrown, but sought to distance themselves from our decadence. Instead they created a lie in a vain attempt to protect themselves. They did not understand the powers they were messing with, nor do they yet comprehend the full complexity of the Gods' position.

As the world united under this lie and then continued to evolve beyond their control they became chained to Humanity even more than we were because they deny their true nature and have corrupted mortal perception.

They sealed away my brethren and persecuted our lineages, locking away magic from Humans. To make them more controllable, how foolish. Without magic they have forgotten what should have been remembered and feared. They have learned to stand on their own."

Sariel sagged to the floor. This was huge, this was unimaginable. Her brain felt like it had just been fried. Everything she had ever known was a lie. Everything about their history, their way of life, their justification for the way they lived. Clearly the Council was aware, or at least the Arch Angels were.

"But how? How did this happen? How is this possible?"

Brigid spoke again with great certainly and age "The world exists in its own right, born from the darkness of Chaos. All worlds are born from Chaos. Each planet has its own spirit or life essence. This is what allows life to flourish and for the planet itself to live. But not all planets have this essence.

The other children of Chaos are the Primordial Gods, Gods of incredible power beyond either your or my understanding. They are born from and return to Chaos or the Lifestream, we were never quite sure which. Or if they are different perspectives of the same entity.

These Primordial Gods allowed life to develop to a point that sentient beings evolved. They had many offspring, many of the Gods that formed the first of their pantheons. Many of which had survived until the War. The mortal's beliefs strengthened the younger Gods while many of the Primordial Gods returned to Chaos. The younger Gods flourished and multiplied as they became altered by mortal belief. They grew strong, they grew weak, ages turned and new Gods rose as old ones fell. Mother Goddesses returned to the Lifestream and were reborn stronger. This happened time and time again as mortals started to build their empires and as their empires flourished. Right up until the War.

As beliefs became longer lasting, Gods grew ever

stronger but they also grew greedy. Their civilisations flourished and grew, conquering weaker nations and absorbing their strength. The Gods continued to breed with each other and also their subjects, birthing Demigods of great power. An age of great magic existed which allowed for magical races to flourish and diversify. One of these magical races was the Angels. They are mostly descended from the bastards of Sky Gods, Zeus particularly is responsible for half the Angel bloodlines.

There was a balance between Man, God and Demons, you could say. Terrifying Monsters and beautiful Angels roamed the Earth providing balance, essential for nature. But everything changes and the Angels grew very powerful while we in our arrogance of our own power never noticed. We paid no attention to the work of Angels, after all they were our servants. We rarely entered Eden nor made any demands to see inside their domains. We were busy with our own power struggles, our empires swallowing others whole. This was the time that the Roman Empire was swallowing most of Europe as well as parts of Africa and the Middle East. In the East the Han Dynasty was swallowing up the Orient. We were very preoccupied with the major world events, and particularly the efforts of many ousted Gods to re-establish themselves.

We never thought for a moment that the Angels would enter our power struggles, let alone imagine they could even have a chance at winning. We were so sure of our absolute power over the world, so arrogant in our assumptions. Perhaps it is our own failings that allowed the Angels to succeed.

As it was the Angels started breeding and training Humans to their will. It is remarkable the patience that the Angels showed in breeding a Human line from their Nephilim offspring. These Humans had never felt our presence, so to them the Angels really were the voice of God. They had no idea that their God was a collection of their Arch Angels. These Humans were eventually released into the Cradle and from there they spread, developed and were enslaved. The Egyptians particularly swallowed up their numbers in droves. We all laughed at these strange Humans with their quaint new beliefs about an unknown God. We thought one of our own was having a joke.

We really should have paid more attention after Moses but we wrote him off as a particularly powerful sorcerer with a flair for theatrics. Soon enough the Roman Empire swallowed up their numbers, but they had diversified. Splintering into different religions and sects they spread and grew. The first time we realised there was a problem was when Jesus walked the Earth, he was no mortal Sorcerer. They were so sure that his death would solve this little problem, but they didn't realise that it was a spark that would ignite to bring down Heaven. Mohammed caused alarm once again but by then we realised there was a problem.

Islam had spread across the Cradle, the Roman Empire converted to Christianity and the scattered Jews clung desperately to their beliefs despite their continual persecution.

From there it was a downwards spiral. Islam spread to Africa and into India, Europe was swallowed whole by the Church even after the collapse of the Roman Empire. The spread of their religions removed the power of many of the Gods as the War started to take its toll. On the outer edges of what had been the Roman Empire, Gods and Goddesses were weeded out and captured. Many Gods escaped, especially those who lived in the Underworld. Some started afresh with other races, only to be hunted down later. Monsters and Divine beings started to decline, many species hunted to extinction. But many races were not eradicated despite the Angels best efforts.

Sects of Pagans still existed throughout Europe and they had the problem of their own people fighting each other. The Crusades started and we laughed from our prisons, excited for their power to come collapsing down. Instead it only strengthened their power, people fought and died for their beliefs, which only grew stronger. Once Europe stared conquering the world we realised there was no hope. Christianity ruled Europe completely and had spread to the Americas, Australia and its Pacific brethren. Islam had spread from the Cradle to most of Africa as well as forming battle lines in Pakistan, where it battled with the Hindu power base. It even reached as far as Indonesia. To this day the only Gods left fighting are the Hindu Gods, their powerbase being the only one strong enough to withstand the incursions of Islam and Christianity."

She laughed wearily "but the Angels had not seen the flaw in their plans, for how could anyone have predicted that Humans would have lost their faith. With the loss of magic miracles ceased, with the eradication of Monsters they stopped fearing, the world became theirs to control. Brilliant Humans started a revolution that is scouring away the Angels' powerbase. Science is Humanity helping itself and seizing control of its own future. Despite the Angels' attempts to stop and control it, science continues to evade religious control. Humans now live longer, healthier and happier lives, due entirely to their own merit, something the Angels' religions do not offer.

While the Angels are still converting the heathens at the edges of their powers and still struggling to wrestle some semblance of control in India, their ancient strongholds are crumbling. Science grows ever stronger in the modern world, and more and more Humans are rebelling against the Angels' decrees. They don't want to think about Sin, or the constraints it sets on their lives. In part it may be the mixing of the bloodlines, diluting the absolute control the Angels enjoyed, that makes them remember their true nature. It is probably more due to them finding scientific evidence about their true natures. They want to live their own way.

This may be the deathblow for Gods and Demons alike. Even the Angels cannot escape this new turn of events. It is too far-gone even for them. They are making various attempts, from migration to war, but it will not work. More is lost to science than gained from it."

Sariel stood up, saying nothing. She was too stunned, now she understood what Patrick had meant by there being no going back. Her mind had been blown, stretched forever beyond being able to resume her old existence. But it explained so much.

No wonder Gabriel and Michael were so desperate for a child, no wonder she was considered valuable despite being powerless. They had won the War, with a few exceptions, but now they were facing a new battle that they were losing. The Gods that were not dead were experiencing continual revivals as Paganism came back in vogue. Science as a whole was the dominant mind-set of Humanity, despite what beliefs they had. The Modern World and the future belonged to Humanity.

The Angels wouldn't die, not entirely, but in time they could end up like the Gods, clinging to the edges of society. Believed only as myth or by the devout few. They might win Humanity back, but she doubted it. Something huge would have to occur for Humanity to start believing in magic again. And it would have to be very widespread as well otherwise the Science Mind would discredit the evidence.

It was strange to think that Humans were unknowingly throwing off the yoke of their masters, the same masters that had over thrown their own masters.

Patrick gently led her out of the room, away from Brigid's paralysing stare. She was magic incarnate from the way she pinned you with those glowing eyes, to the compulsion on her voice. But Sariel knew that every word Brigid had spoken had been true, there had been passion and resignation when she spoke. There was loss in her eyes when she had spoken of the old times, fond memories temporarily easing the pain.

She didn't see the vicious and triumphant smile Brigid flashed at Patrick or the nod he gave in return as he escorted her out. Things had been set in motion, but it was yet to be seen what would occur.

As for Sariel she returned to the Archives and main Library, dusting away in a haze. For weeks she was absent minded, turning over and over everything she had been told. All of Gabriel's cronies reported that she was efficient as ever in her continual cleaning of the library but was very distracted. She had initially been cheerful and chatty but was now withdrawn and vague.

Patrick and Mary were concerned for her, as too were Gabriel and Michael finally. They were worried about her change in behaviour, for different reasons.

She might have been absentminded to everyone else, but her mind was ablaze with hunger and passion. She was throwing herself into her research, unbeknownst to everyone. She was smuggling in and out journals, scrolls and tablets. She poured through journals of Angels, Nymphs and Gods, devouring their tales and histories. Trying to piece together a semblance of the truth.

She was shocked at the decadence and debauchery that had existed before the Angels; orgies, experiments, switching lovers, political intrigue, the list went on and on. The Gods had been so sure of their own power, demanding every little whim and expecting it to be met. Lovers in their bed, cities to be razed, empires to be destroyed, curses on those who had slighted them. Everything was a game to them, with no real consequences.

The Angels initially seemed like a better alternative, they did not condone the lifestyle of the Gods. And yet many happily did. Many Angels had seduced hapless mortals, bringing about more of their numbers and also countless Nephilim. It had gotten to the point the Arch Angels had banned relations between Angels and mortals to deal with the uncontrollable Nephilim.

The edited histories she read were flowery and full of holes. There were gaps that didn't add up, gaps that were filled in by either journals or Brigid. Brigid was quickly becoming her most valuable resource about the Angels and Gods.

Her knowledge of before the War dazzled her with how the world had been, but also her complete acceptance of how the Gods had lived.

Brigid was bitter and angry but she was resigned to her imprisonment. She seemed to enjoy Sariel's company, which may have only been because she could relive the past she missed so much. But either way Sariel found her utterly fascinating. She had lived before the War, had been captured and drained over and over for her powers to empower the Arch Angels. She had seen the world she had known disappear and been transformed into the enemy she hated. She had tales of all mortals, and their transition from cave dwellers into empire builders. Her knowledge of the world after her capture was much less accurate, her understanding pieced together from arrogant Angels drivelling their tales.

There were many gaps in the journals, someone at least had made some attempt to cull them. Though she had found many a secret nook and cranny containing the most startling journal. She read about experiments and breeding programs, of Gods living mortal lives to escape the endless intrigue of Heaven.

She also read about the change in the Angels after Gabriel and Michael had come to power. The slaughter of traitors, as well as the eradication of any undesirables. Which had then extended to mortals- the Angels had hunted many species to extinction, forced many races into hiding, culled off Humanity's magical abilities and tried to eradicate its more promiscuous behaviour and sexualities.

She had hoped initially to try and adjust the Council's perceptions but now that seemed useless. In their eyes she was just a girl who had never known about any of their atrocities.

But what was there for her to do? She had expectations from the other Arch Angels and the council and she felt sure that Brigid was grooming her to a certain mind-set. She also felt sure that Patrick, Mary and John were also grooming her to a certain mind-set. She really wanted to talk to somebody about it all but she had no one. She never got to visit the Citadel to make friends and there was no one else anywhere near her own age in the palace. She was alone and friendless as she had been for all her life.

Would it ever change?

Chapter 5

It had been several months since she had first seen Brigid but she had continued to meet with her, as well as Patrick and Mary. Her behaviour had caused alarm not only for Michael but also for the rest of the Council. She had been taken off her humility cleaning in the hopes that that would correct her behaviour. But the Sariel everyone had known seemed lost. Instead was a vacant girl who did exactly as she was told but didn't seem to be inside any more.

While Gabriel was both pleased and concerned by these turn of events the other Arch Angels were getting really concerned. With the exception of Azrael who had not been in Heaven for several months. It was Uriel most of all who was concerned about her, having always had a soft spot for her.

It was his concern that had caused him to seek out special Council permission to escort Sariel into the Citadel. Which was why this morning he was knocking on Sariel's door once Michael and Gabriel had gone to the Surface to deal with a civil war, to sow the seeds of religious control.

Sariel answered the door, her sleepy eyes acknowledging him. She shuffled backwards to allow him in. He was surprised to find her room cluttered with various books, scrolls and tablets. A casual glance told him she was reading up on everything from architecture to warfare to weather patterns.

"Your tastes seem rather eclectic Sariel"

"My interests vary depending on what I'm reading." She had recently been reading journals by the numerous servants of Athena, Sekhmet, Odin and Anu. It was fascinating reading their collective views on similar events. Most of their servants had been content with their place and treatment. Both Lucifer and Michael had served under both Athena and Sekhmet at the same time. They had once been comrades.

"How can I help you Uriel?"

"I'm here because the Council has granted you permission to be escorted around the Citadel today." She squealed in delight. He was surprised by the absolute shock and wonder that flashed across her face. Was it really so rare for her to get to leave the palace?

She dashed away, the sounds of running water, splashing, muttering, clattering and flapping echoing back to where he waited. He sat down next to a pile of books, curiously looking across them. She did seem to have very eclectic taste, piles seemed randomly chosen; there was a pile made up of books on blood, fermentation, insanity and ancient Egyptian wars. Another pile was made up of books about spiders, weaving, engineering, warfare, Athenian Naval tactics, swords and olives. The one on his other side had books about ravens, horses, warfare and storms.

There was an even weirder collection on her coffee table. Books and scrolls about death, diseases and reaping. There were a lot of books, scrolls and especially tablets about magic. Littering across the whole thing were texts about Angels.

His attention was drawn to a thin red book poking out from under some scrolls. Intrigued he pulled out the journal to see who she was reading about. The crest was burned on, a flaming sword beneath a halo. She was reading one of Michael's more recent journals thankfully. He should mention it to Michael.

He looked up as she walked in. She was a vision. Ornate white over robes, decorated with gold, bronze and metallic pink. She looked every inch the Arch Angel, when in Heaven. Her black wings caught the reflections well, making them shine with a pink iridescence. It was a pity she had no access to her magic, her innate beauty would match Gabriel's.

He felt suddenly underdressed in his armour, being so used to the other Arch Angels living in their armour. Well except Azrael but he always wore his long black shroud. Gabriel and Ariel were really the only ones to wear anything other than their armour and then they tended to look imperial.

Sariel simply looked delicate and beautiful.

He wondered how the Citadel would respond to her. The powerless Arch Angel looking neither soldierly nor imperial.

They stopped underneath the grand statues guarding the palace. They were of two Elder Angels, male and female. Surprisingly they didn't look like any of the Arch Angels, but were rather generic.

She had recently read that before them had stood statues of Oranis and Nut, both had claimed to have built Heaven and had left the statues as a reminder. Both Primordials had long since returned to Chaos. She wondered how either would feel to see what they had created ruled by Angels.

From where they stood she could see straight down the Skybridge that connected the ancient palace to the main square of Citadel. She could see the bridge disappearing into the tall cluster of towers that dominated the heart of the Citadel, and the sprawling manors beyond.

All had been constructions of the Gods.

The Palace which now housed the Arch Angels, the Elder Angels and their servants had originally been used only as a meeting place. It was where the Gods had chosen to meet and play their game of empires. It had been neutral territory, belonging to none and everyone. It was why it was so stunning, generations of Gods and other Divine had added to it with constructions, decorations and artwork. It was the one place they worked together cohesively.

Despite the Palace being large enough to house all the Gods, they had all preferred living in their own manors. Most of which were within the Citadel but there were others scattered across the various islands that made up Heaven. Most had lived in the Citadel, it was the only city in Heaven.

Not all the Gods had lived in Heaven though. Most of the Mother Goddesses tended to live on the Surface in their garden; Eden, Avalon, Tír na nóg or Arcadia, to name a few. They preferred living on the Surface or floating in spirit form in the Lifestream. For they needed the connection to life to be nourished and give back to it. They had a special relationship with the environment.

Then there were the Underworld Gods, who lived in their ethereal domains. Some by choice, some by punishment. Usually most had been shunned by the Divine that lived in Heaven. Ironically enough they had escaped the Purge of Heaven, they might be trapped in the Underworld but they were presumably still alive.

As Uriel led her out onto the Skybridge she felt a sense of loss and freedom. Loss at what Heaven must have been like when the Gods ruled and all the Divine lived in relative harmony. Many things had been mentioned in the journals in passing, she had had to piece together what they must have looked like.

But more than anything she was feeling delight at being allowed into the Citadel. The Skybridge she had always loved for its incredible beauty. It was a long gentle slope that connected the Citadel to the palace, cutting straight through a wide stretch of sky. It was made of long spans of arches, floating on nothing. It was wide enough for several elephants to walk abreast along, apparently how it had been designed. It looked as delicate as spun glass and porcelain but was as strong as any other building.

The final touch as they walked down it was the streams of cloud ripping themselves against it. She laughed in delight as they walked through a patch of cloud.

She turned her head about, this way and that. Watching Angels flying away from the Citadel and walking back up the Skybridge. Due to some ancient magic no one could approach the palace except via the Skybridge. You could leave anyway you wanted.

They passed numerous Lesser Angels and Ascended but there were only a smattering of Elder. All nodded respectfully at Uriel, was it just her or was there fear in their eyes? When they saw her on the other hand their faces lit up and she smiled back warmly.

Her breath hitched in excitement as she stepped onto the solid pavers of the Citadel. The base of the Skybridge had always been a favourite of hers. It was hectically busy with all the traffic heading towards the palace, threading through the crowds of the Citadel Square. Angels swirled about their business, coming and going, through the marketplace.

The Lesser didn't need to eat but the Ascended and Elder did, and there were plenty of Ascended these days. She wondered if the increasing numbers were in any way related to the talks about the Apocalypse. The air was rich with the perfumes of exotic foods and the not so pleasant smells of animals. It was so different from the palace. She loved it.

Uriel led her through the market, along its many streets, under spiralling arches, through the shadows of towers and mansions. Along wide boulevards that were lined with the manors of forgotten Gods. The Citadel was beautiful in its diversity. The Palace was amazing but had a tendency to be white or gold. The Citadel on the other hand was decorated in the colours of the sky- azure blues, sunset oranges and pinks, sunrise reds and yellows, soft indigos and violets and even the occasional splash of rainbow green. There were even places dedicated to the night and storms- muted whites and greys, bruised blacks, blues and purple, deep dark blues and indigos that blended into black with sparkling lights. It was stunning, and complimented by the variety of plants, entwining themselves around the buildings.

"These are where the Gods once lived. You can tell which region of the Earth they came from based on the architecture. This boulevard encircles the whole of the Citadel, beyond these manors and palaces is the edge of the island.

"What happens if you fall off?"

"You plummet to the Surface far, far below. Of course this was never a concern for the Gods or for us Angels. However there was a time Gods found it amusing to push mortals off of the Citadel."

"That's horrible."

"Indeed, but it was one of the Gods lesser crimes."

"Does anyone live in the manors or are they completely abandoned?"

"Completely abandoned. No one wants to live in them. There is the palace and the apartment towers near the Skybridge."

It seemed like such a waste. The buildings though showing signs of battle and ruin were still beautiful.

There was one manor that particularly caught her eye. It was huge, a sprawling frame that dominated the street and the skyline. Much of it was hidden behind lush gardens, but it was its sheer size and unique beauty that struck her strange. Was it a statement? Why did a God need a manor so big? It was pretty much a palace in itself.

It was also black, jet black. The building was entirely dark, even the silver or gold window frames held dark windows. The roof was made of black tiles and the door looked to be ebony. Even some of the trees were black.

"This house once belonged to Hera. She was locked up by her husband to control her rage."

"How barbaric"

"It was justified. Zeus was a philanderer and his own manor was huge to hold his many children and their mothers. Hera was a loyal and a jealous wife. She was the Queen of Heaven, with all the powers connected to that, and his infidelities drew her into a monstrous rage. She slaughtered all his living children and lovers then turned her attention to his palace while he was on the Surface mourning the loss of his mortal families. Little did he know that she was annihilating all trace of them from ever existing.

His palace had been burned to the ground, every city that had housed a lover or child had been bombarded with meteors, lightning, floods and Monsters. Her rage was unlimited, her wrath ferocious and undeniable. All the other Gods would have no part in it. They all sat back to let Zeus deal with his mistake.

In the end he chained her to her own manor, with the strongest spells he could find, forged into the strongest chains ever wrought.

She was still chained in her manor when the War broke out."

"What happened to her?"

"She is still chained in there. She is of no harm to anyone. She is bound and her powerbase of followers is long gone. All she had left are a few priestesses that light the Olympic Flame. She is of no threat to us, she lives there alone to atone for her sins."

"She must be terribly lonely."

"It is a fitting punishment. The Gods were cruel."

She couldn't help but feeling sorry for Hera. She knew how loneliness felt. The Gods may have been cruel but the Angels were the fitting heirs of that cruelty. What had she ever done to be all but a prisoner in the Governing Palace?

He continued to lead her along empty boulevards of abandoned manors. Some were sprawling palaces, others were smaller houses belonging to Demigods or Gods who spent more time on the Surface. She saw into forgotten cultures and beliefs.

She learned that Heaven had a lot of scars from the War, many of which had not healed. Cracks divided some of the boulevards, ruins of once grand manors teetered on the edge of gaping holes. Even parts of the city centre showed damage that had not been repaired.

She saw monuments to those lost during the War and he explained them as best he could. Nowhere did she see either of her parents' names. She even saw statues of Humans, though they did little to sate her curiosity.

She was having a lovely day when they were suddenly surrounded by a full contingent of guards. And not just any guards but Michael's personal guard.

"What is the meaning of this? How dare you raise a weapon at an Arch Angel." He roared. People stopped to stare. Sariel bet this was the most excitement that had happened in ages for them. The Cherubim had not been sent to the Citadel to bring in someone in living memory.

"Sorry my Lord but the orders are from the Council and Arch Angels. Lady Sariel must return to the palace immediately."

He was furious, he looked like he was about to strike Peter, which was not a good thing for anyone. Peter was one of the most powerful Ascended in Heaven, magically and politically. He was one of Michael's favourites, Captain of the Cherubim and led his men into battle in Michael's absence. She didn't want things made difficult for either Uriel or Peter.

"I will comply with the Council's request." She had no choice anyway, it was this or be dragged back.

Peter nodded to her respectfully before his men fell in around them for their walk back to the palace. Her heart sank with every step, spoiling her joy of the day. She didn't even enjoy walking back across the Skybridge, where they had absolute right of way. All other Angels quickly scrambled out of their way.

They were escorted right into the Council Chambers. All of the Council members were attending, as were all the other Arch Angels- even Azrael. This would be no ordinary meeting.

Michael and Gabriel sat on their high thrones, their eyes slitted in disdain. Sitting below them in their own thrones, sat a confused looking Raphael, a resigned looking Azrael and a smirking Ariel. But then she was always smirking.

Uriel spoke first, he was really annoyed "What is the meaning of this? This morning the Council ordained Sariel's trip into the Citadel as a means to snap her out of her current state. She has spent the whole day learning about her own culture which she is shockingly ignorant about."

"The Council has changed its decision Arch Angel

Uriel and you will comply with the majority. Sariel is not to leave the palace under any conditions. She is very academically minded, the library will provide her all the knowledge she needs about her culture without the stress visiting the Citadel induces in her." Gabriel's imperial tone brokered no argument."

But Uriel pressed on "Stressed? Sariel was delighted in the Citadel. She mingled with the people, and showed a remarkable level of concern for all the Angels. She has displayed a mature and conscientious mind that should be nourished not stifled. She is an Arch Angel and should be seen by the people. What kind of Arch Angel is confined to the Palace?"

Sariel was still trying to grasp what they meant about her condition and stress when she heard him say that. She along with everyone else in the room took a sharp intake of breath. Gabriel was not one to be spoken to that way, unless you wanted to be all but banished.

But it was Michael that spoke while her eyes bored into Uriel. Sariel was surprised he didn't spontaneously combust under that glare. "The Council's decision is final. You have been over-ruled. Sariel's health is of the utmost, we cannot waste her potential by having her distressed in such a manner. She will not leave the palace without my permission. I am her Guardian and the Council agrees with me. We cannot risk her."

His shoulders had slumped but he wasn't quite done "What does she need a guardian for? She's 1800 years old, you're only 700 years older than her. You were younger than her when you served in the Armies of the Gods, when you fought to overthrow them. The world is different, she is at no risk."

"Maybe if you thought with your head instead of your cock you might see what the rest of the Council sees Uriel. Sariel is a fragile young girl in dire need of protection. She has so much potential, we cannot risk her!" Her scathing yell tore the last defence he had. He had nothing else to say in her defence, but it was the most anyone had ever said.

She looked up at them all, studying each of the Council members. Old fools that had survived the War but were too scared to live. Instead they hid behind the Arch Angels' shadows. They had all condemned her to a life of imprisonment, it didn't matter that it was in a palace. It was still only an ornate prison. It was so unfair of them to lock her up like this.

"If I may speak?" She asked.

"Denied! Escort her to her rooms, the Council has more important matters to attend to."

Peter and his crew instantly fell instep around her, ready to escort her away when Azrael stood up, instantly drawing all eyes to him "I will escort her."

No one argued as he descended from the steps and approached her. He didn't seem to walk so much as glide, and soundlessly. People shied away from him or averted their gaze. She saw flashes of pity as he escorted her out of the room.

After the doors boomed shut behind them the only sound was her sandals hitting the floor as she walked. Despite him wearing a long black cowl there was no noise, no swishing, no footsteps. Nothing.

They walked in silence, it continued to draw out until Sariel had to speak "Uncle why do so many people seem scared of you?"

"Because they are scared of me."

When he didn't add any more she asked "But why are they scared of you?"

His gaze flicked towards her then back to straight ahead "Even Immortals are scared of Death. Mortals have always feared it, though there are some who embrace it.

Immortals may not be susceptible to the ravages of old age or disease but we are not endless. Divine can kill Divine.

Death is always feared in some way, or viewed with suspicion. Those who deal with it are feared as well."

"But Michael and I are Angels of Death too, why do they not shy away from us?"

"Michael does not embrace his power, it is but one of his gifts he uses as he needs them. He is the Flaming Warrior, one of the heroes of the War. He rarely reaps or guides the dead on their way. As for you Sariel you have been stripped of your potential. Denied your birth right and your right to be an adult."

What did he mean by that? Stripped of her potential did not sound like being born with very little powers. Had something happened to her as child?

"Of the Elder Angels only your father understood what it was like to be feared for being who you are. But he was different from me, he thrived and challenged himself. He became feared for other reasons than being a son of Death."

A son of Death? That sound familiar and yet the Angels never said it. It seemed an odd turn of phrase, almost like he hadn't used it in a long time. Was it a term the Gods had used? Wait her father had been feared? For things other than being an Angel of Death. What had he done?

"What reasons were those?"

He said nothing seeming to ignore her question. She knew better than to press him, he would say what he wanted to only when he wanted to. Not even Gabriel or Michael pressed him, nor did the Council. He was the most autonomous of all the Angel Factions. He dealt with death, he had his own Angels to assist and that was that.

Now that she thought on it perhaps fear had allowed him his independence.

He surprised her however once they were back at her rooms "There were many reasons why Samael was feared. His powers rivalled the Gods, he was a Son of Death, he had a cunning intelligence, was a brilliant general, a friend to many Monsters and Demons, mortals and immortals alike revered him, feared him, wanted him, wanted to be him. He was a law into himself, but he met his match in your mother."

"They were both feared?" why had she never been told any of this before?

"Yes they both were, still are. Even mortals still fear and revere them. And they had two powerful Angelic Children, each with a unique combination of their powers. Michael and Gabriel are powerful Angels in their own right, but their powers exceed that granted to them by faith."

He snatched her hand into his own, his were glowing black but what surprised her more was that hers had started to glow brown, no not just brown, there was a whole kaleidoscope of colours, mixing and flaring.

"Just as I thought, your powers are not miniscule at all. Who ever heard of a powerless Divine, and with your parents? The sins of our family only continue to grow, but against an innocent..." he trailed off lost in some memory.

He snapped back instantly, his eyes turning black "Once I leave this room it will be magically locked. There is however an escape through the secret tunnels. You need to escape Sariel, run away as fast as you can."

She stared at him as he left, too stunned to react. By the time she jerked forward after him, her door was covered in a black shield. She walked out onto the balcony, sure enough she could see a black tinge to the air, but there was also the blue and pink of other Angels. She had been sealed in by the whole Council.

She ran to her closet, closing the doors behind her. She pushed through her clothes, using her still glowing hand to find the catch to the panel.

It slid open to reveal the unblocked passage behind. She smiled in satisfaction before running down the corridor.

Chapter 6

Sariel was glad she had walked these corridors so often the past several months. Her feet automatically took her to Brigid's prison. She was deeply troubled by everything that had happened today on top of everything she had learnt over the last few months. What was really going on in Heaven?

She rushed into the prison, startling Brigid enough that she jumped.

"Are there other prisons behind all these doors? Filled with Gods like you?"

"Not like me, but weakened nevertheless. We are kept in a state of permanent weakness. Drained of our powers to supplement the powers of that wretched council. We are sustained enough to keep us alive and useful, but kept in a state of starvation."

"What would you do if you were free?"

Brigid laughed "an impossible dream. I will never be free, the Angels are too strong. But if I were free I would go back to my beloved Islands. It has been so long, it needs me. The land cries out for me, it is sick. The Fae they call for me. It is not well" a tear rolled down her cheek.

Sariel walked a little closer, what she was about to do would probably condemn her and she doubted Azrael had intended for her to do this. But he had told her to run and Brigid was her only ticket to the Surface.

The room filled with a strange sizzling, they could both taste the lightning in the air and saw the pink flares and blue sparks flickering between them.

"What's happening?" She hadn't expected any resistance spells, she didn't know how to counteract them. She had thought the touch of an Arch Angel would have been enough.

Brigid's eyes opened in surprise before slitting in speculation "So the Council even binds its own. You Sariel have had your powers bound and siphoned away."

"What?"

"This reaction only happens when two containment spells come into contact. It is one of the reasons we have all been contained in our separate prisons. Too much contact and they both react with each other."

"I have powers that have been kept from me" She slumped to the floor "But who would do such a thing? And why?" she whispered to herself.

"It is an Arch Angel spell, like the one that contains me."

Sariel's head snapped towards her, Brigid saw her assessing her. But she spoke the truth.

Sariel's mind was busy sorting through all the stray bits of information she had picked up over the last few months. Both Azrael and Brigid had said she had been cut off from her powers. She had seen her powers because of both of them. Suddenly she remembered Gabriel and Michael's conversation. She was the spell they had been worried about. This was why she had never been allowed to the Surface, why she had been confined to the Palace. Her life of imprisonment had been so that Gabriel and Michael could continue to steal her powers.

They had denied her, her birthright. So that they could have extra powers, so that she could not contest them. Because of them she had lived a life of isolation and she had accepted it. They had been protecting her from her own vulnerability, a vulnerability that they had brought upon her. It was all their fault. How could they have done this to her? She hated them! They would pay.

With a sudden scream that made Brigid jump Sariel lunged forward, sparks and lightning flaring everywhere. For a moment Brigid thought she was planning to attack her, but she lunged for the golden chains. Sariel screamed in agony and frustration, her anger driving her forward as the two spells reacted, trying to drive them apart.

Brigid started screaming as soon as Sariel clamped down on the chains, magic racing up and down both of them, burning them. The room was ablaze with pink and blue magic reacting violently. The chains flared intensely before they exploded. Everything disappeared in a blaze of bright light.

Brigid's eyes fluttered open. Her prison was dark, it was never dark. There was someone else in the room, she could hear their breathing. Without thinking she called in a light, a reflex that hadn't died despite centuries of imprisonment. She stared in surprise at the faint glow of her hands. It was faint, very faint, barely enough to see beyond herself but it was more magic that she had used in centuries. It also showed her a dark shape slumped against the door.

Hesitantly and shakily she stood up, stretching out limbs long unused. For once she was thankful of the Angel's conversion of her, because she was a powerful Saint she had weathered much of her imprisonment. And now she could feel that magic returning to her and giving her strength to move. She still had her natural Mother Goddess powers but they would be far slower in returning to her. But she had all her own knowledge.

She staggered over to the door to discover that it was Sariel slumped against the door. Using her divine strength she pulled Sariel aside and opened up the door.

The air beyond was stale but fresher than what she had breathed in a long time.

She was free. After all these years she was actually free.

The corridor was darkened beyond her prison door. The glow she had remembered was gone. Had it been changed since her imprisonment?

She started to close the door when her gaze fell back on Sariel. She should leave her here. She was after all not only an Elder but also an Arch Angel. But she had freed her of her own volition. And she had much to loath the other Angels for, most of all her own brother and sister-in-law. An Arch Angel who had been imprisoned and stripped of her power would certainly be dangerous to the other Arch Angels. She could be useful in freeing other Gods and Goddesses.

Against her better judgement Brigid laid her hands on her and gave her a light healing. It wasn't much with her powers so weakened but it was enough. She hoisted the girl up, glad for her inhuman strength.

At the very least Sariel would be free from the clutches of her family. She owed her that much for freeing her. If Sariel was found in Brigid's prison she would be imprisoned herself. She couldn't leave the poor young girl to that.

She ran through the darkened corridors, which quickly turned into the lit corridors she remembered. She ran through corridors she remembered from earlier days, not much had changed except some of the decorations. Thankfully she came across no one, carrying an unconscious Sariel would have been difficult to explain. Her own brown wings would have been impossible to explain.

Within very little time she had jumped off a balcony and was soaring towards the Citadel, long before anyone even realised she or Sariel were gone.

Michael knocked on his sister's door fully expecting her to start screaming at him. They had done a horrible thing to her, and for what? He had been surprised with how well she had taken the Council's edict, well really his and Gabriel's. The Council were their fearful puppets. The Council did not have the power to rival Gabriel alone, let alone the full force of the Arch Angels. Unfortunately for the Council the Arch Angels tended to get along.

It was a cruel predicament for Sariel but they could hardly let her powers go to waste, it was for the greater good. They could use her powers effectively, she would take centuries to learn to control them. Especially considering she was surprisingly strong. In time once the Apocalypse had been released again it could be made to look like Sariel had suddenly broken some seal on herself. No one would be any wiser, least of all Sariel.

The world would be back under their control, Humanity cleansed and Sariel could get the life she craved and so rightly deserved.

He entered her room when he heard no sound. Was she sleeping? Perhaps her day of excitement had exhausted her. Or perhaps she was too angry to bother responding. He would hate to find her crying into her pillow. She wasn't in her receiving rooms, nor was she crying or sleeping in her bedroom. Confused he looked through all of her rooms, growing more and more uneasy. He checked in her closet, her bathroom, her balcony. The containment spell was shining lightly, it had not been broken.

Finally he started yelling for her, but there was no answer. Sariel wasn't in her rooms.

He contacted Gabriel with a thought *Gabriel*

What is it? she sounded irritable.

Sariel isn't in her rooms. She's missing.

What? her voice thundered in his head. She was going to be furious, no one would be safe from her anger tonight. *how is this possible? She has no magic to aid her, she can't break the containment spells.*

The spells are still intact. But there is no trace of her.

Inform the guards and the Council. We need to find her. I will join your search once I have dealt with this disturbance.

Disturbance? What disturbance?

Apparently the prison corridors are darker than usual. Apparently it is important enough to need my assistance. He could imagine her rolling her eyes as she spoke. *I will join you soon*

Brigid landed lightly in the shadows of the Divine Boulevard, thankfully the sky was darker than usual, heavy rain clouds hugging the Citadel and palace. It seemed the Fates were working in her favour, she wondered what had happened to them.

She set Sariel down as she tried to get her bearings. It had been so long since she had been in the Citadel, and it looked very different in ruin. She had one chance to escape Heaven, but it all counted on her finding her.

"Thank you for bringing me"

She turned around to see Sariel scrambling up.

"I could hardly leave you after freeing me. I know Angel cruelty, you would not survive it Sariel. Surprisingly for a Divine you are innocent."

She started crying. Her life had fallen apart in the spate of a day. She had been condemned by the Council to imprisonment, her uncle had told her to run, she had found out her own brother and his wife had stripped her of her power and to top it all off she had freed a Goddess. She could never return, she had committed high treason.

Around them thunder boomed and the rain started to pour.

Great just great Brigid thought to herself, she had a crying girl to deal with and it had started to rain. Just her luck, it rarely rained in Heaven, but it least it was gloomy.

"There, there Sariel we'll get out of Heaven and you'll be free. You'll finally get to see the Surface." She awkwardly patted the girl on her shoulders. She had never seen an Angel cry, let alone felt the need to comfort one. They had been servants and then enemies. "Come Sariel we need to keep moving otherwise we will be caught."

"Why are we in the Citadel? Shouldn't we have just teleported to the Surface?"

"Neither of us have the power to teleport at this time and I presume you've never been shown how to teleport" She shook her head. "That leaves us with the use of the Portals, naturally we can't use the one here in the Citadel, that leaves one of the others. Unfortunately they have all fallen into disrepair and the only person who can activate them is the Queen of Heaven. Fortunately for us she is imprisoned in her own house. But it has been so long since I walked the Citadel that I can't remember where her house is."

Sariel perked up, wiping away strands of hair plastering her face "are you talking about Hera?"

Brigid's head snapped around "Yes"

"Her house is two streets away."

Brigid jumped into the air, Sariel following and they very quickly located Hera's house. As they landed on one of the balconies Brigid whistled in approval. Hera was no fool, Zeus might have imprisoned her in her mansion but she had turned it into a palace. The bigger her domain was, the more she could roam.

They walked out of the storm into the silent halls of Hera's palace. As Brigid had expected it was tastefully decorated, but no longer was it the soft pastels it had once been but now was at the darker end of the spectrum. She had heard it once said that it was to reflect her mood after her imprisonment. It was a hauntingly beautiful palace, the black was mixed in with indigo, violet, blue and green. The walls reminded them both of the iridescence of a raven's wing. Ebony tables and stands decorated the sides of the halls, both decorated with white and black marble statues and sculptures. White rugs ran the length of the hallways and there were occasional paintings framed in gold or silver.

The palace was dead silent.

Sariel followed Brigid as she walked along the hallways until they came out into a foyer. It was as tastefully decorated as the hallways. Brigid stopped and looked around, unsure where to go. She had only been in Hera's palace a couple of times. Hera was the Queen of Heaven, while she had been a Goddess from a forgettable set of islands. It was funny that those same islands had at one stage been the biggest and most powerful empire the world had seen to date. It killed her that she hadn't been part of it. So much of Britain's history she had been excluded from. How she wanted to see how it was faring. She was impatient to feel the land's embrace once again, and to restart building her domain.

"Hera" she called out, sending it out on a mental thread as well.

There was a clinking noise that they both turned towards. They followed where the noise had come down the stairs of the foyer. She called again and once again the clinking noise responded. They followed the noise through long corridors and staircases, moving through many wings until they found an internal amphitheatre. It was made entirely of black marble, even the ceiling above. Flecks of metal and diamond set in the marble reflected the soft light. The high arches on the stage hid something from sight, but the soft glows showed something was down there.

Brigid called out again putting her hand on Sariel's shoulder as she started walking down the steps "We do not know what is down there."

"Whatever it is, is suffering. We need to help it."

Brigid fell in step behind Sariel as she descended the stairs, her senses alert for Scorpio or Argus. Both of them had scared her half to death, and they weren't the only pets Hera had kept.

Sariel walked slowly down the amphitheatre steps, her eyes casting about cautiously but always being drawn back to the glowing and slight noises coming from the stage. As she got closer she noticed an unpleasant smell she had never come across before. "What is that awful smell?"

"Decay" she replied with confusion.

"Decay? But nothing rots in Heaven."

"No it doesn't" Things that died automatically broke apart into their base compounds, unless they were preserved in the case of books or leather armour. To smell decay deeply troubled her, and she was worried about what they would find.

The closer they got the stronger the smell got, until they both wanted to gag. They jumped up onto the stage and what they saw made them want to vomit.

A pale skinned woman lay chained to the floor, bound at her ankles, wrists, her major joints and her neck. The metal was dug into angry red flesh blistering around sickly grey skin. She was an absolute mess, covered in dried blood, horrific scars, filth and muck. She was covered in all manner of burns. Brands, crucibles and jars of sizzling acid a testament to how she had been burnt. Someone had hacked into her hip then poured boiling metal into it, the metallic clump clung to the festering mess. Someone had carved sigils and symbols of containment, malady and death into her skin, then rubbed them with filth. Their festering lines, dark and angry among otherwise pale and grey skin. To top it off she was attached to a strange machine neither of them had ever seen before by thin clear tubes. Large vials of fluid sat atop the machine and every time it beeped and whirled a small amount of the fluid trickled down the tubes into her veins.

"This is horrible. This is beyond disgusting." Sariel exclaimed as she fell onto her knees beside Hera. She gently started pulling out the tubes. She gave the metal clump a gentle tug, but it wouldn't come out, either it was stuck in the flesh or it had cooled onto the bone. She placed her hand above Hera's heart and hoped for the best. She knew she had powers and could access them, she didn't have a clue what she was doing but hoped Hera's body would use the power.

Her hands started glowing a soft green, then it started flowing from her hands into Hera's body.

Brigid stood horrified at the mess that was the Queen of Heaven. No wonder the Angels had the full run of Heaven, its Queen didn't have a hope of controlling it. Who would do such a thing to another living person? She understood why it had been done. With Hera powerless, she could be drained and her powers used to control Heaven. That explained why it was never dark since the Angels had seized control.

But it was the sheer brutality of it that had shocked her, it was pure sadistic torture in its purest form. Whoever had done this had taken a perverse pride in their work. The sigils had been carved with delicate care, the diseases injected into her had been sourced from all over the world. Immortal beings might be immortal to disease and aging but this amount of torture, continuously took its toll. Even a strong Goddess could not withstand this abuse and remain healthy. She had never seen a sick Divine, not even the Angels or Nymphs had suffered from sickness.

Hera was even more disadvantaged, with so few believers left she had nowhere near the power she had once enjoyed. But she was still frighteningly powerful.

Brigid watched in fascination as Sariel healed her. What was most surprising was that it wasn't some botched job. Without any prior experience, and only having been freed to use her powers about an hour ago, she was showing incredible aptitude.

The green magic flowed through Hera's body, first of all searing along the sigils, burning them out of existence. Sizzling and soft thunder filled the amphitheatre as her magic overwhelmed and broke the spells. Once the symbols were broken her magic flowed throughout Hera easily, flowing through her blood vessels, searing out the contamination. It pooled into the countless cuts and burns, healing the devastated skin and pushing out pus and filth. There was a metallic ring as the metal clump hit the floor. The green glow filled Hera, chasing away the grey tinge to her skin, her cuts and burns turning into faint silver scars that were quickly disappearing on their own accord.

Her violet eyes flicked open, pinning Sariel with that legendary gaze, then slowly she raised her hand to cup Sariel's face. Her eyes flicked to Brigid and she was relieved to see the flicker of recognition.

"Brigid it has been far too long."

"It has Hera, the Angel's reign has not been kind to

us."

Hera's mouth twisted in disgust "except this one" her eyes flicked back to Sariel "this one is different. Unique."

"She has compassion. And she was also held prisoner by the Arch Angels and Council."

"But she is clearly a pure blooded Angel. Why would they do such a thing to one of their own?"

"It was my brother and his wife. They did it to steal my powers from me, so that they could use it for themselves. They kept me hidden away so that the spells couldn't break. I was but a source of power to them." A tear slid down her face as she realised that was all she had been to them."

"They did not wish for her to make her mark on the world, as she surely would have. I heard Uriel saying once that she could lead them to a new era if she were set free on the Surface. But Michael and Gabriel refused. Gabriel clearly saw the threat to her own power."

"Then it would be most fitting that we set her free to make her mark, with no Angelic control." Hera's smile was chillingly malicious. "I gather neither of you can teleport to the Surface and so need a portal."

"The Angels have changed the nature of Heaven too much, Sariel doesn't know how and my powers are much too weak."

"I'm not strong enough to teleport but I think I can activate a portal." She stood up, her hair falling down in a shiny dark brown curtain. A simple dress grew across her skin and all the muck coating her flaked off. She once again looked like one of the living. She held out her hands to them both, the silver scars on them still fading away.

As soon as they both took hold, everything disappeared in a blaze of golden light.

Chapter 7

Gabriel was in a foul temper as she stalked through the prison corridors. She was personally going to hunt down the fool that had set her on this wild goose chase, string them up then condemn them to cleaning the sewage system of every Human city that took her fancy.

She shivered against her nature, there was magic lingering in the air. What moron had been practising magic down here?

She was about to turn around in disgust when she passed a darkened corridor. Her shield sprang up automatically as she raised her glowing hand to flood the hallway with light.

She walked slowly down the hallway, her senses alert for anything out of the ordinary. She was wondering if the light spells had just faded with age. It had happened before, few ever came down here and not regularly enough to notice when spells were fading. When the Gods had first been captured these halls had been walked often by the Elders, but with their dominance the need to drain the Gods to use their power disappeared. She and Ariel occasionally came down for experimental reasons but few others were likely to.

She had relaxed to the point that she had accepted it as simply the fading of ancient spells when she discovered one of the prison doors hanging ajar. The room within was completely dark. She thrust her hand and light into the prison.

It was completely empty.

Where was the prisoner? The chains? The containment spells? There was no trace of the room's purpose. The lingering magic she had sensed was from the broken containment spells. The prisoner was long gone.

She rushed back to the door to read its plaque, swearing when she did. Brigid was a converted Goddess, she would have a ready supply of powers and could blend in with the Angels.

She called out to all the Arch Angels and the whole Council *Raise the alarms! Brigid has escaped and she's kidnapped Sariel!*

She felt minds probing her, to which she readily showed the images of Brigid's empty prison. She heard the palace bells peeling in response.

As she rushed back up through the corridors she was left thinking how could this have happened. It just wasn't possible. How could Brigid have escaped?

Ariel walked through the gates hanging on their hinges, barely registering the destruction she had wrought once upon a time to the palace grounds. Much of the gardens were recovering but the front of this palace never would. Demons and pretenders had once lived here, just like the rest of Heaven before it had been scoured clean.

She had once worked in this palace, had once fought battles for its owner, as well as for other Gods and Goddesses. The Gods had trained the army that had overthrown them. Her one time mistress still resided in her palace prison. All that had been required was an adjustment to her chains. Were once she could not leave the palace, now she couldn't move at all.

Which was why she was here. Sariel had been kidnapped by Brigid, but it was unlikely Brigid had the power to currently teleport to the Surface. She couldn't use the main portal in the Citadel, which left her one of the smaller ones scattered across Heaven. They had all closed and the only one who could open them was the Queen of Heaven. If she was going to use a portal she would have to come via Hera.

Unless she was desperate enough to try and fly down to the Surface. A dangerous task for anyone, irrespective of how powerful they were. It had been done many times during the War, but legions of Angels were safe enough from the natural hazards between Heaven and the Surface.

She passed through the dark corridors with ease, having treaded these halls thousands of times before, alone and with her Inquisitors. Hera had been an excellent subject to relearn their earthly skills and refine them for a Divine audience.

The Inquisitors were uniquely hers. They were her spies, informants, warriors and above all else loyal servants. They were in essence the secret police of Heaven. They didn't officially have any standing in Heaven, other than publically being recognised as her personal guard, much in the way the other Arch Angels- excluding Sariel- had their own guards. But like the other Arch Guards they had their own special purpose.

By all rights none of them should have been in Heaven, barred for their disgusting actions while alive. In life they had also been Inquisitors hunting down people in the name of God- the deluded fools- to cleanse the Earth. Their actions while in the name of God broke all rules- torturing, raping and generally being completely sadistic to defenceless people were not acceptable actions by anyone's stretch of the imagination.

She had however seen their value and after seeking Gabriel's agreement had started bringing them into her fold. She had of course let them go to Hell for their actions, let them suffer for at least a century, if not more, before calling them up through Purgatory, to really make them grateful for her. Without her they would automatically go back to Hell.

They were not allowed into the Citadel unless accompanying her, so instead they lived on her island, which had originally been part of Asgard. It was there they lived out their sick desires of control and torture. Gabriel gave them a regular supply of people who had pissed her off enough- Humans, Jinn and Lesser Angels. Naturally all captured Demons were given to them after Gabriel was done with them, and there had been times she had even given them Ascended Angels.

When she came out into the amphitheatre the first thing she noticed was that there was no clinking or moaning. Her footsteps echoed loudly as she descended, and there was no answering whimpering. But then again last time Hera had barely been able to move at all. Hera had been dying, or as close as a Divine could get to it without being stripped of their power and Lifeforce by another Divine. Ariel regularly had the urge to do so, but she was more valuable alive. Even without her followers she was a very powerful Goddess.

The stage was empty. Her chains lay shattered on the floor in puddles of filth and acid. The IV machine whirred away, its tubes dripping toxic bacterial solutions all over the floor. She kicked the clump of metal which had a few days ago been festering in the hip bone of Hera. She cast around with her powers but felt nothing but the usual haze of the palace. She was gone.

Gabriel

She felt Gabriel's mind turn its focus towards her. Felt the full irritation focus on her. *What is it Ariel?* she snapped.

Hera has escaped.

What!

Brigid has freed her to access one of the portals.

There was momentary silence, probably while she spoke to Michael.

Gather all your nearest Inquisitors and head to Mount Olympus. If Hera is likely to go anywhere it's there. Some of my Seraphim will join you.

That scared her a little. Gabriel's Guard was probably the most feared in all of Heaven, not because they were excessively violent or cruel- as was the case of some of the guards- but because they were Gabriel's. They were the most dedicated of the lot because if they failed, they failed Gabriel. If Gabriel's Seraphim were ordered to kill you, they would with absolutely no hesitation. Some people whispered that they were little better than Automation, but they did so very quietly.

We will find her.

Gabriel broke the line turning her mind to others clamouring for it. She pushed them all aside to reach the other Arch Angels and their Masters of the Guard. Heaven had to be scoured and the two Goddesses captured.

Sariel gasped in awe as Mount Olympus materialised around her. This was the power base of the Greek Pantheon, where all the Greek Gods had ruled over the ancient Hellenic cities and empires. It was here mortals had been summoned before the Gods, and where the Olympians had gained victory over the Titans.

The actual mountain was miles below, they stood on its ethereal peak high up in Heaven. And it was stunning.

The mountain was a light grey-blue, clothed in cloudbanks of soft pink and orange. The morning sun was spearing through the cloudbanks, seemingly setting the whole mountain on fire. Mighty palaces dominated the edges of the square they stood in. Magnificent plants seemed to explode upwards in a blaze of colours, many similar to the ones in the palace and Citadel but many not. Where these Surface species?

Quick glances showed shrines and temples hidden amongst the foliage and standing atop ridges. She would have loved to have explored them, but it would have to wait for a time when they were not being chased by Heaven's Guard.

In the middle of the square was a crumbling open air shrine. It was perfectly circular, with steps descending into its heart.

Hera led them over to the shrine, glancing about with longing. This had once been her home, before becoming Queen of Heaven and permanently relocating to the Citadel. How long had it been since she had walked on Mount Olympus?

In an instant her attire changed, from ragged escapee into the Greek Goddess she was. Rags gave way to an elegant purple chiton tied with a golden chord. Gold and silver bracelets grew up her wrists and ankles. With a flick her long brown hair hung clean and shining across her bared pale shoulder.

She sighed as she stepped down the steps, lights flaring softly under her bare feet. The whole shrine gained a slight glow.

In the middle of the shrine was a circular pool of clouds. For what reason Sariel could not fathom. Hera stopped on the very last step above the clouds, turning back to them both.

"Brigid I presume you wish to return to Avalon."

"Aye I would, Avalon's Isles are now Great Britain and I missed it all."

Hera nodded in understanding, her whole empire had been converted to Christianity before slowly decaying, leaving both of her civilisations to be ravaged by war. Both were quite firmly in the hands of the Angels but at least she had got to see the peak of her empires. Brigid had missed out on her land's violent and grand history.

There was a ringing noise, Hera's head snapped around before she dropped to her knees. "The Angels come, we must hurry."

The clouds shimmered multi-coloured before darkening quickly. They started to swirl around, taking on the bruised colouring of violent storms. Lightning flashed and thunder roared. Suddenly the lights turned amethyst, its light shining upwards into the gloomy sky. They were a beacon for the approaching Angels.

Hera raised her slender arms upwards, raising the vortex upwards until a miniature hurricane whipped the shrine.

Hera stepped backwards up the steps, before dropping down her arms. The whole maelstrom collapsed inwards, making the ground shake. The clouds drifting across the square were dragged in, forming rivers of clouds.

Hera cast her eyes through the pillars seeing the Angels scrabbling against the defensive spells she had awakened. "They are here you must leave now before they see you." She yelled at Sariel above the roar of the vortex. Without further ado she pushed her into the vortex, her shriek short lived above the roar.

Hera spared her a fleeting glance before turning to Brigid "This is farewell for now, I do not know where you will be spat out but I wish you well dear Cousin. Find your Great Britain and make the Angels pay."

She gave Brigid a quick hug before pushing her into the vortex.

Hera turned back to face Ariel as she and the other Angels poured through the columns of the shrine. She raised burning hands, her face twisted in loathing. Her fury was legendary, her powers beaten only by the oldest Gods and they thought they could take her on. A wall of fire and lightning exploded out from her, clashing against the Angel's magic. Both felt the clash, the slight resistance before Hera's magic burned through theirs. Suddenly they were on the defensive, scrabbling backwards and uniting their shields.

The Angels greatest asset was the ease in which they blended their magic with each other, allowing them to achieve incredible power. Hera was not waiting around for them to complete it. With a maniacal laugh she plunged backwards into the vortex, its magic reaching out to cocoon her and sealing the path behind her. Then the entire world went dark as she left herself to the mercy of the portal.

Chapter 8

The vortex roared around her, spinning her around and around as she tumbled down its height. She had no idea which way was which any more, and despite her Divine nature was in real danger of vomiting everywhere. She had tried to gain some control by using her wings to steer, but she had nearly broken them. She kept them clutched in around her, shielding her from the worst of the vortex.

Lightning flashed all around her, starting to increase in its intensity and frequency. Somewhere far above there was a roar that shot down past her. The vortex shook violently. Lightning flashed past her, striking down further in the vortex. Shot down through this dark gaping maw.

As she looked behind she saw the swirling vortex just disappear. There was no way back.

Michael stared at the cloud covered surface of the Olympus portal as though it would suddenly open up. Behind him stood Ariel and Nuriel, both cautiously hanging back, while he was not as aggressive as Gabriel he was well feared for his slow burning fury. Considering it was very possible his sister had been kidnapped through this portal it was a surprise he hadn't tried to destroy it.

Around them milled all sorts of Angels. Her Inquisitors were busily 'investigating' all the buildings, just in case any of them had any clues- or long forgotten artefacts. His Cherubim stood at the ready, perhaps he was about to explode. Gabriel's Seraphim stood awaiting orders, they had done a preliminary search of the area and turned up no clues.

Now they all stood awaiting his orders.

"Nuriel" he summoned. She stepped up beside him. She didn't cringe like many of the Inquisitors did in his presence. She was a full-blooded Elder, with considerable power. She had once served in his Cherubim before being promoted. Now she was in charge of Divine Investigations. She and her underlings scoured the Heavens and Earth for traces of magic, Divine and pretty much anything else Michael or Raphael asked her to. "Yes my Arch?"

"I want this mountain scoured and searched for any trace of Sariel. Use every skill you possess to prove whether she was here or not. Also check the signatures of both Hera and Brigid, when you have a trace notify me immediately. We need to track those two down." He turned to Ariel "call off your Inquisitors" he laced the word with so much scorn that all the nearby Inquisitors cringed.

"But they have already begun their investigations, they can be of assistance to Nuriel."

"Nuriel needs no assistance. She is thoughtful, methodical and completely efficient. If something needs to be found she will find it, anyone else will only get in her way."

Ariel raised a burning pink hand, immediately all the Inquisitors teleported away to their island. Michael was in no mood to put up with argument, Ariel had no desire to be in the firing line of his anger. Putting up with Gabriel's was bad enough, but she was used to that. Michael was a blank book on dealing with while this furious.

He turned back to Nuriel "Some of your people are on the way, but they may not be what you need. Half of Gabriel's and half of my Guard will stay behind to set up a defence. While here they are under your authority."

Nuriel nodded, Michael was leaving nothing to chance. He wanted things done fast. "Then with your permission I'll begin"

"Thank you" he nodded before turning to Ariel "Come we are needed in the Council."

They disappeared back to the Council, and to crisis control. Michael hoped Gabriel had had more luck tracing Sariel. They had never had any of the Divine escape, and now two had very likely kidnapped an Arch Angel and were now on Earth. They would not last long, the might of Heaven would crush them.

She had walked for ages and ages. She had glided and flown across vast chasms, she had thought about flying down into the chasms, but was scared of what could be down there, or if she would get more lost. She had thought about flying upwards but the darkness above was more oppressive.

She knew she was in some vast cavern system but she had found no signs of life. There was occasionally mist and fog, but otherwise nothing other than rock and darkness. There was nothing to suggest any trace of Humanity; no extinguished torches, no fences, no forgotten belongings, nothing to suggest that Humans even knew about these caverns. She was lost and had nothing to help her find her way out onto the surface.

She was completely and utterly lost.

She slept when she grew tired, but her sleep was restless. Strange dreams invaded her mind, all she saw were ghosts and spirits. Awake she always felt the oppressive weight of the darkness above her. She wasn't used to such darkness, it played tricks on the mind. There seemed to be things at the edges of her vision, but when she investigated they were never there.

Her sporadic sleep became increasingly needed as hunger and thirst started to build. Elder and Ascended Angels being Divine did not need to eat or rest anywhere near as often but they did sustenance. She was starting to get worried, she didn't know how long she had been down here, but it had to have been some time for her to start feeling so tired and hungry. She was really beginning to fear that she would collapse and be lost forever down here, a petrified shell that would be utterly defenceless. She shivered at the thought of an eternity trapped in such an existence.

Perhaps immortality wasn't all it was cracked up to be. It had its own flaws. She presumed the Gods would fall into a similar existence but she wondered what would happen to a Primordial. They weren't quite like their offspring, she had come across little about them. They seemed mysterious shadows more often than not, not really concerned with the power plays of the other Divine. Most of them just seemed to disappear. She didn't think it was likely they were trapped in some dead flesh shell, someone would have found one of those by now.

She perked up when she heard the sound of running water. She sighed in relief, drinking water would revitalise her significantly. She could go without food as long as she had a reasonable amount of water.

She had to pass through several small tunnels, her heart running wild with the thought she was going to get lost but she thankfully came out onto a small ledge.

Underneath was a vast chamber, surprisingly well lit by spots of sporadic fire dancing along the surface of a black river. She stared in amazement at the first river she had ever seen. Its water was glassy black- was water only clear in Heaven?- and thrashing about violently. She was instantly reminded of storms, was nature always so violent? It roared through the cavern, splashing over jutting rocks and the dancing flames.

It all seemed very foreboding.

On one bank of the river were dozens and dozens of tunnel mouths all with sandy trails leading to a small ancient looking wooden wharf. It looked like it was about to collapse at any moment. But at least it was her first sign of Humanity. For people to have built it they would have needed access to trees and they only grew in the sun.

Feeling optimistic she glided down to the bank directly underneath her. It also had a wharf, made of stone and looked far sturdier. It was even decorated with worn carvings and sturdy spires of stone with fire burning out their tops. This was a definite sign of Humanity. Rocks didn't just naturally form such formations. This had been built and decorated, somewhat simplistically but it had been worked. Behind the jetty was a huge gaping tunnel that swallowed up the light. Faint eerie sounds emanated out, probably the wind playing tricks on a bizarre crevice or something.

She landed on the wharf glad to feel that it felt as solid as it looked. She looked about in wonder, the fires allowed for a very unique view of the world. Some things were cast into stark relief, every fault and crevice visible, and yet the fires seemed to create as many shadows as they dispersed.

She leaned carefully over the edge of the wharf, using her hand to channel her magic. She raised her hand and with it rose a black bubble she could hold in both hands. She stared at it once she grabbed onto it. It was bitingly cold and solidly black. How was it possible that water could be so different on Heaven? Did Heaven really make everything so light friendly?

She drank the water, its biting cold spreading from her mouth all the way down her throat and into her stomach. It tasted strange, almost familiar but not something she had tasted for a very long time. She continued to drink, feeling the cold starting to spread throughout her body. Death had touched this water.

She had a moment of panic before she remembered she was an Angel of Death. If she hadn't been she might well have been dead. This was no ordinary river, this was a Divine River overflowing with the powers of Death. It had the power to snuff out Divine life. That was truly terrifying, she hadn't known that natural features could contain power let alone strip Divine of their Lifeforces.

It was strange to think that death felt familiar to her, a long lost memory of the powers she had once enjoyed. This was one of her dominant powers, inherited directly from her father. And denied to her for so long.

From somewhere there was a ringing noise that echoed around the cavern, bouncing unevenly off its walls. She turned around fascinated by the echoing, flinching back when the flames suddenly roared upwards. Everything danced before her eyes. Fire was rarely used as a light source in Heaven, they preferred the constant light of sunglobes. She could understand why, in the flickering light it seemed the shadows were alive.

She stood looking around the cavern, her wings twitching more and more with her increasing uneasiness. She felt sure someone was watching her. She slowly turned around, scrutinising the shadows for any sign of movement. As she did so she came face to face with a nightmare.

A gigantic three headed dog stood there, its pure black body seemingly growing out of the shadowy tunnel behind. Each of the heads were her size, the powerfully built body behind them even larger. Drool pooled from three sets of mouths full of razor sharp teeth, beneath three pairs of burning red eyes.

She was held by those eyes, their predatory gleam paralysing her. There was clear intelligence in those eyes, there was also what could only be described as hatred. She stood perfectly still, barely daring to breath.

She jumped back in fright when it snarled before lunging for her. She had never met a dangerous animal before, she didn't know how to defend herself. Her magic was untrained and untested, and she had no weapons. Her only option was to flee.

She jumped up into the air as it lunged for her again, its snapping jaws just missing her feet. She had a moment of relief as she flew out of reach of the snapping jaws before she screamed in horror as it sunk back on its haunches and launched forward. She darted out of the way, barely missing those snapping jaws as it sailed past her into the river.

She watched transfixed as it sunk beneath the waters of the raging river, only to scream as it jumped out of the water at her again. It barked as she darted out of the way, setting the little fires ablaze. She screamed again as fire roared past her. She started darting back and forth, weaving her way through the raging firestorm. As she glanced over her shoulder she saw the dog soar through the air, passing right through the columns of fire. They turned blue as it soared through them, seemingly untouched by either flame or the death properties of the river.

She flew upwards seeking one of the tunnels that she had come through, it wouldn't be able to fit through it, and hopefully wouldn't be able to jump that high. She was wrong, it jumped nimbly up after her, soaring from ledge to ledge and scrabbling up sheer cliff faces. Behind it trailed those strange blue fires. It was easy to trace its path, blue fires marked everywhere it had landed, blooming outwards across the barren rock face.

She scrabbled up the rock face to find the ledge she had come out on. Only to stare in horror, the tunnels were all gone and in their place stood walls of blue fire. She jumped back off the ledge as the Monster landed, fire bursting outwards across the ledge.

She dove down, plummeting towards the river her keen eyesight searching for any semblance of escape. The tunnel the Monster had come out of was now a raging inferno and the tunnels on the opposite shore were pouring out flames. She swooped along the river top, darting in between the growing plumes of fire.

Her eyes picked out a narrow fissure that the river had carved out downstream.

Her heart was in her throat as she shot along the surface, she heard the splash as the Monster landed in the river. She could hear it splashing along behind her, growling and snapping.

She flew along the twists and turns of the river as they zigzagged through the sheer crevice. Behind her she could hear the Monster gaining on her and also the increasing heat of flames. She used flying skills she had never used before rushing around corners as the river lashed up the sides with ever increasing violence. Blue flames were creeping along the crevices marring the cliffs, bursting outwards in small blooms causing her to swerve from her course.

She heard the Monster behind her, could feel its breath and the heat of flames on her, all seemed lost before she shot out of the cliff face into the vast void beyond. Beneath her the river and its flames disappeared in the vast darkness beneath her.

She flew a safe distance before turning around. The Monster stood at the opening in the cliff face, smaller than it had been. Fire bloomed out all around it, its blue light fading into an eerie glow that was swallowed up by the darkness. Even the howling of the Monster was swallowed up, fading into distant echoes.

It stood there barking and howling until there was a distant roar. A roar that was not swallowed up by the vastness, it swept past shaking the cliff. Great chunks of rock fell off, splashing into the waters far below. The Monster shrunk back into its tunnel, his fearful whimpering echoing out as it ran back up the river.

She was left completely alone in the gloom.

She wanted rest, she wanted food, but most of all she wanted warm sunlight to chase away the creeping cold. She missed Heaven, she missed the palace, she missed safety.

She had never been so scared or in such danger in her entire life. She had never been injured, but now her scorched feathers were regrowing and her burnt feet were healing over.

She started crying, nothing was this bad. She wanted Michael to find her and save her. She didn't like the Surface, there were dangers everywhere. She wasn't prepared for this, she had had none of the training of any of the Legions, let alone the advanced training of the various Guards. She was completely naive to the dangers with little way of defending herself.

She landed on a rock spire jutting out of the gloom, collapsing roughly. She curled up sobbing, wrapping her wings protectively around herself. She was scared and alone. So very alone.

Michael looked up from Sariel's things when there was a knock on the door. He was relieved when he called out for them to enter and Nuriel walked into the room. He had been anticipating her assessment ever since Sariel had been kidnapped. His guard as well as the Legions had scoured all of the Citadel and Heaven for her, even the obscure islands mostly forgotten about. No one had found her.

"You have information?"

"I do my lord. As we had expected Hera opened the portal to the Surface, there are two trace signatures that we are tracking down to the Surface but it will take us a little longer.

Hera was freed after Brigid, probably for the sole purpose of activating the portal. Now it seems they have gone their separate ways, most likely to try and elude us. Your Guard are currently setting up watch on Ireland and Greece. Uriel and Gabriel's Guards along with the Legion are scouring all of the British Isles and the full extent of the Roman and Hellenic Empires. If we locate the traces I'll pass it on immediately."

He nodded "Thank you Nuriel, and what of Sariel?"

"We aren't picking up on a trace for her yet, she's probably been eclipsed by either Goddess's power. In which case it seems likely Hera has taken her prisoner. She is the more powerful Goddess. Sariel was however in all three locations. My concern is that someone either coerced or manipulated Sariel into Brigid's prison. There are lingering traces of broken spells. I presume that one of Sariel's protection spells reacted violently with Brigid's containment spell. The only magical traces I found in her prison was her own and both your's and Gabriel's.

It is clear cut from there, the blast would presumably have rendered Sariel unconscious, and for whatever reason Brigid has taken her with her.

Brigid fled through the palace before flying to Hera's mansion. Once freed Hera teleported the three of them to Mount Olympus with the sole purpose of activating the portal there."

"Someone set Sariel up?" his voice was a cold as ice.

"I believe so, what other reason would Sariel have for being in the prisons? And the pain of the backlash would have rendered her unconscious before the spells were broken. Someone was there with her, someone pushed her into Brigid."

"Do we know who?"

"Unfortunately not. The backlash has covered all trace of other magics, we will have to wait for it to fade enough for other presences to be detected. I'm sorry but it may be a long time before I have anything else to give you."

He nodded, deeply troubled. Someone had deliberately used Sariel to free a Goddess. There was a traitor in Heaven!

"Have you told anyone of this?"

"Only you my Lord, there are only a handful of my people and yours that have enough information to piece together the evidence. They are dependable people but I have written the names down for you. What do you wish me to tell the other Arch Angels?"

This was why he liked Nuriel, she was intelligent, dependable and completely loyal. It was a pity she wasn't still in his Guard, but her promotion suited her well. He now also had first access to all her information. "Tell them a revised version, make no mention of the traitor. Sariel was kidnapped by the Goddesses and now finding them all is paramount. I'll fill in Raphael, his Guard can try searching for flares of Sariel's magic. As for Gabriel, it is better for all of Heaven if she is kept in the dark about the traitor."

Nuriel nodded in understanding. There was a reason Gabriel was feared, her anger was legendary and merciless. Something like this could cause her to purge

Heaven. If left to her own devices much of Heaven would probably be slaughtered. If however she was given the traitor, then her fury would have one sole receiver. There would be no mercy, but it was what they deserved.

Yet Nuriel had a suspicion that it would be Michael's wrath that the traitor would feel. Gabriel's wrath was legendary, but Michael was just as merciless- he had after all imprisoned the Goddess of Mercy and torn the Goddess of Love apart- and Sariel was his sister. She felt sure that Michael would reveal his merciless fury to the whole of Heaven.

Gabriel was not the only dangerous Arch Angel.

Sariel woke up tired, grumpy and sore. She had fallen asleep exhausted from crying, but had tossed and turned all night. She was not used to sleeping on solid rock, or shivering half the night. She was filthy, ash, sand and dust coated her liberally. Her white robes were ruined, her gold make up had rubbed and run off her face onto her sleeves. There were long tears and burn holes all over the outer robe. Her hair and wings were just as disgusting. She needed a bath.

She looked around scowling at the gloomy darkness. Little had changed but there was a softer grey light from above now and there were bluish glows from the dark waters far beneath. There were far too many shadows. She was used to the vast expanses of sky and streams of light that made up Heaven. Or the occasional thunder storm that turned the sky dark then lit it up the whole sky for seconds at a time.

She sighed looking into the gloom, her only marker was the waterfall and tunnel she had come out of. She wasn't going back up there, but everything else faded into the gloom. With another sigh she launched herself off her spire, sending up little clouds of ash as she flapped her wings. She headed off with little direction other than as far away from that Monster as possible.

She flew for hours, losing herself in the simple joy of flying for so long, gliding and swooping above and between the many rock spires. Skimming across the dark river with is occasional blue glow.

She had just flown above the rock spires again when she heard an eerie cry that sent shivers down her spine. She was not alone. Suddenly very scared she landed on the nearest rock spire and sent out her senses. But her senses slid and slithered through the gloom. She sensed spirits all around her, but they were lost and forsaken. There were quick flashes of vibrant spirits, but they were gone as soon as she detected them. None of them were of any harm to her.

But there was something else. Something she could just sense but kept sliding over. The strangest thing was that it felt like Angel Magic, Elder Angel Magic, similar to the spells that had bound Brigid.

She heard a whoosh and a swish, something was flying around her in the darkness. She called to mind the bright sunlight of Heaven, and with a flick of her wrist summoned light to her hand. The whole cavern was bathed in bright sunlight as far as the eye could see. Above her soared stabbing stalactites and gigantic columns of beige rock. Beneath her the misty gloom turned into clouds of rainbows dancing across the dark surface of the river. Its watery arms reaching up to grab the hapless souls stuck floating among the mist, their soundless screams made her blood run cold.

A fluttering shadow at the edge of her vision caught her attention. This time her blood ran colder than ice as she turned to look at it.

A man made of shadows flew towards her. He was a sick parody of an Angel, six tattered wings made of shadows, shiny grey-black skin like insect armour and long grey claws reaching out to her, stained with blood and embers. Each time it flapped its wings a strange grating noise followed. It shot straight towards her, his burning red eyes paralysing her where she stood. His mouth showed black teeth/fangs but while his face had been distorted she could see the clearly Angelic features. He collided into her, his claws ripping through her robes and flesh.

She screamed as they tumbled down into the darkness, her spell ripped from her control. She couldn't see, she couldn't focus, couldn't feel her magic. All she could feel was pain tearing through her. The Demon screamed in fury before it bit down on her neck, they both screamed as he bit through the flesh and blood filled is mouth. She scrabbled at his neck, her strength fading fast. She didn't know how to fight. It was far stronger than her.

Her whole world narrowed down to the utter agony of her neck as the Demon chewed through her flesh. She wanted it off of her, she wanted the pain gone. She had magic but she had to focus and get it right. This might be her only chance. Demons were creatures of darkness and feared the sun. She thought of the power of the sun, feeling it infuse her. She sent it all through her blood into her neck and into the disgusting creature's mouth.

His pain racked scream rent the air as he pulled away from her throat. One of her hands flew to her neck to heal, while the other grabbed his throat and poured forth the power of the sun. He screeched again as his shadows surged in to fight off her magic, but her power was stronger. His skin crackled and pealed, burns spreading across the strange armour. It started to flake off revealing flawless bronze skin beneath. The tattered mess of his wings burned off in a blaze of light to reveal white feathers beneath. The light flowed all over his body burning off the shadows, finally chasing to his burning eyes. The light surged into them washing away red to reveal glacial blue eyes beneath. His scream changed from something unnatural to something that belonged in a throat. He shuddered before he passed out.

She yelled as she suddenly got pulled down by his dead weight. Adjusting she wearily flew them both over to the nearest outcrop of rock. She dropped his dead weight roughly onto the ground. She used her magic to check that he was still alive them collapsed down next to him.

She was in Hell. She was actually in Hell. She had to be. She had been attacked by a Demon, she had been flying over rivers of the dead and had encountered some sort of Demonic spirit guardian. How had Hera gotten it so wrong? Were both her and Brigid floating around in Hell also? She didn't understand how she had missed the Surface.

She was in so much danger. She was prepared for none of this. She wasn't ready to face Demons, she didn't know how to defend herself or fight effectively. She had gotten lucky with this one, next time she may not. And there would be others far stronger.

He had also once been an Elder Angel, he must be a Fallen Angel. But what had been done to him? Did Hell turn all its occupants into Demons? Was she going to turn into one?

She wondered who he was but didn't care enough to not roll over and fall asleep.

Sariel woke up groaning from her aches and pains. She had healed her neck after the Demon had attacked her but she hadn't been able to heal away all trace. She was weakened after so long without sustenance. Angels still needed to eat and it had been too long for her, her powers and natural healing were being affected. Even her skin was looking sallow after everything she had been through.

She suddenly remembered the Demon. How had she forgotten him! She was instantly relieved to find him still unconscious and in his Angel form. But her relief was short lived and tinged with fear. Splotches of grey-black armour were slowly growing across his bronze skin. One of his wings was shedding its feathers.

It seemed that Hell reclaimed its possessions.

She was nearing starvation, but now she feared to eat anything in Hell. Was that how one became trapped, by consuming part of Hell? It turned you from within. She had to keep moving, she had to find some sustenance otherwise she would start to lose her physical body to wasting. She was not going to be trapped down here, to be lost forever.

"The transition will not last for long. You have not broken the spell Arch Angel." Was it just her or did he spit that out with contempt. It was hard to tell with his harsh grating voice.

"Do you know what will break the spell?" she asked as she turned to face him. It was unnerving meeting his gaze. He held one Angelic eye, while the other was losing its blue and starting to burn red. The skin around it was corrupting into its shadowy exoskeleton. It was a bizarre fusion of Heaven and Hell.

"All the spells are connected to Lucifer. All of Hell's bindings are tied to him in his corrupted form. Until it is ripped out of him and broken then not one citizen of Hell will ever be free. We are forever trapped in the forms Michael and Gabriel gave us."

He turned his unnerving gaze over her "And who

are you Arch Angel and why are you in Hell? What trickery is Heaven using to win the war?"

"Win the War? The War ended a long time ago."

He laughed humourlessly as he turned pitying eyes back towards her "When did Heaven start deluding its own children? The Elders let alone the Arch Angels were always overly knowledgeable about the affairs of others. How is it that you are so naïve and clueless?"

She looked away, out across the spirit river feeling even more vulnerable than she had been. Even the Demons laughed at her naivety. How had her brother been so cruel?

"All my life I was raised in the palace and with the rarest exceptions never allowed to leave. My parents were killed not long after I was born so I was raised by my brother and his wife. They bound my powers and raised me as their personal power source. I escaped with the help of a Goddess and had thought I was merely stuck underground until you attacked me. It was then I realised I was in Hell.

He gave her a scathing look, made all the more scathing by its burning red glow "and they think they can win the War with the likes of you." He laughed cruelly, as he did so both his canines grew longer and turned black. He spat his black-silver blood out onto the ground when he bit himself. It sat smoking on the rock, slowly corroding it away. "You had best leave soon otherwise I will revert back to my Forsaken form. And from the looks of you, you wouldn't put up much of a fight."

"Can you tell me the way to the Surface please?"

"Fly downstream following the Acheron until you reach the Crater. From there you just have to access the Portal at the centre. But be careful to avoid the Guardians Leviathan, Ziz and Behemoth." He unconsciously rubbed his heart.

She smiled at him as she turned to take off "Thank you. Are you sure you will be alright?"

He smiled, but it was now a sick parody of a smile. Black teeth poking out of a mouth unsuited to them, blood running down his jaw. "I will exist as I have done for millennia. Go quickly Heaven's Child, Hell is no safe place for you."

With a quick nod and an awkward smile she launched herself off the rock spire and flew as quickly as she could downstream. She did not want him following her.

Kokabel watched her go, rubbing his heart again. He felt a twinge of pity for his lie but it was soon consumed by the Curse, leaving instead satisfaction. She was now headed straight for the Beast's lair, a place where even the Greater Demons feared to go and not even a God would dare venture. If she somehow survived Hell's Demons then the Beast would feast on an Arch Angel's blood.

It seemed only fitting for an Arch Angel to meet Heaven's greatest injustice, it was about time they paid for their sins.

Chapter 9

Brigid wondered where she was. She couldn't seem to move, her limbs all seemed impossibly heavy and were trapped about her in weird angles. Her eyes were sealed shut and her mouth was completely dry.

She was underneath the earth. Somewhere hot and dry. She could feel the land's parchedness, greedily sucking out what she had only to lose it to the heat. Was she in the Egyptian or Mesopotamian Deserts? Not a place the Angels would initially look. She sent a silent thanks to Hera.

She used a small amount of magic to transition herself closer to the surface before scrambling out the last bit by hand. She wanted to leave as little a trace as possible for the Angels to track.

The first thing she noticed as she cleaned out her eyes was that she was in neither Egypt nor Mesopotamia. She wasn't anywhere she had been before. Perhaps it was the lands south of Egypt, she had never seen any other part of Africa. The earth was a strange red-brown colour that she had never seen before, and while the land was dry she was not in a desert. Scrub and spiny grasses covered the land as far as she could see. On the horizons sat some unusual rock formations, her senses told her that they contained residual power.

She was somewhere the Angels had conquered.

It was a strange place. Nothing like her beloved Isles, there the plants had been so green, here they were greyish and nothing she recognised. The strangest thing perhaps was the dryness of the land and yet its abundance of life.

There was a noticeable lack of people, she felt them

at the edges of her sense but they were so few. Even all those millennia ago Britain had been a populous island heading towards development and change. The Angels had told her of its power rise, she could only imagine the population now. But this land was so empty of people.

There were also powers she didn't recognise and had not encountered before. It felt akin to her own earth powers, as twisted as hers had become. This land was ancient, but it had only recently been touched by civilisation. The edges of her senses told her there were settlements, but her powers were so rusty she couldn't sense any more.

She felt relieved, this land had very little feel of the Angels but their touch had tainted the ancient feel of the land. Now both of them were fading, not gone but not strong either.

The Lifestream of the planet held a similar feel. The planet was not healthy, something was affecting its ability to flourish. The world felt aged and weakened. It had never felt like that. It had always been vibrant and powerful.

She was weary, so very weary. She had anticipated being restored by the Lifestream but in this state it needed more help than she did. It was well overdue that she slept in the Lifestream. She summoned her powers, slowly remembering the transition into the Lifestream. She gradually lost her physical sensations, becoming aware of new sensations.

Life was all around her, flourishing and developing as it was always want to do. Life was a miracle, it was incredible and so often over looked. Life was one of the children of Gaia, it was manipulated by the Gods and their offspring but it was not their creation. They were as much its tools and servants as it was to them. But life could exist without the Gods or Angels.

Earth was a testament to that. The War and the Angels neglect had not impeded life's ability to flourish, even the waning Lifestream was not holding it back.

Though if it were to cease so too would life. She embraced the Lifestream losing her conscious mind into the collective sensations of life.

She breathed in deeply as she clawed herself out of the red earth once again. She hadn't shifted back successfully, instead ending up underneath the dirt. She turned to face the sun, feeling it beat down on the land around her. She smiled at it, feeling the power of it flow through her. She wondered what had happened to the Sun Gods and Goddesses.

She stood up shaking off dirt and leaves, laughing at her new found freedom. She still had no idea where she was. She didn't think it was Egypt or Mesopotamia. Perhaps it was Judea or the Gobi Desert, or perhaps she was in the lands of the long dead Aztecs. She didn't know.

But most importantly she was not in Avalon or any of the other Celtic lands.

She suddenly realised just how out of sync with reality she was when she sensed sentient life behind her. Three black skinned and haired women stood there. They were of short stature with very wide noses, they were dressed in a strange combination of clothes and plants. Her first instinct screamed Africa, they were the only people with skin so black but they did not look like any of the Nubians she had seen before.

She spread her wings wide using Angel magic to mesmerize them. They were transfixed and defenceless. With great care she probed through each of their minds, following through every synapses and memory. They had no term for her, no notion of her type. To them she looked like a white woman, but with wings. They had never seen an Angel, they did not belong to them but instead to the long dead spirits that had once roamed this land.

Australia. She was in Australia, not that that helped her much, the name meant absolutely nothing to her. She had never heard of it until now. But she did learn that it contained cities. Not of these people, but others who built buildings reaching into the sky. Strange things she had seen in their mind, most of it incomprehensible.

But the most useful thing she had learned was that the largest nearby settlement was a city called Alice Springs, there she could hopefully learn something more valuable.

She released them as she took flight. The Angels had not touched these people, there was hope yet. Perhaps this country held promise until she was strong enough to return to her home. She was no fool, Europe would be under close guard as the Angels hunted her and Hera.

Alice Springs turned out to be a small city in the middle of Australia. Its size was hardly impressive compared to Babylon or Persepolis but it looked nothing like any of the ancient cities. There were no walls, no soaring palaces or temples. No Human made mountains of rock. Nor was there the squalor she remembered. Streets were not made of stone, buildings were made of metal and glass. Glass! So much of it, it was an utter decadence to the age she remembered.

There were no monuments to the Gods or kings. No temple precincts and only a handful of churches. There were no horses or livestock to be seen. Only these strange machines called cars. They moved on energy the car produced itself. Incredible! The car took oil and turned that into energy to propel itself forward. The amount of energy flowing over the place was incredible and the strangest thing was that it was all Human made. The Lifestream was as weak here as anywhere else. There were no mages, Demons or priests to channel various magics but there was electrical energy flowing through every building, under the roads. The people even had it in their pockets or plugged into their ears.

And the people!

She couldn't comprehend just how much things had changed. Everybody was clothed. Not in furs or even leathers but in synthetic materials they had created themselves, blended with natural fibres. Women walked around on miniature stilts, men looked like women and women looked like men. Most people had some form of jewellery, such an abundance of gold and silver just scattered over the populace. And as for the clothes the variety was incredible, the colours- purple and blue!- the styles varied from nearly all skin covered to women parading around in very little at all. Not that that was surprising, the hotter climates had often had nudity, but never had there been such a variation.

And that wasn't all most of these people were descendants of her Britons, but there were also other Europeans, Asians and Mesopotamians. Not that they were called that any more. Middle Eastern was their modern name.

Unfortunately the Angels' presence was noticeable here. People wore crosses or concealing headdresses. But she did not sense any Angels nearby.

But the most confronting of all things was Humanity's development with technology. The things they had done was incredible, all without magic. She was currently sitting on an aeroplane. An invention that allowed lots of people to fly, without magic. It was mind boggling but that was not the only thing, they had the upper hand against disease, they made light without fire or magic, they turned oil and coal into energy, they could communicate vast distances with things called phones. They could travel vast distances with relative ease, they had ventured into space and landed on the moon, they had submarines to navigate under water, hospitals to heal the sick, no slaves only free people, there were no swords or spears or arrows, but they had learned to make bombs, some so powerful as to destroy whole cities. The amount of power they had at their disposal was amazing and horrifying at the same time.

Life had changed as it was want to do, Humanity had advanced without guidance or magic. They had excelled and destroyed, their nature reflecting all of evolution and Divinity.

She turned her head from such vast notions instead looking out the window at the clouds soaring by, before she took another bite of an amazing creation. Chocolate. It was like an orgasm in her mouth, the chemical rush of endorphins running over her akin to sex. It was miraculous what Humans had come up with.

"Another coffee miss?"

She looked up at the stewardess smiling "Please" another miraculous delicacy. The buzz it gave Humans. They had such variety of foods and drinks, and their tastes were so varied.

"Certainly miss" the young girl gushed. Brigid had read her mind already, she thought that she was a model or movie star. Her Divinity made her a rare beauty to them. She continued to skim others' thoughts, amazed at the differences and similarities. People were still stressed, not about food on the table but money to live. These people were so vain in this day and age, and sex wasn't just on their minds it was in their magazines and shows.

It was everywhere. The thoughts that she alone was inspiring in others minds was shocking. It had been so long since she had immersed herself in Humanity. They had changed so much, the things they got up to and the secret fantasies they actually lived out were incredible.

It was too much to take in, but she would be in Sydney soon and she had decided to stay there for several weeks until she adjusted to the modern age. She had so much catching up to do. Especially with the food.

Once she grew bored of mind reading she turned to normal reading, she couldn't believe the availability of books and paper, picking up the *Da Vinci Code*, a story about the lies of the church. It would be a pleasant way to bring her up to date on one of the Angels' religions and the problems plaguing it. She smiled, Humans so easily mimicked their masters.

There were so many things to discover and there was very little chance of her being found by the Angels. Australia was literally on the other side of the world.

She wondered how Hera and Sariel were faring.

Hera turned her violet eyes over the statue of herself. While it looked very little like her at all, she did like the power and strength the artist had captured in stone. She idly wondered how the artist would feel to know that she now looked over his statue of her. She turned away from the window and continued down the snowy streets of New York, it was a bitter winter in the city that never sleeps.

What a city! She never would have thought it possible, one city containing more people than all the city-states of Achaia and Thrace. It even made Rome, Alexandria and Carthage look small. Well the ancient ones, she didn't know if the modern ones had changed or not.

But the most interesting discovery for her was not the sheer amount of Humans but the vast numbers of Daemons living in the city. She sensed Vampires, Werewolves, Sirens, Maenads, Incubi, Succubi and a couple of species she hadn't encountered before. She saw straight through their pitiful illusions, designed to hide from each other and Angels. Their spells did not hold up under her eyes, she smiled at them knowingly.

She got looks everywhere she went. Mortals turned towards her because of her Divine beauty, mortals always unknowingly craved Divinity. The Daemons eyed her up warily, sensing her powers flowing all around them. Her powers were so vast she couldn't contain them within her skin. But their senses were so diluted they had no comprehension of what she was. She had not been forgotten and she lacked the imbuement of faith but she was still powerful and still the Queen of Heaven. Though that was currently an empty title.

She loved New York, she felt strangely at home in it. But then it was barely touched by the Angels, not a single Angel, not even a Lesser could be sensed in the whole city. Their absence was keenly noticeable by the sheer diversity of decadence within the city. There was such extreme vanity, pictures of beautiful mortals abounded everywhere selling all sorts of products, there was such greed, powerful men and women owning vast tracts of the city with its monolithic towers stabbing into the sky. The sheer abundance of resources and luxury items was surprising. Then there was the blatant sexuality of the city, something completely at odds with any of Michael's commands. This was a city that had legalised homosexual marriages, had hundreds of brothels, strip clubs, fetish clubs and porn stores. Everyday life was hyper-sexualised from the nearly naked models plastered all over the city, to the TV shows and movies. Trawling through people's minds showed an abundant craving for sex.

That alone was the highest indicator that the Angels' control of the world was severely slipping. Then there were the scientific advancements going on in the city. Genetic Engineering, Stem Cell Research among the most prominent Human manipulations of life. Gabriel's domain. While she was very good at manipulating life and creating new species, she considered it something exclusive to her family. Most of her creations had long since been hunted to extinction, and she apparently had not made any more but she had been very active in keeping the control of life in her hands only.

New York was a city abandoned by the Arch Angels. A refuge of the Daemons, and a bastion of Human development and advancement. It was the perfect place to become her powerbase.

Modern day Greece was her original home, then Rome and its empire. She had had temples and orders spread across the 'known world', but they were all but dust. Only a few temples still stood but surprisingly she still had priestesses who lit the Olympic Torches. She would reconnect with them later but for now she would build her power in secret. New York was one of the biggest, richest and most powerful cities in the world. Where better to start.

She wondered how Brigid would react when she discovered how much her little island had changed. The far flung Roman city of Londinium was now one of the largest and most powerful cities in the world. As for the islands, it had survived invasion after invasion to develop into several different kingdoms that were eventually united into Great Britain before going on to become the biggest empire in the world.

She hoped Brigid wouldn't be foolish enough to go

rushing back to her islands. She idly wondered where she ended up. She had crash landed into the Grand Canyon and had been swept along the Colorado River before she recovered from the shock and asserted her powers. Unfortunately her natural storm powers had cocooned her and inadvertently caused intense flooding. There had also been an interesting reaction with the lingering traces of past Gods and spirits.

She had unconsciously bonded with the land, claiming the whole Grand Canyon. She had left a blazing signal for the Angels to follow. She hadn't formally claimed the land, so at least the Angels didn't currently know about it. But she had fled as far east as possible, going to ground in New York.

She hoped Brigid was safe, but it was far too dangerous to risk contacting her.

Hera lounged across her Roman style couch, looking around her new lavish apartments. Using her magic she had procured several properties and a mass of wealth to go to ground with. It was so easy to get what she wanted from these mortals, they had absolutely no defence against her. Her inner economic tycoon was coming out with her rapidly growing understanding of modern economics. Wealth was the main power in the modern age. And she was going to use it to her advantage.

In doing so she had awoken and angered the Daemon inhabitants of New York. They had no idea who or what she was, to them she was a powerful enigma that had broken all their rules. They lived in the shadows, trying their best not to draw the Angel's eyes to New York. The amount of magic she had been using far exceeded New York's usual levels. The Angel's attention would be drawn here once the flaring power in the Grand

Canyon receded.

So she waited for them to come to her and learn their lesson.

She had adorned herself in a long white dress, ironically the Grecian style was in vogue, it seemed prophetic. It had been far too long since she had enjoyed the feel of expensive cotton on her skin, or adorned herself in jewellery. Now more than ever she looked like an ancient Queen.

She felt them coming, some were climbing the stairs, or riding in the elevator. Some were descending from the roof and a few were landing on the balcony outside.

With a thought all the lights went out instead replaced by hundreds of burning candles. The speakers started playing in the background, the classical music the closest thing she had found to the music she remembered. She gave the winds a slight empowerment, making the curtains gently drift in and out of the windows and doors.

She watched as the first came through the balcony doors, apparently growing out of the shadows. That had been his aim, but the eyes and senses of a Goddess were not fooled but such things as the play of light. She let him approach as he gathered all his powers, using his glamour and enchantments to overpower her. He was completely foolish.

She smiled at him and used a far more potent form of the same magic to overpower him. She felt his fear explode as his glamour and enchantments were ripped away, leaving him completely trapped by her small enchantments. He was down on his knees, in a position of worship before he had time for his body to protest.

He was so afraid, she could see the question in his eyes that he could no longer voice. She had complete control of him. She gently stroked his cheek, coursing more powers into him with such a simple action. He couldn't understand how she could have powers that far outstripped any Incubus or Succubus.

"Release him" yelled a Succubus as she ran across the room. She made no attempt to confound by seduction instead lashing out with fire. She was flat on the floor in a heartbeat, her flames extinguished, her power beyond her control. She trembled at the power before her.

The next to appear were a pair of Maenads who entered through the front doors. They at least had sense to recognise her as Divine. They fell to their knees upon seeing her. She smiled in satisfaction. This would be easier than she thought it would be.

"Come forth my daughters" she said gently to them gesturing the forward. They rose hesitantly to their feet before approaching. She rose to embrace them, both of them falling to their knees again, each of them grabbing one of her hands in reverence. Tears fell from their eyes, the joy they felt upon feeling her magic overwhelming them. The Gods were back to end the Age of Angels.

Hera leant down and kissed them gently of the forehead, leaving a slight green glow behind.

Others had joined them by now. The Siren had also prostrated herself, recognising her for what she was. One gesture from Hera had her racing across the floor on her knees to grab onto Hera's hand.

The Werewolf and Werecat stood in the shadows watching warily, but ready to defend the Kitsune a step in front of them. They didn't understand. The four Vampires stood at the ready, guns and swords in their hands but they made no actions. The remaining species she did not know but they too stood hesitantly in the shadows.

She could feel their confusion. Nymphs were usually considered intelligent and responsible, Sirens less so but they were close relations and they were among the best suited to blend into Human society. They had avoided being hunted for centuries while most of the other races were still being hunted to this day. To all intents and purposes they were presumed extinct or hiding far from civilisation.

For three of them to drop to their knees crying at the feet of the very woman they had come to deal with was a perplexing situation. What made it even more incomprehensible was that the three of them had started to glow softly. It might have been centuries since it was last seen but they instinctively recognised the Divine glow Nymphs had once had.

The very same glow was emitting from the woman, it flared brightly blinding them all, wrapping through their senses and giving them a taste of the powers she wielded.

As one they fell to their knees, horrified, amazed, joyous and overwhelmed. A Goddess walked the Earth once more.

"You all know me for what I am. I am Hera, the Queen of Heaven and I am here to bring about your freedom from the tyranny of the Angels. It is time that your true natures were returned, so much of your nature has been forgotten. It is a crime for which the Angels will pay."

Magic danced all over her, fire, lightning and darkness swept over her skin, her hair floated around her, her eyes blazed violet and her voice thundered through their bones.

"Grant me your loyalty and you will rise, do not and you will fall to the Angels. The War will continue, it is coming soon and with it the world will be remade. Go now to your own kind and pass on my ultimatum."

They all staggered to their feet, leaving as fast as they could to report to their leaders or councils. She smiled once they had all left. That had been far easier than she had thought, the Nymphs and Siren had been an unexpected boon in recognising her power. Their actions would carry considerable weight with the others.

She felt that this was a good start to her empire building. The Daemon races of New York had been given their warning, she doubted any would be foolish enough to stand alone. Which left the Human population which had retained its strong attachment to the Angels. Then of course there was the rest of the USA but for now she had her first step forward.

Brigid was far more subtle in her movements through Sydney. She was doing her utmost to avoid all detection from Humans, Daemons and most importantly the Angels. She was but one among millions, insignificant to those around her. She had used magic sparingly to grant her access to basic commodities. Some things were essential but she wanted no trace for the Angels to follow. She knew of Nuriel's skills.

It might have seemed demeaning to other Gods and Angels but she had no qualms living like a Human, working for money to get food, clothing and other Humans needs. But she had been a prisoner for centuries, she had no pride or arrogance unlike the other Divine. It had been ground down by the Angels, and she hadn't had much to begin with. She hadn't gotten to enjoy her civilisation at its peak.

As a Fertility Goddess she was quite at ease working for a living. Most of them were far more down to earth than the other Gods, uncaring of the difference between gold and flowers. She had lived with Fairies and

Nymphs. She had worked in the Gardens of Gaia, Eden, Avalon and she had even tended the Hanging Gardens of Babylon.

"Oh Brigid this is beautiful"

Brigid turned to face Eleanor LaClarke, matriarch of the LaClarke family, one of the richest within the Sydney area. She had extensive gardens open to the public and was generally a patron of the arts. She had hired Brigid as a gardener, mostly due to Brigid's compulsion but she was a shrewd and sharp mind that instinctively fought compulsions. She had been the most surprising find.

She was a woman in the dusk of her looks, their striking echo a stark reminder of what she must have looked like as a young woman. She was still lean, and still stood above most women. She was a gracefully aging woman shunning all cosmetic surgery and accepting her wrinkles. She dressed well and was one of those woman who wore only simple makeup to accentuate.

Her mind was as sharp as it had ever been and she was an extremely busy woman who stood for no nonsense. She still ran several businesses, attended multiple charity events, looked after her numerous grandchildren and spent a great deal of time attending to her gardens. She would have made an excellent High Priestess or Queen.

"Thank you madam" and she genuinely meant it. She was far more in touch with simpler emotions like gratitude than she had been before. What Goddess was touched by a mortals' opinion? How the other Gods would laugh.

"It was a risk hiring you but I have to say you have exceeded all my expectations. This garden is looking lovely."

Which was true. The English style garden was

exploding with rose blooms, their vibrant colours splashed everywhere and their rich heavy scent hanging in the dry summer air. Compared to the other nearby gardens that were browning as they did annually these gardens looked fresh from Europe. It helped that she had magic to counteract both the dry hot Australian summers and the rising levels of toxicity that were the greatest threat to any Australian garden, park or farm.

The rest of the garden paled in comparison next to her creations. There were two reasons for its lush fertility. She was pouring her magic into it and she had claimed the land as her own, binding it to her powers and widening up the Lifestream passing through the region.

"You'll have to work on the rest of the gardens Brigid, this is simply marvellous. It is miraculous, I've never seen roses so stunning, and the colours. I haven't seen gardens this vibrant since my youth. You can stay can't you, I know you're working to get back to London but I'll pay you well. You simply have to work on my other gardens."

Brigid glowed at the compliments "Of course I can stay a while, London can wait." And it could. As much as she wanted to see how much London had changed for herself she had studied it well. She just had to see the physical changes to her islands. But she knew that the Angels would be crawling all over them. The longer she took to get there the less of them there would be.

The darkness was near complete, the nearby street lights had been magically extinguished long before the meeting started. So it was on a frozen winter's night thick fog clung to Central Park as the representatives of each Daemon race met with each other to discuss Hera.

The Matriarch of the Maenads stood next to the Siren Queen, both were surrounded by their honour guards but stood contently in each other's company. On this matter they were united and it had strengthened old relations.

Sarah Appel was the most powerful Maenad in the whole of North America, magically and politically. She had been the Mother of New York for over a hundred years and the Matriarch of the United States for nearly fifty. She was a wealthy woman, with Human political clout who was always looking out for her Maenad brethren. She blended into the respectable elite of New York, avoiding the occasional Angel by regularly attending temple and living a lifestyle that she resented.

Belle Aurora on the other hand lived a lavish lifestyle which directed Angel attention away by living a debauched Human lifestyle as an international supermodel. But her lifestyle in no way reflected her ability as Queen of the Sirens, she was new to the post, her mother only dying two years prior but she had learned quickly from Sarah and strengthened Nymph relations. She had also made overtures to the Lilin to strengthen relations with them.

Many of the other leaders were slowly appearing out of the shadows flanked by their own guard. Some were blending in as Humans, other had made no attempt.

Akiko Sumatsu stood in her Human form, her tails hidden beneath her long dress. There was nothing to suggest she was a Kitsune. She was the Diplomat of the New York Were, holding considerable weight in the Were Council and was usually the one who dealt with the other species. Her honour guard consisted of both the Alpha of the Werewolves and the Werecats as well as several others all in their animal form. A light illusion made it look like a lady out walking her dogs.

Standing beside her was the Encantado High Priestess, also in her Human form, enjoying the protection offered to her.

The Temptress of the Lilin arrived on foot, looking for all appearances like a gothic teenager out with friends, but each and every one of them was more than capable of defending themselves.

The King of the Vampires chose to arrive in his stylish black car, his attendants rushing to open the door for him and assist him out. He was the oldest of them all, being nearly 900 years of age, the other Vampires were all under 200 years. The last Angel purge of New York had been very efficient, nearly eradicating them all. Since then they had hung more to the shadows, being silent hunters and trying to avoid publicity.

The strangest arrival was the Tsarina of the Wild Ones, for they rarely came. They were the blended descendants of Fairies, Elves and Nephilim. Their powers were wide ranging and highly elemental. They were a secretive lot that rarely interacted with the other species. They had rejected their earlier roots, having left the confines of the Old World. No one was quite sure how they had managed to get Nephilim in their mix but it was easy to see from their blended wings. One pair feathered the other pair dragon like. They floated in the air watching all before them.

"The Goddess Hera has returned to Earth and now we have but two options, join her or face annihilation from two fronts." Sarah said as she stepped forward, her voice ringing clearly through the fog. "The Nymphs and Sirens will stand with the Goddess, she was one of the Gods that made us and shaped us. We have a debt of duty to her. The rest of you have the freedom to choose as you will but I do warn you. It is far better to have Hera as an ally than an enemy, her wrath is legendary, her revenge inescapable, her powers without match."

"If her powers are without match how was she

defeated in the War?" retorted one of the Succubi.

"The War changed many things, the element of surprise and the extra powers the Angels had stolen from imprisoned Gods gave them the upper hand. Hera was imprisoned in Heaven by her own husband fearing her."

"If that doesn't say something about her then I don't know what does. The Shapeshifters acknowledge Hera as protector and absolute authority." Akiko said stepping forward, one hand raised up.

Your pledge is accepted little fox, you are most wise. She heard whispered into her mind. She glanced around but saw nothing and none of the other leaders acted like they had heard anything. Hera was listening and no one realised it. This would not end well.

Tsarina Sophia Ben Sarah was no fool, she knew the Goddess was around, and felt her communicate with the Kitsune. She didn't know what was said, but she felt the subtle power of the Goddess suffocating all other powers. Her eerie melodious voice rang out "The Gadawsant bow before the Goddess"

And they shall stand above their ancestors. Hera whispered back.

Sophia gasped quietly, she knew their past, knew their dream, their driving need. They had broken their Oaths to the Seelie Court and the Light Court, fleeing their ancestral homes when the Angels attacked. They had fled to France discovering and breeding with small pockets of Nephilim, only to flee once again when the revolution started and the Angels eyes were drawn to France. They had fled to America seeking a new start and a new identity. And Hera was going to give it to them.

One of the Succubi spat "I refuse to bow before her. The Gods abandoned us to the Angels and now they reappear. Let her fight her own war." She was cut off suddenly as violet fire engulfed her. All watched in horror as she writhed in agony for minutes as her skin blistered and burned, peeling off from blackening bones, but she was not allowed to die. Her reddish spirit was trapped to the dead body until it was completely consumed. A slash of violet ripped the spirit apart, fragments of green magic splashing across the park and sinking into the ground.

"Anyone else of the same opinion?" came Hera's disembodied voice, rolling like thunder.

The Temptress and King dropped to their knees instantly "In the name of Hera we are reborn."

"Good" she said as the materialised in the space between them, her predatory smile bright against the shadows. "Then it is time we started claiming New York as our own. We can't build an empire if we don't have a city. We need to remove all power of the Angels."

"We could burn down all the mosques, racism is more prominent than people are willing to admit. Muslims are hated and distrusted universally across the States, if we target them first then the Angels will not take much notice." King Joseph offered from his knees, she had scared him badly. To so easily and cruelly kill an honour guard showed just how much power was at her disposal.

Hera whipped around, evaporating and reappearing next to him smiling. Her long pale fingers lifted his chin, raising his blood red eyes to meet her violet ones.

"An excellent idea Joseph, let us tear it apart from the foundations. We will divide and conquer on a purely Human level. Let it be done."

With a clap of thunder she was gone, leaving behind dozens of Daemons wondering what they had gotten themselves into.

Chapter 10

The whole council was in session, every single Elder Angel, with the exception of Sariel sat in their seats. This was a closed session, none of the Ascended or Lesser were allowed to attend. The Ascended would be allowed in the second sitting and the Lesser would be informed later on. This was a matter of Heaven's security, Heaven had been fought for by the Elders. It was their magic that had combated the Gods.

Nuriel stood waiting to be called to the centre, her nerves frayed and her wings twitching. Gabriel was not going to like what she had to say, the other Arch Angels would understand. But Gabriel was a loose cannon.

Those legendary violet eyes pinned her where she stood before calling for her "Nuriel step forward and report."

There had been other reports, some from Ariel's Inquisitors, some from Michael's Cherubim and some from Gabriel's Seraphim, each providing evidence on the Goddesses' activities that they had discovered. She of course had the fullest extent of the story, but she had not had time to pass it onto Michael.

She stepped forward, pushing her nerves away and trying to ignore the two hundred odd eyes watching her.

"Much of the early stage has been well accounted for. Brigid once escaping helped Hera escape and the two of them fled to the Mount Olympus Portal to descend to the Surface. Traces of Sariel suggest she has been kidnapped and is either contained or unconscious."

"This has been covered"

Nuriel imagined gagging Gabriel just to make this

easier. "From the portal the two Goddesses were separated. Hera I have tracked to the Grand Canyon in the United States of America. It seems like she inadvertently claimed part of the region, leaving a clear signal for us to track. Since then she has apparently disappeared. There have been some magical traces found in the Gulf Stream but it seems unlikely she is hiding in it. A rough estimate places her most likely on one of the cities on the East Coast."

"Could you be any vaguer Nuriel, the point was to pin point them."

"Nuriel has identified a clear region which is more than any of the Guards or Legions have managed. While we have the Legions scouring Europe it would appear Hera has had the intelligence to go to ground in the New World. Clearly she is trying to be careful and Nuriel should be congratulated on narrowing it down to one country." Raphael added in her defence. She felt her heart flutter a little, he was defending her.

Gabriel's gaze flicked from Nuriel across to Raphael and if looks could kill he would have been dissected on the floor.

"Hera you have tracked to the east coast of America what of Brigid?" Michael asked, he knew the best ways to direct Gabriel's mounting anger. Her eyes swung back to Nuriel with increased fervour.

"We have managed to track a small trace near Uluru, Australia but she seems either more skilled or more careful than Hera. What few traces we have found have been miniscule and old. There was a feel of her across Australia suggesting she is using the Lifestream. We have no clear position of where she might be. Several unusual events in both America and Australia could be blamed on them or they might be natural events."

"So no one has any idea where Brigid is. One of

the most powerful Goddesses the world has ever seen can only be guessed to be on the east coast of a huge country and the other Goddess, not a weakling by any standards cannot apparently be traced at all."

Everyone fell silent at the cold fury in Gabriel's voice, not even Michael was foolish enough to speak. Nuriel wished she could run away or hide in the shadows.

"Have there been any signs from the Underworld?" Everyone jumped as Azrael spoke, even Gabriel looked a little stunned.

"Presently there are none. Your Reapers have not mentioned any changes, Hell and Purgatory appear the same. However change might come. It is clear Brigid is utilising the Lifestream, Hera may as well. Quickening the Lifestream could have unforeseen affects upon the Underworld."

There was a moment of silence as the implications sunk in before Michael asked "has there been any sign of Sariel?"

"I'm sorry my Lord but there have been no traces of her at all. It is as if she has vanished into thin air. There are no magical traces anywhere on the Surface that we have found. We are scouring everywhere we can, but either she is being blocked by one of the Goddesses which seems unlikely considering the small amount of traces or she remains unconscious."

"Is it possible that she is in the Underworld or on the moon?" All eyes turned to Ariel with her unusual suggestion.

"I can have Angels check the moon as soon as we are done, but as for the Underworld there is no way to check. If she is down there then she is trapped." Her words hung in the air, there was nothing anyone could say. If she was in the Underworld there was absolutely nothing anyone could do to help her.

Chapter 11

The Underworld was darker when Sariel moaned herself awake. She was utterly exhausted, on the verge of starting to Desiccate, Angels were after all living Divine, they didn't have the benefits that the Gods did.

What was the point of doing anything anyway, if a Demon attacked she wouldn't be of much use. She might as well lay here and listen to the gentle lapping of the river against her island or the rhythmic sloshing...that was getting closer.

She gingerly stood up, turning around to face the approaching noise.

A woman stood in the river, wearing darkness like a cloak. She was stunningly beautiful in a way she wasn't used to. Exceptionally pale skin that looked finer than porcelain, long flowing black hair that swept over bare shoulders. Amethyst eyes that seemed to glow in a striking face with amethyst lips. She wore a black dress, exposing her shoulders and with long slits that revealed her legs as she walked. Knee high boots sloshed their way through the river, before crunching on the island.

She was like something out of a story, an Underworld Nymph or Demon.

"When the spirits said there was an Angel near Hell we thought they had been deceived. I feel as though my senses are fooling me, for I cannot believe that an Elder Angel would be so foolish as to venture into the Underworld let alone approach Hell."

Sariel blinked back not comprehending "It wasn't my decision to come to the Underworld, Hera was disturbed when opening the Portal."

The woman's eyes widened and her whole manner

changed "Hera opened a portal?"

"Yes she opened the Mount Olympus Portal when we fled from Heaven but we got separated and I don't know where the others ended up."

"The others?" More than one God had escaped Heaven? The Fates be praised!

"Brigid and Hera"

Two Goddesses free from the Angels, pity the girl didn't know where they were, but if they were on the Surface there was hope yet. This Angel surely had more information, but she looked about ready to keel over. What kind of Elder Angel went wandering around the Underworld in such a state? She looked on the verge of Desiccation, then she would have been of no use other than a power source.

"I am Hecate and I have been asked to escort you back."

She started crying "thank you, I've been so lost and hungry and I was attacked by a Demon and it's been absolute Hell and it's been scary and" she trailed off crying, her rush of words touching a soft spot in Hecate. Hecate gently pulled her into a loose embrace, what was a girl doing outside of Heaven? She lacked the usual mettle of an Angel, and it seemed like she had had a rough ride. For some reason she felt compassion towards her.

"What is your name?"

"Sariel" she felt her blood run cold and her compassion wither.

"The Arch Angel Michael's sister?" she was absolutely horrified, Sariel was the famous sister raised by Michael and Gabriel. She had never been seen outside of Heaven and was rumoured to be providing him with powers. It certainly explained his legendary powers during the War. Which meant she had the potential to be an Arch Angel.

"Yes Michael is my brother, do you know him?"

Her question asked so innocently re-stirred her compassion. But how had Michael's enigmatic sister gotten involved with Hera and Brigid?

"Not personally" and for that she was thankful, it hadn't been a personal betrayal nor had he had a personal reason to track her down. He had literally ripped Aphrodite limb from limb, beating her to a pulp before finally draining her Lifeforce and giving her the final release. Then again she had been cruel and unusual in her treatment of her servants. He hadn't been the only one attacking her, but the others were no match for his power or fury.

"Where are you escorting me back to and who asked you?"

She hesitated wondering if Sariel would know any of the names or connotations. "Back to Erebus" Her vacant look was answer enough "There is a castle there, come on you look ready to keel over."

"Is it far" she wouldn't be able to go far, her body was beginning to run on her magical powers just to keep her standing.

"Distance is relative in the Underworld, to those who know how to use it great distances can easily be traversed. Only within each domain are distances set." She held out her slender hand for Sariel, she took it surprised that it was warm.

Hecate laughed "I'm not dead, I can resist the chilling of the Underworld easily"

She took a step supporting Sariel as the whole world suddenly lurched. Hecate continued to take steady, even steps, her iron grip holding Sariel up as she staggered. Sariel couldn't keep her balance as rivers, tunnels, chasms and cliffs surged past her. She saw flashes of orange fire and white-blue spirits. Suddenly they all stopped solidifying back into the current world. They stood on the stone jetty she had seen not so long ago.

"Sorry Travelling can be very disconcerting, especially the first time. I'm so used to it I forget about the side effects."

"Why are we here? A giant Monster tried to kill me. It had three heads."

"Oh so you were the one that got away from Cerberus. He was riled up for days over the Angel that had escaped him. He moaned about how it had ran away into the Borderlands, cheating he called it."

"He tried to kill me!"

"Well naturally he is a guard dog and he has no fondness for Angels."

"Because of the War?"

Hecate stopped herself from spluttering, she had said it so casually like it was some small event. Was she so naive that she didn't grasp the complexity of the War? The Angels had destroyed the Old Order, confining what remained of her brethren to the Underworld. Never to feel the sun or the rain, to never feel fresh air running through her hair or the living strength of the Lifeforce.

There was a loud creak followed by heavy padding, out of the darkness glowed six pairs of red eyes all fixed on her. His teeth bared back in anger, his serpentine tail flicking back and forth like some great weapon. She felt his anger as though it was a solid and living thing, tangible between them.

"Sit" Hecate snapped.

Within an instant the snarling Monster became a simpering puppy, his shoulders hunched and his heads hanging. Sariel understood, she had to resist the urge to sit herself, such had been the commanding tone in

Hecate's voice. A thunder clap combined with the roar of the ocean.

Hecate sighed "You are so skittish Cerberus, I sometimes wonder if you remember the power you have at your disposal." She reached up, scratching under his middle chin. A low growl echoed around the cavern as his hind leg started to quiver.

Sariel hesitantly stepped forward, angling herself behind Hecate's comforting presence. Instantly his hackles were raised and his teeth were bared. Those glowing red eyes paralysing her.

"Cerberus be nice. This is Sariel she may be staying with us for a while" she glanced back at Sariel "hold out your hand for him to smell."

She stared at the Monstrous dog then down at her hand. With the greatest trepidation she held out her hand before three sets of jaws almost bigger than she was. The middle snout gently sniffed her hand before her started to whine.

Hecate gently rubbed his head "it is okay I know she smells but a wash will solve that"

Sariel hesitantly sniffed herself. She hadn't noticed that she smelled. Hecate's eyes were watching when she looked back "You smell like Heaven, down here that is a bad smell."

"Oh" she hadn't realised that Heaven had a distinct smell.

Before she could ask any questions Hecate snapped her fingers and Cerberus was off bounding down the tunnel. She steered Sariel down the tunnel, gently supporting her.

The tunnel was very long and dark, it felt very foreboding. There were the occasional blue-white flash or amethyst flame but otherwise the darkness was unbroken. From what she could see in the small pockets of light the walls were decorated with carvings. Many looked like they represented Gods, at least she presumed they were Gods. The other figures were often bowing or praying before them. There was one image of a man wearing a helmet that kept reappearing again and again. She guessed he must be important, or had been.

After a time they came before a colossal door. It was a construction unlike any she had ever seen before. Not only in its design but its materials. It appeared to be made from granite and steel but was highly decorated in inscriptions of gold, silver, copper and platinum. There were also the occasional flash of cobalt blue and red, their colours so stunning in this realm of ever grey.

Hecate waved her arm, dark purple flames burning in its wake. The same flames seared along the crack of the door before it started to groan open. They swung out leisurely to reveal only darkness behind. No not just darkness, living darkness, it was like looking at a pool of tar or ink.

Sariel instinctively feared it, she was a creature of the light. It would consume her, destroy her. She started to step back but Hecate steered her forward again. She tried to hold her ground but she had no strength. She might as well not have been trying for all the notice Hecate took. She wanted to scream but it was trapped in her throat.

Then she was being swallowed by the darkness, it reached out to embrace her, wrapping around her. There was nothing but darkness. She could not sense or feel a thing. Temperature, light and sound had ceased to exist. The only thing she felt was Hecate's hand.

She fell to her knees blinded by the light. Behind her Hecate laughed. She gasped for breath not understanding where the darkness had gone. It had been swallowing her, she had lost all sense of everything then she was in a brightly lit meadow with the light hurting her eyes. Once her eyes adjusted she looked around at the gently rolling green hills, some had laughing people running across them or lazing under the shade of a tree.

They stood on a road that wound down between the hills to where lines of people stood before an open air classical styled building. Behind it there were three distinctive lands. To the left were skies of fire and smoke, sharp black mountains pierced the sky, some even reaching up to the ceiling far above. To the right stood serene glades, rivers and healthy looking fields. In the middle were shadows and light, it seemed about balance. Fire raced along parts of the sky beside dark clouds releasing rain and rainbows. The land was both gentle and harsh, sharp pine trees stood next to stout oaks, raging rivers and gentle lakes.

She glanced behind her to look for the door of darkness, but instead there just seemed to be a portal of blinding light. Instead of the wispy spirits she had seen in her travels through the Underworld there were bronze skinned people walking out of the light. They looked at them both curiously before following the road down the hills.

"Welcome to Hades" Hecate said smiling, she looked glad to be back.

"What is it?"

Hecate looked at her funny, did this girl know nothing? "It is the realm of the dead, the afterlife for those of the ancient Greek or Roman colonies and empires."

"What about those that just entered, surely they can't be from ancient empires?"

"You would be surprised how long some people get lost in the Underworld. Generally though they are likely to be unclaimed spirits that have found their way here."

"What are unclaimed spirits?"

"Did they teach you nothing in Heaven? Your ignorance is astounding for an Elder Angel." She shook her head sadly at the girl, starting to feel sorry for her, how much of her ignorance was intentional.

"With the spread of the Angels religions; Christianity, Judaism and Islam, there also spread the Angels influence. Their influence includes the claiming of the spirits that belonged to them, either up into Heaven or for the sinful cast into Hell or Purgatory. Up until the last century it was very rare for there to be unclaimed spirits, but now Humans are turning away from the Angels' religions. With no claims they are at the mercy of the Underworld. They might be lucky to stumble across one of the realms or be unlucky enough to be swept up in the rivers to Hell.

"It has been a pleasant change having new faces."

They turned when they heard screeching. Several bird women were chasing a running man out of the fiery landscape and onto the hills. They screeched again before diving down and attacking him. His agonised screams reached them, cut off by a faint gurgling sound. Hecate stood watching passively while Sariel stared in horror as they dragged the pieces of him back towards the fiery landscape.

"What are they?"

"Oh them? Harpies. They stop people from escaping their punishment."

"Punishment? Punishment for what?"

"They truly taught you nothing." She shook her head sadly "The actions of mortals during their lives affect their afterlives. Those who lead good lives end up in Heaven or similar places, those who don't end up in Hell."

"But that seemed so brutal, like it was a sport to them."

Hecate turned those ancient, haunted eyes to her "Harpies gauge their actions based on their victims. He was a rapist who murdered his victims, he has a long time to pay off his crimes."

She turned and headed down the hill, leaving Sariel to chase after her.

Hecate pointed to the building as they passed the lines of people waiting outside "In there the spirits of the dead are judged based on their actions in life. It is a place of great power, the judging is final and cannot be overturned unless by a God."

"Why would a God overturn a judgement?"

"Was there ever anyone in Heaven who you thought shouldn't have been there?"

"I don't know I was never allowed to leave the palace. Though Ariel's Inquisitors always gave me the creeps."

Well that explained a lot about her naivety, if she was never allowed to leave the palace then what information she came into contact with could be easily controlled. But why would Michael of all people keep his sister so much in the dark?

"That might explain why both Michael and Gabriel barely tolerated them in the palace. So you're saying that they belonged in Hell but Ariel saved them?"

"It is very possible" and very likely, Ariel was very similar to Gabriel but of a crueller nature, she didn't have the same self-control Gabriel had. The fact she had spent a lot of time with the Aztec Gods and spent a considerable time as Ares' lover said a lot about her sadistic nature.

"Where are we headed?" Sariel asked full of

curiosity, her time in Hades was revitalising her, she didn't look quite so ready to keel over and was walking on her own.

She pointed at the border of the fiery landscape and the balanced landscape, the shape of a tower could just be seen between the clouds and smoke "There to Hades' palace." Damn she had been avoiding mentioning his name. What would Sariel already know about him? What misconceptions had she been spoon fed?

"There is a palace down here?" She hadn't even blinked at the name, it meant nothing to her. The name of one of the oldest and most feared Gods meant absolutely nothing to her. What the Hell were the Angels playing at?

Hecate laughed "Of course, where else would a ruler live but in a palace."

"I don't know where else would they live?"

She laughed again the girls naivety was surprisingly endearing. This could work to their advantage. "Rulers usually live in palaces or something similar as a mark of their power. It has been proven time and time again by mortals and Divine alike. It is a symbol of their power, it is also a deterrent against rebellion. But here in Hades no one would dare, this is and always will be his realm.

"It must be comforting for him to know that."

She laughed again, its pure melodies drawing the attention of the dead "I imagine it must be, you should tell him that. It might take the sting out of ruling here."

"Why does it sting to rule here?"

"Never mind that is a story for a different time."

Walking in the borderlands was daunting for Sariel, it quickly sapped what little strength she had gleaned from the hills. Hecate was completely used to the whole realm, but deflected much of its brunt away from them. She once again had to support the poor girl, she was looking ready to collapse again. She needed food and rest to heal her body. How long had she been in the Underworld to be on the verge of Desiccating?

The land was dark and stormy, holding the threat of wrath and vengeance in every inch of it. The sky was a maelstrom, lines of fire stretched across it like rivers, lighting rent the air in bright flashes. Bruised clouds fed on the plumes of smoke and behind it all flittered shadows. Some were Harpies, the others Sariel had no idea what they were.

They had walked onto a long causeway leading to the palace that was currently obscured by a storm. On their left lay lakes and rivers of lava that continually spat sparks and smoke into the air. Sharp black rocks dominated the landscape, they seemed inclined to keep breaking, always leaving their edges sharp. The land was so smoky it obscured most of the people.

She wished it had obscured them all. People were staked out, chained up or fleeing their pursuers. Strange creatures of nightmare were torturing the inhabitants, rending them into pieces. It left her feeling cold despite the heat pulsating out of the lava.

On the other side stood a storm blasted forest, dark with twisting mist and low clouds. Strange forms moved within those shadows, but were they spirits, guardians or torturers? She didn't know.

White flowers grew everywhere, among the trees, in the meadows and even on the sheer cliff faces where rivers cascaded into the magma under the bridge. Occasionally something would pick one of the flowers, but she never managed to see what, only mist and shadows.

"Those are asphodels, they have a special meaning in this place, you'll find them quite abundant everywhere"

Seeing the landscape and having lived in the governing palace of Heaven she thought she would have been prepared for Hades' palace.

She wasn't.

It was intimidating. It perched on a rock outcrop in the middle of a lake of lava. Steam and smoke rose from the lake, twisting and twirling around the palace as it rose, casting strange orange rainbows between the dancing sparks. Asphodel grew liberally all over the outcrop, every nook and cranny, every patch of earth had an explosion of the flowers, glowing pale white.

The palace was built from the same black rock as the bridge and outcrop, it seemed to absorb the light and reflect none of it back. It blended into every shadow cast across it from the smoke and clouds.

The palace soared up off the outcrop as though it was trying to stab the sky, the soaring central tower was lost in the clouds above. The palace was all about sharp angles, high walls and soaring arches that all seemed to blend into the shadows. It was as though the palace wanted to become shadows.

The portcullis was raised but she could see the lethally sharp points of black metal as they walked underneath it, through the thick walls and into the courtyard beyond.

Walking into the courtyard was hardly better, it just seemed to breathe shadows. The grand scale was imposing without the comfort of light that the governing palace had to balance itself with. Macabre statues adorned the courtyard, seeming to jump out of the many shadows. In the centre stood a grand fountain, pouring forth black water. The only break to the shadows were the asphodel plants in the fountain, their white lights stark against the black water.

Hecate led her unerringly up to the looming black double doors that swung open as they approached them. A much smaller Cerberus greeted them, his tail wagging contently. Sariel almost laughed in here he was a comforting sight, strange to think that the Monster that had tried to kill her gave her comfort.

She looked around as she followed Hecate into the corridors. They all had high vaulted ceilings, some had triangular windows looking out onto the magma lake. Each corridor seemed stark and bleak, their only adornment more statues or suits of armour. Hecate led them through side corridors until they entered the grand entrance hall.

Sariel stared in amazement at the white marble staircase covered in luxurious red carpet with gold designs. Bright green and blue tapestries hung from arches, though their design was completely alien to her she found them comforting. Cerberus jumped around Hecate as she led her up the stairs, like everything else it was on a grand scale but she found it strangely comforting, she was used to white staircases. It led up onto the next level, ending at imposing ebony doors.

They opened silently as they approached, Cerberus rushed in before them.

Sariel followed into the room staring about in awe. It was a huge hall with a high vaulted ceiling, all composed of black rock. Large glass windows graced the walls letting in streams of light that couldn't be coming from outside. It was bright enough to belong in Heaven. The floor was all white marble, its veins all pointed towards the raised dais of grey marble. A long black carpet led up to the dais, on which sat two black marble thrones, inlaid with gold and ebony.

As impressive as the room and thrones were her eyes were drawn to the two people sitting on them.

One was a beautiful woman with long brown hair wearing a classical style dress of grey and midnight blue. She wore silver bangles on her arms, silver sandals on her feet as well as long delicate earrings. She wore an iron crown, decorated with silver and black pearls, while a large amethyst hung between her breasts. She was pale skinned from lack of sunlight, looked delicate but had fierce silver eyes that pierced her like a hawk's.

The man sitting next to her held the same strength she did but of a different kind. While she was delicate he was quite muscular. He wore a black toga with gold trimming, golden sandals but no jewellery graced his pallid olive skin. His hair was short and black, as was his beard and upon his head he wore a bronze and black helmet. He was the man from the carvings, but he looked very different.

She had never felt so out of place in her life. She stood in torn and dirty robes while the three of them were stunning in their dark clothing. For once in her life she was glad her skin was pale and that her hair and wings were black, it gave her the smallest sense of not being completely alien. At least her eyes were similar in colour to Hecate's.

The two people on the throne stared at her for a long time before he spoke "Hecate why have you brought an Arch Angel into my domain? His voice gave her the creeps, there was something not all together natural sounding about it.

"I'm hardly much of an Arch Angel" those black eyes flicked to her, glaring with the full might of undiluted rage. His queen placed her hand on his arm to calm him.

She stood up fixing her silver eyes on Sariel "You two have matters to discuss I will attend to the needs of our guest, she looks the worse for wear. We will re-join you for dinner" She swept down the dais, her train making soft musical noises behind her "Come child" she ushered Sariel along in front of her. She cast a worried look over her shoulder at Hecate who simply smiled at her.

Hecate turned back to face Hades when the doors snapped shut. "She is a special case. She is Michael's sister and you could say Gabriel's protégé"

"Michael's sister! You brought Michael's own sister into my domain. Are you trying to kill us all? We will have all the Legions of Heaven pouring through our gate. You have brought our destruction upon us."

"Stop being so dramatic Hades, the Angels are not going to come into the Underworld, they would be stuck here just like we are. Michael's sister is the key to our salvation not the harbinger of our doom. She has been horribly mistreated by her family, kept as a prisoner and power slave. She escaped and in the process freed Brigid and Hera. Hera opened the Portal for them all, helping Sariel flee. If that isn't the highest recommendation then I don't know what is."

"Hera is free? My sister is alive?"

"Yes I believe that she is on the Surface."

"Then she is sowing the seeds for the Gods return, let us hope she has avoided the whole Mediterranean region for the usurpers will surely look there first."

"I believe they will have their hands full looking for Brigid, Hera and Sariel."

"And what are your plans for this Arch Angel?"

"Sariel is young and naive, she has been sorely mistreated by her brother. She barely knows how to use her magic but she has incredible potential. She has no notions of our names or any of the other connotations attached to us. We are a blank slate to her, she has no preconceptions about us. She has no reason to distrust us, no reason to fear us. I believe we can use her to break the stalemate."

"And how do you propose to do that?"

"She has the powers of an Arch Angel, untested yes but she can break the Curse on Lucifer. She can open up the Underworld."

He gasped "If she can free Lucifer we may stand a chance at winning the War."

"If she can break the Curse"

Sariel sighed as she slipped herself into the bath. She groaned in pleasure as the hot water rose up over her breasts and neck, the cleaning agents stinging the fading scars. She had had a small amount of food to tide her over to dinner, but it had not been enough to fully recharge her healing abilities. The water eased stiff and sore muscles while the dirt slowly slid off of her. She needed to scrub but lacked the energy, instead easing back to think.

She had been incredibly lucky that Hecate had found her, another day or two and she would have been unable to move and would have been easy prey to any Demons. And if they hadn't found her she would have become little more than a Divine corpse, a true power slave for whoever happened to find her. The body is weak but the power is strong. She suddenly wondered if Heaven contained Desiccated corpses of Angels, had they been returned to their living state or were they simply being tapped. Did any of the Demon races do the same thing?

Desiccation had been staved off with a visit to the kitchens where she had been introduced to Persephone's mother, Demeter. She had stared at her for a long time her green eyes cold and calculating before Persephone had laid her arm on her. Sariel wondered if there was some special significance in that action for both Demeter and Hades to suddenly capitulate their unguarded anger. She seemed universally hated for being an Angel.

Her small lunch had given her a glimpse into life in the palace. Demeter and Persephone had the relationship she had always longed for with her mother, though she was dead. She could tell they were guarded around her, though Persephone seemed to warm to her. She took her out on a tour of the palace, it was a truly impeding building, it seemed to live and breathe darkness and it cast long shadows over the landscape around it. It was nowhere near the size of the governing palace in Heaven and it lacked its delicate beauty but it had its own dark beauty. And its views were truly amazing.

She saw the Shadowlands or more correctly the Asphodel Fields, the flowers glowing like stars in the mist and shadows. It was where most people went. In the distance she saw Elysium with its sunlight and beautiful trees, the place for those chosen by the Gods and for heroes. Then there were the fiery lands of torment which stood above the Gates of Tartarus.

As beautiful as the views from the walls were she was stunned by the views at the top of the central tower. She had seen for miles in every direction, the views so different and striking. It was so different from Heaven, she found she loved it more. Variety and change were interesting, fascinating. Everything was so different from Heaven.

There was even a limitation to the skies, up this high she could see the great doming of rock that encompassed all of Hades. There was no endless airspace leading up into the Darkness Beyond. No one dared venture there. It was weird to know that everything she saw was under the Surface. It certainly didn't have the claustrophobic shadows she had gotten lost in.

Finally Persephone had led her to her rooms. They were beautiful in a completely alien way. Her rooms in Heaven had been the standard gold, white marble and golden woods. Looking back it seemed a very sterile and empty arrangement. But in this palace darkness was the dominating feature not light. A hearty fire burned in a macabre fireplace, casting its strange dancing light around the room. In Heaven most things had the delicate look or it was made to be impressively intimidating. Things had been grand and soaring. Here there was a sense of strength, solidly built, sharp angles and even the hint of malice.

All the furniture was made from either ebony, darkwood or wrought iron, the bathroom was stunningly all black marble. The little veins of white and the gold and silver accents stark and yet beautiful at the same time. Her room despite the sense of strength and solidness held warmth something her rooms in Heaven had lacked looking back. Sure they had been bright and airy but these rooms were sumptuously decorated with violet carpets, upholstery, bedding and tapestries. It complimented the black so well that it gave a sense of ease to her.

She had found it surprisingly easy to have a nap before her bath.

She opened her eyes when she heard the bathroom doors open. Persephone walked in carrying a long black dress, which she laid across the backless golden armchair. Following her into the room were several women with very pale lilac skin and long pale grey hair. They all carried various flasks, boxes and pots.

"Time to get you clean little Angel" and with that said they descended on her despite her protests. They scrubbed her skin until it glowed, her hair until no more dirt came out. They rinsed her over and over until even her feathers had no dirt in them. She felt like she had been drowned in a whirlpool.

They helped her out of the bath, once again ignoring her protests, indeed they seemed amused by her modesty. In Heaven one did not see others naked unless they were married and here she was with six different women seeing her completely naked. It was beyond shameful.

They dried her before helping her into the dress. They ignored her protests that she was perfectly able to dress herself. Her joy of being dressed was short lived, the dress was the most revealing thing she had ever worn. It was nothing like the heavy ceremonial robes of the Arch Angels. She could see not just her cleavage but ample amounts of it, one of her shoulders was completely bare and the arm it belonged to. She saw slithers of her calves and thighs and it clung to her like a second skin. She felt highly exposed.

They then led her to the chair and pushed her down into it. Then they started opening all the pots and boxes that sat amongst the candles. From the pots came creams and powders while from the boxes came jewellery. She watched in the mirror as they applied makeup to her face.

She quickly didn't recognise the face staring back at her. She looked older and more mature, no longer the child's face she seemed trapped in. The makeup accentuated her sharp, delicate features, the eye shadow emphasising her violet eyes. Her hair had been styled in a graceful tumble that fell across her shoulders and framed her face. A large amethyst on a golden chain hung between her breasts, even drawing her eyes to them. The black dress clung to her developing womanly curves while perfectly complimenting her wings and hair. It was hard to tell if they were separate or one and the same.

She looked beautiful. Her violet painted lips parted in amazement, giving her the look of a seductress.

"You look like you belong here" Persephone whispered.

She did. She genuinely looked like she belonged amongst these people. She was one of them. At least in looks.

Persephone held out her arm "come we have dinner to attend to. It is time you met the other inhabitants of the palace and we are all interest to know how you ended up in the Underworld."

Sariel was led into a smaller banquet hall, designed for cosier dinners. There was a wide circular darkwood table, around which were numerous darkwood chairs with high arched backs. Several fires burned in the fireplaces, the natural fires giving warmth and cheer to the room. The strange blue-white fires added a brighter but colder light to the room. Making the shadows longer and more imposing.

At the table were several people. Hades sat pride of place with one space on either side of him. The space between him and Demeter was clearly for Persephone, while the other space was between him and Hecate. She had no idea who the other people were.

There was a fierce looking woman with one white wing and one black. Was she a special type of Angel she had never heard of? She had clearly been in the Underworld for a long time, her skin had that pale pallor the rest of them had. Her red glare was enough for Sariel to falter in her step, it was pure hatred and malice.

There was a man wearing a flowing black shroud with only his skeleton hands poking out the end of his sleeves. They had no flesh but they moved just like regular hands when he picked up his goblet. Next to Hecate was a woman who didn't quite look solid. Her pale skin fading in and out of what she thought was spirit. She had two long canine teeth like the Vampire Demons she had read about in the library. Was she a Vampire?

There were three Human looking men clad in white togas with golden laurels on their brows. They looked at her in fascination. There were also three winged women, fierce looking and dressed in short red robes but their red eyes held no malice when they looked at her.

There were two shadow men, more shadows in the shape of men than flesh and bone. They looked at her with burning eyes sending shivers down her skin. She had never seen anything less mortal looking. Next to them sat two pale skinned men, Angels perhaps? They both had one pair of glorious black wings, and matching black hair. One was asleep while the other stared gloomily into his goblet. They matched each other in loose grey robes.

As she had thought Persephone sat between her husband and mother but indicated for her to take the seat between Hades and Hecate. She was here to be witnessed and analysed. All eyes watched her as she sat down, but turned away as she struggled to adjust her six wings comfortably against the back of the chair.

Everyone turned back to their own conversations leaving her out of the loop. She glanced around the table trying to discreetly study everyone. She noticed there was one empty chair left.

Time began to pass and Sariel felt politely ignored. She looked like she belonged but she didn't really. She grew quickly bored of studying the cutlery and table top and just wished the last person would turn up. She was getting fed up of ignoring the fact she was being studied by all at the table.

As though summoned by her thought the doors opened as the last person entered. She was a strange looking woman. Beautiful, oh so beautiful, but stunning in a completely unnatural and entrancing way. Her long black hair floated around her head unworried by gravity. Her skin was the same pale as everyone else but all her veins were traced in black. Her fingertips, lips and eyes were completely black. It was as though she was darkness itself housed in flesh. Sariel wondered if it was true. The Angels had always said the Underworld was populated by creatures of Darkness.

Most alarmingly she sat down in the empty chair directly opposite her. Her eyes flicked to Sariel as she sat down, holding Sariel transfixed by those dark pools. She was powerless before this woman.

Then she spoke breaking the spell on Sariel "Well it has been a long time since an Angel was allowed in these halls. Or dared to. But never have I encountered an Angel so innocent."

"Nyx this is Sariel, Michael's sister. She is herself an Arch Angel that has somehow happened upon the Underworld. She was just about so share her story with us all." Hecate said for her.

"And here I was thinking that the entertainment was her execution" said the red eyed woman with the malicious glare.

There was an awkward silence as Sariel looked from her to Hecate before Nyx spoke again "One so innocent cannot be deserving of an execution. She has no crimes to answer for." The woman snorted in disdain before Nyx continued "if I did not see her wings I would doubt she was an Angel at all. So innocent is she that I would question she was even Divine if it was not so clear."

"Why? Angels are pure beings who guide mankind to a brighter future"

Everyone laughed at her, cruel and humourless. "My poor girl you are so naive. The Angels have never been guardians of mankind. They are the bastard offspring of the Sun and Sky Gods who usurped Heaven. They brutally killed, enslaved or trapped their rightful masters. You would do well not to mention the lies you have been fed down here otherwise you will find all hostile to you." It was one of the strange shadow men that spoke, his voice was husky with great age but the enormous power it held pounded against her.

"She is young and naive, mistreated and deliberately lied to by her own kind. She is unlike any Angel we have ever met because she herself has been mistreated by the Angels." Hecate snapped at them all. She felt strangely defensive of Sariel.

"Curiously Sariel do you know who your parents were?"

It was pretty standard for Angels not to know who their fathers were in the Age of Gods and sometimes not even know who their mothers were.

Sariel sighed then swallowed as her throat threatened to dry up "I was born as the War was starting to turn in the Angels' favour. My parents were killed shortly afterwards leaving me in the care of my brother and his wife. My mother was the Arch Angel Lilith but I know very little about her, it was rare to find any mention of her in the library. And the other Angels shied away from mention of her. From what I gather her pregnancy of me was highly unexpected to the other Angels. I think she had left Heaven by then. There appeared to be some incident in Eden."

"She married Adam but refused to submit to him. It was a highly strange arrangement considering she was still married to Samael at the time. We were never quite sure why she did it, and yes after she left Eden she seemed to disappear but it appears she bore at least one more Angelic child." Hecate interjected.

Sariel nodded silently thanking her, at least she had another piece in the puzzle that was her life and lineage. "My father was Samael," there was sharp intake of breath "as you mentioned they were married, though it does seem a very strange marriage by any standards. I do know more of him though. He was the first to test Man's faith. He was also the first Angel of Death, both Michael and I inherited some of his gift. It has been said Lucifer was his Protégé and there are hushed whispers about his name. All I know is that he died in the War.

I do not remember either of them.

I was given into Michael and Gabriel's care and raised by them. I led a very lonely childhood, contained within the Governing Palace. In my 1800 years I was allowed into the citadel six times and never allowed to leave Heaven. I had very little magic to my name, though I was still crowned as an Arch Angel. I spent my life thinking I was a freak only to discover that they were the reason, they stole my powers to use as they wanted. My uncle made me leave and I'm worried about his wellbeing in case they figure out it was him that allowed me to escape.

Perhaps the most important discovery was of the Goddess Brigid imprisoned in the bowels of Heaven" there was much stirring and many looks exchanged between the Gods "she had been transformed into an Elder Angel. I'm not sure what happened but when I went to free her I somehow freed myself of my curse."

"Containment spells are rather volatile to each other, I imagine the process was quite explosive" Nyx added.

"Yes it was. I was passed out when Brigid decided to save me. If I had been found in that cell I dare not think what would have happened to me. We went to Hera's palace to seek her assistance in opening a Portal. What we found was sickening, unimaginable cruelty. She was still chained by the chains of her husband but she had had extra containment spells applied to her. They had tortured her again and again, her fire of Divinity was but a flickering ember such was the torment they had applied to her. They had tortured her for century after century with ever increasing acts of cruelty." She fell silent shaking in anger. The Gods all looked around at each other, while they were concerned for Hera such actions did not overly concern them. Such acts of cruelty had been very common place amongst the Gods, and such acts had not been uncommon against other Gods.

Sariel continued on "I freed her and healed her, then we all fled to Mount Olympus to use its Portal. But we were followed by the Angels, Hera threw me in early to protect me, but we were all separated. I hope they are okay."

"Believe me Hera can well look after herself. She is one of the most naturally powerful Goddesses the world has ever seen. Plus she has a brilliant mind for scheming. It was through fear that Zeus chained her to her house. Brigid I do not know of but as an Angel/Goddess hybrid I imagine she will be safe no matter where she goes to ground." Demeter said to her across the table "Both are also Mother Goddesses, they can ask the earth itself for protection. Have no fear of their wellbeing Sariel."

Sariel relaxed feeling a knot of anxiety she hadn't realised unwind in her.

"Samael was your father?" someone suddenly asked her. She leaned forward to look. It was one of the pale skinned men with the black wings and hair looking at her with wide black eyes. He was clutching his goblet as though it was trying to kill him. She missed the worried looks the Gods shared with each other. Nyx and the red eyed woman were watching her intently.

"Yes. He was the first Angel to have black wings, a trait of our family alone. I would guess it was a gift from Samael and Azrael's father, that was then passed onto Michael and I."

"Samael and Azrael are my sons" she dropped her goblet with a clang, the dark red drink splattering across like blood.

She stared at the man. Her grandfather? "What?"

"Samael was my son by an Angel, I think she was one of Zeus' brood but I could be wrong. As you said he was the first Elder Angel to have black wings and pale skin much like myself. He held considerable power for a Demigod with a wide array of skills. He was instrumental in the overthrow of Heaven, but he and Lucifer were also instrumental in the proposed peace between Gods and Angels. That was until Michael and Gabriel betrayed them, casting Lucifer into Hell and sealing shut the Underworld. It would seem betrayal runs thick in my lineage." He hung his head in shame.

"He was young and power hungry, something encouraged in the Gods. Who can blame him for his Divine heritage? If we had not been affected we would have praised him. Indeed we did praise him for his successes in Persia. He has mortal weaknesses in his Divine mix to make him far more volatile than other Gods."

"He still betrayed us mother" said the winged woman.

"And yet sister he pushed for peace, he and Lucifer reached out to us before they themselves were betrayed."

"This argument has been going since the Underworld was sealed, save it for another time. The more pressing issue is what do we do about Sariel? She has committed no crimes, lived a life of isolation, freed two Goddesses, one of them our own." Hades ruled over any argument.

"We accept her into the family of course. Blood is thicker than water, and our blood thicker yet. We have lost so many of our family members in the War. It is heartening to find her, a sign of destiny. The prodigal son's own innocent daughter has returned in his place. Samael is still Thanatos' son and she has committed no wrongs against us. Indeed she has helped us and I welcome my great-granddaughter into the family." She suddenly appeared next to Sariel, pulling her into a hug. Sariel sat there stunned. She and Michael were not alone, Azrael was not their only family, they had a whole clan.

"Mother you cannot expect me to accept an Angel as my great niece" the red eyed woman was absolutely horrified.

"Nemesis you will accept my granddaughter. She is so lost and alone, mistreated by her own brother. She needs us and I recognise the call of blood." Thanatos snapped at her.

Apparently what he had said was final, no one offered any argument, though some looked appalled.

"I believe that introductions are in order." Nyx turned to point to each person in turn "I believe you know Hades, Persephone, Demeter and Hecate. That is Thanatos your grandfather the God of Death, next to him asleep is his brother Hypnos the God of Sleep. Someone will have to fill him in once he awakens." She pointed to Nemesis "That is my daughter Nemesis the Goddess of Vengeance. That is my son Charon, who is the Ferryman for the dead. Cerberus is also a family member, he is my niece's Echidna's son. The two shadows are my brothers Tartarus and Erebus, our sister Gaia slumbers within the core of the planet unable to rise. You will find many relatives among Gaia's descendants, Hecate, Demeter, Hades and Persephone are all distant cousins of yours. Sadly so many were lost during the War."

She then pointed to the three red robed women "They are the Erinyes, family members as well. They once had free reign to chase criminals across the land for which they were widely known as the Furies. Sadly like the rest of us they are wasting away down here." She pointed to the vampirish woman "That is Mormo an old friend of Hecate's. The three men are the Judges of the Dead; Aiakos, Minos and Rhadamanthys. Don't worry they're not related to you" she smiled, encouraging a smile from Sariel.

Nyx stood up, pulling Sariel up with her "Come child, you need your rest and today has been full of surprises. It is a lot to absorb." Shadows engulfed them both then they were standing in Sariel's room. Nyx gently kissed her on the forehead sending her to sleep. She used magic to lift her onto the bed and wrap her up in the covers.

So one of Samael's brood had returned home, life was full of unexpected surprises.

They all watched Nyx and Sariel disappear into shadows before the room brightened again.

Hades was the first to break the lingering silence "What do we do with her?"

"We admit her into our fold, she is my granddaughter. The call of blood has been recognised."

"She could be used against us, a spy from Heaven. She may be on a scouting mission, can any of us actually verify her tale." Nemesis countered.

"Mother recognised the blood. She is our kin." Charon finally spoke in his deep haunting voice "And there are ways to prove her story as either fact or fiction. Hecate has the gift of seeing, mother has mastery of shadows, combined they can see all that shadows have touched."

"That is of no use in Heaven, they've swamped that place in light since the War."

"But the Surface belongs to both day and night, light and shadows. We can find either Hera or Brigid."

There was a murmur of appreciation at his wisdom.

"What if they have remained in Heaven though, throwing down Sariel as a distraction? My sight does have limitations, even with Nyx's help."

"Hecate it is worth a try. Not only could it verify Sariel's story but we can see that Hera is actually well. To think Demeter one of our sisters still lives." Hades gave his sister a hopeful look which she returned. Family relations had not always been the best but they had missed their brothers and sisters since the War, presuming they had all been slain.

""Yes it is worth a try, what harm can it do? If she speaks truth then she can stay and be of use, if she speaks lies then I'm sure we all have suggestions of what can be done to her" her smile was cold and savage. The cruelty of the Gods was legendary and with their powers they were limited only by their imagination.

"You speak so candidly of my granddaughter's life."

"A granddaughter that you have only just met and known of from today. Where is your Divine sense? She means nothing to us, she is our enemy, the spawn of our enemy. The daughter and sister of our betrayers Samael and Michael. She has been raised by him and that viper

Gabriel, how can we accept anything about her. She is the epitome of everything we hate about the Angels. Her sole use lies in the fact that as an Arch Angel she has the potential to break the Curse on Lucifer and free us all from our imprisonment." She snapped her wings wide, her blood red eyes blazing with her anger."

"She has great use either way. Regardless of whether she is trustworthy or not her only possible way to the Surface or Heaven is by descending through Hell and breaking the Curse on Lucifer. She is the tiebreaker to this stalemate we are stuck in. If she speaks true then Hera sent her to us exactly for that reason. Heaven certainly wouldn't willingly send one of their Arch Angels into Hell if there was the slightest chance they would break the Curse. I am inclined to believe her but that doesn't change her worth." Hypnos finally roused himself enough to join the conversation, stunning them all. Then his head lolled back on his shoulder as he fell back asleep.

They sat there in silence. He spoke the truth, they finally had a way to break Lucifer's Curse and free them of their own imprisonment. The Surface and Heaven had never felt so close before, their revenge was at hand and then the Angels would truly learn the full might of the Wrath of the Gods.

Chapter 12

Hera walked along the streets of New York, one in the midst of millions. But not just anyone, a Goddess walking amongst mortals again. Such had not happened since before the War of Heaven, they had no notion of her existence, no understanding that they should be afraid. She was the lion amongst the lambs, the weakening of their magical bloodlines made them so vulnerable to the Divine. They could not resist.

People stared at her as she walked past, though they had no real notion as to why. She was stunningly beautiful, most Divine had a certain degree of natural vanity but it was more than that. Her physical appearance gathered their looks but it was her magic and power that drew their curiosity. They were drawn to her as the moth is to the flame, but they could not comprehend why they found her so fascinating. Magic wasn't on their radar so to speak, its existence was but a quaint childish notion to them in this age of science and reason.

They were in for a rude awakening. She smiled imagining how Humanity was going to cope with the return of magic to their everyday lives.

She came to a stop in Times Square fading out of physicality feeling the rhythm of the place. It was one of New York's many hearts, iconic the world over and a place of pride for not only New Yorkers but for all the United States. It had a very modern beauty to it, especially when the sun set and all the lights came on. The Coca-Cola, Samsung, theatre and store displays. It was a place that called to her because it was so alien from her memories of cities. It fascinated her. It also called to the mortals. They left their imprint and unknowingly drew from it.

As though it were a place of worship.

New York was diverse in it ethnicity and religions. It had a strong presence of the Angel's religions but also Hinduism, Buddhism, Voodoo, Shamanism, Taoism, Confucianism and most interestingly Neopaganism. Their presences were weak compared to the Angels, but she was here and they were not. It was a challenge she had faced before, the conversion of whole cities and peoples to her own religions. It was a task she was up to, certainly each of the religions offered their own challenge in weaning away their followers, unbelievably some of the Neopagans worshipped her already. They were but a vision away from being completely hers.

The greatest challenge however was the atheists. People who didn't believe in the Gods or spirits. What a novel concept. It was nothing she had ever heard of before but then in her day the Gods' presence had been keenly felt. There was no denying their existence, but with their presence gone and the Angels barely visiting the Surface anymore a more rational way of thinking had evolved. They were a challenge worthy of her. Until of course she was free to declare herself to the world, there could be no denying and their quaint little beliefs would be completely broken.

She pulled forth the essences swirling around her, the millions of imprints left by the millions of visitors and travellers passing through over the years. She spun it into the smallest thread wrapping it around her wrist. She felt the beat and thrum of the place keenly and she gave back her own trickle of essence. The key was to attune the place to her without throwing out its equilibrium, for each person passing through to gather a small aspect of her power. To slowly be attuned to her.

For once she was getting to test her abilities with subtlety, something she certainly hadn't needed to do with the Roman Empire.

A city's heart was a place to win over its inhabitants, but modern cities had many hearts, each beating their own tune and essence. She had others to attune to in New York but she had plenty of time. Each spell would be slow acting.

But New York would be hers. Completely.

And then a statue of her would stand in Times Square for all the world to see. And this one would show her at her full glory, perhaps with a couple of Angels underfoot. It seemed a fitting tribute. She smiled as she phased back into reality. There were other hearts to find and attune.

"I would say that proves Sariel's story completely. Hera is perfectly safe and busy in some city. By the look of things she is well on her way of claiming the city as her own." Hecate wiped her hand over the surface of the scrying pool turning the water black once again. Nyx slowly removed her hands from the pool, allowing it to return to its bright blue glow.

She became less solid, more flitting darkness "Sariel has spoken true and freed one of our own. She is blood of our blood and Thanatos has recognised the call of blood. She has no crimes to pay for, and her actions speak enough for her. We accept her."

Nemesis sighed, she had seen this coming "With our numbers so small can we really afford to be picky, but she is still our key to the Surface. Let us not forget that, she has a purpose to complete before she can ever truly be one of us."

Nyx created a shadow of the Beast on the wall, they all watched its seven heads silently roaring "Sariel will free Lucifer" the Beast transformed into the shadow of an Angel "but each of us will need to play our own parts, she is horribly naïve. She was nearly killed in the Borderlands, she won't survive more than five minutes within the borders of Hell."

"Then it is our duty to prepare her for the trials ahead" Nemesis did always have a warriors honour that cropped up at peculiar times.

"It may be prudent not to inform Sariel of our plans. She is innocent yes but is likely to have her own sense of conscience. She may baulk at unlocking Hell and freeing Lucifer, but may otherwise contently make her way through Hell healing its victims."

"You understand her the best at the moment Hecate, I would agree. She is likely to have an odd sense of conscience. Let her training begin but keep her in the dark"

All present nodded their agreement with Nyx. They all wanted to be free, and with the exception of a few they had no qualms about using Sariel to do it. Even if the cost was her life.

Brigid stepped through the security gate fighting the childish urge to set it off. She quickly gathered up her possessions from the tray before continuing along the terminal. This was it, she was leaving Australia and was heading to India. She had a strange sense of pride in working her way to earn her ticket. She had earned her money through hard work alone. Her presence in Sydney was restrained to a few public gardens she had worked on.

None of the Daemons of Sydney had even known that she had walked amongst them. She had sown the seeds to return to Sydney but she had not made any overt attempts to attune it to herself. It was far too dangerous.

Australia was a mostly Christian country and she had felt the presence of Angels in Sydney. Whether they were passing through or staying for a longer visit she hadn't known and had had no desire to find out. She had had a few weekends in some of the other capital cities to sow similar seeds. Her powers would slowly grow there, her passing not being known until she had long gone.

But it would be well prepared for her return. Australia after all was a British colony, a territory of the Empire she sought to resurrect.

She had researched the British Empire, feeling great pride over its achievement. Sure they had conquered weaker nations, killed thousands if not millions in their ever growing hunger for land and wealth but what Empire hadn't. The only thing she regretted was that they had spread Christianity with them. Still that could be rectified by the New British Empire.

Which brought her to her current task. Britain would surely be under intense surveillance by the Angels, the British Colonies were far less likely to be. She planned to cast her net wide, and leave her subtle impressions all over the past territories of the empire before she returned to her isles. The strength it would lend her would make her stronger than she had ever been. And make it perfectly safe to turn Britain into a battleground against the Angels. She had missed out on its glory days, its brutal and dynamic history while she had been a prisoner. Britain would be glorious once again, but under her control not the Angels'.

It would take time to nurture the colonies but it would allow her to leave only passing traces for the Angels instead of any beacons. She would soon be able to teleport between the colonies with ease, giving her extra safety against the Angels. Fortunately she was a patient person, even by Divine standards.

As she settled into her seat she turned her thoughts to India. It would be a dramatic change from Australia. Australia was a sunburnt land, if the War hadn't happened it would have belonged to a Sun god or Goddess. It was a uniquely beautiful place, with its plant and animal life being incredibly unique. She had all but forgotten about monotremes and marsupials.

Despite the age of the land, its settlement was fairly recent. There had been tribal people with loose claims on the land but nothing significant until colonisation. The Angels had left their imprint with the British, but both were fading as Australia continued to make its own identity.

India on the other hand was an ancient land that had been cultivated and settled for a very long time. Its civilisation was ancient, its Gods had been very powerful, being the last pantheon left against the Angels. She didn't know if they were dead or imprisoned but their religions were still very strong. Hinduism was the dominant religion of the region, stripping the Angels of power on the Indian subcontinent.

It was a region lacking much of the Angels' presence but it would not be an easy place to claim. While the faith did not belong to the Angels it was certainly strong. It was a unique challenge, and was technically an affront to those Gods. But if they were the last pantheon to fight the Angels then it was likely the Angels had made an example of them by executing them. She would be able to tell once she got to India.

But it was a prize too good to ignore. India was one of the two most populous countries in the world, with numbers of people she had never seen anywhere except Atlantis. That many people believing in her would make her an extremely powerful Goddess.

She turned her attention back to the present as the

plane started moving. This would be a novel experience flying for hours without even flapping her wings or even using magic.

"Have you seen Eleanor LaClarke's new gardens? They are absolutely stunning." A woman behind her said.

"She has really outdone herself this time. I tried to find out who her gardener was but she would give nothing away. If you ask me though it was probably a hippie." Her friend responded.

A hippie? What the Hell was a hippie?

"What makes you say that? Hippies don't design European Gardens."

"Well one of those Pagans then. There were a lot of statues of Goddesses in the garden. Gaia, Brigid, Hera, Leto, Isis, Cailleach. There were statues of Fairies and Nymphs, Satyrs and Sirens. Even something about the Tuatha something or other."

"Tuatha Dé Danann, the Irish Pantheon to which the Goddess Brigid belonged" a male voice added.

She smirked as she felt the ladies irritation "Thank you sir" her voice was icy.

"No problem ladies" he responded politely before continuing past.

"Can you believe the nerve of some people, eavesdropping and interrupting?"

"Well Jenny you at least know what the Tuatha Dé Danann are now." She sounded more amused than anything.

"What has society come to, people butting into conversations, children drugged up to their eyeballs in orgies, heresy common knowledge. I swear sometimes God has abandoned Australia." Strange that they concerned her more than the environmental ruin plaguing the entire world.

Brigid smiled to herself resisting the urge to

interrupt the conversation. They would learn who Australia truly belonged to soon enough.

"I see I'm not the only one amused by their conversation" She turned to the male voice surprised to find he had sat down next to her. He had long blonde hair bright blue eyes twinkling with what could only be described as mischief and a wide white smile. He wore blue glasses and a well-tailored business suit. He looked too relaxed and cheerful to be a proper business man. Was he a millionaire, merely dressing to impress or an Angel in disguise. They always had a sense of propriety.

"I believe most of the plane is listening to their conversation, but when you're that loud what do you expect?"

He chuckled "So true" he looked at her tilting his head "You must get this a lot but you look very familiar. I'm Ryan by the way." She had found Australians to be uniquely direct in their conversations and likely to jump from one tangent to the other with no notable pause.

"Actually I don't." Smiling she added "Brigid"

"After the Irish Goddess?" Her blood ran cold. He had to be an Angel, but why couldn't she sense his Divinity or powers. Was this a new trick of theirs? Had they developed assassins undetectable to traditional God powers?

"Yes my family were quite entrenched in Irish mythology" that was completely true.

"Fascinating, usually it's a mythology few beyond Ireland know of. If people have any interest in Mythology its usually Egyptian or Greek."

"My family is Irish that's our excuse" the modern way of being so direct still felt rude to her but he didn't so much as blink.

"I'm a professor of Celtic Mythology and Irish History. I've always found it fascinating, and so different from Mediterranean Mythology."

"That would be because it was. Less interference from nearby cultures."

"Until the Catholic Church came along that is and started changing and destroying the truth. Did you know they actually made the Goddess Brigid a saint in an attempt to convert the people because they were so loyal to her?"

"Really? I knew she was sainted but I didn't know why." Perhaps she could learn more about what had happened to Ireland after her clan was lost.

"Yes it's a fascinating story. Brigid was a truly fascinating Goddess, a personal favourite of mine, especially considering her influence extended well beyond Ireland and the British Isles but even throughout Gaul and the north of Europe.

Her eyes widened in surprise even as her mind started turning. She knew her influence had been surprisingly large considering she had been imprisoned while it spread but she hadn't known she had reached mainland Europe.

"Tell me more I fear my knowledge is patchier than I thought it was"

"Gladly" he smiled back, she could feel his sexual interest in her, see his eyes light up at being allowed to talk about what he loved.

Modern men were far more interesting and honest in their approach.

Sariel groaned as she pushed the bed covers away. She felt strangely out of sorts, as though she wasn't properly recovered. Then again considering she had almost been at the state of Desiccation two meals and a night's sleep would not be enough to fully heal her.

She froze when something moved on her bed. She

desperately cast out a frail attempt at sensing, cursing her brother for not properly training her when three sets of tongues started licking her face.

She rolled off the bed onto the floor laughing in a heap of wings and bedding. Cerberus jumped down after her trying to lick her again as she squealed and rolled about the floor. He was much smaller, friendlier seeming and less dangerous.

"He decreases in size when within the castle, makes it easier to navigate the halls. His large size is only really needed at the gate." Said a sorrowful voice. It was though all the sorrows of the world had been distilled down into that one voice.

She pushed herself up past the bounding Cerberus to see Thanatos standing in front of the window. Instead of the unnatural sunlight shining through it was a void into darkness, flashes of white and blue showing crying people running through the darkness. It was clear his powers weighed heavily on his spirit.

He looked wearied, heavy bags under his eyes, messy hair dropping off his head and his skin was exceptionally pale. Paler then the other Gods. Surprisingly he was the same height as her, and she was still stuck in her child body.

His wings were the most vibrant part about him, gloriously glossy black, iridescent with green, blue and purple. But it was his two toned eyes that were the most striking, violet near the pupil and jet black edging the whites. At a glance they appeared dark blue or purple. It was unusual but striking.

He didn't look old, most Gods were very vain about looking in their prime, but he looked world weary. As though he was ready to give up on it all.

Just as she had studied him, he had studied her "You don't look much like Samael, you must take after your mother. But your eyes are definitely his, and your wings."

"I do not remember him. They both died not long after my birth."

"I wonder why he mated with Lilith, she seems an odd choice for him. But then they are both Fallen so there is some sense to it."

She stepped back stunned "My parents were Fallen Angels? No they can't have been, they both died in the War. If they were Fallen Angels then I would not have been accepted into Heaven, I could not have become an Arch Angel. They were heroes of the War."

"And who told you that? Michael or Gabriel? Neither would admit to the fact that they betrayed him and Lucifer and cast powerful spells on them and their followers. Their spell was a stroke of genius that took everyone by surprise. It locked down the Underworld completely, threw out Lucifer and all of their enemies, casting them into the depths of Hell." His voice grew distant.

"That day Angels fell from Heaven like rain, they darkened the sky over Eden, their shrieks of agony reaching as far Alexandria. They transformed as they Fell, twisted by the Curse. But none so much as Lucifer, he bore the full brunt of his sister's wrath. His roars rent the Heavens, out rivalling the fiercest storms. His Fall was mighty as his form twisted into the Beast, it was so powerful it ripped through the Surface into the Underworld. That is how Hell was formed, and he has been trapped there ever since."

"Michael cursed our father?" it seemed so unimaginable. Michael was honourable. Wasn't he?

"It is very possible, those of Divine blood are capable of anything"

"I do not find that comforting, that blood runs in

me."

"Yes very strongly. Your lineages are quite remarkable. Lilith was the daughter of Anu, a Mesopotamian Sky God, who was born from Primordials. Her mother is unknown, presumably some Angel or another, nevertheless Angels usually carry strong bloodlines. Your mother was an Angel but started out as a handmaiden of the Goddess Inanna. Over the centuries she has been many things, Angel, demigoddess, Mother Goddess, the first wife of Adam, and an incredibly powerful Demoness not constrained by Hell. She is considered to be the first Succubus, Vampire and Demon by many mortals. And she is actually the Sacred Mother of the Lilin as well as being believed to be the mother of Leviathan and many other Demons." He paused "it would seem she was more fitting to Samael than I had first thought. They are actually well suited to each other."

"My mother is a Demoness? She was a Goddess?" she staggered backwards until she collapsed in a chair. Painfully catching her wings in the process. How had her mother become a Goddess and then a Demoness? Did that mean she had Demonic siblings. She shuddered at the thought.

"Samael was much the same thing, belonging to both Hell and Heaven, Life and Death, Light and Darkness."

She just stared at him appalled. Her father had been an Arch Angel who had been friends with the Arch Angel Lucifer, both of whom where Fallen Angels. He had been the son of a Greek God and had married her mother who was some sort of Mesopotamian demigoddess Demon who for unknown reasons had then married Adam the first pure Angel Human. She had been an Arch Angel at the time. Now she was hearing that her own brother and his wife had Cursed them both and been solely responsible for the Fall. She didn't know what to believe any more, or if she wanted to hear any more about her family.

"Look on the bright side, there is great power on both sides of your family. Lilith was the demigoddess daughter of Anu. He was once the King of Heaven, he also was one of the oldest Mesopotamian Gods and extremely powerful. I do not know who her mother was but she inherited great power over the skies and death. Perhaps her mother was a Death Daemon or Lampade.

As for your paternal side, there is myself, the God of Death. I do not remember your grandmother but she was an Angel and as such probably the daughter of some God or another. Most likely Zeus, who was the King of Heaven when the War broke out. Then there is my mother Nyx, the Primordial Goddess of Night, and my father Erebus, the Primordial Darkness. Both were born from Chaos. Great power runs through our bloodlines, power you have inherited but as of yet not used."

"Wait. Erebus is your father, but is he not Nyx's brother?"

"Yes, all the Primordials are brothers or sisters of some degree. It is a complicated system that only they seem to understand"

She gagged "my family is inbred?"

"Different times my dear. It happened a lot among the Primordial Gods, after all, all they had was each other. It was also reasonably common among their offspring. Persephone is Hades' niece, the daughter of his sister Demeter and their brother Zeus. You will find a lot of the Gods have parents who are siblings."

"That is disturbing in so many ways." She stared at him horrified.

He walked towards her, making no sound as he moved, before gently kissing her on the forehead "Be at peace Sariel, it is all in the past. Only a handful of the Primordials remain, most of the Gods have been killed or imprisoned and most of their offspring hunted to extinction with only the Angels to carry on their bloodlines." Then he walked out of the room, the door sliding silently behind him. Did he make no noise at all? He reminded her a great deal of Azrael.

Cerberus sat down next to her and she absently stroked his heads while her mind was racing at a million miles per hour. She finally knew some of her family secrets but she gathered there would be many more. Probably far worse. But things finally made sense about her own powers and nature. Was it any wonder that both she and Michael were Angels of Death when their mother had been a Demon of death and their father the Son of Death? But there were also other powers she was likely to have inherited. Thanatos had said she was likely to have powers over air and she had felt at home in Heaven, but she equally felt at home in the Underworld, the realm of darkness. She belonged to death and darkness but also to the light and sky. It made her wonder what else she was capable of. What powers were uniquely her own?

She looked down at Cerberus, doing his darned best to look sad and woeful, though his red eyes gave it a strange cast. "Wait aren't you the son of Echidna? Does that not make you a relative of mine?"

He whined softly. She laughed, kneeling down to hug him. You'd think he was neglected by his expression. He might be a three headed Monster that guarded the Gates of Hades but he was still a dog through and through.

"Well it's just another thing I suppose I will get used to" she muttered to herself as she looked out of the window at the fiery landscapes that held the Gate of Tartarus. So many things had changed, her naivety had been stripped clean and her powers were actually her own. If unknown to her.

She wished she could tell Michael about their family and everything she had learned about them. They had known so little about their parents. Or had he just kept it from her? She realised she didn't know her brother anywhere near what she thought she had. Had he really cursed their father?

Samael was trapped in Hell, but what of Lilith? Where was their mother?

She had circled around New York feeling the different hearts, it had so many. Times Square, The Statue of Liberty, The Empire State Building, The Rockefeller Centre, Grand Central Terminal as well as several others she had left alone. There was the Empire State building, no longer the tallest building in the world, but it was iconic and still retained a place of pride for New York. Times Square symbolised the bustling lifestyle of New York, its dynamic strike forwards.

The Rockefeller Centre had called to her because not only was it iconic, a symbol of the world's richest man, but its ice rink particularly captured the hearts of young and old. It also happened to have statues of Atlas and Prometheus. Fitting places.

Grand Central Terminal was a thoroughfare of thousands, a good place for her magic to spread not only throughout Manhattan but to the rest of New York and the other states and cities.

Her final decision of its biggest heart had been torn between two. The Statue of Liberty was iconic the world over, stained with the hopes of hundreds and thousands of migrants coming to New York. It had been a symbol of hope and dreams. But for New Yorkers it was beaten by the largest Heart; Central Park.

It was perfect, not only spiritually by physically the heart of Manhattan, it was a place of many aspects. But most of all it was a special symbol for New Yorkers, it was somewhere to escape the city and its hustle and bustle. A place to unwind and relax. It was a place to escape the environmental ruin of the world, somehow the city had kept it remarkably alive. It was a beautiful place that called not only the people of New York but to her own nearly forgotten Mother Earth powers.

It was the final heart she would claim, it also contained some of her oldest and dearest animals. Central Park Zoo, and also the Bronx Zoo had peafowl and they called to her. The eyes of Argus continued to look across the world, her gift to one of her most loyal servants. There had been escapes from both Zoos but now Central Park would have more than just a stray peafowl here and there, it would be her gift to them. And her statement of ownership to the world.

She walked across the red pavers surrounding Cleopatra's Needle, running her hands along the surrounding barriers before walking through them. This seemed a fitting place to claim the Heart of New York. One hand on the past the other grasping out for a new future. It was remarkable really to find an Egyptian Obelisk in the middle of the park, but New York was continuing to surprise her with its dynamics.

She raised one hand flaring violet. Across the night came the distinctive call of the peafowl. With that one act she had broken the displays containing them in not only the Central Park Zoo but the Bronx Zoo. Though the latter would take a while to get to Central Park.

She closed her eyes as she heard the call again, answering it with her perfect imitation. These were thankfully hers and did not belong to any of the Hindu Gods. Then again they might simply be responding to a void left from the War.

It felt liberating to make the call, so basic and animalistic. It was apparently time that she had to get back to her roots. Her greatest successes so far had been using her initial Mother Earth powers. She had only used her Queen of Heaven powers on the Daemon Races. And that was still a work in progress. Though the Maenads were eager to please and currently had several projects in the works.

The call came again closer as they came running through the vegetation and others even flew in their eagerness. They came out of the darkness, their blues and greens reflecting the lamplight brightly.

One landed on the barrier in front of her, she reached out and stroked its' neck remembering times past. They had been a symbol of her ever since Argus had died, it was the symbol mortals had come to associate with her, to fear and revere. It was time their memories were refreshed.

She reached down into the earth with her powers, reaching for both the earth and the oceanic powers surrounding the city, pulling them back up, feeding their strength through the park.

New York City shook violently as the magical backlash washed through the earth. Hera smiled to herself. She hadn't claimed the land formally but it knew who controlled it. To further confuse the Angels she summoned a tempest to descend on the city, growing around and above the city. She would stain the city with her magic, covering all trace of her being here.

The Angels would come, but they would leave empty handed and none the wiser. The rush of magic would cover all trace of her smaller acts, hiding the fact that she was laying claim to the city.

Besides she had her eyes on the whole of the

United States not just its crowning jewel. She would leave and make her mark on other cities. Washington D.C. for its political control, New Orleans for its high level of Daemons (it was an army waiting to happen), San Francisco for its high level of homosexuals (another army waiting to happen), as well as the various regional centres. There was so much to do, much of it very time consuming. But she couldn't come back to New York for a while.

She cast a protective spell over the peafowl "Hide my little ones the storm will be fierce." Violet lightning rent the sky as the ground shook again. The rains started to fall even as the sea began to swell. Let the rain cover the city with her essence, let it wash away all the pollution and taint of the Angels.

She disappeared as she sensed the eyes of Heaven turning towards the city. She laughed as she went, they wouldn't understand and they would not be able to tame the storm. It was feeding on the natural powers of the planet.

Chapter 13

Michael stood on the bottom Terrace of Purgatory ignoring the Excommunicate and the Angels purifying them behind him. Instead his attention was solely focussed on the great crater below, stretching away as far as he could see. He could see the souls trapped in Limbo, or those desperate enough to throw themselves into Hell. The great stalactite reached down from the Surface Gate, stabbing into the thick cloudbanks of the Lust Level. Towards where Lucifer was trapped in his lair.

All was as it should be.

Heaven's greatest enemy was still trapped. They could easily overcome two weakened Goddesses. Even if they couldn't track them down. Brigid seemed to have completely disappeared, while Hera seemed to be playing a very different game. First the flaring of the Grand Canyon now the tempest that had savaged New York. Why had she done it? Had someone offended her in New York or had she encountered an Angel? It might be impossible to tell, Nuriel had said the amount of magic she had unleashed on New York would make it damn near impossible to notice other spells. The Demons could be having a field day and they wouldn't be able to tell.

Perhaps that was why. Well the legions of Angels in New York would stop that.

How far the Gods and their brethren had fallen. Two stray Goddesses struggling to avoid the gaze of Heaven. Their kin lay imprisoned in Heaven or trapped in the Underworld, hidden from Heaven but scrabbling around in the dark.

The only true threat to Heaven were the Fallen Angels, they had access to the same powers as the Arch

Angels and unfortunately they had been empowered by Human fear. But thankfully Lucifer and all his followers were trapped in their twisted forms, savaged by madness, unable to escape Hell. Lucifer suffered the most, his mind was shattered across the seven heads of the Beast. There was no chance of sanity ever returning to him.

His father was also trapped in a similar form in Hell. He absently wondered what form his mother now wore. She would be Demonic, but so had she been before, would it be one of her old shapes or a new one imposed by the Curse. It still seemed odd to him that she had became Adam's first wife. For some unfathomable reason the Governing Council had insisted that one of the Arch Angels was to be his wife for his short life. She had rebelled against him, refusing to be submissive to him, even though he had been taught his wife was his. It had been the first fracturing of the Council when she left Eden and did not return to Heaven.

What on earth had possessed Samael to track her down and resume their marriage? Though admittedly the result had been Sariel and despite Lilith being a Demon Sariel was born an Angel. She was still the youngest of all the Elder Angels. If she still lived.

After she had been born Lilith was not the only one to change. She never returned to Heaven, Samael after becoming Demonic at the request of the Council tested Adam as had been asked. He had been the serpent to test man and have them cast out. If anyone could be convincing it was Samael. But then he had mated with several Demonesses, Lilith included. He had no idea how many half siblings he might have, didn't care either. If they weren't Angels he would still kill them.

But then the worst thing happened. Samael who had been so crucial in the overthrow of the Gods had started talking about peace. He and Lucifer had become diplomats between Gods and Angels, they had begun brokering a peace deal. Everything the Angels had worked towards had been threatened.

So he and Gabriel had taken their concerns before the Council and convinced them of the danger. The fear of the Gods was there, and the memories of serving them were still fresh. Many had not been convinced, they had paid the price.

Gabriel was the most powerful Angel that had ever lived, and he was second only to her and her brother. Their control and understanding of power was exemplary. They had laid their trap well. In one act they had cast out two thirds of Heaven making them rain down over Jerusalem. In one magnificent stroke they had removed all the peacemakers and fence sitters, condemning them to Hell or Purgatory. Lucifer in his twisted form had smashed through the Surface, creating the crater that was Hell. All the Fallen Angels had been dragged down with him. And the greatest success was that they were all sealed up in Hell and had incidentally sealed the whole Underworld.

To finalise their success and compound their power they had unleashed the Four Horsemen of the Apocalypse. The world had finally belonged to them. Sure the Roman Empire had been crumbling, but Christianity had spread throughout Europe. Then Islam had spread far and wide as the Caliphate conquered the Middle East and North Africa. Behind it all the Jewish had spread far and wide through many lands, mostly ignored. As the European nations had started to conquer the world so too did Christianity. Faith had been strong and the faithful had stamped out all traces of the Gods and their creations.

Most of the world had been theirs except for India, China and the lands between them. They had been the only resistance against the spread of the Angelic religions. But they had been patiently undermined. The world was going to be theirs.

But then the world had changed. Their numbers had been weakened to the point that they could not effectively rule over so much. two hundred Elder were not a lot when it came to ruling most of a world. The Ascended helped supplement the numbers but they were very careful how much power they were given. They needed greater numbers of the Elder with their potent magic, but unfortunately the Elder rarely bred. While the Elders' attention was spilt across so many fronts some of Humanity had started to turn away from them.

It had seen the rise of science and the birth of the Atheists. It was also likely many of the Demons had a role in it. Magic became a quaint notion, abnormalities became explainable and Humanity effectively sheltered the Demons. As science thundered along, giving first the Industrial Revolution, then the Electrical then the Nanotechnological. With each step up of science, each progression for Humanity more started to turn away or question their faith. Some even turned back to older religions. As tolerance and understanding progressed through Humanity, they became more difficult to control, more assured in their own power.

Oh they had continued to spread the religions through Africa, the Americas, Asia and Oceania but their original strongholds in Europe had continued to decay. Controlled immigration had not strengthened these bastions as they had thought they would.

Their innate powers had not dwindled, and their supplemented powers were still very strong. As Sariel had matured they had grown more hopeful of reasserting their rule on Humanity. There had been serious discussions about unleashing the Apocalypse or having the Second Coming. As powerless as Sariel had thought herself she was invaluable to both.

Now she was lost.

They could find no trace of her in Heaven. Nuriel and all the legions she had been given control of were scouring the Surface but they had found nothing so far. Hope was withering. There were but two possibilities left, she was either in the Underworld or dead. He shuddered at the thought of her in the Underworld, prey for Gods and Demons alike. There was also the highly unlikely but terrifying thought she could inadvertently break some of their Curse.

He knew which option he preferred. Better she was dead than Hell was unlocked. Besides if she had ended up in the Underworld she was likely dead, the rivers having stripped her of her Divinity. The Underworld was a cruel place.

There appeared no trace of her in Hell, no disturbances to Limbo or Purgatory. No one had felt her presence. The cold reality was that one of the Goddesses had probably consumed her strength. If only she hadn't been powerless, it was his fault. She was dead but perhaps that was for the best, her powers had hardly seemed Angelic at all. She might have Fallen. It was probably kinder this way.

Sariel as it happened was running through the palace corridors laughing with Cerberus bounding at her heels. His joyful barking mingled with her musical laughter ringing along the hallways. It had been so long since there had been truly genuine laughter heard in Hades' palace, it was usually bitter and regretful. The dead were noted for their lack of humour, the Lampades were a fairly serious bunch and the Gods' joy was long lost. But her innocent laughter was music to their ears, even to the coldest and angriest heart. Even Nemesis found her mouth tugging into a smile.

She watched her run past with Cerberus, all innocence and joy. What had happened to make her so happy? What in Hades could cause such joy? Or was it that they had all sense of joy leeched out by overwhelming bitterness and resentment to the point they could no longer find joy in the little things like her. They planned to send this girl into Hell. What was she going to do? Laugh the Demons away?

She felt a strange sensation, she wanted to say it was warrior's honour but really it was her long dormant conscience. How ironic that it was an Angel that had awakened it. She couldn't justify sending Sariel into Hell with no prior training, she needed to be able to defend herself. Physically as well as magically, and who better to teach her fighting than herself. Hell was probably the most dangerous place in the world, even more so for an Angel.

She needed training.

What concerned her more than Sariel's complete lack of worldliness was Thanatos' growing attachment to her. Gods and Goddesses rarely showed much attachment even to family and lovers. Its rarity for their species made it all the more valuable, to be loved by a God was truly rare. If it happened it was only ever for lovers, close siblings or between a parent and child. The level of attachment Thanatos was showing for his granddaughter was unheard of. Even Nyx was showing an unnatural level of interest in a great-granddaughter. Admittedly she had no others to be involved with, but it was still troubling. Even near comatose Hypnos was drawn out of his dreams to spend time with her.

She had an uncanny ability to pull the heartstrings. Among the Divine it was unheard of and deeply troubling.

"You do not trust her sister" she nearly jumped out of her skin, Thanatos was lucky she hadn't automatically attacked him. How did he never make any noise? She turned around was even more surprised to realise that it was Hypnos and not Thanatos standing next to her. He was always sleeping, feeding on the dreams of mortals, for he was the only one who had any true access to the world even if it was only through dreams.

"No I do not trust her. Everyone is enchanted by her, it's not natural. We are Gods not mortals, we don't behave like this. Our heartstrings are cold and barely played. Something is different about her to pull us all."

"Always suspicious Nemesis, and yet even your own heartstrings are being pulled. We have never met a Divine being so pure and innocent, is it any wonder we respond as we never have before. More so she is Samael's daughter come home, the prodigal child's child if you may. She is nothing how we expected, we expected her to be another Michael or Gabriel, or be similar to Lilith or Samael but she is truly unique. Such innocence and power are a heady combination for us to handle."

"I think I like you better when you are sleeping."

He smirked "because I can't prove you wrong."

"Exactly"

He turned to her again becoming more serious "do you know what she dreams about?"

"She dreams? But Divine don't dream."

"By choice not by nature. She was never trained how to block out dreams. Her dreams are so simplistic. She is content, joy soaks through every image, though sorrow also lingers. She is happy here, happier than she has ever been before. She has freedom to live, learn, play and explore. No one is telling her where she can and cannot go. Her thirst for knowledge is not being knocked down, Nyx and Hecate have encouraged her to read the library and will begin training her soon."

He eyed her up "You are going to train her" it wasn't a question, he already knew her intentions.

"I cannot send a defenceless girl into Hell."

He hugged her. Out of the blue he actually hugged her. She couldn't remember the last time he or anyone else had hugged her. Had he ever hugged her before? "See even your ice is melting Nemesis. There was a time you would not have hesitated to send defenceless mortals into the same situation."

"But she is no mortal, she is one of us."

"It is good to hear you say that. Yes, she is one of us."

Sarah smiled as a peafowl landed next to her. Despite all efforts to recapture them they remained roaming Central Park. Both zoos were at a loss to explain their behaviour. The official story in the news was that someone had broken into first the Bronx zoo, then Central Park Zoo. On their escape they had ditched the birds to evade capture.

Their brilliant ability to avoid recapture was something of a local amusement. The news had a running day count of how long since they had been set free and how many had successfully been caught. So far it had been a week and they had only captured one. But now they were out on mass to lend their current celebrity status for advancing Hera's cause.

She stepped forward when the mayor called out her name, smiling at the crowd and camera's, thanking them when she reached the podium and microphone. Now the real danger began, Hera had left New York to avoid the Angels and infiltrate other cities. In her wake she had left a magical beacon that had convinced the remaining Daemons that she was not to be messed with. Her power was extraordinary. But the Angels had also come to New York.

Everyone was able to camouflage themselves amongst the Humans, it was one of the benefits of a big city. Plus the amount of magic floating around the city made it easy to avoid magical detection. Well no war was won without causalities and for the freedom of her kind she would give her life.

"Welcome all and thank you. On behalf of the New York Historical Society I would like to thank you all for your time and support. Today is a somewhat prophetic day considering our new guests." She smiled gesturing at the peafowl.

"Today's statue is of one of mythology's least understood characters. She has evolved with the times, starting off from Mother Goddess roots until she was the consort of the most powerful God in antiquity. She was feared, revered and envied. As the Classical Age passed into antiquity her time waned but she was not forgotten. In the Renaissance she enjoyed a revival, and in these days she enjoys much more. For women she is a symbol of strength, endurance and suffering. She is worshipped again by many Neopagans as well. But today we are here to celebrate her for her symbology."

She paused looking around for Angel attack.

"Hera was born from her Titan parents Rhea and Cronus, eaten at birth by her father. She was freed by Zeus the youngest off all their siblings. The Olympians overthrew the Titans, casting them down into Tartarus. What was her thanks? She was raped by her brother and forced into marrying him to avoid the shame. She endured her marriage as a symbol of what was expected of a woman. But she could not avoid the shame. Zeus was a constant cheater, with strings of lovers and children. Hera is famous for hunting them down and killing them, for her cruelty to Leto and Heracles

She is remembered for her part in the Iliad. Her unwavering demand to destroy it, all for the affront Paris made to her and Athena. She evolved as Roman culture expanded throughout Europe. A symbol of matrons, how a mother and wife should be. All the while her husband's affairs continued and her dedication in hunting them down. Which brings us I guess to the peafowl.

Io was a Nymph and priestess of Hera, unfortunately belonging to the Gods was no protection from the others. The story of Medusa attests to that. Io was seduced or raped, it is hard to know, but to protect her from Hera he turned her into a heifer. She sent her loyal guardian Argus, the ever watchful, to keep her but he was slain by Hermes. To reward him for his duty she placed his many eyes into the tail of the peacock. It has been one of her symbols ever since.

Enough with the history lesson" She smiled "let us reveal Central Park's latest addition" she pulled the sheet off the statue revealing it to everyone present.

It was a larger than life casting of Hera. The Maenads had used their very best skills to capture as much of her Divine beauty as they could. They had opted for diluted strength, giving her a more demure look. She stood against a marble pillar, one hand supporting her against it, the other hung behind her back holding peacock feathers. She was dressed in a chiton and wore a simple diadem. Surrounding her were her various loyal servants. Little Carcinus by her feet, several peafowl surrounding her.

Many of the living peafowl called out before fluttering down amongst the bronze statues. One landed on top of the column, looking down at them calling out almost angrily.

"Well we have one seal of approval, let us hope that the Humans like it half as much."

She walked off the stage after a smattering of applause as the mayor reclaimed the spotlight he loved. A couple of news reporters hurried up to her, her senses told her one of them was a Succubus.

"You have mentioned that this is but one in a line of public ventures for the Historical Society, Women's Society and your enterprises. Tell us is this a public ploy to gloss over the allegations made against your company?"

That surprised her "what allegations?"

"Your dealings with the devil, your anti-Christian statements."

She rolled her eyes "Having a higher degree of Jewish people within my companies are not a reflection of anti-Christian views, just those individuals meet my requirements and happen to share the same religion."

The Succubus spoke pushing aside the annoying man. Such was her force he actually fell over "What is the next public venture, as you have said this is but the start."

"Our next venture is a hospital, named in the honour of Hera."

"But why Hera, she wasn't particularly associated with healing."

"No she wasn't but Hera was the agreed upon Goddess for our public ventures. Some she will fit better than others, some less so."

"Why the interest in a Greek Goddess? Why not the use of an Angel from your religion?"

Both Sarah and the Succubus turned to the new man in the crowd, he screamed Angel. His power was not even hidden from them. This was it he was here to kill her.

"Not everyone is Jewish, and the use of religion complicates so many issues. The use of an ancient Goddess has no connotations to it."

She could feel him studying her glamour, please let it hold up, probing her on her apparent Jewish faith.

"Fair enough" he said after what seemed a hundred years, then he slinked back into the crowd. She tried not to stare after him, to do so would scream Daemon.

"No more questions" one of her security detail said pushing his way through and clearing a path for her. For a Human he was surprisingly sensitive to magical influences, and he was utterly efficient.

She felt the warmth returning to her veins as she gulped down her Scotch. That had been close far too close. She was officially under the Angelic radar. But had she passed or not?

Her day had been ruined. The unveiling didn't hold joy for her and when she found out there had been a court case lodged against her company she barely registered.

To anyone that knew her she was the strangest she had ever been. She was always so on the ball, meeting every challenge with poise and authority. She had cancelled all her meetings and now sat in home drinking herself blind drunk. It felt as though the Star of David she wore was burning, but it was merely her imagination. She had sent home all her servants, Human and Daemon. If the Angel came back for her she did not want them in the crossfire.

He didn't come back that night, but her fear didn't go away. Angels were a patient race.

Chapter 14

Sariel sat on the fountain trailing her hands through the black water creating little white whirls in their wake. It was thrilling to do this without being told off, in Heaven she had had to be so dignified all the time. Here she was allowed to be herself.

And she was being trained to use her magic. It was going to be a long path, she was having almost no success with trying to order her magic. She was so ignorant about so much of her power, but then that was Michael and Gabriel's fault. Hecate and Nyx were giving her lessons here and there, giving her time to practice what she could. She was still struggling to grasp her magic at all without heightened emotions.

Thanatos had also started tutoring her about the nuances of death, Hypnos about sleep. She had thought Michael so wise about death but in reality he had been nearly as ignorant as she was. She realised now the true understanding of death in Heaven belonged only to Azrael.

She had stood in awe of Michael and Gabriel's power for so long, in awe of much of the Governing Council and their various abilities. She had never questioned their power. Their decisions and actions certainly but never their magic. They had always seemed so wise about their magic but now she was beginning to question that with but a few lessons. Michael had not accepted his natural strength, he was an Angel of Death but it was the least tapped of his abilities when it was his major strength. He was rejecting his own magic, a dangerous thing to do.

They also lacked the refinement that her family

used so skilfully. Many of the Angels magic seemed ham fisted. She had seen so many beautiful displays of magic since being here and she had felt truly terrifying power wash through her when one of the Primordials touched her. They held truly unfathomable power, the essence of creation itself. She knew the Angels' strength lay in their solidarity and ability to meld their magic together but she still wondered how they had succeeded in overthrowing the Gods.

She looked up to see Nemesis striding towards her, her hair whipping behind her, her wings held close against her body. She was wearing a short blood red tunic with a bronze cuirass over the top as well as bronze greaves and bracers.

She came to a stop in front of her "Sariel" she nodded.

She glanced up meeting that hardened gaze "Yes Nemesis?"

Why did she always manage to look so vulnerable, simply sitting on a fountain she managed to look like the most fragile thing in the world? It had to be the child body she hadn't progressed past. "It is time you learnt to defend yourself Sariel. Magic is not everything and it can be blocked as you are well aware. Being able to physically defend yourself is essential." The little twerp just looked at back her mouth hanging open.

"An excellent idea Nemesis. Life is dangerous, the Underworld essentially so" Sariel jumped as Nyx materialised next to her. Nemesis showed no surprise, she was used to the sudden materialisation of her brethren. "Honestly I'm surprised your brother didn't train you himself."

"As am I. He was a gifted fighter." Nemesis grimaced.

Sariel turned to look at Nemesis funny "Did you

train him?"

"No I did not but I did follow his training with interest, being accepted into the Legions of Athena, Sekhmet and Kali is an incredible achievement. I was considering offering him a place when his time with Aphrodite finished but then the War broke out." She paused "if you have half his talent you will be able to defend yourself sufficiently against even most Divine."

She held out her hand, light blazed as a sword grew from the handle in her hand, the long blade pointing back at her. She offered the handle to Sariel "First you will learn the sword. It is among the oldest and most diverse of weapon skills. There are a variety of swords and you will learn them all. Once satisfied you will progress onto axes, spears, nun-chucks, maces, daggers and the wide variety of bows. When you find a weapon that you like you will train until it becomes an unconscious extension of yourself."

Sariel's eyes widened as she took the handle, her hand dropping suddenly at the unexpected weight of the sword. Nemesis rolled her eyes at her meekness, gliding effortlessly out of the way of the falling sword. Sariel steeled herself, gripping the sword she struggled to stand in what she thought was a suitable position. Nemesis laughed at her, it was the most pitiful and awkward attempt to hold a sword she had ever seen. "This is going to take longer than first anticipated. First we shall start with holding a sword."

Sariel fell into her bed exhausted, she couldn't even be bothered undressing or showering. And she really should clean herself she was covered in dirt and blood. A bath would be better, it would be amazing to soak away all the dirt and ease away the pain in muscles she didn't know she even had. Nemesis was a sadistic maniac, she had worked her worse than a slave driver. A picky obsessive perfectionist who had made her repeat stances and actions over and over until some minute problem changed and she was finally satisfied.

She had lost her entire day training and she was still pathetic at sword fighting. Clearly she lacked even a drop of Michael's talent.

She was Divine, an Angel/Goddess hybrid, wasn't that supposed to grant legendary abilities. Shouldn't she have picked this up as soon as she had picked up the sword? Then again she had severely tested her Divine abilities with the amount of healing she had had to do. As far as Nemesis was concerned for the Divine pain was the best deterrent to bad swordsmanship. As it was her muscles ached unbelievably. How was it possible to hurt this much without being lethally injured? Her arms were quivering in exhaustion, she had been worked until she had actually dropped. Silver blood had spurted from her hands and fingers, from her feet and ankles and even along her arms and legs. She had screamed in pain and agony as her muscles had torn themselves apart in the frenzy.

And yet she hadn't even sparred with Nemesis or anyone else, just exercises. It had been exercise after exercise, punishing her until her body adapted and healed before starting the cycle again. There had been such pain, driving her to her knees only to have Nemesis hauling her to her feet again. She had been driven beyond her natural abilities or motivation. Had it been a spell of some sort? She wouldn't put it past Nemesis, from what she gathered Nemesis was capable of anything. But then her nature demanded it, she was the Goddess of Vengeance. But then again it seemed her entire family was capable of anything, God or Angel. The only exception was herself, but that seemed to be on the change. Whoever would have thought that she could ever lift a sword let alone begin to use it?

"She pushed you hard today. You bled, which is a good sign." Nyx had appeared again, but her presence was a comfort, her shadows wrapping around the sore muscles, slipping deep within them to ease the pain. Her hands were warm as they slid along her back, flitting between her wings with efficient ease.

"She cares. It is why she pushed you so hard. She is not used to attachment and the few that she is attached to are very powerful. We are all ancient Gods of great power and physical strength. You disturb her because you are so untested. You powers are so new to you and currently unshaped and your physical strength or lack of it annoys her the most. You are so weak, so...Human. And yet she strives to improve you, to quicken your Divine blood. She will continue to push you hard Sariel, but she will not be alone. Hecate and I will push you hard in your magic training when it properly begins. But remember love drives us."

Sariel gave a sudden gasp as she was transported into the bathtub. The warm waters swirling around her and pulling her down into its embrace. She opened her eyes to see Nyx's shadows were in the water, twisting around her muscles drawing out the pain. She saw swirls of silver blood in the shadows but she wasn't worried, she at least knew her Divine blood healed haemorrhaging if not aches. Her concerns faded away as the water and shadows helped her drift off to sleep smiling. Her great grandmother's words had truly put her at ease.

She was loved.

Nyx watched as Sariel drifted off to sleep, her heart heavy. She loved her great granddaughter, against all reason and Divine nature. She was truly attached to Sariel, but she knew what had to be done. Sariel had to go into Hell. It was why they were all training her so hard, they all loved her, an Angel, and wanted to keep her safe but she was the key to winning the War.

The Old Order had failed, the Gods had been blind in their power and games. The Angels had taken advantage of these power games to conquer Heaven and cast out the Gods. The New Order of the Angels had been strong but they had become weak from within, the Fall had devastated their numbers and powerbase. The New Order was weak with their lack of numbers but they too had fallen into the same traps as the Old Order. What was needed was something new and different from what had been before.

Sariel offered a new future. She was an Angel, the daughter of Demons and Arch Angels. She was a demigoddess, descended from different pantheons and even held Primordial blood. She pulled on the heartstrings of Gods and Monsters, unsure of her power but she had managed to temporarily lift the curse on a Demon. She represented something new yet still held her innocence.

She would shape the world, Mortals and Divine alike. Sariel held possibility, her young powers resonated with her own ancient Primordial powers. They also resonated with her brothers' Primordial powers as well. The three of them were ancient and strong, yet she enlivened them, making their magic quicken. She was an oddity that fascinated them.

With her magic she lifted Sariel from the bath, dried her then deposited her gently onto the bed. She settled down next to Sariel brushing her hair and preening her feathers until both shone glossy black. The night was coming, she could feel it as she had not in hundreds of years. It had been so long since she had felt the night in the Underworld, it was a place of perpetual twilight and darkness. She felt the need, the drive to celebrate the night, to join with it, such as it was in the Underworld. How she longed to join with the true night, to see the stars, to feel the sun set and the light fade. To encircle the skies in glorious soaring freedom.

She kissed Sariel on the forehead before dispersing in a drift of shadows.

Hecate stood on the battlements, feeling her powers wax as the realm descended into darkness. Sweeping across the 'sky' of Hades was as close to true night as possible, that black-indigo, spreading shadows and darkness over everything. The lights faded until they were but soft pin pricks of torchlight or flowers. Even the magma's glow was banked down low.

It had been centuries since Nyx had given herself into the night, true night had not touched Hades, or the rest of the Underworld, for a very long time. She had a feeling that night would spill out of Hades and throughout the whole Underworld.

She raised her face to the night as she felt the power wash over her, it had been so long since she had embraced the night. It was a part of her own powers, tonight they would be the strongest they had been in a while. Fortunately much of her power was tied to the Underworld, being sealed within it had not overly affected her powers. But she would be revitalised and stronger after this night.

But what had caused Nyx to recognise and embrace the night?

Sariel. It had to be. She was the only thing different. Something she had done had affected Nyx enough to be able to sense the night despite the spells separating it from the world above.

She turned when she heard footsteps. Erebus

walked out onto the battlements, more darkness than man. A moving patch of darkness, darker than the night sky. He nodded to her and she to him, then he walked forward his arms raised to the sky. His darkness swirled around him, drifts and tendrils bleeding into the night. "Drink well tonight Hecate" he whispered as his form blended into the night, darkening the night sky, overwhelming the torchlight. Now the only lights were the asphodel glowing softly, just like stars would be in the sky.

There was a noise, one she had not heard for a very long time, of gates grinding slightly open. There was a screeching of rock, metal and souls. Fire bloomed from the magma fields in great plumes that suddenly turned dark. Tartarus had opened his Gates to the under-darkness of his realm, his true essence. He too would join the darkness of the night.

For the first time in a very long time three of the children of Chaos would dance together. All that was missing was Gaia who was trapped in her sleep. For she was the Earth itself, Chaos' oldest child and its only possible heir. She held more powers of Chaos than any other, and more than most of the other Primordials combined. But she was trapped until the Curse was lifted and the Lifestream quickened once again.

There were more footsteps as Persephone, Demeter, Hades, Thanatos, Nemesis and even Hypnos walked out onto the battlements. Racing behind them was Cerberus and Charon, not exactly Gods but Divine nevertheless. All of their eyes were wide in wonder at the deepening darkness. The last time the three siblings had danced was before the Fall when Nyx could still embrace the real night sky.

The women raised their arms to the sky, baring their necks in an act of offering as the darkness thickened and even the lights of the flowers were overwhelmed. As one they poured forth their magic into the darkness, sensing it drift around them lazily. Then the dance changed and the powers were washed away, blending into the swirling ocean that was the three siblings. Yet their actions were not in vain, for they had all been Mother Earth Goddesses at some stage of their lives and their powers changed the rhythm. Green lights flared in searing lines across the ground. Sigils of life bloomed in ornate dances before fading into the darkness.

A softer tone filled the air as there was a deep resonating shudder from the ground. Every Divine being, with the exception of the slumbering Sariel, was amazed and stunned. For the first time in eons, Gaia had added to the dance. She hadn't risen from her slumber and she had not physically joined the dance but parts of her magic had seeped out of her confinement to join with her younger siblings.

How was it possible? Had Brigid and Hera sufficiently quickened the Lifestream enough that some of Gaia's powers could leak out? Had it been the three of them adding to the darkness? Had it been the siblings dancing for the first time in centuries that had called to her?

Who knew but it had happened.

The darkness deepened, from black to ebony, swirling like a storm. Green flashes streaked through the darkness before disappearing. There was great joy among the siblings, it had been so long since they had danced and even longer since they had felt Gaia's magic. Their powers blended and intertwined, feeding each other's strength and building upon it. The dark maelstrom rolled around all of Hades, pouring through the Gates of Tartarus and into the Underrealms before roaring back up and out the Gate of Hades, intertwining with the

Rivers of Death before surging through them like blood in veins.

Darkness poured through the whole Underworld, invading each of the other realms, even Hell. Its powers enough to overwhelm all light, even the bright lights of Purgatory. For the first time since the Fall the Angels of Purgatory were embraced by Darkness and they sighed in relief. Even in the depths of Hell the burning lights were overwhelmed temporarily.

It even had such strength to escape the constraints of the Curse and flow out onto the Surface.

The last vestiges of light disappeared as twilight turned into night over Greece and all the countries sharing the same longitude, but if was from Greece the darkness spread. From the Surface connections to the Rivers of Death poured forth the dark power, swirling up into the sky and empowering the night. It shot north and south, blanketing the lights of Egypt and Russia as it went. As the planet turned the darkness spread west as more of the Earth turned to night, and was plunged into a darkness it had not seen for a very long time.

As it swept across Europe and Africa the night stripped every light of its power. Whole cities fell into darkness, every TV screen, computer screen and mobile screen fell dark, their noises still continuing. Every light, electrical or flame fell dark. Far above the satellites orbiting saw whole sections of the earth turn dark. The bright lights of the hundreds of large European cities disappeared. Even the lights on cars, planes and ships fell dark

Humanity for the first time since centuries before the War lived in true darkness and they were afraid. The Daemons took to the streets, opening themselves to the darkness and adding their powers to it urging it onwards.

And so it rolled ever westwards across the Atlantic Ocean sweeping over the islands and plunging the Americas into darkness. In New York, the city that never sleeps, darkness fell. Times Square fell dark, all its iconic screens still. The Humans were afraid because they didn't understand, this was no ordinary blackout. But it was nothing compared to the fear the Angels that had invaded the city felt. Thousands of Lesser and hundreds of Ascended were plunged into a darkness they didn't understand. They couldn't reach Heaven, for its portals were made of light. They were left cowering in the dark fearing for their lives.

It swept further west darkening the bright lights of hundreds of cities. Even Las Vegas for the first time in living memory was plunged into complete darkness. In San Francisco Hera felt the darkness rolling past her, felt all the lights be swallowed. Tonight belonged to complete darkness but she couldn't fathom why. Nyx was trapped in the Underworld, how was she bonding with the night? Surely Sariel hadn't already unlocked the Underworld, she felt sure something more dramatic would have happened. She also added her powers to the darkness but with a twist using it to spread her essence all over the United States, spearing all the way back to New York. San Francisco to her surprise liberally lapped it up, this city was desperate for her. Its demography unknowingly hungered for her attention.

The darkness kept on rolling westwards, swamping the bright lights of Tokyo, Seoul, Beijing and Shanghai. Even the technological powers of Japan and Korea were no match for the darkness. Their brightly lit city streets and shopping malls were plunged into complete darkness.

Everywhere the night touched complete darkness fell, Angels cowered in fear while the Daemons flocked to the streets to add their powers to the rolling surge. It swept over India, darkening its bright lights and reacting with the lingering traces of the Hindu Pantheon. They had been the last of the Gods to fall and their people had not turned away from them, indeed faith was very strong despite the Gods being dead. In the Sacred Rivers the darkness flowed awakening powers long latent.

Above India Brigid sat in the aeroplane, amused at the Human panic resulting from the darkness. All lights had gone out but the plane was still flying, everything else worked, though they would have to stay in the air until day break. She too added her powers to the darkness, hoping for much of her powers to rain down on India. It would be so much easier if it was primed for her claiming.

As every minute passed the darkness retreated from the rising sun and chased the setting one. The Darkness did a full circle of the Earth plunging nearly half of it into utter darkness until the night and the Darkness once again returned to Greece and the three siblings were released from their dance.

Heaven was not untouched either by the night and Darkness. Heaven was in a state of ever day, keeping back the natural tide of night but it was not designed to withstand such an attack by the night. Darkness crept around the edges of the sky forming long shadowy fingers into the floating islands that made up Heaven. All of the Outer Islands fell into darkness, but most of them had been abandoned since the War. It was only the Citadel and Palace that held back the night.

But not without a fight.

Gabriel marched along the corridors separating the Divine prisoners. Not all of them were Gods, there were many Angels, Daevas, Nephilim, Nymphs and even some

Monsters imprisoned in the bowels of the palace. Each corridor housed beings of particular natures. The corridors she sought were the sun, moon and light. The Citadel would not fall to darkness. What in the name of Hell was going on? The entire Surface was shrouded in complete darkness at night-time ending only at daybreak. Scared Angels had started appearing as soon as the light returned and they were able to teleport back up to Heaven.

Fortunately the Citadel was relative to the Middle East region on the Surface, as such they had had time to prepare for the rising darkness. Nuriel had been sent out on mass with as many of the Seraphim that were not Elders to find the source of this aberration. All the Elder except Nuriel and those currently trapped on the Surface had been summoned to the Palace to receive the gift of light.

Which was why she and the other Arch Angels were currently racing along the three corridors.

She stopped at the door reading the plaque *Helios*. She smiled despite being mostly forgotten Helios was still very strong. He was one of the first Gods to attune to the sun, but his Roman name lived on in everyday life. Sol formed the basis of the name The Solar System, a fact most Humans were completely ignorant or the fact that they empowered him with such open use of his name. It was one of the reasons he would not be executed. He was far too valuable.

The doors swung open as she marched into the room. As she had expected he sat bolt upright waiting for her presence. All the Sun Gods and Goddesses had been the same. As the darkness spread people prayed for the return of the sun, not to God but for the sun. Such open prayers were empowering all the Sun Gods.

"Back so soon Gabriel, this is a pleasant surprise"

the man breathed sarcasm because he knew his value. She regularly robbed him of his excess power to supplement her own. It was the right that only the Arch Angels had, to strip a God of their power to supplement their own. There had been incidents in the past of Gods being lost because of overzealous Angels.

"Of course Helios I just couldn't stay away."

"Like the flame to the moth. But this time you have a desperate reason. The Darkest Night is coming to the Citadel and you want to stop it." He sneered "do you know the power behind this night?"

No she didn't but she was going to damn well find out. This couldn't be either Hera or Brigid. Neither of them were Sky or Chthonic Goddesses. And this was beyond their power limits even if they suddenly had a whole nation praying to them.

He smiled savagely as she walked forward "You don't do you?"

"The threat to Heaven is irrelevant but it will be dealt with" she grabbed his head roughly, he was starting to annoy her.

"Not all the Primordials faded back into the Lifestream. Nyx is once again one with the night." Her blood ran cold even as she savagely pulled out his magic, she felt the heat rise through her, coursing into her own power.

Damn it a Primordial! That was the last bloody thing they needed. Was she in the Underworld, did the Curse even contain a Primordial? There was no telling what could contain those freaks. Power beyond reasoning but so undefined, so narrow in its application and yet so amazingly broad. Their powers were immeasurable though highly unpredictable, they were even less predictable than their progeny the Titans or the Gods. They had no need for prayers, their powers naturally waxed and waned, a gift they had passed onto many of their offspring particularly sun, moon, sea or seasonal Gods.

If Nyx was once again with the night, what did it mean? Was she going to attack Heaven, was the darkness a build-up of her power before she was going to smash against the strongholds? The Citadel had been built by some air Primordials and their air gifted progeny. Could it withstand a direct assault from undiluted Primordial power? She had no idea, they had to keep away the night.

She had a sudden thought sending it to Michael *Raid the fire corridor, fire fights back the night*

She felt his amusement come back through the thought thread *Already done and I've just finished off Theia and the other Sky Lights.* Oh how she loved her husband sometimes, it was rare for anyone ever to be a step ahead of her but if anyone was it was Michael. *And Raphael has finished with Hyperion and the lights, Ariel just finished with Selene and the moons and Uriel has finished the Star Gods. We are all ready to meet when you are.*

I've just finished Helios, the suns are done. Meet in the audience chambers. She paused before adding *anything from Azrael?*

Outside of the Citadel it became far more difficult to communicate telepathically with other Angels. Beyond a certain distance it became increasingly difficult and could only be overcome by the strengthened bonds of blood or love. Only Michael had the blood connection to Azrael, but he spent so much of his time transferring the dead into Purgatory and Heaven and was often beyond reach.

Yes he is in Iran, apparently there has been an earthquake so many of his Reapers are there. They are stranded in the darkness but otherwise calm and unaffected.

Well they would be calm, they live in the darkness so much of the time

She felt his silent agreement and his reluctance to comment on such things. He was naturally an Angel of Death, a point that was rarely mentioned by either of them. She wasn't overly concerned, power was power, but he was more comfortable in the light than shadows.

All five of them materialised before their respective thrones in a blaze of light. Assembled in the wings were all the Elder Angels currently in Heaven. The five Arch Angels raised their arms in a blaze of light sending out their combining powers to wash through the whole room bathing the Elders with the magic. In its combined form it was far more accessible and controllable for the weaker Elders.

Light blazed out of the crystal roof blazing up into the darkening sky, punching a hole through the fingers of darkness reaching over the palace.

Materialising all around the edges of the floating island that held the Citadel were blazing pillars of light, each one an Elder Angel infused with the power of light.

Steadily with the progression of nature the sky fell to night, the twilight growing long and thick. As the sun disappeared behind the horizon the light of Heaven started to flicker and fade. Darkness progressed around all the horizons, slowly reaching inwards to the Citadel.

It rolled in slowly as though it were a cloudbank composed of pure darkness. The Angels made no move to stave it off, even as the lights surrounding the island flickered, faded then were swallowed by the darkness.

The lights of the Angels wavered as the darkness rolled upon them, before each of them blazed brighter, connecting themselves to each other with rays of blinding light. Rays of light formed a graceful dome over the

Citadel as each Angel became connected to each other. From the palace blazed out pure light, its whiteness blinding, turning the whole palace into a lamp that held back the darkness.

It rolled up to the lines of light then went no further, but nor did the light pierce into the darkness. An equilibrium was reached. The Darkness didn't have the strength to challenge the Citadel of Light but it surrounded it until day broke over the Citadel and the sun rose once again, chasing away the darkness and empowering the weakened light spells.

Each of the Angels returned to their usual tasks while the Arch Angels gratefully collapsed onto their thrones. They knew Nyx was behind it, but they would wait for Nuriel's assessment before they made any actions.

One by one they all left leaving behind Michael and Gabriel. To his great surprise she took his hand in hers when they transported. And he was even more surprised when she teleported them both to their bedroom.

Gabriel was in a very good mood.

Sariel climbed the tower feeling her way with her hands alone. She could not see in the utter darkness, nor had she been able to summon light of any kind, though there was a faint reminder of her natural glow. The entire palace was dark, all the halls and corridors but she had felt the pull and followed it to the steps of the tower.

The complete darkness should have scared her, she was after all an Angel, a creature of light and skies but she was not afraid or even concerned. She felt amazing, all her aches and pains were gone, all her muscles healed. She was the healthiest she had been since she had arrived in Hades. She was stronger than she had been in Heaven and she could feel her powers. Not actually use them, but she could feel them.

She had walked up the stairs hesitantly but she didn't fall or trip. It seemed her other senses were far stronger in the darkness. When she got to the top she felt the presence of the others, but no one was speaking. She felt sure they felt her presence, just as she felt theirs.

She stood there, for how long she didn't know. Hours perhaps, but eventually the darkness began to fade on the horizons. It was odd as though the sun was rising as a horizontal line from every direction. Slowly the darkness retreated as the light speared towards them in all directions. The darkness rushed past her, revealing her family on the tower top to condense until it floated formless a little above them. From there it split into three forms that flowed into the shapes of people. These then gently floated down to the ground shifting into the recognisable forms of Nyx, Tartarus and Erebus.

Nyx seemed more beautiful than she remembered, her skin seemed even paler and the darkness of her veins seemed even darker. Her hair lay as a pool of ink all around her head. Her brothers looked less shadowy and more like her. Both had dark skin and shadowy hair, one shoulder length the other short.

There was something different about them all, a green mark that ran from under their right earlobe down their necks, winding across their collarbones to then curl down around their left nipple. Before all their eyes the marks grew little leaves and drifted gently back and forth as though a vine in the breeze.

As one they all opened their eyes, black pits but with green irises separating the pupils from the blacks. It was completely alien, starkly beautiful and wholly unnerving, especially when all three of them fixed on her own violet eyes. They remained fixed on hers as they rose from the ground, shadowy clothes forming around them. She was relieved, it was highly awkward having family members so unbothered by their own and others' nudity. She had never seen another naked person until she had come to Hades.

"Blessing of Gaia on you Sariel" they said in unison, their voices blending together in a highly unnerving fusion of noises.

She nodded back to them unsure of what to say.

Nyx walked the few steps to Sariel and embraced her great-granddaughter "it has been so very long since I last blended with the night, the Underworld is a pale comparison of the true night. It is my true nature, the very essence of my spirit but so long have I been denied. Last night was the first time I felt the call or had the strength to return to the night. It has been even longer for my brothers and yet they eagerly leapt into the dance. It has been millennia since Gaia joined the dance and yet last night her powers reverberated all around the Underworld and the overflow allowed us to taste the Surface.

We saw it all, our combined consciousness was spread all over the world, how it has changed so much. The Daemons are so very weak but Hera and Brigid are strong and they are determined. The Angels powers are still strong, but only the Citadel held back the night. How unnatural but they are not as weak as we would have hoped."

She paused before asking "Do you know what was different about last night?"

"Gaia's powers? Is that why you have green in your eyes and a green vine on your skin? The three of them glanced at each other with some surprise, each touching the vine on their neck, chest or collarbone.

"Yes this is the mark of Gaia and once her powers

joined the dance there was little stopping it. She slumbers deep, trapped but her powers are so very vast. She was the first child of Chaos and its only true child, the oldest of all the Primordial Gods. She has only grown stronger, each Mother Goddess that returns to the Lifestream in turn becomes part of her, even their memories. She has been reincarnated herself but retains all her past memories. She is the essence of the planet itself, and the life that depends on it.

But no, the difference was you."

"Me? What did I do?"

"I'm not entirely sure but your powers had a strange effect on me, and they are highly unique Sariel, even Gaia noticed. She marked you as her own."

She held up her hands before Sariel, their surface turning into liquid silver for her to look at her reflection in. Sariel looked in wonder at the vine winding up from under her clothes, across her collar bone and up under her right ear. As Nyx touched it, it flared black-green and there was an answering rumble from deep in the earth.

"Gaia has risen in her slumber, you, Brigid and Hera have quickened her blood. This is the most activity we have seen out of her in nearly three thousand years. She went to sleep to rest, her age and all she has seen wearing on her but because of the Curse sealing up the Underworld she is unable to rise from her slumbers. She cannot awaken or take physical form but her magic has quickened the Lifestream for the first time since before the War. You Sariel are the catalyst for change. You will change the world in ways that we can't even begin to guess, but Gaia can." As she finished she and her brothers disappeared in a haze of shadows. The other Gods just simply faded away leaving her all alone of the tower top. Apparently massive declarations meant everyone left. Or perhaps it was just so that they didn't have to clarify what they had said.

Her hand still pressed to her new mark she wondered, was it true? Was she really going to affect the world or were they just saying that? No there had been similar things written in journals she had read. It had been mentioned in both her parents' journals documenting her birth. She had also found her name mentioned in a journal by somebody called the Norns.

But then Michael and Gabriel had had similar predictions said about them when they were born. Was she going to start a war, the thought seemed ridiculous? Who would take over Heaven? The Humans and Daemons left on the Surface?

Yet somehow Nyx's words felt utterly true. She just wondered her part in it all. And why had Gaia blessed her with her mark? She wasn't a Mother Goddess, she was an Arch Angel, such as she was now, still trying to get a basic grasp on her powers. And her sword skills. She sighed at the thought of her next fighting lesson.

Chapter 15

There was a general sigh of relief as the plane was finally cleared for landing, they had had to stay in the air all night as the strange darkness rolled by them all. Most of them were looking the worst for wear, with the noticeable exception of Brigid. A whole extra night on an aeroplane and she was as stunning as ever, she didn't need sleep like the mortals did.

Not that she would have gotten much sleep if she had. Most of the night had disappeared in a blur of stimulating conversation. Darkness made everything so much more personal, flirtation took on a whole new meaning. Things could be whispered in the darkness but not in the light. People truly did belong to both the light and the dark, something she had never truly appreciated before.

Life was all about balances.

Humans being the instinctive animals that they were had felt all sorts of emotions in the darkness. Fear certainly, anxiety yes, but also lust. When people and even animals are scared they turn to each other for comfort. Combine that with the secretive and yet liberating effect of the darkness and you have people finding comfort in each other sexually.

She was no exception. She certainly wasn't scared but it had been so long since she had felt the touch of another person. It was nice to kiss and forget about the world. She was amazed at the audacity of some people though, like no one could hear them moaning and grunting. The worst had been that stupid shrieking bimbo. She would never experience another orgasm in her life.

The Gods were cruel.

As the plane touched down on the runway Brigid was hit with the emptiness of India. She had thought that it would be vibrant and overflowing with magic, it had had so many deities, Divine races and Daemons. It had been a truly magical place, a melting pot of magic and divinity helping civilisation out of its cradle. Just like China and Mesopotamia. How she missed the good old days.

There was truly nothing in India, it was desperately hungry for magic of any kind. The country's dwindling Lifestreams started coiling around her as soon as her shoes hit the ground of the terminal. Grumpy, tired and worn out people poured off the plane all around her, each unwittingly walking through these starving Lifestreams, unknowingly having some of their Lifeforce drained away.

What was wrong with India?

It was so desperate to bond with her, already coiling around her skin, trying desperately to extract some of her power. Australia had not been this desperate to bond with her. It had seemed rather ambivalent about her presence. Oh Sydney had started to respond like a favoured pet, becoming increasingly more eager, but on the whole the country seemed neither eager nor displeased by her presence. She had just been there to it.

India was a like a starving pet, doing everything it possibly could to get food. It would seem the Angels' cleansing had left a power vacuum that had not been filled. How very fortunate she was the first God here. Areas of settlement were used to not only Human and Daemon magic but Divine magic as well. They became accustomed to the magic being pulled out of the Lifestream, they became dependent on it. In many cases magic had dwindled over a period of time, allowing the land to adjust. India had been, and still was, a deeply mystical land. The amount of magical energy flowing through its cities had been phenomenal even back then. To suddenly have the Gods killed and the Daemons hunted to extinction in a very short amount of time had not given the land time to adjust. It wanted power any way it could get it.

It was no wonder the world was starting to fall apart. The Angels had left voids like this all over the world. Without the calming and nurturing influence of a Mother Goddess the Lifestream was turning feral. Damaging not only itself but the life it was meant to be supporting. If this kept up the planet would extinguish the higher life on its surface, eradicating all but the strongest extremophiles. All animals and plants would die, all Daemons would die, even most of the Divine would die as the Lifestream collapsed under its own ineffectiveness.

The Lesser and Ascended Angels would be destroyed and many of the Elder Angels and Gods would have their powers burnt out. Doomed to fade away on a lifeless planet.

What Earth needed was the Mother Goddesses free to heal and nurture it. What it really needed was Gaia, she could heal the world in an instant, for it was her and she was it. But she was chained down in her slumbers, unable to rise while the Underworld was still contained. If the Angels weren't careful there would come a day when all they had worked for had died, their powers failing the Underworld would be unlocked and Gaia in all her fury would rise to wreck vengeance on those who had damaged her planet so much.

The Angels had given her and Hera an unexpected blessing. Claiming and bonding with lands would be ridiculously easy for them, there was no one they had to pry it off of first.

Smiling she opened up her powers to the Lifestream. She staggered as it ploughed through her, greedily twirling around her streams of magic that were haemorrhaging at an alarming rate. But she could now taste the life in the air, underneath all the pollution. The few plants she could see looked healthier, stood a little straighter and looked a whole lot more vibrant.

Thankfully she had staggered as they walked out of the terminal. Ryan gently stabilised her "The humidity is a shocker, especially if all you've known is London's weather."

She felt like snorting, she was a Goddess, menial things like heat and humidity had no effect on her. "It is certainly different from the dry heat of Australia that's for sure.

He smiled at her encouragingly as he hailed a cab for them. Who would have thought they were both staying at the same hotel. She loved her powers, they were just so useful. Since Sydney she had opened up several bank accounts under different aliases and propped them up with magic. She was now one of those secret millionaires just quietly going about her business. If the Angels had the wealth of the Catholic Church then why couldn't she have a small comparison? She'd actually been quite disgusted when she found out how much money they hoarded. They were like Dragons, no Dragons were magnificent creatures, Goblins they were like Goblins.

She climbed into the taxi next to Ryan feeling quite content at the moment to be near him. She hadn't had a lover in a very, very long time and he was refreshing. He challenged her intellectually and he had such a warped sense of humour. She also felt sorry for him, cancer was eating its way through his vital organs. In a few months he would be dead. She could at least offer comfort to a follower of Brigid.

That amused her, he had no idea that the Goddess he prayed to was the same woman he kissed.

He looked at her and smiled, she smiled back laying her had on his. She felt her pulse quicken at his touch. Was it just him or had most modern Humans progressed to the stage where they could quicken the pulse of a deity? Even the Daemon races had struggled to do that. Had the Nephilim, Demigods and Divine Daemon races interbred with Humanity so much that the difference wasn't noticeable. Did traces of Divine blood race through his veins? What would happen when the Lifestream started reactivating those dormant genes?

The world really was in for some interesting developments.

"I have the results of your tests Kyle"

Kyle held his breath as his doctor slid the test results out of the yellow envelope, he shuffled the paper before meeting his eyes "What do they say?"

"Your T cell count is severely low. You have HIV and your tests indicate that you may have developed AIDS"

His eyes widened "But AIDS takes years to develop"

"Not always, the virus has a rapidly mutating genome that dramatically changes its behaviour from person to person. It is possible to have several different strains within the one person."

He sat there completely crestfallen, he had always been so careful his entire life. Always using protection and always getting both himself and his partners tested. That was up until he had been date raped.

It was so unfair, it wasn't his fault, he had always

been careful and now because he had been drugged and raped he was paying the biggest price.

"What can I do?"

The doctor sighed "There are several different drugs treatments you can be placed on. They can extend your life span far longer than it would be untreated but there is no cure for AIDS Kyle. Unfortunately you are paying the price for someone else's actions."

"If I take the course how long will it give me?"

"It is hard to tell exactly but Kyle you have to understand the strain you have contracted is incredibly destructive, your immune system is already dangerously low. If I didn't know better I would say the tests belong to someone at the very end of their struggle with AIDS."

"I'm going to die soon."

He sighed again "Yes Kyle the cards you have been dealt are completely unfair."

Tears started pouring out his eyes, he was only twenty years old and he was going to die soon. He was already dying of AIDS. There was so much he wanted to do with his life, he hadn't finished collage, he hadn't really been in love, he hadn't gone to Europe, heck he hadn't even told his parents he was gay.

It was so unfair.

A box of tissues was pushed towards him, great consoling skills.

"There is something I can suggest considering the uniqueness of your situation."

What the Hell did he mean the uniqueness of his situation?

"There is a new hospital that for some reason or another is highly selective. Have you heard of the Imperial Hospitals?"

"It sounds vaguely familiar"

"They are controversial hospitals being set up all

over the country, by some mysterious benefactor. Medically they've attracted some attention for choosing who they treat, non-medically they've attracted a lot. Many claim they're part of a cult and their loudest critics are the church. However medically they appear to be making great breakthroughs, though not without controversy."

"What has that got to do with me?"

"The San Francisco Imperial has recently had many patients discharged apparently cured of AIDS." He hurried on before Kyle could jump to any conclusions "These have not been greatly substantiated but tests by independent clinics and laboratories are supporting their claims."

"They could cure me"

"Only if they admit you, as I have mentioned they are surprisingly selective for whom they treat."

"Those who can pay" how on earth was he going to afford a cure for AIDS?

"Surprisingly no, indeed many are being selected from the gay community. Whoever the mysterious benefactor of the Imperial Hospitals is, they certainly support the gay community."

Kyle left his doctor soon after, not really sure if his life could take any more turbulence. AIDS, he had AIDS.

Yet there was the possibility of getting rid of it, if the hospital would admit him. Only one way to find out.

The Imperial Hospital of San Francisco was not as he had expected. It stood imposing on the hillside, hugging well to its contours. Despite only recently being opened there was an abundance of plant life, the trees certainly did not look like they were new saplings.

The main drive circled around a peculiar fountain. A beautiful woman stood holding a wide shallow bowl with a real fire burning away. Strips of black material and red ribbons had been thrown in the bowl to burn, though some had slipped out onto the marble steps leading up to the bowl. Spurts of water rose around the woman and the steps leading up to her.

It certainly seemed like the rumours of curing AIDS was true, he recognised AIDS symbols.

The place seemed oddly deserted as he walked through the electric doors, the soft voice of *Enya* playing through the empty corridors. The desk seemed strangely ornate for a hospital, no imposing. It was grand, meant to intimidate those approaching it. Kyle certainly felt very intimidated as he walked up to the desk, under the dismissive glance of a brunette woman. She seemed cut straight out of a magazine, she seemed far too perfect, she almost looked like she glowed.

She focused her stunning grey eyes on him "Can I help you?" she asked in a completely pretentious and dismissive manner.

Taken aback he stared blankly at her before answering "My doctor recommended I come here for treatment"

"We have a very specific clientele here" she dropped a clipboard onto the wood, before pushing it across with a perfectly manicured hand "fill out these forms"

She promptly turned her attention back to the shiny silver screen in front of her.

He was used to gay men, but she brought abrupt dismissal to a whole new level.

He grabbed the clipboard before looking around for a seat, finding none he settled for leaning against the wall. What kind of hospital was this anyway?

The first question simply asked about his medical condition. The pen was a dark purple, the paper was a light gold. This place seemed more like a high flyers spa than a hospital. The second question asked him about his religion. Why was a hospital asking about religious beliefs?

Then he remembered what Doctor Patterson had said about them possibly being a cult.

The third question asked him about his sexuality. He wanted to demand why this was relevant but remembered about them being quite pro-gay, and the black strips that had once belonged to pride flags burning out the front.

The next question was his date of birth, then any allergies he had.

That was the whole sheet

Only two of the five questions had been significantly medical.

"Done" he pushed it towards her.

She flicked her eyes towards him as she snatched the paper out of the clipboard and slid it into a small slit on the desk. There was a slight whorl and a blue light illuminated the opening.

"Mr Cho this way thank you"

He jumped out of his skin at the voice. He spun around to find a mature woman in a doctor's coat. Her brown hair had the slightest streaks of grey, her impassive face slightly lined, but her eyes they were old and studious.

"Excuse me?"

"I presume you want treatment? We can't very well treat you in the foyer." She turned abruptly on her heel and started walking without checking if he was following. He hurried after her to find she was talking to him "If you have any commitments for the next few days cancel them, your cell phone will need to be turned off once your treatments begins. You will have limited access to the outside world until your risk of contraction is eliminated. Your early treatment will make you highly contagious and we cannot risk you infecting other patients"

"But AIDS is only passed on via fluids"

The look she gave him could have peeled paint "Are you a medical professional, developing an experimental cure for the world's current pandemic?"

"No"

"Then don't question me. Our treatments dramatically alter the behaviour of the virus allowing your body to effectively track it down and eliminate it. Hence why you become contagious."

Could this place be any worse at its bedside manner?

She led him to a room and bade him enter "Shower and change into the provided clothes, you'll receive yours again once you leave. You have the next hour to contact anyone and cancel prior arrangements. Then your diagnosis will begin."

"But you already know I have AIDS"

She just looked at him before leaving.

His room was surprisingly spacious, with its own ensuite. It was sterile, practical and yet comforting all at once. There was a bed, a TV, a bookcase with a selection of books, a table with tubes coming down from the ceiling and a couch. All were white. The only colours were the green or violet lights of appliances.

What had he gotten himself into?

She lay in the massive bath, allowing her wings to flex under the water. She could make them disappear but because of her transformation they were now as much a part of her as her arms or legs. She supposed she could re-sculpt her body if she wanted to, it had been vogue at one time to re-sculpt Divine bodies. The Egyptian Gods had all done it as had the Erotes, it was this genetic re-sculpting that had resulted in the Angels, Naga and many of the Monster offspring of the Gods.

But the process was painful, despite the Divine immunity to physical pain. It was also a lengthy process and a waste of magic in her current predicament. It was something the Gods had done to reinvent themselves or distinguish themselves at the height of their power.

She was neither at the height of her power nor looking to reinvent herself. She was just trying to survive.

Besides there was a novelty in having six brown wings. None of the Angels had brown wings and none of the Gods had six. She supposed it made her some kind of Angel/Goddess hybrid, she certainly had powers she had never had before and many of her lesser aspects had been greatly enhanced.

She was also getting used to having them there, sleeping was a bitch with wings but she loved being able to fly. So simple but so wonderful. She now understood why the Angels had always returned to Heaven, they were creatures of the sky.

She wondered if her children would have wings, and if she had any demigod offspring if they would be Angels.

She pushed such thoughts from her mind as she glanced at the clock. An amazing invention, Humans were so ingenious. They were far more reliable than sundials. She stood up, letting the water run down her body before snapping her wings several times. She absently dried herself and the sopping wet room as she walked up to the full-length mirror to look at herself.

She was pale skinned like the pantheon she had come from and the people who had worshipped her. She had been tall for her time, but now was average height, she would have to fix that she liked being taller. Her long hair fell as a curtain of rich, warm brown, glowing from her divinity. Her eyes were greener than she remembered, but they adjusted before her own eyes into the richer dark brown she remembered. On a whim she changed them to bright emerald.

She felt sure she was far more beautiful than she remembered, this modern age was so vain. Even their perception of the past bled through with vanity. She loved this era. It was amazing. Even her body had taken on a changed physicality, everything was more toned. She looked less the warrior she had been and more like a delicate princess.

Her silken dress slid up off the floor, rippling across her smooth skin and conforming to her figure effortlessly. She was glad she had changed her eye colours, her dress matched them perfectly. The dress was low cut at the back, but more conservative at the front. She touched her neck and an emerald choker grew around it. She lightly brushed her wrists and golden bracelets grew. As a final touch she added a touch of green eye-shadow.

She smiled at herself in the mirror as there was a knock at the door. "Coming" she yelled snapping her shoes and purse into existence. Magic was just so convenient. How did Humans live without it?

She hurried to open the door, remembering at the last second to vanish her wings, to find Ryan standing at her threshold looking very handsome in his tailored black suit. His mouth and eyes flew open when he saw her. She felt fantastic as she tapped his mouth closed "could your eyes grow any wider?" she laughed.

"I'm sorry but you look incredible"

She flashed a smile as she flicked her hair "Why thank you, you look very handsome yourself."

He stared at her slightly dazed as she linked her arms into his "Come on you, we'll be late for dinner."

She walked with a spring in her step. She had never felt this amazing before, she had always felt in the shadow of so many of the other Goddess's beauty. It was odd how one mortal man's delight and attention was worth more than the devotion of thousands she had once enjoyed. She didn't understand it but she was certainly enjoying it.

The night had been wonderful, the food had been amazing, an explosion of flavour and spices. But more than anything it was Ryan's company that made the evening for her. It had been so long since she had any real sense of companionship. Her captivity had afforded her very few chances of socialising, other than the occasional Angel coming to gloat. There had been Patrick though who had given her some small companionship, and there had been Sariel whose innocence had touched something in her. Her time in Sydney had been mostly spent alone reacquainting herself with the world and all its new wonders.

But now she was back amongst society and she had a man that delighted her. Now he was walking her back to her room, conversing about the Goddess Brigid and her progression into Saint Brigid. It fascinated her to hear about herself from the Human perception. Humans had a great many perceptions about their deities, and such perceptions had incredible control over them. Mortals had never comprehended the power they wielded over the Gods. This modern fascination with the past and correcting misconceptions had changed not only her. She felt sure any of the surviving Gods would all have been changed.

With a quick flick of the card the door was opened,

technology was its own magic. She turned back to him, he was busy admiring her figure before he flicked his eyes back to hers. She smiled mischievously before leaning forward to kiss him, there was surprise before he surrendered to the kiss. Such fire and passion, she felt her loins stir and her pulse quicken. When had she ever felt like this, she struggled to think of any, Divine or mortal?

Finally they broke apart, both breathing heavily. She smiled as she instantly regained her breath "would you like to come in?" His kiss was all the answer she needed, before she pulled him into the room. Suddenly dynamics changed, he had her against the wall, holding her hands above her head. His mouth moved from hers over to her neck and she gasped in pleasure. He was in control, though it was but a ruse, she could break free of his hold and rip his head off with her bare hands, but the woman in her submitted to his grasp.

It was incredibly arousing but as soon as she felt his hold waver, she had him up against the other wall. Such a simple act that awakened all the primal instincts in her, the woman in her was more alive than she had ever been. She moved her lips to his neck, resisting the urge to bite him, keeping her touch gentle. She was rewarded with a sexual moan. She let go of his arms and slide her hands up to his collar, slowly unbuttoning his shirt as he shrugged out of his jacket. Her mouth followed her hands down his chest and his breathing picked up a hitch.

The dance changed and once again he was in control. He picked her up and carried her over to the bed, lowering them both onto the bed as she wrapped herself around him. She groaned in surprise as his hands slide up her legs, before flying to her shoulder. They gently pulled down the zip and slide the straps off of her shoulder. The silk dress slid off of her as she pulled him out of his shirt. She straddled him as his hands ran up her back, slow and warm leaving a trail of heat in their wake. He unclipped her bra, and she moaned in pleasure as his mouth closed over her nipples. She lost herself to a haze of pleasure as his mouth and fingers trailed all over her body. But for all she received she gave in return, his moans often in unison with hers.

She didn't remember when their underwear came off, but the next thing she knew was the increased pleasure of him sheathing himself in her. After that she had no time for conscious thinking, there was only basic instinct. For every drop of pleasure she gained she returned. They rolled back and forth across the bed, neither of them staying in control for long. Power was a fluid dance between them. Magic swirled uncontrolled around them, seething in her every pore.

She felt her body start to shudder, her pleasure peaking. She felt something stirring deep inside her, more than just pleasure.

As she lost herself in her orgasm, something shuddered deep beneath her, resonating with her own shudders. If she hadn't been so distracted she would have trembled in fear and longing. But she didn't notice the swirling Lifestream surging beneath Delhi, nor the latent powers being awakened all over India. If she had she might have been more careful when delving into the powers of India later.

Kyle stared at the glittering pool before him confused. He had been led to this room, told to enter then the door had promptly locked behind him. They weren't ones for social niceties in this hospital.

The room they had led him to once again looked like it belonged to a science fiction spa. Marble floors and columns, with metallic and glass tubes leading in and out of the pool. The down lights above filtered through different colours as he moved across the room. The water itself seemed to have a changing iridescent sheen. Healthy looking plants sat in marble containers giving the room a faint scent of perfume.

A blank TV screen on the wall blinked into life with instructions to remove clothes and climb into the pool. He waited for a few minutes to see if anything else happened but it didn't.

He removed his strange white clothes, loose pants with a loose gown on top. He suddenly felt highly self-conscious being completely naked in the room. Especially after the instructions changed from remove clothes and get in pool to just get in pool. He walked down the steps encircling the pool, pleasantly surprised to find the water wasn't cold. It was strange, the water touching his skin started to turn black, slowly diffusing away. The more skin in contact with the water the more black that drifted off him.

He stood with the water up to his chest watching as the water around him turned first smoky then solid black, with drifts of black spreading outwards until the whole pool was black. He had no idea what was going on but it was freaking the crap out of him.

There was a whirring noise followed by the sound of sucking water. Several of the shiny tubes spaced evenly around the room had turned black as water was slowly sucked out of the pool. The empty tubes interspacing them turned red as red water started flowing out into the pool. At least he hoped it was water, it bore a strikingly disturbing resemblance to blood. As red patches started to bloom on the surface of the pool he couldn't help but think this wasn't real.

He turned back to the screen which was now flashing submerge yourself. He looked back at the black water surrounding him with the streaks of red near the edges. The last thing he wanted to do was submerge himself. There was a faint buzzing noise, then the next thing he knew he was collared by cold metal, with an air-tube running its way into his mouth. The he was pushed under the water.

He struggled in vain, whatever was holding him down was stronger the he was. His struggles only resulted in him swallowing lots of water before he remembered to use his air tube. Slowly his heart rate calmed as he focussed on breathing through the tube. Despite its relatively small size it was like breathing normally. There wasn't much else for him to focus on, all he could see was darkness.

There were strange tingling sensations all over his body, not dissimilar to pins and needles. Time seemed to stop, he had lost most of his senses, only the subtle tastes of herbs coming through the tube and the feeling of warm water on his skin reminded him he was still in existence. He just floated until he drifted off.

He woke up as someone was fishing him out of the water. He shut his eyes against the light it was far too bright, he tried to cover his ears the sound of footsteps was even too loud. How long had he been desensitized? He just lolled against the step as the person hauled him out. He felt so unbelievably weak.

He was left lying on the floor, it seemed so cold after the bath, but it was strangely pleasant having something solid against him.

Then the next thing he knew someone had stabbed him in the bottom with a needle then were giving it a brief rub. He tried to roll over, all he managed was to turn his neck. Kneeling over him holding her syringes was the strangest woman he had ever seen. Dark forest green hair, even her eyebrows and eyelashes were the same green, with eyes and lips also the same colour. A faint light green leaf had been tattooed next to her eye. She picked up another syringe, pursing her lips as she drew out the drugs from the bottle. This time she gently injected it into his arm. He felt a strange electric feeling flowing through his arm, fading the longer time passed.

"How does he fare?" came a male voice. Deep, sensual and cultured. Even in his current state it did wonders for his libido.

"Better than most, his vital signs are strong and he is responding to the treatment very well. The virus is already diminishing and his genes are more active than I would have anticipated. Perhaps we have one of the ones she is looking for. Too soon to tell yet."

"Better to be sure, he could yet perish."

She stood up and left, her high-heels clicking on the tiles. There were other footsteps as the man walked towards him. There was a gentle brush of his hair before the man gently tilted his head with his hand. Except Kyle wasn't sure if he was a man.

Electric eyes, he had electric eyes. His irises were literally blue electricity, they were stunning and terrifying. Those blue eyes were set in the most perfect man he had ever seen. He looked Latino, beautiful coffee skin, straight black hair that hung down to his cheeks, black stubble lightly covered his perfectly angled face.

He picked Kyle up with ease, carrying him back to his room. He was strong, so he must be muscular and he reckoned that the guy was quite tall. Could he be any sexier? Then he remembered that voice. He felt sure he would let this man do just about anything to him and he would be completely willing.

Before long, too short a time, the man laid him down on his bed. He quickly and efficiently dressed Kyle and tucked him into the bed. He disappeared and the sound of buttons being pressed and whirring occurred. Then he reappeared with a glass of water. "Here you'll need this when you wake up, you'll wake up really dehydrated."

Then he left, the door sliding shut behind him, leaving Kyle with his image dancing across his eyes. What he wouldn't do to be with a man like that.

Chapter 16

She opened her eyes into thin slits, why was she naked on the floor? She couldn't even remember what she had been doing beforehand. She could only remember snippets of her entire life. It would take some time for them all to realign enough for them to make sense. Which meant she had been unconscious for quite some time, but why and what had woken her?

She opened her eyes wider as she awakened all her other senses. She could hear gentle breathing, she smelled a great deal of decay, the room was dark but she sensed others nearby. A quick if haphazard probe identified her family. She must have been out for quite some time for her magic to be so heavy handed and incompetent. How embarrassing, she was the Goddess of Magic, well she used to be.

What was she now, she had passed on the privilege and duties as Queen of Heaven onto Hera when Egypt had been swallowed by the Roman Empire. Her own Empire had become nothing more than a province in an Empire that dominated that side of the world. But still she had survived with cults throughout the Empire. Until the conversion and the War started.

So much had been lost, her followers, her people, her nation, her pantheon, her freedom, her son. Now she was trapped in the Underworld, in the empty realms of Duat and Aaru. Oh they had once been busy, the scales that weighed the heart had been forever swinging back and forth determining people's fate while those waiting watched in apprehension.

Then the numbers had started to decrease more and more, the halls falling emptier and the six of them growing bored and weak. They were all that was left of a once great pantheon, they had been one of the oldest surviving. Then people had ceased to come at all as Islam and Christianity spread their vile clutches up and down the Nile. Trapped in the Underworld they could do nothing to protect their beloved Egypt.

Time had passed and they had sat still on their thrones as the centuries rolled by. They had all Desiccated she realised with horror, she hadn't thought it possible for a God to become Desiccated. The other Divine sure but the Gods were the essence of life and vitality. Then again she supposed it was only logical when trapped for centuries in an empty realm of the dead. They had been dead in all but their immortality as even the strongest of spirits had faded back into the Lifestream.

She stirred more, flicking her wings as she became aware of their presence, using her now functioning legs and arms to push herself up into first kneeling then standing. She stared in disgust as dust poured off of her as she moved, her wings were filthy, a disgrace. She was covered in layers of dust and her wings were literally caked in it. She realised that her wrap had rotted away long ago. She looked at her family in disgust, they all sat slouched on their thrones or the steps, barely moving. But their features were healthy beneath their layers of dust.

What had given them back their vitality? What had woken her from her slumbers? She had been asleep and Desiccated so long she had ceased to dream. What could wake anyone from that kind of slumber?

Looking around she realised the hall was completely dark. The hall had never been dark, Ra's own essence had given it light even after he had returned to the Lifestream. They would not have faded, not even in a million years. Something had overpowered them. What could overpower the power of the sun, the power of a

Primordial Sun God? Only another Primordial and it would have to be a Primordial of Night or Darkness.

But surely there weren't any Primordials left? Wouldn't they have overthrown the Angels? Gaia she knew slumbered deep within herself but she couldn't think of any others that still existed.

She flicked her magic at all the lights, making them blaze into life as she reactivated Ra's essence. So they hadn't been destroyed merely suppressed. No Primordial had been through here, but their powers had been. Which meant they had to be in one of the Underworlds.

She cast a glance back at her family, her pantheon, they were all that was left to her in the world. She was awake and yet they still slumbered, why? Her husband Osiris was slouched on his throne, his bandages all but rotted off, but there was little trace of his once corpse-like appearance. He looked nearly healed apart from the hairline scars running around his neck and limbs. Was he no longer the God of the Dead? Only Gaia had that kind of power, but surely her power would have no effect on Ra's lights.

Slouched on the steps before her throne was her sister Nephthys, her arms and wings clutched protectively around her son Anubis. His jackal ears twitched ever so slightly, drawing her attention to the fact he was far more jackal than she remembered. Before he had merely had the head of a jackal but now most of his torso looked jackal. On the other side of the steps slouched ibis headed Thoth and his wife Ma'at, her now white and black wings half wrapped around them both. Both looked far more birdlike than she remembered. She was a little surprised to see that Ma'at's feather had survived, or had it been revitalised as well?

She thought about waking them but decided against it, better to leave them. If she only had bad news it would break their hearts. She couldn't do that to them. She used her magic to clean herself, it took longer than it should have. Her magic still wasn't back to normal. That would never do.

The hall shook as she grasped her magic, sending it shooting outwards in every direction. She felt the resonating answers of her husband's realm, well she had lived here long enough for it to be hers. Besides he was still slumbering, she had woken for a reason while the others had not. She felt sure that it was because she was more powerful.

It all came rushing back towards her, swirling around her mimicking the natural patterns of the world above. One should not forget that the Underworld and Heaven are but reflections of the Surface and are often bound by the same rhythms. That was something very few Gods had understood, it was one of the reasons that she had always been respected, even after Egypt had been absorbed into the Roman Empire.

For the Underworld to be so active meant that the Surface was once again stirring, and she knew just who to visit to find out about the Surface. Hecate was like herself, very aware of the nature of the Underworld but she was also able to see up to the Surface. Plus it would do well to mix her powers with another Mother Goddess. It was time to get back to her roots.

She was a Mother Goddess, a Goddess of fertility, childbirth, protection, power and magic. But she was also the first child of Nut and Geb and was the strongest of her kin, now that most of them had faded or died she was the most powerful. And she would do whatever she had to, to break the Curse trapping them all in the Underworld.

Mortals would once again whisper her name in reverence and the Angels would whisper it in fear. Yes it was time the world remembered and that the Angels were made to pay.

Isis was not the only Goddess to be awakened from her Desiccated slumber by the lingering darkness. In all the remaining Realms of the Underworld Gods and Goddesses had been revitalised and awoken by the passing of Nyx's night.

Hel sat alone on her throne, the very last of her family and pantheon. Not that she really cared, they had cast her into the Underworld seeking to get rid of her. They had not anticipated on her carving out her own realm. She had not fallen into the squalor of the Egyptian Pantheon but her cold realm was thick with ice.

Erishkigal also sat alone in her decrepit realm Irkalla. She had been slumbering for so long even her throne had decayed. Mesopotamia had fallen long ago and her brethren had all been killed in Heaven. She had been forced to live down here by them, it was ironic that it was her salvation. But her realm was in a terrible state, not a single spirit lingered. Everything that was not stone had rotten away. Well it could certainly do with some renovations to make it suit her but she intended to fill the halls once again with the spirits of the dead, and she knew hundreds of ways to get the living there.

Far away in forgotten Mictlan sat Mictlantecuhtli and his still slumbering wife Mictecacihuatl. They were but skeletons, wearing crumbling headdresses. They too were alone, the last of their kind, nearly completely forgotten by Humanity and Daemons alike. Mesoamerica had been scoured clean by the Christian conquerors and the Angels in their wake. Almost all the native Daemon races had been eradicated.

Circling further around the Underworld was the realm of Yomi or Yin Jian depending on who was talking about it. Within lay the Goddess Izanami-no-Mikoto, before the darkness she had been just another rotting corpse, no more significant than that of a Human or Daemon. She had died in childbirth, a bizarre occurrence for a Goddess, and her spirit had fled to the Underworld where the only form it could inhabit had been a corpse. In the rotting land there had been no escape, her spirit unable to heal the rotting flesh now housing her. Even her husband had not tried to heal her, he had taken one look at her form then fled and blocked the passage back up to the Surface.

She had found a small sense of justice that he and all their brethren had been destroyed by the Angels, while she remained alive, such as it was.

But now she no longer inhabited a rotting corpse, now she was once again a full bodied Goddess, her skin golden and flawless, sensitive to the touch and robust to the scrutiny. She didn't understand it but somehow she was whole again, she just wished she knew who to thank.

The last remaining Underworld Realm was Naraka ruled by Yama, the God and judge of the dead. While the other realms had been holding places for the spirits to slowly fade away into the Lifestream Naraka was an active realm, meant for only temporary holding. There was a set ordeal, unlike the ongoing torment of other realms, before the spirit was allowed to reincarnate. Of all the ancient realms it was the only active one, and while it had nowhere near the traffic of Hell it was a very busy realm. As such there was no hint of ruin or Desiccation.

Yama was the only God outside of the Greek pantheon that knew what had happened. He had witnessed and embraced the darkness as it had flooded through his realm. Many of the spirits had been washed away but he recognised the power of a Mother Goddess, those spirits had been returned to the Lifestream to be reborn.

He was curious as to who but he knew his patience would be rewarded with that knowledge. She would eventually make her presence felt more, and she would come here at some point. It was after all the only active non-Angel Underworld.

The thirst was insane, he felt like he was drowning in sand as he desperately reached for the glass of water sitting on his bed stand. It felt ridiculously amazing to drink it. But it was gone all too soon and he desperately needed more. On trembling legs he staggered his way into the little kitchenette. There it was the sparkling chrome tap, giving forth beautiful life giving water. He could only wait for it to be half full before he was guzzling the water down.

He still felt so parched, it was insane, his legs and arms were trembling so much he felt like he was in an earthquake. Why was he so thirsty? How could he have been so dehydrated? He decided he didn't care, the need was driving, he thrust his mouth under the tap and held it there for a very long time gulping down as much water as he could

He kept going until a strong hand on his shoulder pulled him back.

"You'll make yourself sick if you keep this up"

Kyle stilled instantly at the deeply cultured voice. He knew instantly who it was.

"Your blood has been cleansed but in the process you have lost not only a lot of fluids but a great deal of nutrients as well. You must eat to build back up your strength."

"I'm not going through all that again am I?"

His silence was answer enough. He turned around to meet that unsettling gaze, he couldn't turn away. All else faded as he focused on those eyes, in that face, he wanted to kiss those lips, to run his hands through that gorgeous black hair. It felt so wonderful running through his hands. That black stubble felt nice under his hands and against his chin. Those lips were soft, but turned controlling, his tongue was suddenly in his mouth and he was surrendering to him.

Alejandro smiled as Kyle surrendered to his powers. He might be starting to gain his own Human powers, but he had no defence against the powers of a fully-fledged Incubus. And he had been around long enough to be in complete control of his powers.

It was funny to watch such shy and controlled Humans turn into writhing animals with just a brush of the Lilin magic. It's what made them the best lovers.

But that was a side note, the only reason he was even using his powers was to distract Kyle enough to lead him back to the awakening chambers. He wouldn't willingly go otherwise. The fact Kyle possibly held huge potential was just an added benefit, why not lay the groundwork now.

Kyle was putty in his hands as Alejandro led him back along the corridors and into the pool. Taking his clothes off and convincing him into the pool was easy, he wanted to be naked with him and he held the fantasy of pool sex.

As soon as Kyle's skin touched the water the spell was broken but he continued into it, red drifting off his skin, staining the water. This time however the tubes started whirring long before the pool was anywhere near completely red. Green fluids started pouring into the pool, as well as some purple and some clear but sparkly fluid. They all lazily started to mix and spread throughout the pool, even as the red drifting off of him was still reaching towards it.

227

Kyle looked around in confusion feeling as though he had just woken from a dream. He was in the empty pool room, treading water as a similar situation to the last time replayed itself. He wasn't doing this again, last time had been bad enough, this time the machine wasn't going to get him.

A few quick strokes and he was near the pool edge, he could feel the steps beneath his feet and was starting to climb out when the piping went berserk. Coloured water blasted him backwards into the pool, then a deluge of water rained down from the ceiling pushing him under the water. He was struggling to swim in the onslaught as it pushed him down deeper into the pool. His vision was obscured by the swirls and clouds of red water still coming off of him.

Then suddenly out of the blood red water came the breathing tube, forcing its way into his mouth, along with the collar clamping onto him. But unlike last time it continued to push him down into the pool.

Beneath him the bottom of the pool opened up, revealing a greater depth that he was slowly but surely pushed down into. Above him streamed the blood red swirls and beyond that he could see the swirling green mixing with the red and purple to create shimmers of colour. Beneath him loomed only darkness.

The collar came to a stop, he was suspended in dark water, the light from above blocked. He had no idea how deep he was but he guessed it wasn't anything significant. He could probably swim back up to the surface.

His collar illuminated with a soft green glow. It was eerie in the darkness, especially as it only highlighted the blood red water around him. What kind of fucked up medical treatment was this anyway?

Light flickered slowly awake beneath him, in

jolting blinks until it stayed on, before slowly strengthening. A huge crystal sat beneath him, formed out of the crystal network surrounding it. He was in some sort of underground cavern made entirely of crystal, its focal point being the massive diamond shaped crystal rising out of a cluster of crystal needles. It was beautiful, hauntingly so as the whole cavern started to illuminate from the spreading light.

The water turned from black to rosy red as the light started to penetrate the swirls of red water. Why was that still gathering around him? To his surprise he also saw swirls of purple sinking down from above.

The collar shoved him down again, pushing him down until he was within reaching distance of the crystal. It was stunning, pulsating and sparkling with iridescent light, spreading from the heart of the crystal outwards then shimmering down the outside and spreading out into the rest of the crystals.

He reached out to touch the crystal, curious and fascinated.

As soon as his hands connected light flared and his hand sank beneath its surface before solidifying. He was trapped while light blazed, making the whole cavern shine, chasing away all the shadows. His hand and heart grew warm, he saw green lights flowing from his heart down his arm and into the crystal which had started to glow a soft green, brightening until it shone with emerald brilliance.

Streams of emerald light danced through the cavern shooting light lightning through the crystals and dancing like oriental Dragons through the water. The heat and light intensified. He couldn't look at the crystal any more, even with his eyes closed. There was nowhere to turn as the whole cavern grew to such intense brightness that his eyes started to hurt. His hand and heart felt like they were on fire. He was screaming, for all the good it did him, water just raced in but still he screamed at the agony of it, trying to yank his hand free from its surface.

It was just too much to bear.

Then everything disappeared.

He woke up groggily as once again someone was stabbing his ass with a syringe, followed by the several others into his arms and neck. Blessed coolness supported him, holding him up as the air stole his burning heat away from his wet body.

"All is in order Mistress. His body has been completely awakened and he is indeed the strongest we have found." It was that doctor's voice, the green haired one.

"Excellent I was beginning to think that all the sorcerers' bloodlines had been lost. And one so strong, when he is fully in his powers he will be more powerful than a demigod." The voice was strange, beautiful but not all together Human sounding.

What on earth were they talking about? Sorcerers and Demigods, God this was a cult.

He felt his body lifting up, he opened his eyes to see that he was floating in the air before the doctor, her helper and the most stunning and terrifying woman he had ever seen. Some instinct told him she was more than dangerous. She could have had red and yellow markings and that still would not have been sufficient warning to the world.

"Welcome Kyle to your true nature" she said, smiling with a predator's smile.

"My true nature?"

She flicked her eyes at the others "Has nothing been explained to him?"

"This is only his second treatment, there hasn't been the time, we did not expect such a violent reaction, or such a successful re-awakening."

She smiled in satisfaction "Then he is even more powerful than anticipated, it must be the blending of European and Oriental bloodlines. Such a fusion was beyond rare in the past but I have a feeling it is common in this day and age."

"Yes mistress, there are all manner of mixed race Humans, the potential is vast."

"What the Hell are you lot on about?"

She turned her attention back to him "You have had your latent genes and talents reactivated, oh and your disease cured. You now have powers, beyond even your own comprehension. You have the power to change the world and believe me you will."

"Powers?"

"Magic, you now have magic."

"Phht you expect me to believe in magic, what kind of moron do you take me for?"

"Then explain how you are floating in mid-air."

He looked around "Some form of strong anti-gravitational field."

She looked amused before she suddenly burst into violet flames, she stood up and walked towards him.

"Think whatever you like Kyle but magic exists, it always has it has merely been suppressed under the Angels' rule, but it is a natural part of the world. Some people only have the merest taste of it, the Lifeforce that gives them life and keeps them alive. Others have more, they can touch a power and use it to affect the world around them, some like you have the power to reshape the world, the innate ability to resonate with the natural forces of the planet. Then above you lies those with powers so vast their battles tear the world asunder and destroy entire empires." She smiled "Gods and Goddesses, but your time without us has made Humans forget us, it is long overdue that you were reminded."

Lightning surrounded her in a nexus of fire and ice, blooming outwards as though it were a magical flower. She spoke with a voice made of pure thunder "Magic exists Kyle and you have it"

He collapsed to his knees shaken to his core. This was too much to take in, this wasn't right, this couldn't be happening.

"And what do you plan to do with me? What if I refuse to be trained?"

The two mortals gasped but she simply smiled at him "You are under no obligations to remain but I do warn you that without training you powers will be wild and erratic, flaring at the worst times. How long until you inadvertently kill someone, or destroy part of the city due to uncontrolled powers. Do you really want that on your conscience?"

He didn't and they both knew it.

Hera owned him now, she finally had the sorcerer she had been looking for. She had the Maenads completely, as well as the Sirens, she had most of the Lilin and more than half of the Were. Now she was awakening the latent powers within the genes across all species and her current focus was on Humans. They were the largest percentage of the population, and Humans often had the strangest mix of powers due to their excessive breeding with the other species and across their own races.

New York she could pass off as her own, even in her absence it was converting to her, San Francisco was now a stronghold of hers, and now her attentions were turning towards New Orleans. A city still rich in magic, especially of the Daemonic kind.

It was time she started raising her army. The War

was coming again and this time all the races of the world would be involved. And this time the Angels would not succeed by surprise, this time she would. They had done their best to eradicate magic from the world, it was why she was going to such pains to reactivate magical genes. The magic left to mortals was pitiful, the Angels eradication efforts had been most effective. They would not be prepared to face a sorcerer led army of fully powered Daemons.

And with the increasingly powerful Lilin inserting themselves into all levels of business and government she was now becoming the unknown puppet master all across the United States. Things were going accordingly to plan with only the merest of stuff ups. The Angels truly had no idea what was coming their way.

A meeting had been called between all the Arch Angels and the Governing Council was waiting in trepidation on the results of their meeting. Nuriel on the other hand was fearing to enter the room. They were currently busy interrogating the Captain of Gabriel's Seraphim. She had much to report about the magical state of the world, as did all the other Captains. She had waited as one by one they were all called in. But she already knew what most of them had to say. She had already seen the evidence of what they were reporting.

The darkness that had tried to engulf Heaven had not actually been some form of Divine attack, it was a side effect. Something had allowed Primordials Gods to unite with the night sky and blanket the Earth with darkness.

In doing so it had saturated the planet with magic. All traces of lesser magic, even the powerful traces of Brigid and Hera had been completely smothered. Even New York City which had been a brightly burning beacon of Hera's power had been silenced. All their traces had been lost, all leads covered over. The planet was currently a blank slate, magically speaking, the only detectable magic being the Lifestream or the blanket of darkness magic.

Of course each of the captains would only have a fraction of that knowledge, they didn't have her skills, connections or access to information. And she was still scared to face the Arch Angels.

Zerachiel was probably one of the strongest people she knew, and one of the few who casually withstood Gabriel's temper. It seemed she and Michael were the only two who did not cringe at Gabriel's rants. She certainly needed a strong stomach and will to be Gabriel's Captain. It also made her one of the most politically powerful figures in Heaven. Her loyalty was unquestionable, her manner unshakable. And yet even she walked out of the chamber looking shaken. Not as bad as some of the others, she did after all have an iron will, but she looked worn out and worried.

It did not bode well.

She smiled at Zerachiel as she stood up to answer her summons, the pitying look she gave back did nothing to comfort Nuriel. Still she walked in with her head held high right into the tensest room she had ever entered. Lightning sparked along the length of Gabriel's hair, fire was sparking over Michael's wings, Ariel's hair was bathing in flames, Uriel's feathers were richly covered in both electrical and fiery sparks. Even unshakable Raphael's hands were clenched tight, a sure sign of anger and irritation.

The only Arch Angel showing no signs of anger, irritation, annoyance or impatience was Azrael. Nuriel sometimes wondered if his death magic had killed all his expressions. She quickly silenced such thoughts. He might be able to read her thoughts, there was no telling what other powers he held.

Michael urged her to start with her reports while the others watched her like she was prey. She recounted the Darkness, what she had concluded from it and all the subsequent effects. As expected none were happy with the loss of the traces on the Goddesses. Even less so when she told them about New York City. That had been their best chance at catching Hera, so much magic had meant a Divine trace was easy to construct, and had been in the process. They were unhappy that all traces of Brigid had vanished.

They were even less happy with her research.

Since the Darkness even more people had turned away from the Angelic Religions, sin was on the ever upwards rise, lust and greed had Humanity firmly in their grips. But even more worrying was the sudden spike in Demonic races. Vampires and Were had started increasing their numbers through infection, the Lilin were on a breeding rampage, feeding off their desires and empowering themselves. Even the remaining Maenads would be looking for mates. There was no telling what else could come out of the woodwork.

But it was worse than that she had finally managed to trace Nyx's powers using some forgotten artefact, but she had also discovered that she was not the only Primordial that had infused the darkness. When she had said four Primordials had infused the Darkness she had been met with stunned silence. Listing Nyx, Erebus and Tartarus had concerned them but it was the mentioning of Gaia that caused an uproar. The other three Primordials were unusually gifted, lifted by their nature's, Gaia was not. They had all read that she was the first child of Chaos, that her powers were beyond reckoning and imagination. She had created life, she was the accumulation of every Mother Goddess that had ever returned to the Lifestream.

The Myths about her were many, and what was actually known to be true was surprisingly scarce, even in the records of her own blood children. But if she was freed she could wipe out the Angels with ease. She had the power to force extinction in any way she thought of.

It had taken a long time to settle them down enough to explain her conclusions. The three Primordials were still safely locked away in the Underworld otherwise they surely would have pounced on their opportunity. The main question that had concerned them all was Gaia. What had caused her to rise from her slumbers? Could she rise further? She wasn't awake yet, the whole world would feel when that happened. They all agreed to check the spells binding her and the entire Underworld. For if she awoke she could destroy them all.

Her conclusions told her that all four of them were still bound deep in the Underworld but their powers could leak out, but they had limited control over them. Their powers simply following their own natures.

What was more troubling were the flavours of the darkness she had felt. Hera and Brigid were not the only Gods to lend their powers to the darkness. Apparently there remained quite a few still alive, though they too were bound in the Underworld.

But it was the Angelic flavouring that had her and the others most worried. Sariel's as well as a surprisingly large number of Angels' magic had been in the darkness. Most had been the Fallen Angels, there were some who were not. Had their powers been willingly or forcefully added to the darkness?

She had then been dismissed while they had turned to each other in concern. She had walked out with her head still held high. She walked with a spring in her step along the corridor, despite the concerns going on in the world she had survived a meeting with the Arch Angels when they had all been in a foul temper.

The Arch Angels waited until she was gone before they resumed their discussion.

"If Sariel's magic was in the darkness it means one of the Gods have her"

"Which means they have access to her powers"

"And can use them to their own means"

"But that means they have access to an Arch Angels powers"

"Who has her? Hera or Brigid?"

"She may be in the Underworld at the mercy of any one of them. Which means that an Underworld God has full access to the key of Lucifer's Curse"

That struck the wrong note. If Lucifer's Curse was broken, the backlash would be horrific but the consequences even more so. Not only would Lucifer and his two hundred odd Elders be freed, but so would the two hundred odd Fallen Elders in Purgatory who would presumably join him. There would be twice as many enemy Elders for the two hundred odd Heaven Elders. Never mind the Ascended and Lesser Fallen Angels.

Lucifer's powers would be stronger than a God's, being the focal point of evil in three dominions of religion was sure to have empowered him beyond any of them individually.

But it wasn't just that, all the Demons of Hell would be released, as well as the trapped Gods and their servants but so too would be the three Primordial Gods. Also the last binding keeping Gaia in her slumbers would be gone.

All Hell would break loose, quite literally.

Humanity needed to be forewarned and the masses put back on the right path. If the Arch Angels were empowered more than they could affect the Curse, perhaps sense where Sariel was and make Hell more dangerous. In order to break the Curse an Arch Angel would have to be in close proximity to Lucifer, which meant whatever God was controlling her would have to take them both through the levels of Hell.

They decided that Azrael would scour through Purgatory for any intelligence on the Underworld. Uriel and Ariel would continue in the searches for Hera and Brigid. Gabriel would visit the Pope and make him aware of his duties. Raphael would visit the Patriarchs and Michael would scour Islam for a suitable Prophet. It was time they got the world back in order and they would start from the top down.

They had their strongholds; pretty much all Arab nations or what was left of them, the Vatican, the United States of America, Israel and a handful of other deeply religious countries. There was a strong presence in South America they decided they should encourage more. It was time science was reigned back in and Humanity once again put back under the yoke.

They needed the power.

Chapter 17

"Why are you taking me to Agra?"

"To see the Taj Mahal, the most iconic building in all of India. It is also said to be one of the greatest symbols of love in the world. It is said to be the finest example of Mughal architecture and is a jewel of Muslim art."

That caught her attention, the love part was quaint but an iconic Muslim structure now that grabbed her attention completely. An icon renowned worldwide was also the perfect place to start laying her spells, though she would need many if she was to claim India.

She had discovered that India and Pakistan had once been united under British rule which initially had her hopes high on claiming one of the most populous nations in the world and its neighbours easily. Much to her chagrin she had also discovered that India, as a whole, had a rich and vibrant history of changing between Hindu and Muslim rulers and that it was patchwork of the two conflicting religions. British rule had merely united various kingdoms left over after the Mughal Empire had fallen apart. Granting it its freedom had divided the country into the countries of India, Pakistan and Bangladesh.

She would reunite them all.

The land and the people needed it. The land was dying, it needed her desperately if it was ever to flourish again. Pollution clogged their rivers, clouded the air and shrouded their cities. They were a lost nation, worshipping dead Gods. They were without any guidance through no fault of their own. Or even their Gods, their Gods had been overthrown by the bastard children of other Gods. It reminded her of her own land, well the rest of the world really. The Angels were the progeny of the Mediterranean and Near Eastern Gods.

She looked out the window at the brown pastures, skeleton jungles and toxic wastelands flashing by. The land was dying, the Lifestream sinking deeper into the earth and most life couldn't reach that far. If it sunk further very few things would be able to reach it. Then Humanity was really in trouble.

How she longed to return to Britain and walk its hallowed earth, to hear the whispers of Fairies and druids, probably all long gone. To quicken her land, to pull the Lifestream back up above the surface, to flood the land with its power. To watch Britain explode with life and magic. To quicken her own blood.

Her people were so lost without guidance for so long. They had succeeded incredibly well on their own, the Angels had done very little controlling since the Middle Ages, but they had lost themselves again. But they had cast their net wide and now she would pick up all those threads, all the colonies of Britain would become her domain.

She would claim British India, modern day India, Pakistan and Bangladesh, and finalise her claim of Australia and its neighbour New Zealand. But she had done her research and her hunger for power had grown. She would claim Canada, South Africa, Singapore and Malaysia as well as the myriad of African, Caribbean, Asian and Pacific Island colonies. Then there was Palestine and Israel, a land she had every right to claim as a former British Mandate and yet she was scared to. Jerusalem sat unknowingly over Hell, it sat next to the Dead Sea the very place where Lucifer and his brethren had crashed through the Surface and into the Underworld. It was also near Jerusalem that Eden had sat before it had been hidden.

She could claim it if she dared. But it was also the original Angel stronghold on the Surface. Would she try and claim it and threaten the Angels' foothold on Earth?

She would. When she was far more powerful.

Through the old British Empire she would have control over a quarter of the world's land, never mind the billions of people that would come with that. If she succeeded she would not only have the largest empire the world would ever seen, she would also become the most Empowered Goddess that it had ever seen. The possibilities to destroy the Angels were limitless if she succeeded with the British Empire alone. Never mind any future conquests.

But for now it was still very much baby steps. She still had to make her mark on the Taj Mahal, and claim Agra. From there it would be the Ganges and Indus Rivers. She allowed her powers to flow all around her as the car drove on, feeling the taste of the land and letting it drink in her powers. Normally she would be worried about leaving such a mark but currently the world was under a blanket of magic so thick no one had a hope of tracing her.

She felt the land resonating with her, accepting her. From here on in there would be no hesitation. She would claim all of Britain's territories and when she returned to her homeland she would be a Goddess worthy for them.

Hera slipped out of the bed and walked out onto the balcony heedless to the biting cold or the occasional snowflake falling on her naked skin. She breathed in the cold as she breathed in the power that New York was emitting. New York was safe once again, there was certainly a strong Angelic presence but her trace had been obliterated by the darkness. New York was soaking up the magic slowly, it didn't have a strong history of magic, the land while fertile had never been abundant with the Lifestream. But that was changing, it was fortunate the Angels couldn't sense where the Lifestreams passed through, otherwise they would have noticed it was now moving ever closer to New York, drawn by her presence and the strengthening powers of her Daemons.

Even the Humans were starting to notice a difference, there were cheerier and they didn't know why. They had no idea that one of the most powerful Goddesses in antiquity had made their city her powerbase. New York would be the capital of her new empire. As her powers flowed through the city, the Daemons went about their daily lives adding their own essence to the mix. And with a new Lifestream rising from within the planet's core, New York was about to become abundantly magical. She absently wondered which directions the Lifestream would go.

As she reflected on her continuing small successes in New York, California and Illinois she wondered how Brigid was doing. It was still far too dangerous to contact her. She hoped she had avoided capture and was doing well. She was a cautious one, Hera felt sure she had squirreled away safely somewhere, probably some small town or village. She would be pining to go back to Britain. Maybe she had gone to the Falkland Islands, they were very British and safely at the other end of the globe. It would make sense, Brigid had never been one for big empires. How would she adjust to learn that Britain had been the biggest empire in the world, in her absence?

The Angels were still scouring the British Isles and Mediterranean in case either she or Brigid were stupid enough to return to their old stomping grounds. They would also be looking for Sariel, she was too valuable to their plans and too dangerous to be used against them. They didn't know that she was in the one place they didn't want her, the Underworld. The only way they could get her out was through Lucifer's Crater.

She touched her chest in surprise when she felt a twinge of guilt. How many centuries had it been since she had felt something as useless as guilt? Far longer than her imprisonment. Had she regained a shred of Humanity? That was highly disturbing but perhaps it was long overdue. She had been out of touch of the world for so long, all of Heaven was so out of touch from the world. Was it any wonder that they had been overthrown or that the Angels might well too? Heaven desensitised the Divine to the rest of the world.

Well she couldn't be in a more different situation to the last time she had walked amongst mortals. Back then she had walked among them blazing with her power, inciting wars and conquests, making great men bow before her. She had been a beautiful Siren commanding them to do her bidding, demanding their sons and daughters, their very hearts and souls. And still she had demanded more while they had done everything within their power, and outside it, to achieve it. She had demanded everything and taken it all. They had been but pawns in the Divine Games, and she had used them all ruthlessly.

She missed those days.

Now she lived among them. Most had no idea she even existed, the Daemons knew her and revered her. Humanity as a whole though were nearly completely oblivious to her presence. Since her confrontational arrival she had settled to living in the shadows. She lived in her apartments and she stalked through the city, pulling the strings and soothing the way with magic, seen and yet unseen, always searching and feeling. She hadn't even formally claimed Manhattan yet, never mind the rest of New York City.

One of her peafowl fluttered clumsily onto her arm. He was taking well to the transformation. She hated having to be subtle about everything, in the old days the transformation would have taken seconds and be complete. Unfortunately transformations left quite a magical trace, so she had to do this one slowly. But it was vital to her needs.

She stroked his reddish head and neck, finding some comfort in the action. Had her heart really thawed?

If it had that created new problems for her future plans. If she cared more could she be as ruthless as she had once been? And if she couldn't did she stand any chance at winning? There were so many new problems, Atheists were incredibly resistant to Divine persuasion, many of the races she had once controlled had long since been eradicated, magic did not work as it once had, the planet and her own powers were weak and sluggish, though starting to quicken, and she was alone.

Completely alone, she had no pantheon to back her up. No family, no friends, not even any rivals to compete with. All she had was a life and death struggle with the Angels.

She didn't have any fanatical believers or powerful sorcerers at her disposal. She had one incredibly powerful sorcerer and a handful of others but they were useless at the moment. They had to be trained and made completely loyal. The world was so different, so very different from what she remembered and she was still adjusting to it.

She was living her life hiding in fear. Deny it all she might but she was afraid. She was afraid of being found by the Angels, they could imprison and torture her again or this time they might just execute her. She was struggling to build her power base, she was having small successes but nothing significant, she couldn't even call a single city her own. The land was more difficult than she remembered, very unresponsive to her powers. Its pulse was very weak and there were vestiges of Gods that had once claimed this land. They might be long dead and obliterated by Christendom, but the land still remembered, it couldn't forget when it was still dreaming.

She had been so sure of her abilities and of herself. She had truly believed that within days of being in New York it would belong to her completely, with every citizen a devout fanatic. But times had changed, Humanity had changed and the world had changed. She was uncertain what the future held for her. Heaven was her home, she was still its Queen, perhaps it was time she returned to it. She shook her head at her own foolishness, it was more than suicidal to return to Heaven.

If she was going to have any chance of surviving and hopefully living then it was here on the Surface. For better or worse she had chosen New York. In time she might claim the rest of North America, but for now she would struggle with New York.

Pope John Paul V was a weak man, frail of health and body, and he had never been a strong or charismatic leader. He knew that his election as pontiff was merely the result of a stalemate between conservatives and progressives. He had been their answer, a leader who would not make changes, would not stand up against the groups of cardinals and in all likelihood would die reasonably quicker than any other cardinal.

He was there to buy time for both sides to strengthen up their planned electives. It was going on while he was still alive. Sometimes he wondered if they would do him in when one group finally gained their majority. He had achieved very little in his five year reign and expected that to remain the same until he died. He was a Pope that would become mostly forgotten, except in name.

When he had first been elected he had honestly thought that he had been handpicked by God to lead the Church. He had known about the factions within the Church when he was elected, how could he not? But he had believed that he could move the Church forward and help heal the rifts. He had long prayed for an Angel of the Lord to answer him and help him heal the Church, but Heaven had long been silent.

He sat at his desk absently reading through reports, his heart no longer in it. He waited for the day he would die and be relieved of this task. He only hoped Heaven was different from Earth and that the Angels truly knew peace.

"You would doubt Heaven? You the leader of the Catholic faith doubts Heaven, what hope is there for your religion and followers? What hope is there for more than a billion true believers?" sneered a hauntingly musical voice.

He jumped out of his chair falling to the floor as he saw the Angel. The Angel was nearly eight feet tall, graced with six golden wings and wore heavy Roman style armour. He raised his helmet, the golden eyes within pierced him to the ground. Tears rolled down his cheeks, his prayers had been answered, the Lord had listened.

Gabriel grimaced to herself behind her glowing glamour as she read his thoughts. She had always disliked Humans, her own subjects the most, for they did not believe in her but in the Lord. They were such easily swayed beings, so weak compared to the Angels, or any of the other Demon races for that matter. They were so foolish, the men so patriarchal, it annoyed her to act the messenger. Though she always did to make sure things were done right.

"You are a Servant of the Lord and yet you question his ways. Have no doubt Human when you see the light. Your task is to keep that light strong and let that light spread through all the faithful. The time of Judgement is coming and Humanity needs saving for it is lost. Faith weakens the world over, Demons walk among you, rule corporations and control governments. Sin is rampant, spreading like a disease and the Demons only grow stronger off of Humanity's weakness. Hell grows fat with the souls of mortal sinners while Heaven grows lean."

The Angel raised his sword, which was ablaze in brilliant golden fire "Your doubts feed the darkness and weaken the light." He lowered it until it was centimetres away from his chest "You will spread the light John Paul V or you will earn your place in Hell."

He cowered under the Angel's vehemence.

"But how am I to achieve this?"

The Angel turned the full force of his burning gaze on him, paralysing him and depriving him of rational thought. The Angel stepped forward and grasped his face with burning hands, the pain seared through him but he could not pull away.

"That is the merest taste of what lies in Hell if you fail me. You will use the scant brains you have to unify the Church once again. If you have need of me, call for the Arch Angel Gabriel and I will come to your aid." His voice turned deadly "but do not summon me without due cause, I am not to be trifled with and I am extremely busy. Understand?"

"Yes, perfectly"

Suddenly Gabriel, his light and his pain were

gone. John Paul lay panting on the floor. He was meant for something, he had been handpicked by God. He had been visited by one of the Arch Angels, by Gabriel no less. He was meant for something, he would be remembered as the last Pope. Judgement Day was coming.

He barely noticed when the door swung open, no announcement, it could only be Cardinal Benedict, leader of the conservative faction.

"What are you doing on the floor? Did you have a heart attack?" He heard the lack of concern in the Cardinal's voice.

He stood up a new man, blessed by the Angel. Benedict looked at him strangely, there was a bearing to him that was different.

"No I did not have a heart attack, I was visited by the Arch Angel Gabriel and he gave me a holy mission. It is long overdue that the Church sorted out our problems." He raised his head smiling before turning his attention back to the cardinal "And while we are at it Benedict you will address me with the proper respect I am due." With that he swept out of his office leaving behind a very surprised Cardinal.

Chapter 18

The ring of metal striking against metal filled the courtyard. Nemesis lunged forward with lightning speed and precise calculation. Her face was completely devoid of emotion, only a slight frown marring her perfect features. For her fighting was an intricate dance, a celebration of violence and skill, an acknowledgement to the Chaos that lived in them all. Every fight was calculated and invigorating, and she had not had fights of this intensity in quite some time.

Sariel mirrored Nemesis, her own perfect features scrunched up in concentration, a few stray drops of sweat ran down her brow- extremely rare for any Divine being, an indicator of just how much strain her body was under. She darted back and raised her sword deflecting Nemesis' blow and quickly raised her other sword to deflect the low stab. They jumped back from each other, both using their wings to aid their movement. To those who watched they were like darting shadows.

Nemesis jumped up into the air, cart wheeling towards Sariel. Sariel rolled forward, snapped her wings wide and jumped free of the two swords that speared the ground. Nemesis didn't even pause, as soon as she missed Sariel, she pulled the swords free spun around and cut off a strip of Sariel's flowing top. Both watched the strip of white material as it floated slowly to the ground.

As soon as it landed, they were fighting again, metal ringing out again and again around the courtyard, interspaced with the occasional screech of a sword hitting the marble. They were like lightning, with just as many sparks. Nemesis was like a viper always striking at Sariel.

But Sariel was like the wind, whipping out of range of each and every strike, or countering them.

Sariel launched herself into the air and Nemesis followed like a striking falcon. Up in the air they became as quicksilver, flashes of black and white blending together. The sound of swords clashing became faster and louder. Up in the air they were both in their element.

Sariel flicked out with both her swords, catching one of Nemesis' swords and wrenching it out of her grasp. Sariel gasped in surprise as she watched the sword clatter on the courtyard below, while Nemesis' other sword snaked across her throat.

They both landed in the courtyard and bowed to each other. Nemesis called her sword back to herself while Sariel magically mended her top. "You should always watch your enemy, not their disarmed weapon" She was frowning but despite the rebuke Sariel could tell that she was proud. Suddenly Nyx appeared next to them in a flutter of shadows.

"Well done Sariel, it has been a long, long time since anyone disarmed Nemesis"

"I hardly disarmed her. She still had her other sword and she still beat me. I still have much to learn."

"To disarm me, even just one sword is a major accomplishment Sariel, your brother never achieved it. No Angel has ever achieved it. As for beating me, it has been so long since I lost a fight. The last time was nearly three thousand years to Sekhmet, and that fight went on for nearly a month. You have learned well Sariel, there is very little for me to still teach you." She grasped Sariel's shoulder, like comrades in arms. Sariel looked at her in surprise and she nodded to her before disappearing.

"Your physical fighting is complete and your magical training is done as much as we can. Now we need to know what your truest powers are, it is time we knew the full extent of your unique blend of powers."

Nyx took Sariel's hand and the next instant they were standing in a dark gothic styled room. The floor and walls were all black marble veined with white and silver. The veins were the only colour. There was no furniture or decorations, only a pool taking up most of the room. Strange geometric shapes stabbed up out of the water. There were no light sources, only a soft predawn glow, her eyes quickly adjusted to the near absence of light.

Nyx led her to the edge of the pool and they both knelt down. "Magic is the lifeblood of the planet, it runs in our blood and some believe it is the blood of our spirits. Magic is incredibly varied and it can respond differently. The best way to think of magic is as something living, if you use it according to its nature it will respond and if you use it against its nature it will backlash. It can be unpredictable and it can become your greatest weakness."

Sariel nodded, she had learned as much. Magic was very enigmatic.

"You must learn to understand the nature of your own magic, to embrace it in its entirety. Mine is of the night, everything that belongs to the night is within my power. From the sky to darkness to dreams."

She studied Sariel "your powers are incredibly varied. You have the powers of the Elder Angels, you are in your own right a powerful Arch Angel and as such have a rare and powerful type of magic. But you also have the powers of death and night from this side of your family. We don't know the specifics of your mother's powers but from her father you have inherited powers of the sun and sky." She stopped and looked at the water before continuing "your strongest trait will either be your Angel powers or your death magic. You will explore all your facets in due time. I have taught you about the sky and shadows, Thanatos has taught you about death and Hecate has tried to help with those in between. But there is still much undiscovered about yourself."

She held out her hand, it was slowly lost beneath thickening shadows. "This room is a focus for the shadows, within here you will find it exceptionally easy to reach your powers."

She dropped her hand "You know how you reach your powers, it is especially easy in anger or desperation but you still find it difficult without that emotional help. Knowing your powers will make it far easier."

She placed her hand over Sariel's heart "this is where most agree magic starts in the body, it is believed that our heart and mind is where our spirits are tethered to our bodies. The mind stores our memories but our hearts give us our emotions and our magic. It is within your heart that the core of your magic exists." Her clothes vaporised into black mist, not so very long ago Sariel would have been horrified, but living with so many of the Classical Gods and their subjects had desensitised her to nudity. She was no longer the little sheltered Angel she had once been.

Nyx pointed to her own heart, it could clearly be seen as a black branching blob on her pale skin. She blanked her skin, ensuring that is was unmarred and then allowed her magic to spread. Sariel watched as the darkness quickly spread through the blood, veins and capillaries being traced by darkness across her ivory skin. "It is by our blood that magic infuses our entire body, and we as Gods can control and change our bodies based on our powers. We are less physical than mortals, we are more magic than body, whereas mortals are the opposite, their magic conforms to their physical forms."

She was suddenly behind Sariel, her hands gently grasping her shoulders as she whispered in her ear "To know your magic you must know yourself and open up all your heart." She pushed Sariel into the dark water, the splash was loud but short lived. She barely registered that her clothes were gone as she struggled to roll over. Wings were more of a nuisance in the water. She floated in the dark water, looking for her great-grandmother, but she couldn't see her. Slowly the grey light started to darken, the strange geometric shapes started to move, sharp shadows at the edges of her vision. But she was unafraid, even as the water started to move.

"Open you heart Sariel, within this place you can safely dive within your core. Remember who you are, live your past and dream your future. Know your heart as no other possibly can, embrace the inner darkness." She heard the whisper but the room had fallen into darkness with a few soft lights. She saw darker shapes moving and knew they were the statues. She allowed herself to be swept this way and that, allowing herself to relax as her body adjusted to the rhythm. She breathed deeply and closed her eyes, focussing on her heart and its constant beat.

She slipped down to her core, surprised at just how easily she did. But then she had used her magic many times before, the path was now there to follow. Slowly she felt her powers unfurl from their containment, both her tentative control and the lingering traces of Gabriel and Michael's spells. She drew out tendrils of power and directed it back into the path, opening it further. In the darkness of her core she was suddenly bathed in light and radiance, warmth flooded her and she was awash in power.

Let your power flow through your entire body Sariel, direct it along the natural pathways.

Hearing Nyx's voice Sariel rose slightly from her core, her mind was with her heart, and her magic was brimming over. She held it back, hesitating for a moment before she gradually released her hold, pouring forth into her bloodstream. Another part of her mind registered that her body was filling up with power, her senses growing stronger.

Then she let it all go, a tsunami of magic erupted from her heart along her arteries. Every drop of her blood became infused with her magic, and her mind spread throughout all her magic. She was everywhere within herself, part of every cell and fibre of her being.

Light flooded her senses as darkness swallowed them. She was lost, everything was happening all at once, she couldn't tell which way was up or down, where she was. She was awash in her powers, flooding along her own body, losing senses.

Suddenly her consciousness slowed and stopped in a dark space. She could feel her magic and her blood flowing around her, but she floated within a void. She was in the eye of the storm, the very centre of her being, where she could direct all her magic without being washed away. She realised her magic wasn't raging any more, it was unfurling, growing, building, she wasn't entirely sure what it was doing but it seemed to be getting stronger and vaster.

Colours came back to her, was she seeing this or was her mind filling the details in with other senses? Bright sunlight invaded the space, pushing the shadows away to the edges. She floated halfway between bright sunlight above her and darkness below. Wind blew around her bringing with it the eerie song of the dead, it was stunning. Stars started to twinkle in the darkness below, she smelt rich loam and sea spray. A rhythmic thrum filled the space, was it a heartbeat? Flowers and leaves danced past on the wind, adding their scents to the mix. Thunder roared as lightning rent the air, fire bloomed, lava erupted from the darkness, blood splattered through the air staining white clouds. There were the sounds of screams blending into beautiful songs. She felt power, ancient power stir and shake her. She should have been scared seeing the maelstrom of her magic but she was unafraid. This was everything she was, and she would not be denied her birth right again.

She summoned all of her powers, flooding the eye of the storm with her magic.

Nyx crouched at the edge of the pool watching as Sariel started being consumed by her magic. Darkness flooded the water, she had expected no less, her and Erebus' blood ran strong in her veins. The darkness wrapped itself around the statues, smothering and choking them, only to shy away as they were suddenly flooded with brilliant sunlight. This room had never seen the light of day, those with sun magic only ever managed to make the statues glow, they were composed of darkness. And yet now they could have belonged in Heaven, light speared the shadows in the furthest corners but it could not pierce the darkness of the water.

Then to her utter surprise green lights started shining from within the dark waters, green vines growing upwards from them and twining around the statues. The statues quivered, flashing between green and white light, struggling to reflect which magic. Why was Sariel exhibiting strongly the powers of Gaia? Clouds grew across the water, lightning dancing between them and the statues. All the colours of the rainbow flickered across the water's surface and the statues'. Then the statues went berserk trying to reflect the kaleidoscope of Sariel's powers.

Nyx stood transfixed as she recognised the powers of light and darkness, life and death, air and earth, fire and water, Heaven and Hell, Angel magic, God magic, Primordial magic. She could feel the Apocalypse and the Chaos that had birthed her. The room shook with undiluted powers, then it shook violently as the statues burst into flames. That couldn't be right, the statues had been consumed by her magic, they were now purely magic.

The water swirled, drawing Sariel along with it. She floated around and around, passing through the magical statues. Above the light and clouds mirrored her passage. Nyx crouched transfixed as she watched primal powers condensing in the room. A crash of thunder and the water was heaving upwards, throwing Sariel upwards into a mix of water, clouds of fire and lightning all wrapping around her. Shadows and rays of light added themselves to the mix.

There was a pressure building in the room, bearing down on her, causing Nyx to start laughing maniacally. Why did Sariel feel a Primordial Goddess? She and her siblings were the last Primordial Gods, how was it possible that her own great-granddaughter, an Angel demigoddess at that, could have these powers?

There was a deep rumbling somewhere and everything exploded. Nyx was swept away in forces she had not felt in over a million years, she surrendered to Chaos.

Sariel groaned as she rolled over, everything ached and her mind felt stuffed with cotton wool. She heaved herself up gasping at the pain in her arms. As she stood up she wondered vaguely why she was naked. Then she looked around.

She stood in an empty semi-spherical pool ringed irregularly with glowing pillars. She remembered that the room had been a bastion for darkness and true enough it was thick and deep beyond the pool. The ceiling however and the space above the pool was awash in a rainbow of lights pouring off of the magical pillars. Soft dappled sunlight appeared here and there across the pool. It seemed completely different and yet she knew this was the same room she had come in with Nyx.

She glanced around looking for her great-grandmother. She spotted her crumpled against a back wall, dark tendrils reaching out from the thicker shadows to caress her. She ran over to Nyx ignoring the aches and pains to kneel down next to her. What had happened to her? She looked almost dead, there were no black tracings over her pallidly pale skin. And her hair hung as normal hair, Nyx's hair was always shadows. She shook her gently but she didn't respond.

She was worried now, Gods never passed out against the walls, let alone Primordial Gods. Desperate she grabbed her, haphazardly teleporting out of the room and into a suit of armour. Her screams quickly brought people running, Nemesis and Hecate easing Nyx out of her grasp and took her to her rooms. Hades followed with an incoherent half unconscious Sariel.

"What in the name of Hell happened?"

Nemesis and Hecate both shook their heads, they had no answers to his questions. They had never seen Nyx like this before, they wouldn't have thought it possible. She hadn't even been this bad during the War.

"Could it be something Sariel did?"

"I doubt it. She doesn't contain the powers to match a God, let alone a Primordial Goddess."

"Then what happened to the both of them? Something happened, we all felt it. The whole Underworld probably felt it. The castle felt like it was going to collapse."

"There is no logical explanation"

"There is" the three of them looked up from Nyx as Erebus and Tartarus glided into the room, they were even more darkness than they usually were. "The power that shook the realms was the power of Chaos. That is why she lies prone like that, she has been exposed to the raw powers that birthed us."

"Chaos? But that has not been seen or felt since well before Gaia entered her second most recent slumber."

"Indeed Chaos itself or channelled through Gaia has not been felt, but its power is everywhere. No this is different, someone else was able to channel the powers of Chaos."

"Channel Chaos? Even the Primordial Gods trembled before the power of Chaos, who could possibly channel it?"

They both looked pointedly at Sariel.

"No she couldn't, she is only an Angel."

"That is where you are wrong" they all turned as Nyx opened her eyes, they were glowing with speckled light, they looked akin to black opals. "Sariel is more than an Angel, she is more than a Goddess. She has within herself the nearly undiluted powers of myself, Anu and Gaia. She has the undiluted powers of both her parents and their parents. She has the power over everything, she is a supreme Sky Goddess and has within her magical spectrum all the basis of life and death, creation and destruction. She actually has the powers of Chaos deep within her core. She has full access to the powers of Chaos."

She turned to look at her great-granddaughter, sleeping peacefully next to her on the bed "She is unlike anything before her, Elder Angle, Arch Angel, Daemon, Demigoddess, Goddess, Primordial Goddess and other.

She undoubtedly has other untapped potential the result of her strange breeding."

"But it isn't possible. No one holds that much power."

"She does"

Hecate studied Nyx, there was something she wasn't sharing "What are you not telling us?"

Nyx sighed and looked Hecate in the eyes "She can summon the Apocalypse by herself."

That caused an uproar, people were yelling and screaming. It was chaotic, everyone was scared and confused. And rightly so. The Apocalypse was a power unique to the Angels, such was its power that it required the Seven Arch Angels to release it and once released it was beyond the realms of control. The Angels had used it in the War to horrific effect.

"Silence" Erebus roared. It rocked the room into silence. He then turned to his sister "How can you be so sure Nyx?"

"Because I felt it in her magic. It is there imbedded in her rage. I was testing her in the Dark Sanctuary and it was unlike anything I have ever seen before. She opened up quickly, reaching into her magic and embracing it utterly. Light was cast from the statues themselves, pure sunlight and rainbow."

"But they are composed of shadows."

She nodded "I know, imagine my surprise to find one of my Dark Sanctuaries flooded with not just sunlight but fire and lightning, so much light and yet the shadows were always at the edges. The light could not pierce the dark water. Many things flashed before my eyes, talents we all hold in this room but the most surprising was Gaia's, Chaos and the Apocalypse"

"She can channel Gaia?"

"Yes, it is why she is marked like us brothers. Gaia

awoke enough to quicken her spirit."

"What do we do with her?" Hades asked.

"Love her" Nyx looked around the room keeping their gazes until they turned away. "She is our family and has accepted us. It is time we accept her, completely. Whatever the future may bring she is part of the family. She has powers we can only begin to comprehend and with them she will be a force to be reckoned with but she has no reason to strike out at us. We had better not give her a reason, for she is probably the single most dangerous person on this planet. But she is still a very naïve young woman."

She nodded her dismissal to them before she slumped down into the bed. Sleep was quick in coming for her, she was still so weak. She readily fell into the shadows of her mind.

Next to her Sariel opened her eyes to look at Nyx. She was scared and worried, she was a dangerous threat to the world. She could summon the Apocalypse by herself. Heaven would hunt her down for that. Her family spoke of Chaos, she knew little about it other that it was the powers from which Gaia, Nyx, and the other Primordials were born from. It was the parent of the planet, a force beyond understanding. She could channel its powers, it chilled her to the core.

She pushed away such heavy thoughts and snuggled up to Nyx, who loved her without reservation. She felt safe next to her and she fell quickly into blissful sleep.

Something was different, something in the feel of the city. Hera climbed out of her bed, calling in a thick fur coat. She was somewhat unused to this cold weather of New York, and she drew strange looks if she wasn't properly attired. The weather shouldn't bother her as a

Goddess but she had to remind herself that the city wasn't hers and was currently feeding upon Primordial magic. This cold would affect everyone less powerful than a Primordial.

But something had changed. It was as though the city was giving her more power.

She walked out through the balcony door, looking through the masses of falling snow to try and pinpoint the source of the change. But in reality she didn't know the city well enough, and it was too big to try and analyse with her current amount of power the city was giving her. Her interest quickly waning she turned back inside and was surprised to find a Maenad approaching in the elevator.

With the vanity of most Goddesses she eyed herself in the mirror before adjusting her appearance. Her hair fell sleek and shiny, her skin glowed, her nightgown and coat turned into an elegant dress and a small circlet appeared on her head. She relaxed regally on one of the couches and magically opened the door as the Maenad approached.

Slightly surprised she walked in and bowed deeply to Hera. The loyalty the Maenads gave her was deeply heartening. Hera inclined her head and beckoned the girl.

"My Goddess the Matriarch sends her regards and hopes the current actions are to your desire."

"Which actions are those?" She calmly tried delving through the girls mind but it was a whirlwind of activity. Some people naturally were difficult to read because their minds were always jumping between several topics at once. She could freeze them but it would hurt the girl.

The girl ran over to the TV, turning it on and flicking it through the channels until she found the news feed. Sarah stood there, smartly dressed as usual, among a group of mostly elderly women and few younger ones. One was a Senator, another a movie star. All were Daemons, mostly Maenad or Siren but there were others.

The headline flashed by again. The Imperial Hospital of New York had been officially opened this morning bringing new hope to New York about the successful treatment of AIDS. Sarah made some comments about it being a great asset for the city, and then Dr Connor spoke about the increasing success of the trial cure and that she was optimistic about continual success and opening further hospitals across the country. Then Senator Gilmore spoke of her support for the hospitals and the good it was doing for the country. And her continuing support of the hospitals, then she took a dig at some Senators and the church members denouncing the hospitals.

Some denouncers were interviewed yelling about Hell, and sin and homosexuals, and surprisingly about this fake Goddess Hera.

The reporter, a Succubus, then finished off with a sneer about the denouncers and a little side note about New York being fortunate to attract followers of Hera. In this economic turmoil having a Goddess of Power had to be good for the city.

Hera used her magic to flick through several other new feeds and depending on their own agendas. Christian and anti-gay denounced the opening of the hospital going on about how it was encouraging and naturalising their abnormal lifestyles. Daemonic or gay were openly complimentary of the opening of the hospital and the good it would bring New York. Neutral were more middle of the road, complimentary of the curing but negative about the selectivity of patients and the fact that Dr Connor had not shared her cure with the scientific and medical communities. The Scientific community was quite negative about the fact she had not shared it or had it peer reviewed. Several doctors did add personal comments complimenting her on actually achieving a cure.

The girl turned back to her, Hera looked at her "Tell Sarah she has done brilliantly and that I will visit her shortly." The girl ran out, being near her scared her.

Hera smiled to herself, she had made a beginners oversight. She had forgotten just how influential mortals were on each other. It showed that it had been a long time since she had properly played the power games. No wonder the Christians had had such a sudden success with the Roman Empire.

Sarah was probably her most useful asset to New York, left to her own autonomy she was achieving more than she herself was. For each major city she would have to have at least one person, an overseer to be left to complete tasks while she was busy across the country.

Sure she was a Goddess but she couldn't be everywhere at once. She had been trying to do too much herself. And achieving very little.

She already had all the Maenads across the United States loyal to her, she had a network of very influential women in business, government, science and entertainment. It was time she started utilising it. Never mind the fact she had the Sirens on side as well as ever increasing numbers of the other Daemon races spreading across America.

She had been such a fool.

Gabriel watched the Council for once being rather quiet. They were completely unconcerned about Brigid and Hera still being at large. The Darkness had given them a fright but that had quickly passed. They viewed the two Goddesses as harmless.

The fools. Hera had never been harmless. She was one of the most naturally powerful Goddesses around. She had carved out not just one but two huge empires. She had replaced several pantheons, and left her mark for centuries. Mortals and Divine alike had rightly feared her. Her own husband had chained her to her house because he was scared of her power and fury. She could take out any number of Arch Angels if they were not working in unison. Her roaming the Earth was a disaster.

As for Brigid, she did not elicit the same level of fear. She was reasonably powerful, but her powers where surprisingly wide ranging. No the greatest concern for her was the loyalty she incited. While she had been one of the earliest to be captured, her worship had lasted for centuries afterwards, only stopped with some clever marketing. She was dangerous, such loyalty especially on a large scale would empower her to terrifying levels. Especially if she managed to set up in the UK, its population giving its faith to her. It was a nightmare not worth considering.

Fortunately neither seemed to be making any successes.

She rolled her eyes as many of the Elders started discussing the merits of the search. Many encouraged the conversation. They were actually considering pulling off the hunt and leaving it to Nuriel and her team. Like she wasn't busy enough. But leaving the hunt for two Goddesses to anyone who wasn't an Arch Angel was potentially suicidal.

The fools they were so self-assured of their own importance. Most of them so easily forgot the cost of the War and Rebellion. Their numbers had been decimated, so many of their strongest Elders had been lost. They would never be in the position they were currently in if they had survived. There would always have been seven Arch Angels at any given time.

The Angels were weak, but too proud to realise it. They relied too much on their Arch Angels. They had been spoiled. Perhaps having Hera or Brigid do something significant would be a good scare for them.

Chapter 19

Brigid breathed in deeply, feeling the rich magic of the Ganges filling the air. There was the fetid smell of decay and refuse also filling the air, as well as the smell of the populace but despite that she could still smell the potent magic of the river. It thrummed, flowing into the city of Varanasi, infusing the people who bathed in its sacred, if heavily polluted, waters.

She could feel parts of her own powers too, flowing down from the Yamuna River and mixing with the surprisingly potent powers of the Ganges. Her initial steps had proved successful in Agra. As expected the land was crying out for the magical touch of a Mother Goddess. She had effectively claimed it without officially claiming it, important if she was to continue to avoid the Angels.

But India was full of surprises, while the land was screaming out for her magic, for any Mother or Father to nurture it, the rivers were contently singing away. They still had some of their own magic. India was a patchwork of screaming need and contentment.

Within the city there was an old and strange magical feel that had grown tainted, for lack of a better word. She hazarded that it was the river. It might be singing but it was sick, very sick with the sheer number of pollutants raging through it. It saddened her that in this age such beautiful and magical things as rivers were treated this way. But her research had shown her every nation in the world had various levels of pollution.

She filtered out the Ganges and focused on the smells of Varanasi, the spice and the sweat, the perfumes and the toxins. It was all so alien to her, but she could feel the ancient beat of the city, ancient and weak but firmly entwined with the Ganges. It was here that millions had descended the steps into the sacred waters to bathe and pray.

This was the best place to claim the Ganges, but also the most difficult.

She hooked her arm around Ryan's as he led her towards the river. They stopped at stalls to admire knick knacks and food. They chatted absently as they moved through the pressing throng of people but gradually they made their way to the steps. And with each step closer she felt the potency of the river's magic assail her. Her own magic swirled around her in response and as she glanced around she saw flowers burst into bloom.

She vanished her shoes at the top of the steps and slowly descended towards the dirty water. Shimmers of rainbows played over oily sheens and between plastic bags, bottles and rotting leaves. The river was so very sick and yet people continued to bath in it. She had to fix it, they were endangering their health.

Ryan watched as she slowly descended the steps like a vision from Heaven. How had he ever gotten so lucky? Her hair and green dress were floating around her in a gentle breeze that seemed to be coming from nowhere. The day had been a little overcast but now there were shafts of sunlight spearing through the clouds. It added an ethereal quality to the steps and river as the shafts raced across and around. Bathing Hindus looked up at the shafts of sunlight.

He turned back to see Brigid stop on the last step above the waterline "are you sure that it is wise to get that near?"

She whispered something he couldn't hear except "it will be mine" he shook his head, he must have heard wrong. Then she took the last step, as soon as her skin touched the water it blazed to life with light. People everywhere turned to look in fright and wonder. The light rising out of the river intensified making Brigid and the others in the river little more than dark pillars.

Brigid gasped as she felt the river react to her presence and interference, its powers coiled around her, ensnaring her and trying to draw her in. She felt all the latent powers of ancient India awaken at once. They were far more powerful than she had realised.

She focussed her powers on shielding and slipping between the Ganges' powers.

Ryan staggered back as plumes of water suddenly shot out of the water, all of them aimed directly for Brigid. They twined around the pillar of light encasing her, like snakes winding around prey. Was it an illusion or did Brigid have wings? People were screaming in terror as they rushed to get out of the water and away from the river. The steps were already covered in terrified people and more were coming. Yet Brigid moved deeper into the river.

The water boiled around her feet, she felt the tightening of magic around her, she let go of her illusions. They were a waste of her magic right now. The magic of an Angel might work in her favour. And it did she felt the powers hesitate and in that instant she fed her powers through the river. Years of British rule and Muslim rulers had undermined the strength of the Hindu resistance. Like everywhere the Angels' religions had touched the old powers had been weakened. The rising numbers of Muslims in Pakistan and Bangladesh only undermined the ancient powers that they had one belonged to.

She now walked a dangerously thin line between Earth Goddess and Elder Angel. She wondered if she could qualify as an Arch Angel with her powers. What an abstract thought. It galled her that she had to use her

Angel powers at all, let alone to defend herself. She poured forth her Angelic powers, driving back the powers attacking her and at the same time she flooded her Earth Goddess powers into the river. She felt it respond, it still held far too much power of its own to accept her. She summoned up more power. She felt a small unfurling from nearby, her efforts in Agra were already paying off and she was surprised just how much was coming to her from Australia. She had to return. But her greatest surprise was the fragile amount she received from her ancient homelands.

It still accepted her!

Then everything went berserk.

Ryan scrambled back up the steps as fast as he could when the water started to boil. He hoped that no one was stuck in the river. He couldn't tell if the screams were in pain or terror, but there were so many people surging up the steps it was hard to tell.

Great plumes of steam and water burst out of the river and up into the quickly darkening sky. Brigid moved further into the river, towards the centre, as a large whirlpool started to form around her. Other noises filled the air competing with the screams. Boat horns, sirens, the crunching thud as a boat crashed into stone.

But the screams went from scared to complete terror as fire rained down from the orange clouds. Each droplet of fire that touched the glowing river exploded in a bolt of lightning and a small fireball. Beyond the river the city was quickly set alight. It was something out of the Apocalypse.

And yet Brigid and her column of light did not waver.

The ground started to shake, the sounds of groaning and grating rock ominously filled the air, even over the frightened screams of the populace. Somewhere a great plume of dust shot up as a building collapsed. Then another and another.

Along the river a bridge collapsed, taking with it cars and people. The waves crashed viciously against the river steps, dragging people into the water. They all disappeared beneath the glowing surface and did not reappear. Water surged everywhere. Real rain outnumbered the fire rain, banking many of the fires low and making the streets run brown as all the dust and refuse was washed into the river. He struggled to stand let alone move as every street became a stream, the steps had become a horrific water feature as the water started to drag parts of the city with it. If this kept up the city wouldn't burn to the ground it would be washed into the river.

Then he heard a rumbled that chilled him to the bone. He looked upstream and all wit left him, his body froze with fright. Coming around the river bend was a wall of brown water carrying the debris of the dams that had once contained it, and the cities it had passed through. He was going to die, there was nowhere to run. He couldn't get up the steps, and had luckily avoided the cars and people being washed past him in a deluge of muck and churning water.

Was he hallucinating or were there now bright lights in the sky, they looked almost Human. Maybe he was seeing things funny through the water that was now covering him. If he didn't let go he would drown. Well at least it wasn't the cancer that had killed him. Though a bizarre natural disaster in India hadn't even been a potential thought. He sent a quick prayer for Brigid before he let go and his world disappeared.

There was water everywhere, pulling her and

assaulting her from every direction. Light pierced the water, like a thousand swords stabbing at her shields. She felt the power wrap around her in a smothering cocoon.

She was no longer in the physical realm, but within the spiritual essence of the Ganges, or possibly for all of India.

There was chanting, lots of chanting in languages she didn't know and didn't have the time, or spare magic to make herself understand. Elements flared past her, there were comets and stars. There was smoke drifting lazily past, little flares of light flickering within. It was ethereally beautiful, hinting at a memory she couldn't remember.

There was a flash of dark blue and screams filled the air/water? Thousands of swords suddenly shattered against her shields, but doing their intended work. She responded with her Angelic powers, raising powerful shields one after another while she lashed out wildly. Her magical senses were of less use than her eyes and ears.

She felt something give way under one of her flailing tentacles. The shock passed back up and crumbled against her outer shield, destroying it completely. The world rocked in reprisal, the water flashing from its natural blue to a fiery orange. The flickers of light bloomed into shining spears and swords. Green and purple flashed wildly around her as the weapons started moving. Out of the thickening smoke drifted shapes of Beastmen striking her outer most shield. She intensified her assault with her Angelic powers, while she started cocooning herself inside her Angelic shields with her Mother Earth powers.

She felt a resonance from outside her shields, even hidden behind so much powerful Angel magic the spirit realm still recognised her natural powers. Nature and the elements had always had a strong allegiance to the

Mother Goddesses.

She felt the tides around her changing. Life was breathing through her Angel shields as though they didn't exist to hug her Mother Earth powers. She felt the land's magic and her own entwining around each other, wanting to unite, needing to unite.

She felt the consciousness of India- all of ancient India, the modern states of India, Pakistan and Bangladesh acknowledge her powers. She felt their hunger and thirst for what she could offer. They were starved by centuries of Angelic onslaught. The same magic she had used to defend herself.

There were more screams as her Angelic powers continued to cause devastation beyond her vision. Drawing the ire of Divine powers. She felt herself being smothered by ancient and decayed magic. She heard their whispers, of what had once been Gods but were now nothing more than lingering shades, caught in between the natural states of Gods. Gods did not become shades, they did not enter another state. They simply were drained and absorbed or they willingly chose to relinquish their essence back into the Lifestream.

She had no real way of telling but she felt certain that they were the remains of the once mighty Hindu Pantheon. Bound tightly to the land they had loved, they had weathered the incursion of Alexander the Great and the assault of the Olympians empowering him. There had been various incursions but they had weathered them all. Except the spread of the Angels' religions. They had been slowly poisoned by the continued growth of Islam in the region, but the final death had been by Christianity brought by the British Empire.

Her people had unknowingly assisted in the killing of a once great pantheon. Their legacy so great that they still had millions of worshippers centuries after they had ceased to have any impact on the planet. India was unprotected, and in part it was her fault. Her people had been used by the Angels, but it was the legacy of the gifts that she had once given them that had allowed them to succeed so much.

Britain was her child she would not make excuses for it but she would fix its mistakes. After all India was essentially one of her progeny, the product of Britain's once great empire.

And the only way she could begin the healing was to formally claim India. It could not heal, she could not control it, the shades could not be released and the land made bountiful again until she stepped up to the mark and made a commitment.

She felt sure that these thoughts were not her own, but encouraged in all likelihood by one or more of the shades lingering at the very edges of her sight.

She stilled herself and her powers, allowing the external magic to continue to entwine itself around her own. Then she summoned up her powers, spreading them outwards in all directions, entwining and embracing all magic that they encountered. As she spoke she spoke with voice, spirit and magic. A binding commitment to the land "I, Brigid formally claim the ancient lands of India, no other claims are stronger and there are no contenders bar decayed shades. Rest in peace your lands are now in good hands. In the name of the Great Mother Goddess who gave us life and Chaos who gave us existence I fully accept these lands as mine and mine alone." She hoped that was the ritual saying, she had never formally claimed a land. Only offered her name when her pantheon had settled in Ireland.

She was suddenly assaulted by a barrage of new powers, ancient and Primordial, but these were not weak or decayed like the lingering shades bound to the Sacred

Rivers. These were violently real. All her Angelic shields and spells were ripped away from her in seconds, Angel magic no matter how powerful was no match for Primordial powers. These powers had to belong to Brahman, that had been the source of the Hindu Pantheon but only the strongest among them could be wielding it still. It was most likely to be Kali, Shiva or Vishnu.

She had to admit she was more than surprised to feel a Returned Primordial God's powers still being wielded. But she supposed India was such a unique place that things were more than a little different. It had to be the rivers, they were usually the first claimed and settled areas, sacred and life giving until the cities flourished and the river's importance was forgotten. Except in India, especially the Ganges was sacred. Such strong belief would keep deceased powers alive.

She had been a fool to think that a dead pantheon would mean the land would be easily claimable. Lands were loyal to those Gods and Goddesses who tended them. A fact that had been forgotten by many younger Gods, and the Angels too. It was why Ireland had never relinquished her and why many Britons still exhibited many of her gifts.

But she too had forgotten it. India was no ordinary place, it was like Mesopotamia or China. It was a cradle of civilisation, the birthplace of many races, a region so steeped in history and magic that a Returned Primordial's powers were now assaulting her. And those ancient powers bore only hatred for the Angels that had stripped her of its power and magic. All semblance of her Angel magic was gone, attacked from every aspect and angle. The only thing protecting her was her frail and underdeveloped earth powers. They were the only things that stood between her and death. Those powers held her in a death grip, ready to crush in an instant.

"Who would dare claim my lands from me with Angel magic? It was said as a whisper but it roared through the waters with those Primordial powers. Brigid quailed blind to the voice as she was swept along in the waters. It was a terrible voice, powerful and demanding infused with death and destruction. It reminded her of Hera at her mightiest.

"I dare! The last of my kind, possibly among the last of our kind. I bear the burden of saving the Earth from its own destruction. I will make the Angels pay but the land needs help too."

Her powers were no longer paralysed but they were not under her control either. They were spreading out all over physical and spiritual India, entwining with those ancient cosmic powers lying dormant in all those sacred rivers.

Someone was holding her face, and slowly sight was returned to her. Before her stood a truly terrifying woman. She was more than a shade but not alive, but she was stunning. Her skin was as black as pitch, her lips and hair blood red, her eyes a red-violet. Blood decorated her black skin in symbols. Strangely enough Brigid felt like she could see right through her. As though all of her secrets were being analysed by this shade.

She smiled "You will do Brigid" she said in a voice so worn Brigid didn't realise that she had spoken at first.

"Who are you?"

"Kali, or more correctly the last remnants of her and her brethren. My powers allowed me a bit more strength in this state. But too long have we been denied our return to the wheel, trapped in this indeterminate state. Trapped by the very nature of our worshippers beliefs. Ironic. Now it is finally ended and you have set us free young Brigid."

She couldn't remember the last time she had been called young, but compared to the Hindu Gods she certainly was.

"And so our great dynasty finally comes to an end, just as yours is about to bloom. And yet life is full of cycles, who knows if this is really our last meeting or a final farewell. But you will grow strong Brigid, if you incite the loyalty you once did you will become one of the most powerful Goddesses to have ever existed." She placed her hand over Brigid's heart and abdomen "Break the Angels Brigid, if it is the one thing you do."

"I promise"

She smiled sadly as she touched Brigid's stomach before she faded away. Beyond the other shades scattered as smoke in the wind. They existed no longer, finally allowed the peace they deserved. A slight tug at her heart told her that they had gifted her with powers. She just hoped she would not be tied to the same lingering fate should she fail.

She sighed and relaxed, feeling the realm surge around her, desperate to embrace her, but so was the physical.

With an undignified shriek she was ripped from the ethereal back into the physical. Which unfortunately was a surging waterfront bringing destruction on hundreds of cities and towns along all the tributaries that fed into the Ganges and the Ganges itself. She cast about with her magic, feeling the presence of Angels, lots of Angels. Even Arch Angels.

She cast out with a complex request, fuelled more by desire than any real conscious control. She cast complex shields then joined herself to the river, abandoning the physical and giving the Angels no chance to find her.

She wondered vaguely where she would turn up.

Chapter 20

Hera whipped her head around to face the east as she felt the ripple of power spread outwards. She tasted the surge of the Lifestream as it flowed past her, more active than the whole time she had been freed. For some reason it tasted very strongly of Brigid and the Hindu Gods. But she couldn't make sense of what she was tasting.

Settling for more practical means she flicked on the TV and flicked it to the nearest news channel.

India and Bangladesh are reeling after extensive flooding has devastated the region. The Ganges and all its tributaries have burst their banks suddenly and the reason has as yet been undetermined. The strangest aspect is that there hasn't been a single recorded fatality. We turn now to Kelly Jones in India.

The screen flashed to wreckage scenes. The city had been ripped cleanly in half, the debris scattered far and wide among piles of mud. Flowing through the middle of the devastation was the river Ganges sparkling blue in the sunlight. Kelly Jones waved to the destruction behind her.

The damage is extensive, whole buildings have been swept away, bridges and dams completely destroyed. What caused the rivers to flood so dramatically has not been determined. Initial reports suggest burst dams or a freak monsoon. Though what could cause such widespread flooding over two countries in so many rivers is a mystery.

On top of this bizarre occurrence is the single most amazing aspect of it all. Not a single fatality and only the slightest of casualties. It is impossible to comprehend such a miracle. Hundreds of thousands of people were swept up in the river but none of them where harmed. Not even any animals were harmed. Everyone is at a loss how no one was harmed in such devastation.

On another strange note every person interviewed tells the same story of hearing a woman's voice. The general consensus is that her name is Brigid and that she has claimed India, Pakistan and Bangladesh. Also many of them have mentioned dreams about a woman with six wings. More reports have come in from the city of Varanasi and how the city was thrown into turmoil after a woman entered the river. Thousands tell of pillars of light and firestorms. These tales are being blamed as a mass hallucination.

On a positive note environmentalists are exclaiming over the renewed health of the river. It is the healthiest it has been in living memory, flowing unrestrained and without pollution. Various endemic species have been spotted in regions where they had previously died out. Will this event ever be explained or will it only ever be described as a freak disaster? Kelly Jones for CNN.

Hera just stared at the TV screen in shock. What on Earth had Brigid been thinking, the Angels were as strong as ever? They would descend upon India in all their fury. Tomorrow there might not be an India. Tomorrow the Apocalypse might have been unleashed on the subcontinent. Why would she be so stupid as to make a claim on India? Now was not the age of claiming, not while the Angels were so strong.

But Brigid wasn't stupid, she was known for her wisdom. Tactically speaking it was a fantastic start, India was one of the two most populous nations in the world. India and China were constantly leapfrogging to be the most populous. Bangladesh was also no light weight when it came to population. However Bangladesh was an Islamic country. The Angels would not relinquish it lightly.

Damn Brigid was doing well for herself. She had at her disposal populations that could only have been dreamed of in ancient times. The Angels truly did not wield the power at their disposal. If they had worked together as a unified front the world would have been completely theirs, unified. Instead they had let their petty rivalries get in the way, allowed their religions to fragment. As a result there had been a resurgence of the Old Religions, while Hinduism and Buddhism still flourished. Even stranger was the continual increase of Atheists, the absence of magic had created a void. What a strange notion, people who didn't believe in any Gods, but in this day and age they didn't see the Gods constantly battling. They weren't even visible in this day and age.

But they would remember and fear.

"Good luck Brigid. May Chaos guide you."

She turned to look out the window contemplating if she should make a claim on New York. Though it didn't have any Sacred Rivers to conquer. How could she force it? She had to find New York's Sacred Heart. Ha what a joke!

Fire raged along the banks of the River Ganges keeping away all the mortals. But it was not a natural fire, nor was it the result of Brigid. This was Angel fire burning with all the fury and frustration of the six Arch Angels as they surveyed the devastation Brigid had wrought. The fire was to keep away all mortals from viewing them, but even the other Angels dared not venture near them. Their anger could be felt miles away, mortals were too busy with the wreckage to notice the supernatural unease smothering much of India. But the Daemons could sense their presence and were keeping a very low profile.

Six of the Arch Angels in one place was never good, after a Goddess had unleashed a trapped pantheon and then claimed their land, was the worst possible scenario for any Daemon.

Nuriel, the Guard and Legion Captains landed before the Arch Angels. They showed incredible calm before the burning fury of their leaders.

Zerachiel showed the greatest courage in speaking first "My Arch Angels there is no trace of the Goddess. The river sings emitting so much magic it clouds the air. But as for her trace it disappears out at sea."

"She has vanished without a trace?" Gabriel's voice was as cold as ice, even as the fires dancing over her intensified.

"Yes Mistress. What are your wishes?"

She turned to look at the other Arch Angels, it was clear they were communicating mentally. In times like this Gabriel as the most powerful was the voice and all their discussions were not heard by anyone.

"Nuriel will seek any trace she can of the Goddess. All will aid her regardless of her requests, all Captains will assist her when required. All Captains will use the Guards and Legions to continue observations across America and Europe however the main focus is now the subcontinent." Her voice rang out louder, resonating in every Angel across the globe. "Unless already on a mission already approved by us all Elder, Ascended and Lesser Angels will convene on India. All Elder will work in a minimum of pairs, with four Ascended and a minimum of twenty Lesser. Every rock will be overturned, every Demon eradicated. India will be cleansed, Brigid found and neutralised. All worshippers are to be neutralised one way or another. Such are the Arch Angels commands."

They were released from the spell.

The nearby Angels took flight quickly leaving their masters. One of the Elders was not so wise. He instead landed before them "is this really necessary, the Elder are not bloodhounds, leave it to the underlings."

While Gabriel might share his view on the Ascended and Lesser Angels she was beyond contempt when it came to the Elder's stupidity.

"You dare question your Arch Angels?" Her voice was laced with such venom only a fool would continue.

Jegudiel was such a fool "Your decision is questionable my lords. Heaven is our sanctuary, why should we leave it when there are thousands of servants to scour the Surface for us. Let them catch the two Goddesses, it is only a trivial matter."

She gasped in amazement and she wasn't the only one "Are you really so stupid Jegudiel? This is a God damn fucking nightmare we have not just one but two Goddesses free and claiming parts of the Surface. Hera is the Queen of Heaven and one of the most powerful Goddesses still around. She is at large gathering followers, if she gets a million followers she is beyond the ability of all but the Seven. She can easily get hundreds of millions, even billions.

As for Brigid she has spat in our face and claimed India the one land we have never been able to conquer and claimed two Islamic countries at the same time. She has claimed two of our countries and the faith she has left in her wake is strong. She is in all likelihood beyond the ability of all but the Seven. We do not have Seven Arch Angels.

We are weak while the Goddesses grow only stronger you moron. Do not question us, for we have thought about it more than you are capable of" He collapsed to the ground gasping, clutching his throat. The six Arch Angels stared at him impassively as his physical body was denied is vital breath. Angels didn't really need to breathe but their bodies did, if they couldn't they automatically supplemented their bodies' needs with magic. He could not.

His eyes misted up as his silver blood started pouring out of them. He spluttered between his gasps, blood coming out but no air going in. The ground was quickly splattered with silver blood. Lightning burst from the sky, striking him and sending him flying into the river. His flesh burned as the river turned against him, the Archs had no desire to kill him but the river was now wholly Brigid's.

"How pathetic if this is all Heaven can turn out. Clearly our time of peace has made us soft. Compulsory training sessions will recommence for the whole populace."

The six of them disappeared in a blaze of light.

No one dared help Jegudiel as he struggled to get out of the river. If he died it was of no consequence but to help him might incur the Arch Angel's wrath towards them.

Pope John Paul V had surprised the entire Vatican with his sudden new fervour towards God. He was no longer the weak and cringing man he had been for years, nor was he easily controlled any more. Now he stood in his office but where once he would have hidden behind his desk as the Cardinals made their demands he now stood looking out the window. Behind him were various Cardinals trying to coerce him to their will. But for the first time in years he was agreeing with none of them. He was vehemently ignoring and belittling their suggestions and requests. As far as he was concerned they had to help the world, for the End of Days was coming.

He was looking out the window admiring God's work. He had made such a beautiful world, imperfect for only Heaven could be perfect, but still very beautiful. His attention was caught by the white clouds, blooming and growing across the clear blue Mediterranean sky. By the light striking the different veins of the polished marble and how it moved through the glass. By the wind gently pushing and pulling the leaves on trees and the hair of women.

He turned around and sighed inwardly "How many times do I have to tell you that I am not listening"

"For your sake mortal you had better never say those words to me." Before she had finished speaking Gabriel had lifted him up by the throat. She stood there in full armour again, hiding all traces of her gender with light, spells and metal. "Now you listen carefully John Paul." He nodded as much as he could.

"Good. Now there has been a disaster in India, a miracle some are calling it, and that is exactly what it is not. People heard the voice of Saint Brigid and you will tell the world this, in fact you will immediately propose to visit the devastated region and imprint your faith. Any statues you find of Saint Brigid you will bless. If you play your part well you will have earned you place in Heaven. Understood?"

"Perfectly" he gasped out. She let him go and he crumpled to the floor. She turned to face the quivering Cardinals "You will support his visit, you will support every proposal he makes. It is time your pathetic bickering was put aside and your ambitions given up before the grace of God. Judgement Day is coming and you will all be found wanting."

They all cowered before the blazing image of the Arch Angel Gabriel. None doubted his word, they saw within their own hearts their arrogance and sins. Then as quickly as he appeared he disappeared, leaving behind a lingering glow that slowly faded.

The Pope spoke first "Get me media coverage and

organise my visit to India. The Angel's demands must be completed." Then he swept out leaving behind the Cardinals who had once thought themselves better than him, who had allowed petty ambition and sin into the hallowed halls of God's City. Let the light burn them clean.

Azad Ali was a proud man, a powerful man. He was the kind of man other men looked up to, respected and feared a little. He was ruthless in character and a dedicated man, which was why he had risen so high in the military, he was the Chief of Army Staff. He was the top authority of the Pakistani army and the role suited him well. He was a disciplined man but he did enjoy the power and authority of his rule and was not always so stringent. He had used his power to line his own purse, but that was common for men of his rank.

He stood staring out of the window down on the city of Islamabad. He had had a good life, he had a wife who had given him three healthy sons, the eldest of which had entered the military last year. He also had two daughters that would be married off to friend's sons when they were old enough. He had a grand house, he had power but he also had respect, yet he felt like something was missing.

A direction, a cause. A war perhaps? But the region had been at peace for many years now, the old tensions with India were ever on the mend and Afghanistan was once again a functioning nation having risen out of its squabbling city-states. There was still unrest in the Middle East, and they had given aid to Iran when it had attacked Israel again. That aid was thankfully kept secret especially after how violently Israel had struck back before the United Nations intervened. Israel had destroyed several of their largest cities and nearly all their weapons factories. Iran had all but collapsed into warring city-states, a fate common to the Middle East and much of the world.

He was a military man but there was no good cause to fight for. While he agreed Palestine should be returned to Islamic hands he personally believed the Arabic Muslims were too disordered and divided to successfully achieve it. The Israelis were a strong and united force that the Arabs had little chance of defeating. Because of that fact it made him proud to be Pakistani, they were dedicated Muslims that were more than a match for the Western World or the Hindu might of India. No it was India that was the real temptation. So many sites that belonged to Islam but were under Hindu control. Those animals desecrated sacred sites with their false Gods, they were worse than Jews or Christians who had merely lost their way, no Hindus had never been on the path to Allah. They worshipped women for Heaven's sake. What kind of religion could exist that gave women power over men, women were meant to serve men, it was the natural order. Not only was India a cesspool of Hindu beliefs but it was increasingly being Westernised, turning back many edicts of decency. And that taint was crossing the border into Pakistan. Women were no longer covering up, they held jobs and they thought they could deny their husbands sex. What was the world coming to?

"General?"

He turned to face his Vice Chief, why did the man sound disturbed? Surprisingly enough there was a bright beam of light coming from the ceiling. Without thinking he automatically pulled out his revolver and aimed it at the shape of a man that had appeared. The gun dropped from his hands unnoticed and forgotten as he stared in wonder at the six black wings of the Angel. He fell to his knees before the divine messenger, who carried a flaming sword of light and was adorned in shining armour like the ancients. Fire danced across his wings and arms, flames of righteousness that would strike out at the unfaithful.

"My lord Michael?"

The Angel turned his burning eyes towards him "Yes my faithful servant, it is I. And I bring you a divine command."

"What is Allah's command?"

Michael grimaced behind his helmet, he was beginning to feel as Gabriel did. They should be recognised, not the image they had created. Well they were reaping what they had sown.

"The command of Heaven is that the Ganges be cleansed of the taint it breeds. Demons lure the weak of faith into the waters and claim their souls. Now their chief Demoness Brigid seeks to proclaim herself a rival to God. This affront cannot and will not be allowed to happen." He pulled forth his flaming sword, the globe on the pommel glowing with the light of the sun, and pointed it at Azad "You mortal will cleanse the land of this taint. You will crush the infidels and claim back what has been lost to Allah and his Angels."

He brought the sword down on both of Azad's shoulders, burning through the cloth to leave fiery brands that marked him in the name of Michael. Then as he had appeared he disappeared in a pillar of light. Azad stared at his shoulders, ignoring the pain to read the mark of Michael. This was his calling, this was his cause, his sacred duty. He would cleanse India of its taint, and while he was at it he would cleanse Pakistan and Bangladesh. It was long overdue the countries were reunited under Islam and God.

Ryan knelt before the newly erected statue of

Brigid, despite the wings the resemblance to his Brigid was undeniable. She had somehow ascended, impossible to believe but he accepted it heart and soul. Brigid was now a Goddess, there was now a sect dedicated to her centred in Varanasi, and her image had suddenly appeared in all manner of Hindu paintings and carvings. To many of them she was one of their Goddesses reborn. Those same people were saying that their Gods had all died and been reborn as one deity.

Others were vehemently denying this and claiming that she was a Demon sent to test their faith. The same mumblings were being muttered among the Christian sects as well. The Papal stance was that Saint Brigid had performed a miracle yet many others were claiming she was a Fallen Angel, or a Demon intent on seeking out the weaknesses of Asia. So far Islam had remained quiet, but they surely had their own opinions.

But from all the Old Religions had come many converts to Brigidism, nearly all had been those swept up in the river's devastation. And somehow he had ended up being responsible for them all. Many had seen him standing with her before she entered the river and claimed he had divine favour. He had tried protesting to no avail.

Somehow he was meant to lead a religion in her name, with no Divine help. People were flocking to Varanasi every day, coming to bathe in the sacred waters of the Ganges then flock to the various temples being hastily thrown up all along the river. But as quickly as they went up they came back down, there was a plague of arsonists targeting the Brigidites and all their temples. As well as some of their lives. But it seemed that if they stayed close to the river's edge they were safe, so the banks grew ever more populated.

He found it strange that a religion honouring an

ancient Celtic Goddess had arisen in India but life was currently full of strange things. His vision kept playing up. When he looked at some people their images shifted, some had wings; six, four or two, some had green hair and leaves, others blood red eyes or made him think of Vampires. He wondered if he was being drugged or falling ill.

No he couldn't be falling ill he bathed in the river and that healed all wounds. Those that doubted the power of the river were soon silenced when they saw the sick enter its waters and leave healthy. It was also denied all Human attempts to re-tame it. No dam could be built across it, no canal branching off of it, not even sewage could be discharged into it. It was by Divine favour back to its full glory, and that glory extended to all its tributaries.

But what they all really needed was a visit from Brigid herself, to give them direction. They were building temples in her honour, and he had made some hesitant edicts that had been accepted. But something chilled him, he felt sure they were all targets and that it would lead to civil unrest. If not a religious war.

He looked at the statue for a very long time praying for her to listen and come back. They needed direction. They needed her.

Brigid as it was, was slumped across a piece of driftwood floating amid garbage piles in the Indian Ocean. When she opened her eyes it was only to see the endless expanse of blue sky and toxic sea. Her skin was flaked in salt and chemical residue, her wings were liberally coated in it. When had her wings reappeared? She couldn't remember, she was still piecing together all that had happened.

She sensed along her powers and sure enough she

could feel the very strong presences of India and Bangladesh and the faint whisper of Pakistan. Already there was a noticeable increase in the powers available to her. It was more than just the faith or the powers she had inherited from Kali but she didn't know where else it had come from. She would investigate it later when she returned to the subcontinent, there was still much for her to do there.

Further musing was interrupted when she noticed the massive cruise ship bearing down on her. It was like a building, it was monolithic, she still couldn't comprehend the things Humans could make without magic. Utilising latent memories she had copied she created a flare gun and set it off. She also disappeared her wings when she saw the little boat coming towards her.

She was losing consciousness when they hauled her up out of the water. She wasn't sure why she was so incoherent. She absently nodded her head when they started asking her questions, she wasn't sure what language they were speaking, words were beyond her. She did distinguish Ganges to which she nodded. An awed silence followed, to which she stared wide eyed as she slumped down in the boat.

What had she just gotten herself into?

Several hours later after a conversation with the ship's captain and the presentation of her credit card Brigid was happily bathing in her own first class cabin. It had given her the time to relax, gain coherent thought and control of her body and adjust to the sudden increase in her magical abilities. She still wasn't fully adjusted to it, it made her worry for all the future lands she would claim and the worshippers that would continue to flock to her. Could she handle it?

Her mind might be a mess but she had managed to

get her body back into order, she had to. The captain had invited her to dine on his table tonight and she understood that she was currently the most interesting thing on the ship. It was why she hadn't strayed from her room. She could feel their interest bearing down on her. Sometimes her senses were a curse.

As she allowed her body to soak and allowed all the salt to seep out of her feathers she abandoned her mental constraints and let her mind and powers flow outwards. First she felt the response of the ocean, the still diluting waters of the Ganges still recognised her even as it was bleeding into the immeasurable expanse of the ocean. It made her smile.

She also felt the resonance of her own believers coming from within the ship. She opened her eyes and slowly sat up focusing her powers into precise probes. To her complete surprise nearly half of the passengers belonged to her. She couldn't believe it. In the middle of the Indian Ocean she had more than enough believers to fill a town.

She jumped out of the bath scattering water everywhere as her wings propelled her forward. She ran out into the cabin flicked on the TV to the nearest news channel. It showed the devastation all along the Ganges, the impossible health of the river, the miraculous survival of everyone swept up in the disaster. She saw shrines and temples being built in her honour, and the ruins of the many that were being burnt down. There was also the announcement that the Pope was on his way to India because of Saint Brigid's miracle. That made her grimace. There was also a discussion about the Winged Goddess and the sudden appearance of her image in hundreds of ancient carvings and paintings and how many Hindus were claiming she was the next avatar.

No wonder her powers had grown so much, the

events in India had shaken the world's faith. It explained why she had an abundance of faith powers she couldn't pinpoint. A disaster with no deaths, a voice calling out to millions and a woman ascending from the river. Nearly half the Hindu population were claiming their Gods had died and that she was their reincarnation. She had never hoped for such instantaneous success. Atheists, Buddhists, Muslims and Christians were converting in the Sacred Waters.

She shook herself, she actually had temples now. Then she sobered, the Angels would be on the war path. The arsons and murders were clearly their doing, and that was only the tip of the iceberg. India and Bangladesh could very well soon become a warzone.

The temple was not finished but it clearly had grand designs. People rushed this way and that, some building, others cleaning and even more simply wanting to be in the temple. There was a constant stream leading down the steps to the River Ganges and back. She just couldn't believe the number of people that had already turned to Brigid. Nor the number of temples being erected all along the river. Not just in Varanasi, though it was now decreed the holy city of Brigid, but along its entire length in both India and Bangladesh.

Oh many of them had been burned to the ground, by Angel and Human hands, but still more flocked to the ever increasing number of temples. The Arch Angels were furious but they were also busy dealing with mortal leaders and the stupidity of her fellow Elders.

It was highly ironic that Nuriel found her first moments of peace in days in the temple of Brigid. It was here that no Angels would come searching for her as she studied the Brigidites. They were certainly an odd and colourful lot. But then they had been united in disaster and that always made for strange bedfellows.

Killing them wouldn't erase them or the world's memory. Brigid had outdone herself. Her success was outstanding, on a world scale. She and the disaster was a worldwide discussion topic. Her influence extended far beyond the banks of the Ganges.

It was sad but she felt sure the only way to undo what she had done would be through war. India and Bangladesh would be scoured clean, and Michael would be directing it all. He was very systematic in his eradications. One only had to think of the Cathars, Witches or Nymphs. Oh there was sure to be traces of Demons all over the world but he had hunted down so many of them that they would be nearly Human. His hunting skills, and the skills of his Cherubim had very effectively removed the taint of magic as Michael called it from Humanity.

She wasn't sure what he was up to but he wasn't that far away, he had to be in one of the neighbouring nations preparing for an Islamic revolution and war to come to India.

She felt a moment of pity for them.

But her pity wouldn't save them. There was nothing she could do to save them. They were empowering a rogue Goddess. To the Arch Angels they had signed their own execution. All the evidence she gathered was merely a formality, with the vague hope she could pull a trace on Brigid.

Which was why she was here, word on the wire was that the 'high priest' as some were calling him was the last Human Brigid had been with before she entered the Ganges. Some said he had divine favour, others said he was suffering from a broken heart. One had said that Brigid had cured him of his cancer, because she loved him.

If there was some small kernel of truth to any of them then she might be able to use him to track down Brigid. She doubted it, Brigid was no fool. If she hadn't been hunting her Nuriel would have allowed herself to respect and even revere the Goddess. She had certainly played her part well, avoiding all notice until suddenly she had hundreds of thousands of worshippers, if not millions. It was hard to tell at the moment.

It didn't take her long to track down the 'high priest' a onetime professor of Celtic Mythology. He was a good choice for high priest, educated, charismatic, charming and clearly dedicated. A light probe told her that he belonged to Brigid completely. Heart and soul. So the rumours held truth. Unfortunately there was no connection to Brigid, in fact there was none of her magic on him except a fading healing spell. She would have expected him to have at least been shielded or something.

It seemed Brigid had abandoned him. But why? Or was there more to it?

She should really tell the Arch Angels about his connection to her. But that would only bring more death. Already hundreds, probably thousands had been burned to death, or beaten to death by Angels and their Human followers. It was a far cry from their divine semblance. Immortals were just as cruel and warlike as mortals.

Perhaps they really weren't so different.

She turned around and left, ignoring the other Angels she passed. She was not in the mood to socialise or gather more intelligence. Besides she was stronger than them, they didn't even know she was there.

She paused on the steps, her attention caught by a wayward plant. It and the ones surrounding the temple, and the ones growing all along the river were vibrant. Not just the flowers but the leaves and even the stems. Far more vibrant than any plants she had seen recently.

Was Azrael right in his musings that the earth was failing without some Divine being to nurture the Lifestream?

She hoped there was some other reason otherwise the Angels were slowly killing the planet. For she knew the Arch Angels would never condone using an Earth Goddess' powers on the land. Yet perhaps that was exactly what it needed. Perhaps the Angels had been too stringent in their use of magic and their presence on the world.

Dangerous thoughts. Ones that could potentially see her punished. She pushed such thoughts from her mind as she teleported to Bangladesh. Peter had mentioned that some of the Cherubim had noticed a stronger taint at the river mouth.

If it was true she wondered why? Was it just a focus for an entire river system? Or perish the thought had Brigid been flushed out to sea? She chuckled at the absurdity of it.

A Goddess flushed out to sea. She was starting to have foolish notions.

It was only when she rematerialised at the river mouth she realised she was holding rose petals, bright pink and smelling sweetly. She looked at them in wonder before dropping them into the water. It would not do to be asked why she had them. She didn't know.

Chapter 21

Brigid took a deep breath as she stepped into the heavily clogged river mouth. She was about to piss of the Angels again, to an extent they would not even imagine. But this was more than just a spiteful act it was strategically needed for India and Bangladesh. They needed the Angels' attention divided.

Which was why she was once again in Australia, an ancient land but tenderly young country. It was quite fitting really, the land itself held power but the Angels' hold on it was tenuous at best. It was also hungering to embrace any future than the environmental death it was sliding towards. Already large tracts of arable land had died from salinity or extreme drought. Their largest river, the River Murray was almost dry, and had been running dry for years now. All the way along the Murray-Darling basin was experiencing intense desertification. Once rich farmlands were now dustbowls, a product of Humanity's destructive legacy.

And the failing of the planet.

The whole country was continually devastated by fierce and unpredictable weather patterns. But despite all the recent disasters and trials Australia was a mostly faithless country. They were more pragmatic and didn't see the point of praying for things to change. The weather was after all a natural force. She was going to destroy that notion, but many of them were of Celtic or Anglo-Saxon descent, their blood would resonate with her.

It was fortunate that the *Indian Empress* had berthed in Adelaide, for it was only a short hop to the River Murray, the life river of Australia. And she would claim it as she had claimed the Ganges, bringing

Australia under her patronage. After her success in India she knew she could do it, and she would be so affected afterwards. Australia despite its huge size was a sparsely populated country compared to India. Or any other large country when she thought about it. Even the small island nations of Japan and Britain had populations far in excess of Australia. She would change that.

India was the site of her rebirth, it had to be protected. It was the place where already millions were converting to her, and there wasn't even a real religion in her name. She would need to visit and sort out the problems she had created. But for now she needed to distract the Angels and gather as much power as she could. After this the Angels would be desperate to find and capture her. She needed to be able to defend herself and increase her strength. Which she had, but even with the millions she would never be complete without returning to and claiming Britain. Which had brought her to Australia.

She walked into the deep, thin ravine between high sand banks that were all that served as the river mouth these days and instantly felt the hunger of the river. The closest thing Australia had ever had to a God was the Rainbow Serpent, all rivers were his but the Murray was especially strong with his dead powers. The Angels had hunted him for sport before the British had even colonised Australia.

She unfurled her powers, utilising all the new powers gifted to her. She felt it surge up the river, flowing along the dusty, polluted river bed, up all the hundreds of tributaries. As it went it burst through the dams choking the river, spreading throughout the Eastern states, sinking her claws in very deep. The land sighed in gratitude as she summoned rain saturated with her Mother Earth powers.

She called up such rain unseen in Australia for decades. The very seas around Australia surged upwards to meet the demand for rain.

It didn't take long for people and satellites to notice the strange phenomenon. TV stations quickly started reporting on the strange disaster.

Rain fell. And it fell in a volume the sunburnt land had never seen before. More than the dry earth was able to soak up despite its intense thirst. Rivers swelled and burst their banks, dams and weirs were obliterated as the water surged savagely downstream. Boats, bridges, buildings and people were swept up in the deluge, but as with the Ganges while the devastation was beyond comprehension there was not a single fatality.

Brigid kept rigid control of the river even as it sprayed past her, connecting her to more than half the country.

All over Australia her voice was heard "I claim this land and river as mine with the promise to protect and aid the mortal stewards. I Brigid accept Australia, New Zealand and Papua New Guinea into my embrace. All their territories are mine by Divine law. May my children enjoy this gift of rain.

All across Australia churches, mosques and synagogues shook as though caught in an earthquake. Symbols fell off roofs and walls. Only the truly faithful were not afraid.

Brigid smiled as she allowed the waters to sweep her once again out to sea. The Angels could not find her in an ocean. She laughed, closing her eyes and letting her powers spread out, letting her body combine with the planet. She would spend some time within the Lifestream to strengthen them both. Australia was in dire need of it.

When she awoke she would be intrigued to see how pissed off the Angels would be.

Hera sat glued to her TV screen watching as picture after picture of devastated river basin flashed across the news. India and Bangladesh but now Australia as well. The scenes were of wrecked buildings, clean-up operations, newly erected temples and the sea of tents to accommodate all those that had lost their homes. Scientists were at a loss to explain it but both river systems were the healthiest they had ever been in memory. Torn river banks were already transforming into picturesque swathes of nature, plants growing far faster than their usual pace. Any attempts to dam or build irrigation canals off of either river were failing abysmally.

The two regions were baffling logical scientific analysis. Both had become beacons for occultists and believers. Both rivers had attainted Divine and Demonic connotations.

But connecting it all was Brigid. Both rivers were now hers, not that the Humans fully understood, and along the Ganges banks temples were being erected in her honour. Christians and Muslims were claiming both areas possessed by Demons. The Pope and Catholic church was insisting it was a miracle of Saint Brigid.

Brigid was blatantly pissing off the Angels, she was spitting in their eye, but she was also avoiding them. What had happened to the shy Goddess that had very rarely ventured beyond her beloved isles? She had been a Goddess of relatively little power compared to the rest, but then she hadn't patronised a huge empire. She had never had the powers to compare with Hera, but then Hera had been supplemented by the various Greek city-states, then Alexander's Empire then finally the ever expanding Roman Empire.

Now she had almost no supplementation to her powers. She had been in New York for several months now and had expanded to San Francisco and Chicago, but they were not hers. She had not claimed them. Brigid on the other hand had claimed the holiest river in the world, two ancient countries as well as managing to claim three young countries.

She stood up and started pacing. She had slowly been increasing her presence in the three cities and had been planning on extending her influence to Houston and Los Angeles. Which was why she was currently in Houston.

How had Brigid done so well for herself? This was nothing like the Brigid she had vaguely known. It was so out of character for her, she had always been so cautious. Now she was suicidally reckless.

Yet it was paying dividends. She was managing to avoid the Angels and at the same time gather enough worshippers that temples were being built dedicated to her. Temples in the Age of Angels, she never thought she would see the day. Perhaps she had been too hesitant, too afraid of the Angels' reach and power to truly claim anywhere. But if Brigid could do it she could damn well do it. She was a Goddess of Power after all. It was time she started acting like one.

She would not be afraid of the Angels any more.

She left the apartments with the intent to head to New Orleans and Washington DC. It was time to spread her net wider, particularly over the capital. Houston she could come back to. She wasn't sure why she was really here in the first place, it was incredibly populous but she had felt compelled to be here. She trusted her instincts but apparently she would be empty handed this time.

She descended the stairs ignoring the people she passed but she stopped once she got out onto the street. An ambulance sat next to a truck and a crane. Being lifted into the truck via the crane and several paramedics was the fattest man she had ever seen. He was grotesque, roll after roll, he was a bloated mockery of a man. Completely unable to move himself, unable to fit in the ambulance. He was revolting.

He was why she was here in Houston, this is what her uncanny instincts had lead her to. Her curiosity was spiked and she quickly sent a probe into his brain as she joined the crowd of gawkers. His brain functions were normal, all his nerves were properly working. His circulatory system was under extreme strain, not unexpected, but still functioning. With the exception of his excessive fat and decayed muscles he had a functioning body.

Nothing a little magic couldn't fix.

The paramedics jumped backwards as he suddenly sat up. It was the most movement they had seen out of him. Strangely enough his eyes seemed to have rolled back into his head. With a sudden roar he lurched up awkwardly into a standing position. He then ran, fat rolls bouncing, straight into a brick wall. He fell backwards, dead on the pavement, mortar and brick chips raining down on him.

She smiled savagely in satisfaction. She would have to come back to Huston to experiment further, but now she had a pressing appointment in Washington DC.

She knew her instincts were still sharp. It was the same instincts that had led her to Sparta and to Rome. Her instincts had guided her to have the biggest empires of the ancient world, to train some of the best warriors and generals.

Now she had plans for a whole new type of warrior.

She snapped her fingers and an obese woman walking down the street suddenly screamed and started running. She crashed into a shop front, shattering the glass and battering down the metal frame. She also crushed the several tables and their inhabitants.

Seems she had a new siege weapon. Humanity really was surprisingly useful in the modern era. She wondered what else her instincts would lead her to.

A couple of hours later Hera was reclining as her plane descended into Washington DC, the capital of the United States of America. At least while it was still a free nation. New York would be the capital of her empire.

It was here that she would make her mark on America, where she could leave her marks without the Angels tracing her back to her lair. She admitted to herself that she was scared of the Angels and she was scared even more so of the Arch Angels. She knew what could be done to her again if she was captured. She had suffered for centuries. She especially knew Ariel's taste for cruelty and that of her Inquisitors.

But she was not going to let fear or anything else hold her back.

Which was why she was in the capital, the centre of government was here. She planned to get her claws very deep into Washington and start claiming vast tracts of America. And what better place than a city modelled after Rome. Reading had offered some delightful insights into the modern era. Rome had once been the capital of her biggest empire. To date.

It seemed prophetic that the capital of the country that would form the foundation of her new empire was modelled after Rome. It almost seemed a pity that it wouldn't remain a capital.

Senator John Worthington was flicking through the news feed in the back of his black SUV as it sped through the city streets. It was horrible to admit it but he was glad for the flooding in India and Australia, it had drawn away a lot of the attention away from the government. Unfortunately Americans were very insular, uncaring and ignorant of the outside world, so there was still a strong focus on the latest revelations to shake the government.

And it had not been a good few weeks; Senator Twain had been caught in a sex scandal, the president had insulted the Mexican president, they were still bogged down in three foreign conflicts, the economy was in a mess, unemployment was at its highest and the environmental ruin continued to spread. Yet despite all these other more significant issues the revelations that he was gay were hogging the news time. Ever since he had been outed a week ago the news had fixated on little else. It was the end of his political career, already members of his own party were calling for his resignation. There had also been a public outcry, prayer session and demands for his removal from the bible bashing south.

He looked up as the car slowed to a stop, codes being muttered over his security detail's earphones. They had been assigned to him ever since the death threats had started flowing in. It saddened him, America prided itself on being the land of the free and was obsessed with believing it was the greatest country in the world. But it was such a flawed and backwards first world country. Sexism, racism and socioeconomic inequality were all clearly prevalent. There were such extremes in beliefs and opinions. But what he found saddest of all was the extreme homophobia very much prevalent in America, in its government and in its media.

Outside his house was the usual picket line of bible protesters, with signs saying 'homosexuality is a sin', 'God can forgive you', "Jesus Saves', "Jesus died for our sins', 'Choose redemption'. They all stood there yelling and jeering, waving their pickets around behind the security line. They weren't a very attractive bunch, dressed in fairly horrible clothing. He forgave himself the shallow thought considering they were personally attacking him for something they didn't understand. Why did so many Americans ignorantly believe that homosexuality was a choice?

What was different though was the stunningly beautiful woman standing behind them. She made him think of a Greek Goddess or something similar, dressed in a flowing purple Grecian dress. Her eyes met with his and he felt also though she stared right through him and saw everything about him. Then to his horror she picked up one of the protesters and threw him into the wall.

A woman screamed and jumped at her "burn in Hell"

She laughed as she picked the woman up by her throat. With one hand. "Hell? The greatest torture was being in Heaven with the Angels, Hell would have been a haven by comparison."

The gates finally opened and the car sped in, he cast one final glance back at her as she threw the woman onto the road. Then she walked through the gate, the closed gate. She didn't slip through, she literally walked through solid metal.

"Stop where you are lady" one of the guards yelled.

She laughed, sending a shiver down John's back "Or what you'll shoot me? Go ahead if you have the balls."

Sure enough there was the sound of a single shot being fired. But she didn't collapse to the ground, there was no blood, the bullet didn't even connect with her. It deflected off of some shield or something. All Hell broke loose as more guards opened fire. But she just kept walking towards him.

One of the guards hauled him out of the vehicle, dragged him through the house then stuffed him in the panic room and sealed it. John quickly turned on all the TV screens as the door sealed shut. She wasn't on any of the screens, on one it showed the guards running about and examining a spot on the grass.

"Looking for me John?"

He jumped and turned around to find her lounging across the bed.

"How did you get in here? He gasped in amazement. The room was completely sealed within a metre of solid steel.

I have my ways" she smiled as she sat up.

"What do you want with me?"

She flicked her hair as she stood up and walked towards him with the predatory grace of a lioness. He was prey, he was sure of it.

"I'm here to help you John and make all your problems go away."

"Problems, what problems?

She raised one perfect eyebrow, her violet eyes full of amusement. He had never seen anyone with eyes so stunning. "The lunatics outside, the divisions within your party, the calls for your resignation, your dreams of becoming president."

How did she know he wanted to be president, he had shared that with no one. "How can you possibly help me with those?"

"I can do anything I like John. After all I managed to get within this room." She did have a valid point.

"Who are you?"

"Hera" he waited for a last name but she didn't provide one.

"As in the Greek Goddess?"

She smiled at him "See you do know me"

She disappeared in a coil of smoke and reappeared behind him, her fingers walking up his shoulders "See John you already know of me, I can see you know my myths. And I already know everything about you." She put a distinct emphasis on everything which left him with no doubt that she did. "I'm offering to help you and in return you will give me what I require."

At last the catch "What do you require?"

"To break the Angels' hold on the world, to destroy their religions, to break Christianity's stranglehold on America?"

"Break Christianity's stranglehold?"

"It hasn't done you any favours, or America for that matter. It has held back this country, stagnating progress and development. The power of this country is being decayed by traditionalists who hate change and hate difference. They are still caught up in their sexism, racism and their homophobia. It is time for change and you John are the president that will lead America into a new future." Its days of freedom were limited. Her empire would be born from the ruins of old America.

"How do I know that you're all you say you are?"

She gently kissed his neck and to his utter surprise he was instantly aroused and erect. He had never been aroused by a woman, had never been erect for a woman, had never slept with a woman. This wasn't possible.

"I can do anything John, remember that" then she disappeared but her voice lingered "I will find you again soon my dear. Do not resign, you hold so much potential."

He was nervous waiting for his press conference. Everyone was expecting him to resign but he couldn't Hera had forbade it. While he was still in doubts about her being a Goddess he was sure that the power she had could help him. Or harm him.

He had done some research on the Goddess Hera and what he had read made him very wary to anger her. Her husband had chained her to Mount Olympus because he was scared of her fury. But the old philanderer really had it coming. Even if she wasn't actually the Goddess then she clearly had an affinity for her. Hera had been a powerful, cunning and wrathful Goddess. Paris had pissed her off and the city of Troy had paid the price.

It was evidently clear no one should ever anger her.

"It is good to see that you understand who you're dealing with" he jumped out of his skin when she appeared next to him. "Oh did I scare you?" she didn't seem sorry in the least.

"Now John today is the first step in changing your future and achieving what you deserve" there was a solemness to her words, the weight of destiny. It was weird the way she spoke changed so often. Maybe he was imagining it but he heard other things than just her unusual accent when she spoke- soft thunder, rain, fire, the crack of a whip, the baying of hounds. Perhaps she really was a Goddess or some powerful sorceress.

No magic didn't exist. He was imagining things.

"Doesn't it John? The world is a miracle that science struggles to explain and even the Gods cannot explain. All that we know was that it was birthed from Chaos, there are physical laws in the absence of magic but there is also magic. Humans are not the only species that inhabit the Earth, there are Vampires, Werewolves, Incubi, Succubi, Maenads and Sirens all walking through these city streets. There are places where the unexplainable happens, when you feel someone watching you but no one is there, when you are drawn to a person for no reason other than they aren't Human. Of course you wouldn't know that."

"Not human?"

"See that blonde reporter over there in the second row?"

"Sally Blackheart?"

"Hmm fitting name. She is a Succubus, women who can enter your dreams and feed off your sexual energies. They can do it in the flesh as well. Some may even kill you with your own pleasure. They live for sex and the energies it provides them, as such they are built for seduction and enchantment."

"You expect me to believe that?" he turned to face her and was horrified at what he saw. There stood a stooped old lady wearing rags, her skin was sloughing off, pus oozed from between cracks but it was her eyes, they held the greatest despair he had ever seen. The next instant there was a young boy with blonde curls, white wings and pouting with gold lips. Then what he guessed Medusa had looked like, hair a coiling mass of snakes. Then Abraham Lincoln, Judy Garland, his mother then finally himself.

"Anything is possible with magic, I can turn into anyone and anything I want" she returned to her usual pale skin, large brown eyes (for public appearances), flowing brown hair and a black power suit. There was a peacock broach on her lapel.

"Several of the people in this room are not Human, one of your own security detail is a Werewolf, half the reporters are either Sirens or Lilin, and Senator Clare, your greatest support is a Maenad. Underneath those brown curls are natural green, under her clothes are leaf birthmarks. Once they know for who you stand for they will lend you their support."

She pushed him through the door, then fell back to the edge of the stage with the security detail. He made his way up to the podium ignoring the glare of the flashing lights. His nerves were racing until he felt a cold pass through him leaving him calm. A quick glance at Hera and she smiled. Magic.

"Following recent events there has been a great deal of unrest within the government and we are trying to limit the damage and do what is best for America. We must do what is best for the people. Recent revelations about my sexuality have arisen and yes I am gay. I always have been but have hidden it for most of my life. In some ways I've been ashamed and have denied myself happiness as a result. But being gay is political suicide and I had my ambitions.

Many people are calling for my resignation, even from within my party. And I am here to meet the needs of America."

He paused and took a deep breath, he felt the magical embrace of Hera making him feel calm. "As such I will not be resigning. I was voted in for my politics, not my private life and I will finish my term. It is then in the voters hands whether I will be re-elected. In my own beliefs I help reflect the diversity within America, and our diversity should be seen in our government, even though it so often is not."

There was a stunned silence, everyone had presumed that he would be resigning. Sally Blackheart was the first to jump forward "Sally Blackheart for CNN. What does your party have to say about your decision?"

He glanced at Abigail Clare who smiled at him "The party is divided on my decision but I do have the strong support of several senators and the majority of the party respects my decision."

"Senator Clare this is an unusual act on your part.

Your policies tend to be very conservative."

Abigail stood up, glanced at Hera then squared her shoulders "We are a democracy and are represented by a full spectrum of people and the Senate should reflect the people. Senator Worthington is an outstanding politician and while we may have different views on policies he is a true party member with the best interests of America at heart."

"Will there be any changes to your policies now that you are openly part of the gay agenda?"

He almost snorted "What exactly is the gay agenda? I don't know what it is. For Heaven's sake my sexuality does not instantly change my politics. Yes I might have personal ideas on what should happen but I am part of the party and I will remain within line of the party."

"But can you be absolutely sure this is for the good of America?"

Hera stepped forward instantly drawing attention to her, with her looks and presence it was instinctual to all the mortals in the room, "The Senator has answered all questions he is willing to. He has other commitments he must attend to. Any further questions will be resolved during a special interview" that drew mutterings, they wanted answers now.

She steered him out into the corridor, the security following them. He wondered what they thought of her, did any of them recognise her as the woman who had stormed his residence. That had caused a media sensation.

"Interview? What interview?"

"Your interview with Kelly Lee. Your story is the hottest thing in the tabloids, and she is the undisputed talk show queen since Oprah. Her opinions carry remarkable weight. She is going to endorse your run for presidency."

She put her hand on his shoulder, her eyes reverting to her stunning violet "You will be president and you will be a damn good one John. It will happen." She pushed him into the car "Stay safe John I'll return shortly."

"Where are you going?"

She raised an eyebrow "New Orleans, I've got a king to bring into line."

"King? What king? America has no monarchies."

"Not for Humans but for Vampires they do."

Then she was gone in a flash of darkness and the car was pulling away. What a strange place he was in."

Hera stood outside the old mansion, cloaked in darkness as her instincts flared. Something huge awaited her here, more than the obese soldiers, more than just the Vampire king and his brethren or even the discovery of the Forsaken. There was something in this house, waiting for her, silently, unknowingly calling for her.

She glanced around the street crawling with Vampires. To the normal eye it looked just like a busy street that celebrated a lot of parties but she saw past all glamour and illusions. The Children of the Night had always placed too much faith in their own glamour, they had ever been arrogant. Semi-immortals who fed on the blood of the living to sustain their undead state. Most were strictly nocturnal though some could endure the twilight. It was midnight, every Vampire was in their element.

Despite the variations within their species all American Vampires paid homage to their local monarchs who sometimes in turn paid homage to more powerful state or regional monarchs. Currently most of the eastern states were ruled by King Valentine. Which was why she was standing outside this colonial mansion in New Orleans. On a flight of fancy he had moved his entire court to New Orleans after *An Interview with a Vampire* had been published. Which made sense for it had always had a very strong Vampiric influence throughout its entire history.

She dropped her cloaking darkness gradually as she stepped forward. To the Vampires around she walked out of darkness, coils of it lingering around her. She had always had a flare for the dramatics when it would work the most. Vampires were instinctual creatures, they responded to power. Those in power she found easy to mould with fear. By the time she got to King Valentine his dead heart would be racing faster than a cheetah.

It was time she started living up to her reputation.

She walked through the ornate silver gate, designed to ward off the Were, darkness spreading in every direction from her. Every single spell designed to confuse, scare and keep people out was obliterated. Within their lair the court suddenly lost all contact to the outside.

She felt every eye in the street and within the mansion turn on her with predatory intent. But she was not prey, she was the apex predator and they would learn that. The gates exploded around her and the Vampires went wild. They launched themselves at her from every direction, using every ability and skill at their disposal. She merely raised a hand and sent them all flying.

As she climbed the steps of the mansion she called fire to her arms, coiling it around her like playful pythons before surrounding her in concentric spinning circles. Fire was one of the few thing Vampires feared though that was not common knowledge. Fire was the element of transformation. Transformation for Vampires meant death. Then she summoned sunlight- the most feared thing by Vampires. With very few exceptions sunlight was utter death for Vampires. Using the sunlight she blasted a hole through the front door of the mansion, leaving a slightly smoking crater as the entrance to the building. She simply air walked over the crater, deeper into the mansion. More and more Vampires were pouring into the corridors.

Using her magic she probed the area and easily located King Valentine despite the layers of protective and illusion spells. She sealed him to his throne before he thought to leave. She didn't feel like a wild goose chase. She felt a thrill as she sensed his fear climbing. She threw more Vampires out of her way as she walked into a large room.

Vampires stood at every doorway, their teeth dripping with saliva, their eyes glowing red. These were the mortal converts, used as foot soldiers. They were wildly dangerous, usually beyond reason, controlled by instinct and the minds of those who had turned them. The others had started hanging back as soon as she had summoned sunlight.

She stopped in the middle of the room and raised her arms. Green fire bloomed out from under her in a perfect circle. There were many screams as an explosion shook the house. She had blasted straight down through several layers of the house and under tunnels straight down into the throne room. Slowly with great composure and grace she descended down through the hole.

As she did she summoned the night once again, forming living clothing that drifted and cocooned her, its smoky tendrils floating aimlessly around her. Looks were important in any setting, the darkness made her more ethereal and accentuated her pale skin. She had planned her entrance well.

The first King Valentine or his court saw of Hera was her descending in a halo of bright sunlight. Yet it became evidently clear she belonged just as much to the night, with darkness weaving its way all across her form. It literally clung to her like an affectionate pet. He was no fool, she was powerful beyond his understanding, more powerful than the combined court. That horrified him, it titillated him. Perhaps finally the tide was beginning to turn against the Angels.

Whoever and whatever she might be was becoming increasingly irrelevant. Most things did when you saw your own death coming towards you. What other reason did she have for storming the house? He spared a fleeting thought for his court. He genuinely loved some of them.

More Vampires threw themselves at her, to end up floating in the air constrained by her powers.

She stepped forward once she reached the ground, revealing beautifully long, pale legs. Strangely enough she was wearing no shoes. Even stranger were the scorch marks she was leaving behind as her footprints. They were glazed with gold. She came to a stop before him eying him up as her dress resettled itself. Black and gold peacock feathers branched out from behind one shoulder.

"Who are you?" he asked quite civilly, far more than he usually would. The balance of power was completely out of his favour though. He was more than anything else curious.

"I am the answer to your dreams, your most desperate desires." She certainly was beautiful like a Goddess of the Night. "Not quite Valentine, I am not only of the night" He started a little "Yes Valentine I can hear your thoughts and the thoughts of every mortal in this room." Her gaze swept the room, even taking in the couple of Succubi acting as ambassadors in his court.

He laughed "Mortals, most Vampires are immortal."

"Not like I am. Your kind can be killed by sunlight, fire, a stake through the heart, Phoenix tears and feathers or being taken into any of the Angels' places of worship."

"That might be so but we are stronger than most, they cannot force us into a place sacred to God against our will, we are too fast for them to catch and burn or stake and some of us can even walk in the sunlight with no harm. As for Phoenixes, well they are long extinct."

She smiled knowingly "Are they?" she raised a burning hand that quickly bloomed with fire. From the fire rose several birds, some looked like peacocks, others birds of paradise but they were all composed of living flame. Their eyes were the bright blue at the heart of any flame, their bodies were the reds, yellows and oranges that usually composed fire, but some of their decorative feathers were the bright greens, purples and other colours seen when chemicals were added to flames.

He did not seem overly impressed "Illusions do not undo the past"

She simply smiled indulgently. The Phoenixes spread their wings, flames fanning out, sparks rained down on the floor as each of them took flight with shrieks. Each of the Vampires shrunk back into the retreating shadows, their instincts reminding them what they had long forgotten. Even Valentine could not doubt their existence, its shriek brought such instinctual fear to him, the sparks burned his flesh.

"What is your point? Why are you here?"

"Ah I'm so glad you have asked young Valentine" She suddenly appeared at his shoulder, looking out across the throne room. Her voice rung out clear and commanding "The Age of Angels is at an end. Their tyrannical rule which has seen the slow and continual extinction of the magical races will be turned back. Heaven will burn. The Age of Gods will rise once again."

"Who are you to make such claims? The Angels have been unopposed since the War of Heaven. The Gods are lost and the Angels rule with an iron fist, eradicating all the Daemon races they can find." She reappeared dressed in her purple Grecian dress, a golden diadem and peacock feathers in her hair, she was about to speak when another voice answered.

"She is Hera the true Queen of Heaven, Goddess of Power."

A very ancient woman walked forward from the shadows. Her skin was paler than marble, her hair was just as faded in colour. She showed no other signs of Human aging, her skin was smooth, her muscles still toned but to a Vampire she looked ancient. There was a solidness to her features, a steady grace in all her movements. There was an air of great power about her. She could easily be a queen, she was the oldest Vampire in North America, was probably one of the oldest in the world. But she had no desire to rule, she had once had power beyond that of petty mortality.

Hera looked at her, her senses reeling at what she felt "Ariadne?"

She looked up, her once captivating eyes devoid of all colour. "I am honoured you remember me Hera, it has been so long since I have been in a temple of yours."

"It has been a long time since I was in a temple of mine. I fear they were all destroyed a long time ago by the Angels."

"You are wrong Goddess, one still stands and still has priestesses who light the flames of the Olympic Torch." She stepped forward and raised her hand to the Goddess's face, far over stepping the mark of any mortal. But Hera rewarded her. As soon as their skin connected

Ariadne changed. Her skin regained its once olive colour, her hair as black as night, her eyes became their once legendary midnight blue. She no longer looked like a Vampire, she wasn't one any longer.

Hera took her by the hand "Come we have much to discuss" and together the two old souls left the throne room. No one spoke until Hera released all her spells which unceremoniously dumped all the Vampires on the floor.

Hera studied Ariadne while she prepared tea for the both of them. It was remarkable to think that this minor demigoddess had survived. She returned with the tea and sat down. "It has been a very long time since a Goddess walked the Earth. How is it that you are here?"

"Do you remember the Goddess Brigid?"

"No but she was a Celtic Goddess from Ireland so adored by her followers that the Catholic Church had to make her a saint to try and convert them."

That surprised her, she hadn't known that. But that explained Brigid's wings. "You are well informed."

"I have spent my very long life researching each and every Goddess I can."

Hera nodded before continuing "She was freed by an Arch Angel, a very bizarre Arch Angel. Running for their lives she sought me out but could do nothing to free me from my imprisonment. I might be an immortal Goddess but I was closer to death than life. Life was but the faintest flicker in my soul. The same Angel freed me and healed me. Together we fled to Mount Olympus but were followed by the Angels. In the descent we were separated and I have been in America ever since trying to build up my followers...while once shy Brigid has claimed both India and Australia. Thankfully it has drawn attention away from me."

"We have been wondering about the international headlines, we had begun to hope. But we never thought one of the Gods would come to America."

"All the Native American Gods were slaughtered by the Angels, but that is what makes America safe to claim. The land cries out desperately for the Lifestream and someone who can wield it. The Angels have been busy watching Europe for me and Brigid while both of us set out for new lands. Neither of us could safely return. America is something new, and this as a new age. I love New York, the power there is intoxicating and once it is mine I will be as powerful as I was when I was patron of the Roman Empire. But this time I do not have to share or stand in Zeus' shadow." She accidently crushed the cup in her hand. She took a deep breath, she was free of her husband and would never have to submit to him again. The silver lining of the Angels' Rebellion.

"What about you Ariadne? How did you end up as a Vampire in America?"

"When Dionysus was killed and absorbed by the Angels his gift of Divinity was stripped from me. Fortunately because I bore him so many sons, and it was within my genetics I remained immortal but was stripped of all my Divine power. I was then unfortunately captured by Persians and sold as a concubine. Later I was shipped off for the Orient but on the way the caravan was attacked by young Vampires. Their efforts to eat me were met with great difficulty, so instead they took me to their king.

He decided I was too beautiful to be left as a mortal so he decided to turn me but things did not go at all as he expected. The infusion of semi-Divine blood, dilute to what I used to have, was enough to awaken some of my cells. That began my very slow return to what you see today. Because of my past I was not cursed as other Vampires, but I still became one. I can wear the signs of the Angels and walk in the sun.

Vampires visited from other covens and I drank their blood, gradually increasing my strength and the Divine memory of my cells. I gained all their strengths but none of their weaknesses.

In time I left and none could stop me. Since then I have lived in temples or palaces across the world learning and watching as the world burned under the Angels' Command. At some stages I even joined convents to elude their detection. Their brutality was horrendous to behold. Their desire to weed out all traces of the old religions was fanatical and ruthless. There was so much bloodshed, so much wasted life.

Have you heard of the Crusades? The Angels' religions attacking each other, but then that is the region. Between Eden and the Gates of Hell, it has never known peace except fleetingly. But the whole thing strengthened the power of the Angels so now they encourage bloodshed in the region.

But as time passed science and the desire for freedom eroded the religions' control over Humanity. As they forgot magic, they forgot the Angels. Now the Angels have nearly lost control and yet they seem even more desperate than previously to reassert their authority."

"Because now two Goddesses walk the Surface again. Heaven is weak, Michael and Gabriel still rule with an iron fist but the power the Angels once wielded is no longer there. They were stealing the powers from Michael's sister to supplement their own."

She shook her head in disgust "Michael had a sister?"

"Yes the very Arch Angel that set Brigid and myself free. Her name is Sariel and she was completely denied her powers. Told she had almost none."

"Where is she now?"

"She is in the Underworld, possibly in Hell and hopefully going to break the Curse binding Lucifer and the whole Underworld."

"You would wish to unleash more Arch Angels?"

"Fallen Arch Angels that will rise up against their traitorous brethren. Besides Lucifer was willing to make peace with the Gods, that was why he was punished. He has no love for Michael or Gabriel, they betrayed him completely.

"And if she does not succeed?"

"Then between us I feel confident that Brigid and I will gain enough followers to empower us enough to avenge our lost brethren." She turned her predatory gaze on Ariadne "Which is where you come in, you were once a priestess of mine, now I want you as my High Priestess."

She instinctively wanted to say no, but she was no fool. Those who said no to Hera died. Horribly. She remembered what had happened to Paris and Troy. "Of course my Goddess. I will do all that you ask.

Hera smiled "Excellent New York I believe is in need of the Mistress of the Labyrinth." Ariadne's eyes flashed in fear at her old title but it was a position of great power, especially if translated to the modern age. New York had a lot of underground tunnels.

For Hera it was all starting to fall together. For Ariadne it seemed as it had all suddenly fallen apart.

Gabriel sat on her throne, her face set in a permanent frown. The hunt for Brigid was not going well at all. The Legions, the Guards, even five of The Seven had scoured India and Bangladesh for any trace. Nuriel had her people encouraging the smallest trace of Brigid's magic to lead some clue. Angels walked along the banks of the Ganges, burning what temples they could. Infuriatingly some of them were protected from Angels. Some dark powers must have lent them protection.

Michael was now preoccupied in Pakistan stirring up a civil war and inciting Muslim hatred for Hindus. If all went according to plan he would ride the war machine that would scour across India and Bangladesh finally wiping the subcontinent clean of a religion they had never succeeded in removing.

Brigid had pushed their hand, now all her followers would pay, as would both countries.

Thankfully Michael's reports were increasingly positive. Pakistan was becoming ever closer to becoming an absolute Muslim stronghold. Religious tensions were coming to the fore and the military coup was within the near future. Yes it was time the world was reminded of the Arch Angels' wrath and might. With such a strong presence in Pakistan it would make it far more difficult for Brigid to gain followers in the region.

It was infuriating that they hadn't found Brigid but at least she was showing herself. She had balls, balls of steel as men would say. Hera was the one she would have expected to have already reignited the War of Heaven but she was hiding. Uriel and Raphael had scoured Europe, especially any country that had once belonged to Rome or Greece. But she wasn't foolish enough to return. Her remaining active temple was under constant watch by Elders. That should have been burned down long ago but the Olympic Games were important for the sharing of culture and religions. Though in latter decades it did not seem to spread religion, but hinder it.

Indeed much had not been as it should have been in latter years. Their control of Humanity had been lax, many had slipped the lead and now they were dealing with the consequences. The world had also fallen into ever greater ruin and chaos. Keeping an eye on Sariel had become increasingly more time consuming, the damn girl was having her rebellious stage at the worst time. Add to that her powers had been flaring wildly. While they had been glad for the power it had actually corroded through her confinement spells, only adding to her erratic behaviour.

The Council too had started becoming rebellious. Now that the two Goddesses were on the loose, one of them actively claiming land, total power had been returned to the Seven. Well six, Sariel was still missing. It was becoming increasingly evident that they would need to choose another Arch Angel to replace her. Not that she would mention that to Michael. He was still desperately searching for her. Nothing had been found.

The balance was being returned finally in their favour. They had lost Sariel and her powers but they didn't have to keep an eye on her. The Arch Angels were free to once again incite Humanity. Ariel was smart enough to stand with her cousin, it was where she got her leniency from. Raphael was kept manageable by his friendship with Michael, and Uriel was also one to fall in line behind them.

Azrael, well he did as he always did. His own thing. He kept to himself and his Reapers. Performing a necessary task that took up most of his time. He never spoke out against any of the Arch Angels unless something way out of line happened. He was the silent presence of the Seven. And she liked it like that.

She was busy analysing maps and reports when one of the Ascended Council members came running in.

"Arch Angel Gabriel" he came to a panting stop before her. She hid her sneer, real Angels didn't tire easily. They were the children of Gods not pathetic mortals raised above their station. Only the Elders had any true right in calling themselves Angels. The rest were merely servant spirits given flesh again.

"What is it?" she snapped. She had no patience and was horribly busy trying to find a pattern for either of the Goddesses actions. Brigid's pile was huge, her actions clear. Hera worried her, there was very little trace of her at all. A few spells across America. Not a comprehensive picture at all.

"It is Brigid! She has just claimed Australia, Papua New Guinea and New Zealand."

"WHAT!" she screamed. The whole palace shook violently with her rage. All over Heaven Angels turned to face the palace as they tried to maintain their balance. Thick, dense thunder clouds instantly formed around the palace.

"How the Hell did she claim Australia?"

He fell to his knees cowering in fear and pain as her voice lanced through his mind "She claimed the River Murray as she claimed the Ganges. Exactly the same as last time, massive flooding but no loss of life."

She lashed out at her throne, smashing the top right off. It flew into the wall and exploded in a shower of marble shards. They crackled under her boots as she paced back and forth "it would seem I have misjudged you Brigid. You really do have more balls than most men. Hmm if we can capture her before she shakes off the Angelic ties then this could be advantageous." She stopped and turned back to face the Angel "You said New Zealand as well, what major river is there for that country?"

"None, she claimed it by default when she claimed Australia."

What was happening to the world? "How is that possible? They are two separate countries."

"Lord Raphael said that New Zealand was once under the authority of the colony of New South Wales and the two countries enjoy various partnerships across a great many areas. He also said to pass on that Papua New Guinea had once belonged to Australia."

She ground her teeth, Humans were more hassle than they were worth. It was the same unity and divisions that had allowed Brigid to in essence claim India, Pakistan and Bangladesh. What did she do, study countries that had belonged to each other? She was far cannier than had been imagined.

"I want a list made of every country that might as well be part of another, we cannot have this occurring again. You will bring me this list"

He nodded before running out, red-silver blood pouring out of his ears.

Dear God what if she claimed the Roman Empire? That would give her most of Europe. Or the Mongol Empire, that would pretty much give her Asia. There were just so many empires to think about, Humans had changed their borders as often as their clothing. And some of those empires had been huge and far reaching. What if she claimed any of the Colonial Empires; the Spanish, Portuguese, Dutch, French or Heaven forbid the British. What if she claimed China, it was ancient, large and hugely populated.

No that was not the way to think about it. That would only lead to panic.

She angrily flicked her hand sending a summons for Ariel. She paced impatiently, crumbling the marbles shards to powder as she sent a probe for Uriel.

Uriel

She felt his startled fear *yes Gabriel*

I want security all around Europe increased. I don't care how, use as many people as you need. Brigid is on a claiming frenzy, the last thing we need is her gaining access to all the Empires Europe birthed.

Sudden understanding dawned on him, she cut him off before his panic spread.

"You summoned me cousin?"

Gabriel spun to look at her cousin, she was dressed ready in battle gear but that wasn't new she was always dressed in battle gear. Actually with the exception of Sariel and Azrael all of them were always dressed in armour.

Ariel's name suited her, she really was the fire of the Gods, she was the second most feared female in all of Heaven. After herself of course, easily explained by their similar lineage. Her own father, as loath as she was to think of him, had been from a very powerful family, Ariel's father had also been from a powerful family. And while Horus was more impressive than her own father, it was the comparison of the previous generation that really set the difference. Actually both of their paternal pedigrees were impressive, but her own grandmother was the more impressive of the four grandparents. Gabriel was a throwback to her paternal grandmother.

As for their shared maternal bloodlines, they too showed a remarkable pedigree. Both their mothers had been sired by Hermes, who had been sired by Zeus. Funny how often his name turned up in genealogies. She supposed the Angel Race owed him thanks for giving them their numbers and power. Yes he was an interesting family member to have.

"Yes Ariel I have a special task for you, which will require all your cunning and rage."

She smiled at that, it was Gabriel's way of letting her use any means necessary "What has happened Gabriel?"

"Brigid has claimed Australia and New Zealand

and potentially a third country."

"How did the bitch manage that?"

"A quirk in history, seems we have to be far more careful of old colonies and empires. She has pulled the same trick she did in the Ganges. I want you to scour both countries for her, take your Inquisitors, do as you must. Do what you need to draw her out of hiding. She will come to her worshipper aid."

"What measure do I use for her followers?"

Gabriel fixed her with cold calculating eyes "Whatever means necessary, their loss is of no consequence. They chose their allegiance now they can pay for it."

Ariel smiled savagely and gave her a smart salute. She turned on her heel and was nearly out of the throne room when Gabriel called out "And keep an eye out for Sariel."

"I will search for any trace of her" She marched out of the hall, and through the corridors. This was an unexpected turn of events, she was even getting a longer leash than usual. Things were going to burn.

Gabriel turned her mind back to Sariel, where ever could she be? What exactly had happened to her? She wondered if she missed the girl. She wasn't sure how to classify or read her emotions. What was left to feel when you had effectively killed your own parents, destroyed your family and cursed your own brother to madness in Hell? Then encouraged your husband to strip his sister of her powers. She certainly didn't have the usual measuring stick to compare her emotions to.

She vaguely wondered how Lucifer was doing, she should visit Purgatory and view his crater when she got the time.

But first they had to capture two missing Goddesses. Ariel was on the hunt, Nuriel was on the search, the Legions of Heaven were scouring, her own Seraphim were tracing. It could only be a matter of time. Couldn't it?

Chapter 22

When Sariel first entered the dining room she started in surprise. A Lesser Angel stood next to Nyx, then she turned around and Sariel realised she was no Angel. She was clearly a Goddess from the nexus of light around her. She had long white wings, they reminded Sariel of herons or ibis, very dark olive skin, long flowing black hair and shining eyes heavily edged in kohl. She wore a simple golden crown and a style of dress she had not seen before, it looked like a linen wrap with straps at the shoulder. It was plain white but embroidered in gold. Gold bangles graced her wrists and ankles while she was barefoot. Apparently a common trend among the Gods.

"Isis this is Sariel, my great-granddaughter." She indicated Sariel "Sariel this is my dear old friend and pseudo-cousin Isis. She is the eldest of the remaining Egyptian pantheon." Sariel nodded gracefully to her while Isis studied her acutely.

"She does hold more than a trace of Chaos, it is easy to see Nyx." She stepped forward and took Sariel's face in her hands "You look a lot like your mother, but with the darkness of your father."

"You knew my parents?"

"Everyone knew your parents, living lives like that draws attention."

She noticed Sariel's blank face and realised she had no idea what she was talking about "I knew your father when he was young, he worked for many Death Gods and Goddesses. He probably has one of the most thorough understandings of death among the Divine. He was the obvious choice to make the Angel of Death, of course back when it was a specific task not a common title. He stayed with my husband and I for several decades when he was your age before moving onto other Underworlds. But it was in Aaru that he met your mother.

He was enchanted by her the first time he saw her. Understandable considering the powers she wielded and her looks. She was beautiful with sun kissed olive skin, flowing golden hair with coppery highlights, whenever the sun caught it, it looked like her hair was living flame. She held an exotic beauty for him, being of the skies and brightness, but she was serving Inanna when she descended to the Underworld in her idiotic quest. When her mistress was killed Lilith stayed with Erishkigal for a time to appease her before joining us. She was an amazing woman, bright, shrewd and willing to learn anything. It was what got her into the Angels' plans. Her wide range of abilities were useful for stabilising and hiding Eden once they took over. Nephilim powers are erratic making it hard to hide but her abilities allowed Eden to remain undetected as they bred more Nephilim. She married Adam, for reasons unknown, perhaps to have some semblance of normality. Either way it ended when she was expected to be subservient, she fell straight into the arms of Samael.

Many things happened, your brother was born and much later you were, but they had parted ways before the end of the War, though I do not know why. By that stage she had abandoned Heaven, living as a powerful Demoness in her own right and proud of it, while he was still a powerful Arch Angel. The last I heard before the Fall was that she was in the Underworld.

She glided over to sit next to Nyx "it would seem that you have inherited the full range of both your parents' powers. Unusual but not uncommon, I wonder if your brother did as well. It is strange to think your mother was a child of Heaven and the sky, and both of them were Arch Angels yet now both of them belong to Hell."

"You know where my father is?"

"Of course everyone does. He is in the Beast's Crater. The Curse of the Fall changed him from an Arch Angel into a Greater Demon. I think you will find Hell and the Underworld contain more family surprises for you. You found in the realm of Hades your father's family but there are more. Indeed there are a great many Demons your mother has birthed or your father has sired. The Lilin can trace their bloodline back to her as one of the first Succubi, though their bloodlines have been strengthened by others they still call her Mother. They took their name from hers. Some of the Vampires also call her Mother, among other Daemon races. Indeed she is sometimes referred to as the Mother of all Evil or the Mother of Demons."

"My parents are evil?" she was horrified.

"Sariel my dear you are far too old to hold onto the archaic belief of good and evil. That has been over simplified by your Angelic upbringing. Evil is a Human conception, Gods and the other Divine are not good and evil, they act according to their natures. Humans have made them good or evil. We so often forget for all our grandeur and powers that we are but animals, Divine, evolved and empowered yes but still essentially animals and especially citizens of the planet.

To some your parents could be classed as evil, specifically by the Angelic classification but to others they are not. Your mother in her younger days represented fertility and was a minor Mother Goddess. To the Lilin and Vampires she is not evil, but the first of their kind. They are not inherently evil, they have as much choice as the rest of us. What they eat might class them as evil, but does that make a leech or mosquito evil? No it doesn't because it is what they evolved for, it is simply animal instinct and we do not assign evil to basic instincts in animals.

You never knew your parents so you question everything about them. They were diverse, powerful and intelligent Demigods who grew disillusioned with the old structure and successfully brought in a new. But then they realised it was no better. Your parents have committed crimes no worse than any other God and they have done great good as well. You are both Heaven and Hell, life and death, light and darkness. You have inherited a huge range of opposing powers, you can easily be good or evil, but you have the choice and your actions will speak louder than words.

Just remember that as a Divine your understanding of good and evil will be vastly different from a Human's which is what you are judging them by."

Nyx laughed gently "Isis my dear you have turned into a philosopher in the time we've been apart."

"I have watched many I love die, I have watched the empire I built be conquered and converted and my powers fade. I have had a long time to reflect trapped within the Underworld, yet my powers are strong again. In part due to whatever you did and the touch of Gaia's power but also because my name is invoked again. We are on the brink of change."

"Tell me why did you come Isis?"

"You disturbed my slumbers and I was curious as to what had stimulated the remaining Primordial Gods to cast out such darkness. My pantheon remains asleep" she laughed bitterly "our once great pantheon sleeps in rotted clothing on dusty thrones." She pointed to Sariel "I must admit I was more than surprised to find the source of all the strange occurrences to be the result of an Arch

Angel."

"Oh I'm not really an Arch Angel"

"My dear the fact you had your powers stolen does not change the fact you were crowned as an Arch Angel. Your brother is an Arch Angel, you parents technically still are. You are far more powerful than any simple Elder." She studied Sariel "if you don't believe me there is a simple solution, walk among the Humans and see how they respond to you. Without even trying they will fall at your feet."

"I have never met any living Humans, only the Lesser Angels and the Shades."

"Then it is well overdue that you did. You have never been to the Surface have you?"

"No I was never allowed."

Pity crept into Isis' eyes "You have missed out on the most important aspect of any Divine being's existence, the interaction with mortality."

Oh how she wanted to see Humans and the other mortals, to walk among them and learn what her purpose in life was. "I do want to, I have wanted to ever since I was a child."

"Then it is long overdue that you did."

"It is far too dangerous for her." Nyx said calmly, now was the delicate game to convince her to want to go on her accord. She needed her own drive is she was to succeed.

"Dangerous? How can it be dangerous? I am an Arch Angel/Demigoddess. I have spent the last several months honing my skills and powers. How could it be dangerous?"

"Because the only way to the Surface is through Hell."

"I thought there were many entrances to the Underworld?"

"There are but because of Michael and Gabriel's Curse they are sealed shut. The only entrance that acts as an exit is in Hell, above Lucifer's Crater. The Angels do keep a casual eye on it though, but have been increasingly lax in later centuries."

"Why has it lessened?"

"The Greater Demons no longer terrorise the earth as they once used to, the spells that contain them have warped them in suffering and madness."

"So I would have to venture through Hell to reach the Surface."

"You would and by yourself, we cannot enter another's domain without their permission and Lucifer is incapable of allowing us."

"They why can I enter?"

"Because you were not here when the realms were sealed down here. Out of respect we have always asked permission to enter another's realm, but you are not a Goddess of the Underworld, so you have the freedom to pass into other realms." She glided over to Sariel "we will not stop you if you wish to go, it is important that you do go. We all have powers over mortals and we should understand them before we start using that power. However you must understand that we will be unable to help you. Think of it as an ordeal that mortals do to make themselves men or women. Once you complete it you will have great ease moving between the Surface and the Underworld."

Isis and Nyx watched her as she thought over all they had said to her. She had never had the option to choose, it had always been denied to her. She loved it here but she wanted to see more, she wanted desperately to see the Surface. And her family was allowing her, giving her an ordeal to prove herself.

"I want to do it. I want to go to the Surface. I want

to understand mortals and I also want to see if I can find Hera and Brigid."

"Oh I wouldn't worry about Hera, a more resourceful woman I never did meet." Isis said over her goblet "if they want to find you they will, otherwise they will be hiding their trails from the Angels.

"Nevertheless I would like to see the Surface and do something on my own for once."

They both nodded to her "it is settled then, you will leave for the Surface and when you come back you will be a true demigoddess. When will you leave?"

"Tomorrow"

That stunned them both, they had expected her to wait. She was clearly far more determined than either of them had thought. Nyx stood up in one elegant movement "then we shall have a sending off party for you tonight."

And just like that she was back to the wide eyed girl they had all come to love "A party? For me? I've never had a party." Then she rushed out of the hall and bowled into Cerberus. Nyx smiled as she heard Sariel gushing to Cerberus that she was getting a party.

"She really is still a child" Isis observed.

"She is a child in terms of Gods and Angels. She has also been so secluded for most of her life, she is more a child than anyone her age. It shows in her physicality. Add to that all the lies and half-truths she has been spoon fed and she has an innocence and naivety never seen in an immortal."

"Do you think she will manage?"

"She better or Hell will feel my wrath. I don't care how powerful the spells holding Hell are, if she dies down there I will rip it open and kill all the Demons myself."

"I don't think she will die, she is extraordinarily

strong, if she were far older I would say she was a Primordial Goddess. She won't die Nyx, but will she break the Curse?"

"I hope so, I'm fed up living down here. I want to embrace the true night. I want my sister to awaken. I want to feel mortals and the strength they give."

"Don't we all"

They both looked up, lost in their memories of when they had been patrons of tribes and empires. When mortals had given them strength and their numbers had been vast.

The Lampades had done a thorough job of her again, Sariel thought as she looked at her reflection. She had been clothed in an elegantly flowing violet dress of a design unfamiliar to her, it left her creamy shoulders bare before flowing down and out into a small train. The colour complimented her violet eyes and the black of her wings and hair, which had been pulled into draping curls. She smiled at herself, she liked what she saw, a happy young woman. Her face had changed in her time in Hades, she looked noticeably older. Yes she was starting to look like a woman, her cleavage now testified to that.

Her vanity done and satisfied she opened the door to find Cerberus waiting for her. Delighted she dropped down to hug him. They had developed quite a close relationship in her time here. Cerberus was not alone in his fascination and attraction to her bright innocence. She was a flame that called to them all. He led her thought the various corridors to the throne room, it was the biggest hall in the castle. She was excited and a little bit nervous as the doors opened before her.

The sight that greeted her astounded her. Purple streamers hung from the high ceiling and from the numerous arches, little violet globes floated around the room providing little pools of light. Jasmine, roses and lavenders sat in large black pots, their scents filling the air. She breathed in deeply smiling. Little fairy lights of various colours skittered around the room, while all the windows had been attuned to Earth. Real cities sparkling away in the night, streams of smoke and vehicles moving during the day. She was awed but didn't have the time to reflect on them, her attention was taken by her family standing prominent in the crowd of Lampades, Harpies and Shades.

Nyx was radiant in a figure hugging black dress, her brothers had donned black togas. Hades wore a black robe accentuated with bronze. Persephone wore a long grey dress, it hinted at other colours that had faded and was decorated in a variety of pale pearls. Demeter was dressed in a darker version of her daughter's dress. Hecate had gone for simplicity, a black and grey dress with a long split up to her thigh. Even the Furies had given up their standard red tunics to be dressed in black tunics that somehow looked feminine. Nemesis was the real surprise, stunningly beautiful in a black dress accentuated with white. She looked nothing like a warrior but Sariel was not fooled. Thanatos and Hypnos wore black togas akin to their father.

It seemed of all the Gods only Isis did not wear black or grey, dressed in a different version of her Egyptian wrap, heavily decorated in gold.

Everyone in the room was barefoot in honour of Gaia who could not join them.

Nyx was the first to speak "Sariel my dear you look absolutely stunning."

"Thank you" she gushed, trying to hide her desire to blush. She was used to attention for having no magic, but she had never realised that it might have also been because of her looks. She had never realised that she was beautiful. All it had taken was time with a loving family.

Hades stepped forward, because it was his realm he held the right to speak first "Sariel my dear, it is with sorrow we anticipate your departure in the morning but with the best wishes we wish you well in your ordeal. You will always have a home here and will always be welcome but we do not wish to hold you back. Fly free and high, but before you do we have parting gifts for you."

"Oh you didn't half to"

"We do Sariel honour and blood demands it. We cannot send you into Hell unprepared." Ironic that that was what they had initially intended.

Persephone walked forward with a mahogany box "For you Sariel, so that the whole world knows who you are."

Sariel lifted up the lid and gasped. Sitting on black velvet was an ornate circlet made of gold and silver, with a black metal intertwining them both. It made her think of the rising or setting sun."

"Silver and gold compliment your hair, the gold is for your affinity to the sun and the silver your affinity to the moon. Nyxite shows that you are descended from Nyx. Only those of her blood or blessed by her may wear the metal." Persephone explained as Hades lifted the circlet and placed it on her brow. Cold rushed through her before disappearing.

Then Nemesis and the Furies stepped forward, the three of them were carrying black sheaths. Nemesis smiled at her "no warrior should be without her own weapon. It was a difficult task to choose for you, despite my gripes you were an excellent student and you were proficient with many weapons." She turned to the Furies, two of which handed her sheathed swords. "These are katanas, typically two handed for mortals but our superior strength allows us to wield them one handed. You excelled using two and this is our gift to you."

Sariel accepted the swords with reverence before pulling them out of their sheaths. One was black, Nyxite, with silver guard and handle. The other was white, platinum, with gold guard and handle "You could say they are day and night. They will negate all the natural shields given to the denizens of the day and night. You will not be disadvantaged in a fight." The third Fury handed her two small sheaths, each containing a dagger matching the swords. "You never know when you will need a dagger."

They stepped back as Isis and Hecate stepped forward, they held between them a belt of black leather. It was decorated with silver and gold around panels of black opal. "Every warrior needs a belt for their blades, but any sorceress needs a store of extra magic. We are Divine and do not need such things, but we have imbued it with the strongest protection spells we know. And black opals represent Chaos, who has marked you as its conduit."

Silently Sariel put it on and attached her sheaths. The opals began to glow softly with a dark fire.

Next were Nyx and her brothers. Sariel was expecting something marking the night or darkness, she was very surprised when instead they gave her a green bracelet. "Because Gaia has marked you" They slid it onto her wrist, where it started to wriggle and warp. She watched in fascination as it grew into a vine that wound its way up her forearm.

Lastly Thanatos and Hypnos stepped forward but instead of offering any gifts they dropped to their knees and grabbed one of her ankles each. It felt like fire was racing up her legs. It was over in seconds.

"We have given you the same gift we gave your father. You will not be weakened by the presence of the dead and they will head your call. You will stay easily beyond the call of death, and death's powers will not easily touch you."

"Thank you" she said solemnly, it was a huge gift to be bestowed upon anyone. Even more so because it was a connection to her father.

She had no idea how many times in the future she would have cause to thank them.

She turned when she heard movement behind her, it was Charon and Cerberus. In his skeletal hands he held a wooden box. It was simple pine, seemingly so bright in the room when everything else was in the dark end of the colour spectrum. She looked up and was surprised to see that he had eyes today. Usually he was little more than bones but today he had piercing blue-grey eyes that seemed to catch the smallest amount of light. She had never seen him with eyes before, they were beautiful and belied his emotions.

"Everyone else has given gifts of practicality but Cerberus and I searched but could not find anything else that would aid you. Our gift to you is purely aesthetic." With one elegant movement of his fingers he lifted the lid of the box to reveal a necklace lying on violet silk. It looked vaguely of Celtic design; gold, silver, Nyxite, platinum and copper twisting around each other. The light caught on the metals in different ways and directed the eyes down to the jewels. They were set in long rectangles or triangles, overall it looked like a rising sun, just upside down. They were mostly black opals, cut to catch the dark fires within, but there were also smaller shards of diamond. She also noticed that there were strange reflections, but she couldn't pick the source.

"It is beautiful" she gasped, staring at it in awe.

Charon carefully picked it up and put it on her, his touch was so light she only felt the necklace. At first it was freezing cold against her skin, she thought it was going to brand her, but it quickly warmed. She idly thought it felt like it was waking up.

She turned to face the nearest window, it instantly changed into a mirror. She gasped when she saw herself. She was stunning. She stood there in a beautiful violet dress with her black opal belt holding her weapons. Her hair seemed to almost blend into her wings. Black marks entwined around her ankles, shifting slightly just as her Gaia bracelet did. Her circlet sparkled brightly, as for her necklace it drew the most attention, reflecting light and shadows across her skin. She looked out of a fairy-tale, a warrior princess, an avenging Angel, a heroine, a demigoddess. She looked complete.

Her violet eyes started to water, then she started crying. Hecate was next to her in an instant "Sariel whatever is the matter?"

She sniffed and wiped away her tears "nothing, I'm just so happy. These are the only gifts I have ever gotten, I never even got birthday presents, it was below an Arch Angel. You have all put so much effort into them all. They are so beautiful and thoughtful. All my life I've dreamed of a true family to belong to and now I have it. You are all so much better than I dreamed. And you're letting me go to the Surface under my own steam. A journey you have all worked so hard to prepare me for. I don't know how I can ever thank you all for it."

The Gods shifted uneasily, casting their eyes at the ground or each other. None of their actions were as selfless as she believed, their gifts were a means to alleviate their guilt. Something many of them had never felt before. Guilt was primarily a Human emotion that rarely affected the Divine.

Surprising everyone it was Nemesis who spoke first "we believe in you Sariel and we believe in what you are capable of, far more than you believe. Michael and Gabriel may have clipped your wings, extremely, but you are meant to soar. Life is dangerous, we all know it well. And make no mistake Hell is no playground, right now Hell is the most dangerous place in the world. But you are not some weak mortal and if they can make their way through the various Underworlds then surely you can. It will be dangerous, your life will be at risk but there is nothing to be gained in keeping you under lock and key."

Sariel raised her eyes to Nemesis, smiled and then hugged her. Nemesis stood there stunned before awkwardly patting her shoulder. Sariel just laughed, stood back and gently punched her in the shoulders. With raised eyebrows and a smile she asked "better"

The others laughed at her dismay. It had been a very long time since they had a ray of sunshine in the Underworld, and Sariel was the brightest there had ever been. She lit up the whole room with her bright, inquisitive nature and her naivety always brought a smile.

Thanatos watched as she made the ever stoic Nemesis laugh, something the rest of them could rarely do. In their long imprisonment in the Underground they had faded, the vibrancy that the Surface and Heaven had imbued them with had long since disappeared. Sariel was the very essence of vitality. She was so unlike anyone else in his family, she lacked calculation. Gods and their progeny had it by nature, it was almost instinctual. His son had received it by the bucket loads, and Michael was cut from the same cloth but not Sariel. Everything she did was impulsive, selfless or for the sake of it. She did things the rest of them had never considered, simply to see if it could be done. Her laughter was like music through the ancient empty halls of the castle.

He belatedly realised everyone was looking at him "what is it?"

"You have to make a speech" Nemesis said with glee, calculation plain in her eyes.

"Why do I have to make a speech?"

"Because you are her closest blood relative." Hades responded, he looked thankful more than anything, probably because he didn't have to make another speech.

He sighed. Then he turned to Sariel who watched him with innocent eyes and a slight smile "In the morning one of our own leaves to prove herself, on an ordeal of adulthood and Godhood. The path will be long and difficult but I truly believe that nothing will get in your way. I have only known you a short time granddaughter but you are the most amazing person I have ever met. You are like pure sunshine in this realm, you brighten our days and remind us to live. You make us believe and hope, you make us smile and laugh. You try our patience, you pull our heart strings, you make us feel again. You are like a tonic. To you Sariel." He raised his goblet and the others followed suit cheering. She ran forward and hugged him beaming widely. He hugged her back, breathing in her scent and feeling her warmth. She was vibrancy encased in skin.

Her attention was caught by fireworks in one of the cityscapes and she darted off to gasp in delight, while Hypnos explained the modern world from what he had learned in dreams. She was very quickly laughing and gasping in awe at his stories.

"That was a beautiful speech" Hades came to stand next to him.

"It was heartfelt."

"We've all changed so much in the time she has

been with us. When was the last time a phrase such as heartfelt left our lips? When did we start feeling guilt for using one of our own? Who would have ever thought it possible that one day we would call an Angel family again, and not just an Angel, an Arch Angel?" He sighed heavily, his years were like a burden these days "I feel guilt for sending her off to solve our problems, I feel we should tell her why we are allowing her to venture into Hell but then I fear she won't break the Curse."

"How do you think I feel? I'm allowing my granddaughter to be used by all of us."

"Is that not what we have always done? We are Gods it is what we do?

"But before we never cared or felt guilt. But now..." he trailed off looking at Sariel as she pulled Charon into a dance. Her laughter was melodious, her joy infectious. She pulled him around and around, his robes swishing faster than they probably ever had before, his feet slapping the ground with a rattle of bones. And while he looked exasperated and awkward he was smiling. Even Nemesis was smiling widely, even when she too was pulled into the dance. She was more graceful than Charon.

Part 2

Descent into Hell

Chapter 23

She was nervous, but very excited. Today was the day she ventured into Hell. She should be frightened, she should be wary. She knew the stories of the Demons, they were the Fallen Angels and Monsters from the Age of Gods. She remembered Michael and Gabriel having to fight Greater Demons when she was younger, they had somehow escaped from Hell. She had also been attacked by a Demon in the borderlands of Hell, and he had been but a minor Demon. There was far worse within the depths of Hell, but she just had to avoid them before she could sneak out the top of Lucifer's Crater.

She was brought back to reality when Charon extended his skeletal hand to help her in to his ferry. Hades had insisted on helping her as much as possible. Charon was ferrying her through the rivers Styx and Acheron, which bordered Hell. She had been surprised to learn that he ferried souls into both Hades and Hell. Apparently mortals had not given up their notions of the world despite the spread of the Angels' religions. As such many of their old beliefs had merely been incorporated. Hecate had taken the imagery of witches and Demons, much like Lilith. They were well remembered but changed. Charon had merely had his job updated while Hades was half remembered as ruling the Underworld. The rest of them had been forgotten, becoming myths of the past or in Hypnos and Nemesis' case simply words. The only one of them who had maintained their power was Gaia, she is more commonly called Mother Nature these days but her various names were thrown around commonly.

Charon's ferry was surprisingly large. From the references to him she read in Heaven's library she had expected a simple row boat. This was a fair sized vessel as far as she could tell, not that she had any experience what so ever. It was several metres long which easily accommodated herself, Hecate and Isis, plus their wings. It was an age darkened ship, smoke and water had stained the outside of the boat. The inside was clean and neat, though Spartan. There were a couple of wooden benches. They were the only decorations.

He caught her looking at his boat "sorry, I keep it sparse for the souls. They only damage finery in their denial." He waved his hand and the whole vessel started to change. The ship revitalised itself, age peeling away as gilt spread along the pristine wood. Cushions bloomed along the benches which themselves became sturdier. Where had sat an aged and weather beaten boat, now sat a beautiful example of fine workmanship. She smiled at Charon as she settled onto the silk cushion "thank you".

Instead of the skeleton she was used to stood a youth, with not a hair on his face. He was almost Angelic in beauty, delicate features and slim limbs. His hair was jet black, his eyes were a startling blue-grey that flashed in the slightest light, his finger nails were black, his skin a shadowy grey. In this form it was very easy to see that Nyx was his mother. He smiled at her, flashing very long canines "this is the form I assume when ferrying Gods, Demigods and heroes. My form changes on what task I have."

"Like us all he is subject to mortal belief. Their perceptions become facets through which our powers are filtered." Hecate assisted Isis into the boat and they settled gracefully. Sariel wondered how they both managed to so casually be graceful and seductive in their every movement.

"So if mortals were to believe that I had golden hair then I could change my hair to gold."

"You can do that anyway, it is more along the lines of if Christians believed you had golden hair then it would automatically change to gold when you entered a church. The perception of Gabriel is that she is a man, so she and the other Arch Angels appear to mortals as shining warriors from above. If you had met mortals with your fellow Arch Angels you would have appeared the same.

I on the other hand have become a shadow of the night, something to be feared. I have become associated with Demons and witchcraft, one of my forms is Demonic. Just like Charon. The closer we get to Hell the more Demonic we will appear. Perception is the one thing Gods are powerless to fight against. We can control mortal perception but it can easily run away from our control."

"But you appeared now as when I first met you."

"That was at the edge of the Borderlands, we will take you almost to the edge of Limbo."

"Don't worry while these two turn into Demons I will remain the same" Isis smirked.

"She was forgotten, or not considered a threat. Either way the Angels and their religions did not slur her name like they did ours."

"Is that a good or a bad thing?" Sariel asked.

"Definitely good" Isis said at the same time Hecate said "Horribly bad"

Sariel laughed as they glared at each other.

"Only time will tell whether it is good or bad" Charon added absently.

A long wooden pole materialised within his hands and with obvious ease he pushed it into the water and the boat started to move forward. Sariel cast a final glance back at the entrance to Hades, and waved when she saw Cerberus in his giant form watching them leave.

She glanced about taking the time to actually look at the Underworld now that she wasn't being chased by Cerberus. It held a strange quality, eerily beautiful in its own way with the sense of danger pervading everything. The River Styx was different to what she remembered, it was far wider and while there were still plumes of fire they were nowhere near as numerous. The river was completely dark beneath the boat, not even the flames were reflected in the water.

"This is different from the last time I was here"

Charon glanced back at her "The Underworld is not like Heaven. It is not stationary but always dynamic and changing. It is unpredictable. The rivers that flow through here follow set paths and as though to make up for that one piece of order they are forever changing. Their width and speed change all the time, the only certainty is that the dead cannot cross the waters without being drawn in and the living are stripped of their lives. Even the Divine."

"What about Achilles?"

"He was the son of a Nymph, they are kin to Angels semi-Divine by nature with the potential to Ascend to being Gods. She was also unique in her genetic powers. That same blood ran in his veins, so the waters reacted differently for him. The Styx is alive, which people forget, it has its own alien intelligence, which is why strange miracles and oddities occur."

They passed out of the wide cavern into the smaller tunnel she remembered "So when I was last here it was trying to contain me, which was why everything was so violent?"

"Yes that is exactly it."

"Does that mean that the waterfall will not be there

this time?"

"It is always there, for that is the end of the Styx. The borders of the rivers are always dramatic because it is essentially where two entities are blending into each other. At the bottom of the falls is the Acheron which will take us into Hell. It surrounds Hades on all other sides and it is also the water source for Hades."

"I thought there was only one entrance to Hades."

"There is, with the exception of Hell, the Underworld realms have only one entrance in the form of a gate. It makes it easier to direct and contain the dead. But the rivers themselves are not stopped by such boundaries. Hell is the one exception, it is where all the rivers of the Underworld congregate. The Acheron has grown very powerful fed by all the other rivers. When Lucifer and his Angels fell from Heaven they created a massive crater. The spells that Gabriel and Michael cast reshaped the dynamics of Hell. It is the focal point of power in the Underworld.

Now the dead can enter Hell from any direction. All the rivers feed into the Acheron which encircles all of Hell before feeding through Limbo and falling into the crater. I ferry some of the dead to those shores, most though are caught in the current and swept straight over the waters into Hell."

"What happens to them in the crater?"

"We have little understanding except that it is a place of torment some of us are pulled in and out of. Their memories are broken and fragmented though, but we do know it is a terrifying place."

There was something ominous in that warning and she sharpened her gaze at him.

"Some of us venture through the Borderlands and as such we do have some understanding of the Demons but we know little about the Greater Demons. But none of us can truly venture in. We have no understanding of Lucifer since the Fall. The only person I can think of who may actually know is your mother. Because of her nature she can traverse all boundaries of Heaven and Hell."

"I wouldn't even know what she looks like."

"I have no idea what she looks like now, the centuries would not have left her unchanged. The Human perception of her has changed dramatically and the Lilin and Vampire beliefs will have only strengthened her Demonic side."

"It is so great to know that both my parents are Demons"

"It is not the Demons that you should worry most about but the spells. The very nature of things have been changed with those spell, nothing will be as it seems."

She was about to ask him more when they shot out of the tunnel and the roar of a waterfall eclipsed all other sounds. This time the waterfall was wide, curving around as far as the gloom permitted her to see. But her attention was immediately directed to the empty void in front of her. Within the gloom she could see the pillar she had slept on.

She was on the verge of screaming but Charon simply waved his hand as the boat shot out into the air. She grabbed the edge of the boat and peered over the edge to see the boat was slowly gliding downwards. She was enchanted by the slight hints of rainbows in the spumes of water and within the smoke fire of different colours danced like will-o-wisps.

She turned back when she heard stifled laughter, Isis was watching her, a hand covering her mouth. "You really thought we were going to fall. We are Gods, you really have no faith in our powers."

Sariel decided that being quiet was better than responding.

The boat gradually eased back into the waters of the Acheron a long distance from the falls. Their drone gradually receded as the strong current pulled them away. Sariel suddenly noticed that Charon was changing. The youthfulness was fading out of his features ever so slowly. She flicked her eyes to Hecate and saw the same change occurring.

As the boat thundered along the now raging river, another roar started to grow. It was a distant but ominous sound. Something big lay ahead. But as they shot along the river it was the changes to Charon and Hecate that fascinated her the most. Charon's skin wrinkled and greased, aging until he became a hunchbacked old man. A long white beard grew down into the river as his skin took on a sickly grey tone. He was old and weak looking but his eyes had started to burn brightly casting their own strange grey-blue light.

Hecate on the other hand had taken the opposite direction. While his fearful form was from age and deformity, her fearful appearance stemmed from the fear of lust. Everything about her seemed sexually charged, from her hair forming seductive curls over her now pale shoulders. Every feature on her face sharpened and became more alluring, but her eyes were cold, she now wore the face of a predator. Her clothing had changed from Greek style to black witch's robes with long wide sleeves, skin hugging around an increasingly ample amount of exposed bosom. Her lips were now blood red as were her fingernails that had grown into what could only be called talons or claws. Even her eyes had turned blood red. She instilled a sense of longing that greatly disturbed Sariel, she was Divine, how on earth would a mortal feel?

In complete contrast Isis was completely the same, no not completely. Her bright aura now shone even brighter as though to fight off the shadows pressing in. It was the brightest source of light in any direction. Sariel couldn't help but feel she was a beacon for Demons to zone in on. She suddenly felt very vulnerable.

Her feelings only increased when she saw Charon's back rippling. She covered her gasp when a pair of bat like wings erupted out of his robe. She didn't manage to hide her scream when a black pair erupted out the back of Hecate. They both absently flapped them as they turned to regard her.

"You really do startle easily. We may be Gods but we are slaves to the power of perception and Hell is perhaps the strongest place for mortal perception." Her voice sounded ancient, haunted with a seductive huskiness. She seemed to be caught between being a figure of fear and lust. The combination didn't sit well with her. She grimaced at her voice.

The boat gently scraped up onto a long sand bank. Charon turned to her, his appearance was even more unsettling "this is where we part Sariel. Any further and we risk becoming stuck in these forms and being dragged into Hell." He held out his hand to her and she carefully allowed him to help her out onto the shore. He leaned in close to her, catching her attention with his burning eyes "Remember that things will not be as they seem. We believe in you Sariel and wish for you to succeed. You must slowly descend through each Level of Hell until you reach the final Level, it is only from there that you can ascend to the Surface."

Hecate and Isis stood and bowed to her "Farewell and good luck."

Sariel stood waving to them as they faded back into the gloom. The last she saw was the bony arm of Charon waving beneath his flaming eyes and the nexus of light that was Isis long after they had been swallowed by the mists.

She looked around herself for the first time, taking in the sheer emptiness of the Borderlands. There were long sandbanks all leading towards Limbo. The River Acheron branched between the many sandbanks and if she understood it correctly would then plunge downwards into the second Level of Hell. For now she had to make her way into Limbo.

And what a bleak landscape it was. Apart from the sand banks and the towering pillars of rock of which some rose all the way up to meet the ceiling far above, there was only the ever shifting curtains of mist. There was also the river, which strangely enough wasn't as dark as the Styx. It was much greyer in colour, often lit by flashing streaks as souls were dragged with the waters into Hell. None of them had a chance of fighting the river.

This place seemed to leach out all joy and colour. She wondered if she stayed long enough if her hair and wings would lose their gloss and her eyes would lose their colour. She imagined it must be worse in Hell. Speed was of the essence she decided. And with that she set of at a brisk march down the sandbank towards Limbo.

"We have just sent her to her death"

"Hecate she knows what she is doing. She wanted this."

"She does not know that the only way she will get out is to break the Curse and that the only way for her to do that is by fighting the Beast."

"She will figure it out for herself."

"And she will believe that this is a betrayal."

"Nonsense we told her time and time again that we do not really understand or know what happens with Hell. We can simply say we had no understanding that for her to escape required the breaking of Lucifer's Curse. If she survives then she will probably have other concerns, probably having to deal with Lucifer. And if she does not then we do not have to explain ourselves."

"She is not going to die!" Hecate shouted.

"You must consider that it is a very definite possibility. This is Hell we are talking about. Right now it is the most dangerous place in the entire world." Isis replied calmly "She may die in there, but you did do your best to prepare her. After all you saved her from going in there herself. You trained her up to defend herself and make her capable. She stands a far higher chance than she did before. She is armed with swords of light and darkness. She now knows how to access and use her powers. If she remembers to use them. And she can channel Chaos, if she uses that power there is nothing in Hell that can stand up to her. Not even the Beast. If she channelled that power against us we probably wouldn't be able to successfully defend ourselves. I don't know about you but I only inherited a small trace of Chaos from my parents and they were Primordials."

"I had even less, my quantity is only what I have absorbed from my ventures through the Underworld or what Tartarus infused into me."

"Exactly we have only small quantities and yet we are ancient Gods. I am the daughter of two Primordial Gods, you have ventured where few have ever dared to. The small amounts of Chaos we do have is far more than any non-Primordial ever accumulates. She has Chaos that eclipses every Primordial other than possibly Gaia. She has more than Nyx, Erebus and Tartarus combined."

"How on earth did an Angel get such powers?"

"Who knows, perhaps it accumulated along the bloodlines. Both her parents were exceptionally powerful, she comes from both Nyx's and Anu's bloodlines. The combination of her powers is certainly unique. Nyx said she has never seen anyone with such contrasting powers. I can understand the balance of the four elements, but the balance of light and dark is far rarer. The combination of the balanced elements, shadow gradient, adding in her powers of life and death...is it any wonder she has Chaotic powers?"

"What if Michael holds similar powers?"

The boat slowed as Charon and Isis whipped around to stare at her "It is something we may have to consider. He is her brother, he may have similar powers."

"Hopefully we can count on the Divine tendency for siblings to have different powers."

"Or does that mean he is equally powerful in other ways?"

"What is equal to Chaos?"

She let her gaze fix on the distance before turning back to face them "The powers of Creation and Destruction. What if he merely has another aspect of Chaos?"

"That does not bare thinking about" Charon muttered as he started poling again.

"But it must be considered. Michael and Sariel are dangerous, even more so than their parents. Imagine what could happen if they were to use their combined powers."

Isis shuddered and turned away to look into the mist, thinking she had seen something. She shook her head as she turned back, only her mind playing tricks. The Underworld had that affect.

But it hadn't been her mind. Isis had glanced right over the Greater Demon that clung to the rock edge. It turned its red eyes from the boat to the direction it had come from. Its nostrils flared and it flicked out its serpentine tongue to taste the scent of an Angel. Its black wings twitched in anticipation. They were a strange aberration, bat-like as Demons had been deemed, but there were black and gold feathers covering the bone edging and the feathers continued along its sinuous spine. It looked more reptilian than anything with a distinctly serpentine twist to what had once been an Angelic body. Long black hair hung down as a curtain of darkness over its reptilian face and the long fangs dripping venom. The body was much longer than any humanoid's body, serpentine with a long black tail tapering to a sharp point. Where once there had been fingers and toes there were only long, wickedly sharp talons. Despite its horror it was a fearful example of the terror lust could induce. It was unnaturally beautiful, terrifyingly so considering its appearance but the powers of enchantment and seduction were very strong, assets to its predatory nature.

It was what the Angels had made it become, fuelling the mortal fears of who it had once been.

Its tongue flicked again and it caught the Divine scent that was driving it wild. Angel blood was so rich and potent, and they were all such prudes. It smiled revealing sharp teeth next to its fangs. This Angel held a scent unlike any it remembered, and it was nothing like the wasted Angels trapped in Purgatory.

It slipped down the cliff face and broke the water without a single splash. The tide was strong, stirred by the Demon's strong Lifeforce but the Demon could easily handle the currents and was immune to the leeching nature of the water. It flicked its tail back and forth, propelling itself easily through the dark waters.

Lilith tasted the air again before she swam deeper into Hell after her prey.

Chapter 24

Brigid walked along the street invisible. No one could see her, touch her or sense her. She was but a mere presence in people's subconscious as she probed them all on her way to the river. Humans, Daemons and even Lesser Angels had no clue to her passing or probing of their minds. It was most remarkable that even here in Pakistan how much she was on people's minds. Most didn't think on her so much as her actions. Her actions were in the minds of everyone, from Christians to Hindu whom she had taken on new qualities for, to the Muslims that viewed her as a Demon. That made her smile. It was time she shook up their delicate sensibilities. She was a Western Woman, a warrioress, a scholar, an increasingly powerful Goddess, she was going to impose her style of thinking upon all her countries. Though she still had to get to Britain, it was the corner stone, the foundation, the centre of this vast web she was constructing.

It was fascinating how much she was on their minds considering they had just had a military coup. Then again military coups were extremely common in Pakistan's history so she guessed for them it was nothing new. Their president was in prison and now their military leader was now their ruler. And interesting changes he was bringing in. His first few acts other than consolidating his power had been stripping Hindus of their rights. Pakistan was on the brink of civil war between Muslims and Hindus, she was going to force their hand.

It was fortunate that she needed to return to Australia to consolidate her power. This would distract the Angels enough to leave Australia unwatched.

357

She reached the edge of the Indus River, feeling its ancient, faded powers. Until she properly claimed it Pakistan would never truly be hers, it was the ancient heart of modern Pakistan. It had once been part of India, so her claim on the Ganges and India had given her an automatic if tenuous control but she couldn't actually enforce her rule without claiming the Indus. Oh how the Angels would be furious. She knew Michael and Raphael were in India searching for her, she could sense Ariel in Australia. She couldn't sense Uriel, Gabriel or Azrael but they were not in her domains so she was unconcerned. She guessed at least one of them must still be in Europe in case she or Hera were foolish enough to return to their ancient lands. She would but once the Angels' attention was firmly directed elsewhere. Claiming Pakistan would be the final straw. Her return was imminent.

She wondered were Hera was these days.

Right now the Indian subcontinent was the most contentious place on Earth, for once Israel and Palestine were being eclipsed by greater civil and religious conflicts. Pakistan had just had a military coup and more was sure to come, India was birthing more and more religious conflicts between the established religions fracturing and the new ones shooting up. Religious hate was mounting, Muslims and Christians had been caught murdering Brigidites along the Ganges. Hinduism was starting to show the signs of tearing apart. The new leader of Pakistan had called her a Demon and anyone that followed her an infidel. He was also openly encouraging persecution of any Brigidite.

Added to that two Arch Angels and their personal guards as well as the Angelic Legions walked the subcontinent. She knew worse was yet to come, she accepted the sorrow that had appeared within her, she knew her actions were going to cost lives. Possibly millions of lives, but the Angels were a cruel tyrannical oligarchy and had to be overthrown. Yes she knew the Gods had been little better, they too had been a cruel oligarchy but they had created as much as they destroyed. Life and the diversity of life had flourished, the world had flourish. The Angels eradicated all those that would not submit or had magic. The Lifestream needed magic to draw it to the surface. During the Angels' violent reign the Lifestream had receded to a point that the Surface was dying in vast amounts. The greatest rivers in the world were running dry most years if not permanently, vast tracts of arable land all over the globe had turned into desert wastelands. There were also vast tracts of poisonous wastelands from mortal conflicts and industry.

It was time for a change, if nothing else she was doing it for the planet. If something wasn't done soon all life on land would cease to exist except the hardiest extremophiles.

She smiled as she dropped all her spells hiding her from others. People turned and gasped as in a blaze of light a beautiful European woman with six brown wings appeared on the river bank. There was instant shouting as soldiers within the area converged on her. She knew that they were yelling at her to stop, and she felt for them, she really did. Most of them would die. But how could she stop at the edge of this ailing river, only flowing because of the sheer amount of pollutants in it and stop? As an Earth Goddess she had a duty to the Earth, and she did not shirk her duties. What was it with these modern Humans? Why did they pump so much pollution into the vital arteries of the land, vital arteries they depended upon themselves.

The crack of a gun and the flare of light from her shields encouraged her to step into the water. As soon as her foot touched the disgusting water the pollution shot away, just as oil on water does when detergent is added. Her foot slid into the cold clean water, allowing it to take her magic into itself, to heal itself. There was a violent explosion and orange flames surrounded her. The soldiers were using incendiaries now. They were no match for her shields. Claiming a world without magic was just so simple, so very easy. They had no defence against magic.

She reached out into the river with her powers as she continued to walk deeper, well as deep as she could go. The river slugged by no higher than her thighs. The river started to glow, the oil slicking it starting to burn off, the other pollutants breaking down under the river's onslaught aided by her powers. She heard gasps and screams, but she tuned them out along with the gun fire and explosions. Mortal concerns were currently beyond her. She had so much that had to be done. She was thankful that the British Empire had spread so widely around the world. Awakening the Lifestream in all its countries would in effect heal much of the planet.

Just as before her powers shot both directions along the river and up every tributary, cleansing it of taint and destroying dams and irrigation canals. From far upriver came a thundering roar as all the dried up tributaries as one filled up and flooded. The flood raced downstream wrecking devastation in its path. Ripping through bridges, towns, cities, boats and dams as though they were nothing.

Brigid smiled as she pronounced "I claim the Indus River and with it full control of Pakistan. Long last the rule of Brigid." Her voice thundered through millions of peoples' heads spreading wide out from Pakistan. And in every country she had claimed so far people heard her speak the words. Then the ferocious river roared past her and once again she blended into it, becoming immutable from the water and Lifestream. Completely undetectable to anyone, least of all the Angels.

Ariel was in Adelaide, Australia, the so called City of Churches. It had once borne that title truly, now many of the churches had been turned into houses, nightclubs and stores. It was becoming increasingly obvious they had been far too lax with Humanity. They should have ruled with an iron first, would have too if not for the divisions Lucifer had created. Weak hearted fool, he had fought so hard in the War then he had turned into one of the loudest advocates for peace. Like they could live alongside the Gods without being treated as less. Now they ruled in their own right, owned by no one.

But now that rule was coming increasingly under threat by one backwater Goddess. True her backwater island had come to conquer a quarter of the world, but not because of her. Because of them. Now all their other concerns had taken a back seat and she was now their number one priority, even more so than Hera. Which was the most surprisingly thing. Hera a patron of ancient empires, the Queen of Heaven, once one of the most feared females on the planet had not so much as made one formal claim. Brigid the sly little bitch had claimed a subcontinent, and a country that liked to claim it was a continent. She officially had control of India, Bangladesh and Australia with nominal claims on Pakistan, Papua New Guinea and New Zealand. All within less than a month. If she wasn't so ready to kill the upstart bitch she would be impressed.

Thankfully while she may have claimed the lands and been acknowledged she still had to claim the people. That was where the greatest effort was required, and the greatest time. With their plans for Pakistan and India nicely coming along that dealt with the subcontinent. As for Australia well it was a Western Nation, increasingly atheist with the continual leaps and bounds in science Humans made. Christianity still had a nominal influence, but science had won. Brigid would not get a foothold.

When they unleashed the Apocalypse then all these scientific countries would be made to heel again. That she was looking forward to. Perhaps they could get it right this time and have one united religion, the world order, along the lines of the Middle East and its religion dominated society. Yes that would be a good model. What did she care for the lives of Humans so long as they obeyed and worshipped.

She stood on top of Saint Peter's Cathedral in North Adelaide watching the small city start to awaken for the day. Yes this would be a good start to reclaim Australia. Small and backward enough to retain a high level of unconscious faith without so many of the vices the larger cities offered. The fact it was a state capital was of extra merit and the fact it did have so many churches was of further benefit.

She sent out her powers wide through the city and her suburbs surprised to find such a wide array of the Angelic Religions. There was a vast array of Christianity; Catholic, Greek and Russian Orthodox, Anglican, Lutheran, but there were also sects of Judaism and Islam. Perhaps there was something to be said for Australia's multi-ethnicity, it was going to be far easier to asset her control. Her brow snapped down in annoyance when she picked up the scents of Neopagans, Buddhists, Hindus and those Chinese religions she had never even bothered to learn about. Hindus were a long standing thorn in her side but the revival of Pagan religions had gone mostly unnoticed unfortunately allowing it to spread, and it was about to gain considerable momentum because of bloody

Brigid. Curse the bitch, she would smite her down.

There was also the feel of homosexuals. Damn liberal countries allowing them to live as they pleased. She missed the old days when they were hunted down. While she did not have the burning hatred for them that Michael did, she certainly didn't see any merit or worth in them. They were a dead end, despite their noticeable presence. Perhaps it was time she visited the Middle East, their barbaric practices had always sat better with her than the other Arch Angels. She did so enjoy a good witch hunt or gay bashing. And then there were the stonings.

Not for the first time she wondered at Michael's unwavering hatred of homosexuals. His hatred of magic wielders was practical, it had removed opposition to the Angels. The extermination of the Demon races had removed any threat to the Angels. Even the patriarchal nature of their religions cleverly played on Human divisions and natural strengths. Perhaps it was part of that divide, conquer and suppress regime that had worked wonders for their religions and various empires and societies.

She sent her search wider, feeling along the small country communities which she was glad to note were still very set in their Christian ways. But much to her annoyance there was a strong feel of Brigid along the River Murray. There was also the feel of her converts. So Brigid had done well in sowing her seeds, but she would not reap the power of her crop.

The magical energies of the world suddenly flexed. She was no Earth Goddess, or descended from one but she knew what this meant. No it couldn't be, she wouldn't dare. But sure enough she heard Brigid's voice speak within her head "I claim the Indus River and with it full control of Pakistan. Long last the rule of Brigid."

She felt the earth shift away from her and her brethren, turn to and accept instead Brigid. She screamed her fury, her power exploding outwards as raging electrical storms and wild fires. All over Adelaide people shivered or jumped for no reason. But her Inquisitors and the other Angels cowered and tried to cover their ears, to them her scream burned. Then she raised her voice in a roar "To Pakistan, every fucking Angel to Pakistan. Find that fucking bitch. Kill her" She exploded in a flash of sunlight, leaving behind a sense of unease in the city.

Ariadne looked around the colonial building as people started to filter up into the top floor. Hera had done a remarkable job in removing all the rooms to create a single upper story room that while perpetuating her personal Hellenic tastes were blended smoothly with the French style building. The wall had been decorated in friezes of Heaven, with the images of a wrathful Hera slaughtering Angels. A prophecy she meant to live up to?

There was an altar made of white marble, the underside carved into cows with extremely long horns, their heads raised to hold up the altar. It was mostly bare apart from a few peacock feathers flittering in the slight breeze. Behind the altar was a frieze of a peacock, its fully exposed tail taking up most of the wall. The many eyes of Argus watching all those gathering in their seats. Now that dark was falling the Vampires were quickly filling in the empty spots.

Everyone was curious to see the new High Priestess of Hera, especially now who she was, and what she had been had spread like wildfire. They were also curious to see what was being offered. Vultures the lot of them.

They didn't remember the Age of Gods. To them they were just stories. They hated the Angels, granted they were worse for the Daemon races than the Gods but they didn't comprehend the nature of the Gods. They were selfish and demanding, they always got what they wanted and if they didn't they got highly destructive. Hera had been among the most fearful with her ferocious temper.

She turned to face the garden as the scent of jasmine and the other twilight flowers started to fill the air. Out of the window she could see St Louis Cathedral, one of the most iconic buildings in all of New Orleans. She wondered if Hera's choice of view had a meaning, knowing Hera it did.

She gently touched her dress for comfort, Hera had decided to resurrect ancient styles of clothing for her, but thankfully with modern twists. It was cotton, so it thankfully breathed in the humid air, and it was violet with gold trimming and belt. She almost felt like a demigoddess again. It was beautiful and she was very thankful for that fact. The modern age perpetuated vanity, and Hera had always been more than a little vain. She was an intelligent woman though and knew that beauty was a one of the ways a woman could control men and even other women. Which was why many of her priestesses had been beautiful. To top off the outfit was a small fan made of peacock feathers settled at the back of her head. Thankfully it wasn't ostentatious but actually completed the whole image.

She felt like a High Priestess. She almost felt like a demigoddess. And if she did all Hera asked, she would be again.

She walked into the altar room from the antechamber she had been waiting, a couple of people stood up but most didn't. They would soon learn their mistake. She was surprised at who stood up; King Valentine, Matriarch Sarah with Senator Clare, and even most surprisingly Senator Worthington. It was only then that she realised there were several Humans scattered amongst the magic races. Important Humans of industry and commerce. Hera's reach was spreading deep through America and it didn't even know it.

More people were trickling up the stairs to lounge at the back of the room. They were waiting, watching with intense gazes. They had come to make a decision, fools didn't realise they had no choice. They would either join Hera or be removed from her way.

"I welcome you all in the name of Hera, Queen of Heaven. May you all prosper in her bounty and power." God it had been so long since she had partook in any rituals let alone had to lead them. She couldn't remember much of what she was meant to say or do. Plus most of it was obsolete in the modern world. That was one thing the Angels religions had never realised. So for the most part she was winging it "Today marks a new era, when the Gods will rise once again and the Angels will be cast out of Heaven for their blind arrogance and finally made to pay for their atrocities. An age where we Daemons and magic wielders can walk the streets we helped create as who we are, unafraid of watching Angels."

She shifted to a more sombre tone "but we have a long path ahead of us, we have to debase the power of the Angels and strengthen ourselves in preparation. We must turn to what Hera offers us."

"Why should we do anything for her? We are the ones who have suffered not her." Some fool yelled from the back.

"I have suffered more than you will ever know or comprehend mortal. I have seen my entire family slaughtered, my children, my husband, my parents, my siblings and their children. I have seen my friends driven out into the streets of Heaven only to be brutally slaughtered by those upstart bastards. I have been tortured for centuries under the cruel tastes of the Angels. Believe me I have suffered." She had appeared next to the fool, her fingers wrapping seductively around his neck, before she snapped it clean. The Incubus fell to the ground, but with a snap of her fingers he was standing again. His eyes were wide open in abject terror. "If you ever question me again that is your fate." She said contemptuously as she walked up to the altar, sitting down on it to face the audience. She had their undivided attention.

"We are at war and you have but two options, the Angels or me. That is the harsh reality." Lightning danced along her skin as she cast her eyes across the crowd.

"It is time for change, it is time for war but we cannot run in foolishly. We cannot make mistakes for we will get but one chance. We must damage the Angels' powerbase as we build our own. Some of you may not believe in who I am or what I can do, but I will change that. America will be remade in the image of my choosing. Those who are loyal to me will do well, while those who are not will perish." She swept her hands and several phoenixes appeared, their haunting song filling the air and raising the hairs on everyone's necks. The Vampires shrank into their seats.

"It is a time of change and rebirth, what has been destroyed will be again. Phoenixes now fly, sorcerers are embracing their powers and the Daemons are finally awakening their legacy. But there is more that has been lost and will be reborn, who will offer themselves willingly?"

A female Vampire spoke "will I be able to walk in the sun?"

Hera smiled, she had them "indeed you will love

the sun very much"

She stepped forward, trepidation and want written clear across her face, before she dropped to her knees in front of Hera "Then I am yours to command"

Hera reached out and touched her lips, green spreading from the finger tips, turning those blood red lips a brilliant forest green. The green continued to spread out across the sallow black skin, creeping across her face. "Then you will be well rewarded Catherine" she said as she stepped back from the Vampire.

Everyone watched in awed silence as the green spread throughout her, tracing along her veins and spreading as a gradual wave down from her head. Her arms twisted, her fingers grew longer before ending in sharp claws. Her Vampire fangs shifted further apart as they grew longer and curved, while her whole face underwent a restructure. Rounding and sharpening of various features, giving her a distinctively reptilian cast. To those watching it looked painful, her skin rippled as her bones reforged themselves, but she did not cry out. Her legs snapped together, the limbs rippling and twisting from the skin down, as skin and muscle fused together. She fell forward as her leg strength gave way, Hera caught her in her Divine grasp. Her fused legs stretched out longer and longer, twisting and flexing into a long serpentine tail then spread backwards for several metres. Her frizzy black hair rippled, smoothing out into a black curtain before clumping together and rippling. Her hair looked like a nest of vipers, as the green spread up through the hair it transformed it into living snakes.

They let out several low hisses as her green skin took on a reptilian sheen. There was a louder hiss as her tail flicked. Hera lightly touched her neck and she slid upright, with a new air of confidence. Catherine looked over her body with intense curiosity before asking "Am I a Gorgon?"

"Indeed you are but in the modern image. In my time they walked on legs and had tusks. Since then they have undergone an evolution in the Human mindscape until they believe Gorgons appear as you do now. An improvement I have to say."

Hera left Catherine to adjust to her body "Now I need another volunteer."

People looked around at each other but none offered themselves. She raised an eyebrow, a dangerous sign. Finally an old werewolf came forward "If the Children of the Night take up such an offer so should the Children of the Moon."

Hera smiled and held out her hand to him. He walked forward slowly due to age and his face crinkled in pain as he knelt to take her hand.

Instantly he transformed into his other form. But his shaggy grey fur shortened to short black hair. His snout widened, two long horns grew from his head, his tail thinned and shortened. His hands grew shorter, more humanistic but his paws changed into hooves. His skin momentarily flashed before growing the short black hair on his bovine face.

"What am I?" he whispered in a low deep voice.

"You Samuel are a Minotaur, the very first of your kind since Asterion was killed. Naturally with some alterations." She smiled as she swept her arms wide indicating Samuel and Catherine "They were brave enough to accept change and they have been rewarded and shall continue to be. They are the first of their kind, not the last. In the days that will follow forgotten races will live again. But now your tasks come into play, you must weaken the Angel's powers.

It was Ariadne that spoke "What would you have us do Goddess?"

Hera turned to face the window and pointed at Saint Louis Cathedral. Violet lightning struck the old building out of the clear night sky. The bolt exploded into the cathedral, shattering the tower across Jackson Square. Violet flames licked up at the building in moments, a blaze that was beyond stopping. She turned to face them "I want every church, every synagogue and every mosque burned to the ground. Every symbol of the Angels shall be destroyed and their taint removed from my empire." Then she was gone, with no doubt that the tasks would be completed.

The congregation sat in horrified silence as one of the icons of New Orleans was steady consumed by the fire. Fire trucks and firemen arrived to fight the blaze but no amount of water could battle the Goddess' all-consuming flames. When the last flame died, there was nothing but a blackened piece of ground, no structural skeleton, even the stones had burned to ash.

They looked amongst themselves knowing that there were hundreds of historic churches across America. For some it was a troubling task but there was no denying Hera, she had stamped her mark on each race, their leaders already fearful to fail her. A well placed fear.

"Well High Priestess what should we do?" Catherine asked.

Ariadne knew she was going to like the direct young woman "We play it carefully and pander to America's hardly disguised racism. We shall target mosques first, there is still much distrust and misplaced hatred directed at Muslims. We can even use many of the churches as our tools. It should not draw the attention of the Angels. But we shall have to burn a church here and there in apparent retaliation. We shall create a religious war under their noses and have them do the task for us."

They nodded their understanding. Despite its

power America was a highly flawed and fractured society. Playing different groups off each other was going to be easy. But most of them knew this was the beginning of the end for America. The Land of the Free would fall, one way or another. Even if Hera had to wipe it from the face of the earth. A prospect all were prepared to prevent.

The black SUV hurtled through the Mexican countryside, all but screaming America. The locals watched it flash by with bitterness, Americans were so proud of their technology and they loved to flaunt their wealth. But they also loved to come to Mexico for their drugs and to party. But they looked down upon the locals, most were rich white brats whose only interactions with Mexicans were with their servants. Which perhaps explained their general behaviour, other than the natural American arrogance and stupidity so many of them seemed to live and breathe.

Much the same thoughts went through the residents of Nuevo San Juan Parangaricutiro when the black SUV turned off of Lázaro Cárdenas and pulled up in front of Iglesia de San Juan Nuevo. The door opened and one long pale leg gracefully landed on the road. It was followed by another leg, before the woman climbed down from the car. To the locals she embodied the very essence of American culture. From her tall black pumps, to her clearly expensive purple dress revealing a fair expanse of her legs to the large black sunglasses and the expensive gold watch on her wrist. Her mass of brown curls caught the sunlight as though she was a picture in a magazine.

She turned her attention to the church, pulling her sunglasses off to study the two star windows before focussing on the clock. She flicked her hair behind her and with long graceful strides walked into the church.

They looked at each other, their expressions grim. This was an opportunity too good to pass up. Times had been very hard, corruption was running wild in the government, the drought was continuing into its fifth year and the agricultural laboratories could not meet the full demand, many had died of starvation. No one was helping them. And now here was this rich bitch flaunting her wealth in their face, a wealth that would see them through the next year if they ransomed her.

Hera slowly walked towards the altar looking over the Angels' legacy. She had to concede they did have a very firm grasp on vast tracts of the United States and Latin America. While the Americans were fanatics, fundamentalist morons convinced of their superiority the Mexicans were not. But they were deeply entrenched in their beliefs in another way, each person was named after a saint. As such saints gained a lot of strength from Mexico and it was the saints that were much of the force behind the Angel's armies. Of course the Elder and the even more powerful Archs were the mightiest but they did not often participate in the mortal world, instead leaving it to the so called Ascended Angels.

But no Angel could replace a God unless they became one. The land needed the touch of a Mother Goddess or even a Nature God to tame it, heal it, enliven it. As it was Mexico had been invaded by the Spanish, the invasion had destroyed the native empires and had weakened the few remaining Gods left to fight. She didn't know what had happened to them, had they been killed or where they merely imprisoned? But the world was very sick, a combination of Human activity but more directly the lack of any Mother Goddesses.

In recent years much of the world had been suffering even more. Desertification was widespread and rampant, destroying huge tracts of arable land the world over. Pollution continued to soar, raining down from the skies into choked rivers and onto piles of rubbish. Sea levels continued to rise as world weather patterns became increasingly erratic, causing widespread droughts and floods and hastening the extinction of ever more species. Mexico had not been spared despite its faith, droughts came and went lasting for several years only to be broken with flooding. Famine had wracked Mexico on and off for over two decades. But their desperation only added to the Angels' strength, the least they could do was reward them for their loyalty.

Which was what she intended to do.

She heard the doors creak open, hushed whispers and soft footsteps. She smiled, foolish mortals. She could sense their intent as easily as she could hear and smell them. They reeked of desperation and under that a very palpable anger with more than a little lust. If she had been a mortal woman she would have feared for her life, of course if she had been mortal she wouldn't have known they were there. As a Goddess she had no reason to worry for her life, except from other Gods and Demigods.

She casually turned to face them as they approached her. They were dirty and ragged carrying guns, ropes and clubs. They were wearied and desperate, outside she knew others were trying to break into her car.

They started speaking in Spanish and she absorbed their understanding. Magic was just so convenient.

One of them started speaking in broken English "You come with us, we no hurt you."

She responded in Spanish "And if I refuse Gabriel, what shall you do then?" she found it odd that he was named after Gabriel then she remembered that the Arch Angels appeared as males.

"How the Hell do you know my name?" His first

thought was that she was a police officer.

"I know all your names, all your parents, all your children's names and all your wives' names."

He grabbed a gun from one of the others and aimed it at her "look lady you are going tell us how you know us or I'm going to fucking kill you"

She gave him a level stare "such language in a holy place, whatever would the Angels think?"

"Look bitch you don't know the first thing about God."

"I know that he never existed. I know the Arch Angels rule in his name and Humans don't know the difference. I know that they are ruining the planet with their tyrannical rule."

He fired at her in impatience, God damn bloody American women were so annoying. Why were things never simple with them?

The bullet reflected off her shield, the only sound was the bullet rattling on the floor. She stood up and looked down on them from the altar "first of all I am not American, if anything I am Greek. Secondly that was just rude and now you have pissed me off and that is never a wise thing to do."

"What are you?" he gasped as all of them started backing away from her.

She smiled cruelly "your worst nightmare"

Flames suddenly erupted next to her and they screamed as a snake woman slithered out of the flames. She was disturbingly beautiful in a non-Human way, but more than anything she was terrifying. She flicked her forked tongue then struck out lightning fast at Gabriel. He fell to the floor holding the bite mark. His eyes went blank within seconds before his body crumpled to the ground.

Hera waved her hand giving Catherine the

permission she was looking for, and as she did so she magically summoned every person in the town into the church.

They arrived in a quick flash to find several of their own kneeling before the altar, their hands behind their heads as a fearsome snake woman was feasting on a body. Behind her on the altar stood the most beautiful woman any of them had ever seen.

"How nice of you all to join us" she indicated with a hand, and all of a sudden they were sitting down in the pews.

"Demon! Diablo! Witch!" the priest started yelling from his position against the wall. She barely noticed him, uncaring of his mortal fears but she was very interested in the massive spike of fear and loathing within the church. She stepped down off the altar, walking through the crowd, ignoring them as she zoned in on a boy. He was gangly, sad looking, barely twelve and yet burning with a hatred that sent a shiver down her spine. Such strong loathing. Her instincts had led her to him.

"Why do you hate him so much Juan?" she asked gently though she already knew.

He looked up at her with his dark brown eyes focussing on her own violet eyes, within them was a kindness and understanding that encouraged him to say what he had never said before "because he touches me. He makes me touch him. He kisses me. He makes me do things and he hurts me if I don't. I can't tell anyone because no one will believe me." Tears had started to trickle their way down his dirty face.

She held out her hand to him, gently pulling him up as she said loud enough for everyone to clearly hear "I believe you, I can see it in you. I can feel your suffering and fury." She led him over to where the priest stood against the wall. Catherine slithered over to join them, tasting his intense fury, to his credit Juan did not cower from her. But then he had dealt with monsters wearing Human masks that had done far worse than she ever would. Hera handed him a long dagger, felt his hatred spike. Oh the rage, it was intoxicating and so surprising in one so young. She had not felt such rage in so long, it was so concentrated, so directed.

He took the dagger in his little arms, they dropped with the weight. Then he squared his shoulders as Hera lightly touched them, giving him the strength to do what he needed to do. With a quick thrust he stabbed the priest in the stomach. Then again and again and again. Hera stood there and laughed as Juan continued to stab the priest screaming and venting his broken childhood rage. He screamed and screamed about every obscenity the priest had ever made him do. Blood and gore splattered all over the boy and the two women. Hera for her part trapped his soul within his body until Juan collapsed to the ground exhausted. He sat there breathing heavily, still clutching the blade.

The priest sighed and coughed, his last breath leaving his body as Hera finally released her constraints on him. But she was not letting him go. She stepped forward her hands blazing red as she pulled his soul out. Everyone saw the white-blue image of him before it flared red and disappeared.

She knelt down next to Juan "Do not worry Juan he can never hurt you again and he will never know release. He will be held with my powers and made to pay for what he did to you." She picked him up, and he cuddled into her, turning his face away from the stares of his town. She gently stroked his hair, using her magic to grant him sleep, as she turned to face the town "Well, well, well, what a terrible little town. Abuse under your nose, planning to kill an innocent woman and stealing from each other. No wonder the land forsakes you. Perhaps the first volcano wasn't enough, perhaps you need another to cleanse you."

They started screaming and wailing as lava bubbled up onto the altar, the crucifix slowly melting into the glowing mass. "No?" she asked "it is not your fault the land starves and the Angels forsake you, for they cannot embrace the earth. So I will call the rains to ease your burdens. But it comes at a price." Thunder boomed outside and the sound of rain pelting down on the roof cause people to gasp in surprise. It had been over a decade since they had had proper rain, they had had to import it in better years. Hera smiled "This land belongs to me, this town belongs to me, and your pathetic lives belong to me." She snapped her fingers and all the crucifixes in the church burst into flame, many people had to quickly rip off their burning necklaces.

Hera turned to Catherine "This land once belonged to the Feathered Serpent and now it will once again be the land of Serpents. Claim what you will but destroy every church."

She smiled "As you wish my Goddess" then with lightning speed she wrapped herself around several of the females, biting them and casting the transformation spell. Hera turned her attention to the little boy in her arms while Catherine quickly started swelling her numbers. She brushed his hair back, surprisingly he was still awake "What should I do with you little one?" she asked gently.

"Take me away from here please?"

"I tell you what I'll make a bargain with you. If I take you away from here you will become one of my soldiers and with that comes the right to choose a new form."

He raised his watery eyes to hers, they were filled

with determination "What do you wish of me my Goddess?" smart kid.

"Well initially learn how to fight, but you shall seek out more of your kind and your numbers will grow. A war is coming and we must be prepared." She had a feeling that empowering abuse victims was going to be a stroke of genius. They burned with a fury and sorrow that would empower them beyond their mortal gifts.

Yes her army was finally starting to take shape. She had all the magical races of America flocking to her, and soon too would the Mexicans. The Gorgons and Minotaurs were automatically hers and as their numbers grew, they would provide a solid support. The victims were going to be another section of Humanity easy to claim. She would give them power and the leash to get their revenge. They would form her Elites. She was also harvesting vast amounts of sorcerers from amongst the homosexuals. Her name and symbol were openly being worn and invoked by magical and non-magical homosexuals alike. They were outcast so easily, but survived with a strength she found valuable. She had also been experimenting with the Obese. Infused with magic they were living siege weapons, disgusting freaks that they were, once under her full control they were useful. Her magic overriding the extensive damage they had already done to their bodies.

Yes it was all coming together.

She cast a final glance back at Catherine, who had now turned ten women into Gorgons, before she snapped her fingers. Fire bloomed along all the pews, violet flames licking hungrily for all traces of the Angels. The town had a new beginning now. She left with Juan leaving the town completely at the mercy of Catherine.

Michael was perched atop the Taj Mahal, Raphael

was crouched next to him as they both analysed the people milling below them.

"She's done something here but I can't pin it down."

Michael nodded his agreement that was exactly what Nuriel had told him. "Whatever it is it is subtle, far more than her efforts in the Ganges."

"That may have lacked subtlety but it worked for her. Varanasi almost completely belongs to her. Even with the spike in murders, religious killings and arsons, people still flock there. We have lost our first city. She grows ever stronger too, her presence spreading. Ariel reports that her influence in Australia is rising sharply."

"It would seem our once shy little Goddess has turned into a Hydra, we cut down one part and she's appeared in several other places with even more followers."

"Do you think she will head for Britain?"

"Who knows what she's going to do anymore? We once thought we knew her, how she would react and she has confounded us time and time again. She's claimed two major river systems, and is ever strengthening her claims on India, Bangladesh, Australia, New Zealand and Papua New Guinea. Even in Pakistan with its civil war and our influence her presence is still being felt.

None of it makes sense, her claiming of the Ganges and India was brilliant. Beyond anything we would have ever accredited to her. How on earth did she convince more than half of the Hindu population that she was the avatar of all their Gods reincarnated? They have been the biggest thorn in our side for millennia. Their faith prevented either Islam or Christianity claiming the subcontinent and spreading further. How did she do it? So quickly?"

"Perhaps somehow the Hindu Gods played a part

in all this?"

"Not beyond the realms of possibility but I would like to know where they have been hiding all these years."

"Should we recall Uriel and his legions to assist us here?"

"No there is always a chance one of them may return to their homelands, we must stay vigilant. It is our own pride that is getting the better of us. We must not be rash."

He had barely finished before they felt the shift of magical energies, felt a wave of potent magic sweep out past them. They felt the world's life currents surge past them, heading towards Pakistan as they heard her voice speak in their heads.

"That fucking canny bitch" Michael snarled but as he said it he smiled. He had always been a warrior and for centuries there had been no worthy enemy. The spread of their religions only intrigued him so much as the powers it granted and that his stamp was made on Humanity. But now Brigid surprisingly enough was shaping up to be more than a worthy advisory. For the first time since the War the Angels were losing ground.

"Get in contact with Gabriel, I'll go and sort out this mess. Keep your Ophanim and the legions here, she'll be long gone from Pakistan but she might revisit here." He gave a half-hearted salute before disappearing.

Great he had to deal with Gabriel. He felt around the Taj Mahal once again trying to decipher the subtle nuances of her spell. He shook his head it was beyond him despite his power. Perhaps Gabriel would be able to help, she was far more skilled in the finer manipulations of magic than any other Angel. If the War had not occurred she would have ascended to the ranks of the Gods long ago to join and thrive in their games.

Gabriel?

Yes Raphael? She sounded surprisingly polite, she couldn't have heard the news about Pakistan yet. He wasn't going to be the one to tell her.

I require you magical assistance and skills. Michael and myself have found something unusual and we believe it may be one of Brigid's spells but it is beyond our expertise.

Even in his mind he could feel her smiling, knew she was delighted that he admitted such limitations to her, but then he was not like her and Michael. He knew his limitations and was willing to acknowledge and accept them.

Of course Raphael I just have to go chase up John Paul and get him to Australia then I will join you.

I'll be waiting at the Taj Mahal.

The connection went out. How would she react when she found out that Brigid had formally claimed Pakistan? He hoped she found out after she had helped him, he really wasn't in the mood to dance around her foul temper.

Brigid pulled herself out of the gently flowing river, not quite sure how she had ended up in Australia or in the River Murray. Apparently the Lifestream had seen fit to deposit her here. She was needed.

She gave a sigh of relief as she felt Ariel leave. She would head down stream and head over to Adelaide to snoop around and sort out whatever she had done. But her attention was drawn to the young girl watching her from in between two red gums. The girl was staring at her wide eyed and Brigid belatedly realised she hadn't hidden her wings.

"Are you an Angel?" she asked hesitantly, awed beyond her wildest dreams.

Brigid smiled "No I am not, I am a Goddess."

The girl stared wide eyed, the term meant nothing to her.

"There is much sorrow in you Rachel. Why such sorrow in one so young?"

"The river went crazy a few days ago, a lot was destroyed. But now the river is healthy, it flows. I've never seen it so full. But now we can't get any water from it. The water just won't go up the pipes or flow into channels. The water refuses to leave the river."

Brigid knelt down next to her "Do you know why that is?"

"No"

"Because it isn't your water, it is Brigid's and you must ask her for it. You wouldn't take something without asking for it would you?"

"No mummy says that's wrong."

"Exactly so you must ask for the water."

"But how do we ask her?" Children were so easy to explain things to, their minds accepted things adults' could not.

Brigid smiled at the girl before saying "You must say to the river Brigid we ask for the gift of water"

Rachel gave her a funny look "is that all?"

"It is, give it a go."

Rachel gave her an assessing look, she wasn't convinced but with that natural curiosity of the young she climbed up onto the nearby irrigation gates. They sat wide open with the river rushing straight past, defying the laws of gravity.

"Brigid we ask for the gift of water."

Brigid smiled as Rachel shrieked in delight as water started pouring through the sluice gate into the irrigation channels behind. Rachel was delighted quickly running to a nearby box and flicking the control for the pipes to start sucking up the water. Their crops wouldn't be ruined this year.

She turned around but the Goddess, whatever that was, was gone. The only trace of her existence being a golden necklace of a six winged woman sparkling on the ground. She picked it up, it looked exactly like the woman she had just seen. Turning it over she found ornate writing that simply said *Brigid*.

This was the Brigid everyone was talking about. The voices in people's heads, the news was always talking about her. She realised that the woman had the same voice as the one that had spoken in her head. And she had come to speak to her personally.

She had to tell her mum. She was going to be so impressed that she had met a Goddess. She could also ask what that was.

Hundreds of kilometres away in Adelaide Brigid smiled as she felt Rachel's heart and spirit align to her. She would spread what she had learned, first to her parents and community and from there by word of mouth it would spread along the whole river basin. As they asked for her gift, she in turn would take their debt. Not that they would realise that asking for the gift of water came with the price of their spirits.

She could now safely say that the whole Murray-Darling Basin would be hers, which was a fair amount of the land in Australia. Now she could turn her attention to the capital cities and also to New Zealand and Papua New Guinea. She hadn't realised she would gain them. The Fates were smiling on her.

First on her list was Adelaide, Ariel had been here she had to fix and heal whatever mischief she had been up to. Plus as the City of Churches what better place to start to weed out Christianity?

She was perched on St Peter's Cathedral, feeling Ariel's strong magic lingering. She would remove that. Taking a breath she sank down through the roof and perched on the ceiling. She gathered that Hera was probably the driving force behind the sudden destruction of so many mosques and hate crimes in America. That or the country was tearing itself apart. Hard to tell in this day and age, so many civil wars had erupted in previously stable countries in the last three decades.

If it was Hera she was dividing and conquering. It had to be, who else would destroy St Louis Cathedral with purple fire? Brigid gathered that Hera's overall plan was to destroy all traces of the Angels and their Religions, presumably from America. Though she had no idea if that was where she was set up. Then again if she didn't know then the Angels weren't likely to either.

But she had other plans for the churches in her domain. She would assimilate them, and then manipulate them as she saw fit. She waved her hand and the whole church rippled. All the crucifixes burst into flames, pooling into puddles of liquid metal. All the stained glass windows exploded inwards, their shards frozen in the air before spinning around and rearranging themselves back into the windows. All throughout the cathedral any images of Jesus, any crucifix, any bible, any symbol of Christian faith and power was destroyed. In their place were the symbols of her. The six winged woman and fire. There were also the symbols of her past scattered about; the cow, the serpent, the ewe and the cockerel.

From here on in she would direct the worship of herself. The church had virginised her and stripped her of her true nature. She was a Mother Goddess and a Goddess of justice, peace, fire, the sun, wisdom and crafts. She would embrace all those again and she would embrace new attributes. But mortality would know her foremost as the Mother Earth Goddess, patron of the British Empire.

Churches ironically enough had desecrated her sacred grounds and groves but were still sacred to her. And with them widespread due to the British Empire it would be far easier to convert them than destroy them and rebuilt them again. What she needed was something that would desecrate the church and its religious ties while consecrating it in her name.

She remembered that there was a congregation beneath her, and realised that they were all looking up at her in amazement. God damn these wings, curse her own stupidity. She should be remembering to hide herself.

The point was moot really considering what she had just done to the cathedral. Many were pointing at the central stained glass window over the altar, the one that now depicted her bathed in flames. Beneath it the Chancel was transforming from dull into a beautiful, lush grove. The altar had been replaced by a simple altar of bluestone, reminiscent of Stonehenge. It was here that she gently alighted, looking over the stunned congregation. The priest nearby was almost comatose in shock. If he wasn't careful the plants would wrap themselves around him.

But how to make the changes permanent?

Then she felt him. Her eyes located the youth, dragged along to church against his will. Behind his bible he was on his phone. His need was palpable, a poor virgin desperate to lose it. The last of his mates and feeling the shame. Poor lad. Yes he would do perfectly, sex was among her greatest declarations of power. The Church valued virginity citing it as purity. Losing one's virginity in a church would be very sacrilegious.

She pointed at him, golden streams of light coiling outwards towards him and playfully encircling him. He looked up, his lust and confusion apparent to all. She beckoned with her fingers. Everyone else remained frozen where they were as he stood up and walked towards her, the golden lights giving him the appearance of divinity.

He was tall and thin, needing adulthood to fill out his figure. His black dyed hair hung as a mop over his face, hiding his various piercings. His clothing while not his usual suited him and were neat and well fitted. He had slid his phone back into his pocket, right next to his game console. He really did not like church.

He walked towards her completely enchanted by her beauty more than anything else. He had never seen a woman so beautiful, even more stunning that those photoshopped images of supermodels. She was slender yet curvaceous, tall, with long legs. She was elegant, her long brown hair floating around her striking face and complimenting her eyes. One emerald green, one warm brown. They watched her with unhidden hunger.

She reached out to him with one of those elegant hands, her fingers tracing the scattered stubble on his chin. She adjusted her position, causing one of her shoulder straps to fall down her arm, exposing her pale shoulder and an ample amount of her pale perfect breast.

He stood there awkwardly unsure what to do, his eyes fixated on the exposed amount of her breast. His breath was racing as fast as his pulse, he was harder than he had ever been and yet he hesitated before this perfect creature. She shifted her head as her hand travelled down from his chin, tantalisingly down his neck and round to his chest. On impulse, he couldn't call such lunacy anything else, he reached out and pulled down the other shoulder strap.

The dress slipped down, flowing off her into a silken puddle of green on the floor. She stood there naked and completely perfect on a pagan altar in a house of God. Her wings only added to her ethereal beauty.

She smiled at him seductively, vanishing his sweaty shirt. He stood topless in a house of God! He ceased caring when she vanished the rest of his sweaty clothing. Her exploring hands were pleasantly cold in the sticky summer heat.

This was the most surreal moment of his life and this beautiful Angel was naked and suggestive before him. Her hands running across his skin and through his long hair. She pulled him close to her, kissing him deeply as her long legs wrapped about his thin frame. Her mouth was like fire, it was beyond any hook-up he had ever had before, he was kissing Heaven. This was pure and concentrated desire.

For each of his fumbling and nervous movements she countered with her own controlled and skilled movements. Time and conscious thought disappeared to him as she pulled him down on her, then rolled over. His last conscious thought before she sheathed him inside her was that he was losing his virginity, in church, in front of lots of people he knew. After that his mind was in a haze of passion.

He let out a satisfied moan and gasped, she arched her back smiling as she felt his brain lose all focus but her. His fumbling hands had taken on more skill, slowing and starting to tantalise. Some part of her was conscious of the people watching, but it was nothing new to her. Gods and most of the Divine were decidedly open about sex. The Angels had turned out to be the strange exception. These people were witnesses to her change.

She let out a startled gasp as he found his rhythm and apparently his skill. Her control on her powers weakened as her mind lost its focus. They shot out in every direction, twisting and winding around her to form a protective cocoon. The whole cathedral became awash in her Mother Earth powers as her pleasure climbed. The building shook violently with each of her pleasured moans, she had never imagine that a virgin could be this good.

The whole church shook as it restructured itself. The crucifix shape was lost, the insides taking on a more circular shape, while the rectangular outside grew larger. The pews shifted about changing as they did so, becoming covered in cushions to ease the sore bottoms sitting on them. All the finery of the church changed into more earthy tones and images. Green was the dominant colour, but it was complimented by red, white, brown and black.

Humans were much better lovers than they had been in the past. Two of them had managed to bring her to the brink of orgasm, his whole body focussed on bringing her pleasure even as his own raced him towards his own orgasm. He let out a strained moan, his back arching, his face scrunching as he ejaculated inside her. She felt a strange surge pass through her which pushed her over the edge and then she too was moaning as she orgasmed, her body shaking. They both collapsed against the altar exhausted. Seconds later she stood up, Divinity was such a gift, looking around the cathedral. It looked decidedly pagan.

She was very satisfied. In more ways than one.

She faced the congregation, still transfixed where they sat, also wrapped up in much of the flora. Her dress flowed upwards covering her nudity, but not their memories. "The time of the Angels and their lies is over. God does not exist, but I do. You have heard me before in your minds, you know my name. This land is mine, this country is mine, this boy is mine and you are all mine. Forget the lies and the sanctions of the church, live life as it is meant to be lived. I see all of you, your wants and desires, your needs. Give in to them, celebrate life, celebrate me.

She touched the chest of Josh, still gasping on the altar. Copper bloomed from her fingers, marking his chest with the coppery symbol of the Six Winged Goddess.

"This boy, nay sorcerer-priest has lain with a Goddess, a great honour. He is claimed in my name, may Hell ravage any who harm him. In my name, Brigid, it is done."

She ascended in a bright beam of light, fire exploding outwards though it burned nothing.

He lay there on the altar watching her ascend as he heard her voice speak in his head. *Great things lie ahead for you Josh Gray, desecrate and sanctify for me. Spread the word, bring down the lies, spread the passion and desire, my chosen one and you will be rewarded.*

"Who's there?" he yelled through the empty temple. The open airy halls filled with columns were beautiful in the day. The unique blend of Celtic and Hindu imagery was stunning, even though the temple was nowhere near complete. It was already setting itself up as one of the Jewels of the Ganges.

But in the empty dark nights it was decidedly creepy. Especially with the strange fog pouring off the Ganges. He shouldn't be on edge but he was, with the targeted murders of his people he had the feeling it was only a matter of time before they came for him.

Being alone in an empty temple building site was more than foolish, it was downright stupid.

"Such dedication Ryan"

He whipped around to see Brigid sitting cross legged on the incomplete altar. So far it was but a round block of white marble. She was dressed in a red dress, pooling about her and yet not hiding one of her long white legs or her bosom and shoulders. Her brown hair hung as a straight curtain over one of her shoulders

"Brigid!" he gasped in surprise.

She smiled at him, beckoning him forward. He ran to her, embracing her, kissing her, exclaiming with a rush of questions. She silenced him with her lips, and began a routine he knew well. As usual his attention became solely focussed on her.

He was awoken in the morning by one of the priestesses. She was staring at his chest quizzically. Looking down he noticed that much of his chest was taken up with the coppery image of the Six Winged Goddess. Touching it he realised his skin was now that colour. He also noticed a slight flaring of light when his fingers touched it. He would examine it later.

Brigid was long gone but her mark was clear, not just on him. The temple was complete, all his grand designs were now real. The blending of her Celtic background and new Hindu claims were unique and stunning. Lotus crowned columns of white marble held aloft arched pastel ceilings depicting both Brigid and the Ganges. The columns were decorated with serpents and Naga, their twining and twisting figures wrapped around and carved with such skill they almost looked alive. The white marble floor was decorated with gold, copper, amber and other fiery semi-precious stones that it looked as though they were walking on fire. The altar he was sitting on, half covered by his robe was now stunning. A white marble carving of Brigid stood behind it, each of the wings gilded in copper. Smaller than her were each of the mortal races still in existence, their unique beauty plain to the world.

With an added twist there were small carvings on the floor throughout the temple complex that was fed by the Ganges itself, before returning to it. The severely damaged steps that had once been the iconic image of Varanasi were now repaired.

He was no longer confused or without direction. He knew what he had to do now. India would stand strong, it would be united completely under Brigid and it would once again be one of the crown jewels of the British Empire.

The Goddess had grand designs. But she had made his come to light so he would help hers come to light. She was making a better tomorrow.

Rachel walked happily along with her full bucket of water. She could finally water her sunflowers and hopefully they would pull through and flower. They had been looking rather dead of late with the strange drought affecting the region. Rainfall might be low but they had always had the river. Such as it had been in recent years.

She had just finished watering her sunflowers when her mother stepped out of the house. "Rachel what did I tell you about wasting water?"

"But mum this isn't from the tap. It's from the river."

Matilda knelt down next to her daughter "Rachel for reasons unknown the river will not give even a single drop of water. I cannot explain it, no one can but we simply cannot access the water we once could."

"I know. Brigid said it was because we didn't ask her for the gift of water."

"Brigid? Who is Brigid?"

"The Goddess of the river. What is a Goddess mum? She showed me how to ask for the water. I asked and was given the gift of water, the lower irrigation canals are filling up. I took the water from there to water my flowers."

"Rachel sweetie Goddesses don't exist. And what have I told you about talking to strangers?"

"But she was real, she had wings and everything. She even glowed."

"Rachel don't lie to me."

Rachel pouted angrily at her mother. It was one thing to be caught telling a fib, but she was telling the truth. "Come look with me" She reached for her mother's pale hands with her own brown ones. Matilda lifted her up, rolling her eyes but as she did so she caught sight of Rachel's sunflowers. They didn't look wilted any more, two of them were budding, one of which was already poking through green-yellow petals.

She walked along with her beautiful little girl, her heart starting to believe even though the sensible part of her mind told her she would find only the dead and dying trees. To her surprise not only were the irrigation channels flowing but grass was already sending up shoots from the parched ground and many of the dead trees, they had been dead, were now budding over with leaves and even flowers.

"How is this possible?" she whispered to herself trying to fathom the impossibility of it all.

"Because I asked the Goddess. See let me show you."

Dumbstruck she watched her daughter run over to the next set of empty irrigation channels, their open sluice-gate showing the river rushing past. A stark reminder of how bizarre their lives had all become.

"See the river goes not give if we do not ask." She turned to face the river and said clearly and politely "We ask of Brigid the gift of water please." Suddenly water was flowing through the sluice-gate, once again adhering to the laws of gravity. The water rushed along the channels feeding the complex system and feeding into the pipes that watered the grounds. But what was even more surprising was that at the water's edge, where once there had been barren channels was now starting to burst forth with greenery.

"See mum she even gave me this" she held out her golden necklace. On it was a pendant of the Six Winged Goddess.

"What did you say her name was?" she asked in a whisper, barely daring to breathe. This wasn't real, it couldn't be.

"Brigid and she is the answer to our prayers."

Michael crouched by the Indus River, invisible to the Humans milling about the edge. Already they held the taint of Brigid. Who would have thought she would have been so successful in a land that had never been hers. But then they had never thought that any of the Gods would ever escape their prisons. And now there were two powerful Goddesses loose and Brigid at least was empowering herself disturbingly quickly.

They really should have taken more efforts to hunt them down initially, but they had foolishly thought that they would be weak and merely hide from them until they traced them. Which had initially been true, especially for Hera, they had found nothing but passing traces of her but there was no knowing her powers. Hera was one of the most powerful Goddesses who have ever lived.

As for Brigid they had severely underestimated her abilities. They had planned on her actions mirroring the past. She had been a quiet Mother Earth Goddess from Ireland and Britain before they ever became important. Even during her long imprisonment her worship had continued to spread, she commanded such loyalty. And the worship had changed from her being just a Mother Earth Goddess to picking up other aspects of power. Which had only increased her power. At the height of her power, thankfully during imprisonment, her powers and skills would have rivalled Athena. Indeed they would have been peas in a pod. Having someone like Athena on the loose was deeply troubling. She had been near impossible to weaken and it had taken the concentrated efforts of nearly all the Angels to imprison her.

He would visit her later to drain off any powers she was gaining from the revival of paganism.

But the time of Brigid's free reign had to come to an end. She was no longer an inconvenience or minor threat. She was now the greatest threat to the Angels since Lucifer and the rebellion. Surprising that they had all feared Hera more. She had to be recaptured and drained of her powers, such powers could help them finally remove the traces of other religions and stamp their across the world. But first they had to destroy her power base, remove the extra power she was gaining. And he knew just the man to do it.

Azad Ali ground his teeth to stop himself striking out at the other men. He still needed them, as frustrating as they were. He was now the President of Pakistan, but the power was not all his, it was still shared with the other generals and they were baulking.

Why could they not see that this was the command of Allah? This was not a personal decision but one given from the Heavens. Pakistan was infested with infidels, undermining their righteous society. There were increasing reports of public nudity while bathing in the Ganges and most disturbingly were reports that it was starting in the Indus. They were starting to build their temples of sin and who knew what went on within them. They were a cancer that had to be removed before it spread. They were a threat to Islam and Pakistan.

He had said the same things to them over and over, but they were not real men, their testicles had shrivelled up. It was why they had mostly daughters. They lived in fear instead of willing to risk life and limb for their country and their God.

"There is nothing that will make us agree to your demands Azad Ali. We will not condone genocide, do you want to call down the UN on us. It is clear the power had gone to your head and it is our increasing belief that you should be stripped of your rank."

Then you are all fools.

Azad breathed a sigh of relief when the Arch Angel Michael exploded into the room in a burst of fire and sunlight. The other generals were slammed to the floor while he thankfully remained standing. With the proper care he bowed to the Angel. He was different from last time, there was more fire to his form. His wings seemed to dominate the room and his eyes were just light that he used to pin them all.

Michael hated dealing with such foolish mortals. They were so set in their ways and so blinded in their own decisions. They refused to see the truth because they constructed their own. He cast through their minds seeing how selfish and cowardly they were. Ah but luck was with him, one of them was a Demon.

With a swift and deadly movement he grabbed the Demon by his throat. *See how Demons hide in your ranks. Even your own power is corrupted from within, blind to the taint and the truth. It is pathetic.*

The Incubus hissed his fury as his Human semblance was burned off of him, leaving only the spirit essence of him within the clutches of Michael's power. The men stared appalled at the black spirit complete with erect penis, luscious lips, pleasing form and red burning eyes.

"You think to stop us Arch Angel, you have already lost. May the Goddesses reign supreme!"

Damn you to Hell Demon spawn. Your Goddesses will be joining you soon. Michael roared, sunlight blazing from his palms rendering the spirit in to mere dust motes as he was banished to Hell.

He turned his burning gaze on the generals as swords of light appeared floating above him. They all shot towards the generals, each sword stabbing a general in the right shoulder before burning up. Each of the generals cried out in pain as they clutched the burn.

We are in a crisis and Azad Ali has been selected by Heaven to lead this nation back to purity. You are on the front lines and yet you would falter. He will lead you back to the path of righteousness. His decisions are final, his requests are the demands of Heaven. Drive out and slaughter these infidels and Demons before they pollute your nation beyond saving. Do you wish to bring the Day of Judgment early?

Woe to any who dare question my authority or the Mandate of Heaven.

Then as suddenly as he appeared he was gone, making the room seem dark without his blinding light. It was hard to believe that one of their own had been a Demon but there was no denying what they had seen.

Azad sent a silent prayer of thanks to the Arch Angel before he turned to face the generals. They were all prostrate on the floor before him. This was going to be easier than imagined.

Should you choose you can kill any of your generals with a thought if they get in the way. The brands mark their allegiance to you. If they break it they will suffer.

He thanked Michael. Yes this was going to be so

much easier. Pakistan would be cleansed of this taint.

Chapter 25

Sariel stumbled out of the thick mists of the Borderlands right into the bright lights of Purgatory shining down on Limbo. She gasped in wonder as she viewed the colossal crater that was Hell. It stretched as far as she could see in every direction, it was impossibly deep, edged in gigantic claws of jutting rock reaching up into the white hemisphere of Purgatory mimicking the crater below. Stabbing down from the ceiling was a colossal stalactite on the far horizon, piercing through the fog covering the whole crater. That was her destination.

The sand drifts had led onto solid rock, through which the Acheron continued to split into a myriad of fast running rivers that spewed forth out into the empty space of the darkened crater before plummeting down into the cloud bank and the next Level of Hell. She could not see through the clouds but she knew that hidden in them was a path leading down into the crater. Flying was ill advised in such magical confines, the combination of Hell and Purgatory's containment spells could literally rip her apart.

She walked to the edge of the sandbank, walking through the wall of light rising up to Purgatory. It was to catch any saveable souls and send them up to the first Terrace. She knew that there were seven Terraces above her and eight Levels beneath her, each representing the Angelic versions of sin. On each Terrace of Purgatory there were Angels condemned to punish the souls of the redeemable in order to purify them. It was a post Hell construction, the Arch Angels' punishment for those who had not taken a side. They were Cursed to live in Purgatory.

Beneath them in Hell were the Fallen Angels, corrupted by Michael and Gabriel's spells. Very little was known about it, other than each Level had to be descended in order to reach Lucifer's Crater. It was just above the lowest point of Hell and harboured the only exit for the corporeal.

What was held within Hell's depths was unknown other than that there were Demons and souls of the Cursed.

Right now she stood in Limbo, the lip of the great crater, the First Level of Hell. It was here that nearly all unsanctified souls ended up, unless they were lucky enough to fall into another Underworld. They did not belong to the Angels and thus could not ascend through Purgatory to eventually reach Heaven, but neither did they technically belong to Hell. They were simply trapped here. It was the final resting place for all Atheists, Agnostics and many Pagans. The Hindus and Buddhists were lucky, their belief in reincarnation negated the need to enter the Underworld. Those who did not end up in one of the Ancient Underworlds were doomed to be left to linger in Limbo for all eternity. Or at least that was what she had been taught.

She turned her gaze upwards, using her keen Angelic eyesight to slightly pierce the rays of light to see the First Terrace and the hundreds of souls being dumped by the rays onto the Terrace. Angels, all three types, milled back and forth picking up the souls and leading them away, or bringing shaking souls back to the rays to ascend further. Every one of the Angels were grim faced with slumped shoulders. They were all the proof she needed that you had to stand up for what you believed, fence sitting would not get you what you want.

She hoped none of them could see her. They held no love for Heaven and would probably attack her on sight. Or report her when one of the Arch Angels came to Purgatory.

She stepped forward looking once again over the edge only to see the water spumes sinking into the dark gloom beneath. The only way she would see what lay within was if she descended, and once she did there would be no turning back. Not that she could turn back now anyway, she was sealed into Hell. At a loss as to where to begin she started walking along the edge of the crater, looking for anything that resembled a path.

She walked for a long time before she noticed a blue-white glow separate from the walls of white light cocooning this Underworld. She increased her pace to discover that Minos stood on a particularly large island. She gasped "Minos what are you doing here?"

"The same thing as Charon or the Furies. Human belief has subjected us to being part of Hell. Normally we are strong enough to remain apart, but we must return to perform the tasks we have been set. The demand overwhelms our powers. The Curse is powerful beyond measure and completely unrelenting. The presence of a living soul will only strengthen it further, awakening its most powerful and dangerous components. Be prepared to face the Demon forms of many of us."

"And what do you do here Minos?"

He shook his head slowly "Why I judge the dead of course. I use this bloody tail to determine which Level of Hell the poor souls will be condemned to. Then the Curse drags them down to where they deserve."

"But where are they all, there are plenty of souls being dredged up from the rivers into Purgatory. Why are there none before you and what about the souls that do not belong to Hell?"

"Firstly I have just finished my judging, your presence empowers the process, secondly many are simply dragged by the river straight into Hell. I am more of a figurehead, Dante's image of me. As for the millions of souls that wash up on the shores and should be stuck here waiting for eternity. Well the place gets so crowded that they end up being pushed into the rivers, islands collapse and yet many more fling themselves into the waters driven to the point of madness that they care not where they end up. Being stuck here is Hellish, there is no change, only the continual drain of one's essence. At least in Hell they can fade back into the Lifestream. Here there is no chance of that."

She stared at him horrified, why had she not been told this before?

"Are you aware that you are being hunted? By a Greater Demon. It has passed through the lights of Limbo recently, following your scent.

"How do I get away from it?"

"You can only out run it, you cannot hide. Descend further into Hell Sariel and be quick." He whipped his tail around him and spread his arms wide behind him. The sheet of water that had been running over the edge of the island dried up to reveal stone steps. She hurried over to the edge to see that they descended while following the edge of the crater's edge. She turned to thank Minos but he was gone. She hurried down the steps, trailing her left hand against the crater wall. Behind her the water started flowing again, covering any trace of where she had entered. She looked up expecting to see a torrent of water pouring down on her, but the water shot out into the void before falling down. The steps were set back from the streams of water. She was hidden from view as she descended into the Second Level of Hell.

Azrael watched her from the moment she entered Limbo until she disappeared down the steps. Good she had made it this far, if she had survived this long then she had obviously honed her fighting abilities somewhere. She would need them in Hell. Now if only she could reach the end and break the Curse, the balance would be returned and the world would be allowed to heal.

He cast a look around Purgatory before he ascended to Heaven. He doubted any had seen her and if they had it didn't matter, it was too late to intervene now.

"If is done Sariel has entered Hell and descended to the Second Level of Hell."

"You have done well Minos."

"I'm surprised I was able to leave. She's is one powerful young lady, Hell will pull out all its worst for her. She breathes power down there."

"She is going to die down there because of you all. She is far too powerful to have entered Hell."

"I have said this before Thanatos she is the only one who can do it."

Nyx interjected "her powers are unique, Hell will respond but her powers are surprisingly suited to battling whatever it throws at her. We can only wait in any case."

"How long until we are free?"

"Who can say, that all depends on Sariel."

A meeting had been called. All the Arch and Elder Angels. It was something that affected them directly. What surprised Gabriel was that she had had no clue one was coming. She always knew when one was going to be called, because usually it was her or Michael that called it. The others at least informed her, which meant only Azrael could have called it.

Sure enough he sat in his throne with the four other Arch Angels. She took her seat confused. Why would Azrael call a Council? He was the least active of all the Elder.

A few more Elders entered then the doors slammed shut. They were all here now.

Azrael spoke in his chilling voice "I have called this session because I have discovered news that affects us all and poses the greatest risk to us, beyond even that of Brigid and Hera."

He had everyone's full attention. What on earth could be more of a risk than those two? Heck the rate Brigid was claiming and converting was downright alarming despite their best efforts to the contrary. It had been decided the only way to counter her insurrection in India was by invading it with Pakistan.

It was Michael that pressed him "What is the greatest risk to us?"

"Sariel"

No one understood. Blank faces turned from one to another. Even she was at a loss as to how Sariel was a threat. Sure she was powerful, but she was naive, untrained and currently missing.

"How is Sariel the greatest threat we face. Is she a power source to one of the Goddesses?"

"No. It is worse than that."

Everyone leaned forward in their seats. He had an annoying habit of waiting before he spoke again. "Sariel has entered Hell"

Jesus Christ! What the fuck had happened for her to end up in Hell. This was a God damn nightmare.

Michael spoke slowly and with great care "In what state was she in? Poor of health? Under command? Is she frail? Will she perish?" Hope was lost for her, he was having to come to that, publically. She could not be retrieved now and she was too much of a danger to be allowed to live. Unfortunately they could do nothing.

"She seemed healthy enough, she didn't look frail

but as to coercion I cannot say. Such spells are beyond the understanding of Purgatory's guards."

There was silence before one of the Elders spoke "Can she not be retrieved like the Greater Demons. They have been summoned to the Surface before to suit our needs could we not do the same for her."

Azrael answered "We can only do that once Hell has consumed her and she herself is a Greater Demon. It is too late for her, there is nothing we can do."

"Is she not a threat being alive, she could free some of the Greater Demons. She has no idea what she is doing but once freed they would. We could have all Hell breaking loose. Can we not eradicate her?"

Michael's glare pinned the man to his chair by fury alone. Even Gabriel was not daring to answer, though she completely agreed. Sariel was now a threat whether she realised it or not.

Once again Azrael answered "The only way to eradicate her as you suggest, to remove this problem, would for one of our own to descend into Hell themselves. It is a suicide mission at best. I doubt any would volunteer."

No one did.

"We will have to wait, it is unlikely she will survive long in any case. She is but a young, naive and untrained girl with untapped power. She will perish soon.'

Michael turned his head away from the crowd as he disappeared. They let him go, there was nothing any of them could do for him. Despite using her, Michael did love Sariel.

Still that answered where she had been. Angels could be redirected into finding the Goddesses without any distractions now. Though she would wait until Michael gave the order. Not even she was willing to anger him so.

Chapter 26

The Second Level of Hell was hidden beneath a thick cloud bank that seemed to absorb any of the ambient light floating around. It was dark and menacing. She stood a couple of steps above it, watching it gently lap against the steps and wall. The rivers poured straight into the darkness, leaving no mark on the surface of the clouds. It was eerily calm, the only sound being of rushing and roaring water from far above. She could barely see the top of the crater, only discernible from by the darkness encircling the lights of Purgatory above.

She took a step down, and then another until she stood one step above the clouds. Hesitantly she placed one foot down onto the unseen step. Her foot chilled but nothing else happened. Perhaps the only danger was falling off the edge because she couldn't see the steps. Carefully she placed her other foot on the next step down. She spent the next several minutes carefully feeling for the next step before she continued to descend. As she lowered herself into the inky darkness she found it akin to stepping through steam, only cold. There were no solid or liquid structures, only the wall to her left and the steps beneath her feet. There was little to suggest to her body that she was neck deep in darkness.

She took a steadying breath before she stepped down the last step, feeling a little foolish for her hesitation. She walked down feeling the coldness spread up her neck. She shook her head at her own foolishness, she would just have to be careful not to fall off while she descended. Clumsiness and blindness were the only dangers.

She discovered how shockingly wrong she was

once she was fully under the cloudbank. There was a flash of white light, the Level above was now sealed shut. Then the illusion wore off. She was in a brutal tempest, violent winds knocking her against the wall, tugging mercilessly at her wings and clothes in an attempt to drag her off the steps. Were there had been very little sound now there was far too much. Winds roared, rain pelted her and lightning flashed constantly, the booming thunder more like an unsteady drum beat. Her eyes were blinded by the flashes of white, grey and blood red lightning streaking through the otherwise impenetrable darkness. While her ears continued to be assaulted by the booming of thunder and wail of tortured winds. They shrieked and screamed far more than could ever possibly be natural.

Then she realised why. With each lightning strike she noticed more and more people being flung around in the storm. Clutching desperately towards each other, reaching out for anyone as they were spun around and around, smacked off the cliffs and each other as the wind changed direction every time the thunder boomed.

She screamed as a body was flung next to her, the soul clearly visible through the corporeal body. This was the Underworld, spirits didn't have bodies. Why did he have a body that bled and bruised? Before she could move it slumped forward and was dragged back into the maelstrom.

She shivered as the cold rain beat against her. She pressed herself as close against the cliff as she could. This wasn't like the rest of the Underworlds. She had seen all of Hades, Isis had described Aaru and she had ventured along several waterways with Hecate. Nothing but the living had corporeal bodies, the spirits of the dead could not interact with the physical world. Why were they in bodies here?

The whole crater shook as an unholy roar filled the air. The rain stopped, the thunder silenced and everything fell dark while the roar went on. Her heart went out to it, whatever it was it was in agony. Then the roar fell silent and in its wake the storm started up. She wondered if that had been Lucifer trapped in his Beast form. What an awful punishment for such a brilliant man.

A screech filled the air. It was close, it had to be within this Level of Hell. The screams of the damned only increased as they were flung about and she quickly started to descend again. Whatever it was she didn't want to hang around to find out what it was. To her surprise the stairs widened out, expanding out onto wide terraces, littered with shifting bodies before returning to thin steps again.

She was running across one such terrace when lightning flashed illuminating the whole area. There were bodies strewn all across the terrace. Curious she knelt by the nearest one. It was a woman with pallid olive skin and ragged black hair. But her brown eyes were wide looking at her. The wind changed and she started slithering across the terrace. Sariel reached out and grabbed her by the hand as the other bodies were blown off the terrace into the storm. As soon as her hand grasped the woman's light moved through her skin from where she held Sariel's down into her heart before spreading throughout the rest of her. The woman looked at her with her dark eyes and gestured down the path.

In silence Sariel ran after the woman, her hand clutched desperately in the woman's. They ran for a long time, through many more terraces, each of them slightly bigger than the last until they came across a massive terrace that stuck far out into the crater. Sariel couldn't even see the other side in the storm but she could tell it was different from the other terraces. The rain fell softly here and the thunder was but a dull distant rumble. For the first time since she had entered the Level she could actually hear other noises, their heavy breathing and the slap of their feet on the wet rock.

The woman let go and turned to stare at her. It was clear from the piercing gaze and air of authority that she had once been an important person.

"How is it that you have a body? You should only be a spirit."

The woman laughed "This is Hell, the Angels' spells changed all the dynamics of the Underworld. Here we are subjected to endless torture for committing sin. We are given our bodies back in order to feel pain and suffering."

"That is horrendous"

"The Gods were cruel but the Angels are even crueller. Which begs the question why is an Angel in Hell?"

"Because the only way to leave the Underworld is through Hell."

How very naive of her, one could not leave Hell without breaking the Curse. Someone had told her half-truths. Still the girl held potential. She had power enough to survive. If she could was another question. "You're an Arch Angel it should be easy for you to leave."

"Hell is sealed shut, the only exit is through Lucifer's Crater."

Which was true but who ever had told her that had neglected to mention she would have to battle the Beast to get past. "Then I wish the best of luck to you?"

"Sariel"

"Cleopatra"

"Why does that sound familiar?"

Cleopatra stared at her in surprise. She had thought everyone knew of her "The Last Pharaoh of

Egypt before it was swallowed up by Rome."

"If you are Egyptian shouldn't you been in Aaru with your Gods?"

"I was until Dante's writings influenced Humans so much that their perception pulled me out of Aaru and flung me into here. Apparently to Christians I am the epitome of the sin of Lust. But I am not alone in my treatment, plenty of us have been pulled from our final resting places to suffer for sins we committed before the notion of sin even existed."

"You mean others have been pulled from other Underworlds?"

"To suffer for all eternity. Or at least while the world still holds up. By the Angels teachings we are Demons, the perception only strengthened over the centuries and we continue to suffer. The injustice of it all completely undermines the Angels' teachings but of course mortals don't know about our suffering. Demons belong in Hell, even if you're only seen as one."

Sariel couldn't believe the injustice of it all. To rip people away from their resting places and cast them into Hell because they embodied a sin that hadn't been a sin in their time. It was barbaric. As for the poor Daemon races they were automatically thrown straight into Hell for being something they could not change. She knew that that included the Lilin, Vampires and Werewolves but there had to be other races equally tortured. Only the Nymphs and Fairies avoided being sucked into Hell because their spirits stayed with the land and never entered the Underworld.

She wondered if there were any Lilin in the other Levels or if they were all in the Lust Level.

There was a loud screech and before she knew what had happened Cleopatra had flung herself off the terrace into the raging storm. At first she thought it the actions of a lunatic until she saw the huge dark shape coming towards her. It was a gigantic bird, a huge dark shape whenever the clouds lit up. A darkness that stood out even against the dark clouds. And it was heading straight for her.

Sariel had no idea what to do. Jumping into the storm was not an option and she couldn't even see where the stairs leading off the terrace where.

She started to run across the terrace casting her eyes back at the creature. It resembled some kind of colossal Griffin landing on its four legs. It was covered in black feathers, right to its reptilian tail that was a mixture of black and grey scales. Even the skin on its feet was black. It looked down on her with burning blood red eyes.

It screeched again, drowning out all other noise as it charged towards her. It took four steps to traverse the entire distance, then its claws were swiping at her and its beak was snapping. She jumped up into the air, using her wings to flit about but she had never flown in a storm before. Her control was weak, her evasions of the creature were more a testament to the storm then her skills.

It jumped forward and because of its sheer size she had no chance of avoiding it. She ploughed into it, hastily gripping onto feathers larger than she was. She turned her face away from the blood and gore that coated it. It turned out to be a mistake. The creature launched itself into the air, leaving far behind the terrace.

It was a nightmare. The thing screeched rendering her deaf. Bodies flew at her, many being cut asunder against the sharp feathers, covering her in their blood. Their screams filled her ears when the creature's did not. She clung desperately to the feathers, ignoring the pain as she cowered against it.

What else could she to do?

It had flown for what seemed like hours. It seemed to have forgotten about her, but she feared letting go. In this storm she would be lost and disorientated in a second. She simply would not stand a chance. But she was fed up.

She shook her head at her own stupidity. Her life with the Angels had conditioned her to a life with no magic. She had magic, a lot apparently. She quickly turned within herself searching for what would help her. She passed by night and fire, Hell was strong in them there was no way she could combat its greater power. She was wrong but she didn't know that. Water would not serve her well nor would death, they both permeated the air. She needed something different, something in contrast.

Light called to her and she beckoned it. It unwound within her, like a flower blooming. A ray of light burst out of her chest, expanding until her entire chest was a blazing sun. The creature screeched as it suddenly became aware of the Angel attached to it. Angels were the bringers of pain. Why was one here? Was it the Apocalypse? They were coming for its flesh to feed their followers. It screamed forth its terror trying to shake off the Angel with all its might.

Sariel despite her Divine strength was sent spinning away, sharp feathers cutting through her hands. Blood droplets flew slowly past her eyes, sparkling with the magic she was using. The whole world slowed down, the lightning flashes lasted longer as did the darkness between. The bodies floated past her slowly, she could see the pain and suffering written all across their face in blood. She could even hear what they were screaming "Beware the Ziz!"

The Ziz wheeled around, its burning eyes focusing

on the streaks of light. It shrieked its fury, how dare they come for its flesh, how dare they invade her last retreat. Ironic that she saw her prison as her sanctuary now. She had been banished here when the Angels took over the world and only summoned occasionally to do their bidding.

They had Cursed her and stripped her of her vibrant beauty. Forced her from the open skies and fresh air, dragged her away from the fertile lands she had cultivated for millenia. They had cast her down into this damned abyss, trapped within the eternal storms born of the fires of Hell and the Waters of Death.

And now they had finally come for to collect her flesh promised to their followers. No they would not have her flesh it belonged to the earth not to domesticated Angel spawn. They would not have it!

She charged forward screaming at the haze of light.

Sariel beat her wings slowly, holding her position with the aid of her magic. She was still staring at her hands, silver blood pooling in her hands and dripping away. Mortal weapons, whether natural or handmade, could not harm Divine flesh. The Ziz had to be Divine.

She realised that the blood droplets were floating in the air about her, sparkling like jewels in the darkness. Even the rain had stilled, reflecting her light into a myriad of rainbows. Everything had stilled and then she realised that the shrieking of the Ziz held magic. It was the focal point of power for the Lust Level. She wondered if the connection was simply because the Ziz was a flying creature or if it had in some way had committed the sin of lust.

Through the twilight she noticed the Ziz charging full pelt at her. She pulled up her magic, feeding the blazing sun of her chest that was spreading throughout her. She was a blazing sun, in every cell from the tips of her toes to the tips of her hair floating around her. She was more light than flesh, stabbing outwards into the darkness, pushing them back. But the darkness was extensive and her light could only probe so far. She turned her attention to the Ziz as it charged towards her, she swung her arm down and a ray of burning light followed. It slashed across its chest, burning away shadows to reveal a line of copper. Just as she had expected the Ziz had been corrupted by the spells of Hell. She could use her Angel magic to convert it back to its natural form.

Then the Ziz was on her, its forelegs clawing forward, the beak following close behind. The one advantage of it being so vast was once she dodged them she was relatively safe. Nemesis had trained her well, she easily dodged talons and beak to grab onto its feathers on its shoulders. She didn't want it to be able to claw at her. Everywhere she touched blazed coppery before the shadows closed back in.

It shrieked its dismay and horror at not being able to reach her. It snapped its wings and rolled trying to knock her off. Then it spotted its terrace in the distance, it would be able to roll on her.

Sariel had other ideas. She grabbed as many feathers as she could and wrapped her legs around them. Not that it did much, she felt as insignificant as a tick. But she was no tick, she was a demigoddess Arch Angel with powerful bloodlines and magic. With a scream of pain her magic exploded out of her into the Ziz. It shrieked in agony, falling onto the terrace and skating across its surface. She tried to reach around to grasp the light and Angel, she rolled over to crush her. But try as she might she could not dislodge the Angel.

Sariel used her magic to bind herself to the Ziz,

reaching into its powerbase, seeking out its core. Her powers flitted across its flanks, black flickering copper before turning back to black. The shadows were strong, so was the spell binding them to her. Already the darkness was smothering them both, reducing Sariel's blaze of light to spears that barely illuminated the terrace. She turned her magic inwards, the Ziz blazed from within with such intensity that it managed to shine through even her shadowy feathers.

Sariel continued to probe and search, shaping her magic within the creature. Ziz tried to struggle, tried to claw and snap, even roll over but to no avail. She just could not dislodge the Angel. It was going to have its flesh, what was taking it so long anyway. Was it just toying with her? The Angels were a sick lot. She shrieked her dismay as she saw light shining out of herself. What was it doing to her? She shrieked even louder when she heard a gentle female voice whisper gently into her mind.

Remember who you are Simurgh

Then she plunged down into memories.

The sun warmed her coppered feathers as she glided through the air, watching the desert people beneath her...ploughing fields with her talons, using her magic to make them fertile, watching her people gather the fruits of their labour...she remembered when she was young, the colours of her feathers, she remembered the destruction of various civilisations, one of the so called end of the worlds. She had lived through several, she had even survived the first Apocalypse...She had seen the fall of kings, of Gods, of Lucifer and his brethren, the fall of her people and their massacre...She had seen the world change, the Gods change, mortal races and civilisations rise and fall time and time again. She was ancient even by the Gods standards...It had all changed when the vicious and conniving Angels had overthrown the Gods and ripped her from everything she had ever known. What had she ever done to them, she had mothered none, she had caused no wars, she had stayed out of Divine politics. She had not intervened. Yet they had turned her into a Monster and cast her into Hell.

Sariel watched the light burn off the shadows from within, the darkness trailed off of Simurgh as thick smoke trails. Light started to burst out from between the swirling darkness. She couldn't see it but Sariel felt Simurgh's heart absorb her powers, pumping them through her body and driving out the last of the shadows. It also unlocked her own true powers for her once again. To her magical vision she saw the chains of Gabriel's spell sliding off of her true form, saw the colours appearing underneath the darkness. She urged her magic along Gabriel's chains, breaking and unlocking them, setting Simurgh free of her Monster Curse.

Further afield they were both watched by the denizens of the Lust Level. In all their time in Hell the storm had never once stopped howling. There had never been any Angels, only Demons moving between the Levels. And the Ziz had never been able to still, driven to the brink of madness by the Curse. But now they watched as an Angel drowned the stilled Ziz in intense light. She had stopped the storm, had driven light into darkness, and even as the Ziz lay twisting on the terrace the darkness of the Level was fading. A soft grey light infused the clouds.

They watched as light exploded out of the Ziz, a circle rippled through the whole level, casting slight rainbows within the clouds. They had forgotten colours.

Shadows retracted from her chest as light continued to pour forth. Where she had been covered and contained within darkness now her true beauty was free to shine.

Her neck was covered in coppery fur that ran under her body and down her legs. The back of her neck was feathered in all the colours of the rainbow, spreading down her back and into her long tail somewhat of a combination between peacock and bird of paradise. Her wings looked more like rainbows than feathers. Her talons changed into shining copper as light danced across her whole form.

Her colossal form shrank, she was no longer the gigantic Greater Demon Ziz but a far smaller animal Goddess. Her eyes opened to reveal brown then closed again as she gave a gentle sigh.

Sariel found it far easier to climb down off of Simurgh. She walked around to look at Simurgh front on. She was a stunning creature and she had felt her heart, she was so kind and gentle. Why had the Angels done this to her? She had done nothing to them. There was no mention of her in the journals she had read. This was not an act of revenge but pure cruelty.

She glanced around the Lust Level in surprise. It looked like a very cloudy day. Grey clouds drifted about and the occasional ray of sunlight streamed through. The violent winds had died down, leaving the bodies to gently float through the air. There was nothing she could do for them but at least she had eased their suffering.

She placed her hand on Simurgh's beak, it was still larger than her, "Sleep well Simurgh, you truly deserve it"

Then she turned away and headed over to the steps at the edge of the terrace. She started following the trail again. She cast one last glance back at Simurgh sleeping peacefully and the changes she had wrought on this Level. She smiled at her achievement before skipping a little bit down the path. Next was the Gluttony Level and the dangers it would hold.

At least this time she knew she was walking into danger, no matter how serene it pretended to be.

The two youths ran through the shadows of the cathedral, keeping out of the streetlights as much as they could. The taller one eased forward, glancing around cautiously. The other gently placed his hand on his shoulder, before slipping around him to try the side door.

The taller shook his head "of course it's locked James" then he pushed him out of the way before lifting a hand shrouded in red shadows. The lock clicked open and the other quickly pushed the door open and pulled the other into the church. "You might have magic Rob but you still need a Human to help you enter a holy place."

Rob grimaced "A place that you as a gay are technically banned from. Seeing as you are damned to burn in the bowels of Hell."

"Phht like Hell actually exists. Christians are deluded, like there is an actual God who sits up there watching us and sending us to Hell. And if there is there is something very fucked up about it. Besides you're an Incubus, you're Demon spawn and cannot enter without my help. You tell me who is going to Hell?"

Rob stared down at him "There was a time that the Gods did such things but then they were killed by the Angels. There is no God but there are Angels, hundreds and thousands of them, and if the rumours are true then we shall sanctify this cathedral in Brigid's name."

"Oh you're actually serious about that. I thought it was just a ruse to make it into a role-play."

"Of course this is very serious James. This could get us killed. You only think about sex don't you?"

James smiled "You say that like it's a bad thing. Where else are you going to get a Human boyfriend with a sex drive to match an Incubus'?" he reached up and kissed Rob, deepening it quickly. Rob soon found himself scrabbling along the walls as James expertly started to remove his clothing. It was a bit of a rush for James but for Rob it was much more serious. He had heard the story of Joshua Brigidsword, or so he called himself now, who had had sex with the Goddess in the middle of Saint Peter's Cathedral in Adelaide. It had caused quite the media sensation. It also would have had all the Angels for miles flocking. It was bad enough there were so many in Australia at the moment.

It had caused claims of mass hallucination to divine intervention. Who knew what had happened in the cathedral. Since then Josh was now the High Priest of the Brigidites in Australia. Their numbers were growing rapidly, thanks mostly to the Daemons but also among the people living along the Murray River. Josh had disappeared, mostly to stop the Angels killing him, but he did reappear for significant events. He had watched the videos on the internet. He was also very active among the magical races.

For it would seem that Brigid had given him the gift of magic, long forgotten to Humans and weak within the magical races. Rumour had it that anyone who defiled a church in Brigid's name was given the gift of magic. He planned to do that to find out. And even if it was fruitless then at least he had defiled a church. But this wasn't just any church, this was Saint Mary's Cathedral, the seat of the Catholic Church in Australia, and one of the many prominent sights of Sydney. It was a miracle combined with his own magic that they had not alerted security.

"This would be hotter on the altar" James whispered into his ear as he raised his face from Rob's body. Amazing that he knew exactly what was needed to defile a church the most, when he was just being kinky. He accepted the fact that there were Daemons but he didn't accept Angels or Gods. Rob picked up James, who promptly wrapped his legs around his waist as Rob carried him up the steps to the altar. They knocked over candles and pushed a bible off the altar in their passion. James giggled as he looked around at the pictures and stained glass windows "They're certainly going to get a show tonight" Even Rob smirked at that before going down on James.

The only sound in the empty cathedral were James' gasps and moans of pleasure, followed by the clang of metal as he knocked something off the altar. He grabbed Rob's face and pulled him back up to kiss him. His spare hand started pulling down Rob's underwear "Take me now. Make love to me"

Rob smiled as he stepped out of his underwear, then kissed him deeply as James wrapped his arms and legs around him, his body arching up towards him. Their love while young was pure and passionate. Strong enough to last a lifetime or to lay their lives down for each other. It transcended the borders of their races.

He dropped down to rummage through his trousers.

"What are you doing?"

"Getting the lube idiot. Don't think you'd really want it dry."

James just watched him until he started putting his penis in. Then his face wrinkled in pain. After a bit it eased up and he started to moan and smile.

They continued kissing passionately while he thrust away into James. Both of their moans echoing through the cathedral.

Their moans intensified in unison as their orgasms approached. This was going to be one of those rare times they both orgasmed together. Both of them arched their backs, Rob flinging his head back as he came while James bit down on his lower neck. To their complete surprise both their chest bloomed with light. They were frozen in place as the coppery image of a six winged woman bloomed between their nipples. Then the light was gone and Rob collapsed onto James.

He pushed himself up shakily to study the image on James' chest. It was smaller than a hand and felt exactly like skin.

"What do you think it means?" James asked quietly. He ran his hand over the image, captivated by it.

"I have no idea but it holds power, lots of power." It flared slightly under his touch.

Bright light flared behind them and they tumbled off the altar. Once they managed to untangle themselves they peeked over the top of the altar. What Rob saw turned his blood cold and made James stare in surprise.

An Angel floated in the air in front of the altar, his four white wings beating slowly. His eyes glowed with light as he looked around the cathedral, his gaze scrutinizing the melting crucifixes and burning bibles. He didn't flinch when the stained glass windows shattered and began to rearrange themselves. Instead his gaze fell upon the altar, with its sweat and sex stains. And the two pairs of eyes watching him, one with horror the other awe.

Rob's worst fears were confirmed when he was lifted into the air by swirls of light. "Demon spawn" the Angel spat, loathing contorting his beautiful face. He raised a flaming sword and pointed at the Incubus "You will die for what you have done"

"Stop" James yelled as he jumped up onto the altar, placing himself in front of the Angel's poised sword.

The Angel turned his burning gaze to the Human before him and somehow managed to express more loathing "You too will burn in Hell homosexual for your unnatural ways" he roared, thrusting his sword forward. James screamed as the sword cut through his chest, shattering his ribs. The Angel looked down at his sword, surprised that he was still there before he flicked his sword to the side. James was sent sprawling across the shaking floor in a stream of blood.

Rob yelled at him trying to reach his magic. Shadows danced around him, wrapping around the streams of light. The Angel laughed as more light flooded the shaking cathedral, banishing all shadows.

"Your pitiful shadow magic is no might for the Light of Heaven." He raised his sword up in a high arch, bringing it swinging down towards the Demon. As soon as it cut through his flesh it would immolate him and send him straight into the depths of Hell.

"NO!" James screamed, Rob had told him about Angel magic, not that he had paid it much heed before now. Rob would be completely lost to Hell. He reached out his bloodied hand straining to reach him. Blood shot through the air, splattering across the Angel's white armour. He didn't notice until it burst into flames and another burst of flames sent him crashing off the altar. James stared at the flames encircling his hand. Rob stared at James in amazement before turning his attention back to the Angel.

He roared his fury as he pushed himself back up. His sword erupted into brilliant white flames as he turned back to face James. Murder and hate were written deeply all across his face. He raised his flaming sword and swung it down, flames roaring out towards James. Everyone stared in shock as they fanned across a shield before twisting around into two streams, wreathing like snakes around him.

"Do not interfere with my followers" A six winged

woman wearing red armour had appeared on the bluestone altar. Her voice sounded like the ocean's roar across a wintery landscape. She raised a spear dancing with lightning and the two fire snakes, then drove it straight into the Angel. The fire and lightning flooded into him. He twitched on the end before he exploded in a flurry of smoking white embers. A flash of silver light flooded up the spear into her.

She turned her attention to James, she snapped her fingers and he was instantly healed. She strode across to help him up. Rob warily rushed over to join him casting a fearful glance at her.

"Who are you?" James asked, she had to be friendly. She wouldn't have healed him otherwise.

She smiled at him but her only response was to tap the image of herself on his chest.

"So the rumours are true, we really did defile a place of God in your name."

"In a manner yes. It would appear my blessing has awakened some forgotten talents of your bloodline. She took his burning hand in her own. He felt a coolness spread through his skin then the flames died. "You will need training." She cast her eyes over Rob "both of you. You have talents that have not been seen for many centuries. Magic has long been forgotten but apparently it has merely been dormant. The blood remembers much."

"Is the Age of Angels really at an end? Are the Gods back to save us?" Rob asked desperately. He had had several family members killed by the Angels.

It was funny Brigid thought. The Age of Gods had hardly been a peaceful period, whereas under the Angel's rule Humanity had advanced and flourished though that was starting to fall apart. Admittedly it had taken them many centuries and it was probably more due to the Humans than the Angels now she thought about it. But for the Daemons it had been a period of brutality and genocide. Many races had been hunted to extinction and Humans had had their magic wielders eliminated entirely.

"Yes Robert the Age of Angels is coming to an end and the Gods will rise again. The Lilin will no longer have to hide in the shadows, nor will any Daemon have to hide who they are." She held out a hand to each of them "Come with me boys, there is much for you to learn." Neither of them hesitated to grab her hands. Then they were gone leaving behind the dramatically altered cathedral, a strange mess of blood, sweat, semen and embers to be found in the morning. A few moments later their clothes disappeared.

The woman walked into Saint Mary's cathedral with the other Sunday worshippers, her clothes properly restrained. Long black trousers, a white blouse and a long black jacket over the top. Her hair was tied back into a ponytail. She was rather plain looking, one people would easily forget. Except her eyes they were a stunning amber colour. She walked with purpose to the front row of the cathedral before taking a seat. The pews still held their cushions.

Her gaze examined the church. All the stained glass windows showed Brigid or her symbols. The bluestone altar had not managed to be removed, instead covered in a robe and crucifixes that had had to have been hastily made. The plant life had been stripped but their signs were still evident.

What had once been a proud declaration of the Christian faith was now a sad vestige in need of repair.

Powerful magic had been used here. She could smell it. And something else as well.

She sat through the mass, but her eyes were rarely

on the bible she held, instead constantly flicking all over the cathedral, picking up every change since she had last been there. She was familiar with the story her people had brought her as well as being on the news. Churches all over Australia and New Zealand were undergoing similar changes. Other than powerful magic being used no one understood why it was happening. This taint was spreading and they were at a loss as to why.

She dropped her bible, the sound echoing throughout the whole cathedral but no one moved. Her spell had frozen them all. She also dropped her illusion, once again embracing her Angel form. She marched to the altar with purposeful strides, the magic was strongest here.

She ran her hands over the altar, ignoring the radiating magic to sense what had happened. Her lips twitched when she felt the lust that stained the altar, among other things. It wasn't just any sexual encounter, it had been two males, one of them an Incubus. And it had been willing. Michael would be furious to learn of this defilement.

She walked around the altar, sensing the magic that had been used here. There had been four wielders of magic. There was the Incubus' and Brigid's so strong that it nearly masked the others. What stopped her in her tracks and sent a chill down her spine was the hint of Human magic. Human magic had been weeded out during the Middle Ages by their religions. True there had remained traces in Asia, Africa and the Americas but they had been dealt with during European colonisation. Even the Demon races could hardly claim to be very magical, too much magic left traces for the Angels to hunt down.

But this was not some weak trace from either boy, both were far stronger than they had a right to be. Michael really would not be pleased to hear this.

Her head whipped around to face the wall. The police reports had said the scene had been covered with blood across the altar and floor. Sweat and semen had been found on the altar. What was odd was that feathers and ash had been found but no bodies. The report had confused her but understanding dawned on her as she finally felt the last trace. An Angel.

She ran over to the wall, placing her hand against it driving her powers into it. She gasped in horror as she felt his death occur. Her knees buckled. An Angel had been killed in a House of God. This was war.

The Arch Angels were not going to like this.

She waved her hands allowing her powers to spread through the cathedral, returning it to how she remembered and cutting its ties to Brigid. Her hold was tenuous at best when it came to churches.

Nuriel swallowed. She had no good news for the Arch Angels. She squared her shoulders before ascending to Heaven. It didn't matter how much Gabriel unnerved her, she had to deal with her. She had to deal with all the Arch Angels, it was her job requirement. But Gabriel was just so terrifying when she got angry.

Matilda ran through the orchards yelling in despair. Rachel had disappeared, she should have been in the house. She had left her there when she went to check on the cows. She should have taken her with her, but Rachel was so difficult to drag away from the animals. She just loved them so much. It had been her bed time anyway.

So she had put her to bed and left her behind. She wasn't going to be long. Only she had come back to find the back door broken down and Rachel missing. It was her worst nightmare, Rachel's father had found them again. She had left Gavin because of his violent tendencies and his general hatred of Australia. He was one of those Aboriginals that believed every non-Indigenous person owed him something. Like his race had anything to do with his standing in life. He wasted his Indigenous benefits on alcohol and gambling, instead of paying child support for his daughter.

His brother Nathan was the polar opposite, he was a lawyer in Adelaide. It was to him that she had ran to for support with her divorce. He was completely understanding and supportive of her. He still came to visit when he could even though Adelaide was miles away. Rachel adored him and he her. He taught her about her heritage which was something Matilda couldn't do. She was an English migrant, she knew nothing of the Indigenous culture, but she wanted Rachel to learn both her cultural identities.

The divorce of course had not been amicable, she had slapped him with a restraining order then ran away to the country to make a new life. She had given up her promising career as a doctor in order to hide, throwing herself into small farming. She had struggled to make friends of her neighbours, they were a racist, conservative lot. Being a single mother of a half aboriginal girl did not place her well in their eyes. But she had endured and tried to make Rachel's life happy.

But she had failed.

She ran along the path screaming out for Rachel, following the many footprints on the path. Why was there so many and why were they all heading back to town? Had Gavin brought his jail buddies with him? She ran as fast as she could, following the footsteps as they headed directly back to town.

She slowed when she saw bright lights. And lots of burning torches. What was this the Dark Ages? There was a large crowd gathered in front of the church, each of them holding a torch. They were all subdued and quiet listening to someone speaking.

She edged forward straining to hear the words. She caught snippets "witch...cleansing...good of the town...unnatural" she didn't hear much but what she did chilled her to the bone. She continued to edge forward, pushing her way through the crowd uncaring of the vacant eyes that turned to watch her. She had eyes only for her daughter, tied up to a wooden stake sticking out of a pile of wood and trash.

They were planning on burning her daughter!

"And so the witch's mother comes for her spawn." Someone spat.

Her eyes flicked over the old priest, there was something wrong with him. His eyes burned with an insane fervour, but it wasn't just that, he didn't look right. His edges seemed to blur, she could have sworn she saw light and wings. It was as though his image was superimposed on another.

"My daughter is not a witch."

"She consorts with Demons and uses magic she is a witch!"

She looked around in confusion at everyone numbly nodding along with him "Are you seriously buying this? Demons do not exist. Magic does not exist. This is insanity, what you are doing is murder. You are planning on murdering a nine year old girl based on the ranting of a deluded old man."

"Heaven is above the law" they mumbled.

"They belong to the light, they do not consort with Demons and pretenders. They are pure. You are tainted. Grab her, she will burn too."

She fought back viciously but there were too many and none of them seemed to notice pain. She quickly found herself tied up behind her daughter. They were actually going to burn them alive! This was insane. This simply could not be happening. Witch burnings did not happen in Australia. They were going to murder them because of the ranting of a deranged old man.

Her heart and mind were in a rollercoaster of disbelief and fear. Rachel strangely enough wasn't crying, she didn't even seem upset. She was far more composed than herself. Matilda stared around at her in silent wonder. She smiled back sweetly as though she didn't have a care in the world.

"It is okay mummy Brigid will save us"

She didn't know whether to laugh or cry at her naive faith in a Goddess that didn't exist.

"Silence whore of Satan. You will not speak your Demon's name."

"She is a Goddess not a Demon and she represents all that is just. She is real while your God is not. She gives us water so that we may live but none of you even thank her. You say her name then go back to your closed minded ways. I have heard you all invoke her name. You are just as guilty as I."

"The witch admits it. She's guilty." In a blind rage he threw his torch at Rachel.

Matilda had a moment to stare in awe at her daughter before she turned back to being terrified as all of the town started throwing torches at them. The heat was quickly intense and it was only going to get worse.

"I'm sorry I wasn't a better mother Rachel and I'm sorry we're going to die like this. But know this I have always loved you."

"I love you too mummy and you were the best mummy in the whole world. Do not fear, Brigid will not abandon us."

It was strange how she flicked between adult and child when she spoke.

"Of course not Rachel, the world would mourn your loss."

Everyone but Rachel gasped at the six winged woman who had appeared in their midst. The flames of the pyre died, their bindings snapped off and the vacant look vanished from people's faces. Except the priest's, his contorted in fury.

Brigid turned to face him "Why don't you show your real face Inquisitor"

She flicked her hand and the old priest collapsed, leaving behind the hazy image of an Angel. But Inquisitors were not stunning examples of Angels, their souls twisted and tainted. Their light was gloomy, their robes dark grey, their eyes cruel and dark. They did not look so far removed from Demons.

He screamed as burning chains of gold wrapped around his wrists "hear me now Inquisitor and mortals. The Age of Angels is coming to an end and the Gods will rise to claim what is rightfully ours. No longer will magic be persecuted or those who wield it. No longer will the land be raped and plundered. Hate will not spread so rapidly. It is time for the truth to be shown and the world to awaken."

He burst into flames as he disappeared. She had learned how to send Angels to Hell, which seemed the most fitting punishment for such depraved spirits.

She turned to the townspeople "Rachel is a priestess of mine, this church is now my domain and will be tended by her. She has the power over the land and the river, to heal the damage you have done. She is your salvation and your only hope. You will listen to her commands and follow them through for they are my desires and they shall be done. Your lives are all mine now."

Then she was gone in an eruption of fire and

lightning.

The entire town fell to their knees as they turned to face Rachel. "What must we do Sacred One?"

Rachel walked forward in a long red dress that fluttered about in the breeze. Where had she gotten that dress? She hadn't been wearing it a few moments ago.

"First of all we shall build a statue for the Goddess, all bibles will be burned and all crucifixes destroyed. You shall give back to the land what you take from it and you will pray to the Goddess for your salvation and her forgiveness. You will also never attempt to harm myself or my mother on pain of death."

Then sweet as a button she grabbed her mother's hand and led her away confused.

Chapter 27

Sariel sighed in relief when she finally walked out from under the cloud bank. She could actually see the bottom of the stairs and what appeared to be swampland at their base. It stretched as far as she could see in the drizzling rain. She sighed in annoyance, yet more rain and it was just as cold as the Lust Level. She knew she was in the Gluttony Level but she didn't know what to expect. Her family had been vague on the details of Hell. She now had a feeling they knew a lot more than they had told her. And from what Minos had said she was going to run into Cerberus and the Furies in their Demon forms. That wasn't a comforting fact.

After her battle with the Ziz she had managed to dry off. By the time she reached the bottom of the stairs she was completely drenched again. Her hair stuck to her neck, her clothes clung to her skin and her feathers clung to her back and arms. Water ran in rivers down her neck. She stood with shoulders slumped as she stared at the swamp just beyond the rock shelf. Terrible smells of decay rose from the fetid swamp. Black and grey plants thrust out their skeletons above the black water. Bare patches of grey earth poked out of the water and all manner of beasts wandered across the islands.

She really didn't want to walk across the swampland in sandals. The thought of getting that mud between her toes was repulsive. If only she had brought boots with her. Then again she really hadn't prepared at all for this journey. She had only really left with the gifts she had been given. Why hadn't she taken more care?

Then it dawned on her she had magic.

She was a demigoddess Angel but she certainly

wasn't that bright. She shook her head at her own stupidity. She had battled the Ziz with magic then forgotten all about it. She smiled at herself as she magically dried herself off, surrounded herself in a bubble shield to hold off the rain and changed her sandals into boots. How Gabriel would laugh at her foolishness.

She ran her hands through her hair before she jumped across to the first island. She fell short, splashing into the fetid water, thankfully held back by her shield. As she struggled to sit up from her tangled wings she smacked herself on the forehead. She was an Angel, she could fly. Was it just today or was she always this stupid? She really wasn't off to the best start for the Gluttony level.

She screamed when something stuck her shield. She struggled to spin around and screamed even louder when she saw the bloated body reach out for her. She hastily scrambled up onto the nearest island only to have one of the beasts pounce on her. She rolled awkwardly over her wings. It sailed past her and started attacking the body that had followed her out of the water. She scrambled upright watching the dog-thing tear into the body, ripping great chunks out of it before throwing it back into the water.

It turned to face her with bared teeth.

She screamed and threw up her arms, instinctively strengthening her shield as the creature bashed against it. It slid down the shield, to warily sit up and watch her. Its eyes glowed with white light when it pawed at the shield. She kept expecting it to do something else but it just watched her.

She stood up. It stood up. She started walking, and so did it. It followed her, right next to her shield, occasionally brushing against it. Testing to make sure it was still there.

There were other beasts around. There were bizarre cats, bears, walking bats, clawed orang-utans, savage armadillos and many other strange variations of mammals. Whatever they had once been had been clearly warped in the Hellscape. They pounced on anybody that tried to clamber out of the water, though that didn't happen very often. She had the impression that it was only the new residents that tried to climb out of the water.

She continued to walk, but only the dog paid her any attention. The others whose path she crossed watched her before resuming their patrols. The only direction she had was the slight current flowing through the swamp and the fact the crater wall was behind her. Ahead she presumed would be access to the next level, not that she could see that far ahead in the gloom.

Nuriel felt her body lose all feeling as Gabriel turned her violet eyes towards her. A cold smile grew as those eyes bored into her. There was never any way to lie to Gabriel, no way to omit the truth, along with her phenomenal powers it was one of the reasons she had risen to be an Arch Angel.

On the throne next to her Michael was completely stoic. The news about Sariel had hit him hard. He looked tired and run down, he was still dealing with the mess Brigid had created on the subcontinent.

On the next tier down were the other thrones. Sariel's sat empty in front of both of them. To Michael's side sat Azrael's empty throne, he rarely joined Council meetings, and Raphael who was also watching her intently. To Gabriel's side sat both Ariel and Uriel, watching her intently as well. Ariel was not going to like the news she bore.

She was part of a long line of Angels bearing bad news. Brigid could not be found, nor could Hera. Churches across Australia and New Zealand were being desecrated. Mosques in America were being burned down. India had become a Demon playground, the civil war in Pakistan was not progressing as fast as it should. There were also peculiar things happening in Mexico. Unfortunately she held all the pieces and had put them together. She was the one they would hear the most from that they least wanted to.

"Ah Nuriel it is good to see you have returned from your investigations. I trust you understand very well the problems plaguing us. I hope you bring some good news for us." Was it just her or did it sound like Gabriel was threatening her.

"I bear only bad news my Arch Angels. No trace of either Hera or Brigid have been found, though Brigid's left enough magic across the planet that we have tracking spells on her. However she seems more than capable of slipping out of detection most of the time.

My investigations into the desecrations of churches across Australia and New Zealand have left no doubt that it is entirely Brigid. She is converting our places of worship to hers through the act of sex. It doesn't matter who does it, Human, Demon, heterosexual or homosexual. They have all tainted hallowed ground with extreme variants of lust. I have also found that in the process Brigid is granting magic to any who desecrates a church."

A deadly silence filled the air and she held her breath. "Are you certain of this?" Michael spoke for the first time in the whole session. His voice was a deadly hiss, he was the driving force behind eradicating Human mages. He had been the loudest protester to the birth of Jesus.

"The signatures are clear. And most troubling I have personally sensed the trace of one who will become a sorcerer."

There was an uproar from the Council, though the Arch Angels remained impassive. Many were calling her a liar or deluded.

"Nuriel is never wrong about these things. She is methodical and vigilant. Her reports are truth without embellishment. If she says it is so then it is." She wanted to throw her arms around Michael and hug him. Not that she would, that would be highly inappropriate.

He turned his attention to her "Please continue"

"This was in Saint Mary's Cathedral in Sydney, it has undergone a full conversion, though I have returned it back to its order. Other than the sorcerer and Demon, Brigid and an Angel were also present."

"We have a traitor in our midst?" Gabriel almost lunged out of her throne.

"No he was killed but I am still working on the identity but it was an Ascended Angel."

Stunned silence met her words. They had not lost a single Angel since the Fall.

"I have yet to ascertain the identity but he was killed by Brigid. He was also sent to Hell."

"When did Brigid become such a fighter?" someone asked.

"Probably two millennia of captivity" someone retorted.

Arial snapped back "Her believers changed her image before Europe fell to Christianity. She is likely feeding off those archaic beliefs of her. The events in the Ganges, Indus and Murray have only increased interest in her. Something should have been done to stop her before she gained such strength."

It was the wrong thing to say Michael turned on

her "And who abandoned their post of guarding Australia therefore allowing her to come back and start making sorcerers?" His voice went from angry to scathing "Do share with us your brilliant plan Ariel which somehow has not dawned on the other five of us on how to suddenly stop Brigid."

She wisely didn't say a word.

He shook his head in disgust before gesturing for Nuriel to continue.

"While I was in Australia I also made another discovery in one of the churches. It is something that concerns you Lady Ariel."

Ariel raised her glaring violet eyes from her glower.

"One of your Inquisitors was killed by Brigid."

There was a horrified silence. One of the Arch Angel's personal guards had been killed.

Her eyes had widened in horror "Who?"

"I'm sorry I do not know but I have passed on all I know to your Captain."

She nodded her thanks, her face taking a slightly vacant look as she communicated with her Captain.

"Have you found anything about Hera?" Gabriel questioned.

"She is still somewhere on the west coast of the United States. Her magical signature crops up from time to time. The most recent being yesterday when she burned down Saint Louis Cathedral in New Orleans."

"These assaults on our churches need to be stopped. We need to make a statement." She turned to Raphael "Can you return the cathedral to its former state, you oversaw its construction if I recall?"

He nodded before asking "Does the recent anti-Islamic sentiment have any connection to Hera?"

"I don't believe so. The destroyed mosques and the

victims have no trace of magic on them. This seems to just be a case of racism boiling over again in America. I will continue to monitor the issue but at the moment there doesn't seem to be any magical influence." She paused for a moment "There has been however some strange incidences across Texas."

"Strange incidences?"

"There have been several instances were morbidly obese people have had their brains and bodies controlled. They seem like experiments but what the goal is I cannot guess. All of them have died in violent accidents. I would hazard it might be the petty cruelty of the Gods but why when it leaves such distinctive signatures. There are other instances where her hand is obvious but nothing can be traced back to her."

"Thank you Nuriel is there anything else?"

"No my Arch Angels but if I find anything else I will naturally report the findings."

Gabriel nodded her head "Continue investigating these strange occurrences, we may be able to flush Hera out. Raphael can assist you while he is in America. Raphael see if you can strengthen the faith in the region. It needs a good injection. Uriel continue watching Europe, I have a feeling Brigid still has her eyes set on Britain. Michael push Pakistan into all-out war, we need to wipe this region clean. I will go to Australia while the Pope is there and see what I can do to counteract Brigid's influence there. Ariel you will spearhead the hunt for Brigid. You yearn for her blood now. Hunt her by any means necessary and bring me her blood or her in chains."

She cast her cold calculating eyes over the Council "For now it might be advisable that our strength is preserved. If Brigid is killing Angels then war has been declared. All Elder outside of Heaven must be in a group of at least four, preferably more. If you encounter her summon help, she is equal to any Arch Angel."

She stood up, Michael following suit and together they descended the dais and walked out of the chambers. It was the signal to allow the others to leave. Raphael stepped down, taking Nuriel by the arm as they left in conversation. Uriel disappeared in a blaze of white light but Ariel remained where she was long after all the Elder had left. She had been granted the honour and the duty to track down Brigid. She would not fail. She could not fail.

She left heading for the cells. She would need strength and she would need to recognise Brigid's scent.

Sariel and her chaperone stopped when a fierce howling filled the air. Her chaperone echoed the sound as did all the other creatures. The waters started to stir, bubbling and emitting dense red vapour. Six red lights appeared on the horizon, rapidly getting closer as a large dark shape separated from the gloom. Two of its heads flung back howling, their red eyes disappearing while two remained focussed on her.

Cerberus had found her.

She simply waited for him to get closer, she could not run away from him so she used the time to study him as he approached. He was far larger and more fearsome than when she had first encountered him outside of Hades. He seemed somehow darker too. But it was his Demon-possessed eyes, so akin to Ziz's or Charon's that told her the most. He was Cursed. And she was going to strip it from him.

Then she wouldn't be alone.

There was an almighty roar that shook the whole Level, many of the islands jumped up into the air. Water splashed up above her head sweeping many of the creatures into the water. What was most surprising were the creatures, they were all cowering in fear. Even massive Cerberus whined and cowered close to the ground, his tail between his legs.

Only a Greater Demon could cause such fear.

She jumped when she felt a head push into her hand. Her shields had retracted to her skin and now the creature was sitting on her foot, his head pushing into her hand for comfort. She knelt down next to it, patting it. It started to lick her face.

As she continued to pat it, it let out a low keening noise. To her horror all the nearby creatures started running towards her. Even Cerberus started running towards her. All of them ran as close to the ground as they possibly could.

She soon found herself surrounded by beasts, all trying to get closer to her for comfort. And to think they had tried to attack her before. Cerberus was meant to be the most feared thing in this circle, what could terrify a Demon-possessed God/Monster so much?

As if to answer her question there was another roar that shook the whole Level even more violently. The mists shifted and she saw a mountain looming in the distance. She didn't remember being told about mountains in Hell. She supposed it was possible that the others hadn't known, it just seemed strange for a mountain to be in a crater. Unless it was the central peak. No it wasn't thin enough.

She was puzzled but turned her attention back to Cerberus as he nuzzled up to her. The Demonic fire in his eyes was nearly dead and what was left was blatant fear. A fear so strong that in combination with this Greater Demon's power had almost eclipsed Gabriel's Curse.

She laid her hand on him, channelling in her magic to soothe him. She found almost no resistance, this was going to be so much easier than freeing Simurgh. The mortal consciousness of Cerberus was still strong and his Demonic form was only an alteration of his natural form. There was not the level of corruption that had created the Ziz. With a sudden flare of light and hardly much magic, she stripped him of the Curse. He let out a painful howl as the last of it was ripped out of him. Light flared then was smothered by shadows as his natural powers once again reasserted their dominance.

The island was swallowed by darkness, their bloodlines reacting to each other's presence and emphasizing the night magic they had both inherited from Nyx. This was one of the reasons why fights amongst the Gods were so catastrophic, if they shared bloodlines their powers reacted in unpredictable ways. Shadows speared through the Gluttony Level, lines of darkness sucking out what little light there was in the twilight gloom. In answer there was another roar that shook the level. The shadows wavered in response to some unknown magic.

"What is that? I thought you were meant to be the most powerful thing in this Level."

Cerberus turned his sad eyes to her. *For a long time Hell was not organised, the current structure is the result of Dante. Gabriel sent him into Hell with the expectation he would organise it with his imagination. He would then document what he saw solidifying the change and giving it power as his books were spread. It was only then that I was dragged into Hell, along with Charon, Minos and the Furies simply because he knew of our legends. He was protected by Gabriel's powers when he walked through here. He gave Hell its first structuring, since then it has evolved with Human belief.*

"So I can expect all manner of surprises in Hell, and the structure might be different from the nine Levels I'm expecting."

No. The Nine Levels have been set, Christianity is after all the most populous religion. It lends the greatest strength to shaping Hell. Plus the Arch Angels are pleased with its structure. No it is the inhabitants you must be wary of, with each Level Hell becomes more dangerous. The stronger the Demon, the deeper it was sealed. Except from the Guardians. They are powerful Greater Demons to which a Level is tied to.

"Like Ziz for the Lust Level"

I presume so, but I have never been. Each Guardian is bound to their level. I was Gluttony's guardian but some of the Greater Demons are free to roam whatever level they choose. In doing so they can replace the old Guardian and become trapped.

"What Guardian is that? What scares even you?"

The Guardian of Eden.

She gasped in surprise. Eden was the first city of the Angels. They had taken over the forgotten garden, abandoned since Eden had returned to the Lifestream. They had hidden it from the Gods and it was there that they had bred the first strains of Humanity loyal to them. Beyond that she knew little else. It annoyed her how little she knew about her own kind.

Behemoth, the greatest creature to ever walk the Earth.

She turned back to where the sound had come from but the shadows lay thick around them. There was another roar, strong enough to rip apart their connection and twilight returned to the level. It was then she saw that the mountain was far closer than it had been. She could see it coming towards them. Fast.

He is the result of Gabriel, Ariel and their mothers experimenting on Monsters of the past. Gabriel was once highly sought after by the Gods to create Monsters for them. She is responsible for a whole manner of Chimeric beings.

For the Guardian of Eden they had to make something truly terrifying. They scoured the world obtaining the blood and genetics of elephants, rhinos, dinosaurs and Dragons before combining it with the blood of the dead Primordial Goddess Tiamat. Then they captured the Primordial beings Bahamut and Kujuta. Forcefully combined them with the blood and spells they had created. There are no words to describe the agony they endured. The roars of agony were heard the world over, such was their suffering and the size of their lungs.

The final product was Behemoth, a kind of mockery of his original name. The creature who had once been Lord of the Seas was chained to the deserts around Eden to guard it against the Gods. Once the War was won and the Angels had moved to Heaven, Eden was hidden away and there was no use left for him. He was thrown into Hell.

The poor creature sounded like it had been through absolute Hell. To have been an animal God then to have been experimented on, twisted and changed beyond recognition. Forced to serve those who had done it then as a reward it been thrown into Hell. She didn't understand why Gabriel had done it. Though after witnessing Simurgh she wondered if Gabriel took joy in twisting the Gods to the forms she believed they should wear. That sounded a lot like Gabriel, the world should be as she saw it.

"Why did they use the blood of Tiamat?"

She was strong in the powers of Chaos, her only equal Gaia.

"Her blood would be rich with her powers and have the capacity to break order. It allowed for the transition to occur."

Exactly. Chaos Blood it is called, it makes many things possible. Even combining spirits and powers. They combined many different living things to create him

She turned back to watch Behemoth thundering towards her. He was truly...colossal was the only word vast enough she could think of. He was the size of a mountain. He walked on four legs, each ending in a strange blend of hoof and paw, each foot being bigger than the whole of Hades' castle. His body was muscular, something of a blend between bull and Dragon, moving with a fluid grace. His tail could only be seen as a swinging light that was the same strange glow as his eyes, each bigger than Cerberus at his largest. His head was wide and heavy, crowned with long vicious looking horns.

All the while he emitted a low moan. He was in such pain. She could feel it.

This was going to be like fighting Ziz. She was too small to be easily caught and could latch onto him where he could not reach. She jumped into the air, a violet spark amongst all the grey drizzle. Behemoth would not have noticed that she had taken to the air except for the flash of colour. He roared in terror, its broken mind remembering its forging. Angels brought pain.

Sariel was flung backwards by its roar alone, the air rushing past her was phenomenal. She had no hope of controlling her flight. All she could do was summon her powers to cocoon herself as she was swept away. Cerberus and the other beasts whined as she was blown away. Then he leapt forward attacking Behemoth's gigantic leg. The other creatures followed suit.

Behemoth didn't even notice, they were fleas to him and his skin was impregnable.

Sariel managed to wheel out of the wind, gliding away just under the Lust Clouds. A surge of her magic had the Level above bleeding into this one. Light burst through the clouds, in wide shafts bathing the gloomy swamp. The Damned, the creatures and Behemoth turned to gaze at something they hadn't seen in many centuries.

She soared down while they were all blinded to land on his head. She felt so insignificant, its hairs were longer than she was. It just seemed unfathomable that something living could be this large. On either side of her, his horns rose up as far as skyscrapers. He didn't even notice that she had landed on him.

Behemoth's great strength and power lay in his

mass, he could devastate cities in seconds, destroy whole empires within a matter of days. Even battling Gods was no issue for him because they met him on his grounds. They became bigger, thus easier for him to fight. She was so insignificant to him, except the vast amount of power she wielded, and he had no way of stopping her.

She pushed aside all fear and took a steadying breath before she once again summoned up her powers. It came to her easily and quickly, her fight with Ziz had paved a direct route for her powers. It flooded through her hands and into his armoured skin.

She fell to her knees as she was assaulted with a backlash of Angel magic. Behemoth was held together with incomplete spells. Gabriel, Ariel and their mothers had deliberately not finished it, it allowed for him to get even larger even as it drove him mindlessly obedient to them. The spells could not be broken without killing him. And underneath all the spells she felt Tiamat's Chaos Blood coursing through his veins. There was nothing to counteract the effects of her blood, but she could finish the spell and in the process hopefully strip him of the Curse.

Cerberus and the other creatures jumped back from Behemoth's legs as soon as they started to glow, thin lines creeping their way across him in curving matrixes. Red, green, black and white lines formed their own distinct patterns, but there was another colour, constantly blending and separating, forming patterns that had not been seen in eons. Patterns that scared even Cerberus. Sariel was attempting to control the Chaos coursing through Behemoth.

Behemoth bellowed in fury as he realised the Angel was on him. He spun around hoping to dislodge her. All he achieved was to send all those beneath him flying in great deluges of water and mud. He moaned in hopelessness, she would not meet him on his battlefield and he had no chance of locating her.

Sariel screamed, piercing through even Behemoth's mournful moans, as Gabriel's Curse swept up her arms, reacting violently with her own powers. She used her powers to push Gabriel's back but she wasn't going to win against Gabriel's powers. One of her hands clutched her necklace. Her family had said she was unusually gifted in the powers of Chaos, perhaps she could use that to tip the scales against Gabriel. As it was her powers were flowing out her at an alarming rate just to hold back the powers trying to surge upwards.

Dark rainbows danced under her hand as the black opals exploded with light. Her other hand sunk beneath Behemoth's skin, her arm following quickly as she lost her balance. Then all of her fell forward, sinking through his skin.

Suddenly light radiated out of Behemoth in every direction, he became a sun shining forth brown, black and brilliant white light. His moans of terror were so loud and powerful that they drove all beings to the ground desperately trying to cover their ears. Even Lilith who was slinking down the final steps to Gluttony. Even the beings in the other Levels heard his moans.

Sariel was surrounded by a blaze of light symbols, forming concentric rings around her as she sank through his skin into his bloodstream. Voices whispered and she felt wild power flowing all around her. She saw strange shapes pushing against her shields. She heard a female laugh and felt the brush of a feminine mind against her hers. Yet the power that surrounded her and continued to attack her was distinctly male.

She pushed everything far from her, flooding her phenomenal powers through his blood. She might be small but she was far from insignificant. She searched for the root of his Curse. It didn't take her long to find it poisoning his heart. But it was layer upon layer of different spells and curses. The final being the corruption of Hell.

One step at a time she thought. But she had the knack of it. With a flood of her Arch Angel powers she ripped the Hell Curse to shreds. Its grey fetters burning up in the maelstrom of magic inside him.

Behemoth's black fur suddenly exploded off of him, like clouds of ravens taking flight. The darkness was sucked up into the clouds above. The fur underneath was revealed to be dark brown to beige. The burning fires in his eyes died, leaving in their wake tearful brown eyes, raining torrents down on the marsh far below. The magic patterns gracing his skin changed their patterns, forming circular symbols of blazing white light.

With the Curse lifting and disintegrating she felt the shift in Behemoth, the distinctive make up of his was no longer in conflict. She searched up Bahamut the strongest of all the minds she could feel. She used it at the spirit to graft the other weaker and broken spirits onto. There were even weaker spirits without form or substance that she wove around them all, blending them with his core. She could almost hear the click as all the masculine flavours were finally connected in a natural way. But then the feminine went wild, attacking the core and Sariel with devastating effect. It was trying to wash her away in the deluge of raw power, trying to resist her every attempt at magic. She was in a magical maelstrom of Chaos powers, everything around her was blood, black opal light and the blue-white of spirits.

On the outside the light flaring out of Behemoth turned blood red. Cerberus and the other creatures howled and whined. This wasn't natural, something had gone terribly wrong. Something had happened to Sariel, this was the Curse clamping back down.

Sariel spread her mind outwards sensing into the dark, Chaotic, feminine powers flowing around her. *Tiamat* she thought with single minded intensity.

The swirling powers and blood stilled. So it was her. Somehow Tiamat's blood had retained not only part of her power but part of her consciousness. There was a blinding flash then Sariel felt like she was falling. When the light faded she discovered she was in a magical void. Around her shifting walls of grey-black power surged upwards like waterfalls in reverse. But she floated in empty space. She turned around and gasped when she saw the being who was trapped within the void.

She was female, with a beautiful face marred by long gashes exposing bone. Her eyes were like burned out fires, with only the faintest glimmer of what had once been there. Her grey-black hair was floating around her long neck and delicate shoulders. But from the shoulders down her body changed dramatically, while her top two arms were Human the next pair down were scorpion pincers. Her stomach was dominated by large udders, her two long legs were Dragon like but the most dominating feature below her waist was her long serpentine tail whipping back and forth. She was a bizarre mismatch of animals. She was something Primordial and very dangerous. To top it off rings and coils of sea water were swirling around her in various concentric rings. The scent of sea water was the only smell in the void.

"Tiamat?"

The eyes looked at her, stray tears forming at their edges. "All that is left of me after my children killed me. My blood used time and time again in experiments until eventually the Angels used just a tad too much, transferring all the power of my blood to Behemoth.

Trapped lingering in a broken experiment, denied from returning to the Lifestream." She glared at Sariel "Your kind did this to me" she roared. Her rings of water and the walls of the void wavered.

"I didn't, I'm here to help you, to heal you."

"What can you do Angel? Experiment on me further, try and fuse me fully with Bahamut. Achieve the blending of male and female, to twist us completely beyond our natures."

"No" She said slowly and carefully "To try and separate you. I cannot separate the souls that now depend on him, they cannot exist on their own. But you two have not been fully combined, you can be separated."

"Lies" she screamed as she flung out her arms. Water raced across the void to smash against Sariel's shields. Tiamat screamed all her rage as she summoned up the full extent of her Chaos magic. They were the powers no one could deflect, except her cousin Gaia and she was long gone.

Sariel watched as Tiamat was enveloped in brown-black flames, her water rings turned into pure Chaos magic, emitting and swallowing all light. The walls of the void shrank back from the Primordial powers, even magic feared Chaos. With a desperate roar Tiamat attacked Sariel with her magic. It raced across the void, splashing, burning, sizzling and crumbling, it was the essence of everything. Twisting, destroying, creating and recreating as it went. It smashed against Sariel's wards destroying them in an instant, encircling her like the death coils of a python.

Tiamat laughed maniacally as she swamped the Angel with her Chaos powers. No one could survive such an onslaught from such pure Chaos.

Sariel felt the power coiling around her, smothering her, burning, drowning, cutting, tearing and ripping into her. She was being pulled apart and crushed at the same time. There was nothing she could do to defend herself, her powers were stripped out of her. She let out a faint scream as the raw power tore down her throat. Then she blacked out.

Ariadne stood at the window looking out over the ruins of Saint Louis Cathedral. There was a sense of satisfaction in seeing the blackened plot of land. It had been enjoyable watching the firemen try to put out the raging purple flames. It had been all over the news, the purple flames had the experts confused. No one had any explanations why all attempts to extinguish the flames had failed or what had started it or why it had been so destructive. She had laughed at the upset priests, they had been distraught over the loss. The Pope had promised to head straight there from Australia.

New Orleans was currently the religious centre of Hera's covert empire. Her capital would be New York, but the holy city would be New Orleans. But scattered all across the USA and Mexico were various cities and towns converting to Hera. In Mexico the Gorgons were growing rapidly in numbers. They were spreading outwards, gaining control of new towns and subjugating them to her rule. Their news was ablaze with the ever increasing numbers of missing people and empty towns. Even the metropolitan edges of cities were beginning to be affected. The Minotaurs had been settled in Colorado and their numbers were spreading up and down the Great Plains. Their actions however were not yet drawing media attention. America was having widespread disappearances all across the nation as the Daemons' power grew.

On the other hand the AIDS cure and the reactivation of magical genes was drawing a huge amount of media attention. Though of course the media didn't know about magic. The Imperial Hospitals were being denounced by conservatives and medical groups alike for their unusual practices. Despite this they continued to be set up in ever more cities across the US. The numbers of mages being gained was starting to dramatically increase though the numbers of sorcerers was almost non-existent. So far they had Kyle who had been a remarkable find and four others. Kyle was by far the remarkable exception, which was why he was here in the temple with her. She was the only one who could effectively teach him.

Then there was Juan who had been personally trained by Hera and set loose. A more disturbed child she had never met, she had met numerous sex abuse victims in her many centuries. They always saddened her, such poor tortured souls. Juan was something different, he had been completely broken, more so than any she had ever euthanized or saved. But Hera had granted him and the others she sent to her considerable power. That much power, their unstable minds and their thirst for revenge scared her.

But Hera demanded that they be trained and the Goddess could not be denied. It wasn't so much their power that scared them but their rage. Magical powers could be dramatically increased by emotion. With the rents and tears to their sanity their powers were far beyond their gifted levels. The news was full of sex offenders going missing or being found murdered.

Their rage was burning unchecked across America. Thankfully it was only directed at those who deserved it. But what an army they would be when the time came. For the time being he was also searching for a home base for them, where they could feel safe beyond the reach of their abusers.

Hera's plans were starting to bear fruit. With very few exceptions the magical races had flocked to her, and the power she offered. The empowerment she offered had given them back their pride and purpose. Those healed from AIDS were forever grateful, while mostly under no compulsion many had joined the masses of worshippers. Formal temples were still in the process of being built away from Angels. But already priests and priestesses were in the process of being trained, just as the process of worship was still being developed.

On top of that her political manipulations were bearing fruit as well. Senator Worthington was doing surprisingly well in Congress, though his admission of being gay had caused an uproar the followers of Hera had swamped him with so much support that his party had dared not cut him loose. Especially considering a fair number of them were Hera's. Ariadne was not sure how Hera would initiate the change from United States of America to her Empire but it couldn't be far in the future.

Her mind drifted off from being overworked when Kyle spoke from behind her making her jump "What is that light?"

She shrank behind the curtains and pushed Kyle behind the other. Rays of light were coming down from the clouds, illuminating the dark ground. Descending in the light was an Arch Angel, his six wings catching the sunlight. He raised his hands high and the ground started to shake. The Cathedral started to rebuild itself, slowly, unburning and uncollapsing, walls and debris rising up. It was as though he had turned back time. Before her very eyes she saw Saint Louis Cathedral standing resplendent once again in the bright sunlight.

People had stopped to watch, and she could see the media coming like the plague. Streams of sunlight at night were not exactly normal, nor was a burned cathedral rebuilding itself.

The Arch Angel descended onto the roof top and spoke "Welcome all to the love of God, see his wonder and know his kingdom awaits in Heaven." Then he shot upwards in a blaze of fire and sunlight. She ground her teeth as she heard the gasps of wonder from the observers. Great just what New Orleans needed, a mass influx of Christian zealots.

She stayed hidden behind the curtain for a very long time, as did Kyle. It was the first time he had ever seen an Angel, but it instinctively made him wary. He knew the stories but his magic feared the Angels. It was this natural instinct that had taken over that could only explain his next actions.

He summoned his powers, still vastly untrained and unrefined and unleashed them on the cathedral. There was no warning, no flash, no visuals but suddenly the cathedral exploded as though a bomb had gone off. The explosion shook the city, the bright light flaring in every direction, the mushroom cloud vivid against the night sky.

Daemons, Lesser Angels and Humans watched on in avid horror and surprise as the newly erected cathedral was eradicated. Then the flames turned a vivid purple.

It was then as the media continued to film that Ariadne spoke, her voice echoing loud across the city "Know that the Age of Angels is at an end. Hera will free us from their enslavement. Heaven will belong to the Gods once again." Then she used her powers to smother the explosion, instantly turning the sky dark once again.

She grabbed Kyle by the hand "What the Hell were you thinking you fool?"

He looked at her in surprise and at his still glowing hands "I didn't mean to, it just happened. I don't even have control of fire yet."

Her anger stilled. He truly was everything Hera had hoped for, he was a true-born sorcerer. He didn't necessarily need training, his magic could respond to want and emotion. He must have Divine blood in him somewhere. He had to be protected. She transported them both to Texas, she had to oversee Hera's experiments with the Obese and see what she could do with them, she also didn't want the Angels to trace them to New York.

They left behind a very shocked city, Daemons cheered but very quickly went underground as the Angels started scouring the city. The Humans simply stood and gawked in wonder. So many things were happening that couldn't logically be explained any more.

By morning the story was not just all across America but the world. Hera sat smiling in New York as the story came on the news. But in London Raphael seethed in fury. It was well played on Hera's part but it wasn't going to save her.

She opened her eyes to complete and utter darkness. Where the Hell was she? She couldn't be dead, could she? She could still feel her pulse, her warmth and the magic coursing through her body. But it wasn't a magic she recognised, she couldn't distinguish the essence. It seemed to hint at everything but had no real identity.

Out of the darkness a faint brown light appeared. In the distance a planet appeared. Its face cracked, the brown light emitting from the cracks, slowly getting brighter. It reminded her of a dying star.

She floated around for a long time with nothing happening. The star/planet continued to slowly get brighter until the brown light was almost white in intensity.

Then it exploded.

She instinctively raised her hands to cover her face, but no shields would rise. Planet shrapnel was sent in every direction. She felt it pierce through her arms, legs, wings and torso. She felt it even stab into her face. Then the light was gone and she was left floating in darkness once again. But it wasn't complete darkness, she was glowing with a faint brown light. Every one of her wounds was glowing, most of all her arms. She turned them over, there was nothing sticking into them, but she watched in amazement as the brown light started to form intricate circles on her arms. She felt something moving throughout her body, a magic she guessed, moving from her other wounds to her arms. Her arms flared painfully bright as the shapes finished and the last pieces of the planet completed the complex symbols.

Understanding suddenly came to her. She had just seen Chaos, at least its representation, and it had just given her more power.

The silence of the void was shattered as her magic was suddenly evaporated. The Angel floated in the vestiges of her Chaos magic, completely unharmed. Her own Chaos was now surrounding the Angel protectively, long forgotten Chaos symbols flaring often. She shrieked in fury then fear when she saw the Angel's eyes. They were glowing with the brown starburst that was Chaos.

The Angel shot towards her and grabbed her around the throat in an instant. Tiamat struggled against the smaller Angel, her various limbs all attacking her to no effect. She was protected by an indestructible covering of Chaos.

"Tiamat, it is time you were set free." The Angel said in a terrifying voice devoid of emotion. The void started to shake, the watery walls collapsing in on them in an unearthly roar.

Sariel held onto Tiamat as she rose up out of Bahamut's core. As she did so she severed all connection between the two. All around them there were screams as the Curse was ripped asunder. Her powers surged through both Tiamat and Bahamut, ripping away their own powers, bodies and their madness. She stripped them back to their spirits, their purest essence. But she could not separate the spirits that had fused into them both. Gabriel's Curse had denied them existence and they had blended completely with the two dominant spirits.

Then her Chaos surged through them, healing and rebuilding them.

Cerberus watched as the magic covering Behemoth suddenly flared brown, no not just brown, Chaos brown with hints of every colour imaginable. There were especially strong presences of light and darkness. What on earth was going on in there? What had happened to Sariel, where was all this Chaos coming from?

Behemoth started to moan and stumble, its massive feet struggling to keep it upright. Each missed step sent damaging tremors across the Level. It collapsed to the ground in a thundering earthquake that shook all of Hell.

Light erupted all over the creature, his hair started to burn off in thick coils that shattered into smaller shards in the sky. There was a deafening scream that tore through the entire Underworld. Then Behemoth exploded.

The chunks of gore vaporised into darkness then swirled around like water, pulling in on itself. It formed a vague swirling sphere that severed in two and formed smaller spheres. Intense brown light and mist poured forth, the amount of Chaos was terrifying. It had to be

Sariel she was the only one who could channel Chaos in any amount, but the amount she was channelling was truly horrifying, she could destroy the Gods.

She could destroy the world.

There was a heartbeat then the darkness evaporated off, revealing two large Dragons that descended to the ground. They were both large even by Dragons' standards, but nothing compared to the Behemoth they had been. One was black the other was ocean blue-grey.

The black one was slightly smaller than the other with red wing membranes. While most of it was black its underbelly was ocean grey, with a distinct line of red separating the two. His claws and the spines running down his back were also red, as were the two long horns on his head.

The other was larger and far more serpentine. Her colouring wasn't solid either, highly iridescent, especially along her neck where there were flickers of the rainbow. Her wings were another matter entirely, they were almost identical to Simurgh's, feathered and rainbow, their brilliance undiminished by the draining effects of Hell. She lacked spines but her claws were longer and platinum white.

Sariel lowered them as gently as she could onto the ground, she tried to keep them out of the water but both were so large they covered several of the islands. She herself slowly floated down from where the darkness had been rent, but she stumbled once her feet hit the ground. Cerberus raced forward to support her.

What did you do Sariel?

She smiled at him tiredly "I gave them peace as best I could, I separated them out as best I could." Then her legs gave way and she collapsed to the ground. She weakly stretched out uncaring as she drifted off into an exhausted sleep. He tenderly licked her face but she was sound asleep. She had done the unbelievable and once she left this Level he would be cast back into Hades, he could tell everyone the good news. If she continued as she had she would easily best and free Lucifer.

He stretched out beside her. There was nothing to trouble them but instincts were hard to break. The various other guardians all lay down, some with heads raised in observation. There was a sense of unease, especially in Cerberus. His instincts told him to be wary. He thought he saw a twinkle in the distance but it was gone before he could focus on it.

Far in the distance Lilith was drooling over the power saturating the air. She slowly crawled forward her eyes fixated on her prey.

Something was happening but she couldn't place her finger on it. Just like Agra. The city confounded her. She could feel that Brigid had done something but she couldn't pinpoint it or counteract it. She had been coming back here ever since Raphael had requested her help. She hadn't mentioned to him or Michael that she hadn't been able to undo whatever Brigid had done.

Now it was a puzzle for her that she kept picking at. Funnily enough it had become the place for her to destress, it was almost a comfort working to undo the Goddess' work. Not that she was succeeding. But it would be eradicated when Pakistan invaded India. That was some comfort.

But now something was troubling her and she really couldn't place it. She got fuzzy feelings, and she hated that she didn't know. She almost felt like she had lost something but had no clue as to what it was. She idly wondered if some of her spells had faded away. Problem was she had that many, of which most were inaccessible.

She could hardly check the ones in Hell, not that she needed to.

Besides she had plastered spells and curses all across the planet, of which most she had probably forgotten. It was likely that one of those long forgotten ones had finally faded.

Putting it aside she emptied her mind as she tried to feel the complexities of Brigid's spell. She smiled dangling her legs off the roof. It was nice to unwind.

When Sariel awoke in the morning she still felt weak but very refreshed. It took her a moment to realise that her eyes were working, she was just staring up at the ever grey of Hell. She quickly jumped to her feet to find both Cerberus and Tiamat watching her. Bahamut was still soundly sleeping, but then his spirit had suffered incredible mutilation.

Cerberus smiled at her knowingly with his three mouths, his tail flicking back and forth. *Tiamat and I have found an interesting family connection, she is Anu's grandmother.*

"Anu as in my grandfather?"

Tiamat nodded her head, creating a nexus of rainbow. Sariel stared up in wonder at her ancestor. It was odd to think that only a few months ago the only relatives she had had were Michael and Azrael. Now she had met much of her paternal side, though still not her father. Her maternal side was much more of a mystery, but at least now she could put a face to one ancestor. She wondered what Michael would think when he found out that Gabriel had experimented on his great, great-grandmother. Then again he probably wouldn't care.

It perhaps helps explain your affinity to Chaos. I was the first in my region, raising lands from the primordial seas. Nyx is the primordial night and Cerberus tells me Gaia herself has marked you. In part it helps explain your strength but only in part and not enough. *Chaos dilutes quickly with each generation, even if both parents are strong in it. You are far removed from your Primordial ancestors, before you there was probably no Angel who could even touch Chaos let alone do much with it. You are perhaps the most bizarre anomaly I have ever encountered in my life.*

"And it is a pleasure to meet you too Tiamat. It is always nice finding out about my relatives and of course you are welcome for being freed." Cerberus smiled at her, she was doing well with her sarcasm these days.

Tiamat laughed, the pure, though thundering note, filled the Level. It had been thousands of years since she had last laughed, or even been in the flesh. *Thank you Sariel Hellbreaker for breaking the Curse binding us together.* She placed her paw on Bahamut gently. *He has suffered so much from Gabriel's Curse, I felt his pain all these years. He has suffered much. And I thank you little Chaos Angel for freeing me from my blood and granting back physicality. It has been a very long time since I had a body of my own. Thank you for giving me back life.*

"I thought that once a God died they could not be brought back to life."

That is true, but everything of them must be lost. Typically when a God is killed their powers are drained, this is what seals their fate. I was not drained and my blood was gathered by many because of its Chaos properties. This was injected into various beings, which in turn gave me a half-life, unable to fade away. Then too much was added to Behemoth and I became concentrated there, trapped within him. Doomed to an eternity of madness and suffering until you freed me. You also gave me a much better body than my last one.

"I just let the magic shape you, it is a combination of mortal perception and your own desires."

Mortals know who I am?

"Apparently, according to the others there has been a resurgence of interest in the Gods of old. But I'm not really sure what that means."

Time will tell little one. What of Bahamut?

"Similar, he too has been shaped by mortal perception but he was far more damaged. I cannot say what harm the other spirits have done to him and combining Kujuta to him was the essence of cruelty. I could not separate them without killing Kujuta.

Tiamat tenderly stoked his snout. *I will remain here and look after him. We will have much to discuss once he awakens. I suggest you continue your journey Sariel, Hell will only continue to weaken you the longer you remain.*

She was a bit cut by the dismissal but she nodded her agreement. She very much wanted to exit Hell. She wanted to feel real sunlight and wind again.

Fear not Sariel when we are free of Hell we will have much to discuss for I am sure you have many questions. But Hell is not safe and there are many who bray for your blood. Speed will be your greatest ally, for we cannot move between the Levels. I can sense Simurgh above, it has been so long, but we cannot transcend the Levels. We are prisoners of Hell but you are not.

"Can I not do anything to free you?"

Tiamat caught Cerberus' head shake, she also sensed the half-truths they had told Sariel. *Not now, you have already done so much but may I ask a favour of you?*

"Of course"

If you are able to free all those that you can, it will clear a path for us. But look after yourself first, do not exhaust yourself. The tip of her tail wrapped itself across Sariel's shoulder in her attempt at a hug.

Sariel smiled "Look after him, he is very fragile."

Of course my dear, as am I. But we will lend what strength we can to you. She carefully stroked Cerberus with one of her white claws. A line of fire raced off from him, deeper into Hell. *This will take you as quickly as possible to the next level, and Sariel.*

She turned back to face the Dragon "Yes?"

Please be careful, you are an extreme rarity.

She smiled again "Thank you"

She set out quickly, following the burn. She was imbued with energy and progressed with great speed. She cast a final look back to see Cerberus evaporate in a nexus of light. He was finally relieved enough to return to Hades, that was until Hell demanded him again. It was so cruel, she had forgotten to break his Curse, but at least she had freed Tiamat and Bahamut.

Tiamat watched her disappear into the distance with a strange feeling inside her. She had a descendant alive, admittedly it was a despised Angel but from what Cerberus had told her and she had sensed Sariel was far more than an Angel. She was a Goddess through and through, she just didn't realise it. And with Chaos powers as strong as her she was born to achieve great things. She felt sure that Sariel would restore order to the ailing planet, but she felt sure it was not in the way any of the Gods were imagining.

Chapter 28

The descent into the Fourth Level was relatively simple. The swamps stopped just short of the edge, forming large rivers that thundered down into the next Level. Carved out by the rivers were easy to traverse steps. She wondered if it was a forewarning of greater trouble that descending was so easy. The drizzle stopped while she climbed down, though the clouds remained. By the time she had placed her feet into the Greed Level she understood the lack of rain. Greed was a desert, with only the occasional river cutting through the many sand dunes.

At first she thought the Level abandoned, there were no signs of life, such as they were in Hell. There appeared to be no souls suffering eternal torment, and there appeared to be no Guardians forced to torment them. She also had no sense of any Greater Demons.

She walked for a time over the sand dunes, but seeking an easier route decided to head to the nearest river. It would be the most direct path to the next level. She was wondering why the Greed Level had no citizens when she crested her current dune.

Spread before her was a wide river carving its way through the many dunes. Along the banks of the river were thousands of people fighting. She instinctively knew that this scene would be occurring along every river bank in this level. She wondered where the Guardian was.

From what she could see there appeared to be two distinct groups, those close by the water who seemed to be fiercely defending it and those attacking them. Whenever it appeared that the attackers got through they rushed to the river's edge and started digging as fast as they could. Sometimes they succeeded in making little channels, directing water into ponds formed in the hollows between the dunes. As they did they scrambled to make more and more channels, intent to spread the water wide. One of the channels poured out into a very large hollow, cheers went up as the water gushed out into it and started spreading through the valleys between the dunes. Their entire intent seemed to spread the water as wide as possible.

Suddenly the river started to boil. Sariel flattened herself onto the dune while she watched. The water speared upwards in decorative sprays. Still the Prodigal, as she believed them to be, continued to spread the water as far and wide as they could. All the while defending themselves from the Avaricious, who were intent on hording as much of the water as they could.

From the water appeared a man or perhaps a Fallen Angel, for he had wings. He walked out of the spray, across the river surface as though it were solid. He was different from the other Demons or Guardians she had seen. He didn't look scary, he didn't induce terror. He stood like a man on two legs and had two Demonic wings, bat like and tattered. The only other remarkable feature was that he was entirely golden. His skin, wings, hair, teeth, even his fingernails were golden.

She wondered who he was.

He raised his hands and in each appeared flaming golden swords. Both of these he swept down on the Prodigal, cutting and tearing with great speed and finesse. The Avaricious cheered, rushing forward to stem the haemorrhaging of the river. Many of them scooped up the water in the ponds to carry back to the river. They worried about a pond when a mighty river flowed past. She couldn't understand it. Even the greediest of people wouldn't worry about the spilt water when they had the river. Would they? It had to be the nature of the Curse or she had a lot to learn about Human nature.

The Demon continued to slaughter the poor souls crowded around the pond, even the Avaricious trying to take their handfuls back to the river. His laughed reached her, it sounded devoid of reason. She lost interest knowing the souls would rise again to resume their task. The Avaricious would fight to keep the water to themselves, even trying to dam it. The Prodigal would strive to spread the water as far as they could, to widen the river, to build as many channels as they could and flood as many hollows.

She carefully slid down to the bottom of the sand dune and walked along the troughs being careful to avoid being seen by the river. This was perhaps the first time she really had the option of sneaking by, and she had every intention of doing so. She also wanted to avoid the Demon, she presumed he might be the Guardian of this Level and if not he was still one of the many Guardians.

Her hopes were short lived though, she walked around one of the dunes to discover that he sat waiting for her on an ornate golden throne decorated with every conceivable precious material. He smiled baring his golden teeth, then she realised they weren't golden, they were diamonds reflecting his golden light. As were his fingernails that had grown into claws.

"What foolish mortal tries to sneak through the Greed Level while carrying precious metals and jewels?" He eyed up her weapons, belt and jewellery "Did you seriously think you could pass without paying a tithe to me?" he sounded incredulous more than anything.

She stood there a little stunned. She was used to Demons attacking her but she had forgotten that most had been Angels. It appeared their arrogance transcended into Hell. "I am no mortal and I may go wherever I please. You might be a Demon but I am Divine and I can easily end your existence."

"I was once Divine and that means that I can kill you. Which brings us to an impasse. A change of tact is needed." He smiled "I am Mammon the Fallen Angel of Greed and you would be?"

"Sariel the Angel of Death and Chaos" that sounded impressive, it also made her sound like a Fallen Angel. But both were her birth right, though Chaos was by far the more impressive. She wasn't quite ready to drop death from her title solely for Chaos. It was still so new to her.

"Hmm impressive, though I guess you are referring to Primordial Chaos as opposed to the disorder we Demons are so meant to thrive on."

"Yes that Chaos."

"Interesting" he really drew out the word "I have never heard of an Angel being able to utilise the power of Chaos, indeed there have been exceptionally few Gods who have been able to. It is a trait usually confined to the oldest of the Primordial Gods, and you definitely are not one of those."

"No I am not a Primordial Goddess"

"But you are no longer just an Elder Angel, perhaps an Arch Angel or Goddess. Which begs the question why are you in Hell?

"That is my own concern just as the Avaricious and Prodigal are your own concern."

He clapped mockingly "Well done Sariel you understand this Level so well and yet my true concern is wealth. I can't very well let you leave without adding to it, that is a very nice necklace and then there is the belt, circlet, bracelets and swords as well. Do you really think I'm going to allow you to leave with them all?"

"Yes but you might need some convincing." She

grabbed her sword handles and assumed the guard stance. His mocking smile widened at the sound of her swords unsheathing. He felt a faint unease when his eyes fell on the platinum blade.

"That is a beautiful sword, one I will gladly fight to own."

She shifted her stance so that the Nyxite blade was in front. If it was possible the gleam in his eyes got brighter.

"Nyxite, very impressive. Now that is a sword to kill for, pity I'll never be able to wield it. Still what I do with your blades is hardly your concern."

"You'll have to take them off of me first"

"Deal" he yelled as he charged at her, his own swords burning once again. Sariel easily blocked his attack and dodged away. She then stabbed forward before he could recover, drawing black blood from deep punctures on his chest. He stopped and looked down in utter surprise. "You injured me. In one attack."

He looked back up her stunned "Which Angel taught you to fight so well? Michael or Raphael? You are far too young to have been taught by any of the other Angels. It is most surprising, I would have thought they would have gotten lax in their victory. Perhaps it was Ariel, she always had a thirst for violence."

"It was Nemesis"

He staggered backwards as if struck by a blow "Nemesis is a Goddess"

"I am well aware of that fact."

"Nemesis is one of the best fighters the world has ever seen. She is only matched by Sekhmet, Durga, Athena or Odin. They sparred for days on end, their fights sending Gods and mortals running away. In Heaven their fights caused storms and on the land they tore it asunder. And that was without the use of magic, such was their incredible ability. And you say she taught you."

This had to be the strangest Demon she had ever encountered. So much for fighting, it had been laughable. He seemed far more interested in the sound of his voice. Perhaps he was greedy for attention. "Yes she taught me all I know. She said I was one of her best students."

"High praise indeed, there is no way I can win against you. You may pass then." He disappeared in a burst of flame, but not before emitting a high pitched whistle. Once he was gone she could hear him laughing. He had sprung a trap of that she was sure, but what it was she couldn't say.

Cautious she raised new shields and allowed her powers to drift around her in case they sensed anything. She walked for some time with her swords out, before finally sheathing them. Perhaps he was merely playing mind games with her, she wouldn't put it past him. She hoped he was, annoying as it was.

Her hope was short lived. It had been a long while but the dunes in front of her started to shake. She stopped and unsheathed her swords once again, preparing for the attack. At least fighting would be easier in this Level, she could see more and there were not raging winds or vast amounts of water. Besides if this was Mammon again he would be easy to beat. She was thankful yet again for her tutelage, before Nemesis he would have easily beaten her.

The sand dune suddenly jerked up. As the sand drained away it revealed a skeleton, three times her own height. It had two pairs of wings akin to dragonfly's, long but triangular rather than rounded. In patches its bones were covered in what reminded her of insect chitin, it was black and shiny. It was most prominent at the joints and on the spine. His skull was completely encased in it, even the two long horns. Horns seemed to be a prominent feature of Hell's citizens. His mouth was wide open, but the chitin completely covered it, he looked like he was in a perpetual scream, made creepier by the empty eye sockets.

He was ghastly in appearance but she was thankful that he wasn't covered in rotting flesh. In his hands he held a sword to match his size which was made from rusty iron. While it was probably sharp she had no reason to fear iron could not harm her unless it had been imbued with Divinity. She felt a lot less worried about the fight.

It charged towards her and just like Mammon she easily avoided his clumsy attempts. She realised just how amazing a fighter Nemesis was and that she herself was in a different league from most others. She could manage to beat Nemesis a quarter of the time. She had never really thought about Nemesis' abilities, she had just done as she had been instructed. But according to Mammon she was one of the most gifted fighters ever, and the others were probably dead. Did the fact she could beat Nemesis make her one of the best fighters or was she being far too arrogant?

Were all the Demons this slow, or had she just gotten so used to Nemesis' speed that all else seemed slower in comparison? Admittedly the Monsters that had been the Greater Demons had possessed great speed. Would she find victory easy to obtain against other Gods, Angels or Demons? What would fighting a mortal be like? She jumped out of the way of his sword once again before bringing down her own platinum blade on his wrist. It sliced though bone and chitin with contemptuous ease. He jumped back looking at his wrist. She assumed the guard position waiting for his next move.

He picked up his hand and reattached it with a

snap. He then flicked his arms wide hurtling fire at her. She deflected it easily before it even reached her shields. He made some sort of strangled moan, whether in frustration or annoyance she couldn't tell. He then charged her moaning, his whole body erupted into flames as his hands grew into long black claws. She jumped up over him, twirling as he charged, ripping off his skull and blasting her powers through him.

Within an instant she was inside him, flicking through his memories as though he had no defences. He was Abaddon a Fallen Angel who had once been the Angel of Destruction. It was he who had swept through Egypt killing the first born children before disappearing into the east, confusing the Egyptian Gods. He had fallen out of favour before the Fall, his behaviour had grown increasingly erratic. Destroyers needed guidance or they went mad. The only one that really understood that were the Gods of Destruction and their servants. He had voted for peace though, which had sealed his fate.

He had been cast into Hell and Cursed, transformed into this skeletal form. She realised that some of the Greater Demons had been summoned up out of Hell and unleashed on the Surface to bring Humanity back to heel. His mind was a mess, mostly of his own creation. A surge of magic sent him crumpling to the ground asleep. He would trouble her no further, but she didn't have the time or inclination to assist him. She just wanted out of Hell.

She squared her shoulders and started walking again. It wasn't long until she found herself at the edge of the Greed Level, Mammon stood at the edge watching her approach. She had somewhat expected his appearance. He gave her a mocking salute "Well I certainly didn't see that coming. Abaddon has been the bane of Humanity for years."

"I'm not as delicate as I look."

"If you were you would break in the first puff of wind."

"What do you want Mammon?"

"Your sword, but alas that is not going to happen. No I have come to warn you, Hell so far has been simple and weak. The changes in society have weakened them. Lust isn't considered a sin these days by the masses, it is widespread and accepted, just as greed runs riot and gluttony claims more and more. They have become accepted facts but from here on Hell becomes far more ferocious and once within the city of Dis there will actually be Demons. These Levels are sparsely populated by the Fallen Angels, only some of the strongest forming Guardians. But within the city there will be many."

"Why are you telling me this?" her suspicions were running wild.

"Can't I act altruistically?"

"You're the Hell Guardian of Greed."

"Oh you flatter me" he blew a kiss at her as he disappeared "Remember you have been warned. Heaven knows how you snuck past Ziz and Behemoth but you will never sneak past Leviathan" Damn he was irritating. No wonder he had been cast out of Heaven.

The drop to the next Level was hardly anything at all. The rivers all poured out in wide waterfalls. And just like the Gluttony Level the rivers branched out into swamps. Great more walking about in the mud. But there were noticeable differences, fires raged across the surface of the water and there were no distinct islands only small mounds. There were also other shapes lurking in the shadows.

She cast a final look back at the Greed Level remembering Mammon's warning. So far it had been easy apart from the Guardians and Greater Demons. What would she face from here on in?

She spread her wings wide as she glided across the swamps, her black wings blended into the smoke filled air making her look as though she were part of the cloud. Within the water and fire many eyes watched her pass.

She couldn't say what had brought her back to Eden, nostalgia? But she had a sense that her magical unease was in some way related to Eden. It was here she had perfected her various Chimeras and her services had become highly sought after by Gods, all vying to have her enter their service. Others had paid her handsomely for work behind their brethren's back. Few of the Gods really knew how much of her work had covered the world.

She had spent a great deal of time in the Orient, creating such unusual creatures to protect the Jade Palace. When she had returned to the Near East she had quickly populated it with all manner of creatures. But it was the Greek Gods who had paid for her services with all manner of favours. She had created Chimera for them, the Nemean Lion, the Stymphalian Birds, she had imported her Griffins, Sphinxes and Manticores with adjustments. What many didn't know was that she had performed experiments on the Divine as well. It was she who had fused Sea Nymph with avian to create the Sirens, and then the Harpies. She had created the Centaurs though uncredited for it. Indeed many of her creations were uncredited because so many of the Gods had Monstrous offspring. The fact she added to the mix raised no one's eyebrows.

It was she who had taught her people how to craft Golems. They had proved very useful to their protection until the Gods were overthrown. Then she had been so busy she had had no time to experiment.

In the Middle Ages she had once again continued

to experiment, creating such Monsters as the Basilisk, Cockatrice, Hippogriffs, Ogres, Cynocephalus and Tengu just to name a few. She had stopped once she realised Michael and his Guard were hunting them down and destroying them. It was their major disagreement. She believed that the presence of Monsters kept faith strong, he believed that all magic was a threat to them. She felt highly smug that she had been right.

The Demon Races had persisted, some unaware that she had created them even as her husband continued to hunt them down. So her laboratories in Eden had become abandoned. There was no point in creating if it was only going to be hunted down.

Perhaps the last of one of her races had been killed. That would certainly explain her feeling.

She walked through the dusty laboratory using her magic to clean while she walked through absently touching a cage here and there. She had always been very proud of her creations. No one had matched her abilities, the only Monsters to rival had been born from Gods. She had created Divine beings. But that was a fact very few would have appreciated. Divine creatures were dangerous, they could kill other Divine.

She was a little surprised that many of the blood stains were still very prominent, she would have thought they would have decayed after all this time. Then again the laboratory was filled with an abundance of magic, so that had probably kept it fresh.

She used her magic to unlock one of the walls, its image rippling as blue and pink symbols raced across it. Then it vaporised to reveal her precious holdings behind. This was where her greatest assets were stored, which no one, absolutely no one knew about.

Along one wall sat thirty Desiccated Divine. Gods, Angels, Nymphs, Fairies, Naga there were even a

Valkyrie and a Dragon. Some she had forced the Desiccation upon others she had found them over a period of centuries, most before the War and some after. They were trapped forever in this form unless someone ended them or returned them to their former state. She would do neither, their power was far too valuable. No one knew she had access to these extra powers. They were part of the natural defence of Eden, everyone thought it was her powers alone.

True she was naturally the most powerful Angel to have ever existed, a definite throwback to her powerful bloodlines, but it never hurt to supplement one's powers. She was always ready for a fight because she had access to nearly her full amount of powers.

She had the sudden urge to create something, given the current situation she could blame it on one of the Goddesses. Michael wouldn't know. But experiments took time and time was currently a luxury. She sighed in disappointment, duty was a heavy burden. And now was definitely not the time to shirk duty.

She lightly touched each of the Vestiges, feeling the power flare beneath, and their resentment. They hated her, it amused her. There was nothing any of them could ever do.

She then turned her attention to her work tables and their priceless collections. Gems, minerals, stardust and a variety of other non-living matter essential in empowering life. Various plants, herbs, rare specimens with unusual properties. She even had golden apples from the Hesperides' Garden, a most magical plant that had been Gaia's wedding gift to Hera. The apples held Chaos properties in trace amounts. She had tried growing them in Eden but while they held Divine properties they lost the Chaos.

The third work desk contained all the animalistic

materials she had gathered. Bones, heartstrings, horns, teeth, hairs and blood of various creatures and beings. She had Unicorn horns, Dragon bones, Gods' blood, Nymph blood, Fairy blood, Banshee tears, Gorgon and Naga venom. She had an amazing collection but her prize glory was Tiamat's blood, Chaos Blood as it was also called. Many had collected it from her dead body. She had managed to track down many of the collections and obtain a considerable quantity. It was essential in balancing Chimeric organisms.

But to her dismay all her bottles lay shattered, their contents having apparently burned up, if the strange scorch marks were a testament to how the blood had destroyed itself. What on earth would cause such an occurrence? Tiamat had died a long time before she had been born, it was remarkable that the blood had held her powers. Perhaps whatever had anchored her strength to the blood had given out, or been destroyed.

With Tiamat's blood gone and powerless what did this mean for her creations? Would they survive, would they burn up or would they slowly die as the Chaos faded from their bodies and their opposing natures destroyed each other? The species she believed would be fine, this far down the generations they had to have stabilised themselves without Chaos.

But what of the Greater Demons?

What of Behemoth whose entire existence was dependent upon Chaos Blood. She had used so much to stabilise him, he went against so many of nature's laws. She had worried over how much she had used fearful that that much Chaos might destroy him. But it had worked and Eden had had its Guardian, keeping away even the Gods.

Still he had outlived his use, the Gods had been destroyed, Eden hidden away and Humanity brought to heel. It didn't really matter what happened to him in Hell. Still it was a pity he had been such a useful Demon to summon. No one did destruction on such a massive scale like Behemoth.

Well at least she knew why she was having odd feelings from her magic. Chaos Blood had expired, those that were dependent on it had probably died.

Now if only she could solve the mystery of Agra.

Nuriel moved among the police officers and crime scene investigators. They all moved readily out of her way, one rushing forward to walk with her.

"What do we have Tom?"

"A mess that's what we bloody have. Bloody media filmed nearly the whole thing. I would think it a hoax if I didn't see the ruins myself."

"A miracle and counter-miracle it would appear. But who would burn down a Cathedral?"

"Muslims"

"Tom how many time do I have to tell you the actions of September 11 and fundamentalists are not the beliefs of Islam. They distort their own teachings. The Quran clearly states suicide is a crime against Allah. It may be fundamentalists but I doubt it, far more likely anti-Christian protesters. But what are they protesting against and why not claim responsibility."

"There have been a spate of Mosques being burned down, perhaps it is in response to the flaring anti-Islamic sentiment sweeping the south. You know you sure do know a lot about Islam." He eyed her up with distrust.

She pulled out her crucifix on her necklace "I'm Catholic you idiot, we've been through this before. It doesn't hurt to understand other religions, it is the only way peace can ever occur. Now has anyone claimed responsibility?"

"No one has and there are no markings either."

"Hmm" was her only response as she stopped at the edge of the Cathedral ruins, at what had been the front door. This had once been a beautiful building that she had visited many times before. Poor Raphael, he had only raised it hours before it was destroyed again. It could only be Demons, they were the only ones to magically burn down a cathedral. They had to be powerful to counteract the still strong Angel powers remaining after it was resurrected.

She stopped as she let her senses open. Yes magic had been used by two people. Both were remarkably strong. They held a similar flavour though distinctly different. The feminine had the sense of Vampires to it. But that couldn't be right, Vampires hardly had any magic at all.

She placed her hand on the charred pillar. She could sense the lingering strength of Raphael, the destructive powers of Hera then underneath she felt the sharp sting of Demon magic. But it was laced with great age and power, it wasn't purely Vampire power. Somehow a powerful sorceress had survived all this time as a Vampire. Not a good sign. Worse yet the male sense was nearly as powerful, though very young. Hera was recruiting sorcerers, young and old. She had to be empowering mortals.

"Any conclusions Detective Kelly?"

"The same accelerant was used as the last time, though there was less used. Keep any eye out for any active anti-Christian groups in the area. Perhaps check the Voodoo. After all Mosques have been getting burned down, perhaps churches are next and they are connected. Check in with neighbouring districts and states, see if this is an isolated matter or part of a pattern."

He nodded as he rushed off. She felt eyes watching

her, someone knew she was an Angel. She looked around casually trying to locate the source, but it eluded her. However she did notice Hera's lingering powers, it blanketed the whole city effectively making any attempts to pinpoint others useless. Hera had a presence in this city, she was interested in it. Which meant the Angels would be too.

She pulled out her phone and called the station.

"What can I do for you Sarah?"

"Do a search across America for any unusual activities. Any unexplained absences, damages to religious buildings or so called miracles."

"Do you believe it has a connection to the arson?"

"Yes" Why did Humans ask so many questions, couldn't they simply do as they were told.

"You're in luck there have been a spate of Mosque burnings all across Louisiana, Mississippi, Arkansas, Texas, New York and Chicago. There have been incidences of church burnings in San Francisco and New Orleans. There have also been a massive surge of disappearances in New York, California, Louisiana and Illinois. There have been noticeable spikes across all the states.

As an aside there have been reports of whole towns disappearing in Mexico. But we don't have access to that data. And there have been a spate of strange seizures occurring to overweight people in Texas."

"Thank you Jean you have been most helpful."

"Glad to help detective."

She hung up deep in thought. Hera had to be here, it explained so much. She was digging her claws into America, and apparently Mexico. She had clearly aligned herself with the Demon races, not unexpected and was empowering them. She had at least two powerful sorcerers, very troubling. She was also destabilising faith in the States. The missing were either being eaten or turned, which either way meant their numbers were increasing. She would have to investigate Mexico when she got time, she would get a legion to go there for their own safety. It sounded much worse there.

"Victoria what are you doing out here?"

Victoria turned to face her cousin Margaret, dressed in all the finery that was the birth right of the British Royal Family. Margaret looked far more the princess than Victoria did, she also behaved like a spoiled princess. Everything had to be her way, she was the centre of attention at any party and regularly used Victoria as some sort of limelight attracter. She got very annoyed because Victoria was forever slipping away for peace and quiet.

Victoria might be the Princess of Wales, the next in line for the crown of the United Kingdom of Great Britain and Northern Ireland and what remained of the Commonwealth but she was not like the rest of her family. Perhaps that was why the British public adored her. Even the government and politicians liked and respected her, she was often requested for public events. She was respected because she was currently studying medicine with plans to go into the defence force. She was often compared to her great-grandfather and his sister. It wasn't a comparison she was easy with but it was high praise indeed.

They had been among the last royals eagerly embraced by the public. Her father and Grandfather were not cut out to rule, even self-governing Britain. Royalty was nearly purely ceremonial these days, just like the other European royal families but it was a tradition such countries were proud to have. But Britain disdained their wild royals. Her grandfather had partied hard into an early grave at thirty, it was just as well he had married young and produced an heir. Her own father was not long to follow. He had never been comfortable with the media's attention and invasion or the expectations of him.

While she didn't love the media's attention she could deal with it and she had an active interest in running her country. She attended parliament and was welcomed by the politicians. She was an intelligent young woman whose opinions were well respected, and who measured all sides of an argument. Her humanitarian work had won her public appeal. She worked tirelessly among various charities within Britain, seeking to improve her country. Her favourite being the RSPCA, she had always had a soft spot for animals. She donated a lot of her personal income to her charities. She also assisted in aid work to Africa, that had become part of her family's duty, not that she minded.

She didn't really enjoy partying, she enjoyed it occasionally for it was nice to let off steam, but not the parties the other nobles and royals attended. They were but a few articles of clothing away from a drunken orgy at all times. And the amount of drugs disturbed her. They were so frivolous, spending their millions on parties, ships and other material possessions. She felt sorry for their accountants. Hers on the other hand loved her, she had a canny business sense and had turned her own inheritance into her own billions. The public didn't know it but she had major shares in over half of all British companies, and had lesser amounts of shares in the rest. She owned vast tracts of land all over the UK of which quite a few had been turned into nature reserves. The public loved her and yet they remained unaware of all she did.

To top it off were her horse riding skills, something the royal family said marked her as one of them. Quite a few of them had won various awards and she was not the first princess to win gold in the Olympics for equestrian. All of which made her cousins very jealous. She had everything they envied, money and the public love.

"I'm just watching the moonlight on the glaciers."

"You watched them all day Victoria, come and party."

She sighed. That was exactly why she was out here, she didn't feel like drinking and being sober she couldn't stand them. They were all pretentious pricks boasting about who had the best bloodline or greatest wealth. She beat them hands down, not that she joined such stupid conversations. She couldn't wait for this cruise to be over. "It's nice out here."

"It's cold. How are you not freezing without a jacket?"

She glanced down at herself, dressed in a long emerald dress, then glanced at Margaret's skimpy little black dress. The answer was pretty obvious, she was exposing nearly all her skin to the brisk arctic night. Inside Victoria was overdressed, out here she felt comfortable. She was not some slut to have her dress finishing millimetres below her privates and just above her nipples. Sure she showed off her assets but demurely. There was that old saying about legs or breasts but never both.

Ironically her designer was called London Victoria, she found it amusing his parents had actually called him London. But he had the most fascinating designs, old style elegance it was pegged as. He had all sorts of olden twists that resulted in stunning creations. He found it amusing that she was his best client, and had often said it seemed his whole brand seemed perfectly suited for her, even the name.

"Because I don't dress like a slut Margaret"

Her face twisted in fury as she slapped Victoria.

She resisted the urge to grab her face, Christ that hurt. "Feel better now? It isn't going to change the way people see you or what they say about you. If you want that perhaps try closing your legs sometime. With all the activity it sees I'm surprised it hasn't been closed for maintenance. It definitely needs it."

"You're just jealous you frigid bitch. They all call you a prude." She spat back.

Victoria laughed with genuine amusement "Frigid? The sheer fact I've had sex means I'm not frigid."

Margaret gawked at her.

"Oh you were under the quaint notion I was a virgin. I've travelled the world. I've enjoyed beautiful men from Australia, Canada, Scotland, Ireland, France and even Africa. I just don't flaunt the fact that I've done them."

She sneered "Oh so perfect Victoria isn't so perfect then."

"I'm just not a drunk slut who throws herself at every man at a party. I prefer to actually know someone before I sleep with them, and you know what it works. I don't have bad sex stories, I've had amazing sex with hunky, smart and sensual men. I've not had nights I can't remember, never worried that I might have slept with someone I shouldn't have or wondered whether I used protection or not.

Nor do I live in fear that the family will find out about my drug habits. But then you, Henry, Catherine and Andrew all worry. Don't complain that your parents wish they had had me instead. Don't complain that the media splashes your vagina and drug fucked face all across the globe. Grow up Margaret and actually take some responsibility for your own actions."

"You're just a snotty bitch who thinks she's better."

"No you are and a slut to boot."

She slapped Victoria again then smacked her shoulders. She had been standing against the railing and with the shove toppled half over, struggling to grab onto something to support her.

Margaret stopped shocked before a vicious smile grew. She glanced around, there were no witnesses, before savagely pushing Victoria over the edge. As soon as she heard the splash and Victoria's scream cut off she started screaming "Help! Help! Somebody help! Person overboard. Victoria's fallen in."

She took great satisfaction in the amount of time it took for people to come running and for life rafts to be thrown out. Someone wrapped her in a blanket and she gratefully sank into their embrace all the while forcing out tears.

Well that was one way to solve a problem.

Victoria fell backwards her eyes locked onto her cousin's victorious smile, before she hit the water. The initial hit stunned her, then the cold took away all her breath. It was fucking freezing. She had minutes until she died from hypothermia, if she didn't drown first.

She struggled to swim but her legs got ensnared in her dress. She desperately pulled at her dress, trying to rip it open. She continued to sink as the ship got further away. She was going to die, she knew it. She was sinking unable to swim and was losing feeling in her limbs. She was still ripping at her zipper and her petticoats to no avail. She vaguely registered that one of her high heels had come off. Her hair wound around her face, obscuring what little she could see in the black waters.

She was so cold, so desperately cold. She couldn't

move her arms or legs any more, she couldn't even feel them anymore. Her lungs were on fire, her body demanding air, but it would find none. She was going to drown.

Somebody help me, anybody please find me she thought desperately knowing it was completely futile. In these black waters they wouldn't be able to find her. Her time was at an end anyway. She reached up desperately, trying to kick her numb legs as her mouth opened involuntarily and the ocean rushed in. She felt the raging cold rush in, felt herself choke on it and felt it extinguish the burning in her lungs. It was all fading away so fast.

Then suddenly there was air, blessed air to breathe in as she coughed up the contents of her lungs all over her hands. How was she on her knees? Why was she dry? Was she dead? Was this the afterlife? She struggled to straighten but she was so weak. She pulled her hair out of her face so that her eyes could focus. Maybe she was dead and you started death completely weak. It made sense in a way. She had no idea what she was thinking about anymore, it made no sense to her anymore.

"You are not dead Victoria. You very nearly were but you haven't died yet." A woman said to her, she had a beautiful voice, she found it very comforting.

Finally her eyes started to focus. There was light and in front of her was a huge black window, a curved black window. With fish swimming past. Where the Hell was she? She managed to stand up and look around. She was in some kind of bubble, completely surrounded by the Atlantic Ocean. It was darker than the night. She looked down at the water she had coughed up, it hadn't pooled on the floor but drained through it. How was this possible, was this some sort of high tech material? Did the government really have access to technology like this? She was definitely going to have to examine that once she got out of here.

The woman laughed, it was musical but for some reason reminded her of Britain and warm fires.

"No government has access to such technology. For it does not exist to them, they do not accept magic."

Victoria was about to laugh, magic ha, but then glanced around herself. She turned around, there was only the bubble, no submarine dock, nor a single sign of technology. Only the bubble and the strangest woman she had ever seen lounging on a white sofa. She had six wings!

"You certainly make a convincing argument."

She laughed again seeming to fill the air with warmth "You are certainly an interesting character Victoria. It would be appalling if I didn't make a convincing argument for magic considering I live and breathe it. Besides this is nothing special, more visual than anything."

"I don't understand."

"Humans so rarely do. Magic simply doesn't exist in your world any more, you explain and rationalise everything with science. But magic is real Victoria, very real."

"So I'm alive, in a bubble under the Atlantic Ocean due to magic?"

"Precisely"

"And are you some kind of sorceress, benevolent spirit, Nymph, Sprite, Fairy..?" she waved her hands about running out of ideas.

She laughed again "No they are far too weak to describe me. I am Brigid the ancient Goddess of Britain and Ireland."

That sounded familiar "Brigid as in the voice people in Australia heard when the River Murray flooded?"

"The same one."

"But Gods and Goddesses don't exist, I don't even believe in God."

"As well you shouldn't he does not exist. He is a lie the Angels made in order to strengthen their religions. The world and Heaven are ruled by Angels not Gods. They slaughtered and imprisoned my kind in a war long ago. Since then their religions have spread across the world, rewriting history and spreading their lies."

"Wait what? So God doesn't exist, but the Gods of myth and legend did, or may still exist. But the Angels of the Abrahamic religions overthrew them and have since ruled the world. Where did you come from then?"

"I was imprisoned in Heaven, but an Angel set me free."

"So why are you here? Why save me?

"Would you rather I had let you die?"

"No. But why save me?"

"You are the heir to the British Empire."

"The United Kingdom. The Empire was granted its freedom a long time ago."

"You are heir to the British Empire. Britain is my land and it will be truly great once again. I have already claimed several colonies and I will claim more. I will reclaim my homeland. With mine and Hera's release the War will break out again. The world will know the truth."

She ignored the reference to Hera, though she knew who she was. "You want to resurrect the British Empire during your war?"

"Not just my war Victoria, the world's war. Dormant powers will erupt. The Daemons will be given hope, no longer will they cower from the Angels. Humanity has been under the Angels' control for far too long."

"Demons? As in from Hell?"

"No Daemons, as in non-Human mortals. Nymphs, Vampires, Fairies, Werewolves, Sirens, Lilin, the list goes on."

"Vampires aren't real, they're just stories."

"And yet you accept the truth of Gods and Angels. Vampires are very real, as are sorcerers, mages, even Cerberus is real.

She was lost, too many names, too many truths and misconceptions turned over. "I still don't get what you want from me Brigid."

"All I want from you is your loyalty."

"My loyalty?"

"When you are crowned Queen of the United Kingdom, you will invoke my name. You will rule the British Empire as I recreate it. You will make an excellent Queen, you will live up to your namesake. And in turn I will offer you my patronage and protection. I will answer all your questions and offer you power beyond your current understanding."

"You're to be my patron?"

She smiled "You do understand. Do we have an agreement?"

"And what if I say no?"

"Then I will leave you here to save yourself" She said it in complete seriousness that Victoria had no doubt she would. If she remembered right from the myths and legends she had read, Gods were remarkably uncaring of mortals.

No choice at all if she wanted to live "Then I accept Brigid"

Brigid smiled brightly "Excellent"

Then there was water everywhere, but she broke the surface to find a searchlight beaming straight in her face. There were gasps and surprised shouts and hands were hauling her out of the water. She wasn't even cold, and was surprisingly coherent. People were yelling and asking questions, there was too much noise after the calm of the ocean. She was bundled up in the foil stuff she had seen on TV. It was all a bit surreal, but she felt perfectly fine.

As the lifeboat started to drive back to the cruise ship she whispered "Thank you Brigid" and she meant it. Without her she would have been long dead. Just for a moment she saw to large green spots on the water. Brigid's eyes. Then they were gone, but she knew she hadn't dreamed or hallucinated it. She belonged to Brigid now and in return she was going to be Queen of an Empire. The British Empire would rise again.

She smiled, it held great appeal for her.

"Here drink this" Michael placed a chalice in front of Raphael.

"What is it?" he asked picking up the crystal chalice and examining the golden fluid inside. He sniffed it and was surprised at the orange and saffron smell "Surely it can't be Lightningsun?"

"It is. Drink up it will do you wonders

"But this was made by the Satyrs. How on earth did you manage to get some? Have you got a stash of it somewhere?" He took a swig, swirling it around his mouth. The rich golden flavour suffused his mouth, its sweetness perfect on his tongue. As he swallowed he felt warmth spread through him and his tight muscles relax. He looked at Michael in surprise "This is fresh"

Michael nodded in agreement.

Raphael was confused. Satyrs and their Nymph lovers had made Lightningsun for thousands of years for the Primordial Gods and their progeny. It had adorned the tables of every banquet in Heaven and had been given as a special blessing to mortal rulers. It was one of those special drinks made by Daemons for the Divine. Its only matches were Earthlaughter made by the Fairies or Paradox made by the Naga. None had been made fresh since the War. The Naga and Unicorns were extinct, both vital to the production of Paradox. Satyrs had also been hunted to extinction. Fairies and Nymphs had been hunted down to near extinction, forced to reside in remote places and dilute their blood with Humans to avoid detection. The ability to make Earthlaughter and Lightningsun surely would have been lost.

"How did you get fresh Lightningsun? The Satyrs are extinct. Did someone else discover how to make it?"

"No only the Satyrs can make it, nor are they extinct."

He didn't like where this was going "Michael what are you telling me?"

"There are a group of Satyrs and Nymphs living on Djerba. In exchange for my protection they make Lightningsun exclusively for me. But this secret does not leave this room, they are a weak and harmless lot who would be easy victims for the likes of Ariel."

"I'm not a fool."

They both smiled. First wind of a Demon colony and Ariel would descend with the fires of Heaven. Neither were quite sure what Gabriel would do. She had never really cared about the Demon Races or Mages.

They both jumped when there was a knock at the door, both hastily casting glamour spells on their chalices. They narrowed their eyes before the door swung open. To their surprise Nuriel walked in

Beautiful, methodical Nuriel. She was a favourite of the Arch Angels, even Gabriel had warmed to her. She did what was asked, her ability to gather intelligence was unrivalled even by their own guards. Raphael was aware she had a crush on him, and looking at her now, stunning and radiant, he couldn't think of a reason why he hadn't returned her feelings. He would have to remedy that as soon as the fiasco with Hera and Brigid were sorted out.

She smiled at him "Lord Raphael" then she turned her attention to Michael "My Lord Michael"

"What is it Nuriel we are extremely busy." Michael spoke harshly, highly unusual toward Nuriel. Raphael guessed the Lightningsun had him on edge. To her merit she merely glanced at the two chalices before returning her gaze back to Michael.

"Believe me my lords you will wish to know what I have found out, though I can go to the Lady Gabriel instead."

Michael sighed, rubbing his forehead "What have you found out Nuriel?"

She smiled in victory "I have found Hera."

Chapter 29

The Fifth Level of Hell was as dreary as the Second and Third but had the violence of the Fourth mixed in. It wasn't as dark, the various fires illuminated the bleak swamp. What little land there was was covered in bodies fighting each other. Whether it was by tearing each other apart with their bare hands or utilising any weapons they could find, be that rocks, planks of wood, swords, axes and even guns.

There was very little vegetation and what there was was clearly dead.

The other landmarks were just as cheery, rusting tanks, cars and trucks. Crashed fighter planes stuck out of crumbling walls, suits of armour and rotting catapults were heaped on top of rusting submarines. Skeletons of bunkers stuck up out of the dark water, dead creepers wrapped around them and the missiles sticking out of them. The deeper she got the more features appeared. There were the occasional streets, with wrecked cars and checkpoints. Skeletons of rusting skyscrapers sat next to the ruins of castles and palaces while crumbling walls stained with blood and twisted railway tracks cut randomly through it all.

In the water floated the bloating corpses of the Sullen, their bodies barely moving as they were knocked about in its currents. Some climbed up out of the water to join the Wrathful fighting on any available scrap of land, building or vehicle. Those that fell into the water either struggled to get back out or simply fell into their morose brooding. The fires that raged across the water's surface forced many of them to scramble into the waters until it passed only to struggle back out.

Sariel felt very glad she was flying. There was no discernible path through the ruins and wreckage, she would have had to fly from island to island. And she would only enter the water as a last resort. It stirred with strange ripples that could not be explained by either the Sullen or the currents. Something dangerous was in there, every time the ripples neared the Sullen even they scrambled out of the water. She also saw vehicles and buildings move about, their inhabitants doing everything they could to stay out of the water.

Mammon's warning was still ringing in her head. From here on in it was only going to get worse. The previous Levels' inhabitants had mostly ignored her, while the Wrathful below watched with such hate filled eyes it made her skin crawl. She was glad she was flying, she felt sure they would attack her if she landed on any of the islands. So far her greatest danger had been the Guardians, which would only continue to get worse. She feared to think what the other Guardians would be like. She had lucked out with Mammon and Abbadon. She doubted she would be so lucky again.

She flew for a long while, the ruins beneath her growing ever more numerous. The weight of loneliness continued to press down on her increasingly. She still had so far to go but no one to talk to, strange conversations with Demons notwithstanding.

This journey was shaping up to be an excessive task just to reach the Surface. Mortals had better be interesting otherwise she was going to return to Hades in a foul temper. Which wasn't fair on her family after all they had done for her. There surely had to be a simpler way to the Surface, bloody Gabriel making life hard for everyone. She made a mental note to check the spells once she had snuck past the Beast and see if she could use her Chaos powers to create a back passage.

She had flown for so long that she felt the need for a break. It could have been days for all she knew, she had no idea just how long she had already been in Hell. Flying in Hell was nothing like flying in the Heavens, it was a joyless task.

Spotting a cored out skeleton of a particularly tall skyscraper she glided down to the crumbling roof. The Damned were contained to the bottom floors, at least a hundred storeys away from her, she would be safe. But as soon as her feet touched the metal an orange light flared then plummeted down into the water where it flared brightly. Her shoulders slumped as a surging wave of water started moving towards her. It would appear that she had fallen into the focus of Wrath's Guardian. She called up extra wards and shields, it didn't hurt to be prepared. Not that she was worried. She had survived the previous Guardians, she would survive this one.

Beneath her the Damned had completely abandoned the skyscraper, they were all trying as hard as they could to get at least several blocks away from her. Not that she noticed from her vantage point.

She squared her shoulders and faced the wave as a large sucking noise filled the air. Water was being pulled from in between the ruins, rising up at least twenty floors. Whatever was approaching was big, very big, whole ruins were being smashed by the surging wave that was only growing taller. It was only then she realised she must be near the end of the Level, the area was incredibly dense with ruins and distinguishable streets. All of which were rapidly being destroyed by the approaching tsunami.

Then from the wall of water rose the head of a Monster. It was a gigantic serpent, its head a sharp triangle to slice through the water opening to reveal a many fanged maw. Its eyes burned ruby red, glowing brightly through the darkness and water. They were the only mark of colour on the creature, its skin was black as the water, the sharp fins running along its length and armouring its face were darkest grey.

It lifted its head fully out of the water, its long sinuous neck following as it grew rapidly closer. It was truly colossal, larger than even Ziz, though nowhere near the mountain Behemoth had been. This could only be Leviathan.

Whole city blocks were swept away in a deluge of destruction as in approached, its head and neck were now fully raised out of the water, its mouth level with her. From its fangs dripped black venom, falling down to sizzle in the water or corrode the buildings. The wails of the Damned, Wrathful and Sullen alike, filled the air as they were swept away in the deluge surrounding Leviathan.

In a disturbingly short amount of time it had stilled before her ruin, the tsunami before it shaking her perch. The sound of crumbling concrete and screaming metal filled the air as first the tsunami crashed into her skyscraper and the surrounding buildings and then Leviathan's coils constricting around them. She tried not to flinch as drops of venom hurtled past her. They were as big as she was.

She raised her gaze to its. She was pinned with the intensity of hate within those eyes. It loathed her, it despised what she was, hated what she represented and hungered for revenge against all Angels.

The skyscraper swayed violently as his coils crushed the base to powder. She jumped backwards and moved with the building as it started to fall. His head smashed through where she had been seconds prior. She could not fight him as she had Ziz and Behemoth, he moved like lightning.

She dove downwards with the rubble but she had only covered several metres before his gaping maw was underneath her. With basic instincts she spiralled out of the way, only to almost be ripped to shreds by his fins flying past her. She was very thankful for her wards. Then his head was shooting towards her again. She created a blazing blast of light to blind him as she dove into the nearest building hoping that he hadn't seen her.

She pressed herself against the wall, trying to catch her breath and calm her racing pulse. Damn he was fast, all her prior confidence had evaporated. She wasn't prepared for this. Ziz and Behemoth had been colossal also but she had easily outmanoeuvred them, avoiding them easily and not meeting them on their battlefield. She had easily latched onto them, well beyond their reach to attack them with her magic. Leviathan was supernaturally agile for his size, he didn't attack with claws but with his gaping maw and lightning fast coils. His fins had already tested her wards.

She couldn't believe just how fast he moved. Coils that had been in a death grip around her skyscraper had been seconds later knocking flat whole blocks as its head seemed to soar in every direction.

She was just beginning to think she had succeeded in hiding from him when his face smashed through the wall opposite her. The only thing that saved her from being swallowed, wards and all was a chunk of rock that knocked her out of his mouth. His whole gargantuan body shot past her in a time far too short, the building was only just starting to collapse under his weight when all of him had disappeared out into the wasteland. But she was no fool, she had shot far from where she had been, luckily enough for he smashed though where she had just been standing.

The whole building collapsed, its structural

integrity completely destroyed from above and below. She allowed herself to fall with the rubble, using a bubble shield to attach and cover herself in the falling ruins. It was strangely fascinating to fall within the skyscraper, all her instincts yelled out for her to fly. But she fell in the knowledge she was perfectly safe, so long as Leviathan didn't attack. She saw his black scales shoot past her again, she saw concrete literally turn to powder, and the metal skeletons within twist beyond repair. In the moments it took for her to plummet the hundred or so floors she saw surprisingly much.

Then she crashed into the rubble below, only to be rained down upon by the rest of the skyscraper. She was thankfully untouched within her thick layering of shields, feeling safe from his ability to locate her. She was buried beneath quite a substantial amount of rubble. She could imagine thick dust clouds rising up from the pile, obscuring that burning gaze.

She strained all her senses to tell if Leviathan was near or not, yet was hesitant to use more than a drop of magic. It would only act as a beacon for him. Moments past and she could hear him slicing through the water, getting increasingly distant. His shriek of fury seemed to indicate that he had thankfully lost her. She breathed a sigh of relief. That had been truly terrifying.

She continued to wait as the sounds of Leviathan got more and more distant but his frustrated shrieks easily penetrated the rubble forcing her to cover her ears. He had lost her, now she had only to wait until he was completely gone before she could quickly sneak her way down to the next Level. She might not survive another encounter. She had already used quite a bit of her magic just in her shields alone.

Her waiting was cut short by the water rushing up past her and her shields. There was no stable land in the

Swamps of Wrath. The ruins seemed to offer the only stability, but once destroyed they apparently just sunk beneath the water. No wonder there were so few islands.

Her heart sank as the water around her blazed orange, while the rubble that had hidden her sunk out of sight. The surface was some distance above her, and it was hindered by more rubble sinking, forcing her downwards as it hit her shields. She was now completely within Leviathan's element, his preferred battlefield. And to boot she was lit up like a Christmas tree.

In short she was doomed.

Physicality had failed dramatically, now all she had left was magic. She hoped it was enough. Light exploded out of her, the heat she was generating causing her bubble to rise. She cast out her magical senses wide, and sure enough Leviathan was heading straight towards her. He was a truly terrifying creature, far more dangerous that Ziz or Behemoth.

He shot towards her streaking out of the darkness, all she saw coming was his gaping maw. And she couldn't fly away this time, not that she would have been able to, he was utterly pissed and completely focussed on destroying her.

Darkness fell around her and her light faltered. She was inside his mouth, her light struggling to reflect off his fangs and black tongue. She killed her light, fused her shields to his tongue then waited as water rushed past her. The sound of his swallowing stopped, then all that was left was the drip of water and venom.

She dropped to her knees, her hands already starting to blaze with her Chaos magic, the symbols flaring across her arms glowing amber. It knew what she needed to do. The instant she touched Chaos to Leviathan she was pulled away into his consciousness.

Leviathan was rising to the surface, searching for

more food when light flared out of his mouth and magic started wrapping around his tongue. He went to shriek his fury but his mouth would not open, it had been bound shut. He shot to the surface, breaking through what had been several city blocks, sending rubble and Damned in every direction as he started to writhe about. Then his mind was pulled away from his body.

Leviathan was a poor tortured spirit, just another of Gabriel's experimentations. His true core was the Divine creature Jörmungandr. He had been bound by the Norse Gods in preparation for the day that he and Thor would fight in Ragnarok. After the Gods had been defeated he had been left chained until Gabriel had found him in the seas surrounding Midgard. She had broken the spells and taken him to the now abandoned Eden to conduct her experiments on him. She had felt that she needed a sea monster to compliment Ziz and Behemoth. While he had been in Eden he had suffered many experiments. The glimpses Sariel saw in his memories horrified her. All manner of creatures and Demons, blood covering everything.

But even before Gabriel had found him and conducted her experiments he had hardly lived a pleasant life. Odin had taken him as a child and chained him in the seas that surrounded Midgard. He was to be contained there until the day he was to fight Thor, not that he didn't try and fight him before the prophesized day. He had lived his lonely life chained in the seas, growing bigger and avoiding Thor. He had grown up with the knowledge that he would die by Thor's hands.

He had been separated from his brother and sister, never to see them again. Hel had been thrown in the Underworld because the Gods were disgusted by her appearance. Fenrisúlfr had been chained like him, prophesised to die by a God's hand when Ragnarok came.

It had meant nothing when the Angels had overthrown the Gods, they had never treated him or his siblings well. His ambivalent feelings towards the Angels changed very quickly to match his feelings for the Gods. The Gods had been scared of them and generally left them alone, Gabriel was not afraid. The only positive to his imprisonment in Eden was that he had seen Fenrisúlfr. He had also been experimented on. He had no idea where he had ended up.

Sariel sifted wider. Gabriel's experiments on Jörmungandr echoed the experiments that had resulted in Behemoth, but she had not fused the spirits together. She had wanted a reliable thinking creature that she could bind to her will. Behemoth while the destructive force she had desired was not really controllable, nor could he be relied upon. Madness filtered out orders and compulsions. There was but one intentional spirit to Leviathan, but there was also an unintentional one.

Jörmungandr had been bathed in the blood of two other Divine creatures, the God Quetzalcoatl who was still alive, chained up in Heaven and also the blood of Python, slain by Apollo. Naturally the two bloods had reacted very differently. Quetzalcoatl's blood had infused him with extra strength, power and magical resistance. Because he was still alive there was no risk of his spirit attaching to Jörmungandr's. However Gabriel had also used the blood of Python who had been a powerful earth serpent. She had been slain by Apollo because he had wanted Gaia's oracle in Delphi. He had killed her but he had not drained her, a small offering to the earth so that it would accept him.

Gabriel was unaware of this, she had only known that her blood had been strong in Chaos. Python's blood had completed the experiment, increasing his speed and magical abilities. Though bound as he was he could not access it. Unbeknownst to Gabriel Python's lingering spirit had attached itself through blood to Leviathan increasing his power and strength. Leviathan was among her greatest achievements, more powerful than she had intended and sane enough to be controlled.

He had been unleashed on hundreds of helpless ships and ports at her command. He was Wrath incarnate for the poor God fearing people, yet how had she repaid him once Humanity was firmly under their control? She had thrown him into Hell along with so many of her other creations, he had fallen to the Wrath Level, his fury burning brighter than the rest.

Now it was time for her to set him free and Python as well, but her spirit was anchored to his, it wasn't going to be a pleasant experience for either of them.

Leviathan crashed through the Level, his thrashing body laying waste to everything around him. His body threw up waves the size of buildings causing widespread destruction in every direction. The air was thick with the dust clouds thrown up from the collapsing buildings.

From the iron walls of Dis watched the eyes of dozens of Demons, once Fallen Angels and now the Guardians of Inner Hell. It was behind these walls that the greatest number of Demons lived in torment. Forced by their nature to torment others. It held a far more violent nature than Upper Hell and had procured a wider variety of denizens. Along with the Fallen Angels along the wall top were also the Hell Cursed Furies as well as Medusa, the mortal Gorgon.

Atop the wall they watched in confusion as Leviathan thrashed ever closer towards the wall, his many coils a whipping frenzy. Tons of rubble was sent flying, much of it smashing against the magical shields extending from the walls.

"What is wrong with him?" one of the Demons asked.

Medusa turned her burning eyes to his before extending one blood red arm, to point with her talons as the beams of light emitting from Leviathan's mouth. "Something he ate" she said in a harsh sibilant whisper. He backed away from her, using turning back to face Leviathan to cover his actions. Even the most twisted of the Fallen Angels feared her, Gabriel's Curse had only expanded upon her ability to petrify others, literally and figuratively. It was more than just her strange appearance with snakes for hair, or the cold fury burning in her eyes or even her ability to transform others into stone. It was more than that, it was the ancient feel of her magic mixed with the cold fury within her spirit, it emanated out through her strange appearance.

She was one of the few Demons who did not resent being confined to Hell. It had brought her back to life and empowered her. It was in Hell that she had embraced her powers and nature, she was no longer ashamed or scared of what she was. She had learned to embrace the terror she created.

She wondered what the arrival of the Angel meant for her. If she could cause Leviathan such pain then what could she do to the rest of them? Leviathan was one of the most powerful Demons in all of Hell. Yet he lay thrashing about in the Swamps of Wrath because of an Angel.

She rested against the wall watching him. The others kept a clear distance around her, though the Furies came to stand behind her, their burning gazes fixed on Leviathan as well. They were not afraid of her.

Memories flooded her mind as she cocooned

Jörmungandr with her powers, lancing the pain and suffering that had tainted his spirit to the core. She also cocooned the fragments of Python's spirit, drawing upon the strength of Quetzalcoatl to put the shattered pieces back together. She drew out the remnants of his blood and hers, forging them together to give Python's spirit flesh.

She felt Jörmungandr silently sigh in relief as the burden and strain of her spirit was drawn away from his own. She smoothed over the cracks in his mind, allowing him to finally know peace. She also felt Python's mind suddenly become conscious, raging in terror and confusion. She had spent the last several millennia as little more than an apparition in his mind and body, the poor thing had no idea what was going on. Sariel had to soothe her mind and fill in the various blanks with Jörmungandr's memories.

She felt both of them relax, so she let them go. Her Chaos dividing them from each other and finally giving them back their own bodies, minds and consciousness.

Medusa watched fascinated as Leviathan's tail smashed against the shields, light flaring from its tip. The whole wall was shaking despite the shields, it was fortunate that they were protected otherwise the wall would be little more than flattened iron.

The light in his mouth flared along his sides to his shining tail, from these direct lines flared curving circular symbols that gradually turned a strange brown colour. Soon all his flesh was lost beneath the lights.

The landscape of Hell was cast into stark relief as Leviathan blazed bright as the sun. The serpentine shape of Leviathan split into two, a small slither streaming off of him. Compared to the size of Leviathan it was small, which wasn't hard but it was easily the size of several small buildings.

The slither slowly darkened to reveal a forest green serpent. Other than its monstrous size there was little to mark it different from an ordinary snake. That was until it opened its eyes, they shone bright green in the twilight. Power permeated its very essence to shine from its eyes, and that green spoke of ancient earth powers.

What had just been born?

Then the light of Leviathan shimmered and faded in surges to reveal his new form. He was no longer black but a grey-green reminiscent of wintery seas, his fins were white like wave crests. Every time he moved he shimmered aquamarine, ocean blue, stormy grey, wintery green and vivid icy blue. His eyes no longer burned Demonic red but they had not returned to his natural blood red either, instead they were now a deep blue.

The last light did not fade but continued to burn like sunlight. It alighted gently onto what had been Leviathan then he surged towards the battle scarred beach that sat before the gates.

Chapter 30

"So why are you accompanying me on a plane? Couldn't you just appear in Britain?" Victoria asked while gazing out of the plane's window at the clouds streaming past. She looked like any other young woman, comfortable in jeans and a jumper, her feet were resting on the chair opposite. She had forsaken elegance, sophistication and class for simple comfort while flying. Today she wanted to feel like a normal girl.

Margaret was being extradited back to Britain to be charged with attempted murder. Miraculously video evidence had been provided categorically showing Margaret pushing her. She felt sure that was Brigid's doing.

Since that fateful day she had formed an interesting relationship with the Goddess. She came and went all the time, transporting all over the globe for her various reasons but she kept returning. Despite their start they seemed to have formed a strange friendship. Victoria had to admit she found her utterly fascinating and strangely amusing. Who would have known that the Gods had a sense of humour?

Brigid smiled, Victoria was a queen she would be happy to give the reigns of an empire to. She was forever asking and seeking, she would not leave the empire to be run by others.

"I could but that would alert whichever Angels are watching Britain and there are bound to be many. My presence will also excite what remains of the Fair Folk for they will not have felt the touch of any Gods since the War finished. They have been hiding ever since the Angels started massacring them."

"But you have made yourself known very blatantly in Australia, New Zealand, India, Bangladesh and Pakistan. And you have said yourself that you have been empowering many races. What makes the Fairies so different?"

"The other Daemon races have diluted their bloodlines over the centuries to hide themselves from the Angels. Their powers are weak which is why I have been strengthening them. Yes I have made my presence known, but initially that was not intended but what is done is done. Claiming land is always public, but my connection to the lands allow the Daemons a margin of safety from the Angels. With so many countries now claimed the Angels have to split their attention quite wide trying to outmanoeuvre me.

The Fairies on the other hand are semi-Divine. You could say Angels and Nymphs are sibling races, cut from very similar cloth. Fairies are their cousins, made from a slightly different design. All three races have been around for millennia, serving the Gods in various ways, often being their lovers and bearing offspring. Before the War Angels, Nymphs and Fairies were more Divine than mortal.

The other Daemon races are mainly deviations from the Human blueprint but Nymphs and Fairies are special, they evolved from the spirits of the earth. Their connection to the land is incredibly powerful. When they die they return to the earth or the Otherworld. There is no Heaven, Hell or Underworld for them."

"What is the Otherworld?"

"It is hard to explain. For mortals their spirits or souls usually go onto the Afterlife or are reincarnated, depending on their beliefs. Most spirits are too strong simply to fade back into the Lifestream, the Afterlife which usually occurs in the Underworld is where they live out the rest of their strength before fading into the Lifestream.

For the truly Divine we are absorbed back into the Lifestream as soon as our tenuous connection to our flesh is destroyed. We are but pure magic contained within a magically constructed shell of flesh. Sever that connection and we are swept up into the Lifestream.

The realms of the Living and the Dead rarely cross over. Sure you have ghosts, Angels descending from Heaven and Spectres ascending from the Underworld but generally they are separate and distinct. The Otherworld is a realm of the dead inhabited by both the dead and living. The Veils are particularly thin allowing both the dead and living to easily traverse between the realms. It is also why Britain has so many unexplained phenomena.

The Fair Folk, the Fae, the Wee Folk, the People of Peace, the Old People, whatever you call them are an extraordinary collection of species, living and dead, all united by their differences not divided. They have a huge range of remarkable powers available to them that easily transcend mortal limitations. One is Fairy if they live by the creed of the Seelie Court and accept the queen's authority, which is the limiting factor. In the past their numbers swelled as other Daemon races interbred with them, they have never been stringent about pure bloodlines or other such nonsense.

They always regularly interbred with the Nymphs and Satyrs as fellow nature spirits. Through the centuries they have bred with both genders of the Lilin, Werewolves, Vampires, Naga, Merfolk, Sirens, Jinn, Demigods, Gods, Humans whether magical or not. Any species you can think of they have interbred with, even the Angels."

"Wait they've interbred with the Angels? But don't they hunt them down? And how did they breed with

Vampires? Aren't they undead?

She smiled at her intelligence "Yes Vampires are undead but the oldest of their kind, their nobles and royals, do have the capacity to breed. It is however an exceptionally rare event and common Vampires do not have the gift. As for the Angels well that is an interesting tale. Not all the Fallen Angels fell straight into Hell, those that were not on Heaven to be cast out but were on the Surface sought out refuge. Those who sought the Fairies help were welcomed with opened arms, and legs you could say.

There were of course those sent to hunt them down who let them free for a price" She raised her eyebrows at that.

"But that's forced sex, its rape."

"Yes Humans would look at it like that, the Angels and Fairies however did not. The Fairies saw it as trading one commodity for their life, something they were more than willing to do. If they got pregnant, more so the better for it introduced new bloodlines.

Because of this mixing of their blood they are incredibly powerful with access to nearly all types of magic. They have the power and capacity to render the whole country a wasteland. If they were ever to use their powers beyond defence they would truly be a force to be reckoned with."

"But weren't they hunted down by the Angels?"

"Yes which is why I am unsure of their numbers or strength. But their response to my presence on British soil will be immediate and very noticeable, which is why I'm trying to sneak in under the Angels' radar."

"Are you not expecting a warm welcome? Will they not be glad to see you?"

"Considering I was among the very first to be imprisoned they will be very understanding." She raised her hands to cut of Victoria. "Your cynicism is noted Victoria, it is so prevalent in one so young. But you will see once we have landed. In less than ten minutes you will see your first Fairies."

Despite her cynicism she was curious and excited. She had thought she had outgrown all the childish notions of magic. But when faced with it she was as excited as any child. It seemed fitting that the first Daemon race she would meet would be Fairies.

She looked out of the window as the plane came hurtling down on the runway. The weather suddenly changed from a fairly nice spring afternoon to something out of a horror movie. Think fog banks were rolling in from every direction, it was just as well they had just landed otherwise they would have been stuck in the air for hours. Heathrow would not be able to land any more planes until the fog cleared. It was going to wreak havoc on air travel. It was still a point of pride that Heathrow was still the busiest airport on the world.

"Luckily we landed when we did, fog is rolling in deep."

Brigid had faraway look "The Fae are coming to greet us."

Brigid was up and waiting by the door as soon as the plane had stopped. The staff had all been frozen where they were. Victoria passed her frozen staff and security "What did you do to them?"

"This is the Fairies, it is their trademark. This way they don't have to talk to those they don't wish to."

She was surprised "They want to talk to me?" She was quite chuffed.

"No I stopped them from freezing you. You need to attend this." She cast a thoughtful look over Victoria and herself "but not dressed like this, we'll fail to make an impression." Victoria watched wide eyed as her clothing transformed into a floor length emerald green dress. It was beautifully elegant but simple with an unusual design. It came to mid-thigh at the front, before falling further at the sides and ending up floor length at the rear. It was practical, allowing her to easily move her legs. It was held up by thin golden straps that wrapped around her neck in Celtic designs. Brigid wore exactly the same dress.

Brigid snapped her fingers and the door opened without a sound. She then descended down a staircase made of shining light. Victoria hurried after her, watching in wonder as Brigid stepped onto solid ground. Light flared underneath her before spiralling outwards in fluorescent symbols of plants and animals. They spread like wild fire, their glows visible beyond the thick veil of fog.

Brigid helped her down the last few steps as the stairs evaporated. Together they watched as fairy lights grew and danced about in the fog. Victoria gasped as several floated beyond the fog to reveal fist sized lights bobbing around. Within could be seen the silhouette of people with butterfly or dragonfly wings.

The first lights to descend were blue and they came by the hundreds. Where they descended fully armoured people erupted in blue flames. What they were Victoria had no idea, they looked humanoid but any other details were hidden beneath their armour. It was made from some blue metal she had never seen before, trimmed with gold and silver. Their armour was very angular and reminiscent of birds. Their variety of weapons were strapped to their backs. They ringed a wide area that she and Brigid stood in, their ranks disappearing back into the fog. Their presence seemed foreboding.

"The Atlantean Guard" Brigid whispered in her

ear.

"Atlantean Guard, but Atlantis is just a story?"

"It was real but that's a story for another time." She pointed.

Several lighter blue lights landed revealing strange insect like people. They were blue skinned with four transparent blue wings. Their limbs and bodies were very thin and long, their limbs ending in four digits. Their large indigo eyes lacked any whites or pupils. Their gaze on her was most unnerving.

"Sprites"

There were brown lights with flickers of blue that landed within the fog. From the afterglow and fog walked several black horses, their manes running with water. Riding bareback were several brown skinned women with short brown hair. Their lower arms, hands, calves and feet were covered in short brown fur, they also had several whiskers. Their lips were dark brown as were their nails. Both types of creatures had liquid brown eyes sparkling with swirls of blue.

"Kelpies and Selkies"

There were more blue lights, this time tinged with grey, floating around the edge of the clearing. Closer inspection revealed people within though they had no wings. Their forms also appeared fluid though it resembled Human form. "Nixies" They were joined by pink lights that joined them in intricate dances around the edge of the clearing. Within these lights were petite little beings with antennas, butterfly wings and stingers. "Pixies"

Four other large lights joined the rest but they had no corporeal bodies, remaining instead as floating and writing flames, water, earth or wind. "Elementals, very powerful, very dangerous"

More shapes were walking out of the fog

"Korrigans, Leprechauns and Clurichauns" The Korrigans had long flowing hair that floated around them, red eyes, long red fingernails and what appeared to be red tattoos all over their bodies. They seemed to hold a very seductive nature to them, and several of them even had feathery wings.

The Leprechauns surprisingly conformed to common beliefs she had read. They were little men wearing red or green olden style clothes decorated with gold and completed with their little black shoes with big golden buckles. They might only be knee height but they were full of life and spunk, smiling at her knowingly.

The Clurichauns were the same height but completely different. They appeared very animalistic, covered in their thick fur of black, brown, grey or forest green. They had paws instead of feet and their hands were remarkably paw like. They even had snouts with moist black noses. Their eyes were bright green fires. Some of them wore blue or purple waistcoats while other wore nothing.

The last of the nobles to arrive, that's what Brigid had whispered they all were, were the Banshees. They were spectral women with no corporeal form. They varied in blue-white to grey transparency. They were clearly defined from the shoulders up, from their shoulders down were ill defined dresses that were severely ripped along the bottoms. Each of their eyes held cold calculation.

The very last lights to appear were three green lights that landed together in a smaller ring of the Atlantean Guard. The first one landed, and as the light faded it revealed a Human sized woman of extraordinary beauty. She had snow white skin, green curls that fell to her breasts which were all that held up her green dress. Silver and gold bracelets adorned her arms and a garland of flowers crowned her head. Her green eyes twitched into a smile as she looked at Brigid.

Two other green lights landed next to her, the people who grew from them could only be her children. Their resemblance to her was completely obvious, though they had brown hair as well as the green and their skin was not so strikingly white. The son was also a little bit taller than his sister and mother, but all three were beautiful creatures.

"You brought the nobles to greet me, I am most honoured Sorcha."

The Fairy Queen nodded deeply "And I am even more honoured you remember who I am Brigid."

She laughed a little "But of course, you were Mòr's long awaited daughter. Your conception was a miracle of my own creation to repay your grandmother Dáirine's loyalty. Though the last time I saw you, you were but a child."

"Before the War destroyed the world. We had feared you killed, but are most relieved to find you alive."

"I am still surprised I am alive and even more so that I am free after all these years. How I wish I could be a fly on the wall when the Arch Angels discover it was one of their own that set me free."

There was a collective gasp from all the gathered Fae before Sorcha asked "An Arch Angel set you free?"

"Indeed. She was the youngest of them all, cut off from her powers so that her family could use them. We helped each other escape, then we freed Hera to escape Heaven. We were lucky to have escaped at all." She shuddered "The power of the Angels is truly terrifying." They nodded in agreement, the Fae long knew the powerful reach of the Angels. "How has the Seelie Court fared since the War? How many have been slaughtered by the Angels?"

At this Sorcha smiled "Not as many as you would fear or expect. The Otherworld has proved invaluable in hiding our numbers. Our protection spells have only gotten stronger and subtler, remaining undetected by the Angels. Our blood and theirs have gone into those spells but the price was worth it. The Seelie Court has continued to grow as our powers have diversified. Among our numbers we have the descendants of Nymphs and Satyrs, still breeding true. They would be here but as yet none of the others have agreed on their nobles.

Within our numbers we have the bloodlines of Gods and Angels. Our powers cover the whole British Isles and not a single one of our number has been persecuted in over 500 years. Our powers and spells allow us to completely avoid Angel detection. With your awakening Goddess we have the power to completely prevent them entering the British Isles entirely. Avalon will be beyond the Angels."

Brigid was surprised, the combined powers of the Fae was enough to rival a God or powerful Angel. With her addition they could have a completely Angel free homeland. "I am impressed, you have the largest concentration of Daemons in the world. Naturally I will grant my patronage, protection and power. It is long time we wrested control back from the Angels. And to that effect I have our Human Key." She placed an arm around Victoria's shoulder as she pulled her forward.

"We were wondering why you had brought a Human with no magical powers."

"Not powerless for much longer. I present to the Seelie Court the Princess of Wales Victoria Windsor, Heir of the United Kingdom of Great Britain and Northern Island and soon to be Queen and Empress of the British Empire."

That clearly surprised the Queen but a gleam filled

her eyes "You're planning on resurrecting the Empire?"

"Indeed and expanding on it too. This time the magical will walk openly in the streets, our enemies will fear our military and magical might. Our lands will flourish like never before."

"You wish us to pledge our allegiance to a powerless Human?"

"This Human, the Key and heir apparent. And she will not be powerless for long, as the Key she will be imbued with the powers of the land."

"I have a condition."

Victoria was surprised, for a race so enamoured with the Gods to make demands of one seemed sacrilegious.

Brigid nodded for her to continue.

"We demand an assurance in our allegiance to this Human, an agreement bonded in blood. She will marry my son."

Victoria gasped, the son whipped around to glare at his mother. Brigid on the other hand clapped her hands together "What an excellent idea. A union to truly herald a new beginning."

Sorcha motioned her two children "Princess Victoria I present my daughter and heir to the Seelie Court Princess Aisling and my son Prince Cathair."

He was still spluttering "Mother I must protest, she has no ethereal sense whatsoever."

"Well I hardly want to marry you either" Victoria retorted.

Brigid and Sorcha continued on as though neither of them had spoken. "They will not be wed before she is crowned in her own right."

"She will also spend time in the Seelie Court, my people will need to adjust to the idea of her having power over us. She must also learn our ways. But in the meantime Aisling and Cathair will both attend her, they are ignorant of Human ways and it is better they learn it now before the world becomes aware of them."

"That is an excellent idea. I believe Victoria has many country estates where they can reside and learn from each other."

Sorcha smiled "Then we are agreed, this calls for a drink" with a wave of her hand a crystal decanter appeared filled with emerald green liquid that shone brightly as it swirled around. It poured itself out into five crystal chalices that floated their way to the four royals and the Goddess.

"Is this Earthlaughter?" Brigid asked in amazement. It had been millennia since she had drunk it.

Sorcha could only laugh "It certainly is, the best in the land. Though I presume it has been forever since you last tasted it."

"Aye but you never forget it. Victoria you are in for a rare treat, few Humans have ever tasted Earthlaughter."

Victoria took the chalice that hovered before her. As flustered and annoyed as she was with Brigid and the Fae she had to admit she was curious about the strange liquid, especially if it could delight Brigid so much. "What is in it?"

"A secret the Fae will not disclose. The only others that come close are Lightningsun of the Satyrs and Paradox of the Naga. Drink it, believe me you will enjoy it."

"We have Lightningsun but the secret of Paradox is forever lost with the Naga and Unicorns being extinct." She smiled at Brigid's raised eyebrow "The Nymphs and Satyrs that joined our numbers kept the secret to themselves but they share the drink."

"You have done well"

Sorcha smiled "A toast to a brighter future" They raised their glasses and drank.

For Victoria it was unlike anything she had ever drunk before. It smelled strongly of mint and lavender but the taste was something different. It was as though they had captured the essence of the forest, meadows, rivers and earth then distilled them down to capture their strongest essences. She gasped after she swallowed, it was very potent, she felt empowerment after one sip.

"This is amazing" she couldn't wipe the smile off her face.

"She is coping far better than most for her first taste." Aisling deigned to speak for the first time.

"She will do well, I have never seen a Human handle it so well. There is hope for you yet. Welcome to the Seelie Court Victoria Windsor. It has been a long time since a Human has seen the Court, what a stir it will cause when you come to greet us all." She turned back to Brigid "I like her, I can see why you have chosen her as your future empress." She stepped closer to Victoria turning her unnerving green eyes over her.

Victoria was surprised, she was a full head shorter than herself, but Sorcha's presence more than made up for it. There was a regal air and poise to her that Victoria could only envy. Adding her beauty, grace and presumed powers she was the image of a fantasy queen.

Sorcha looked over the young Human "Well I guess by Human standards she isn't unattractive, but Cathair is right she lacks any of the ethereal to attract the magical. I doubt the Elementals will even acknowledge her. They have always been against the Human stain. Will she be able to handle the responsibility, she looks like she would be crushed beneath the weight of responsibility, and the Human monarchy certainly isn't what we are. I'm beginning to feel sorry for my son, he is marrying far beneath his position."

He perked up hoping for his new betrothal to be broken.

Victoria spluttered in rage "There is nothing wrong with the way I look, just because I don't look like I've rolled around in pearls. I couldn't give a damn about some pretentious elementals if they're so close minded I couldn't care less. Human stain! Well sorry if we don't dance around the forest naked bathing in moonbeams while we're busy discovering space travel. My family may have made mistakes but I am far better suited to ruling Britain than they are, my people love and adore me, I will make a fantastic queen. They love me because I'm not a pretentious bitch as your son's Fairy wife would be. I've lived with responsibility all my life, I know my country, I own over half of it, I have regrown forest all over the country just so you can have your toadstool parties.

Your son is marrying up, I am the best he will ever get. Don't look down your nose at me, you're looking up it shorty."

There were many gasps from the Fairies. The Elementals all pulsed with their powers and there were hisses from behind her. Sorcha on the other hand surprised everyone by laughing, she clapped Victoria on the shoulder "Oh yes Brigid I like this one. Welcome to the family Victoria, I like a daughter-in-law who isn't afraid to speak her mind. And with my son you'll have too, I'm sorry to tell you both my children are spoilt and arrogant. He is certainly lucky to have you, and you'll be lucky to have him, once you've whipped him into shape of course."

Both her children glowered at her. Victoria burst out laughing, she wasn't happy that she was somehow suddenly betrothed but she could work on changing that but she had to say she liked and respected Sorcha.

Sorcha nodded to Brigid as the colourful symbols on the floor started changing. All the Fairies stepped back while Brigid steered her into the middle of the symbols. They changed green as Brigid channelled her powers through Victoria. The three Fae Royals stood in the next ring out, the symbols swirling about them turning blue. The other Fairies all assumed various positions, the symbols swirling between them turning into a kaleidoscope of colours.

To Victoria it all seemed so surreal, other than that night in the Atlantic Ocean she hadn't seen magic. If it wasn't for Brigid being a fixture of her life she would have thought she had dreamed it.

Everyone had their eyes closed, slight smiles on their faces. This was their lifelong dreams, what they had striven for, for so long. She felt like an interloper, she didn't understand their need or desire, it was still all so new to her. She had never been persecuted by the Angels. She had lived a fairly normal life, well as normal as could be for a princess.

But it was more than that. They all seemed to be enjoying sensations she wasn't aware of, their eyes fluttering away behind their lids. It had to be magical and she couldn't feel it. Cathair was right she had no sense of the ethereal. She felt like she was in a room where everyone was speaking another language. She didn't have the slightest clue what was going on. She had a brief moment of paranoia when she thought they could be sacrificing her for all she knew.

Brigid's hands on her shoulder started to glow, the light was also spreading into her own skin. Everyone around her was a blazing beacon of magic while she was the shadow on the glass. She knew that around her the world was changing, she knew it but she couldn't feel it.

Suddenly Sorcha plunged her hands into her chest, Victoria stared down in horror and the glowing arms sticking out her chest. This really was a sacrifice! She felt the hands clasp her heart, felt its racing beat within its new cage.

Then she heard the voices in her head, the hundreds, no thousands, no the millions of voices all calling out to her. Was this magic? Where were these voices coming from and who did they belong to?

All the voices of the Fae. Every living and Spectral Fae within the British Isles and Otherworld. Within every facet of Avalon. We are many voices but we speak as one, our unity binds us together and makes us stronger.

Her vision darkened, she couldn't see the airport or the thick swirling fog. She couldn't see the Fairies anymore or Sorcha with her hands in her chest. She was surrounded in darkness, everyone else had disappeared. She could still feel Brigid's hands on her shoulder and Sorcha's around her heart, but she couldn't see them.

Tonight the Fae make our stand. We shall no longer hide in the shadow of Heaven. Tonight Brigid lends her strength to us and we will be completed. Our fates forever intertwined. But fate is at the crossroads. Tonight a Human dares enter our world.

"I was brought here by Brigid." Her voice sounded weak, even to herself. What the Hell was going on?"

The Goddess brought you here? Why would the Goddess bring a Human to the Sacred Isles, their infestation is bad enough.

She couldn't believe what she was hearing.

"Human infestation? We were once the greatest empire the world has ever known and we are still one of the richest countries in the world. We have millenniums of history, culture and conquest. Who are you to question my worth on this earth?"

The voices roared at her. If she had been standing

in the physical world she would have collapsed to her knees clutching her ears.

Who are we? We are the voice of the Land. We are the Fae, the Fair Folk, the Old Ones. We were here before Humans came from across the sea. This land is ours, you are but trespassers who rape our land. Our history is far longer than yours, our culture more diverse, our power greater.

"You might have magical powers to make things easier but my people conquered the world on people power and technology alone. You need me, you need my people. You have lived so long in the shadows that you are afraid. You envy Humanity's ever present courage and resilience. We traversed the world with no magic, we ventured into the unknown time and time again. We have shaken off the Angels' shackles on our own accord and you hate that."

Light burst from her chest, illuminating the darkness. But she barely noticed that she was lighting up the darkness. But she did see faces in the darkness, a mob of faces, a faceless pack working as one to tear her apart. It reminded her very strongly of the media.

It made her more certain of herself "I have been chosen by the Goddess to rule my nation and to revitalise and resurrect my empire. You are living in shadows but crave the light. For once in your lives you want to live in the open, to walk down the streets as you are, free from Angelic persecution. You want, no you need to be part of my empire and yet you would have me beg for your assistance. You would make me feel inferior for my lack of magic, but that has never held back Humanity. We rise every time we fall. Brigid is the patron of my empire and she is your last surviving Goddess but that does not automatically grant you a place in the new world order.

You have to fight and work for what you want. If you want any place in my empire you must work for it, do not try and scare me into granting it. I am the empress and you need to be a part of my empire. Prove your worth to me and you can hold your heads high in an Angel free Britain."

Heat flooded her heart, pressure started to build, there was a ringing in her ears and her sense went spiralling. There was light and darkness, heat and biting cold, she couldn't make sense of anything anymore. Then something exploded out of her chest, there was fire, ice, lightning, wind, dirt, clouds and green lights. She stared at it wide eyed then she passed out.

"It is done"

"Yes Avalon is now officially an Angel free zone. I wonder how long until the Angel fire covers the skies."

"Not long I imagine, though only time will tell. But now we are safe from the Wrath of Heaven."

"I wouldn't say that but we are shielded from them. Remember Sorcha the Angels play by a different set of rules, whatever they did to themselves is unique and unknown. Their powers and capabilities are beyond our current understandings. Oh we know what they've done but not what they're capable of. But at least the lines have been drawn and we have our weapons out."

"You think Victoria is a weapon against Heaven?"

Brigid shook her head "Not against Heaven, against the world. It is time for change."

"And for rebirth. What have been will be again. The Empire will be resurrected as will many extinct species. Hera has resurrected the Phoenixes and there are rumours of two new Daemon species in America.

"It is the era for new discoveries." She reached down and picked up Victoria. She carried her over to the awaiting car and placed her in the back seat. She smiled down at her with pride, she had done better against the Fae than any mortal ever had before. She was shaping up to be more than she had ever hoped for, she had chosen well. She had only just been exposed to the Fae but already her lips held a tinge of green. She would be extremely powerful if it was showing already.

She caught Cathair in her gaze when she stepped back out the car "You make sure you treat her right, if you break her heart then I will condemn you to Hell. Aisling you will teach her how to use her magic, it will be growing in leaps and bounds. You will both use your glamour and learn to live in her world. She is the single most important person in these entire isles, do I make myself clear?

The nodded sullenly, their lips turned red, and their green parts of their hair turned brown. They lost their ethereal glow but maintained that unique beauty. They bowed to their mother and their Goddess before climbing into the car.

Brigid and Sorcha hid their smiles while they watched the two royals. Their resentment was thick in the air.

Sorcha sniggered as she hugged Brigid farewell "this will do them well, I fear we have been out of touch with Humanity too long. I doubt many of us could pass as Humans in this age. She glanced around as the nobles and guards started to alight into fairy lights again. Even the fog was starting to tear and drift. "What of you Brigid? Where are you off to?"

"India. You've given me an idea and I have a mess to try and sort out, especially with Pakistan erupting into civil war. I fear the Arch Angels have come to play in Pakistan, it certainly explains the eruption of religious hatred in the region. The same madness is threatening to burn through India and if the Angels truly are involved there will be none of my followers left. I cannot allow this to happen, Kali gave me the last of her powers to protect

India. I have a sacred duty to protect it."

"May Gaia be with you"

"I hope so, she's the only one more powerful than the Angels. If only she could awake from her slumbers our problems would be over. Farewell my friend and may the fates be with you." Then she was gone.

Sorcha walked over to the car and put her head through the window "You will stay with her until I recall you. You heard the Goddess' demands, do not draw her ire." Then she disappeared as the wind tore the fog apart and the whole airport came to life again.

The two royals sulked in the back as Victoria's staff resumed moving as though nothing had happened and they were not completely new. He wanted to spar with someone, she wanted to blast something to smithereens. Here they were stuck in the Human world, pretending to be Humans. What was worse they had to look after a child while the whole Fae world was changing.

Chapter 31

Sariel jumped down from Jörmungandr's neck, who was still glowing slightly. Her boots crunched on the crumbling pavers that formed the ruin of a road that led out of the swamps to the gate of Dis. She looked down at herself in disgust, she was absolutely covered in blood. It took her several attempts to clean herself off, her powers were worn out from unwinding Gabriel's Curse.

She patted him affectionately on the neck, sending a wave of goodwill into him. He was still fragile and probably would be for a long time, but for the first time in his life he had a taste of freedom. He also had a companion, Python was curled up beside him, both lost in the first peaceful dreams they had had in millennia.

She watched them hoping nothing would be so foolish as to attack them, even without their Demon Curse they were extremely dangerous. She was worried what she may have unleashed but she could not allow Gabriel's cruel torment to continue.

It felt right to undo Gabriel's Curse. How could it not when the poor souls were so tortured and tattered? It did however make her fear what Gabriel would do to her when she found out that she was the one who had undone her Curses.

She turned to face the nearest gate of Dis, somewhat disappointed at its plainness. The gate was not particularly wide, six carriages could ride abreast which was probably quite large but she was used to the grandeur of Heaven.

She had at least thought that Hell would be on a similar scale to Heaven if not in appearance. The Gates of Heaven had been made of gold, ivory and platinum while these gates appeared to be made from nothing but plain iron. While Heaven's gates were ornate and intricate these were simplistic but functional. She wondered if they contained spells. The gates of Heaven were open to the sky, these were crowned by thick and menacing walls that had a touch of erosion.

Atop the battlements she spied the familiar shapes of the Furies though twisted by Hell's Curse. They were truly terrifying, their feather wings twisted into Demon wings, long bloody talons in place of fingers. They seemed shorter, more predatory. To top it off they were bathed in flames.

Next to them towered a serpent woman, with a writhing mass of snakes for hair. Even from this distance her eyes burned with Hellfire. She had normal looking arms that gripped the battlements as she stared down.

All along the wall top were Demons who had once been Angels. Their anorexic bodies were black, red or grey, having matching tattered membranous wings. How many wings they had depended on what they had once been. Horns grew from their heads, spines covered their shoulders and wing joints, they all had spikes on the ends of their tails and instead of fingers they had claws or talons. These were what had become of the Angels who had stood with Lucifer.

They were what she might become if she faltered.

"Send out the Guardian" called a harsh sibilant voice, it didn't sound natural. No mortal could have made such a noise, it could only have come from the serpent woman.

The portcullis started to rise, screeching and groaning the entire way as showers of rock and dust fell. It was followed by deathly silence. Even those on the battlements were silent.

Then she heard claws scraping on rock and the

rasp of scales.

She unsheathed her swords, the action comforting her. Then she waited.

Out of the gate walked a Greater Demon. He radiated power and moved with a deadly fluid grace. At first glance he appeared similar to a monitor lizard, even having the same swinging walk. His long tail swept back and forth behind him, tipped in a ball of empowered metals that could harm immortals.

He stopped and stood up on his hind legs, towering over twice her height. He was muscular and yet she had a feeling he would be even stronger than he looked. His face vaguely resembled the Angel he once had been, though with much blunter features. Long red-metallic teeth poked out from his gums, his claws were the same metal. His skin was beige colour with red marks running all over his body in intricate symbols. He even had strange red appendages that reminded her of dreadlocks, though made of scales. Even his six vestigial wings were red, they were thin and serpentine. He wasn't flying anywhere.

He turned his blood red eyes towards her, his pupils were but large vertical slits. He closed his eyes as he held out one of his paws. Blood pooled from his paw as a long red spear grew out of it. With his other paw he clutched it with proficiency. The bleeding paw he shook, splattering blood between them.

He adjusted into the guard position, she mimicked his stance with her own two blades. So this was to be a weapons fight, which was some small comfort. Her magic was still recovering.

Jeering rained down from above when she didn't instantly attack. But she remembered Nemesis' teachings, let them make the first move. It gave you slightly more time to analyse their fighting style, not much but it could be just enough.

He brought his spear swinging down towards her which she easily darted out of the way of before swinging her swords in front of her to block his uppercut. Silence fell upon the watchers, there was rarely anyone who could survive the first attack.

He started to circle her and she moved with him, watching his walk and the movement of his muscles. She had long learned that they showed intent even before they had consciously decided to attack. Sure enough she dodged or blocked his few probing jabs. She realised he was testing her.

Then his tail swung at her while he stabbed forward with his spear where she was dodging to. She avoided his tail but was nearly impaled upon his spear. Damn she had forgotten about the tail and had been unprepared for it. A foolish mistake.

She continued to dart and dodge around his spear thrusts and tail swipes with ease once she realised his tail was dangerous weapon. However when she darted under his spear his spare paw slashed across her chest, she had forgotten yet another weapon. His claws dug deep, drawing silver blood before the wounds healed over.

He stopped and raised his claws to his mouth, his long tongue snaking out to lick the blood off.

Pissed off she stabbed in with both her swords, causing him to scramble backwards but he had underestimated her speed and skill. As she stabbed she spun inwards, raising her swords. They battered against his spear with the distinctive clang of metal striking metal. But with practised skill she used one of her swords to follow through, as the first sword struck the spear the second stabbed forward to his exposed belly.

He darted backwards howling as black blood poured from the wound, before it slowly healed over. He had definitely been Divine before his Curse. Most likely an Elder Angel, but possibly a demigod or minor God. That would explain his useless wings.

He rushed towards her, using his spear and tail to trap her swords while he pushed forward with his weight. She somersaulted over him, stabbing him in the shoulder as she passed over. As soon as she landed she spun around, slashing with her swords catching him across his wings, severing four of the creepy limbs. He roared his fury striking out with his tail, again and again, driving her backwards to the water's edge.

Then she struck back, spinning towards him, her two swords swinging at him in paired upper and undercuts driving him back until he was against the wall. He swung down with his tail, smashing against her swords. She jumped backward to avoid being knocked out.

They resumed circling each other, both were surprised at the other's skill. She was actually enjoying the challenge of the fight, then he spoiled it by using magic.

A blast of red magic exploded against her shields. Thankfully they had not been depleted despite her magical efforts. She glared at him as she raised her hand, it was glowing green. Vines jumped out the ground at him, wrapping around his limbs and throat. He tried to fight off her magic, but like everything else in Hell he had severely underestimated her powers.

She wasn't fully aware of it but her own phenomenal powers were increased by her affinity to Chaos, as well as supplemented by Nyx and Gaia as well as all the Demons she had freed.

She drove him to his knees as she walked forward. Her powers flowed over him but as it did it told her something different. This was not Gabriel's doing this was Michael's, and it was extremely strong. What on earth was Michael hiding in Hell?

She sent surge after surge of her powers down into the Demon, watching in fascination as section by section the Curse was peeled off of him. First of all his eyes changed from glowing blood red to beautiful violet. Then his strange hair like appendages separated into strands of shoulder length black hair. His vestigial wings started to grow black feathers, ever so slowly. From around his eyes the scales started turning into pale white skin, and as it did so his facial structure readjusted.

She gasped when his face had completely changed, he looked disturbingly like Michael, though with subtle differences. In fact he looked even more like Thanatos or Azrael. Unlike either of them though he had striking red lips, with a slight purple tinge.

This could only be her father Samael.

She faltered, shocked beyond reasoning. The Curse started snapping straight back, crawling up his neck. She fought back with her magic, struggling to send more into him. There seemed to be a limit to how much she could throw against the Curse at a time.

The Curse continued to be stripped away revealing the pale skin of his neck and shoulders, they were liberally covered in black symbols. The same symbols that covered her legs. There was no denying that this was her father.

She stepped forward and held his chin in one hand, she looked into his eyes watching as they slowly gained lucidity.

"Samael"

His lips twisted up ever so slightly before he replied "Sariel" His teeth were surprisingly white and more surprisingly black symbols covered the inside of his mouth. He really was the Angel of Death. His violet eyes were exactly like hers and the rest of the family. They flicked back and forth absorbing the features of her face.

His bulging muscular neck gave way to a more slender Angel neck. The overzealous Demon muscling gave way to far more natural Angelic muscles. She realised that even his physique was the halfway step from Thanatos' slim frame to Michael's more muscular one. The spear dropped to the ground as his arms twisted. What fascinated her the most, other than the spreading wave of pale and black skin, was the transformation of his hands. They shrank, the claws seeming to melt and flow back into his body leaving behind benign violet fingernails.

He started flapping his wings as they returned to their former glory, and what a glory they were. They were jet black with a lustre that any Angel would envy, they even had a noticeable violet iridescence.

The scales were shrinking down his torso and stomach revealing his lean, muscular physique all the more prominent because of his continuing death wards. She was beginning to understand some of the stories about him. He was a striking man that would draw the attention of men and women alike. It seemed her mother wasn't the only inherently seductive parent she had.

He reached out with one of his hands cupping her face, where their skin connected both their Angelic glows increased. "Beautiful just like your mother" Her breath caught at the compliment. She had always thought herself rather plain by Divine standards. But her mother was an acclaimed beauty among Angels and even Gods.

He let go of her and let out a fearful Demonic roar as a shaft of sunlight speared down from above. She stepped back in confusion, and she wasn't the only one to shy away from the sunlight. Sunlight was unnatural in Hell. It was a realm of shadows and ever twilight. It bleached Samael of all colour except his black marks. All her spells and progress was instantly cut off, the backlash sending her sprawling backwards. The Curse regrew in earnest, reclaiming what it had lost.

His face twisted in fury, but he caught her in his gaze "I am proud of you Sariel, set us free." Then he was gone, absorbed up in a final blaze of sunlight.

Then it was gone and she was left extremely night blind.

She heard hushed whispering from atop the wall and once again the grating noise of the portcullis being raised.

Sure enough she heard the familiar sound of scales scraping the ground and the clip of talons. But there were also noises behind her. The swish of water being broken followed by something hauling itself out of the water. Then there was another set of reptilian noises.

She wiped her vision clean with her magic, raising even more shields. There was the twang of bows releasing a volley her shields easily deflected. But as they continued fire blossomed across her shields as the Fallen Angels savagely attacked her, probing and assessing, searching for any weakness. Their twisted powers surrounded her, competing with each other to eat away at her shields. Two heavy bodies slammed against her outer shields before sliding down.

Then they were slamming against her shield again, smashing through it. They were strong, far stronger than the Fallen Angels on the wall combined. Their strength rivalled Samael, they had to be Fallen Arch Angels. Once again they had the strong sense of Michael. Now what was he hiding?

Strong powers assaulted her, driving her to her knees as her shields buckled and she hastily threw up more. Her magic flared out around her in defence, catching some on the wall, but the attacks only intensified. Her powers were draining away at an alarming rate, she hadn't recovered from her fight with Samael or Leviathan. Now she had to face two Greater Demons together.

She felt her last shield waver under the onslaught. Then it collapsed.

Arrows plunged into her chest, she screamed in agony. Never had her skin been pierced before, only during her training with Nemesis had she ever been cut. These were twisted metals to kill a Divine, she could feel their poison spreading through her as a cold numbness. Her skin was on fire, spurred on by the Fallen Angels, but she ceased to feel it. She was dragged one way then another, whatever those two bodies had been were fighting over her. Surely they were tearing her apart, strange she could no longer feel pain. She could see claws tearing into her shoulder and wings but she couldn't feel it. She couldn't feel anything anymore.

Her hearing faded away, her vision blurred, the sulphurous burn disappeared from her nose. She was losing her senses, she had lost all feeling in her body. Even her magic was sliding beyond her control.

Was she really dying? Was this really all her life had led to?

Chapter 32

"Yes Ariadne?"

"All the mosques on the East Coast and southern states have been destroyed. Their demise is spreading quickly through the northern states and West coast. They've also been completely destroyed in Alaska and Hawaii. The media storm is blaming Christian groups, and we've played our part in them getting the blame. We've also indicated racist groups. We've now started targeting churches and synagogues but we've hit a problem."

Hera turned away from the window and the grey skies beyond. It was spring in New York, the last week of March. The deep snows of February had begrudgingly given way to strong rains. As a consequence New York was remarkably clean. It had been a strange winter, extreme and frigid. There had also been a spike in murders, and targeted attempts on religious groups. Most New Yorkers had mentioned there had never been a winter like it before.

Nor had there been, not since before America was even discovered had such plans for a rebellion been laid, or armies gathered. Nor had a Goddess permanently resided in a Human city since Atlantis had been destroyed.

Now it was spring, and just like the winter it would be unlike anything New York had ever experienced.

"And what problem is that?"

"It is Good Friday, a holy holiday of Christianity. All Churches are under Divine protection until the weekend is over. The Vampires had planned to do something really dramatic, to really drive home a point to the Angels and their believers."

"But it went horribly wrong?"

"They attempted to burn down Saint Patrick's Cathedral and the protections responded accordingly."

"How many did we lose?"

"Twenty and the cathedral's defences have gotten stronger."

Twenty was nothing, Vampires could easily increase their numbers, indeed they had been doing so all winter. "Hmm this calls for a more personal touch after their ineptitude. Really how could they have been so stupid?"

Ariadne said nothing, she didn't know why they had been so stupid. Then again the Daemons were getting increasingly more reckless. They believed with Hera around they had nothing to fear. How wrong they were, Hera was one, the Angels many. She was powerful but so were they.

People had died doing her will, and many more would. They were after all just pawns. Losses were expected even necessary, Christianity had flourished on martyrdom. The Vampires deaths would only encourage others to fight harder and smarter, Daemons would continue to flock to her. Hera knew how to manipulate and control.

Hera patted Ariadne on the shoulder, easily reading her thoughts "Their loss shall not be in vain. I will attend to the cathedral myself."

With that said she turned and glided gracefully out of the apartments. Ariadne was right many more would die. It was a thought that troubled her slightly, her time among Humanity had humanised her, weakened her. True power was only seized by the ruthless. Death was a necessary part of life, and the price of power. And the results were paying off, nearly every major city in United States was suffering an anti-religion assault, or so the media called it.

She smiled as the elevator closed, she had worded her response well. Ariadne would continue to gather followers for her. She really was an exceptional High Priestess, her ability to inspire faith had impressed even her. Then again her reward for loyalty was her Divinity again. Most mortals would do anything for that, a Divine who had lost it would do everything and anything.

She called in a heavy raincoat and umbrella as she walked out into the downpour. It would not do well today to draw too much attention to herself. What a strange city to rain so much, it wasn't so dissimilar to the northern provinces of the Roman Empire. She supposed that was why the Northern Europeans had felt so at home here.

As she cut through the crowds of the Rockefeller Plaza her attention was grabbed by the glowing statue that stood pride of place behind the ice rink. A quick probe into people's minds told her it was a statue of Prometheus. How strange that a Titan was immortalised in their consciousness. Then again he had always loved Humanity, suffering much to give them fire. It was likely they would always have a soft spot for their protector.

On a whim she gave the statue a more realistic fiery glow, drawing fascinated looks to the statue as she hurried out of the plaza.

Her surprise only increased when she stepped out into Fifth Avenue next to the statue of Atlas. How strange that there were two Titans in the Rockefeller Centre. She made a mental note to look up who this Rockefeller was. Who was he to have allowed two Titans to be constructed? Prometheus she understood, Humanity had always had a fondness for him. He had helped shape many of the cultures that had flourished around the Mediterranean. The progeny of those ancients had spread through Europe and beyond, carrying within their racial memory the love for him.

Atlas was different though, he was a Titan through and through. Prometheus along with his brother and Hecate had given their loyalties to the Olympians but Atlas had personally led the assault against them. When the Olympians had won the war and imprisoned them in Tartarus, they had pulled Atlas aside and given him the special punishment of holding up the Heavens. He had later been killed by Heracles, or Hercules as most modern Humans knew him as. That had sent tremors through the Gods, a Titan killed by a demigod. It had been unfeasible.

But she supposed to Man it symbolised their ability to overcome even the greatest of odds. Though she supposed it could represent power, strength and discovery. Books of maps had been named after Atlas. She found European development and expansion a very fascinating thing.

She stopped next the statue, looking across Fifth Avenue at Saint Patrick's Cathedral. It was a beautiful building, a true testament to Human skill in construction. That had always been a remarkable talent of theirs. They were like ants and termites, working away all the time to build remarkable constructions.

As she crossed the street the rings of the globe that Atlas carried started to slowly spin. Tomorrow the news would be ablaze with the loss of the Cathedral but there would be side notes about the two statues. They might be dead, but interest in the two Titans would undermine the Angels' strength and faith.

She walked straight through the closed doors, barely noticing the faintest assault on her shields by the building's defences. She snapped her fingers disappearing her raingear and adjusting her hair and attire. She stood resplendent in a stunning black ball gown rising only to her breasts, her pale cleavage adorned with a black opal cut into a starburst. She wore black gloves to her elbow, leaving her upper arms, shoulders and neck bare. Her intricate brown curls fell lightly across her bare shoulders. Her violet eyes shining like lanterns in the candle lit gloom of the cathedral.

It was only then that she turned her attention to her surroundings. It was truly stunning, her attention drawn along the gothic structures, the windows down the back and to the high vaulted ceilings. This was a beautiful and important building. It was power and strength, covered with beauty but she saw through it to its true nature. It was an impressive and imposing building designed to unconsciously scare followers into line. Of course to their perception they would feel pride, but then they were ignorant to the Angels' powers.

Her attention skipped over the gaudy Easter decorations and worshippers. What did she care for them? Their attention though was naturally drawn to her, mortals were always drawn to the Divine. For better or worse.

She walked down the central aisle, the altar would be the source of power that needed to be overcome. Not that it would take much at all. From the altar would bloom beautiful fire, bringing with it purifying destruction. Eyes followed her as she passed the pews. Many had the vague look of a mortal intoxicated by a Divine's presence.

By the time she was climbing onto the altar all eyes were on her. The priest bustled over to stop her, foolish mortal. With an offhand wave she sent him sailing through the air to smack into one of the columns. Voices raised in concern or protest. What did she care, her spells had locked them in. They would burn in the purifying flames.

Easter worshippers looked about in fear, many started moving about. This woman had sent the priest flying through the air without touching him. The cathedral now echoed with the sounds of slamming doors and the distinctive sound of locks.

She started to glow with white light as she climbed the last few steps of the altar, her powers easily overwhelming its pitiful amount of sacred power. She smiled in satisfaction as the whole altar burst into roaring violet flames.

Light flared behind the flames then they died. She narrowed her eyes in irritation "Show yourself Angel." She started covering herself in the most complex shields and protective spells she could imagine.

"Just like a Goddess to make demands. Seems your freedom has only led you back to your old habits" Michael said as he walked down the aisle. As usual he was dressed in his Roman Centurion attire, blazing like a miniature sun. Even his wings despite being black somehow managed to express light.

"Just like an Angel to lie in ambush."

"I stand before you do I not?"

"And how many others are still hiding Michael? I know your games."

"You speak of other Angels Hera, I am renowned for my truth."

"So then stealing Sariel's powers to supplement your and Gabriel's own was not a deception? Then again I am no Angel, such practices may be common amongst your kind. However I know Sariel would not consider you to be truthful."

"What would you know of Sariel" she had unnerved him and taken him by surprise.

"I know everything Michael, I probed her shockingly undefended mind. Imagine leaving an Arch Angel so weak and vulnerable. You call us cold and cruel but you inherited it undiluted from us.

"We are not like you" he spat.

"No you are weaker."

"We won the War."

"By deception and trickery, as well as our own pride. You played off our rules very well, then you left the world to rot. You are fools, the world was yours, now look at it."

"I did not come here to be lectured about your outdated practices, the Age of Gods is over Hera. Accept it. Now it is the Age of Angels, we are now the masters."

"And yet I sent your sister to Hell. Who is the master now?" her eyes flashed with pure malice.

He pulled out his sword, a line of magic slicing through the air and pews before faltering against Hera's shields. "Such anger for one who claims it is a Deadly Sin, and such waste of your worshipper." She indicated the severed corpses sliding out of the sliced pews.

"Mortals lives are insignificant."

She smiled "A point we both agree on" she flicked her hand and fire shot out in a graceful curve, burning through several rows of worshippers before smacking against his shield.

He responded in kind, fire blazing towards her. It didn't take long for fire, lightning and ice shards to be hurtling through the air between them. Their shields were ablaze with light as they cast aside attack after attack. Underneath each of them started to grow blackened craters, growing faster as their magical onslaught increased.

The once grand interior of the cathedral was now a ruin, craters and huge gashes rent deep in the ground.

Cracks and burns spread ever outwards from them. The columns nearest them buckled and collapsed. The stained glass window behind Hera shattered as an attack was deflected.

Not a single mortal remained alive. Their shredded and burned bodies littered the battleground, occasionally lifted up by an explosion or raging wind. Those that had tried to flee had fared no better, their bodies lay crushed underneath collapsing walls and columns or blown to pieces by a deflected attack. Neither Divine has spared a moment's thought for the mortals caught up in their conflict.

Hera ceased her attacks, smirking as Michael continued to attack her. Slowly he ceased his assaults. He was surprised she had held up for so long, by his approximation more than an hour had passed with them exchanging attacks. He was starting to feel the effects in his magical reservoirs. He had no idea if she had started to notice if she was starting to run dry. She was far more powerful than he had accounted for, damn Demons flocking to her. All of the Demons in America must have flocked to her call, and there had to be more than they thought.

He cast a quick glance around the ruined cathedral, mildly surprised that the outer walls and roof were still standing. Usually battles between the Divine devastated entire cities and deeply scarred the land. Then again Hera was not at her full strength and he was but one Angel. The fight would have been far more savage if other Angels had been present, then she really would have been fighting for her life. Or if she had been at full power, then he would have been fighting for his.

Hera floated up higher, the ruins of the window behind her starting to glow. She pointed to ground, a thin line of lava separated them. Small orange flames licked across the ground, setting ablaze any remaining pews nearby. "A familiar scene Michael?"

"What do you care of Hell Hera? You've sent enough to the deepest bowels of Hades, you even locked away your own father in Tartarus."

"Yes but Hell is your own creation Michael, Tartarus is a natural entity but I digress. I wanted you to see my special addition to your creation." The crack grew wider and within the flames rose an image of Sariel. She lay in chains, her body halfway through the transition to Demon. She was naked and had clearly been raped many times then drained off all her life. She wasn't Desiccated but on the verge of death. As he watched he saw the last spark extinguish as a clawed hand drew the last of her Lifeforce out of her.

She smiled in victory at her illusion, in reality she had no idea how Sariel was faring. She didn't have the power to pry into Hell. Not that Michael knew that.

She stepped backwards at his unnatural roar. He collapsed to his knees, flames and pure power surging around him. This was no longer a controlled attack, this was driven by pure emotion. Uncontrolled powers left to emotions' control were unpredictable and the most powerful magic. She was surprised he still had so much pure power left in him, for this could only be his own powers. But then it appeared rage and guilt had robbed him of his wits.

The ground shook violently sending the roof crashing down on them. It smashed against her shields, sliding down their sides. But it buried Michael. She did not move, she was curious but not foolish. He was still alive underneath the wreckage.

She was not surprised when flames erupted up out of the wreckage. Michael stood at the lips of a great fiery hole in the ground. What was surprisingly was the shaft of sunlight shining up out of the hole and disappearing into the smoke above. The smoke was trapped by both their containment spells.

Divine symbols flared across the floor and up the shaft of light as the image of a man began to appear. Though he appeared to be half man, half Demon. If she assumed right Michael had summoned a Greater Demon to the Surface. It was the Angels' trump card. The Demons they had created had pure undiluted powers granted to them by mortals' fear. They did not have the complex network the Angels did to defend themselves from faith and yet reap the power. They were wholly empowered and controlled by mortals' beliefs.

But to her surprise and especially Michael's he was not wholly Demon. His face was the face of a black haired, pale skinned Angel who bore a remarkable resemblance to Michael. He glared at Michael with unadulterated hatred before his face was consumed by the Demon Curse. All traces of beauty were lost beneath his reptilian cocoon.

Hera gasped in surprise, he had turned his own father into a Greater Demon.

"Now you shall taste Hell for what you have done" he roared at her. Then the creature let out an unearthly scream before launching himself at Hera.

Amid the confusion Michael flew out of the cathedral, cutting through her containment spells with pure power. He landed on the Rockefeller Centre opposite watching the scene below. Emergency services, the media and ordinary citizens stood watching the historic landmark burn. Firemen directed their hoses through the windows at the blaze to no avail. Flames continued to grow higher and higher into the night sky. Amid blasts of lightning, earth shudders and all manner of elements flaring within the cathedral.

Mortals gaped in awed horror at an event they could not, or would not comprehend. Magic had been dead in societies since the Middle Ages and now their minds were now firmly given to science. The paranormal events in front of them only confused them, in time they would deny them or rationalise what they had witnessed.

"She is still alive?" Raphael asked as he and Uriel dropped their glamour.

"Not for long, Samael will finish her off."

They gaped at him "You summoned a Greater Demon? Have you gone mad? The Council will kill you. Have you forgotten the devastation they cause? There will be nothing left of New York."

"It is well overdue that we made our mark on Humanity again. She must be killed and we do not have the Seven to kill her. She is far too strong, the Demons have flocked to her in numbers greater than we feared. As for the Council I will deal with them myself. She sent Sariel to Hell, the least she can do is have a taste of what they did to her."

They fell silent as they noticed the tears on his cheek. They didn't want to know what he had seen of Sariel, they doubted there had been much left of her. The poor girl, a victim to powers far greater then herself.

Raphael grasped Michael's shoulder, offering the only support he knew how to give and drawing Michael into the Angel Weave containing the battle within the Cathedral. All over New York Angels had descended to contain the Goddess. The other Arch Angels descended to stand with them, adding their power to the weave.

Gabriel automatically sensed Michael's pain, coming to stand with her husband, drawing him towards her. He remained watching the cathedral burn. If all New York had to burn to kill her then so be it. It was a price he was more than willing to pay.

Hera regarded the Demon with the interest a Vampire regards a Human, of no real threat but potentially dangerous if not watched. She knew Michael had fled after summoning the Demon, just as she knew he and his brethren now covered the city with their spells to contain her. They were watching her, she would give them the show they didn't want to see.

She slowly descended to the ground and walked across the crater towards the Demon. It had ceased its howling to look at her with weariness. She had the feeling the Demon had no choice but to obey Michael but it seemed unwilling to act upon its orders. Then she remembered that Samael had been one of the Angels vying for peace.

"Samael?" she asked softly as she walked towards him.

He backed away snarling until a collar of light tightened around his throat. It cut in viciously, ripping the flesh even as it healed and pushed away. The agony would drive him mad if he did not complete Michael's will.

He threw himself at her snarling, only to smash against her shields. Again and again he threw himself against her shields. The onslaught was unbelievable, her shields flaring and crumbling beneath his onslaught. He wasn't using refined power but raw, elemental power that corroded through refined spells. Raw power cracked in the air, with each encounter their powers reacted and flared off around them. The Cathedral was so thick with power the air was changing colour.

Uncontrolled magics reacted with each other as Hera met might with might, it rolled around them beyond either's control. This was the battles that levelled cities, raw power that reacted on its own accord, even striking against its own source. Light danced up into the sky in shifting shafts and striking bolts, illuminating the battleground through all the layers of smoke and magic. Fire danced on the air like Fairies and Titans, ice slicked the ruins like the palaces of the Ice Giants, great cracks snaked across the ground as it shook with ever increasing frequency.

Despite the ferocity of the battle and the sheer volume of power being unleashed the Angels were easily containing the errant power. But they were noticing the drain that raw powers caused. Raw power had the ability to corrode through any refined spell.

Samael was driven to attack her again and again. Hera continued to back away from his attacks, still unsure how to drive him off. His powers were completely alien to her, strong in the taste of Angels but corrupted in a manner she could not understand. He did not strike with spells but raw power. Any of the shields she normally used against Angels were near useless. His own shields rivalled hers in strength, made of raw power it was impervious to any spell she had thrown against it, even elemental attacks. It was also withstanding her own raw attacks.

It would seem that the Greater Demons truly were the ultimate weapons.

But they were flawed, despite their strength, despite their powers and despite their ability to rival the Gods they were but constructs that belonged to Hell. And Hell called to them.

More time passed as he continued to assault her, she was really beginning to feel the strain of two Divine battles. It was a sad reflection of the powers she had lost. There was a time she had taken on whole pantheons easily. She was amongst the most powerful Gods to have ever lived. But she was still weak, her own natural powers were nowhere near their peak and she couldn't understand why.

Leaving her powers uncontrolled to defend herself she descended within the depths of her power, seeking its raging core to calm her. It was also within here the memory she sought to use, of actions done long ago. The Underworld was connected to the Surface in all places, but only some places were permanent for the dead to pass through. These passageways could also be traversed by the living, earning their way into myth and legend. Divine beings had the ability to enter and leave the Underworld at will, well the true blooded ones did.

Passages could however be created, temporary as they were.

Mortals had managed it before to send or summon spirits. Some beings, particularly the Lampades and Valkyrie, were adept at traversing between the Surface and Underworld. They could even take spirits and the living with them. In the past Ereshkigal had created a passage for the dead to walk onto the Surface to make the living fear her. In her past Hera and her siblings had created a passage to the gates of Tartarus when they had overthrown the Titans. It was that memory she sought.

Samael continued to attack Hera, driven ever onwards by the mounting agony of Michael's leash. However that same drive allowed Hera to work her will without him noticing what she was doing. She drove her powers downwards, it was easier than she thought. New York was a vast city that had people dying all the time, the sheer volume had made a semi-permanent passageway for the dead.

The Underworld surged up to meet her, she could feel the pressure building underneath her. Huge cracks shattered the floor of the cathedral, smoke and flame pouring out of the earthly vents.

It wasn't just to the Underworld she was making the passage but to Hell. Luckily enough she could use Samael as the anchor. The Greater Demons belonged in Hell, their Curse required their return. She made the connection to Hell, surprised to feel Sariel's power floating about. What had the girl been getting up to?

She felt the ground surge and knew that by now the Angels would start working out what she was doing. She had to do something they would not suspect.

With a last almighty cry she drove home her spell, even as she abandoned herself to the Lifestream. Surrendering all of her to its uncontrolled powers, it was a risk, a literal sacrifice. She may not return but it was a better chance than being sucked into Hell which was her only other option now she had opened it up.

Samael looked around in confusion as his prey disappeared in a flurry of green mist. His confusion was short lived as the ground exploded beneath him. Fire rushed up in an inferno, the screams and sounds of Hell filled the night air, sending the Humans outside scurrying.

Across the street the Arch Angels watched as the cathedral and the Greater Demon it contained were swallowed by Hell. The remaining skeleton of the cathedral collapsed inwards into the raging fiery chasm. Samael gave forth a petrified scream as he was swallowed up by the chasm. Flames leapt as high as sky scrapers before the maw darkened and closed. The flames suddenly died, their absence sending everyone night blind.

All that remained of the cathedral was a bare slab of solid rock.

Chapter 33

In the morning sunlight the Arch Angels walked over the ground, invisible to the confused mortals still milling about. Even the emergency workers avoided walking on the slab.

The Angels scoured every section of the slab and the buckled dirt around it, but there were no trace of Samael or Hera. Had she really been sucked into Hell? Had she been that foolish to believe she could control something she had not created? Did she think she could survive in Hell? Had she forgotten that the Underworld was now a one way passage?

They knew she hadn't escaped. The Angel Weave prevented her from leaving by any magical means. She hadn't ascended or teleported, she hadn't transformed into something else. She hadn't tried to break free. Which meant she was either dead or had been sucked into Hell, which was as good as dead.

Sariel had in some way been avenged though that did little to ease Michael's guilt. The others breathed easily. Now there was but one rogue Goddess.

Ariadne watched them from the street, she could see them despite their spells of invisibility. She was after all Divine, she had just been stripped of most of her powers. But they were returning with Hera's help. She used simpler glamour to hide herself, but it worked. Their eyes did not linger on her when they scanned the crowds. They saw Hera's High Priestess and they didn't realise it. She smirked. She was the greatest threat to their power after Brigid and they didn't even know of her.

She had watched the fight last night, unlike the

Humans and Daemons around her she had understood what was happening. She hadn't thought such power possible, or even imagined such power. The Age of Angels had deluded everyone. The Gods were truly a force to be reckoned with, the Angels Rebellion had succeeded through trickery, luck, using the Gods' rules and their own unique ability to combine their powers. But could they really face Hera or Brigid on an open field as they continued to gain more and more power. It scared her to think just how powerful Hera would be once Humans started worshipping her in real numbers. If she succeeded in converting America and Mexico then how much power would she wield?

She was well aware the entire battle had been contained by the Angels. All magic across Manhattan had been impeded by their Weave. The impact of the battle had been severely reduced. But she has still sensed its power, the amount of power had overwhelmed her senses. Manhattan would be awash with lingering magical energy for weeks, if not months. The residual magic would slowly be absorbed into the living systems. She wondered just how many mortals were suddenly going to start experiencing strange phenomena as the result of their developing powers.

She smiled it would be the perfect time to gather them to Hera's call. She was no fool, she was replaceable. But if she did all that was asked then she would be rewarded. Hera was not Human and lacked Humanity but she understood mortal drives. She rewarded those who pleased her well.

Hera was not dead, though where she was Ariadne had no clue but she would not be idle in Hera's absence. What better way to greet the Goddess' return than with an every growing army of worshippers, Daemons and mages.

Anjali ducked in behind the nearest doorframe, pushing herself as far into the shadows as she could while the military patrol shot along the street ahead. She was tired of running, she was tired of hiding but what choice did she have? Pakistan had gone insane.

No one had though much when the military had overthrown the president, he hadn't done much for Pakistan and it was a fairly regular occurrence in Pakistani politics. But things had changed once Azad Ali had taken control, slowly at first. Islam was the state religion, it had always been but their worship changed. It became enforced. Those who were not Muslims started being ostracised by their communities as ever more restrictions and laws were brought into place.

Women lost what rights they had. They had once been a country who had had Benazir Bhutto as their prime minister, now a woman was not even allowed to leave the house without a male escort. They had degraded quickly into Afghanistan under the Taliban. The men held all the power, the military's rule was absolute. All who did not comply were punished. Those who were not Muslims were enemies of the state.

If she was caught she would be killed. She was a Hindu woman and she wasn't wearing a burqa. She would not wear a burqa. If she was wearing one she might stand a chance, it wasn't like they checked who was under them, but she required a male chaperone to be outside.

She was alone, completely alone. Her father and brothers had been killed in the home invasion. She and her mother had hidden in the pantry and thank the Gods they had been lucky enough that none of the soldiers had checked. They had set the house on fire as they left, uncaring if people were still inside. It had only been a

Hindu house to them.

Her mother had not survived the night.

Now she had nowhere to go, no one to seek sanctuary from. Which was why she was creeping through the city of Hyderabad. It had a long history of fighting and religious hate between Muslim and Hindu. It was a fitting place for her to be, fleeing the Islamic Military regime.

But the real reason she was here was the Indus River. It was a sacred river, and it was calling her. It had been calling her for several days now. It spoke of safety, sanctuary and transformation, strangely enough with the voice of a British woman. What did she have to lose? She had already lost everything. And there was no way she could get across the border into India. Iran and Afghanistan were not choices either.

She crept along the railway lines, glad that the trains were out of service since the bridge had been destroyed in the flood that had devastated the Indus River. That in itself was her greatest hope, much of her banks were ruined wastelands that the government had not gotten around to clearing up.

She paused when she saw movement at the edge of her vision. She started breathing again when she saw it was a family of three hurrying between the rubble. It would seem that they too were seeking the sanctuary of the river. At least she wasn't hallucinating, which had been her greatest worry.

Her hurried movement, fearful creeping and petrified pauses only increased the closer she got to the river. There were hundreds of people creeping through the rubble, darting through the open zones and hiding within the twisted remains of civilisation. It was appalling that it hadn't been cleared. Someone could get hurt, never mind the risk of infection.

She shook her head sadly at her foolishness. The military was hunting all non-Muslims like dogs, what did they care for the state of the cities.

Everything was going well. She could see the Indus, its dark waters reflecting the thin sliver of the moon. She could see people slipping into its waters. Many had managed to bring valued possessions with them. She even saw one family silently push their car into the river. Nothing resurfaced, not a single person yet she did not think they had drowned. She saw a family climb into the water and before her very eyes disappear, they hadn't even fully submerged yet.

She didn't care where it led to or what happened, it offered sanctuary.

Then she heard a noise that turned her blood cold. A helicopter was flying above her, its search light probing between the rubble for people. Hunting infidels. Sure enough it took them no time at all to locate people.

The sound of a machine gun firing filled the air, as did the sounds of screams and bodies being shot at. Somewhere a siren started to blare, drawing the attention of all nearby military units. The only sound louder was the roar of trucks and tanks.

People broke from cover, running screaming as fast as their legs could carry them to the river. It was now or never. The rat-a-tat-tat of the helicopter's machine gun filled the air, obscuring all other noises. It was as though time slowed down, she saw people near her jerk into strange motions as clouds of blood exploded out of them. Their bodies became riddled with holes, the ground before them peppered with bullets and blood before their bodies sprawled unmoving onto the ground.

She ran screaming from her cover as bullets sprayed the wreckage, ripping holes in the ground and rubble. All around her she saw the flash of bullets, then the spotlight flicked back her way as the helicopter turned around. She ran with all her desperation, praying to Kali to be saved and reach the river. Then she heard the machine blaze back into life, as she heard the tank fire its round. The mound near her exploded. It had been covered in children, little children struggling to climb it. The air was filled with short, sharp cries that were quickly silenced. She was flung to the side by the explosion, thankfully just missing the line of bullets that shot through where she had just been.

She struggled to stand up, screaming in horror when she realised she was slipping and sliding on the children's remains. She stared in horror at her bloodied hands. They had been children.

More screams filled the air as tanks thundered over the rubble, crushing people hiding within. The night sky was ablaze with gunfire and explosions.

She ran for her life, scooping up a small child as she ran past. The child would die, it was clear. Her wounds were severe, her legs had been ripped off in the explosion, but those dark liquid eyes caught her. She could not leave her to die when there was still a chance.

The river had started to glow with a white light, beams shining high into the sky. She saw the dark shapes of people diving into the water, desperate to escape the army. Another helicopter was coming from across the river, its machine guns falling silent. Must be more people on this bank. It was flying across the river when a bolt of red lightning shot up and hit it. Its explosion temporary drew the attention of the army giving the fleeing people precious seconds.

She was surprised when she saw a crucifix shining in a puddle of blood. Apparently the river called to all the infidels.

The little girl stared up at her, her small bloodied

hands wrapped through Anjali's long black hair. It was reflected in the little girls eyes that she saw her end. She glanced over her shoulder to see the first helicopter bearing down on her again, its spotlight fixed on her. Its machine gun swept back and forth as it drew closer, mowing down defenceless people.

She sent her last prayer to Kali as the bullets ripped through her body. She screamed in agony but refused to let go of the little girl. She teetered on the edge of the bank, jerking as bullets continued to rip through her. She didn't need a doctor to tell her there was no hope. She had already seen most of her organs explode out of her as mist. In a haze she slipped forward, her arms wrapped tightly around the little girl. If nothing else she would get her to the river.

Another spotlight flicked over her before seeping back. She heard the rumble of the tank as it fired its deadly missile. She was sent flying as the ground behind her exploded. She couldn't feel anything below her waist, she had been paralysed. Time passed slowly as she was flung through the air, she saw part of her leg fly past. She saw why she couldn't feel her legs, she didn't have them anymore. There was no hope for her or the little girl. She was probably dead anyway.

As she flipped around in the air she saw the massacre on the river banks, blood ran in streams into the river but strange enough the river was surging up where the blood drained in. She hoped someone had videoed it all and put it on the internet. The world had to know about these atrocities.

She fell through the shining lights and splashed into the river's waters. Her breath caught at the pain and cold. Then she felt her pain fade away, felt her body fade away. Was this death? She didn't care.

She could no longer see or hear the battlefield. She

was at peace.

Medusa turned her attention back to the body of Sariel as it suddenly flared with light. Both the Greater Demons who had been eating her backed away nervously. The body slowly floated upright, her grievous wounds healing in seconds. Her eyes were a blaze of white light, even the green, black and brown symbols covering her body had all turned bright white. They were also now moving.

White lightning danced all over her body, and even along her black wings.

She flicked her hands at the two Greater Demons, lightning struck them both from above. Their bodies twisted and writhed as they were thrown up into the air. They remained floating in the air as lightning coursed through their bodies, ripping through their Curse and stripping them of their reptilian and Demonic shells. In the two Demons' place were revealed two beautiful female Elder Angels. One had long blonde hair, the other warm brown, both had dark bronze skin. Both had three pairs of golden wings. They bore a strong resemblance to each other, and a resemblance to Sariel.

The Fallen Angels on the wall tops resumed their attacks on Sariel, but Medusa could see it was foolish. This was not an Angel who could be defeated with an onslaught of magic. This was well and truly a Goddess, beyond the abilities of even this many Demons to kill.

Sariel flicked her attention from Lilith and Naamah to the wall tops, irritated by their feeble attacks against her. A multitude of lightning struck the wall in a writhing net, as far as she could see in either direction. Within seconds the Demons were stripped of their Curse, leaving behind their original Angelic splendour. They slumped down exhausted.

The Furies tried attacking her, but she sent them back to Hades. Their thanks echoed out across the wall as they disappeared.

Her powers then swept over Medusa, stripping her of her Demonic guise and leaving instead a strange alien beauty, an echo of the Nymph she had once been. Medusa felt power beyond imagining sweep through her and neatly cut all remnants of Gabriel's Curse away. To her surprise her powers did not disappear, they remained but were now different.

With all the wall's guardians floating in the air, Sariel turned her attention to the closed gate. A massive blast of white light exploded into the gate, tearing it asunder. She floated forward, a nexus of blazing light, through the remains of the Gate to Dis. Each of the once Demons were laid down safely behind the hesitantly regrowing wall. Once again it stood strong, separating Outer and Inner Hell.

Sariel continued onwards.

Victoria flicked the remote, changing the channel onto her father's address. He was currently in France on an official visit, much to the surprise of Britain. He was performing most of his royal duties. No one knew that he was preparing the way for Victoria. They had made the decision that he would abdicate once she had turned 21 so that she could assume the throne. He had worried and argued with her but she was far better suited to being Queen than he was to being King. They both knew it.

So did the whole country.

The three years were to give her time to herself and time to adjust to the hectic duties expected of the ruling Monarch. Being one for the few countries that still had a monarchy Britain expected a lot from their royals. It was only fair considering they paid for them.

She snuggled into the couch under the blanket, it might be March but winter was not letting go. It had rained every day since the snows had stopped falling. Her two Fae shadows had informed her that the land was awakening under Brigid's touch. The Lifestream was quickening and rising to the surface. She was to expect erratic weather patterns, but also an increased fertility all over the country. Plants, animals and Humans would suddenly be abundantly fertile.

As it was the agricultural scientists were glowing at the unexpected growth in their labs and conservation groups were noticing forests were looking healthier.

So far the Angels had not noticed that Britain and Ireland were now cut off to them. But then it had only been a couple of days. It felt like years around Cathair and Aisling. They seemed to cast a depressing shadow over the whole palace. The servants shied away from them. She had no such luck, she had to endure hours of magical training that seemed to be progressing nowhere. They were acting even more snobbish towards her than before, she hadn't thought it possible.

She had managed to extract herself from this afternoon's lessons to watch her father's speech. Their understanding of Humans was shockingly ignorant, a fact she planned to exploit against them. Perhaps she could use it to force an end to this ridiculous idea of an arranged marriage.

For now she was comfortably snuggled up on a couch, wrapped in blankets and sipping hot chocolate as she idly watched the TV. It wasn't like anything exciting was going to happen. The speech was merely a formality, the negotiations had already been made. France and Britain were going to be having shared military practices over the next two years, and there were some changes to commerce and information trade.

Her father was doing well. He looked relaxed and healthy, probably because he knew the light was at the end of the tunnel. These three years were his final farewell, a way to redeem himself to the public and pave the way for her.

He tapered off when a beam of light descended from the ceiling. Everyone watched in confusion as an Angel, a real Angel, descended. Victoria saw two images on top of each other. A Roman Centurion with six shining wings, the guise of the Arch Angels but underneath she saw an angry female with blonde hair and gold and white wings.

"What have you done you foolish mortal?" she yelled in utter fury, before she ran her father through with her sword. Victoria surged forward screaming, entangled in her blankets. She scrambled up to the TV screen.

Her father looked down in surprise at the sword sticking out of him, he looked stupidly back up at the Angel not comprehending what had happened. The French President next to him was similarly paralysed. The security detail was not, they surged forward, guns blazing at the Angel. All their bullets were deflected off her shields. She raised her sword, the king dragged up into the air with it. No Human could so easily carry such a weight in one arm.

"You and your country will pay for this insult, we will raze it to the ground. All your cities will burn. You will become the lesson the world will not forget." Then she flicked her arm and sent the king hurtling into the wall. His lifeless body slid down the wall, his eyes vacant and dull. The President and both their aides were at his side in seconds to give medical help, but they were too late. King George VII was dead.

"Beware the Wrath of Heaven, Britain and Ireland

have forsaken God for Brigid. You will suffer the consequences." Then she disappeared upwards in a shaft of sunlight.

Security had rushed in by now at her screams. They stood awkwardly about until servants came in to attend their princess. Cathair had come with them. It was he who picked her up and carried her to her bedroom. He held her as she cried herself into an exhausted sleep. He then sat in one of the armchairs to watch over her. He too had lost his father to the Angels, he knew her pain.

Chapter 34

Sariel blazed through the burning landscape that was the Sixth Level of Hell. Impatience and her phenomenal powers lending her great speed. The sixth level was for heresy and it was perhaps the most densely populated of all the levels she had seen. It was also a testament to the Arch Angels' utter lack of care for mortals. In every direction, tightly packed together were burning tombs, their inhabitants wailing and screaming from pain. None were able to leave their tombs.

Perhaps the greatest cruelty of the Angels to their worshipers lay in their ever diverging religions and the views each religion took against each other. It was remarkable that there were any Lesser Angels at all, which meant they all had to have been fanatical as Humans. Because Judaism, Christianity and Islam all viewed each other as infidels and heretics, and within each religion there were various sects who saw each other as heretics it meant that nearly anyone could be classed as a heretic. It meant that any believer who was viewed as a heretic by another would likely burn for being a heretic. Unless they were famous or important to the Angels, then they would be dragged up through Purgatory.

Sariel flew over them, feeling their pain and suffering, but beneath it their confusion. Many had lived devout lives only to end up in eternal torment because they had been viewed negatively by others.

Where she passed the flames died, and from her long streams of rain clouds drifted across the burning plains to gently extinguish the fires. She didn't linger to examine her handiwork, instead pushing forward to find the cliff that announced the descent into the next level of

Hell.

When Victoria awoke she was very surprised to find Cathair dozing in an armchair next to her bed. She was less surprised to find her maid laying her breakfast on the table. She jerked her head towards him. "watched you all night he did, even carried you here when you collapsed. I was beginning to think he didn't have a pleasant bone in his body."

Victoria looked back at him in surprise, this was most unexpected. He had been nothing but cold since he had come to Buckingham Palace. She climbed out of bed and pulled on her robe as the maid left. Rumours would be born from tonight but she was over caring.

She hesitantly and gently shook him awake, his glowing green eyes snapped up to her. Her breath caught when she saw his pupils were slitted like a cats and that his whites had entirely disappeared. As suddenly as it had happened his eyes returned to normal "you startled me" was all he said.

She felt awkward with him, she knew they were technically engaged as much as they both disliked it. She had no idea what to say to him, and had never been alone with him before. His sister had always been present before.

"There's breakfast if you want it" she said indicating the table.

He nodded before uncurling and walking to the table with completely feline grace. It was times like this that she realised the Fae were natural born predators. She had initially thought that they would be vegetarian like Buddhists or Pagan, akin in their beliefs about the sanctity of life. They had curtly dismissed such notions, they were part of the circle of life and consumed life just as they gave to it. To their mind vegetarians were imbeciles. Turned out they were proficient hunters who usually turned into animals before hunting. If they did hunt with weapons it was with archery or spears only.

The fact they could commune with animals and turn into them did not deter them at all. The royal family always changed into predators, it was part of their nature. She personally believed it heightened their predatory natures. She also believed that was why they lacked so much Humanity.

"If I may ask why did you stay last night?" she had found being subtle got her nowhere with the Fairies, not even the guards that had been assigned to her. Not that they often took form, she had only ever seen them as blue flashes at the edges of her vision when she left the palace.

"It is never easy to lose a parent, especially at the brutal hands of the Angels. It was clear that you were close to your father, his demise was particularly shocking because you are still so new to the world of magic." He picked up an apple and bit into it, his green eyes fixed firmly on her.

His gaze was so unnerving "My presence makes you uncomfortable" he stated plainly.

"No" she quickly lied.

He merely smiled.

His smile died when she asked "Is that what happened to your own father?"

"In a manner yes. He was hunted down by the Angels and slaughtered just as brutally. He was holding open the passage to the Otherworld for others who could not make a passageway themselves. They butchered him because so many escaped."

"Your father was a hero"

He nodded solemnly "His sacrifice saved thousands of lives." He turned to look at her, piercing her with his gaze "Your father will become a martyr in the coming War." He got up gracefully and gently grabbed her chin with one hand "it will do no good to blame yourself Victoria, remember it is the Angels who are to blame. They killed him, not you, not anyone else. You have the power to readdress justice. You can cut off a great deal of their powers. You also have great potential within yourself."

He casually walked out of the room, closing the door with a final courteous nod at her. She just sat there with her heart racing. Christ his hands were like fire, and he had been so close. She had had to resist with every fibre of her being to stop herself from kissing him. She rubbed her chin, feeling the heat dissipating. She didn't know what to make of it, it had felt like an intimate moment, but she couldn't be sure with him.

Instead she poured herself a stiff drink and sank back into her armchair. Her presence would not be expected for today. Tomorrow she would begin preparations for her father's funeral and once that was done she would have to start planning her coronation. Her planned marriage would be expected after that. She found she was suddenly less angered by it.

She poured herself another drink to stop her shaking hands when she wondered how the decanter had gotten to the table when she hadn't gone to the cabinet to get it.

To Anjali's surprise she was alive. Or at least she presumed she was still alive, for she was still clutching the little girl. But things felt different, she couldn't feel her legs. Then she remembered she had lost them. Just like the little girl.

She realised she was underwater. She strove upwards to reach the surface, suddenly fearing for air. She moved surprisingly quickly, despite having no legs and having her arms full. Then her eyes adjusted to the water.

She nearly screamed, in her hands she held a baby Naga. Then she saw her own arms, her own four arms, holding the baby Naga. The little Naga also had four arms. She was more serpentine than the myths usually said, she was completely serpentine from the waist down, her black-green coils drifting gently in the water. Above the waist the child was distinctly more humanoid, though with four arms. Her skin was also green-black. Her long black hair floated freely in the water, her face despite its colouring looked Human. Her little eyes were closed in sleep.

Then she looked down at herself and saw the same green-black coils, though far longer than the child's. She was a Naga, no a Nagini. One of the legendary serpent princesses.

There were others in the water as well, swimming upwards from the dark depths towards the sunlight above.

She slowly raised her head from the water, worrying that it might still be the Indus, despite the inexplicable changes to herself. It was a bright sunny day, it shone brightly on her dark skin as she looked around at the other Naga. They were not all the same, some had four arms others two. There were also a range of colours reflecting the natural array of serpents. There were very few like herself. She wondered if that meant something.

Also in the water were other Naga, if they were still to be classed as such. They were very large serpents, as long as several men. Their sinuous bodies twisted about in what she thought was desperate confusion.

She turned her attention to the river banks and was surprised to recognise the distinctive steps of Varanasi. She was in the Ganges. Standing on the banks was a six winged woman glowing softly, beside her stood a man in green robes. They both stood out from the crowd because they were both remarkably pale skinned beside the natives of the Subcontinent.

The Naga nearest the stairs climbed and slithered out of the water. As she slowly swam over she watched the proceedings. The Humans stared stunned at the emerging Naga, but their attention continually flicked back to the winged woman. Who was she?

What was even more curious was that the Naga who climbed up out of the water prostrated themselves before the winged woman. She flicked her hands and people came forward to lead the Naga away. They left with blankly awed faces.

She was hesitant to go to shore but what choice did she have.

As she awkwardly slithered up the steps the little girl she was holding woke up crying. She gently rocked the child, she'd had very little contact with children, she had no idea what to do. It did however catch the attention of the winged woman. She pointed at Anjali, then curled her finger, beckoning. Feeling very self-conscious in front of everyone she slid over to the woman.

"Thank you Anjali" she said as she gently lifted the little girl up. It fell quiet instantly, and to Anjali's surprise a hood like a cobra's spread around her neck. It was covered in strange markings. She gently rubbed the girl's chin and she giggled, her forked tongue flicking in and out.

She turned to address the crowd her voice carried to all ears "You may be wondering where you are, how you have gotten here and why you have all transformed."

Heads were nodding all among the Naga.

"You are on the banks of Sacred Ganges, sister to Sacred Indus which has allowed you to be transported between Pakistan and India. As you are all aware of Pakistan has gone crazy, the Angels have stirred up Islam and all those not belonging to the Angels are in danger. Even their own people are in danger.

Now I know you are a mixture of Hindu's, Buddhists as well as my own Brigidites. Your personal views are your own, for you do not belong to the Angels and I will grant you your protection. For the Hindus your Gods have died but I swore to them to protect you. I have accepted the burden of your protection and all I ask of you is to fight against the Angels when they come for us.

You have all suffered for simply being who you are and now your homes and lives have been destroyed by the Angels and their people. The sacred waters have cleansed you, healed you and transformed you. You are now Naga, once extinct sacred beings of water. Immortal to age and bearers of great power.

I cannot give you back your old lives, I cannot give you back your country. But you can claim it back, you can fight for your country. Now as the Naga you have claim to ancient territories crying out for your touch for centuries.

The land, rivers and the world need us. It is not the same place it used to be for it has changed irrevocably. The War of Heaven has started again and this time mortals will be choosing sides. I am the Goddess Brigid, yes I see your surprise and I know many of you have heard my voice. I am as real as you are, and I have suffered under the Angels just as you have. But I offer you a brighter future, one in which your long heritage will be respected.

Come now and rest, have time to think and reflect. Some of you now possess magical powers and many of you will be anxious to reunite with family members. Every person who entered the Indus has washed up on the Ganges, you may find your loved ones."

Anjali looked around in surprise as people started weeping. Perhaps it was just her but she personally blamed Brigid for her current woes. She wasn't sure what to make of the tale she had just been spun.

As the others started being led away Brigid handed the little girl back to her "Stay Anjali I have a special task for you."

Brigid placed an arm around her shoulder "You are a special type of Naga, you are a very powerful sorceress. I am sending you to the Seelie Court in Scotland in order to receive formal training. If you can master your talents then you can teach them to the others of your species, and that is our best defence against the Muslim insurrection. I know you have lost everything, but I have given you the power to claim it back. You can get revenge."

She snapped her fingers and a little pink light appeared "Take her to the Queen and ensures she receives proper training."

Anjali didn't have time to react as the pink orb grew into a woman with dragonfly wings and predatory eyes. She grabbed onto Anjali and they both disappeared.

"Was that a wise choice Goddess?"

"Perhaps not, she resents me but time in the Seelie Court may heal that. It is better than having her here spreading her resentment. She is very powerful and her anger burns strong, and will do for a long time. She has nothing to tie her to India currently, I want to start creating the spirit of the Empire now. The Empire will be reborn, but this time it won't just be the largest empire the world has ever seen but the most magical as well. My hold on India is weak at best but it is slowly getting stronger. The creation of the Naga will cement my claim over the subcontinent and give me a strong claim to

South East Asia. It will also help bring the Hindus and Buddhists to me. My control will spread further and many new countries will join the empire. The Naga are known in many countries."

"What of the large serpents?"

"The Naga will serve the Naga as powerful steeds. Under the combined strength of the Naga, India will become my centre of power in Asia.

Ryan fell silent before returning to his temple. He suddenly had thousands of people to look after.

Brigid watched him go, knowing the questions he had not aired. Where had the serpents come from? Hindus and Buddhists had been turned into the Naga as an honour. But they were not the only ones who had climbed into the river. Those who carried the taint of the Angels could not be given such an honour, nor had they been willing to forsake their faith. Yet she had been hesitant to kill them, life was precious, so she had made them into non-humanoid races.

They were no longer of any use to the Angels.

"I cannot even begin to fathom the stupidity of your actions" Gabriel paced back and forth yelling at Ariel and Michael as they knelt in the petitioners circle. The whole Council of Elders was in attendance to pass judgment on them.

"Your behaviour was utterly reckless. This behaviour in any Angel is unacceptable but in an Arch Angel it is beyond comprehension. Your actions have thrown out centuries of manipulation and destroyed our image to the world. Just when we need to be nurturing our cause with the Goddesses free."

Gabriel fell silent all but spitting like a cat. The other three Arch Angels remained silent, afraid to draw her attention and yet silently condemning both of them.

"Michael explain yourself" she snapped.

He cringed ever so slightly at her tone. He had seen her in many a temper before but this was different. Now she was dealing with the after effects of his actions and she was not pleased. Nor was the Council, his and Ariel's actions within such a short time of each other portrayed the Angels very negatively.

"Following information gathered by Nuriel, myself and my Angels laid a trap for Hera. I chose Saint Patricks Cathedral and empowered it, fully expecting her to intervene over Easter. My predictions proved correct. Within the cathedral we battled each other for over an hour, during which time more Angels descended on New York and strengthened our containment Weave.

She stopped fighting and cautiously I stopped my attacks. It was then that she summoned images of Sariel. She was dying, having been raped and beaten by the Demons in Hell. It was then she told me she sent Sariel to Hell. Before my eyes I saw the last of Sariel's life drawn out of her."

There was a rustling of guilty relief among the Angels, now they had no longer had to fear Sariel affecting the Curse. Things were as they should be.

Gabriel's anger died before everyone's eyes. She had known Michael grieved for his sister but she hadn't known the full story. Political mechanisms be damned some things were more important.

"It was then that my rage overtook me. I am sorry to admit it by my wrath consumed me, it blinded me to all reason. There is no excuse I allowed my hate towards Hera to dictate my actions. It was then I summoned the Greater Demon Samael to fight my battle. It was my only hope for overcoming her. She was beyond my powers to beat."

There were gasps at his admission.

"Are you telling us that Hera was more powerful than you?"

"I am, far more powerful."

Gabriel resumed pacing "We have lost an Arch Angel and now we shall grieve. The cost was heavy but at last the Goddess Hera is gone, either dead or sucked down into Hell."

She glanced around at the Council, most were nodding, as were the other Arch Angels.

"Then your actions are excusable before the Council. The threat of Hera is no more."

Michael stood up, bowed to the Council then walked to his throne, on his way past she grabbed his shoulder.

Then she turned to face her cousin "While the threat of Hera was removed you were meant to be tracking down Brigid's whereabouts. Last we knew she was destroying the Indus and hiding all over Australia. We are all extremely curious as to how you ended up in France killing the British King." Her voice dripped with venom. She was at her scariest when she was this calm.

"Following leads brought to me by Nuriel it was discovered Brigid has been very active across Australia, New Zealand, India, Pakistan, Bangladesh and has started making her presence felt in Canada. Following a hunch I headed to Britain to scout and perhaps lay an ambush. But I was prevented from entering Britain."

That caused a stir.

"Why were you prevented from entering?"

"Because there is a Veil around those islands. No Angel can access Britain or Ireland."

There was a stunned silence to meet her words. A Veil was a powerful act of magic to keep certain types out. They required a lot of magic, the more highly selective they were the more they required. They were usually confined to a single city. A Veil of this size was unfathomable. The power required to keep out all three types of Angels over such a vast area was beyond comprehension.

It worried them all deeply, if it was Brigid alone then they would need the Seven Arch Angels to bring her in. If it wasn't Brigid then there were many questions in desperate need of answers.

"How could this have happened?" someone dared to ask

"Only the ruling monarch of a nation can raise or act as the focus of such spells. That explains Ariel's actions. But the Veil did not falter when the old king died, he was not the foundation."

"No killing him did not release the spell. Which means someone else is the foundation, but whom? It couldn't be his daughter, could it? She's not the reigning monarch."

"Is it beyond reason that perhaps some of the Fae survived and with Brigid's powers act as the foundation?" Raphael asked.

"It is possible, all that we managed to hunt down was one of the princes which means the Queen is still alive somewhere. She could easily act as the foundation with Brigid's powers. But where is Brigid getting such power from, she wasn't naturally as strong as Hera?"

"She has negligible followings in Australia, New Zealand and Bangladesh. Only India has enough numbers to be empowering her. But it doesn't explain the strength required for such a Veil. Her presence in Pakistan has been eliminated with the eradication of non-Muslims. The only explanation for her empowerment is the same as for Hera. The Demons must be in far greater numbers than we thought."

"This is worse than we thought" Gabriel looked at

the other Arch Angels and they nodded their agreement" She turned back to Ariel "Your punishment is yet to be determined. Your actions were ill advised but well intended. You will light the Fires above Britain."

Ariel's eyes lit up with delight and fervour. It was an honour to light the Fires.

"We have been sealed off from Britain, such an event has not occurred since the Fall. It is clear Humanity needs to be reminded of our power and presence. Apparently recent actions have not been enough. As with Pakistan we will deal with Britain decisively and without hesitation. There will be no mercy."

Chapter 35

Victoria looked into the coffin of her father. The embalmers had done an excellent job, there was no way to tell how he had died. Though that image would never leave her, it had played over and over in her head, invading her dreams. Again and again she had seen the Arch Angel Ariel killing her father. Sometimes they spoke sometimes they didn't. Ariel condemned her and laughed. Her father pleaded, told her it wasn't her fault or asked for vengeance.

Clearly her subconscious was trying to tell her something, her father had always said revenge was an ugly emotion.

He looked completely at peace now, his face carried none of the worries it always had. In a way she was glad he was finally at peace. He had lived a troubled life, it was a pity death was the price for peace. At least he could re-join her mother, and together they could be at peace. That made her smile. He had sorely missed her mother, theirs had been a genuine love that lasted until she died, and even beyond.

She would sorely miss him. Now the weight of an entire country rested on her shoulders, a weight that was going to increase dramatically.

She jumped when Cathair placed his hand on her shoulder "Come Victoria"

She looked wearily up at him "How long have I been standing here?"

"Close to an hour"

"I still can't believe he is gone" she said as he led her away. The funeral had been nice at least, the people had come out in droves to mourn their monarch. He had regained their love in past months, and his life had always been a point of interest for them. They had also come to see her, to mourn with her. Or in the media's case to showcase her mourning to the world.

He nodded his understanding but didn't say anything more as he led her away. She held onto his arm feeling lost. All her life her father had been her sun, despite his own problems and hectic schedule he had always made time for her, had always managed to brighten up her day and chase away her woes. He had often told her that she was his greatest pride, and he meant it. He had kept every painting she had ever painted, ever story every written, every award won. He had kept them all. He had truly been a great father.

She had always gravitated towards him, making him happy. He had been a deeply unhappy man since her mother died. And the duties of being a king wearied him. She had figured out from an early age that she was one of the few things that made him smile, so she had worked hard to be everything she could be. She could talk to him about almost anything, and theirs had been a relationship truly envied by most fathers and daughters. He hadn't just been her father, he had been her friend.

Now he was gone, and like a missing sun all that was left was a void.

She came out of her reverie as Cathair helped her into the car. Her eyes picked up the flashes of blue, there were a lot today, but most surprisingly the compassion in his eyes.

She glanced out of the window, for once glad of the dreary English weather. It was fitting that even the weather was unhappy. Even the faces of the people had reflected the loss, he hadn't been a popular king but he hadn't deserved to be murdered. Royalist feeling was riding very high. She had also been told there had been a complete drop in the sales of anything Angel related. The people were rallying behind their royal family.

"Why are you here Cathair?"

He flicked those beautiful green eyes of his towards her "because you need company."

"This goes beyond duty. This is the act of a friend, which is completely at odds with your previously cold behaviour."

If she had offended him he didn't show it. "I am your fiancé" he snapped before sighing "it goes beyond that. Since your father's death a light has gone out in you. There's barely even a spark left. That light is a fire that reaches out to others, an honesty, a compassion, a joy that burns so strongly that others cannot help but be drawn to it. Now it lies in embers. You have no one to turn to, your relatives are worse than a pit of vipers and you have no real close friends. You are alone, bar for me, and I know how that feels."

She was suddenly curious "You had an unhappy childhood?"

"Not as such, I have lived a privileged life and my parents fortunately spent time with me. But when my father was killed no one held me or looked after me. Mother was too busy trying to hold the court together and keeping the spells protecting us from breaking. I didn't have any friends, I had spent most of my time with Aisling growing up but she was safe in the Otherworld. I had no one to turn to, and it has stayed that way. The Fae are respected, feared, revered and loved but very few get close to us."

"You say Fae as though you're something different?"

"We are. Fae can be used interchangeably with Fairy to mean all the races. We are the Fae, Fairy, Fair Folk and a whole manner of other names. But the Fae specifically refers to the royal bloodline, for we are unlike any other race under our authority. We are the mixed bloodlines of them all. We are the culmination of Fairy power. We are the direct descendants of Avalon herself."

"Is that why you look more Human than the other Fairy Races?"

"Yes, but that has more to do with the heavy interbreeding we did with Human sorcerers in order to strengthen our bloodlines. It also has much to do with our interbreeding with Nymphs and Angels. We are far more Human looking than the other Fae races but it does have its advantages. Humans are less scared of us."

"So when the other Fairies look Human it is just spells and illusions?"

"Well certain humanoid characteristics are always there, but we are the flesh bound spirits of the land, we will always be animalistic in appearance. Most of the time we don't bother hiding those, but we can use our Glamour to adjust our appearances for various reasons. With it we can blend in with Humans."

"Are you wearing your Glamour now?"

"Only to make my hair brown and my lips red. Even for the Fae we are remarkably Human looking. My paternal grandmother was a Nymph and my paternal grandfather was an Angel. My near ancestry is rich in the more humanoid races. For the Fae, Aisling and I are remarkably plain. Usually Fae skin colours vary wildly, as do their hair and eye colours.

It is very likely that Aisling's mate will come from one of the Older Fairy races to reassert our Fairy appearance."

She nodded digesting the information "Does that have anything do to with why my lips are now tinged green?" that had been a shock for her, now she had to make sure she was always wearing lip colour.

He smiled "It could be but I doubt you are Fairy. I would hazard a guess that Brigid has activated some latent magical powers in your bloodline and added some extra. She understands that the Fae breed for power and diversity. I imagine that you'll prove to be something new and unique."

That made her blush. "What about the other races?"

"For the most part they're as much a part of Ireland and Britain as the landscape. The Fairies have been around for a very long time, we were one of the very first races. New additions to our numbers include the Were, Lilin, Sirens, and Vampires. But their positions in court were only made after the War of Heaven. It became necessary for all the magical races to band together, for our protection they joined and became subject to the Seelie Court.

There are of course the Nymphs and Satyrs, also very ancient races who we have always long interbred with. They came in large numbers as the War destroyed the Mediterranean. We have interbred with Gods, Angels and even the Naga in the past, though not in a long time. The Gods are dead or imprisoned, the Naga extinct. The Angels for the most part are our enemies, except for the small group of Watchers that sought our protection.

Our races have developed and evolved over countless years, the Elementals gained form, the spirits too. New races and old races became subject to the Seelie Court and its Queen. In the shadow of the Angels we have grown strong, mixing our bloodlines.

In fact the only ancient race that didn't develop their powers here are the Royal Guards, though the land recognised their powers easily enough."

"Where did they come from then?"

"Atlantis. They were refugees who sought

sanctuary. They were fleeing the destruction wrought by their warring Gods and wanted to be as far away as possible. Sanctuary was granted and in their gratitude they became the Royal Guard swearing to protect the Fae with their lives. They are the magical, technological and physical might of the Fae."

"You expect me to believe they came from Atlantis" she chuckled.

"Why wouldn't you?"

"Oh come on Atlantis is just a myth" how gullible did he think she was? He was clearly pulling her leg, then again she had never heard him make any kind of joke.

"Up until a few days ago Victoria you believed Fairies, Angels and Gods to be myths. You have seen all three. Science rejects Atlantis because it does not take into account magic. To science continents do not suddenly sink, that takes millions of years. Magic however changes everything."

"So Atlantis really existed? Do you know what it was like, why it was destroyed?" her eyes were the brightest he had seen them in days. He truly had her undivided attention.

"Atlantis like Lemuria and Mu were islands where ancient civilisations lived with technology that excelled even the technology of today. Their magic rivalled the strength of the Angels today. They were incredible races, and fantastical places created by several Gods or pantheons. When several pantheons work together the results are phenomenal. Those ancient empires flourished while the primitive colonies at the time were still learning agriculture and metallurgy. For thousands of years the three empires existed, trading with each other and even expanding their colonies onto the continents. They found the other races interesting, just as the Gods found them interesting.

But the Gods are fickle creatures and it is sad to say that they were not the first or last civilisation to be destroyed by the Gods' fighting. Mu was completely obliterated, all traces destroyed. Its only remains are the volcanic activity that birthed Hawaii. Lemuria was much the same, though some of its inhabitants survived and settled in modern day India. It used to stand where the Maldives stand today. It seems sad that the Naga survived the destruction of their civilisation by the Gods, to once again flourish, admittedly in much more primitive society to then be eradicated by the Angels."

"But Atlantis was different?"

"Yes it survived a lot longer, in part due to the presence of the Primordial Gods protecting it. It flourished long after Lemuria and Mu had been destroyed, even up until Classical Times. They were a centre of learning for all races, some of our ancestors went there to learn, as did the ancestors of many other races.

But all good things come to an end. The Primordial Gods while unbelievably powerful, and the reason the Gods of Atlantis stayed in line, were ancient and slowly they desired to return to the Lifestream. They craved to return their powers to the planet, and so Atlantis found itself without its greatest protectors.

Thus the balance was tipped and Poseidon claimed it for himself. The people accepted, for what choice did they have, they were an island nation. He was worshipped as the High God of Atlantis, but this did not sit well with the other Gods who had helped create and shape Atlantis over the millennia. War broke out between the Gods.

In the Cataclysm that ensued, Atlantis was destroyed, but Atlantis had spread far and wide, it had colonies throughout the Mediterranean and along the

North African Coast. Knowing their days were numbered they fled to lands beyond the scope of their Gods. A land insignificant to most of the world, a small set of islands they remembered from the strange Fae they had educated over the centuries. Not all came to us, but most of the survivors did, even many who had fled the Cataclysm before it destroyed their homes.

It was then that the peaceful Atlanteans became warriors, never would they have to flee their homelands. They sought sanctuary from us, and it was granted. We hid them away from the Gods until they lost interest and returned to their empire building. For our part the Atlanteans swore a blood oath to serve and protect us. They have been with us ever since, a unique and separate class in the scheme of things but always loyal to us. Their numbers have boomed under our protection, and now Avalon is as much their home as ours."

"Are they willing to return to the Gods? Is it wise to throw ourselves in with the Gods? They seem to cause so much destruction."

"They have always caused destruction, it is part of their nature. Just as it is a part of fire's nature. They cannot change what they are, for they are forces of nature and aspects of the world. However the Angels are no better, the Gods may have destroyed civilisations but they rebuilt new ones, the Angels have eradicated entire species.

If they had their wish only two mortal species would be left standing."

"Why only two?"

"Because only Humans and the Jinn are willing to accept them as their masters. No other species have, or will unless the Angels make new species. But it is more complex than that, we need the Gods, they are necessary."

That was surprising. "Why?"

"Not all of them but we do need the Mother Goddesses and Nature Gods. Their presence and magic quickens the Lifestream, bringing life to the Surface. Without them the planet's Surface has slowly been dying."

"The planet is dying?"

"Yes, but slowly. Remember the world and Gods work in hundreds and thousands of years. The planet had been dying for centuries. World weather patterns have been getting increasingly erratic, once fertile land is now barren. One only has to look at the world to see it is crying out for help.

Mortals and Angels are not powerful enough to draw on the power the Gods can. Even our vast numbers cannot compensate for what one Nature God can do for the land.

The Lifestream has been sinking from the Surface ever since the War. We have all felt its presence fading, though Humans have not. Your magic wielders were culled in the Middle Ages. With Brigid's return Britain and Ireland are already starting to flourish. In the spring it will hardly be recognisable. This will be the best year for farmers in a long time, even mineral wealth will have grown. Once you are crowned and Brigid reinstated as the Goddess your country will have the greatest wealth it has seen in decades."

"So the Mother Goddesses are particularly essential?"

"Yes...especially now the Great Mother is trapped in her sleep. If she could awaken then the Lifestream would not slow, she is the essence of the planet and life. Without her awake it is only the Mother Goddesses that can stop the planet slowly failing."

"Who is the Great Mother Goddess?"

"Gaia, oldest of all the Primordial Gods and first born of Chaos. If she had not been slumbering then the Angels could never have overthrown Heaven. But they timed it well."

"Why doesn't anyone wake her up?"

"She is trapped by the Underworld Curse, it is only if Lucifer's Curse is broken that she will be able to awake. However the Curse can only be broken by an Arch Angel or if the Angels are destroyed."

Silence fell as she sorted through all the information she had learned. It was so much more complex than she had first thought.

She was still milling over the information when the car stopped. He slid out in one elegant movement, then had her door open before she realised. He offered his hand to her. She couldn't help but smile, she felt as though some of his walls had come down.

"Well now I must leave you to get your affairs in order. Do what is essential then remove yourself to your Scottish estates, you need to escape this world for a little while. I have very much enjoyed our talk and look forward to future discussions." He leaned forward and kissed her on the cheek before striding off.

She watched him go, one hand clasped to the cheek he had kissed, smiling. She didn't know what this meant, but she was beginning to think she actually liked him. She allowed herself to appreciate his retreating form before shaking her head and heading inside. She had a lot to do if she was going to hide in the countryside for a while.

Anjali stared blankly out the window. As she had done ever since she had been taken to the Seelie Court. She didn't know these people, didn't know their language. They were stranger than she was, and she hadn't thought that possible.

"They told me you'd be moping in her. If you're going to stare out the window all day the least you can do is go out and enjoy it. The Otherworld truly is beautiful."

She turned around hearing someone speak in what she guessed was English. He was white, white people spoke English. But she wasn't sure, she didn't speak English.

She studied him with interest. He was Human, or at least appeared to be. He was of average height, pale skin and had brown hair. Though it looked like he had died parts of it green. His eyes were bright above his charming smile. He was dressed in the skimpy clothes of half of these beings. He had mischief written all over him.

She stared at him blankly while he spoke.

He stopped his talking to focus on her. He did not show revulsion or horror, only fascination. This was followed by understanding.

James left at a slight jog looking for one of the Nobles, surely they would be able to help.

As luck would have it he ran in front of the Queen and some of her advisors.

He hurried to bow to her while trying to stop himself at the same time. The result was him toppling over into the bushes.

Her rich musical laugh filled the air before one of the advisors helped him up. It was a very old Satyr.

"Tell me James what is so urgent as to have you running through our corridors. The Seelie Court is a place of rest." She asked him.

"It's about the Naga. I think I've figured out why she won't talk to anyone?"

She arched her delicate eyebrows high. He could tell what she was thinking, did he really think he had figured out what they could not? But she humoured him

"And why will she not speak to any of us?"

"She doesn't know English. She must only speak Pakistani or whatever language it is they speak. What do they speak?"

She looked at him with surprise. They hadn't thought of that. The others the Goddess had given to them had all spoken English so they hadn't thought that an issue.

"Come. Let us test your theory." She took his hand, then they reappeared in the Naga's room, startling the poor woman.

Sorcha walked towards Anjali, her hands held out before her facing upwards. She stopped before her waiting for her to take her hand. After some hesitation Anjali reached forward and took the Queen's hand.

"I believe you should be able to understand me now, we have dealt with the issue of language."

Anjali jerked "Yes I can understand you now. Where am I? Who are you?"

"So many questions and yet there is not enough time for them all. Anjali this is James, he is new here also. Ask him all the questions you wish. I have other duties to attend to." Then she promptly disappeared.

"Don't worry she's always doing that. Queen Sorcha is a very busy woman."

She looked up at the boy "That was a Queen? Of where?"

"Why the Seelie Court. She rules over all the Fae and the Otherworld. With Brigid empowering more people and recreating lost species she now has to train vast amounts of us. Which is difficult seeing as we are not Fairies so our magic does not behave as theirs."

He smiled at her "Welcome to the Seelie Court, it truly is a fascinating place." For some reason his cheerfulness was infectious. She suddenly wanted to know more, she had so many questions she wanted answered.

He smiled happily when she started asking. He had his own questions he wished to ask her.

"You would have us risk the Angels wrath when Hera is dead? Do you take us for fools Ariadne? We have no defence now?

Ariadne stopped herself from rolling her eyes at Valentine's comments. Had he always been this stupid? Perhaps working with Hera had made her look down on the intellect of all mortals.

"Hera is not dead we all would have felt it. We are her subjects, sworn to her in blood. We all would have felt her death but not a single one of us did?" She looked around the assorted group "Did any of you sense her death?"

They shook their heads.

She calmed herself by looking out the window onto the statue of Hera that stood at the hospital's entrance. Hera would be back, she was absolutely certain.

She turned back to face what she had to work with. Kyle sat watching quietly, he was her other pair of eyes and ears, watching the others and rooting out problems for her. Hera had gained his eternal gratitude for the healing of his AIDS, the powers he was less thankful of, but now he was mastering them he was starting to enjoy them. He was also enjoying the attraction it leant to him. Many of the magical races that wouldn't look twice at a Human certainly stopped to look at the Arch Sorcerer.

Next to him was Sarah, Matriarch of the Nymphs. Her support she did not have to worry about. Her loyalty was beyond reproach. She too believed Hera would be back and had continued on with her duties.

Standing silently behind her was Juan in the

ghastly form he had decided suited the Broken. The Xenomorphs from the Alien movies had really appealed to him. They were perfect specimens of evolution, or so the movies suggested. The breeding cycle had been changed so that he could transform other Broken into them. Now they were fearful warriors, who needed no weapons, armed with stealth, speed and strength. Never mind their fatal tails, claws and strange mouths. It was unnerving sharing a room with the creatures. They had no eyes but somehow manage to look right through you. He too was continuing on as though nothing had happened.

Catherine and Samuel were no concern either. The Gorgons and Minotaurs were still capturing and transforming towns and cities all across the States and Mexico. Their actions were alarming the police and governments in both countries. Their actions were even alarming the drug cartels, suddenly towns under their control were empty and their own people were going missing.

No it was the leaders that had been forced to kneel before Hera that were the ones trying to go back to ground and reclaim their authority. The pitiful fools, their people would not return to hiding with them. Bloodlust was spreading. People wanted to fight the Angels.

"As I have said Hera is not dead. She will be back and I for one do not wish to explain my lack of action to her." She slammed her hands down on the table "I don't think you quite grasp who you are dealing with. This is Hera, perhaps the most naturally powerful Goddess the world has ever seen with a legendary wrath to match. Her own husband chained her up from fear. She laid waste to Troy for a slight their prince made. She has strung up greater leaders than us for the slightest insult or negligence. She will have no qualms about killing any of us, we are but pawns to her. Our lives are immaterial in her grand plans."

She sat down, everyone watching her movements. Some of them had fear in their eyes, they were finally beginning to understand.

"She battled the Arch Angel Michael alone, besting him enough that he summoned a Greater Demon. He also called upon the other Arch Angels and Council of Elders to create a containment Weave so that she could not escape. She opened the very gates of Hell to remove the Demon."

"Then she herself was sucked down into Hell. Our cause is lost." How she wanted to smack King Roger. She wanted to smack all the Vampire Royals, why couldn't they have a collective High King or Queen like the other races.

"Hera was not sucked down into Hell."

She held up her hand to stop the protests "Many Mother Goddesses have the ability to fuse to the Lifestream, it is part of their nature, something unique to them. In doing so they revitalise the land and the Lifestream. I have seen this happen before and I feel sure this is what Hera has done to avoid the Angels' Weave. I do not know how long she will remain in the Lifestream but she will return."

She stood up and walked to the door "I for one will not be held accountable for sloth, the Goddess will find no fault in my actions to focus her anger on. And remember she will be angry when she returns." Then she left, leaving the others to their own consciences. She would not drag them along if they wished to stop. Besides Kyle was in there to hear their mutinous comments.

There were enough leaders loyal to Hera for her to return to a successful revolution waiting to happen. The

United States of America would fall, the Angels would lose all that faith and Hera would gain it. The Empire would reach as far as the Goddess desired.

And Ariadne would be a Goddess once again.

Chapter 36

It was strangely ironic that Sariel entered the Seventh Circle of Hell in a blaze of dramatic violence. As she floated down the cliff face her powers were already racing ahead of her, sweeping obstacles and Demons out of her way. She burned with anger, frustration, annoyance and impatience.

The first to fall to her magic, with no warning, was Asterion. He was the original Minotaur, born from an unholy mating of Queen Pasiphaë and a sacred bull of Poseidon. He had been locked away in the Labyrinth and fed Athenians until he was killed by Theseus. She stripped the Curse from him, not caring about being gentle for she could feel his violent nature. Then again it had been determined by his predatory lifestyle and a life deprived of love and affection. She laid him to rest where he had stood, giving him gentle dreams.

The Centaurs had some sense of her approach, she burned pure white, a completely unnatural light in Hell. There was nothing they could do to stop her or defend themselves, Hell had afforded them no powers. Their only task was to shoot any who tried to climb out of the boiling river of blood. The stench was horrific.

She was gentler with them, the Curse was stripped from them slowly and carefully. They might be violent by nature but that was born from a warrior culture and the need to protect. She was particularly gentle with their leader Chiron, who was completely undeserving of his fate. The Gods had honoured his life and sacrifices by making him a constellation. The Curse of the Angels had pulled him from his resting place and cast him into Hell.

She swept across the river, extinguishing its flames

and calming the raging blood. She could feel its nature, it was fed by the Rivers of Death but it was a perversion she wished she had the time to fix. It was a waste of time and magic while the Curse remained.

Once she was past the river she entered the next ring of the Violence Level but here she slowed and her powers became gentler. The anguish and sorrow of the field's victims pulled at her hardened heart. She might have covered it in ice to protect herself, but it was still the innocence and caring thing it always had been. She had seen the cruelty of Hell, unimaginable to her in her naivety. She had been horrified at what had been done, beings twisted beyond their nature and undeserving people punished.

Simurgh, Chiron, Bahamut and Kujuta were the innocents that instantly sprang to mind. Poor beautiful Simurgh turned into a monstrosity, poor gentle Bahamut and Kujuta fused together in eternal torment, poor loyal Chiron ripped from his rest. Then there were the countless Daemons and Humans suffering for their natures. The injustice of it all tormented her, she could not leave them trapped within Hell, but how was she to free them?

The field was densely populated, perhaps nearly as densely as the Heresy Level but instead of corpses or bodies there were only twisted brown bushes and trees. They were the victims of suicide cruelly denied their bodies.

For the first time since she had burst through the Gates she stopped moving, overwhelmed by the anguish of these poor tortured souls who had sought death to ease their sufferings. They had not known that greater suffering awaited them.

Tears rolled down her face as she poured her powers through the field. As her powers spread through the field she learned the story of each and every victim, before releasing the spirits from their barky confines. The sorrow and despair of their lives seeped into her, she lived so many of their memories with tears rolling down her face. So many of the victims had suffered rape and abuse in their lives with no hope of end. They had sought the release of death only to be tortured for seeking that release. There were other tales as well; killers who could not bear their guilt, people who had destroyed their own lives through gambling, sex, alcohol and drugs. There were lovers who could not live on without their loves, parents too bereaved and grief stricken to think rationally, many who could not forgive themselves for one thing or another. There were those who had ended up destitute. Those who had been driven to suicide by bullying, harassment, shame and sheer hopelessness. Then there were those who had ended their lives early rather than endure the wasting pain of fatal sickness.

Yet they were all punished eternally, unable to move or defend themselves as they were eaten again and again by the Harpies.

Tears continued to roll down her face even as she saw the trees and bushes crumple as they released the trapped spirits. Their transparent blue-white faces turned to her filled with utter devotion. She could unfortunately do no more for them while Hell was still bound by Gabriel's Curse. But at least for the moment she had given them peace.

Which was all they had ever sought.

She was confused by the presence of the Profligates when their nature was the same as the Prodigal she had encountered in the Greed Level. She seriously began to wonder what kind of man Dante had been and if his beliefs were typical for his age. Then again the Middle Ages had been a particularly violent era in which the Church had only grown in power.

She calmed the dogs tasked with chasing them, buying them some rest also. As for the Harpies that infested the Suicide Woods she was less gentle. Her power slammed through their minds, angry at their treatment of the poor spirits before she realised her error in judgement. They were as Cursed as everything else in Hell. They were a race descended from Divine blood, one of the multitude of semi-Divine races that had existed before the War. They had been exterminated by the Angels then their spirits denied rest within Hell. Their spirits were enslaved to torture the souls of the dead in Hell.

They had been trapped in Hell long before Dante had come through to reshape it.

Guilty of her anger she sent them all to sleep, allowing their bodies to gently land on the ground. She carefully moved through the spells Gabriel had wrought on them, surprised to find older curses on them. Who else had cursed them?

She skilfully unravelled all the curses laid upon them, easy with her powers flowing so freely.

Their change in appearance was dramatic. Their Hell forms were truly Demonic; they had the typical Demon wings but these were fused to their arms. Their hands and feet were long stabbing talons suited only to cutting and tearing. Their bodies were somewhere between reptilian scales and insect chitin, hard flexible and shiny. They ranged in colours from black, grey and purple to red and green. They had truly been terrors of the skies.

Yet the removal of their Curses revealed creatures nearly entirely different. They weren't even Human sized, being slightly less than half her size. Their small bird bodies were no different to any other bird their size, ranging in colours and plumage greatly, but all their necks were crowned by small Human heads. Their faces were gentle and serene, reflecting their Classic Greek beauty. Their brown or black hair fell free behind their heads.

They seemed so peaceful sleeping. Yet she was not fooled, they had always served as the punishers of the truly guilty.

She released her spells feeling far calmer than when she had entered the Level. She had done much good, even if it would not last.

She floated further into the Level.

The third ring within the Violence Level started where the old forest had ended. The flat stony ground changed into burning sand dunes with fire drifting down from above. A quick magical scan revealed three groups of people, those lying in the sand, those sitting on it and those wandering about in groups. Her magic easily revealed their natures.

Those lying in the sand were Blasphemers, those apparently violent to God. It was a varied group of angry Christians, Jew and Muslims who had been unhappy with their lots in life. They were more numerously made up of those who had not belonged to the Angels and were made to suffer for their lack of faith.

Those sitting were the Usurers and she got the distinct impression that there had been a steep increase in their numbers in recent decades. She wondered why charging interest on lent money was a sin before God but she had given up trying to understand the Angels religions and Dante's image of Hell. She felt sorry for them, the modern world was structured around lending money and charging interest on it. She vaguely wondered if every bank owner or manager ended up here even if they had committed other sins. She would have thought they would have been victims of Greed, but here they were in this lower Level.

It made no sense to her.

The last group was far more numerous than the two other groups combined and she found them to be extremely diverse. They were the Sodomites. The vast majority were Incubi and Succubi but all the races were represented. She was disheartened to discover that most of them were simply there for the sin of being Bisexual or Homosexual.

It was unjustly cruel to punish someone for something that was perfectly natural and could not be changed. Yet she knew this to be her brother's handiwork. Gabriel was ambivalent about sexuality, she loved Michael and couldn't care less what others got up to sexually so long as they were married. Michael on the other hand hated any deviation from Heterosexuality. She had never questioned it before, but now she wondered why he hated it so much.

There were a surprising number of Heterosexuals as well, which confused her until she probed deeper. She blushed when she saw people's memories. She had never had sex, so seeing through their memories felt very strange. It was even stranger because she had so little experience with it at all, it was never talked about in Heaven. Though her time among the Greek Gods had taken away the mystery of it. She might be innocent but she was no longer ignorant. They had believed sex was a natural and integral part of life. They had no qualms discussing it.

The memories taught her many things, the overriding factor being that these people were connected by similar sins. The sin of the penis not entering the vagina exclusively. Having spent so much time in Hades she was confused as to why this was perceived as wrong. She had been party to many conversations about the wide range of sexual practices and had accidently seen more than she had meant to on numerous occasions. The Greeks were very open minded about sexuality and sex. To her mind seeking pleasure didn't seem like a sin, but what did she know? She had never had sex to make such judgement calls.

It seemed particularly prejudiced against homosexuals, they couldn't have heterosexual sex. Why was it so wrong to express love in the only physical way available to you? She couldn't understand it at all.

She was utterly repelled by some of the Sodomites though, they had truly earned their place in Hell. She quickly shied away from the memories of the paedophiles, their memories sickening her with the merest glimpse of their memories. It wasn't about love, affection or physical connection. It was horrific and wholly unnatural. Because of them many of their victims were now residents of the Suicide Ring.

It was completely unjust that they had been painted with the same brush as those whose only crime was love.

There wasn't much she could do though. Resigned she simply floated through the ring extinguishing the flames. Then inspiration hit her. She probed back through the Level finding the Harpies, dogs and Centaurs. Speaking to them she gained their assent as she marked the paedophiles for who they were. Flaming collars marked them all from the innocent. She just could not leave them mixed among those who had genuinely committed no crimes.

She extinguished more flames as shrieks started to sound out behind her. She smiled in satisfaction as the Centaurs, Harpies and dogs started rounding up the paedophiles and driving them into the rivers of blood. They did not deserve the respite she had bought the others. What she had seen had truly sickened her to her core. She didn't know if she would ever get the images out of her head, but she had a good understanding as to why so many victims preferred suicide to living on.

Conveniently the Guardians found merit in the new task she had set them. But she also felt the strain of her actions. She had changed so much of Hell but the Curse was not broken and already it was trying to claim back what she had cleansed. She could feel the fear of millions, perhaps billions flooding Hell as they saw the Curse seeking to reclaim her territory. She had over extended herself so much, drawing upon reserves she hadn't even known she had. She was sure she had died in the mortal sense but because she had not been drained she had remained. As to how she had regained consciousness with more power...she was at a loss.

She hurried on. Such strain on her was not good, it made her weak to Hell's attacks. She could feel the Curse bearing down on her. It would do no one good if she became Cursed herself. All her work would be undone and any chance of curing Hell would be lost.

She could not allow that to happen.

The black Bentley roared along the motorway, leaving far behind the city of London and all its duties. Inside sat Victoria II, Queen of the United Kingdom of Great Britain and Northern Ireland. And by Brigid's plan a whole lot more. Sitting wearing mourning black she bore more than a passing resemblance to her ancestor whose name she carried. On either side of her sat Prince Cathair and Princess Aisling of the Fae. All sat in complete silence.

The car was on its way to Victoria's country estates

in Scotland, which incidentally was within Fae territory. They had already argued about whose land it was when they set out.

Victoria sat in silence remembering her father's funeral. She had hated sitting through the Christian ceremony but she hadn't been able to have it changed. He had been blessed by a God that didn't exist in a place holy to those who had killed him. Would she have to endure the same Christian pomp for her coronation? She would have to ask Brigid, surely she had other intentions.

It struck her that what she and Brigid planned to do would divide Britain. Christianity was its major religion with various sects. There was also a great deal of Muslim immigrants. But she would stamp them both out if it was the last thing she did. The Angels would gain no power from her land and people. But that was Brigid's goal also, and she had the powers to make it so. Britain would be free of the Angels' grasp.

But who would crown her instead of the Archbishop of Canterbury? What would she hold instead of the orb? Could it even be held at Westminster Abbey? She hoped despite its religious taint it would still be used. It was where her father and those before him had been crowned. There had to be some way to make it acceptable to Brigid. Yet she knew that Brigid was not the major obstacle. She had the British public, parliament and the Churches of England and Scotland to worry about also.

She was the Supreme Governor of the Church of England, the Defender of the Faith and yet here she was planning on stripping it of its power and banishing its teachings.

She hoped to Brigid that they could pull it off. Otherwise her reign would be remarkably brief. She had no desire to contest Lady Jane Grey as the shortest serving monarch. It was a fitting comparison, England had been torn apart by religious differences and intolerance in her time.

The world really hadn't come that far.

She felt a burning hate towards the Angels, and to a lesser degree the religions that empowered them. But did she really want to ignite civil war by denouncing and banning Christianity? What would happen to the Churches of England and Scotland? All the churches, abbeys and cathedrals? What of the people? What if they refused to accept her decree? What would she do with them? She couldn't very well kill them. It was unthinkable. She didn't want to mount her throne bathed in blood, never mind all the Human rights it would breach.

She hoped Brigid had the answers. Wherever she was.

"Why does the sky look like it is on fire?" she asked of the Fae.

They both snapped around to look at where she was pointing. Up in the evening sky fire was spreading through the clouds and clear sky alike. High in the sky an ominous crucifix burned.

"The Angels have lit the Fires." Aisling muttered before she dashed off. As soon as she was out of the sight of Victoria's servants she disappeared.

Victoria watched her vanish before turning to Cathair. He looked deeply troubled. "What is going on?"

He sighed heavily "The Angels know Britain is sealed off from them. That is why they light the Fires. It is a warning of Divine Retribution that will descend on us. That they have done it so blatantly in the Modern Age shows just how deep their fury runs.

"What kind of retribution?"

He looked at her like she was stupid "The Fires of

Heaven, the Apocalypse and its Horsemen, the Greater Demons and the Demon Horde, or sending Human armies at us. Their options are many and devastating. It is the herald of great death and devastation from the Angels."

"Then why on earth did we activate the spell?"

"Because they would have sensed the spike in power that Brigid's presence is having on the land. It bought us more time and will help shield us. The Fires have been lit but no attack has come yet, nor will it until they are surer of their position."

He wandered off inside the manor and she was left feeling frightened and vulnerable. She had expected the Fae to be steadfast in their resolve but they seemed strangely accepting of an inevitability she had not been warned about. Couldn't they have acted more assured for her sake?

She needed the comfort of Brigid's presence and assurance. She was the patron of Britain and Ireland, she wouldn't let them fall. Would she?

"No I will not allow the Angels to sully my land any further, but it is nice to know I've been missed."

Victoria spun around to see Brigid standing behind her accompanied by the most surprising and incredible thing she had ever seen- real Unicorns. She threw herself into the Goddess' arms, taking Brigid by surprise. Brigid was truly touched. It was her nature that set her apart from the other Gods and Angels, it was also what had made converting her loyal worshippers so difficult. The other Gods had called it a weakness or an amusing temperament, but she had always had far more Humanity in her than any other full Divine being. Even more than the other Mother Goddesses who embodied life, then again life was harsh and some of them were quite uncaring.

Other Gods and Angels waged war with little or no care for the cost in mortal lives. Sometimes they didn't even care for the cost in Divine lives. She knew she could never be that callous, just as she knew that hundreds of thousands, even millions of people were going to die for her. The Second War of Heaven would surely erupt soon, the lines were already being drawn up. Britain was safe for the moment, but Victoria needed to be on the throne for the spell to be at full strength. Once she was crowned Britain and its colonies were in for some turbulent times.

"I am very sorry about your father Victoria, I never thought he would be a target."

Victoria stepped back studying Brigid's eyes. Whatever she saw there satisfied her, and the fact it did troubled Brigid slightly. Mortals were not meant to be able to read Gods. Was it merely intuition or did she harbours skills to tell such things. "The only ones to blame are the Angels. We may have pushed their hand but my father was a complete innocent. They will be made to pay for murdering him."

It appeared she was firmly set on this path, for which Brigid was glad. But it also saddened her, she was to blame. Because of her Victoria's life and world had been turned upside down, and it was only the beginning. "We will make them pay, I swear to you Victoria." She didn't care if feeling made her weak, she considered it a valuable trait. For she felt what other Gods could not, she lived the full emotional spectrum and understood the value of life. Each and every life was unique and precious though they were as common as grains of sand.

"Are those really Unicorns?" Victoria changed the subject unable to stem her delight any longer. There was a small herd of them, most of them were pure white as culture portrayed them but there were also some as black as night, grey as clouds and even two dazzling aquamarine ones. Their hooves and horns were gold, as was the hair of their manes and tails. They were truly breathtaking, their gold reflecting the scant light of the Scottish evening. She felt sure it would reflect moonlight and starlight. For all their beauty their horns were a deadly reminder they were dangerous, they were as long as her forearm.

"Beautiful are they not? I will never understand why they were hunted to extinction, they pose very little threat other than being impaled."

"Did you create them?" she asked in wonder. She had seen magic, had managed a little of her own. But so far it had mostly been lights and fire, this was truly amazing. Being a horse rider she appraised the Unicorns, they were slightly taller than the ones she rode yet they were somehow more delicate. They were also more fleet of foot.

"Yes with magic returning to the Surface and the Lifestream rising miracles become easier. There will come a time when miracles truly happen on their own. So much of what has been lost will be again. If Hera can create Phoenixes, Minotaurs and Gorgons then I need to be equally impressive."

"Believe me you are" she held out her hand to the nearest Unicorn, a black mare with silver eyes. The mare eyed her warily before stepping forward to sniff and lip her hand. "She is absolutely beautiful" she gushed over the mare, the mare looked at her with clear humour in her eyes before nudging her.

"She likes you, it a rare honour for a Unicorn to accept a rider."

Victoria excitedly and ungracefully clambered up onto the bare back of the mare. She squealed with pure delight as the mare pranced about good naturedly before running down the garden stairs onto the lawn beneath.

Brigid watched smiling as Victoria and Starflight raced around the ornamental gardens. When Victoria returned she was flushed with excitement. She slid down off of Starflight beaming "That was amazing, she was so fast."

"I'm glad you like her for she is yours."

She gaped open mouthed until she felt a phantom hand close her mouth "For me?"

"Consider it an early coronation present. You will be one of very few people to have your own herd of Unicorns, and the only Human. Though that might change in time if they grant their blessing."

"The others will go to the Fae?"

"Yes it will be my mark of blessing, they are also better suited to their care than Humans. Unicorns despite their looks are not horses, they are as intelligent as any sentient race. They have their own powers, can understand our languages and can even speak telepathically. It is better to think of them as sentient beings."

"Then how can I own her, that is slavery" Starflight neighed in approval.

It was interesting that she raised such concerns about slavery, clearly the British Empire would not be resurrecting its slavery filled past. She considered that a good thing and was glad that the world had moved well on. She was also proud of Victoria's insight and logic. "Precisely you do not own her. Yes I gifted her to you, this herd was willing to live here but she chose to accept you as her rider. You will look after the herd and in return they will grant you their loyalty. But never forget what they are, they are sentient beings. If they so choose they will leave and there is nothing you can do to keep them. Others may come and go but Starflight will remain loyal to you as long as you treat her right."

Victoria nodded her understanding as she patted the mare.

"She is only new to her powers, in time your bond will deepen as both of you develop your powers."

Victoria smiled in sudden understanding "Your gifting wouldn't happen to coincide with my coronations carriage ride would it? Your plan is to show my reign will start with magic and what better way than with my own Unicorns."

"The young queen is very perceptive" Cathair remarked as he walked out onto the terrace "I also believe that it coincides with your formal presentation at the Seelie Court. What better way to be introduced to the Fae world than entering on a Unicorn."

"I must remember how perceptive you both are" Brigid joked though she was glad both had so easily worked it out. It would not do well for the royal couple to be stupid. Their insights continued to surprise her, or was she just that out of touch with mortals.

"Wait when am I being presented at the Seelie Court?" Victoria asked suddenly wary.

"Tomorrow. You need to serve your time at the Court before your coronation if the Fae are to swear loyalty to you. With your coronation looming we need to get it done now. It is the only time your presence can be excusable from your royal duties."

"But I can't even control my magic, all I've managed so far is some flashing lights. I will be the laughing stock at Court, they'll never take me seriously."

"Not when you arrive with Unicorns, believe me the entire court will treat you with respect. Brigid has thought this through."

"But I'm not ready, I can't go. What will I wear? Cathair what will I wear?"

"You concern is amusing but needless."

"Why?"

"We don't wear clothing at the Seelie Court, clothes are a Human construction that we only wear for their sake. Why do you think there are so many tales of naked Fairies."

"What?"

Brigid laughed "don't listen to him, he's pulling your leg" she raised an eyebrow at Cathair "well, well, well a Fae with a sense of humour, you've certainly rubbed off on him Victoria. Don't worry I will take care of your dress, remember I want you to shine in their eyes. And besides Cathair and Aisling will still be in your service at Court."

Victoria smiled when she saw him jerk. But she was still worried, these were not her people, they weren't even her own species and yet she was meant to impress them enough that they would swear fealty to her. She jerked suddenly, startling the prince and Goddess, when something brushed against her mind.

"Something just tried touching my mind"

Starflight whickered, Brigid smiled again "It is Starflight, she's still new to her powers, she will fumble as much as you do. Try and reach back to her, it is a rare honour indeed to have a Unicorn trying to communicate with you telepathically.

"Oh" Victoria leaned in close to the mare to speak in her ear "sorry and thank you" she gave her a pat.

She snorted and stamped her foot. Not quite sure what she meant Victoria patted her shoulder. She nudged her again. Victoria looked at her not understanding.

"She wants you to ride her again" Brigid said.

Delighted Victoria scrambled back up onto Starflight, barely having time to grab onto her mane before she charged off down the stairs again.

Brigid watched her go "Beautiful isn't she?" she

could sense the prince's attraction to her.

"Yes she is. What an image she makes on the back of a Unicorn, she will dazzle Human and Fairy alike. Does she know they used to be children?"

"No" she snapped "And you will not tell her. I saved their lives and gave them a new one."

"Who were they?"

"Christians and Muslims from Pakistan. It is a war zone there, I can't believe just how destructive Humans are in this age. The Buddhists and Hindu were turned into Naga, I'm sure you are aware there are a few attending the Seelie Court. India needs to be prepared to seize back Pakistan from the Angels. Those who refused to accept me could not be allowed to keep empowering the Angels but I couldn't just abandon them. They cry out in their suffering and it is my fault."

Cathair looked at her in surprise, hesitantly he placed his hand on her shoulder "Most would simply have killed them and not thought twice about it, or abandoned them to their fate. You gave them a kinder fate, a second life and their innocence back. You do not waste life.

Will they remember their time as Humans?"

"No I wiped those painful memories from them. Most of them were but children but what they had seen disturbs even me. Now their spirits will heal in peace."

"You are truly not like the rest of your kind are you? You actually care about mortals, you consider our suffering. You've even eased the suffering of mortals who don't belong to you."

"No I guess I'm not. Life is precious no matter who it belongs to. It was a point of mockery for me but I never cared, my people loved and adored me."

"I am glad you are not like the others for I agree with you." She turned to look at him in surprise, his eyes were unmasked and glowing slightly. "That you are different sets you apart Brigid, it makes you better than them and it makes me glad to serve you. You care about us. You touch our hearts instead of stealing our wits. If any God deserves to rule a quarter of the world it is you because you will look after us and help all your lands flourish. All of it, not just parts."

She made to speak but he cut her off pointing to the Unicorns "your actions speak louder than anything else Brigid. You might be a powerful Goddess but a heart beats within you. Yes war will be waged in your name but you have considered the costs to us. Your heart is what will serve you the best in the future, mortals cannot help but be drawn to you. You are a fitting heir to Avalon."

She had a feeling he was right.

Chapter 37

The drop from the Seventh to the Eighth Level of Hell was far more significant than any prior. The only way down was by flying, or falling. Her senses alerted her of the winged Demonic creatures that lived within the cliffs. It told her that they were the usual transport down the cliff, not that she had any intention of using them.

She stood in the dark looking down, all the power she had been channelling had been released. The strain had been too much and she would certainly need it to defend herself.

Her power had also wreaked havoc on Hell's already bizarre structure. What kind of crater was divided into nine different distinct Levels that had been further divided? And what moron had placed the exit at the very bottom? What she saw and had experienced was merely the strongest aspect of Hell, her presence brought out the strength of the Curse. She had seen within others minds somewhat calmer landscapes. Hell fluctuated.

What she saw was the strongest aspect of it, Dante's imagining of Hell, heavily influenced by Christianity. But Hell was also the vessel for Muslims, Jews and their derivatives. All their beliefs shaped Hell as well. Between the three religions Hell was a nightmare of flame and suffering. She could never have imagined such a place in her wildest and most disturbed nightmares.

What was truly sick was that the most disgusting people could not only share the same Level but the same classification as innocents. People whose only crimes had been love or being viewed by someone else as believing the wrong thing. What confused her was Hell's structure, some of the Seven Deadly Sins were represented. Envy,

Sloth and Pride were absent from its structure and yet it had Limbo, a place for unbaptised babies to linger. Why was such innocence punished?

The religions denounced the Gods of old, claiming the One True God and yet Gods had been condemned to Hell. Their presence strengthened the magic of Hell yet undermined its truth, such as it was told. It was a truth she had once accepted completely.

Hell was a truly wretched place, which made sense but it was the presence of innocents that made it truly abhorrent. Divine Beings twisted in experiments, old spirits ripped from their afterlives, babies and children...the list went on and on for those who did not deserve to be suffering within its confines.

Even belonging to other faiths or having no faith had not offered any protection. Hindus, Buddhists, Atheists, Agnostics and Neopagans had all been dragged into the accursed abyss. The Angels truly had no mercy.

Except herself.

But then she was no longer sure if she was just an Angel any more or a Goddess. She had been told about Angels becoming Gods but had written it off as stories but what if it were true?

She cloaked herself within invisibility, masking her presence to all who would seek to find her. Then she jumped off the cliff. For perhaps the first time since she had entered Hell she felt a mild amount of simple pleasure to be flying down the cliff face. Her hair whipped behind her, as did her dress, or what remained of it. It felt good to pump her wings, temporarily forgetting her troubles.

She landed gently at the bottom of the cliff, conscious of the dust her wings had stirred. She saw Demons turn their attention from the edge of a large ditch, their yellow eyes watching the sand and dust settle. They turned their attention and their whips back to the people within the ditch. Hell had all manner of strange occurrences, what was some unsettled sand?

She walked closer, looking at the two lines of people marching in opposite directions within the ditch. She felt sure that many were probably undeserving to be in here, but she spared them only a passing thought. There were far too many Demons to consider doing anything.

She walked over a primitive wooden bridge, surprised it hadn't burned away long ago. Fire was the most common feature of Hell. Her skin crawled as nearby Demons turned to watch the bridge. It was as though they could tell she was walking over it despite her invisibility. They watched but did nothing, instead returning back to their duties once she was on the other side.

The short trek to the next ditch was across plain sand with little to make it stand out, except for the fires that danced across it. She was thankful for these, they scoured away her footprints. However the closer she got to the next ditch a horrible smell got stronger until it was horrendous.

She understood why when she was walking across its wooden bridge. The ditch was filled with excrement, the smell was utterly awful. She had to cast a filter spell to keep the stench out of her nose. Otherwise she would be vomiting all over the place.

What was even more disgusting was that there were people within the excrement. She watched in appalled horror as a man crawled up onto the stony sides, coughing and puking up faeces before he was whipped back into the fluid. The Demon that had driven him back into the excrement laughed before urinating on the man.

Sariel had to close her eyes for a minute in order to keep moving.

She hurried across the bridge, covering her mouth in the vain hope it would stop her vomiting. Never had she seen something so disgusting.

She was glad when she reached the other side and hurried across the sand to put as much distance between her and the ditch. She didn't pay attention to the sand she kicked up or to the Demons who had turned to watch the small disturbance.

Within the third ditch was more bizarre cruelty. People were buried upside down with only their feet sticking out. Fire burned on the soles of their feet, even as they jerked feebly. She paid them only passing attention as she hurried across the bridge.

They were soon gone from her mind when she came across the oddity of the fourth ditch. It was particularly wide, the wooden bridge disappearing into the gloom. The Damned confined within this ditch all had their heads turned around. In order to see where they were going they had to walk backwards. The sheer creepiness of it made her curious as to what their apparent crime had been.

She discovered that the nearest woman had been a witch, well she had been branded as one. She barely had enough power to be classed as any form of mage. What simply would have been called psychic intuition in the Modern Age had had her burned at the stake as a witch. Another victim of being hated for who she was and could not change.

As much as she wanted to aid her plight there were a disturbing number of Demons watching them. Her actions and battles in the higher levels had left her drained. Now was the time for stealth, she need to regain her strength and get out of Hell. She could feel its magic boring into her defences. If she wasn't careful she would become a Demon herself.

She hurried onto the next ditch, though it could hardly be called that. It was a vast lake of boiling pitch with an immense island in the distance, leading onto the lower Levels. She really didn't understand Hell, or its structuring but she had given up trying to.

There was no bridge over the lake, she had to take to the air once again. She was very careful to avoid the Demons flying about on their black wings. They flew back and forth cackling manically. Occasionally they skimmed the surface of the pitch, pulling up one of the Damned. Their tortured screams filled the air as the Demons tormented them before throwing them away. They landed on the pitch to slowly sink beneath its bubbling surface.

She allowed herself to sigh and shudder once she landed on the other side of the lake before hurrying onwards. She crested some small hills to find the sixth ditch which she was beginning to see as divisions. The ditches divided the different types of fraud.

The citizens of the sixth ditch walked aimlessly around, whipped into continual action by the Demons that watched them. They walked around wearing metal cloaks, there were traces of gold gilt that had long since worn away. There were scatterings of jewels and ornaments, all of which were fake. The new denizens were clearly the only ones that reached for them, only to have them crumble in their hands. It was probably one of the most scenic areas of Hell, fool's gold covered the ground and walls of the ditch. Even the bridge was golden, though she wasn't fooled. She could see the wears and cracks in the gilt, wood showed through.

Once again she hurried on to the next circle, wondering how many circles the Fraud Level had.

The seventh circle was not ditches but sheer ravines. A thin winding path hugged close to the walls of crumbling shale. The ravine disappeared into the darkness, parts of the cliff faces crumbling off and falling down into the darkness. Everywhere she looked there were shards of rocks forming lethal obstacles. But the gorges were not uninhabited, screams and inhuman shrieks filled the air, echoing off the walls. The walls themselves were thick with snakes and lizards of all sizes, regularly snapping and biting the people trapped within the ravine. Every time they bit someone the person screamed in agony, grabbing at the bite, ripping their skin in their desperate attempt to stop the pain.

They didn't succeed.

Those who were bitten transformed as the venom spread. Then they withered into ashes, before finally returning to their original form. Only to be bitten again and again.

She stood transfixed in horrified curiosity as one man changed into a six legged reptile before bursting into flames then reappearing. Another woman transformed into a chimeric being, above the waist she remained Human but below she had developed into an octopus. Her tentacles fought for purchase on the sharp rocks to no avail. She slid down the sharp flint, tearing her soft cephalopod body apart. She slid out of sight as she fell into the darkness, her screams ceased sometime after.

She decided it would be prudent to fly through the ravine rather than traipsing through the writhing forms of tortured souls and reptiles.

She flew through several ravines that intersected each other before several sets of crumbling stairs led back up onto the sand dunes that divided all the circles. She continued to fly over the dunes until she reached the flames of the eighth circle.

She continued to fly over the flames her keen Angel eyesight picking out the bodies in the flames. What stood out the most was the large wooden horse rising above the flames. It was bathed in green flames, the hottest flames bathing the man strapped to its snout. The uniqueness of his torture confused her, what crime was so great that he gained special torment? Curious she probed him. He was Odysseus, an ancient king, a brilliant general, who had had won the Trojan War by using the Trojan Horse. He had endured a ten year odyssey to get home, cursed by Poseidon. He had been a hero. Naturally going to the Elysium Fields where he had resided in peace until he had been ripped out of Hades and cast into Hell. Now he was punished for being a betrayer.

It seemed strange that he should be damned to such a place when back in his time he was applauded as a genius. Even the Trojans had resentfully admitted his plan was brilliant. In the modern era he was revered as a brilliant general. Yet because of Dante he was condemned as a deceitful adviser who had led Agamemnon astray.

He wearily looked up in surprise as rain extinguished the flames that had continuously burned him for centuries. All the green flames licking up the Trojan Horse were extinguished. To his even greater surprise the chains binding him snapped open and he started to fall. Was this it? Was this the end?

He disappeared before he hit the ground. Sariel smiled despite herself, she just couldn't leave an injustice alone. So much for using as little magic as possible. Thankfully she had been able to cast him out of Hell. Hades had a far stronger call on him than Hell, modern thinking did not agree with Dante. He would be able to return to the Elysium Fields, hopefully he would be able to recover from his centuries of torture. He would also be able to tell her family she was still alive.

The ninth circle was filled with sword wielding Demons, their grey hulking forms looming in and out of the gloom. Their great blades swung back and forth, hacking apart bodies as they moved slowly through the masses. What was surprising was that there were notably more females than males in the area.

What was even more surprising was the ray of sunlight that shone on a bare spot of rock that was covered in blood.

Once again curious, everything in here made her curious for so much of it was beyond her understanding, she probed the area. It reeked of patriarchal sexism and female fury. It was the Discord area of Fraud. The sexist patriarchal views of man through the millennia believed that women sowed discord among men. It was a belief firmly entrenched within the Angelic Religions, one only had to look at Adam and Eve. She could not understand how Gabriel and the other female Angels had allowed such sexist religions to spread across the Earth like a cancer. Then again the Elder Angels had no care of Humanity and their plight, it didn't matter what occurred so long as they believed in God.

She felt sorry for the women of the past and those still trapped in backwards societies. She couldn't imagine being held back and always being judged inferior because of her gender. The Angels were completely equal when it came to gender, sure there with differences in body shape but physical and magical strength were not affected by gender. Gabriel was the most magically gifted Angel there had ever been, she had a feeling she was now too.

The Angels were truly equal when it came to gender, though not class.

The ray of sunlight was an even greater enigma. Upon probing the magical signatures she became even more confused. She recognised both Gabriel and Mohammed's traces. How on earth had Mohammed ended up in Hell? He was the holiest man in all of Islam, the one true Prophet and one of the loyalist servants the Angels had ever had.

She landed on the rock, thankful she was still invisible. Her hands traced the old blood stains, pulling out the story within. Once again Dante was to blame. In the eyes of Christians Muslims were lost souls or just plain evil. This was a mindset deeply entrenched when Dante had made his way through Hell to shape it. Viewing Islam in a very negative light he and his fellow Christians had believed that Mohammed was one of the greatest creators of discord. It had earned him special punishment in the Discord Circle. From the magical traces the Arch Angels had expelled quite a bit of power to extract him from Hell.

She wondered that if they knew she was down here if they would be able to do the same.

She immediately felt sorry for Mohammed, his blood had been shed while he had been tortured. She wondered how long it had taken for them to save him. She also wondered if he had sought his revenge on Dante when he had died.

She took flight, flying on to the next Circle. It was merely a downwards slant covered in sick people. Living in Heaven she had never seen sickness or disease, Divine beings were immune to all sicknesses. But her time in Hades had educated her to the troubles of the mortal world. She now knew about various diseases and how they killed. What was before her was a far wider array than she had learned about. There were various poxes, venereal diseases, fevers, cancers and a whole manner of others. People were bent double coughing and vomiting up blood, peoples' legs were slick with bloody diarrhoea, skins were buckled, pox marked, oozing, bleeding. People had blood running from their eyes, skin peeling off, even body parts were falling off of some.

The stench of sickness was overwhelming in the air.

How on Earth had Dante imagined such things? A sweep of the area told her that these were all natural diseases, mortals had suffered from each of the diseases before her. This was a natural part of life. It was terrifying. She was suddenly very grateful to be an Angel, she had never overly appreciated the benefits of being Divine but now she would never forget.

There was nothing she could do for them. They were after all already dead and her own time was running out. Her magic was starting to become erratic and slipping beyond her control. Soon she would probably lose her invisibility.

She flew quickly onwards towards the Ninth and last Level of Hell. She could make it, she would make it.

She flew down a very sharp decline, this was the border between the two Levels as opposed to the usual cliffs. Within the gloom figures loomed and faded but rising above the gloom was a mountain. It was the gigantic stalagmite that was the exit of Hell, it was also the Lair of Lucifer. She could see the gap between the stalactite and stalagmite glowing.

She was so close to the end.

Odysseus slowly came awake and to his complete surprise felt no pain. When he opened his eyes there were no flames, no smoke, no darkness, only soft sunlight. There was not the roar of flames licking over his skin and the wooden horse he had been attached to for centuries. There was only the sound of running water and distant laughter.

He heard footsteps approaching but didn't have the strength to even move. He was exhausted, his limbs and body weight too much for him to move them. He had barely moved them for centuries, only weakly struggling against his chains.

"Odysseus?" a woman's voice asked. He couldn't see her, his eyes were still unfocussed.

He felt a cool and gentle hand grab his face "yes it is" she said more to herself than to him.

He was suddenly weightless and the light disappeared. He was now somewhere different, the light faded to a soft twilight and now there were many voices nearby.

"Why have you brought a shade within the castle Nemesis?" a man with a deep compelling voice asked.

"This is Odysseus, he has returned from Hell." He felt a slight surge of pain from her touch then he could see again. He was in Hades castle, spread eagle across the floor before the thrones of Hades and Persephone. A beautiful black haired Goddess was kneeling over him. "What level of Hell were you trapped in?" she asked him with desperation.

He stared back at her not comprehending what she was saying.

She grabbed his face with both hands, her amethyst eyes pinning him to the floor. It felt like she had stripped him of every defence and was staring right into his soul. She probably was.

"It is very important that you remember where in Hell you were." They had no idea where Sariel was up to, last they had known was that she had passed through the Gates of Dis sending the Furies back to Hades.

"The Horse, on the Horse" he muttered.

Hecate looked around at the others rolling her eyes. A dark shadow swept down from the nearest window, spreading across the floor like ink before solidifying as a shadow cut-out of a woman. She swept her hands across his face then grabbed his shoulders "Where is Sariel? Is she well?" she demanded as she shook him violently.

He mumbled incoherently as she shook him.

"We know she got past the Fifth Level" said Alecto "And believe me the powers she unleashed shook Hell. She stripped the Curse from us, Medusa and the Fallen Angels on the wall top. She had already stripped Leviathan, Lilith and Naamah of their Curses. We have no need to worry about her safety."

They had already heard Minos, Cerberus and the Furies accounts of Sariel's actions in Hell, but her family couldn't help but worry. Thanatos had ceased speaking to them all, his powers a constant blanket around him that no one, not even Nyx or Hypnos were willing to interact with. They all bore his silent condemnation as their long forgotten sense of guilt gnawed at them.

"Fraud" Odysseus muttered.

Nyx snapped her dark eyes back towards him, moving lightning fast to sweep her hands up to his face and plunging her fingers into his brain. He shuddered as she extracted his memories.

"He was in the Eighth Level, Fraud. From his memories and my estimation he was near the end of the Level. He was chained to the Trojan Horse and burned." She fell silent as she moved through his memories "He never saw Sariel, but I can sense her presence. She is strong, so strong. She set him free, she sent him back here."

"Near the end of the Eighth Level, she is close to finishing her task." Hecate mused as she appeared next to the table covered in maps, drawings and lists of Dante's Inferno. Her fingers traced the last descent to the bottom of Hell "That is of course presuming Hell is completely to Dante's design. We could be wrong in our beliefs."

"She has survived every Level so far with a grace and power we could not have believed. Her powers are incredible. She will be fine." Cerberus added to alleviate their concerns. He was of no doubt she would succeed. He had seen her strip the Curse from Behemoth and free Tiamat and Bahamut.

Thanatos turned from the window he was staring out of "She had better be fine or I will never forgive any of you." He disappeared in a burst of black flames.

An ominous feeling settled over all of them. Would any of them be able to forgive themselves?

Chapter 38

She slowed her approach as she neared the final Level cliff. Beyond she would dive down into the last Level of Hell, treachery. Yet it was guarded by giants looming out of the gloom. They seemed impossibly large, for she could only see them from the waist up but then what wasn't possible in Hell? They were formidable looking males, but also wearied. Their bodies were scarred from whips and claws. Being Guardians offered no safety. Their greasy hair and beards fell in a cascade that disappeared behind the cliff.

She flew past them as silently as she could, glad that her invisibility was holding up. They never even noticed her passing.

To her amusement she saw that they were not as gigantic as she had first thought. They were standing on ledges carved into the cliff face. She was glad she could fly down the cliff, she would not have wanted to navigate between their feet during her descent.

She dove down into Treachery, staying close to the cliff before alighting on the outer ring of ice. For some reason she knew that there were four concentric rings, yet she could only see one, the rest must be under the stalactite. The one she was standing on disappeared underneath it.

She eyed up the stalagmite contemplating flying up directly to the Lair but decided against it. Row upon row upon row of Demons nested all over its surface and fierce storms plagued it. She could feel the winds tugging at her where she stood, flying up through that would be suicide. She would have to pass through the whole Level underneath the Great Stalagmite.

A great boom filled the air causing her to jump. Fire and lightning raced around the air, superheating it within seconds. There was no way she could safely pass up that way.

She glided silently over the ice until she passed into the eerie glow of the caverns.

The first zone contained those immersed up to their faces, they were the only part of their bodies showing above the ice. Fierce winds blew across the ice, covering the faces in layers of ice that cracked off, peeling parts of their faces with it. She was forced to land for fear of being blown against the cavern walls. The winds ceased, then resumed. She rushed forward when the winds died and stilled when they blew again. There seemed to be no pattern to the winds, they appeared random.

She hurried across the ice, half running, half slipping and occasionally having to jump over frozen faces. The faces disturbed her, their eyes the only thing that moved, following her as she ran across the ice.

It didn't take her long to reach the second ring, the border between them was only a thin and low line of black rock, akin to the black rock that composed the stalagmite towering over her. The cavern above her flattened, broken only occasionally by a stalactite. The winds however had gotten stronger, roaring through the enclosed space, covering the Damned in fresh layers of ice. It crunched beneath her boots as she struggled against the strong winds.

By the time she reached the third zone the ceiling was starting to curve upwards around another huge stalagmite that broke up from the smooth ice in the distance. Once again the two zones were only separated by a small wall of black rock.

The people of the third zone were immersed in the

ice on their backs, only the thinnest section of their faces were uncovered. Their skin was deathly pale, their lips blue and unmoving. The winds blew harder still, filled with shards of ice that scoured the surface of the zone and battered against her shields. What was exposed of the Damned was regularly ripped to shreds by the ice fragments.

It took her far longer to reach the fourth zone because of the winds, they had gotten stronger the further she had progressed. By the time she crossed the low stone wall the winds were a tempest, raging down from above, winding around the stalagmite before splintering off in all directions across the ice. Each step was a small battle against the winds, and the ice here was smooth and unbroken making it harder still. The Damned were now fully immersed in the ice, their bodies twisted into strange and painful positions.

She spared little thought for them as she pushed onwards against the wind.

She reached the base of the stalagmite, wandering around it until she found crude stairs carved in to its face. Crude was an understatement, they were uneven, crumbling and wound back and forth across the stalagmite in the most demented fashion. They seemed to follow no logical mindset. Whoever had carved them had either been mad or a terrible craftsman.

She squared her shoulders and waited for a break in the wind before she started her ascent. When the break came she hauled herself upwards, clinging to the demented staircase for dear life as the winds erupted downwards again. Painstakingly slowly she hauled herself upwards towards the shaft the stalagmite speared upwards into, the frozen lake falling behind until there was only the black shaft in both directions. It was softly lit from some unknown source. As she climbed the stalagmite fused into the walls, leaving but one thin shaft to climb into. The winds pouring down nearly succeeded on more than one occasion to rip her from the stairs.

She clung to the stairs with all her might as the winds continued to blow, relenting only rarely. It was in these brief periods that she struggled to climb as much as she could before the winds started up again. It was made more difficult by the thin layers of ice that now permanently coated the shaft.

Ever so slowly she continued upwards.

John wandered into his kitchen, feeling more than ever sleep deprived. The election campaign was sapping all his energy, never mind the meeting he had to have with Ariadne and the other Daemon senators.

He stopped when he eyed the Asian youth typing away on a laptop at his breakfast bench. "Who are you?"

The youth raised unnerving amber eyes from his laptop to him "Kyle" then flicked back to whatever he was doing.

"What are you doing in my kitchen Kyle?" this was meant to be a secure area, along with his own security detail he had been assigned magical ones to protect him as well. He was apparently very valuable to Hera's cause, whatever it might be.

He didn't even bother looking up as he replied "I'm your new security detail."

He couldn't help himself, he laughed "You? They've sent a child to protect me?"

Now he reacted, those eyes flicked up in anger as he glared "I'm not a child I'm nineteen and I'm the most powerful sorcerer in the whole of North America so count yourself lucky old man."

"Old man? I'm only thirty five! I'm the youngest senator in the senate."

"Yeah a whole lot of old people."

He really didn't like this kid's attitude. "You expect me to believe that you are the most powerful sorcerer in the whole of North America." He eyed up Kyle. He was thin, almost scrawny but tall, noticeably so for an Asian. He was quite attractive, his face still holding the cuteness of youth, though right now it was all seriousness. The seriousness was undermined by his unusual haircut, long and ragged, but those eyes were nothing but scrutiny. He was well dressed in a suit that was tailored, on his lapel he wore a small peacock pin and underneath a small rainbow flag pin.

He was gay and clearly favoured by Hera.

Similarly Kyle scrutinised him. He was here because Ariadne did not trust the Senator, and he was one of her most trusted aides. It was his duty to spy on the senator and keep him in line. Though admittedly his purpose was not so desperate. With him as president they could do sweeping reforms, without there would just have to be a revolution.

As he had said he was thirty five, still quite attractive for an older man, though Kyle begrudgingly admitted he wasn't that old. He certainly didn't look it. He was only dressed in track pants, not having expected anyone in his kitchen. It allowed Kyle to give him a good once over. His body was muscular and well toned, he looked how he thought a man should. He had a smattering of brown hair across his chest and a snail trail but nothing more. Kyle could see the outline of what looked like his large cock through the track pants. He flicked his eyes back up to the face. Hair just long enough to run fingers through with no signs of grey. Morning stubble gave him a rugged look. There were some wrinkles, but otherwise he was looking good. He found him quite attractive.

"Believe what you will senator but I have been assigned to you and I do my duties. You'll just have to put up with me. Now you better hurry up and get dressed we have a meeting with Senator Claire and McClain."

"What meeting?"

"The meeting on adjustments to healthcare." He jumped up, grabbed the Senator by the shoulders and steered him back out of the kitchen "Now hurry up and get dressed otherwise we will be late." He gave him a slight push, his hands suddenly itching to do more than just push him.

Strange.

He returned to his laptop and coffee, he had a lot to do. He could contemplate this attraction later, in the car.

This assignment suddenly seemed more interesting.

Chapter 39

Sariel climbed up out of the shaft and the blue-green mist pouring down it, her arms aching with exhaustion. How could a mortal ever make this journey, she was Divine and it had nearly killed her on more than one occasion. She thanked her Divinity yet again.

She stood at the lip of the shaft as the mist poured down it. The mist was also the reason for the raging maelstrom at the apex of the stalagmite. This was where the degraded souls were trapped, too weak to do anything but fuse with the others, their Lifeforce released directly into the Lair where it reacted violently with Lucifer's own phenomenal powers.

It was these souls pouring down the shaft that had illuminated it, but she also realised that while they should be seeping back down into the Lifestream they weren't. They were as trapped as everything else. No wonder the planet was ailing. Hell was blocking the natural systems of the planet, it was swallowing up Lifeforce without returning it to the Lifestream.

Above her soared a vast cavern, the bright hole of sunlight far above was the opening to the Surface. Thick coils of smoke drifted through the sunlight, their source unknown. Deep scratches marked the ceiling and the floor. Rubble covered most of the crater, large and small rocks, skeletons of buildings, vehicles and mortals. Beyond the lip of the crater cavern was the raging tempest. It deterred her going anywhere near the edge.

She glanced down as she felt cold spreading up her legs. They were visible within the swirling Lifeforces. It was stripping her spells from her, she was becoming visible within the Beast's Lair. Now was the prudent time to sneak past it but how was she to get up to the shaft far above without being noticed? More importantly where was the Beast?

New winds sprang up forcing her to the ground, being covered within Lifeforce was a strange experience, especially as it stripped the last of her spells away. She was now visible and defenceless within the Beast's lair.

She looked in the direction that the wind was coming from, her rational mind fleeing as she saw the Beast. He was beating his six wings, as he stopped so did the wind. He was the source of the wind.

The Beast was a truly impressive creature. He was a gigantic Dragon with seven heads upon seven sinuous necks. Each head bore a single horn except the middle head which had four horns. It seemed odd to have ten horns for seven heads. He had six black wings, a testament to his true Angelic nature, though they were now far larger and were the membranous wings prevalent on all Demons. His wings were so large that when he beat them he completely blocked out the sunlight from the shaft far above.

His necks were two thirds the length of his body, as was his long serpentine tail. His main body was completely black, and she couldn't tell whether it was covered in skin, scales or chitin. To her eyes it was shiny and smooth like chitin, but it moved like skin. There were ripples of gold within the black. Whatever it was made of it was hard, sharp rocks stuck into his underside, as he moved they were worn down smooth. Was his skin as hard as diamonds? He had only four legs, each tipped with ten golden talons the size of her. Golden spines ran down the length of his spine, some were thick and triangular others were needle thin.

Strangely though his eyes were unlike any other Demons'. They were an icy blue, shimmering with

627

electricity. It was strange to look into eyes that were not burning. Those shimmering eyes watched her with predatory hunger.

In a quick fluid movement he scrambled down the cliff and across the ground to her. Thinking fast she shot upwards, powered by magic as she cloaked herself once again in shields. She flew up like a rocket aiming straight for that sunlit shaft. She was escaping Hell and nothing was going to stop her.

She slammed into a magical barrier, a spider web of blue, pink and bright green magic, shimmering all over the cavern and completely blocking the exit. It was then she realised how little her family had known...or told her. There was no way to sneak out of Hell, there was no escape.

She was trapped in the Beast's Lair!

She fell slightly stunned despite her shields, only narrowly dodging out of the way of the Beast's reaching claws. She flitted away and dove behind the nearest pile of rubble. Her heart was ready to burst out of her chest it was beating that fast. Her pulse continued to race as she heard the Beast move around his Lair looking for her. She screamed when his golden talons grasped the building she was hiding in. She sat paralysed by the sizzling blue eyes that studied her through the windows. There was some lucidity within that gaze, but it was small, very small.

He was mad. Gabriel had driven her own brother mad with her Curse and his confinement.

He flicked his forked blue tongues out, tasting her fear. His long tail waved dangerously out of the side windows, cutting off any plans for escape. She was completely at his mercy.

She glanced at movement, there were Demons creeping into his lair. Their eyes were focussed on her, and all they held was murder. She was going to die, the Beast had her trapped and now his hordes were coming to butcher her. All her hard work, all her trials, all the lives she had changed had been for naught. She was simply going to be Demon fodder.

To her surprise he roared and charged across the lair to attack the Demons that had dared trespass. She sat transfixed as the Beast tore into the Demons. His fury was evident even to her. His madness had apparently made him extremely territorial. While he tore into the foolish Demons she slunk away.

She crawled into a hole in one of the rubble piles, hidden by the Lifeforce mists curling around. She could feel it draining her shields but it offered the best camouflage. From her cubbyhole she saw many more Demons moving through the lair, searching for her. It was completely illogical but she feared them more than the Beast. There was only vicious cruelty in their eyes, and hunger. The strange noises they made only unnerved her more.

She kept quiet even as the Beast clambered over a mound of rubble, his eyes burning with fury before he roared. The Demons turned in fear as the seven heads and the tail lashed out at them. Flames, ice and lightning poured out of his mouths at the Demons. Powerful magic soon filled the air, reacting with the trapped Lifeforce. She watched in wonder as plants bloomed across the floor before they were consumed by the flames dancing across the ground.

She tuned out the shrieks and screams of Demons in pain as plants wound around her fingers. The mist around her thickened, helping to further obscure her from view. She felt alive, strange sensations firing through her nerves. She no longer felt the continued press down of the Curse. It was as though the Lifeforce was protecting her.

She realised the screams had stopped. The Beast had driven them all from his lair back out into the maelstrom. She saw one limping away as fast as it could, the long black tail struck him from behind. He was thrown out of the lair.

Then silence fell.

She kept completely still, she wasn't foolish enough to dare climb out of her hole to see where the Beast had gone. She was more than content to remain within her hidey hole. She listened for sounds of movement.

She held her breath as she saw golden talons through the green mist. They crept closer before stopping near her hovel. Nothing happened.

She was just beginning to relax when his talons ripped off the rubble hiding her. She didn't stop to think, darting out as fast as her wings would carry her, casting the first spell that came to mind to distract him. Flashes of lightning distracted him as she fled.

She rushed behind a crumbling wall, recasting her invisibility. She stood trying to calm her breathing as she watched the Beast purposefully dig through the rubble. She noticed why he had so easily found her. The ruins she had been hiding under were ablaze with plant life. It was a literal meadow in the middle of a desolate wasteland. The Beast was curiously studying the flowers. His talon delicately stroked a flower, the tip of the talon sliced right through it. He watched sorrowfully as the flower wilted. He seemed sad to have damaged it. It was only then he realised he had trampled half of them.

He let out a long, low moan. It seemed he was keening over the death of the flowers. Around him they started to perish, their colours fading before they crumbled into dust. As they did so little puffs of white magic bloomed before being absorbed into the trapped Lifestream. She found it a peculiarly touching moment.

That was until all the flowers were gone, no more than dust in the wind, and he resumed looking for her. To her dismay she realised that flowers were blooming all around her. She was the catalyst, the Lifestream was reacting to her presence.

She ran away to another corner of the lair thinking desperately. She couldn't stay still for very long otherwise flowers would bloom but running made her visible. It was also quite noisy on the broken shards covering the floor.

He had turned when he saw her running only to get distracted by the flowers she had left in her wake. She watched him, slowly walking between the rubble as she did so. He was not what she had expected, yet he was ferocious, territorial and violent, all of which she had expected. But he was also surprisingly tender and sorrowful towards the flowers.

It was almost as though they reminded him of his life before he was Cursed. She knew it to be true, she had seen a small amount of lucidity in his eyes.

She screamed when long grey talons ripped into her shoulder. Her shields had once again been worn away. She grabbed her daggers and stabbed them both behind her. She spun around raising all her defensive powers, her light casting the lair into stark relief. The shadows disappeared but the flowers burst into light, shining like hundreds of pixie lights.

She paid no attention to the roaring Beast, her attention firmly fixed on the Demon standing before her. It was a grey, grotesque being who bore no resemblance to the Angel he had once been. His face looked like an insect's, large beady eyes, mashing mandibles that clicked. It had eight limbs, stick thin and ending in two long talons. Two of his limbs covered the spurting wounds she had inflicted on its abdomen.

Her daggers sizzled slightly as the blood boiled. She sheathed her daggers and unsheathed her katanas. She stood ready and waiting for its next move.

It struck out with six of its appendages, their talons cutting through the air. She flicked her wrists, her katanas cut smoothly through its wrists. It screeched in pain as its six appendages fell to the ground. She jumped back from its flailing limbs and the acidic blood spurting out.

The next instant the thing was crushed beneath the Beast's claws. Its blood spurted out onto the flowers, burning them on contact. She had forgotten about the Beast, he could have done that to her for all the attention she had been paying him. She paid for that negligence when the next second his other paw grabbed her.

He scrapped his dirty paw off on the ground before he lifted her up before the seven heads. She shrunk before the seven pairs of electric eyes boring into her. Seven forked tongues licked the air around her. It snarled at her and she realised she was still blazing like the sun. To him she was just another Angel.

It was the Angels that had sealed him in here.

He roared at her, squeezing his paw. She screamed and struggled to stab him with her swords. He yelped, dropping her as she managed to cut into his paw. She was too slow to get away before his tail smacked her into the wall.

She slid down stunned, powerless to resist him as he used his tail to pick her up. He dangled her upside down before his middle face. She tried summoning her magic, but he easily cut her off. He was fresh and revived, within the full element of his Curse. She was exhausted after battling her way through all the Levels of Hell.

Slowly her light faded and fizzled as he drained

away the last of her magical defences. She had dropped her swords, all she had left were her daggers which she couldn't reach while the tail was wrapped around her. She was completely at his mercy and looking into his eyes she saw none. Only cold rage.

At least he would only kill her, he wouldn't torture or rape her like the other Demons would. He was a Beast, not a monster, with enough of his true personality shining through. She would at least have the benefit of a clean death, small mercy as it was.

He shook her. Her jewellery jangled, reminding her that she still had them. She reached up to touch her necklace and the vine amulet. Green light flared from her right wrist up her arm to just under her right ear. Chaos brown flared from around her neck. Power flooded her and she felt alive. The Chaos sigils on her arms blazed into life.

She heard a heartbeat, deep and distant. Was that the Lifestream or was it Gaia's heartbeat? He dropped her hissing, curling his tail underneath him as though he had been burned. She dropped to the floor, smacking against the stone. She lay there dazed while he sat there hissing at her.

She sat up watching him warily as she recalled her swords to her. She sheathed them as she continued to wrap herself with power. The green mist beneath her feet blazed to life. Beyond the lair she heard hundreds of Demons scrabbling to get away from the lair. Wind whipped in around her, raising the mist in to various shapes and forms. It was as though the mist was coming alive with the spirits within it.

His tail whipped past her but she stepped out of the way. It seemed as though time had slowed down as she called upon more and more power. She blazed with it, the green of Gaia and the brown of Chaos. All around her the Angels' Curse flared brightly, their lights were overpowered by her own. He cowered away from her, snarling and hissing, his tail flicking back and forth in front of him.

The Lifestream surged up from the shaft, wrapping around her like a playful python.

He hissed again and this time struck out with magic. He was strong, far stronger than she would have expected. He would have been nearly as strong as Gabriel naturally, but now he was empowered by the Curse and the Human perception of Satan. She felt her outer shields shatter under his onslaught, but his attack was undirected and uncontrolled. The Lifestream surged around her to protect her.

She wound her own powers around his, snaking back up his magical stream without him noticing.

He shrieked in desperation as he felt her magic coiling around him.

Desperate he charged at her, running through the Lifestream mists that slowed him down, he felt as though he was wading through syrup. He reared up and flapped his wings, the blasts of wind coating the cavern with ice. The mist was blown away before it surged back with a vengeance, coiling up around him.

He roared his fury at his constraint, his magic being taken beyond his control. He struggled against the mist and the nets of power the Angel was wrapping around him. Soon the whole lair was illuminated by the sigils and symbols of the Curse.

Outside the lair the whole of Hell was lit up in the same manner. The divides between each Level were thick with symbols, big and small, moving over each other and blending together. Within the Levels large sigils danced lazily across the landscape while the Damned stilled to watched the thousands of tiny sigils racing across their skins.

Far above in Purgatory the Fallen Angels stilled as the whole of Hell lit up with bright lights, pink and blue symbols dancing across the crater. Then the light spread up each of the Terraces, stone being lost beneath a flood of symbols, some large others tiny, some blazing white, some pink, some blue and some golden. The Angels smiled for the first time since the Curse was laid upon them as the sigils raced up their skin. The time was near, their suffering was at an end. They were no longer force to do the tasks set for them. They could still and rest.

Lucifer was breaking free of his bonds.

Sariel stepped forward, sending out waves of shimmering sigils. His skin shimmered in response, the thick layers of his Curse lighting up. He roared his distress, his heads flailing around.

She snapped her fingers and they all froze.

She stepped under them all, walking forward to lay her hands upon his chest. She had to stand on her toes to reach it. His skin was perfectly smooth as glass but both hot and cold to the touch. The white sigils across his skin flared pink and blue in response, the Angels' magic was now clearly visible. She realised there were burn marks beneath the sigils.

How had Gabriel done this to her own brother? She could never imagine doing this to Michael. She rubbed her hands over the burns, feeling the agony trapped within them. The spells were incredibly vicious, biting down into his burns. Her magic slowly spread through him, in doing so she shared his pain as her own. The pain would have driven her to her knees but her hands had fused to his chest. She screamed in agony at the backlash of power striking out at her. Gabriel's power, and the power of the Angelic Horde burned through her, boiling her blood. He roared in unison suffering the same as her.

He managed to claw his way forward, pushing down to crush her. Lightning struck him down from above, then again and again. A whole matrix of lightning struck down on him. He screamed in pure agony as lightning poured through him, burning his flesh. The air was thick with the smell of burning skin. His tail swished around in anguished frenzy scattering rubble everywhere.

She struggled to move with his body crushing her, the Lifestream came to her rescue, forcing its way under him and lifting him up off of her. He started to roll around, his wings beating.

"Lucifer"

He stilled instantly at his name. A name he had not been called in near two millennia. She pulled her hands away, no longer fused to his skin. She used his many deep scars to clamber up onto his back where his seven necks met. The Lifestream surged up after her, coating his body in the life giving magic. Most of his body was lost beneath the green mist wrapping around him and more was still pouring into the Lair.

He started to moan in pain, Gabriel's Curse had dug in deep over the centuries, wrapping around his very core and bones.

She flew up onto his middle head, grabbing it between her glowing hands. It closed its eyes, feeling the comfort of her magic spreading through it. The pain slowly receded from the central head and with it he regained a grasp of sanity. He was Lucifer that was why he had responded to the name instinctively.

One of the other heads disappeared as she pulled out a chunk of the Curse. The other heads screamed, except the central one. As she unravelled the section of

Curse she had grabbed onto long lost memories flooded back into him.

He had a sister called Gabriel and a mother called Israfel. He also had an aunt called Jehoel and a cousin called Ariel. He had never known who his father or uncle were. He had grown up in a very matriarchal family.

Sariel felt a calm descend on the Beast as the unravelled the last of the memories that had been divided and placed in the head. The Curse had been deliberately designed to make him lose his sanity.

She grasped onto another flailing head with her powers, ripping it away from the Curse as she started to unravel it. As she did so the black started to slough off his massive wings. As it did so white and gold feathers started to grow from the skin.

He had had a friend, Michael who he had grown up loving like a brother. They had learned to fight together, serving in the armies of Ares, Sekhmet, Athena, Guan Yu and Horus. They had participated in various battles the world over, between the Gods and between civilisations.

She ripped of a third head, dismantling the memories stored within and returning them to the central head. The golden spines along his back started to evaporate. His whole body shimmered.

More memories flooded in. Michael's parents had had a little girl, a great celebration among the Angels. Michael had married his sister Gabriel, it had been a wondrous occasion. Their two families had rejoiced, it had been a pleasant interruption to their continual successes in the War. The Celtic Gods had been removed. The Greek/Roman and Egyptian Pantheons had been brought down. The other pantheons had stood back, thinking it merely a family dynasty change. The fools.

The fourth head faded away. The Dragon

continued to shrink and the black faded from his skin, leaving behind grey. More of the sigils covering his body evaporated away.

He had made a friend in Michael's father. They saw eye to eye on the problems the Angels were now facing. The lands without Mother Goddesses had started ailing. Gabriel was power hungry, she was refusing their reasoning. The Gods were willing to parley, peace could be brokered. The War could come to an end. But Gabriel hadn't wanted it, she had liked the power of being an Arch Angel. She did not want to give it up. He had beseeched her time and time again, speaking desperately to Michael. He had even asked their mother to speak to her. But in the end even Michael had betrayed him. Michael had fought him to distract him while Gabriel had used their blood connection to overcome his defences and Curse him.

Sariel ripped off the fifth head. Sigils started to evaporate off in a stream as they raced across his body in a chaotic jumble while his body continued to shrink. Already his wings had returned to their original splendour. They were still shrinking, beating back and forth lazily, catching the light to shine brightly.

He was falling and so were others. There was so much pain, he was burned horribly. He saw Michael and Gabriel's faces shrinking as Heaven grew further and further away. He was falling faster and faster, he couldn't fly, his wings had been pinned to his side. Everything was agony, his body was twisting and writhing, his skin was changing colour. His mind was shattering, there were images everywhere. Hundreds of images, none of them making sense.

The sixth head disappeared as all of Hell started to shake. The cloud banks of the Second and Third Levels started to swirl around. Demons stilled in their torment, the Damned stared in amazement as their punishments ceased. Angel magic flared everywhere sending beams of sunlight spearing through the gloom of Hell. What was left of the Greater Demons and who had been freed turned from their haunts to stare at the Great Stalagmite that was now visible from everywhere in Hell. The Walls of Dis started to crumble, the swamps started to steam and the sand dunes started to whip up. Hell had become a maelstrom of raging magic.

Angel magic was shattering as the Curse was broken out of Lucifer. Chaos magic flared around her as the planet's Lifestream surge upwards to her.

The Beast was nearly no longer the Beast, he had but one dragon head left. His body had nearly receded back to his normal size. His skin was losing its greyish pallor and turning into that beautiful tanned skin she had always envied in Gabriel. His wings were now the same size as hers, his golden talons fusing together and turning into his fingers and toes.

Scattered memories clicked into place. He was holding little Sariel, already showing such promise with magic. Watching Adam and Eve leave Eden, the heavy weight of mortality bearing down on them. Walking through his sister's laboratory feeling pride in her creations. Athena personally asking him to duel, she had beaten him but told him he was the best Angel she had ever fought. He remembered his first drink of Lightningsun, his fist kiss, his first spell, the first sword he ever made. So many firsts. He remembered his late night conversations with Samael on everything from philosophy to magical studies. He had been a wise man, troubled but gifted.

It all seemed so very long ago.

Finally his last head started to evaporate. The horns burned up into a glowing halo as the last remains of his Demonic Curse were pulled out of him. The Dragon head evaporated off of his real head. His tail burned up in fiery haze. The very last of the sigils flashing over his skin exploded outwards in a blaze of light.

Left behind was Lucifer's true form. She looked at him surprised, he was a very handsome man, almost beautiful. Gloriously tanned skin, well-muscled and toned. His skin was warm beneath her hands, which she longed to run through his thick brown hair. She had the strange urge to kiss his lips and the stretched skin of his neck. His exposed chest was smooth and perfect. She blushed when she realised she was holding a naked man in her arms. He was taller than her, with his glorious wings half cupped around her. How she longed to see him in his full glory, he had her full attention and he wasn't even conscious.

"Lucifer" she whispered giving in to the urge to brush his hair from his face.

He opened his eyes, as stunningly violet as her own. They were slightly darker than his sisters, more amethyst than violet. She stared into them, captivated, there was just something about them that drew her in.

He looked up at her who this beautiful creature was. Her long black hair fell down across him, her stunning violet eyes, almost seeming to glow, watching him. Her skin was flawless porcelain, except for the green vines winding down from her neck to her right forearm. Brownish sigils danced across her skin as little more than shadows. He vaguely wondered what they meant. She wore incredible jewellery, the style of which reminded him very much of the Olympians. He had the strangest urge to reach up and kiss those beautiful violet lips. "Who are you?"

She smiled "Welcome back Lucifer, I'm Sariel."

The cavern above them groaned as gigantic cracks spider-webbed across the ceiling and walls. Shouts and screams filled the air. The whole of Hell started to shake. The stalactite above them exploded in a shower of light that was whipped away in the raging maelstrom that was consuming Hell. They stared up in horror at the raging tempest as it savaged the Terraces of Purgatory. The groaning of thousands of tonnes of rock cracking filled the air above even the storm. Large sections of Purgatory had started to fall even as chunks of the Level cliffs were ripped upwards. The waters of the Acheron were caught in a demented dance between the collapsing Purgatory and rising Hell.

They could see for miles in every direction as the Gate of Hell was thrown open, the contents of the Curse breathing in real air for the first time as they were sucked upwards in a raging vortex.

He turned back to look at her "What have you done?"

She knelt transfixed, clutching to him for dear life "I don't know"

What in the name of Hell had she unleashed?

Glossary

Abaddon: Fallen Angel of Destruction.

Aisling: The current Fae Princess.

Angels: Winged Divine beings, separated into three divisions; Elder, Ascended and Lesser. All ruled by the seven Arch Angels.

Angel Weave: The special talent of the Angels to combine their magic.

Anu: Mesopotamian sky god, Lilith's father.

Arch Angel: The seven most powerful Arch Angels, often referred to as the Seven. Current Arch Angels are Gabriel, Michael, Azrael, Ariel, Uriel, Raphael and Sariel.

Ariel: Daughter of Jehoel, Gabriel and Lucifer are her cousins. One of the Arch Angels, her personal guard are the Inquisitors.

Apocalypse: Devastating spell that the Seven can unleash, uncontrollable.

The Acheron: One of the Rivers of Death, all of which flow into the Acheron which flows into Hell.

Ariadne: Demigoddess, once the Mistress of the Labyrinth and wife of Dionysus.

Ascended Angel: Saints who have been granted Divinity. Characterised by their four wings.

Atlantis: Ancient islands ruled by many Gods and Primordial Gods, once a great place of learning and magic before it was destroyed.

Atlanteans: Refugees of Atlantis who sought sanctuary with the Fae, now serve as the military arm of the Seelie Court. Very technologically advanced.

Avalon: Ancient primordial Goddess who created the Fae, also refers to the British Isles which she created.

Azrael: Brother of Samael, the Arch Angel of Death, his

personal guard are the Reapers.

The Beast: Lucifer's Cursed form.

Brigid: Celtic Goddess imprisoned at the start of the War. The Heir of Avalon.

Behemoth: Greater Demon, Guardian of Gluttony.

Cathair: Prince of the Fae.

Cerberus: Divine Monster Guardian of Hades.

Chaos: Refers to the universe and its unfathomable powers, parent of Gaia and thus the planet.

Charon: The Ferryman, transports the dead to Hades and Hell.

The Council: The Council of Elders who govern Heaven and the Angels.

The Curse: The Angels' Curse, Hell's Curse, Gabriel's Curse, Michael's Curse, the spell that caused the Fall and transformed Lucifer into the Beast and created Hell.

Daemons: Magical races throughout the world, hunted by the Angels.

The Damned: The Cursed, tortured mortal citizens of Hell.

Dante: One of Gabriel's favourites, gave Hell its structure.

Demeter: Mother of Persephone, one of Hera's sisters.

Demons: The Angels' term for Daemons, also the Cursed denizens of Hell.

Desiccation: A process in which Divine beings bodies cease to function but the power is too strong to fade away.

Dragons: Divine race of primordial creatures older than the Gods. Hunted to extinction.

Eden: Primordial Goddess, her Garden later became the home of the Angels.

Elder Angel: Divine Demigods, often the bastard offspring of Gods. Characterised by six wings and great power.

The Elites: Terrifying Monsters that Hera has crafted out of children who have suffered sexual abuse.

Encantado: Mysterious Daemon race from the Amazon.

Erebus: Primordial God of darkness.

Fae/Fairies: Divine, mortal spirits that live in Avalon and are descended from her. Governed by the Seelie Court and ruled by the Fae Queen.

The Fall: When Gabriel and Michael cast out Lucifer and his brethren from Heaven.

Gabriel: Daughter of Israfel and sister of Lucifer. The most powerful Arch Angel, her personal guard are the Seraphim.

Gadawsant: The Forsaken, the Wild Ones. The descendants of Fairies and Elves who broke their oaths and thus were cursed.

Gaia: First of all Primordial Gods, she is the planet's spirit and the only true child of Chaos.

Glamour: A spell to assume the appearance of being Human.

Gods: Immortal Divine beings of phenomenal powers that once ruled the world. The offspring of the Primordial Gods.

Gorgons: All female Serpentine Daemon race. Have snakes for hair.

Greater Demon: Extremely powerful Demons created by the Curse.

Hades: Greek God of the Dead, also the Underworld realm he rules.

Harpies: Divine Avian race who torture the Damned in both Hell and Hades.

Hecate: Titaness of Magic.

Hera: Greek Goddess, one of the most powerful Goddesses to have ever lived. The current Queen of Heaven.

Hypnos: Greek God of Dreams, brother of Thanatos.

The Furies: Also the Erinyes, minor Goddesses that hunted down criminals.

Heaven: Magical realm in the sky, home of the Gods and Angels.

Hell: Largest of all the Underworlds, formed when Lucifer fell from Heaven and from the Angels' Curse.

Inanna: Mesopotamian Goddess, considered the mother of the Angels. Once the Queen of Heaven.

Isis: Egyptian Goddess of Magic, once the Queen of Heaven

Kali: Hindu Goddess, the last shade of a once great pantheon.

Kitsune: Magical race of fox shapeshifters, most magical of all the Were.

Lampades: Underworld Nymphs utterly loyal to Hecate. Have the gift of prophecy.

Lesser Angels: Spirits of mortals who serve the other Angels. Characterised by two wings.

Leviathan: Greater Demon, Guardian of Wrath.

The Lifestream: From whence all spirits and souls come from and return. The endless cycle of life magic that keeps the world alive.

Lilin: Daemon race, males are Incubi, females Succubi.

Lilith: Fallen Arch Angel, Michael and Sariel's mother. Considered the mother of the Lilin. Was married to Samael and Adam.

Maenads: Warrior Nymphs once loyal to Dionysus, the only surviving Nymph species on the Surface.

Mammon: Fallen Angel and Greater Demon.

Medusa: The only mortal Gorgon, Cursed into Hell to become a Greater Demon.

Michael: Husband of Gabriel and Sariel's brother. Arch Angel, his personal guard are the Cherubim. An Angel of Death. One time friend of Lucifer.

Minotaurs: Bovine Daemon race. Original was Asterion

in the Labyrinth.

Minos: Judge of the dead in both Hades and Hell.

Monsters: Divine creatures of considerable power, usually the offspring of Primordial Gods and Gods though many have been created by Gabriel.

Naga: Divine beings that once lived in Lumeria and after its destruction South Asia. Hunted to extinction.

Nemesis: Goddess of Revenge.

Nephilim: The children of Angels and Humans.

Nymphs: All female Divine race. Often taken as the lovers by the Gods, usually mated with the Satyrs. Wide range of species with varying powers. Most species have been hunted to extinction.

Nyx: Primordial Goddess of the Night, closest relative to Gaia. Her brothers are Erebus and Tartarus.

Nyxite: Black metal formed from Nyx's blood, an empowered metal that can cause harm to the Divine.

The Otherworld: Magical realm created by Avalon for the Fae. It is a realm of the Dead.

Persephone: The Queen of Hades and Hades' wife.

Phoenixes: Divine avian species. Hunted to extinction.

Primordial Gods: The first of all magical beings, parents of the Gods.

Raphael: Arch Angel, his personal guard are the Ophanim.

Sariel: Daughter of Lilith and Samael, Michael's sister, powerless Arch Angel. The conduit of Chaos.

Satyrs: All male Divine race of wood spirits. Often wild and unruly, usually mate with Nymphs. Hunted to extinction.

Samael: Fallen Arch Angel, father of Michael and Sariel, married to Lilith. Was Lucifer's Mentor. The original Arch Angel of Death. The serpent of Eden.

Shade: Spirit

Sirens: All female Avian Daemon race noted for their

beauty and powers of seduction. Related to the Nymphs.

Sorcha: The current Queen of the Fae, can trace her ancestry back to Avalon.

The Styx: One of the Rivers of Death, flows by the entrance of Hades.

The Surface: the surface of the planet, where mortal life lives.

Tartarus: Primordial God, also refers to the forgotten Underrealms beneath the Underworld. A prison for many forgotten Gods and Monsters.

Thanatos: Greek God of Death, father of Samael and Azrael.

The Underworld: The magical realms beneath the Surface. Typically where the dead go.

Unicorns: Sentient equine Divine species. Hunted to extinction.

Uriel: Arch Angel, personal guard are the Malikhim

Vampires: Undead Daemon race that feeds on blood.

Victoria: The Princess of Wales.

The War of Heaven: Also referred to as the War. The Angel Rebellion that overthrew the Gods and brought about the eradication of nearly all the Divine races.

Were: Daemon race of animal shapeshifters. Include the Werewolves and Werecats as the main two species but there are many more.

Zeus: Greek god of Heaven, fathered many of the Angels.

Ziz: Greater Demon, Guardian of Lust.

CPSIA information can be obtained at www.ICGtesting.com
Printed in the USA
BVOW02s0254141215

430212BV00041B/1419/P